MW00564177

REBEL

DAVID WEBER
RICHARD FOX

Rebel

Copyright © 2024 by Words of Weber, Inc. and Richard Fox

A Baen Books Original

Baen Publishing Enterprises
P.O. Box 1403
Riverdale, NY 10471
www.baen.com

ISBN: 978-1-9821-9360-7

Cover art by David Mattingly

First printing, September 2024

Distributed by Simon & Schuster
1230 Avenue of the Americas
New York, NY 10020

Library of Congress Cataloging-in-Publication Data

Names: Weber, David, 1952– author. | Fox, Richard, 1978– author.
Title: Rebel / David Weber & Richard Fox.
Description: Riverdale, NY : Baen Publishing Enterprises, 2024. | Series:
    Ascent to Empire ; 2
Identifiers: LCCN 2024019307 (print) | LCCN 2024019308 (ebook) | ISBN
    9781982193607 (hardcover) | ISBN 9781625799821 (ebook)
Subjects: LCGFT: Science fiction. | Novels.
Classification: LCC PS3573.E217 R43 2024 (print) | LCC PS3573.E217
    (ebook) | DDC 813/.54—dc23/eng/20240506
LC record available at https://lccn.loc.gov/2024019307
LC ebook record available at https://lccn.loc.gov/2024019308

Printed in the United States of America
10 9 8 7 6 5 4 3 2 1

For Master Sergeant Terry Murphy, a cancer survivor
who gave the U.S. Air Force twenty-two years of his
life and me sixty years of friendship and love.
—D.W.

For Professor Elizabeth Samet.
Thank you for the library.
—R.F.

How it began...

The Great Eastern War, sparked by the Taiwan Crisis of 2057, kills 43,000,000 people. Deserted by all but a handful of its allies/ client states, the Communist Party loses its internal mandate and is replaced with a façade democracy, which the rest of the world refuses to accept as a genuinely representative government.

In 2059, the Federated Government of Earth is created, intended as a multi-continental federal system, not a consultative body. As a major, deliberately unifying project recalling the twentieth century "race to the Moon," the FGE commits to achieving interstellar flight. China, which sees the invitation to join the FGE as an effort to further subordinate it, rejects membership but commits to its own, independent interstellar flight program as part of its assertion of continued political, scientific, and economic power.

In 2082, the first FGE-sponsored Bussard RAIR (Ram Augmented Interstellar Rocket) departs the Solar System for the stars. Additional state and privately sponsored expeditions follow.

In 2086, China launches its first state-sponsored generation colony ship. Whereas FGE-sponsored expeditions are deliberately multi-ethnic, Chinese colony expeditions (like many privately sponsored FGE expeditions), are not. Chinese colony expeditions represent just under thirty percent of all sublight colonization flights and are deliberately sent to star systems well separated from those being colonized by the rest of humanity in a conscious effort to create an interstellar "Chinese sphere."

In 2109, faced with a progressively shrinking share of the international and system economy (and access to the scientific community), China finally (and grudgingly) joins the FGE on its fiftieth anniversary. China-sponsored colony flights continue, however. There is some concern about this among other nation state members of the FGE, but given that the colonies will be light-years (and decades—or centuries—of travel) away from Earth (or any of the other colonies), no formal objections are raised.

The situation changes radically in 2149, when the Fasset drive (originally tested in an extremely unreliable form in 2137) becomes a reliable means of propulsion, allowing an effective velocity three hundred times that of light.

For the next 165 years, Fasset drive-powered colonies spread out not just from Earth but from some of the older daughter colonies, as well. The sphere of human occupied (or at least explored) space expands radically. The FGE assumes responsibility for interstellar survey but sends out fewer state-sponsored colony ships. In partial compensation, private colony expeditions multiply, but the Chinese government continues sponsoring ships which are now predominantly Chinese-crewed but also include non-Chinese Asians who desire to preserve their "traditional cultures" in the face of the Western influence which has inundated them for the last two or three centuries. They continue to seek destination stars well separated from colonies of other ethnicities.

In 2231, the Terran Federation is formally founded, tying its member systems together into a single government. Ominously, despite the fact that all human settled planets are invited to join it, not one of the China-sponsored colonies attends its constitutional convention or ratifies that Constitution as a member.

In 2237, the majority of the Chinese/Asian sponsored colonies create the Tè Lā Lián Méng (Terran League), which is democratic in terms of individual enfranchisement but also highly corporatist and dominated by consensus-building within elite power groups.

For the next hundred years or so, the Federation and the League expand separately. The Federation is more successful in building industrial infrastructure and expands more rapidly. A handful of Asian-sponsored colonies closer to the Federation than to the League become Federation member systems, and a handful of FGE colonies closer to the League than to the heart of the Federation become League members. Other systems, which refuse to join either star nation and instead remain independent, are known as "feral worlds." Initially this is because their citizens refuse to be "domesticated" by either of the interstellar superpowers; ultimately, the term becomes a derogatory pejorative applied to all of them by the League and Federation alike.

In 2340, humanity encounters the Rish, reptilelike, extremely militant aliens whose interstellar empire—the "Rishathan Sphere"—is larger than either of the human star nations, but substantially smaller than their combined volume and, especially, population. The Federation establishes its first embassy on Rishatha Prime in 2347. The Sphere establishes its first embassy on Old Earth simultaneously. The League, which is slightly farther from the Sphere than the Federation, does not establish formal diplomatic relations until 2350.

What neither human star nation realizes is that the Rish perceive humanity as a threat. Humans appear to advance technologically at a faster rate, their populations grow much more rapidly, and they prefer lower population densities, all of which means that the human-occupied sphere is expanding much more quickly than the Rishathan Sphere. Faced by that unpalatable realization, the Great Council of Clan Mothers determines that a strategy to prevent human dominance must be developed and implemented.

For the next fifty-odd years, the Sphere deliberately fosters economic and trade links with both the Federation and the League. They encourage cultural exchanges with humanity, although neither the League nor the Federation is aware that the planets to which human study teams are admitted are "Potemkin villages," carefully designed façades intended to prevent the humans from understanding the true nature of the Sphere.

In their study of their human competitors, the Rish become aware of the original, long-standing animosity which led to the creation of the two independent interstellar human powers they confront. That animosity has died back to little more than a tradition of dislike, but the Rish decide to resurrect it. From 2384, the Sphere's diplomats (and human propaganda efforts *financed* by the Sphere) play slowly and subtly upon that lingering animosity, and it grows steadily more intense.

In 2475, Rishathan efforts move to active covert operations with the destruction of the League passenger liner *Shao Shi* (and all 7,800 of its passengers and crew) in Federation space in what the League insists was an act of deliberate sabotage. The Federation investigates but can find no evidence of any Federation involvement and rules the ship's destruction an accident. It was, however, carried out by human agents of the Sphere (who had no idea for whom they were actually working). They were then *eliminated* by the Sphere...but not until it had anonymously provided entirely genuine evidence of their actions to the League, which thus has "proof" of a deliberate mass murder which the Federation insists was merely "an accident of navigation."

Three years later, the Federation-flagged passenger ship *Sargasso* is destroyed in *League* space in a mirror image of the *Shao Shi* incident. The similarity is not lost upon the Federation, especially when evidence (anonymously provided) indicates that *Sargasso*'s destruction was a reprisal attack by League citizens who lost loved ones aboard *Shao Shi*.

Relations between the Federation and League become increasingly acrimonious. Trade declines, there are other incidents, and while only a few are on the scale of the *Shao Shi* or *Sargasso* disasters, they multiply and accelerate. Many of the more spectacular incidents are orchestrated by the Sphere, but the animosity the Rish are stoking provides ample opportunity for genuine, purely human-on-human acts of violence. And as they continue to increase, both the Federation and the League begin building genuine interstellar navies for the first time in their histories.

In 2565, the League, in response to pirate raids originating from the "feral world" of Cabochon in the Crestwell System, forcibly incorporates Crestwell into the Tè Lā Lián Méng. This is a move of genuine (and justified) self-defense, but the "Crestwell System Government in Exile," operating from the Federation's Heart Worlds, mounts an aggressive publicity campaign portraying itself as an innocent victim. The League designates the Government in Exile as a terrorist organization and demands the Federation suppress it; the Federation cites freedom of speech and refuses to do so. Both sides' naval buildups accelerate.

By 2580, the League and Federation are engaged in a massive naval building race. The huge sums being poured into the effort provide opportunities for enormous enrichment, and the Federation finds its economy increasingly dominated by "the Five Hundred," a collective label for the wealthiest four or five percent of its total population. There are far more than simply five hundred families involved, but the most powerful of all are those within the Sol System itself, where they begin asserting ever increasing influence in the Federation's government.

In 2594, a multi-carrier strike force of the Rénzú Liánméng

Hǎijūn (the Terran League Navy) enters the Minotaur System, a member system of the Terran Federation, in "hot pursuit" of pirates who have carried out a particularly bloody raid on a League planet. Neither the pirates nor the League know that the raid in question was sponsored by the Sphere, which has fed both sides carefully tailored intelligence to create precisely this situation. Nor are the League, the pirates, *or* the Federation aware that the Sphere has inserted a Rish-crewed Q ship under a false Federation registry into the Minotaur System. The League CO has no intention of attacking any Federation planet or ships; he is simply pursuing the pirates. The local Federation Navy senior officer orders him to stay clear of the system's inhabited planet while he investigates the purportedly pirate vessel which has already entered orbit around it. At which point the Q ship launches a devastating strike on the planet, killing almost three-quarters of its total population, destroys the pirate ship, and blows itself up.

The Federation CO believes the League is responsible and opens fire. The League CO knows he didn't do it, but returns fire and destroys or cripples the much lighter Federation naval presence in the system.

Neither side wants to charge into the abyss, but both blame the other for the disaster. When the Rish, as neutral third-parties, offer to conduct an inquiry into what happened, they accept. Both sides believe (since the Rish have been at some lengths to convince them) that the "impartial" investigators are their friends and so, at the very least, won't shade the evidence against them. But after a several-months investigation, the Sphere declares that it is unfortunately unable to determine who actually did what first and to whom in Minotaur. The evidence is simply insufficient to draw positive conclusions, a fact for which it apologizes to both the Federation and the League.

In private, the Sphere suggests to each side that while it can't find conclusive evidence—and so, as an impartial and honest investigator, cannot announce a conclusion one way or the other—it believes the preponderance of circumstantial evidence suggests the other side is lying. The Federation declares the Minotaur strike an atrocity and a war crime and demands the surrender of the carrier group commander, his staff, and his squadron commanders for trial. It also demands reparations. The implication is that the demands are backed by the threat of open war. The numerically weaker League responds with a preemptive attack as a self-defense option designed to cripple the Terran Federation Navy before the Federation can attack it. The preemptive strike inflicts heavy casualties and damage but is unable to prevent the TFN from counterattacking in turn.

The war between the Federation and the League begins in 2595.

Fifty-six years later, in 2651, newly promoted Admiral Terrence Murphy, grandson of the Terran Federation Navy's greatest war hero, is named Governor for the Fringe System of New Dublin. Murphy's wife is a member of one of the most powerful families of the Five Hundred, whose dominance of the Federation's government is now complete. The half-century of war against the League has only increased the Five Hundred's enormous wealth, and the Heart Worlds—the heavily populated, heavily industrialized, enormously wealthy planets near the heart of the Federation—are largely insulated from the human cost of the war, which falls far more heavily on the sparsely populated planets of the Fringe, whose children do most of the dying. The Five Hundred has also used its power to concentrate the vast majority of all heavy industry in the Heart Worlds, on the grounds that it will be safer there from League attacks than it would be in the more exposed star systems of the Fringe. The practical consequence is to turn the Fringe Worlds into the abused and impoverished subjects of a system in which they have no effective voice. Even worse, they are considered less valuable than the starships which might be lost defending them in the face of heavy attack. The hatred and resentment the Five Hundred's policies have stoked in the Fringe is attaining critical mass, but the Five Hundred don't care, because they control all the levers of power, including punitive expeditions against star systems which "go out of compliance."

Unfortunately for the Five Hundred, all of that is about to change.

CHAPTER ONE

RHLNS Cai Shen
Wormhole Space
August 10, 2552

"WE'RE AS READY AS WE ARE GOING TO BE, SIR," CAPTAIN SU Zhihao said somberly.

Third Admiral Than Qiang looked up from his cup of tea and nodded to his chief of staff. His expression was remarkably tranquil, Su thought. Far more tranquil than the man behind it could possibly feel, at least.

They were twenty-four hours by the universe's clock—only three and a half by the clocks aboard RHLNS *Cai Shen*, as the enormous faster-than-light carrier tore through wormhole space at ninety-nine percent of light speed—out of the Tè Lā Lián Méng system of Shanhaiguan.

"The communication protocols are all in place," Su continued. "But you know there are going to be questions about the lockdown from Shanhaiguan HQ."

"You mean there will be a great deal of *curiosity* about it," Than responded. Su raised his eyebrows, and the third admiral chuckled. There was very little humor in the sound.

"The last time we were in Shanhaiguan, we were still Liu's anointed secret weapon," he pointed out. "No one here knows differently. And Duan does know he was deliberately cut out of the chain for Bastion. That he was never even briefed on what it *was*, only that he was to give me whatever support I required and never say a word about it. Do you really think he's going to question any 'security protocol' I want to impose?"

1

Su began to reply, then paused, stroking his goatee.

Fourth Admiral Duan Bao, the Shanhaiguan System's military commander, was junior to Than. Technically, he couldn't countermand any order Than gave to the units of his own command; practically speaking, his authority as Shanhaiguan's "port admiral" gave him more than enough authority to *question* them, however. But Than was correct. Duan was a thoroughly political animal, and Liu Gengxin wasn't simply a senior member of the Accord. He was also the Minister of War and almost certainly the next president of the Tè Lā Lián Méng—the Terran League, to its *baakgwai* adversaries. As long as Duan thought Than was one of Liu's favorites, he would never dream of crossing the third admiral.

"There *is* that," the chief of staff acknowledged. "No, put that way, I don't see him rocking the boat. But what about Xiong?"

Than grimaced. Unlike Duan, Xiong Luoyang, the civilian governor of Shanhaiguan, was a member in good standing of the Accord that ruled the League. That meant that, unlike Duan, he *did* have authority to press Than on any decision he might make. And while he had no authority—legally—to override the third admiral in purely military matters, he was one of Minister of War Liu's toadies. On the other hand...

"Xiong is a *xīxuèguǐ*," Than said. It was a mark of his utter trust in Su that he allowed himself to use the derogatory term. Although, he thought, calling the career bureaucrats and self-seekers who'd sold their souls to the Accord bloodsuckers did a profound disservice to leeches, fleas, ticks, and vampires.

"He's not going to risk putting his oar into anything to do with Dragon Fleet," Than continued, just a bit more confidently than he felt. "Especially if he even *thinks* whatever's going on has the potential to piss off Liu. If something serious has gone wrong, all *he'll* be thinking about is how to prove it wasn't his fault and that he didn't know a thing about it at the time."

"Umm." Su stroked his goatee some more, then nodded with a slow and nasty smile. But then the smile faded, and he shook his head.

"Whether Duan or Xiong or any of their people ask those questions officially, they're still going to exist," he pointed out. "And some of our people will be really unhappy if they can't even speak to their families."

"I know." Than nodded unhappily. "In fact, I've decided you're right. Pass the word that all of our people will be allowed to leave messages for their families before we depart the system. The lockdown on all comm transmissions stands, so there won't be any face-to-face conversations, and I can't allow any messages to be distributed until we're back into wormhole space. But any of them who have loved ones in Shanhaiguan deserve the right to tell them at least something, and how can I deny them that? Especially now."

Their eyes met, and Su nodded in understanding. How could he *not* understand, when he was the one who'd made the quiet arrangements to see to it that Than's family was aboard one of his ships when they left the system? There were arguments against taking them into the range of the Guójiā Ānquán Jú, the Bureau of State Security. There were even more arguments against leaving them behind, under the circumstances.

"I want you to personally tweak the censorship protocols, though," Than continued. "There's no way we can keep this quiet forever, especially when we start staging the evacuees through Shanhaiguan, but the longer we keep a lid on it, the better. And we absolutely need to keep it quiet until we've cleared the system for Uromachi."

"You aren't going to ask Duan to send the rescue ships to Diyu directly from here?" Su asked in a rather neutral tone, and Than grimaced.

"I can't. For one thing, Duan isn't cleared for Bastion or Dragon Fleet. I know—I know!" He waved one hand. "After what Murphy did to us, that's just become a dead letter, but, let's face it, Zhihao. We have enough marks against us on the Accord's ledger without adding 'willful dissemination of classified information' to the charge list. Besides, there won't be enough FTL lift in Shanhaiguan to pick up more than a handful of them, anyway. There probably won't be enough at Uromachi, for that matter! Still, we'll have a bigger potential shipping pool to work with there. I'll have to look around and see what's available. And what Governor Zheng and Fourth Admiral Deng are willing to cut loose."

Su nodded thoughtfully.

Governor Zheng Nuan was well into her seventies, almost eighty, with a political career that had begun even before the war with the Federation. She regarded Liu and Eternal Forward in general as political thugs and they knew it, but she was too good at her job—and too firmly entrenched in the hearts of the citizens of Uromachi—for Liu to get rid of. Or, at least, to waste the political capital getting rid of her would cost. Besides, encroaching age had cost her some of her fire. It was fairly evident she and Liu had arrived at a truce under which she did her job without getting in his way and he left her alone to do it. But she certainly had both the stature and the authority to authorize the evacuation of Diyu.

On the Navy side, Fourth Admiral Deng Zan was ten or fifteen years younger than Than, but she'd had a reputation as a fighter before she got sucked into the administrative side of the Rénzú Liánméng Hǎijūn. As far as Su knew, she was a loyal supporter of the Accord, but at the end of the day, he suspected, her most fundamental loyalty was to the Tè Lā Lián Méng itself, and not to whatever corrupt political clique happened to be running it this week.

If *he* knew that, though, the Accord certainly knew it, too, in which case they'd be keeping her on a short leash. And the fact that Uromachi was both the Di Jun Sector's administrative hub and one of the League's major shipyards—major *known* shipyards, anyway—would only add to the shortness of that leash. In fact—

"You *are* going to tell Governor Zheng about what happened to Diyu, though, Sir?"

"I haven't changed my mind about that. She and Deng both have to know, given what losing the yards there probably means for Uromachi. But the rest of it—" Than grimaced. "There ought to be a balance between what we can tell people who need information without getting ourselves shot and the complete silence you know damned well Liu will slam down as soon as he gets a hint of this. I'll be damned if I know where the balance point is, though! *Damn* Xing!"

Su certainly couldn't argue with his admiral there. Xing Xuefeng had to have been the most narcissistic, sociopathic, *useless* excuse for a flag officer it had ever been Su Zhihao's misfortune to encounter. Just thinking about the disaster she'd engineered—engineered in no small part by systematically ignoring or willfully disregarding every single thing Than had suggested—was enough to turn his stomach. Years—*decades!*—of investment in money, resources, personnel to build what should have been the League's decisive weapon against the Terran Federation. All of it pissed away in the space of months by an arrogant, egotistical bitch.

"At least you told Murphy she was still alive aboard *Nüwa*, Sir," he pointed out. "After Inverness, and what she tried to do in New Dublin, I doubt she enjoyed making his acquaintance."

"*I* didn't much enjoy making his acquaintance," Than admitted wryly. "That man's dangerous, Zhihao! I know the gods themselves must have conspired to give him the intel to pull that off, but he *acted* on it. How many Fed admirals would've had the guts to go that far outside his standing orders? Or the tactical ability to kick our ass so thoroughly when he did!"

"We don't know for sure how far outside orders he actually was," Su pointed out.

"Oh, please!" Than rolled his eyes. "We've known for decades that the last thing any of the Five Hundred want is a Fringe system with the ability to go 'out of compliance' and stay there. Oh, don't misunderstand me—our political elite's done just as good a job of protecting their *families* as the Five Hundred has, but outside those families, the burden of combat's much more evenly shared by our people as a whole. But their Heart Worlds have shuffled the burden of something like eighty percent of the Federation's combat deaths off onto their Fringers, and the total Fringe population is less than a third of the Federation's total population. Think about that. Eighty percent of their casualties out of *thirty percent* of their population." Than grimaced. "That's the real reason we've never had to park as many pickets amongst the Out Worlds as the Feds have to scatter across the Fringe, and you know it as well as I do. All *we* have to worry about is a Federation attack, not whether or not our own people will rebel.

"And there's no way he hauled all of those missile pods—or whatever they were—out from the Heart with him, either. If they'd had that kind of weapon, they wouldn't have shipped it someplace like the Fringe. They'd have shipped it to Beta Cygni and ripped the front wide open. So whatever it was, he cobbled it up in New Dublin, and he *built* it there. That means the New Dubliners can build as many more of it as they want, and you and I both know what he was *supposed* to do was sit on New Dublin and keep it 'in compliance,' not give it the means to go *out* of it!" The third admiral shook his head. "No, he was so far out of official Fed policy he couldn't have found it with a gravitic sensor."

Su saw something very much like admiration, or possibly even envy, in Than's eyes, and he understood it. The number of times Than Qiang had wanted to emulate Murphy's defiance of policies he *knew* were wrong had to be enormous. And, in fairness, for all his lethality in combat, Terrence Murphy was a man of honor, as well. That, too, was something Than Qiang understood.

"The truth is," Than went on now, "that Murphy is probably the only admiral more likely than me to get shot for being the bearer of bad news. Sure, he's got a little better 'job security' than we do, given the fact that he's from the Five Hundred. But if the rest of the Five Hundred decide he's a threat—and anybody who can motivate Fringers to do what the New Dubliners obviously did for him *is* a threat—they'll throw him to the wolves even faster than Liu would throw *me* to the wolves."

"That's too bad," Su said soberly. "I think he was sincere. I think he wants the war to end. And I don't think he's one of those Feds who think the only acceptable peace treaty has to be signed in the rubble of Anyang."

"Maybe not, but he *is* a Fed," Than pointed out. "If he can convince the Oval and the Five Hundred to really look at his evidence—and, gods know, he's got plenty of it from Diyu—they'll have to realize how badly we've been hurt. And now that Murphy's uncovered our little agreement with the Rish, they'll have to wonder if the Sphere might be willing to come into the war openly to support us. If the matriarchs were willing to secretly help us build ships to fight the Feds, will they be willing to send in their own navy to offset our losses in Diyu?"

"You don't really think they will, though, do you?"

"I think anyone who thinks he truly understands how the Rish think is delusional." Than shrugged. "The one thing I do know is that I never believed for a moment that the Rishathan Sphere was helping us out of any sense of altruism. For that matter, they never made any pretense that they were. It was a matter of their finding us less threatening to their long-term interests than the Feds. They weren't helping *us* so much as they were breaking the Feds' kneecaps and using us to do it."

He shrugged again, and Su nodded. As Than had just suggested, the Rishathan matriarchs didn't think remotely like humans did.

But they clearly understood galactic realpolitik, and the Federation's frontiers weren't simply closer to the Rishathan Sphere's borders than the Tè Lā Lián Méng's, they were also expanding more rapidly.

"Unfortunately," Than continued, "the Feds can't rely on the Sphere's deciding to take its toys and go home, and they have to know that if it should decide to double down on its investment in us and commit its own navy, it would tilt the balance of power a lot further in our favor than even the Dragon Fleet could have. That's not something that could happen overnight, though, so even if the Rish are prepared to do it—which I doubt they are—the Federation still has a window in which it will hold a significant—decisive, really—advantage. So I'm afraid it's only too likely that if they believe him, they *will* push for a new offensive, while they have the edge, and equip it with those new pods of his. And if we're *totally* unlucky, they'll put him in command of it, when they do!"

"Then we'd just better hope the Five Hundred *won't* look at it, Sir," Su said hopefully. "As you said, they've got plenty of reason to decide he's a threat. There's a damned good chance they'll act on that instead of listening to anything ° has to say!"

"I know there is. And, little though he deserves it, I can't help hoping that's exactly what they do. But the truth is," Than shook his head, "I'm afraid it's wishful thinking. Given what he's discovered, and what he did to us, I can't really believe even the Five Hundred would be stupid enough not to believe him. And if they do, we—in that so-charming Fed turn of phrase—are toast."

Ithaca House
City of Kórinthos
Planet Odysseus
Bellerophon System
Terran Federation
September 23, 2552

"GENERAL TOLALLIS IS HERE, MR. PRESIDENT," ERASMIA SAMARILI announced, as she opened the door and bowed Menelaos Tolallis through it.

Tolallis had known her for years; despite the fact that she'd just turned thirty-one, and although she was officially listed only as Konstantinos Xeneas's secretary, she'd actually been his personal assistant and aide for over five years. And because Tolallis knew her so well, something about her tone...bothered him. She'd greeted him as courteously as ever, yet there'd been a subtle tension, something he might almost have called *fear*, in her brown eyes, and whatever it was, it shadowed her voice, as well.

"Thank you, Erasmia." System President Xeneas climbed out of his chair, standing behind his desk to hold out his hand. "And thanks for getting here so quickly, Menelaos."

"Your message said to hurry," Tolallis replied, gripping his hand firmly. "And, given the fact that you weren't willing to tell me what's on your mind over the comm, you can safely assume my curiosity's suitably piqued."

"Oh, trust me, you're not going to believe it when I do tell you." Xeneas's smile held a curious mix of bleakness and excitement, and he looked over Tolallis's shoulder.

"Make sure no one interrupts us, Erasmia. Unless it's the Vice President, of course. But give me a heads-up even in her case before you let her in."

"Of course, Mr. President."

Samarili disappeared, the door closed behind her, and Xeneas pointed at the pair of comfortable armchairs in one corner of his spacious office, then led the way to them. He settled himself into one, and Tolallis took the other. The general opened his mouth, but Xeneas raised a "not just yet" quieting hand, and Tolallis frowned as the president opened the panel in his chair's padded arm and tapped the touchscreen it revealed. A musical tone sounded, and Tolallis's frown deepened. He'd commanded the Bellerophon System Defense Force for over ten years, visited in this office both officially and unofficially scores of times, yet he could count on one hand—without using all his fingers—the number of times Xeneas had activated the internal security systems that enclosed this "conversational nook." His office was already proof against every known surveillance system, so why—?

"There," Xeneas said, pushing back deeper into his armchair, and something about his expression frightened Tolallis.

"I'm sure you're wondering what this is all about," the president continued. "Well, you're about to find out. And then you and I have some decisions to make."

"What sort of decisions?" Tolallis asked warily.

"Nasty ones." Xeneas's smile was bleak. "The kind that could get us both killed."

Tolallis stiffened, and Xeneas leaned forward in his chair once more, planting his forearms firmly on the armrests.

"Anthellis got back this morning," he said, and Tolallis's brow furrowed.

Serapheim Anthellis was the captain of the fast freighter *Timoleon*. Technically, his ship belonged to the Calloglou Consortium, one of the Bellerophon System's larger and more successful industrial concerns. Calloglou was not only more diversified than most of Bellerophon's other employers, it also benefited from far more "sweetheart" arrangements with other Heart-owned operations than its competitors enjoyed, since it was the primary local affiliate of the Société Auchan. So it wasn't too surprising that Calloglou operated almost a dozen Bellerophon-flagged freighters. They weren't permitted to encroach on the bigger, Heart

World-owned freight lines' routes, of course, but they handled most of Calloglou's point-to-point transport out in the boondocks of the Fringe. *Timoleon* was a bit faster than most of the Calloglou fleet—in fact, she mounted a milspec Fasset drive, which made her as fast as most mail packets—but aside from that, there was nothing outstanding about her.

Except for the minor fact that she actually took her orders from the Bellerophon System Republic. She did whatever Calloglou told her to do, as well, of course, which kept the Consortium's Heart World "partners" happy. But she also did whatever Konstantinos Xeneas asked her to do, including carrying messages he wanted the federal government to know nothing about.

"He got back from where?" the general asked after a moment.

"Concordia," Xeneas replied, and chuckled humorlessly at Tolallis's expression. "Actually, I never sent him there. It was a 'legit' trip for Calloglou, because their home office found out it could buy refined platinum and rhodium from New Dublin Extractions cheaper than anywhere else, now that the Leucippus deposits have pretty much played out. It's seventy-five light-years, but that's only thirty-eight days for a bulk freighter, and they estimated they could save at least seven percent on the purchase price, which would more than cover any extra freight costs. Actually, the rep they sent out aboard *Timoleon* got the New Dubliners down to over *nine* percent less than any of their other suppliers were offering."

"Fascinating. Why do I think that's not the reason I'm sitting in your office?"

"Because you've known me since we were both twelve. And because you're a very smart fellow. God, I *hope* you are, anyway! Because all hell's about to break loose, Menelaos."

"What?" Tolallis's eyes narrowed. "Why?"

"Because last month, the entire Concordia Sector went out of compliance," Xeneas said flatly.

"*What?!*"

The general came to his feet, staring at the president in shock. Xeneas only looked back for a handful of heartbeats—long enough for Tolallis to realize he was standing and force himself back into his chair. Then the president drew a deep breath.

"I don't have full information. Nobody's going to be stupid enough to discuss even the possibility of going out of compliance with anybody he doesn't know really, really well. So nobody in an official position in Concordia's ever said a word to me about anything like this, any more than I'd ever have dreamed of saying anything to them. For that matter, there's never been that much trade between us and them. From the Heart's perspective, Concordia's purely an extractive operation. Everything it produces is raw materials that funnel straight back to the Heart Worlds. There may be a few instances when someone like Calloglou gets permission from its Heart World management to go platinum-shopping, but aside from that, every scrap of it goes to the Heart. There's certainly not much in the way of heavy industry to use it at home! And when the raw materials play out, like happened to Leucippus, they just cut their losses, yank their investment out, and leave the locals to starve. So, no, we don't have much in the way of contacts in New Dublin.

"On the other hand, I know—knew—a bit about Alan Tolmach, Crann Bethadh's planetary president. So I guess I shouldn't have been as surprised as I was by the news."

"Are you seriously telling me this Tolmach was somehow able to take the entire *Concordia Sector* out of compliance? And that the rest of the people living in it were crazy enough to actually *listen* to him?"

"I said I don't have full information, but I think I have enough to understand—more or less, at least—what happened. Not that I found it easy to believe when Anthellis came by my office to deliver the case of *Craigmore Nua* I'd somehow forgotten I'd personally asked him to pick up for me while he was there. That would have been very clever of me, actually—almost as clever as it was of him—since it gave him a cover story when he contacted me."

Despite his tension, Tolallis's lips twitched at the dryness of Xeneas's tone. But any temptation to smile disappeared as the system president continued much more soberly.

"Basically," he said, "Concordia's had an encounter with a mythological creature: a Heart World admiral—a member of the Five Hundred, no less—who's actually interested in doing his job. Either that, or he's a megalomaniac with delusions of grandeur, and I don't think he is."

"Why not?" Tolallis asked skeptically.

"First, because he's Henrik Murphy's grandson. Second, because he diverted his entire task force to the Scotia System to save what he could of the planetary population after the Leaguies K-struck Inverness." Their eyes met bleakly. Even in Bellerophon, they'd heard about the Inverness strike. "He couldn't do much, but off the top of your head, can you think of any *other* Heart admiral who'd divert from his orders to do something like that? Third, because after Inverness, he took that same task force off across the Blue Line somewhere 'hunting slavers,' and came back with word that the League was about to hit New Dublin in strength. And fourth, because he drafted two other task groups to reinforce his task force and proceeded to kick the League's ass right up between its ears when it did attack New Dublin, exactly as he'd predicted. I don't know if the people Anthellis talked to were exaggerating, but if they weren't, Murphy took out at least ten League FTLCs."

Tolallis's expression had segued deeper and deeper into astonishment as Xeneas went on. Now astonishment became pure shock.

"*Ten* Leaguie carriers hit someplace like *New Dublin*?"

"No, a *dozen* of them did. According to Anthellis, he killed eight of them, then chased the other four home to a major shipyard no one even knew the League had. Captured two more carriers when he got there, not to mention the entire yard. Which, according to Anthellis's sources, is—was, at any rate—probably at least as big as Venus Futures' entire Sol operation. And, apparently, the Rish helped build the damned thing."

"Wait a minute." Tolallis raised one hand. "Just... *wait* a minute! The rest of this is all crazy enough without bringing in Rish conspiracy nuts from the gray net, Konstantinos! Whoever Anthellis's 'sources' were, they had to be either drunk or pulling his leg!"

"I don't know about the Rish. And to be honest, that bit sounds shaky to me, too," Xeneas acknowledged. "But whatever else is going on, he'd obviously already scared the hell out of the Five Hundred before he ever set off for this 'Diyu' place. Shortly after he got back to New Dublin, a passel of federal marshals and Capital Division Hoplons tried to arrest him."

"Wait," Tolallis said again, his face ashen. "They *tried* to arrest him? Don't tell me—"

"That they stepped on their dicks when they did?" Xeneas barked a laugh. "Oh, I think you might say that. In fact, the idiots must've had a frigging *checklist* for how to screw up!"

Tolallis stared at his friend in horror, and the system president shook his head.

"They not only tried to arrest him, they decided to do it at the very moment Murphy was being awarded New Dublin's highest medal of valor. Given typical Heart arrogance, I'm pretty sure they saw it as the best way to make their point to the ignorant, dumbass Fringers that they'd better mind their manners. So they waltzed right into the ceremony itself, Menelaos. Walked into a banquet with over four hundred guests to arrest the man who every one of those guests *knew* had gone against his standing orders to save their system." Xeneas shook his head, his own face like iron. "Not only that, Murphy obviously knew it was coming, because he had his own Marine Hoplons present. They had the drop on the bastards—had them *cold*—and the fucking Hearts pushed it anyway."

"And?"

"And only one of the Capital Division Hoplons and two of the marshals survived the firefight. But they did manage to kill the President of New Dublin and four civilian bystanders before they went down."

"Oh, Sweet Jesus," Tolallis half-whispered as he tried to imagine what it must have been like.

"Oh, it gets even better," Xeneas told him bitterly. "Tolmach's *son-in-law* is the President of Crann Bethadh now, and the system declared its independence the very next day. For that matter, it 'just happened' that the presidents and chief executives of virtually every other system in the sector were 'visiting' New Dublin, and *they* all announced their independence right alongside Crann Bethadh.

"And then they hanged all the surviving Hearts for murder."

Tolallis gaped at him, and for once, his brain completely refused to function. Silence hung heavily for endless seconds, and then he shook himself.

"So this Murphy was killed in the fighting?" he said, and his eyes widened when Xeneas shook his head. "Then what the hell was *he* doing while all this was going on? He was the goddamn *system governor!*"

"Technically, he still is, but he was present for the executions. The bastards were sentenced by a New Dublin court, but he *authorized* the hangings."

"He's insane! He has to know how the Heart's going to react to this!"

"I don't think he had much choice," Xeneas said flatly.

"Choice?"

"Use your brain. All the heads of government from the Concordia systems were already in New Dublin, Menelaos. *He* didn't invite them all over for a quick cup of coffee! The only way this could've happened was if they'd already been planning it. Sure, when he went 'out of compliance' with his own orders—and when they knew he had—and stood his ground against the League, it was probably the last straw they needed, especially when the frigging idiots tried to *arrest* him! But Murphy didn't plan any of this. *They* did, and Murphy was smart enough to realize he couldn't shove the genie back into the bottle once it was loose. Not unless he wanted to K-strike the very planet he'd just finished defending!"

"Sounds to me like the man wants to play warlord," Tolallis said grimly.

"Nobody in Concordia seems to agree with you. And Murphy's official position is that while he's willing to 'present their grievances' to the Assembly and back their demands for constitutional reforms to address them, he's still an officer of the Terran Federation Navy and he doesn't recognize the legality of their secession. He recognized the authority of the Republic of Sliver Tree to try and execute the Hearts who killed its president, but he recognized its right to do that as a member system of the Federation, applying its local jurisprudence within the Federation's recognized constitutional framework, not as an independent star nation. Concordia's organized into something called the Free Worlds Alliance, and apparently he's willing to regard that as an association of member systems of the Federation who have banded together to 'petition' Olympia for redress, but he's not prepared to recognize them as an independent star nation. That's why he's still officially Governor of New Dublin."

"Well he'd better *get* prepared," Tolallis said even more grimly. "Nobody else in the Heart's going to 'recognize' them as anything but rebels and traitors. And the only response they're going to get from Olympia's a goddamned fleet with orders to turn their planets into billiard balls!"

"I'm pretty sure anyone as smart as Murphy seems to be has to recognize that, too, deep down inside." Xeneas's tone wasn't grim; it was sad. "I think he's entirely serious. That he really wants to save the Federation. But I also think his dream of somehow resolving this is...quixotic, at best. And either way, I doubt he'll just stand there with his hands in his pockets when the Heart moves on New Dublin."

"And exactly what's he going to do to stop it?"

"He came home from Diyu with seven carriers. By the time *Timoleon* pulled out, two more had come in. Their crews mutinied, Menelaos, and from the sound of things, they won't be the last. I won't be a bit surprised if the majority of the Concordia Sector pickets come over to him in the end, and a force that size, under an admiral who's already beaten twice his own number in *League* carriers, isn't going down easily."

"Maybe not, but in that case, they'll pull in however many ships they need to take him down *hard*."

"If they can."

Tolallis's eyes narrowed at those three softly spoken words.

"Why shouldn't they be able to?" he asked after a moment.

"Because the entire damned Fringe is about to blow sky high," Xeneas said flatly. "God knows you and I've talked about this often enough, Menelaos! We've always had it easier here in Bellerophon because we're the closest thing the Five Hundred has to a golden goose in the Fringe. Economically, we've had a hell of a lot more comfortable ride than systems like Scotia or New Dublin, so that hasn't been part of the equation here. It has for other systems in Cyclops, just not for us. But what *has* been part of our equation is the blood price. The fact that it's *our* sons and daughters the Heart sends off to die in its goddamned war! You've lost two brothers, I've lost a brother and a son and a niece, and I doubt there's a single family here on Odysseus who hasn't lost *someone*."

The system president glared at his boyhood friend.

"Now the dam's broken. Concordia's come out into the open, and you're right—the Feds and the Five Hundred will do whatever it takes to crush them. To *smash* them. To turn them into the object lesson that will terrify the rest of the Fringe into meek obedience for generations! And do you know what will happen when they try to?"

"They'll smash hell out of the poor bastards," Tolallis said.

"They'll try. And they may manage it...for Concordia. But this is going to spread, Menelaos. We already know about it; by now, especially if this Free Worlds Alliance is half as smart as

I think it is, they've commandeered every FTL courier they can find to spread the news. I don't plan on letting a word about this leak until we've decided what we're going to do about it, but eventually it *will* come out. And exactly how do *you* think our most bitter, angry, pissed-off fellow citizens—and especially our pissed-off *vets*—will react when it hits the feeds?"

Tolallis's jaw tightened, and Xeneas nodded.

"Damn straight. *Best*-case scenario, a huge chunk of the electorate goes up in flames and we—you and I, Menelaos—crush it before it gets out of hand. We make enough examples, break enough heads—and necks—to satisfy the Five Hundred that the situation's safely under control, and the Feds let that be enough."

He paused, his expression the most bitter one Tolallis had seen in all the forty years they'd known one another, then shook his head once, hard.

"I don't think I could bring myself to do that. Not really. And even if I could, it wouldn't matter. Not this time. Because this time, the Five Hundred's coming for all of us. We won't have to actually do a single, solitary thing. All we'll have to do is *be* here, and the bastards will absolutely find some reason, some excuse, some . . . imagined threat to turn us all into Gobelins. And that means that no matter how hard we come down on any expressions of discontent here in Bellerophon, it can't possibly be enough to keep them from using it as their pretext.

"And even if it would, every other Fringe system's going to know what's coming. They'll know that trying to keep their heads down to avoid the Hearts' hammer won't work, this time. Oh, it might work for a handful of systems—maybe even for *us*, given how much of our infrastructure the Five Hundred owns outright—if they're willing to shoot enough of their own neighbors before the Hearts get around to it. But it won't work for the rest of the Fringe, and when the *rest* of the Fringe goes up in flames, the fire will burn Bellerophon to the ground right along with it.

"Unless we do something about it."

"You're talking about Thermopylae."

"That's exactly what I'm talking about."

The two of them sat looking at one another, and the silence was heavy about them. Finally, after a seeming eternity, Tolallis stirred in his chair.

"That was never a real possibility," he said softly.

"You put a hell of a lot of thought into something that was never a possibility, then," Xeneas replied with a crooked smile.

"I—"

Tolallis broke off. He closed his eyes, and his nostrils flared as he sucked in oxygen. Then he opened his eyes and looked at his friend again.

"I did," he admitted, "but I never thought there'd be one chance in a million of actually pulling it off. It was...It was a last-ditch stand. Something to try only if they were already coming for us and we didn't have anything left to lose. Why the hell do you think I called it 'Thermopylae'? You know what happened to Leonidas!"

"Of course I do. But I think they *are* already coming for us—or will be as soon as they find out what's happening in Concordia. And that means we *don't* have anything left to lose, really. We're damned if we do, or damned if we don't, but think about it. They may be coming, but they won't be able to concentrate just on *us*, Menelaos. That's what's changed. I don't see any way in hell other Fringe systems—hell, *most* of the Fringe systems, and pretty damned near *all* of them in the southern lobe—won't sign on with this Free Worlds Alliance. And a lot of their picket ships will do exactly what seems to be happening in Concordia. So when the time comes, the Heart's going to find itself up against some *significant* military opposition, and it still has the League to worry about. For that matter, how do you think Heart public opinion will react when all of a sudden it's *their* kids—their husbands and fathers and mothers and wives—out there getting killed in the Five Hundred's war?"

"Are you honestly telling me you think we could pull this off?"

Disbelief, fear, and a strange, deep longing mingled in Tolallis's voice, and he stared almost pleadingly at Xeneas.

"I'm telling you I think we don't have any choice but to *try*," the system president said compassionately. "I'm telling you that if we can make Thermopylae work, and if we can get word to this Free Worlds Alliance that we want *in*, we'll have at least a chance. And I'm telling you that whatever we do, the Fringe is going to *burn*, Menelaos. We may not have all that great a chance, but you and I both swore an oath to protect and serve the voters and people of Bellerophon—*our* people—and that means we have to try. God help us, we *have* to try."

CHAPTER THREE

City of Korinthos
Planet Odysseus
Bellerophon System
Terran Federation
September 25, 2552

"THERE YOU ARE!" ISADORA TOLALLIS SAID, BESTOWING AN ENOR-
mous hug on Captain Achilleas Rodoulis. "You'd better have an
excuse for how long it's been since we've seen you here!"

"Misery," Rodoulis said promptly.

"Misery?" Isadora was a slim, attractive woman, twenty
centimeters shorter than her towering husband, and she stood
back, hands still on Rodoulis's shoulders, to raise both eyebrows
skeptically.

"Of course misery!"

"And just why should that be?"

"Because of the way you feed my worthless cousin." Rodoulis
put on his very best woebegone expression and managed a fairly
credible sniff. "Every time I do come over, you put all that delicious food on the table. And I know, even as I'm eating it, that
no one *else* is going to feed me that well. So it's better if I just
stay away and stop tormenting myself with such brief, fleeting
moments of epicurean bliss."

"You're a lunatic. Did you know that?"

"I understand that's been said by some who fail to appreciate
the true keenness of my trenchant wit. By the way, where's my
favorite first cousin once removed?"

"Unfortunately—or perhaps fortunately, given what you two

are like whenever you get together—Grigorios is visiting with friends in Égina. Which is just as well. They're studying for their finals, and they *don't* need the distraction."

"Distraction? What distraction? The only thing for which I am more famed than my trenchant wit is my academic brilliance. As long as it's not math. Or physics. Or geography, come to think of it. But for anything else, I'm your man! Except for spelling."

"Oh, my God." Isadora looked at her husband and rolled her gray eyes. "Do you *believe* this guy?!"

"You should have tried growing up with him," Menelaos Tolallis said dryly.

"By the way, what's for dinner?" Rodoulis interjected hopefully.

"Kleftiko, feta salad, and spanakopita, although I'm really, really tempted to not share it with you," his hostess replied.

"I'll be good!" he promised. "At least till we're done eating."

"Idiot!" Isadora swatted him, then shook her head. "Well, it won't be ready for a while. I knew you and Menelaos's other lowbrow friends were going to be playing cards for at least a couple of hours first. But if you're *really* nice to me, I might just see my way to laying out a little tzatziki for you in a half hour or so. Purely to stave off starvation while you deal."

"Bless you, my daughter!" Rodoulis gave her a hug and she laughed, then headed for her kitchen.

Rodoulis smiled after her...until the instant the door closed behind her.

"She doesn't have a clue, does she?" he asked then, frowning at his cousin.

"She knows it's more than just cards, and she knows enough to be worried," Tolallis replied. "I haven't told her anything specific, but she knows me too well." He grimaced. "She knows *something's* up. That's the real reason Grigorios is in Égina. He may be only fourteen, but she knows how he idolizes you, and he's smart as a whip. She doesn't want him figuring out anything it's better he not know about."

"Menelaos, she deserves to know!"

"Of course she does!" Tolallis more than half-snapped. "But we're not telling *anyone* unless we absolutely have to. That was the President's call, and I think it was the right one. But I can't justify making an exception for my wife when there won't be one for anyone else's!"

Rodoulis started to say something even sharper, but then clamped his jaw. The iron code of personal honor which refused to make an exception even for the woman he loved was one reason Menelaos Tolallis was the Bellerophon System Defense Force's CO. And it was also the reason his other guests might just trust him enough for them to pull this off.

Or die trying, at any rate.

At the moment, he suspected the odds favored the latter.

"Come on," Tolallis said after a moment, twitching his head towards the stairs, and Rodoulis nodded.

He followed his cousin down the interior stairs to the spacious rec room Isadora Tolallis insisted on calling her husband's "man cave." One entire wall was glass, looking out over the dark waters of the Thálassa Krasioú Ocean from the house's clifftop perch. The Kórinthos city skyline caught the golden afternoon sunlight to the east, on the far side of the Bay of Kórinthos, but clouds were rolling in on a brisk northerly that sent waves crashing steadily higher on the rocky beach at the foot of the cliff.

A pair of card tables sat in front of that wall, surrounded by comfortable chairs. Decks of cards, glasses, bottles of whiskey, and even a bottle of Bellerophon retsina had been set out, but none of the five men and two women occupying seven of those chairs seemed particularly interested in them. Their heads snapped around as Tolallis and Rodoulis walked in, and the captain felt the tension level ratchet even higher.

"Find a seat, Achilleas," Tolallis said, pointing him at the chairs as he continued across the room to the smart wall at its end. He tapped the master screen alive, then entered a complicated code. Nothing happened for a moment, and then an odd, eye-twisting shimmer seemed to flow down the glass wall.

"There!" He smiled thinly. "Some advantages to having a home office when you're the defense force CO. I got really good security systems on the taxpayer's credit card."

"Which I'm sure is very reassuring," Commissioner Lazaros Ganatos observed. The commander of the Bellerophon Unified Police Force was tall, heavyset, and gray-haired, with a lined face whose expression fell well short of cheerful. "I'm sure any of my people who happen to be looking this way won't feel at all curious as to why you've turned them on for a friendly card game."

"But it's *your* card game," Tolallis pointed out. "I'm sure the UPF wouldn't be spying on its own chief!"

"Not officially, no." Ganatos shrugged. "I can't promise there aren't a few *ochiés* carrying water for the Hearts buried in the Force, though."

"We'll just have to hope none of them get curious in the next week or two, then," Tolallis said. "In a lot of ways, I'd rather not have pulled you out here for this, Lazaros. You're not part of my usual card-playing circle, so having you join us might raise an eyebrow or two. But we've got to have you on board, and this isn't something we can afford to discuss—especially at this level—any way except under four eyes. Even if we do happen to have *eighteen* eyes present at the moment."

Ganatos grimaced in unhappy agreement, and Tolallis considered his other guests.

Yeorgia Elitzi, his own executive officer, was brown-haired, gray-eyed, and petite. Like him, she was a veteran of the Federation Marines, but while he'd been medically retired with an artificial left calf, she'd managed to hang on to all of her original parts. And, aside from Rodoulis, she was the one person in the room he already knew was absolutely committed to what they were about to discuss.

His other five guests all wore the uniform of the Terran Federation Navy, at least when they were on duty. In point of fact, three of them were the commanding officers of TFN carriers, and people didn't get picked at random for those billets.

His cousin Achilleas, only a centimeter or so shorter than Tolallis himself, was TF 1709's senior captain and commanded the *Baldur*-class FTLC *Freyr*. Captain Madelien Hoveling, CO of TFNS *Perseus*, was ash-blond, aqua-eyed, and twenty-four centimeters taller than Elitzi. Captain Khairi al-Massoud, *Ninurta*'s skipper and the most junior of the task force's COs, was of only medium height, thin and quick-moving as a whippet, with dark hair and eyes. And Commander Lloyd Marchant, the only one of Tolallis's commissioned guests who didn't command his own ship, was seven centimeters shorter than Tolallis, with brown hair and brown eyes. A totally unremarkable-looking fellow... until one looked into those mild eyes and saw the dagger-sharp mind behind them.

Then there was the only person present who wasn't an officer.

Senior Master Chief Weldon O'Cahill was a square-shouldered, square-faced fellow with a shaven head, a hooked nose, and the hard, competent features of a noncommissioned officer who'd served the Federation for going on forty years. And if he felt the least uncomfortable in his astronomically senior company, there was no sign of it.

"All right." Tolallis pulled out a chair of his own, sat, and began idly shuffling a deck of cards. "I guess we should get right down to it. Lazaros and Yeorgia, I know you're up to speed because I issued the invitation directly. But I want all the cards on the table—you should pardon the expression"—he flipped an ace of spades face-up on the table—"before we go any further. I won't have anyone involved in this unless he—or she—knows exactly what we're getting into."

"I think you can assume Achilleas brought us pretty much up to speed, General," Madelien Hoveling said dryly. "He's not a lot better at lying to people or double-dealing than you seem to be."

"Hey, I can lie with the best of them!" Rodoulis objected.

"I didn't say you couldn't lie. I said you couldn't lie *well*. There's a reason you never leave a poker game with as much money as you had when you came," Hoveling pointed out, and looked back at Tolallis.

"I can't say I didn't think he was out of his mind when he started sounding me out," she continued in a more serious tone. "But assuming President Xeneas's intelligence from New Dublin's solid, maybe he's not totally crazy."

"Not as crazy as *I* am, anyway," Tolallis said. "But, just to make sure we're all on the same page, let's be clear that what I'm proposing here is an act of mutiny and arguably an act of treason. That's certainly how Olympia will regard it, at any rate. And that means that if it goes south on us, the consequences not just for us, but for everyone we care about, will be... extreme."

"Actually, General, that's more likely to be true for the native Odyssians in the room," Marchant pointed out. "You've all got family right here in-system. If it falls into the crapper, you're the ones with the most to lose. The worst any of us 'foreigners' has to worry about is getting killed."

"I know. Believe me, I know!"

Tolallis's face tightened for a moment, then his nostrils flared and he shook himself.

"I know," he repeated, "and Isadora and I have three kids right in the line of fire. I'd do just about anything to keep them safe, but the more I've thought about it, the more I've come to the conclusion that Konstantinos—I mean, the President—is right. Whether we do anything to prepare for it or not, the shit storm is coming. I wish to hell we had more information, but what we already know is more than bad enough."

"I have to say I wish New Dublin hadn't gone off the deep end," Elitzi said. The others looked at her, and she grimaced. "I'm not saying they didn't have plenty of cause. Hell, I don't think there's a single Fringe system that *wouldn't* have plenty of cause. But they've lit a fuse—all of us know that!—and God only knows what's going to happen when it reaches the main charge. I'd really have preferred to have a little more time—you know, like maybe an entire month—to plan something like this."

"What we've got is what we've got," Tolallis replied. "Not that I don't totally agree with you. It's just that what we'd prefer doesn't mean squat compared to what we actually have."

"We could take a little longer than you and Konstantinos are contemplating, though," Ganatos pointed out. Tolallis looked at him, and the police commissioner twitched a shrug. "We only know about it because *Timoleon* happened to be in New Dublin and came straight here and her skipper told him about it. It'll be a while before anyone else in Bellerophon, much less the rest of the sector, finds out. So it's not like we have to pull the trigger tomorrow to stay in front of the news."

"You're right, at least in some ways." Tolallis nodded. "But we all know damned well the news will hit Olympia and the Oval like a sledgehammer when *they* find out about it. And if this business about the marshals trying to arrest Murphy's accurate, they already knew they had a problem building in New Dublin. That suggests that as soon as they have confirmation it's hit the fan, they'll at least send out precautionary warnings to the other Fringe sectors. Including Cyclops. If that happens, the chance of our pulling off something like this at all will nosedive. And the chance of our pulling it off without a *bloodbath* will dive even faster and deeper."

"And there's another factor," Rodoulis said. Eyes turned towards him, and he shrugged. "President Xeneas can't send word to New Dublin until he knows what word to send, and the communications loop isn't really on our side. We're eighteen light-years closer to New Dublin than we are to Sol, but we're almost a hundred light-years closer to Sol than New Dublin is. If Schleibaum and Fokaides decide to start flinging around orders—or task forces—they can get them to Bellerophon a hell of a lot faster than to New Dublin. And Admiral Murphy isn't between *us* and Sol. If we're going to do this, we need to get it done and get word to him and this Free Worlds Alliance as early—and as fast—as we possibly can."

Ganatos didn't look any happier, but he nodded heavily, and Tolallis leaned forward in his chair.

"I don't have anywhere near as good a feel for the Navy side of things as I'd like," he said. "As far as the System Defense Force is concerned, sure, Yeorgia and I can lock things down. Our people trust us, and we know exactly who to bring onboard when the token drops. But Achilleas tells me it's likely to be more of a crapshoot from the system picket's perspective. And that a lot of it will depend on you, Commander."

He looked at Marchant, and the commander shrugged unhappily.

"He's probably right, General. About its being a crapshoot, I mean. Sure, sixty or seventy percent of our personnel are Fringers, and the Heart doesn't have a lot of friends among them. But we'll have to be insanely careful about who we approach."

"Well, we can start right out by crossing Admiral Adamovič off our Christmas card list," Hoveling said dryly, and al-Massoud cracked a barking laugh of agreement.

Rear Admiral Arshula Adamovič, who commanded both Task Force 1709 and FTLC Squadron 62, was a hard-bitten, not particularly imaginative officer. But she was also related to at least a half dozen Five Hundred families, and none of them needed to guess how *she* would respond if she heard about their current tête-à-tête.

"And, unfortunately, Captain Aguayo," Marchant said heavily. "I hate that. Pascual's a good man in an awful lot of ways, but he's a Heart to the core."

"I know." Rodoulis's expression was even unhappier than Marchant's. "I've known him since the Academy. Hell, I'm his daughter's godfather!" His jaw tightened for a moment. "I know exactly how he'll react to something like this if he has time. That's why you were one of the first people I talked to, Lloyd."

"I wish I could think you'd been mistaken about that," Marchant said. "But you're not. Which means I have to figure out a way to neutralize both of them. And, God help me, so far I haven't been able to come up with a...nonlethal approach. Or not one without entirely too much potential to *turn* lethal, anyway."

"I *may* be able to help a little with that," Tolallis said. Marchant looked at him, and he raised one hand in a tossing away gesture. "The President's planning on inviting Ramsay to a meeting at Ithaca House to discuss certain 'troubling indications' he's heard about Fringe unrest. If he phrases it right, and if I sign on with him, we can probably convince her to bring Adamovič along with her and have both of them sitting in a conference room with him."

"That would help—a lot," Marchant said.

Mollie Ramsay was the Bellerophon System Governor, which meant Adamovič came under her orders. If she invited the admiral to a conference with the system president, Adamovič would damned well be there.

"Yeah." Al-Massoud nodded feelingly. "Still gonna be tricky, though. Especially setting up the conduits to the lower deck. Be kind of hard for one of us to sit down in the chiefs' mess and just start shooting the breeze."

He was looking across at SMCPO O'Cahill as he spoke, and O'Cahill looked back steadily.

"Which, obviously, is the reason I brought the Senior Master Chief along, Khairi," Rodoulis said just a bit testily.

"I know that." There was a genuine, if faint, note of apology in al-Massoud's tone, but he didn't look away from O'Cahill. "And I know you and he have been together a long time, Achilleas. But I don't know him as well as you do, and a lot's going to depend on him."

Rodoulis opened his mouth, but O'Cahill held up a hand before he could speak.

"That's a fair point, Sir," he said. "And can't say I blame you for raising it. On the other hand, you might want to ask Charlene Dabrowski about me." He smiled very faintly. "She's an old drinking buddy of mine."

"You and Senior Master Chief Dabrowski?" Al-Massoud raised his eyebrows.

"She was Spacer Third-Class Dabrowski when I first met her, Sir. You might say we go back a long way."

Al-Massoud regarded him very thoughtfully indeed. SMCPO Dabrowski was *Ninurta*'s boatswain, the ship's senior noncommissioned officer, the same post O'Cahill held aboard Rodoulis's *Freyr*.

"I was wondering how I might approach the Boatswain," the captain said after a moment. "Obviously, I need her onboard for this if I expect the enlisted to go along with it. Should I take it you don't think that will be quite as much of a problem as I was afraid it would be?"

"You're worried because she's a Heart, like me," O'Cahill said calmly.

"That...and the fact that I've known her for less than two years, standard," al-Massoud admitted. "And now that you brought it up, that *is* one of the reasons I mentioned the fact that I don't really know you, either."

"*I* do," Rodoulis said flatly. Al-Massoud looked at him, and he snorted. "I met O'Cahill on my snotty cruise, Khairi. I've known him for damned near twenty-five years. That's why I specifically requested him for *Freyr*."

"Skipper," O'Cahill gave Rodoulis a crooked grin, "don't worry so much! I know exactly why Captain al-Massoud's sweating it, because I *am* a Heart. At least—" he looked back at al-Massoud, and his grin vanished "—by birth. But I've worn the uniform since I was twenty-seven, and that's forty years standard next month. I've seen a *lot* of this war—I signed up right after the Brin Gap—so I know *exactly* how fucked up it's been for the last thirty years. And my wife's from Hathaway. We've been married for thirty-two T-years, Sir...and our daughter Kimberly was killed in action four years ago. For that matter, we've got two boys still in uniform. Trust me," he shook his head, "I'm over being a Heart by birth."

"I see." Al-Massoud nodded, slowly at first, and then more briskly. "I see, Senior Master Chief. And I'm sorry to hear about your daughter."

"So were we. And a hell of a lot more Fringers than Hearts get the same letter we got. I don't know what kicked them off in New Dublin any more than you do, Sir. But I do know it's been too damned long coming. And I know exactly which 'troublemakers' in my ship to approach. I'll damn straight bet you Charlene knows which ones to talk to in *Ninurta*, too. I wouldn't get Senior Master Chief Silvestre involved, Captain Hoveling. She's not a big one for sticking out her neck, and I figure there's a fifty-fifty chance she'd rat you out the minute you approached her, but Master Chief Jahoda's a good man. Charlene and I could work with him. And Brewster's as solid as they come, Commander Marchant. He's been with Captain Aguayo a while, but he's got a nephew and three cousins who never came home again."

O'Cahill looked around the circle of monumentally senior officers, and his eyes were hard.

"If you're serious about this, I can get the ball rolling tomorrow below decks. Probably faster than you can do it in officers' country, really. But this is all or nothing. Even if we pull it off, we all know the Oval's gonna send some hardass Heart out here with every ship they can scrape up. Aside from the ones this Murphy may have distracted, at least. A lot of what you people are talking about is above my pay grade, but I think President Xeneas is right that the entire Fringe is going up in flames, one way or the other, when it hears about New Dublin, and the Five Hundred're going to put it down *hard*. They won't give a single, solitary damn who gets ground up in the process, either. Hell, the more examples the better, from their viewpoint! It's gonna be Gobelins all over again, only worse...unless we stop 'em. So I don't see where we have a lot of choice. But I'm not gonna go and talk to any of my men and women and invite them to step out the lock without a suit with me unless we *are* going all the way. So, are we?"

He looked around the suddenly silent rec room. No one spoke for several seconds, and then al-Massoud inhaled deeply.

"Yes, Senior Master Chief," he said into that silence. "Yes, we are."

CHAPTER FOUR

Bellerophon System
Terran Federation
October 7, 2552

"MORNING, LLOYD." ACHILLEAS RODOULIS LIFTED HIS COFFEE CUP in salute to the comm display. "What can I do for you this fine day?"

"Nothing planet shaking," Commander Marchant replied. "The Captain just asked me to give you a call about that exercise Admiral Adamovič was talking about day before yesterday. He says she's planning on bringing it up at tomorrow's CO's brief, and he wanted you to see about getting a memo together covering the points you and I talked about. Right this minute, he and the Admiral are both headed planet-side for a meeting with President Xeneas, but he'll be back in two or three hours—four, at the outside. You think you can get it all organized in that window?"

"Not a problem," Rodoulis said. He sipped coffee, then smiled crookedly. "Not a problem."

"Sublight in ninety minutes, Skip," Antonia Michaels said.

Captain Tobias Echols looked up from the chess game on his smart pad and checked the astrogation display. The Devinger Lines freighter *Lucille G. Anderman*—known somewhat irreverently to her crew as the *Lucy Anne*—was twenty-five days objective and three-point-five days subjective outbound from the Espeadas System, approaching Bellerophon, where she would arrive in the aforesaid ninety minutes. Of course, that was ninety minutes by *Lucy Anne*'s clocks; by the standards of the rest of the universe, it was well over eleven hours. Not that it mattered particularly to Echols or his crew.

What did matter to them was that as too infrequently happened—*far* too infrequently, in Echols's opinion—this time Devinger's Bellerophon office knew *Lucy Anne* was coming. The system wasn't on *Lucy Anne*'s regular route, but the Espeadas agent had known for at least two months that someone would be making the trip, and Echols and his crew had drawn the lucky number. At least the layover wouldn't put them too far behind on their scheduled run to Centauri.

Unless, of course, the Bellerophon office had screwed up, which also happened more frequently than he could have preferred. In fact, he had a bet with the purser over just how FUBARed the paperwork would be this time. Which he would be learning sometime in the next fifteen hours or so. In the meantime, all he could do was wait for the inevitable, and he nodded acknowledgment of Michaels's report, then looked back down at his pad.

Surely there had to be *some* way he could save his queen's castle!

"Hi, Alaksiej," Captain Viktor Nedergaard said as Alaksiej Litvak's image appeared on his comm. "What do you need?"

"I'm afraid we're running a little late, Vic," Litvack said.

"Oh?" Nedergaard cocked his head with a merely inquisitive smile, but it wasn't easy to smile naturally. As the head of Konstantinos Xeneas's personal security detail, Nedergaard really disliked hiccups in the president's schedule at any time, and especially today. "How late do you think?"

"Probably less than fifteen minutes," Litvack replied, and unlike Nedergaard, he allowed an edge of disgust into his grimace. "The hangup's at Admiral Adamovič's end."

"I see. Is it anything serious?" Nedergaard asked as casually as he could.

"No. Just between you and me, I think Adamovič's dragging ass because she's pissed the Governor is 'dragging her down' to Kórinthos. As a loyal member of the Federation Marines, I'll deny that under oath, you understand."

"Oh, I understand!" Nedergaard said with a chuckle that was only slightly forced.

Litvack might be a Marine, but he'd headed System Governor

Mollie Ramsay's security team for almost three years, and he and
Nedergaard had established a solid, professional relationship that
had segued into personal friendship. They understood one another
well, and Nedergaard wasn't at all happy about what was about
to happen. On the other hand—

"Okay, I'll advise the front gate that you'll be a little late," he
said. "Just make sure you get here before the baklava gets cold!"

"*Cold* baklava?!" Litvack shuddered. "Talk about a way to
motivate somebody! See you in a few."

"Don't forget the *Lucille Anderman* is due in today, Angie,"
Quincy Rogers said, and Angelica Lewis hid a smile.

She really liked Rogers, and for a Heart, he was easy to work
with . . . usually. He was a worrywart, though, when normal shipping routes were disordered. A certain degree of that came with
his job as Devinger Freight Lines' VP for Freight Management,
but he was one of those people who always had trouble delegating,
and that could get out of hand when his routine was disturbed.
As DFL's Warehouse Manager, Lewis got a better look at that
than a lot of their people did.

"I haven't forgotten, Quincy," she said. "In fact, Jordan pinged
me about an hour ago." Jordan Dupree was DFL's chief communications officer in Bellerophon. "System Command just put
out a routine notification that there's an incoming wormhole
signature. A little early for our girl, but I'm willing to bet it's
her." She shrugged. "In fact, it's just about got to be, since it's the
only signature out there at the moment. She should be dropping
sublight in about another four and a half hours."

"Good morning, Mollie," Konstantinos Xeneas said, rising
along with everyone else in the briefing room buried under
Ithaca House, to greet Governor Ramsay as Erasmia Samarili
escorted her, Rear Admiral Adamovič, and Captain Aguayo into
it. Major Litvak, the Marine commander of Ramsay's protective
detail, trailed along behind.

"Good morning," Ramsay replied as she crossed to the table
to shake Xeneas's offered hand. Samarili waited till the president
had waved for Ramsay and all the others to be seated, then
poured a glass of ice water for the system governor, and Ramsay
smiled at her.

"Don't forget dinner Tuesday," she said, and Samarili nodded with a smile of her own. Then she withdrew, and Ramsay turned back to the system president with a politely raised eyebrow.

"Your memo said it was urgent," she said.

Ramsay was ten years younger than Xeneas, with the slenderness of someone who'd grown up on a low-grav planet, and her brown eyes were dark with obvious concern. Her family was well placed in the Five Hundred, but she was both a naturally compassionate woman and one willing to see what was before her own eyes, and she'd been the Bellerophon System's governor for almost eleven years. She'd put down deep roots here, and she knew as well as any native Odyssian that even though Bellerophon was an atypical Fringe system in a lot of ways, it still had far too many bones to pick with the federal government and the Heart Worlds in general. She'd done her best to ameliorate the more egregious abuses, but she was only too well aware that the situation in the Fringe in general had grown steadily worse with each passing year.

"I'm afraid 'urgent' is probably putting it lightly," Xeneas said heavily.

"Why, if I may ask, Mr. President?" Admiral Adamovič asked. She was twenty years older than Xeneas, silver-haired, with a stocky build that looked almost chunky beside the taller, slimmer Ramsay, and her blunt features reflected her bulldog attack mentality only too well. "There wasn't a lot of detail in the memo Governor Ramsay shared with me," she added.

"I didn't want to put too many details into it, Admiral," Xeneas said. "For a lot of reasons. Including the fact that I wasn't too sure you'd believe me."

"Believe you about what?"

Adamovič sounded more than a bit impatient, and Xeneas suppressed a grimace. The Admiral was unfortunately well aware of her own connections to the Five Hundred, and *her* attitude towards the Fringe was markedly different from Mollie Ramsay's. She seemed to feel that spending her valuable time to grant a mere star system's president the opportunity to address her was an enormous—and totally unwarranted—sacrifice.

Captain Aguayo, her solid, muscular flag captain, was as much a Heart Worlder as she was, but a flicker of distaste chased itself across his expression as his admiral's tone registered.

"I'm sure President Xeneas is about to tell us that, Admiral."

Ramsay's tone was ever so slightly but unmistakably repressive. She held Adamovič's gaze with her own for a moment, until the Admiral's nostrils flared and she gave a curt nod. Then the governor turned back to Xeneas.

"You were saying, Konstantinos?"

"I was saying that I think this is going to be one of the unhappiest conversations we've ever had," Xeneas replied. "I don't know what messages you may have received from Sol, but we've recently had word from New Dublin, and it's not good."

"Meaning what?" Adamovič said sharply.

"Meaning, Admiral, that New Dublin's gone 'out of compliance,'" Xeneas said flatly.

The admiral's eyes flared wide, and Ramsay sat back in her chair in obvious surprise.

"I knew there were some...concerns about Governor Murphy," she said after a moment, her tone as troubled as her expression. "I had no idea it might have gone *that* far, though!"

"I certainly understand that." Xeneas tipped back his own chair and shook his head, his expression grim. "I don't think anyone ever really 'expects' something like this. But I'm sure you can understand why I might be concerned about the repercussions beyond just New Dublin and Concordia."

"Why should it have any implications for Cyclops?" Adamovič's tone was barely short of peremptory as she threw out the question. It was an obvious challenge, and Xeneas didn't try very hard to hide the contempt in his own expression as he gazed at her.

"Because New Dublin and Concordia aren't the only parts of the Fringe that are more than a little unhappy with the status quo, Admiral." *His* tone was that of an adult explaining something to a particularly slow child. "One may debate the reasons for that, but only a fool would try to pretend it's not a fact."

"Are you—" Adamovič began sharply.

"Admiral!" Ramsay said even more sharply, and Adamovič's head snapped around towards her. From her congested expression, she hovered on the brink of a furious outburst, but Ramsay's brown eyes nailed her.

"You will remember the courtesy due to President Xeneas's office," the governor continued coldly. "There may be sharp differences of opinion, but that doesn't mean those differences aren't *legitimate*, and the President has only stated the obvious. You've seen the same briefings I have, and probably purely military ones I *haven't*. And that means you're as aware as I am—or damned well should be—that what the President's described as 'unhappiness' is rather stronger than that. And, frankly, for quite a few of the Fringe systems, that sentiment is completely justified!"

Adamovič's outraged expression segued into one of shock.

"We're both Heart Worlders," Ramsay told her, "and all too many Heart Worlders never bother to listen to the Fringe at all. I've mentioned the... unwisdom of that attitude in my own reports, and I sometimes wonder if anyone's bothered to review them at all. But if New Dublin's gone out of compliance, I doubt it will be the last system to do so."

"Then the Navy will just have to teach them the error of their ways, Governor!" Adamovič said harshly.

"That may be true," Xeneas said. "For the moment, however, Governor Ramsay has a point. In fact, according to the information that's reached me here in Kórinthos, other systems *have* gone out of compliance. In fact, by the time my informant left New Dublin, virtually the entire Concordia Sector had declared its secession from the Federation and the formation of something called the Free Worlds Alliance." Adamovič looked as if he'd just punched her in the belly, and he continued coldly. "At least a handful of systems from the Acera Sector have announced their intention to join that alliance, and I strongly suspect more will follow."

"And what were the sector pickets doing while all this fucking treason was going on?" Adamovič demanded.

"Mutinying," Xeneas said flatly.

"What?!" Adamovič surged halfway out of her chair, and Aguayo looked as if Xeneas had just slapped him.

"I said they mutinied." Xeneas regarded her coldly. "Apparently, the federal government ordered Admiral Terrence Murphy's arrest shortly after he successfully defended New Dublin against an attack by at least a dozen League carriers. The New Dubliners were... less than pleased by that. They objected, and when they *expressed* their displeasure, an Inspectorate officer sent to arrest him shot and killed the system president in front of several hundred witnesses."

Ramsay stared at him in horror, but he never took his eyes from Adamovič as alternating shock and fury chased themselves across her face.

"After that, it was a bloodbath. Only a handful of the Hoplons and marshals sent to arrest Murphy survived the fiasco—the cluster-fuck, to use my cousin Achilleas's charming phrase—and New Dublin tried them for murder afterward. And hanged them."

"They murdered Federation military and police officers?!"

"No, Admiral. They *executed* them."

"Don't you go splitting hairs with *me*!" Adamovič barked.

"I'm not splitting hairs at all," Xeneas said. "I'm telling you exactly what happened. And that it's spreading."

"Well it's fucking well not spreading *here*!"

"Really?"

Xeneas gazed at her, then tapped his armrest smart screen. Something in his tone caused her eyes to narrow, and Major Litvak's head snapped around, right hand moving towards his hip, as the conference room door opened.

"*Don't*, Alaksiej!" Captain Nedergaard said sharply from behind him. The pistol in the Odyssian's hand was very steady, and the uniformed troopers behind him carried assault rifles.

"I like you a lot," Nedergaard continued. "I really do. But if your hand comes out from under the table with a gun in it, I *will* kill you."

"Are you out of your fucking *mind*?!" Adamovič demanded, surging to her feet. "I'll have you—!"

"Sit *down*, Admiral!" Xeneas snapped. Her head whipped around towards him, and he slammed a hand on the conference tabletop. "Until this minute, I wouldn't have believed you *could* be even stupider than I thought you were! If you can't sit down and control yourself, then Captain Nedergaard and his people will drag your arrogant Heart ass out of this conference room and throw it in a fucking cell!"

Adamovič stared at him in sheer, stunned disbelief.

"Put your ass in that chair *now*!" he barked, and slowly, manifestly against her will, she settled back down.

"As of ninety seconds ago," Xeneas continued then, tapping the earbud in his left ear, "a codeword was passed over the planetary datanet and the Navy's communication channels. That codeword was 'Thermopylae,' and at this moment forces loyal to Bellerophon are disarming all federal personnel anywhere in the system. I can't tell you exactly what's going on aboard your ships, Admiral Adamovič, but given the percentage of Fringers in your ships' companies and how completely and utterly pissed off the Fringe is, I will be astonished if they, too, aren't under Bellerophon control within the next hour or two."

"You *are* insane," Adamovič half whispered. "You have to know how the Oval will respond to this!"

"Konstantinos?" Ramsay's voice was stronger than Adamovič's, but her expression was drawn. "Why are you doing this?"

"Because we don't have a choice, Mollie." He looked at her, his own expression sad. "Because when those idiots killed President Tolmach, they lit a fuse that's about to send the entire Fringe up in flames. There's enough hatred for the Five Hundred and the Heart Worlds out here—enough *well-deserved* hatred—to fuel a hundred New Dublins, and when the rest of the Fringe hears about this, Fringers everywhere will know it's all on the table now. This isn't a top-down rebellion. This is driven from the bottom, and it's only going to spread, and it's only going to get worse. Whatever I might want, I can't stop that, and you and I both know the Five Hundred will respond exactly the way *she*—" he jabbed an index finger at Adamovič "—would have. And this isn't just another Gobelins. This will be entire sectors going 'out of compliance,' and the only answer the Heart will come up with is the iron boot. They'll kill and terrorize anyone who gets in their way, and they'll turn all the rest of us into examples. Tell me you don't know that's what they'll do."

She stared at him, lips trembling ever so slightly, and he shook his head.

"I don't want to kill the Federation," he said softly. "I don't want to shatter its cohesion while we're still at war with the League. But I know what's coming for my star system and my people if I don't stop it. It won't matter what we've done or not done. What will matter is that the Five Hundred will make damned sure no one in the Fringe thinks any 'uppity thoughts' for at least the next two generations, and they will *crush* any semblance of self-rule or freedom we might have clung to.

"And if that's the way it's got to be, so be it. If they're going to hammer us no matter what we do, then I am going to do my damnedest to protect my star system—my *home*—from the barbarians out to burn it to the fucking ground. From what I'm hearing, we aren't the only star system and hers—" he jerked his head at Adamovič "—aren't the only carriers who'll be signing up for the same fight. It's possible, maybe even likely, some or all of us will get smashed flat for the temerity of defending ourselves and our homes and our families. I'm sure quite a few of us will get killed, along the way. But if we do, we do, and there are a hell of a lot worse reasons for dying."

His eyes bored into hers, and he drew a deep breath.

"I'm not going to ask you to do anything that would violate your own conscience," he said. "But you know as well as I do what the balance of power between the local authorities and the federal organs here in Bellerophon really is. I'm asking you to ask your people to stand down. We don't want anyone injured or killed if we can possibly avoid it. I promise you, on my personal word of honor, that none of your people will be mistreated if they do stand down. If they don't, though, I'm afraid it will get even uglier than it has to. So, will you accept that we *are* going out of compliance and work with me to maintain domestic order here in Bellerophon, at least until we find out how Sol is going to react?"

Quincy Rogers frowned as his desk comm warbled a priority attention signal. The initial signal transmuted into a sharp, syncopated five-note chime, and his frown abruptly deepened. That was the personal comm tone of Senior Vice President Timothy Lattimore, the most senior man in the DFL's Bellerophon hierarchy. That made Lattimore a very big fish in the sprawling transstellar's upper echelons, but he seldom bothered himself with Devinger's day-to-day routine. His background was more fiscal than operational, so he left most of that to Rogers. Besides, like too many other junior members of the Five Hundred, he preferred wining and dining the local bigwigs to anything remotely like work.

All of which meant Rogers could count the number of times he'd received a priority call from his boss on his thumbs.

He stabbed the acceptance, and his eyes widened abruptly as Lattimore appeared on the display. The one descriptor he'd always applied to Lattimore was "well groomed," but today he was in a T-shirt and exercise shorts, and the hair that was normally perfectly coiffed looked like a hayrick. More to the point, his regular expression of genial arrogance looked more like a mask of terror.

"Rogers!" he snapped as soon as the image stabilized. "What have you heard from Traffic Control?!"

"Nothing." Rogers shook his head, his own expression confused. "Why?"

"Jesus! Don't any of you have a news channel running over there?!"

"No, of course not," Rogers replied. That was a point Lattimore had made in his initial "I'm the new hardass in charge" memo to all hands when he first arrived in-system. Devinger Freight Lines wasn't paying its people to sit around watching entertainment or newsfeeds on office time.

Rogers considered mentioning that, but only briefly.

"Why?" he asked instead. "What's going on?"

"The entire goddamn system's gone insane, that's what!" Lattimore bared his teeth in a grimace no one would have called a smile. "The UPF and the SDF are taking over every federal office and agency in the system at gunpoint! And Xeneas's gone on an all-feed cast and announced Bellerophon is seceding from the Federation!"

"*What?*" Rogers stared at him in disbelief for a heartbeat, then shook himself violently. "They have to be crazy! Admiral Adamovič and Governor Ramsay will never stand for that!"

"Adamovič's in custody," Lattimore grated. "And they may be crazy, but that doesn't mean they didn't think this shit through. It sounds like Xeneas invited her and Ramsay to an 'emergency conference' here in Kórinthos specifically to get Adamovič planet-side when her fucking ships *mutinied*. According to Xeneas, all of the carriers, at least, have gone over to the rebels!"

"That's . . . that's impossible," Rogers stammered while his brain sought to grasp the enormity of what Lattimore had said.

"The fact that there are no K-strikes headed for any of the System Defense Force's bases suggests it's not!" Lattimore snapped.

"Wait. Wait. You said Xeneas had both Adamovič and the Governor? He's got proof of that?"

"I don't know about Adamovič, but he's damn straight got *Ramsay*," Lattimore snarled. "The traitorous bitch's gone over to *his* side!"

"What?!"

"Listen for yourself!"

Lattimore tapped his own comm and a recorded newsfeed replaced his image. Mollie Ramsay looked out of the display, her expression taut and strained.

"I urge all citizens to remain calm," she said. "As President

Xeneas's announcement indicates, events here in Bellerophon are moving far too quickly for anyone to be able to control or predict at this point. I fully understand that there are deep reservoirs of frustration and, yes, anger here in the Fringe. And, to be fair, many Fringers are fully justified in feeling both frustration and anger. But I ask all of you, those who might support the notion of secession and the many loyal citizens who might oppose it, to show restraint. I have no idea where this may all end, or whether or not some... negotiated solution can be reached. But this I *do* know: killing one another will solve *nothing*.

"In order to prevent any avoidable bloodshed, I am ordering all federal personnel in Bellerophon, military and civilian, to stand down. All any of you can accomplish at this point is to die for the Federation, and I would vastly prefer for you to *live* for it. Obviously, when Prime Minister Schleibaum's government learns of events here, she will have to determine policy going forward, and I am as anxious as any of you could possibly be about where that will end. But I don't intend to rush to meet that moment, either. So, I say again. Stand down. Somehow, someway, one way or the other, we will get through this, and I pray it can be accomplished without mass bloodshed."

Her image disappeared, replaced by Lattimore's, and Rogers rubbed his mouth numbly, trying to process what he'd just seen.

"Well?" Lattimore demanded. "What are we going to do about this?!"

"I don't see anything we *can* do," Rogers said after a moment. "We've got maybe sixty armed cops for warehouse security. That's *it*. If the Governor's ordering all of her people to lay down their guns, there's not a damn thing our people can do!"

"But... but they'll seize the company!"

Rogers stared at him in disbelief. Seize the company? *That* was what the idiot was worried about?!

"If they do, they do," he said after a moment. "And, with all due respect, I'm a little more worried about the other places this could go. Have none of these people ever heard of Gobelins?!"

Lattimore's face froze. Then he swallowed visibly, and Rogers shook his head. Jesus. The idiot hadn't even thought about that!

"But—" Lattimore swallowed again. "But... surely there's something we can do," he said almost feebly.

Rogers glowered at him, but then his own eyes narrowed.

"I don't see anything we can do here in Bellerophon," he said. "But, maybe..."

He punched the screen, cavalierly dropping Lattimore's call, and tapped another comm combination. A moment later, Angelica Lewis appeared on the display.

"Hello, Quincy," she said cheerfully. "What can I do for you?"

"Get on the news channels," he said tersely. "Pull down a record of everything from the last... two hours. Then zip it and get it to Jordan. I've got a signal to send!"

"Skipper, I think you'd better hear this."

Tobias Echols looked up sharply. He'd never heard quite that note in Trent Hollis's voice before, and he spun his command chair towards the communications officer's station.

"Hear what?"

"Hear *this*, Skip," Hollis replied, and the main holo display flicked alive.

"This is Quincy Rogers," the man on that display said. "I'm attaching critical news footage to this message. You are instructed to divert immediately—I repeat, *immediately*—and transit directly to the Sol System. The instant you arrive there, you will relay this message to the federal authorities. I cannot overstress the importance of this."

He looked out of the display grimly, then closed his eyes.

"The Bellerophon System has gone out of compliance," he said flatly. "A far as I know, all federal organs and agencies in the system have been taken over by the system government, and the picket task force has apparently mutinied in support of the Bellerophon government."

Echols felt his own expression congeal like cold gravy. Rogers couldn't have said what he'd just heard! He just... couldn't have. But—

"You're the only ship in a position to get out of here with the news. Don't blow it!"

The screen blanked, and Echols shook himself, then looked back at Hollis.

"That was tight beam, right?" he demanded.

"There's a limit to how 'tight' *any* transmission can be at this range, Skip." Hollis shrugged. "It wasn't omnidirectional, if that's what you mean."

"That's exactly what I mean," Echols replied, and looked at Cordelia Turner, his first officer. She looked as stunned as he felt, but unlike Tobias Echols, she was also a Fringer, and he watched as emotions raced across her face. Then she closed her eyes. She sat that way for a moment, strapped into her bridge chair in *Lucy Anne*'s zero-gravity, then inhaled deeply and looked back at her skipper.

"I guess we have it to do," she said heavily.

"Sorry, Cordy," Echols said as gently as he could.

"Not your fault they've all gone crazy," she sighed.

"No, but still."

He shook his head and looked at Antonia Michaels.

"What do we have, Antonia?"

"Been crunching the numbers," she said, "and I think we're good."

"Even if the carriers really have gone over and one of them tries to intercept?"

"Unless they're way the hell and gone out-system and started the instant Bellerophon Astro picked up our footprint, there's not much way they could," Michaels pointed out, and Echols grunted.

Lucy Anne had gone sublight two and a half hours ago. Her commercial-grade Fasset drive's normal acceleration rate outside a Powell Limit was 750 gravities, although she could hit 925 if he maxed the nodes. Because it was so low, she had to begin her deceleration run from farther out than a warship would have, and the Bellerophon Powell limit's radius was a hefty 58.3 LM. So she'd come out of wormhole space 391.43 LM from the system primary, 333.13 LM from the Powell Limit and 378.43 LM from Odysseus. At the moment, she was down to a velocity of 230,805 KPS and still over three and a half light-hours from the limit, which meant Rogers's message had been sent six hours before she went sublight. Outside a Powell Limit, a TFN carrier's maximum acceleration was 1,800 gravities—more than that if she redlined her nodes—but at six and a half light-hours, a star system was a *very* big haystack. So Michaels was right. Unless they'd happened to have an FTLC right on top of them, relatively speaking, there was no way anyone could intercept *Lucy Anne*.

"Trent says it started out as a laser, not a general broadcast," he said. "So unless someone strayed into its path, they don't even know he sent it. Or they didn't *when* he sent it, at least. If we go back to max accel, how short of the limit do we break back into wormhole space?"

"About two light-hours," Michaels replied, and Echols nodded. It was remotely possible that an FTLC that had headed out to intercept them the moment their footprint was reported could generate an intercept, but the odds against it were astronomical. Of course, they'd be on completely the wrong heading for a least-time course to Sol. They'd have to decelerate back into n-space, find the right vector, and accelerate again, which would delay their arrival.

One the other hand, they *would* arrive, and he was willing to bet no one in Bellerophon had factored *that* into their planning when they set all this up. And that meant . . .

"Do it, Antonia," he said flatly.

CHAPTER FIVE

TFNS **Ishtar**
Wormhole Space
October 13, 2552

"TWO MORE SHIP DAYS TO JALAL," A VOICE OBSERVED QUIETLY, and Terrence Murphy glanced up at the auburn-haired Navy captain floating beside his command chair. Harrison O'Hanraghty looked back expressionlessly, and Murphy snorted silently.

It was quiet on TFNS *Ishtar*'s flag bridge as the four-kilometer-long carrier tore through wormhole space, but he could feel the tension hovering about him, and he understood it perfectly.

Ishtar wasn't alone. Eleven other faster-than-light carriers shared her pocket of subspace, and that was the reason for the flag bridge's tension. Technically, every single crewman and crewwoman aboard those ships, and aboard all of the sublight warships riding their parasite racks, was a mutineer. Or, at least, they were there obedient to the orders of someone they knew would be *declared* a mutineer—if he hadn't been already—as soon as the Federation learned about what they were about to do.

Two more ship days. Fourteen days, by the rest of the universe's clocks. That was how long they had before the Federation officially pinned the traitor's label upon them all.

Twelve carriers and almost a hundred and fifty sublight capital ships represented a massive concentration of fighting power, far greater than anyone had seen in one place in the Fringe in generations. There were, however, two hundred and ninety FTLCs—and enough sublight warships to fill their racks thrice over—on the Federation's order of battle. At any given moment, a quarter of those carriers were in yard hands for repairs or scheduled maintenance. Another forty-five percent were deployed to the battle line systems of the Beta Cygni Line, the 470-light-year "front" along which the Federation and League had been locked in combat for decades, and ten percent were retained to cover the Heart World systems and serve as the Federation's strategic reserve. The remaining fifty-odd FTLCs were deployed as picket forces covering positions in the Fringe, mostly in the enormous hemisphere on the far side of the Federation from Beta Cygni.

Ostensibly, they were there to protect the Fringe Worlds from the ships of the Rénzú Liánméng Hǎijūn, more commonly known by its foes as the Terran League Navy. In fact, that was a purely secondary function in the eyes of the Federation government and the Five Hundred, the Heart Worlds' political and economic elite who controlled that government. The pickets' true mission, from the Five Hundred's perspective, was control. To ensure that the numerous but sparsely populated Fringe Worlds who possessed precious little economic and even less political power yet provided the bulk of the Federation's military manpower—and had done most of the dying in the Federation's six-decade war against the League—stayed "in compliance." Oh, those pickets had been expected to fight, even die, in defense of *some* Fringe systems. The beta and gamma-tier systems that housed nodes of industrial power, orbital refineries, shipyards owned by absentee Heart World landlords. The ones that were *important*. But the other Fringe systems? The ones that housed not valuable properties but only the odd million, or even fewer, Federation citizens?

The enormous carriers were strategic assets, and those assets were worth far more than *those* systems. Their standing orders were to withdraw in the face of any powerful attack. Just as Captain Yance Drebin had, when he'd left three quarters of a million men, women, and children to die on a blasted, wintry world in the Inverness System. A world whose infrastructure had been reduced to rubble by a League raiding squadron he'd refused to face, even though his own ships had actually outmassed it. Indeed, Drebin hadn't simply used that standing order to justify his cowardice in the face of the actual attack. He'd used it again, even after Admiral Xing Xuefeng's withdrawal, when he'd abandoned the system entirely.

And left the survivors of Xing's bombardment to watch their children freeze to death in front of them.

Ninety-six percent of them had done precisely that.

If not for Terrence Murphy, *all* of them would have died. Murphy would never—ever—forgive himself for the fact that he'd been able to rescue fewer than fifty thousand people, but at least he'd managed that much after Drebin abandoned them to slow, lingering death. And, again if not for Terrence Murphy, none of Drebin's superiors would have faulted his actions. Especially not if condemning those actions might have drawn his carefully never discussed standing orders into the public's view. Besides, it wasn't as if a marginal system like Inverness had *mattered*.

Murphy knew how that worked, knew how the Five Hundred thought. He was a member of the Five Hundred, and he had no illusions about the system into which he'd been born. And because he had none, he knew exactly what the Five Hundred most feared. They feared an exhausted, embittered, enraged Fringe, gaunt with starvation and abuse, crushed by the grief of unending casualty lists, fully aware that they and the people they loved were supremely unimportant to a Five Hundred concerned with bottom lines, their own wealth and power and comfort. They feared what that Fringe might do to those who had exploited and abused it for so very long.

And they feared, above all things, the emergence of some warlord who would draw the sword of all that rage from the stone of the Fringe's loyalty and tear the Federation asunder. They told themselves it was because such a rebellion would lead to defeat at the League's hands, but deep in the secret part of their hearts, what they truly feared was the long-deferred, righteous retribution the Fringe would visit upon them.

That was what made Murphy's dozen FTLCs so dangerous to the Five Hundred. They represented barely five percent of the TFN's total carrier strength. But they constituted almost forty percent of the FTLCs deployed to the Southern Lobe, and every single one of them was "out of compliance."

The Five Hundred didn't know it yet. So far as they knew, he had only the seven FTLCs he'd commandeered for the Battle of New Dublin. He'd dutifully reported that battle, and everything leading up to it, and he'd sent a follow-up report after his return from the Diyu System. But that had been before the disastrous attempt to arrest him . . . and before Alan Tolmach's murder.

He was grimly certain how they would react when they did

find out, because those twelve ships, and the sublight battleships and battlecruisers riding their parasite racks, were the Five Hundred's worst nightmare. Not because of their raw combat power, but because of the reason they were there. Because Rear Admiral Terrence Murphy had disobeyed a direct order to withdraw from the New Dublin System and abandon the hundred million citizens of Crann Bethadh, New Dublin's inhabited planet. Because he'd not simply stood and fought but used his authority as system governor to commandeer four more FTLCs to bolster his own three-carrier task force. Because, worse, he'd used that same authority to authorize the shipyards in New Dublin to manufacture thousands of missiles to be used in the system's defense. Worse yet, he'd evolved a new, deadly tactical doctrine to *use* those thousands of missiles.

For the first time in at least two generations, a Heart World admiral had put his duty to the Federation's *citizens* above his duty to the Five Hundred. And in the process, he'd laid bare a fact the Five Hundred had overlooked, an unintended consequence of allowing the Fringe to do the dying while their own sons and daughters evaded that grim toll. More than two thirds of the men and women who crewed *all* of its ships were also Fringers. Fringers whose abused loyalty might prove the whetted edge of that warlord's blade.

No wonder the government had ordered his arrest as soon as it learned about the Battle of New Dublin, ordered that he be returned to the Sol System in chains to face trial on trumped-up charges for his manifold "crimes." That decision hadn't surprised Murphy. Not really. He'd long since learned how stupid otherwise intelligent people could be if their prejudices, their beliefs, their bigotries—or, far worse, their view of themselves as masters of creation—were threatened. Anyone who'd accomplished what he had, who'd given a face and a voice to the Fringe's abuse and anger—who threatened their own power and control—*had* to be discredited.

So they'd sent the orders, only to discover that the Federation—or the Five Hundred, at least—had finally pushed the Crann Bethadhans too far.

The Five Hundred couldn't know that yet. The travel time for any news from New Dublin to reach Earth was just over eleven weeks, by the clocks of the galaxy at large. For the actual traveler, moving at .99 *c*, the subjective time was just under one week, of course. But that meant the Five Hundred had known it would take almost five and a half months for Captain Andrew Lipshen and the Capital Division troopers they'd sent to New Dublin to return to Sol with their prisoner. Until they did, no one in the Heart Worlds could know how their mission had fared.

It had taken far less time for New Dublin's neighbors to find out, however, and *their* reaction had justified every one of the Five Hundred's fears.

Murphy had tried to stop the tsunami of secession declarations, but he'd known even then that he'd have fared better ordering the tide not to come in. He might have refused to acknowledge the Free Worlds Alliance as an independent star nation, yet he had no choice but to admit the legitimacy of its demands. And so he'd become the "Governor" of a breakaway batch of secessionists who were at least willing—for now—to follow his lead. To let him speak for them.

The best he could hope was that he might be able to ride the wave front of the Fringe's totally justified fury, be a voice of moderation that might somehow broker a rapprochement between it and its hated victimizers. But he was afraid, terribly afraid, that even that hope was doomed. And one thing he did know for certain: the creation of the Free Worlds Alliance, including all of what had been the Concordia Sector and a half dozen systems from the neighboring Acera and Tremont sectors, would *not* play well on Earth.

The question—or *one* of the questions, at any rate—burning in Murphy's mind was what other measures might have been put in train at the same time Lipshen was dispatched to arrest him. For all their shortsighted arrogance, the members of Prime Minister Schleibaum's government in Olympia weren't truly stupid. Or, rather, they *were* stupid, but it was the monumentally self-destructive stupidity only otherwise intelligent people could achieve. The sort of stupidity that could almost always make a catastrophe worse by convincing itself of its own cunning and cleverness. Considering the stakes for which they were playing—or *thought* they were playing, anyway—there was no way Lipshen's mission could have been the only string to their bow. They must have instructed Admiral Fokaides and the Oval to take additional "precautionary" measures, and at the moment, Murphy had no idea what those measures might have been.

On the other hand, *they* couldn't know—yet—what measures *he'd* taken.

But that was about to change. Probably for both sides.

Jalal Station, just over halfway from Sol to New Dublin, was one of the five, widely spaced major bases built to support the naval pickets of the Fringe. In particular, Jalal was designed to support operations in the Southern Lobe: Concordia, Acera, Tremont, and the Claremont Sector. That meant Lipshen had staged through Jalal on his way to New Dublin and that the Five Hundred would have assumed he—or any news of his mission, at least—would follow the same path back to Sol.

And that, in turn, meant any naval forces sent to backstop Lipshen would also flow through Jalal.

Murphy glanced at the digital time display.

One more day, and then we'll know, he thought. *Then we'll know.*

CHAPTER SIX

Jack's Steakhouse
City of Olympia
Old Terra
Sol System
Terran Federation
October 15, 2552

"YOU'RE LATE," LEOPOLD OSIECKI OBSERVED AS THE REAL LIVE human waiter seated the attractive Asiatic woman across the table from him.

"So sue me," Kawaguchi Kurumi said sweetly, and Osiecki chuckled. Very few of his employees would have taken that tone with him, but then very few of them had been with him as long as she had or were as good at their jobs as she was at hers.

Of course, there were some additional factors in play in her case.

"Would you care to view the menu, Sir?" the waiter asked, half-extending the slate tucked under his arm.

"Please, Gordon." Osiecki rolled his blue eyes. "*How* long have we been coming in here?"

"Eight years, I believe, Sir," Gordon replied with a small smile.

"I'm pretty sure we have the menu down by now, then. I'll have my usual. Kurumi?"

"I think I'll have the Lomo Saltado today," she said. "And some of those delicious yeast rolls of yours, Gordon."

"Excellent choice," Gordon said with a broader smile. "Salad?"

"Yes, I think. With peppercorn dressing. And sweetened iced tea, please."

"Of course. And just to be sure, Mr. Osiecki, for you braised tenderloin, blue rare, with baked potato—butter, no sour cream—steamed broccoli, a side salad with balsamic vinaigrette, and a stein of Kielce lager."

"Exactly." Osiecki nodded, and the waiter filled their ice water glasses and disappeared, leaving them in the quiet alcove that was permanently reserved at Jack's Steakhouse for Osiecki Enterprises's senior executives.

There were several interesting features built into that alcove, the most important of which were the most sophisticated anti-snooping systems Federation technology could build. Not that anyone would have been surprised to discover that. After all, Osiecki Enterprises was widely—and with reason—regarded as the Sol System's most efficient and effective industrial security firm. Most people knew that. What a much smaller and highly select clientele knew was that in addition to its sterling credentials in industrial *security*, Osiecki Enterprises was also the most accomplished industrial *espionage* firm in the system.

Leopold Osiecki had spent thirty years of his life building that firm, and those who employed him as their industrial spy automatically received the services of his security arm, as well, plus a guarantee that he wouldn't be spying on them. Mostly. There had been occasions upon which one or more members of the Five Hundred had taken umbrage over his...acquisition of proprietary information and processes for one or more of their competitors, but he was far too valuable for them to squash. And he was an honest broker, whose services were available to all.

What not even that smaller and select clientele knew, of course, was that Leopold Osiecki—who hadn't thought of himself as Huang Jiang in almost forty years—wasn't what he seemed. For that matter, despite the splendidly official birth certificate on file for her in the ancient city of Tokyo, neither was Kawaguchi Kurumi, who'd actually been born Ryom Jung-Soo in the Uromachi System.

They were, in fact, the Tè Lā Lián Méng's two most highly placed spies in the Federation.

They made small talk until Gordon returned with their drink orders and their salads. Then Osiecki tapped the smart panel in the tabletop to bring up the privacy systems. All sound from the rest of the restaurant disappeared instantly, and he leaned back slightly in his chair.

"And what brings us here today?"

His tone was pleasant, but his eyes—those blue eyes, which had earned him so much boyhood grief and bullying as a *"gwáijái"* on the planet Tu Di Ye—were focused and intent. One of his ironclad rules was that he never discussed League business in any of Osiecki Enterprises's offices. One of the quid pro quos of his "industrial espionage" activities was that Federation intelligence got to keep an eye on those activities, and he was perfectly happy to provide the Central Intelligence Directorate and the Federal Bureau of Investigation—even the Hand—with complete access. In fact, he'd helped them out on several occasions, including pointing them at more than one anti-war group's efforts to sabotage critical war industries.

All of which, in combination, meant that both CID and the FBI knew exactly who Leopold Osiecki was and what he did for a living. And that Osiecki Enterprises passed its semiannual security background checks with ludicrous ease.

It also meant that anything related to what he *really* did for a living was passed on primarily by word of mouth in public settings no serious spy would ever even consider. There were, of course, conduits for passing electronic messages and even dead drops for old-fashioned physical letters, but those operated through a dizzying level of cutouts with which he never had any personal contact.

"I talked to O'Casey," "Kawaguchi" said now. "He says the leak about Murphy's been confirmed and the Five Hundred's panicking."

"Confirmed?" Osiecki frowned. "Confirmed how?"

Benjamin O'Casey was one of Kawaguchi's crown jewels, although he was also a bit of a two-edged sword. He'd begun working for Osiecki Enterprises as a junior engineer in the powerful Dawson family's Astro Engineering transstellar almost twenty years ago, and he was smart, capable, and supremely unencumbered by anything remotely resembling a principle. He'd also figured out about ten years ago that there was rather more to Osiecki Enterprises than the Federation at large suspected. By then, though, he'd been in too deep—delivered too much proprietary military R&D data that had made its way to the League—to turn state's evidence. Oh, he might have been able to avoid the death sentence by testifying for the prosecution, but that was far from a given, whereas the probability that Osiecki would have him killed if he even looked like talking to the FBI approached one hundred percent. On the other hand, Osiecki was prepared to pay him even more handsomely than before and promised him relocation to a life of luxury on one of the more affluent feral worlds out beyond the Blue Line within the next twenty-five years or so.

Under the circumstances, he'd opted for continued employment, and he was worth every penny Osiecki had ever paid him. Not only was he smart and unscrupulous, he'd also risen to the assistant directorship of Astro Engineering's Energy Weapons Division. The information he'd provided over the years hadn't been spectacular; it had only been priceless to its recipients.

That was what worried Osiecki now. O'Casey was far too valuable—and knew far too much—to be compromised pushing for more data on something as speculative as the rumors about Terrence Murphy.

"We're talking about O'Casey, Leopold," Kawaguchi said dryly. "The next time he sticks his neck out for us will also be the *first* time he sticks his neck out for us."

Osiecki snorted, because she had a point. In truth, O'Casey had put his neck on the line at least half a dozen times over the years, but only after careful thought and very, very cautiously. And for *extremely* high bonuses.

"All right, that's a given," he acknowledged. "But the question stands: What kind of confirmation are we talking about?"

"It's—"

A buzzer sounded quietly, and Kawaguchi broke off, glancing over her shoulder as the alcove's privacy curtain opened and Gordon walked in with their salads, her tea, and Osiecki's beer. After so many years, Jack's staff knew the drill as well as Osiecki and his senior employees did. They wouldn't have dreamed of interrupting such old, valued, and high-tipping customers without first warning them.

Food and drink transferred smoothly from Gordon's tray to the tabletop. He glanced around, double-checking everything, then withdrew, and Kawaguchi picked up her fork.

"He and Kleinmueller were called in to brief Dawson personally on the grav-lens focusing project," she said then, and Osiecki nodded.

Judson Kleinmueller was O'Casey's boss over at Energy Weapons, and if they ever got the bugs out of the gravitically focused lasers they'd been working on for the last six years or so, it would increase energy engagement ranges dramatically.

"Anyway, they were briefing Dawson when she got a call. It was from one of her contacts in the Oval. Somebody in Fokaides's staff, if I had to guess. And she didn't bother to shoo them out of the room when she took it."

Kawaguchi scooped up a forkful of salad, chewed, and swallowed. Osiecki was fully aware that the delay was deliberate. The twinkle in her eye would have told him that, even if he hadn't already known her so well. And, since he was aware, he simply waited as if he'd never noticed a thing.

"Anyway," she said with a smile that acknowledged he'd won the round, "apparently Murphy's official report's come in. O'Casey didn't get a look at it, of course, but Dawson was excited enough—and kept interrupting whoever had called often enough—that he thinks he got most of the high points."

"Which are?"

"Which are," Kawaguchi's smile disappeared, "that, according to Murphy, he defeated an attack in strength on New Dublin. If Dawson's informant's to be believed, Murphy claims to have defeated a twelve-carrier task force . . . and destroyed at least eight of them."

"What?!"

Even Leopold Osiecki's formidable self-control could waver on occasion, and Kawaguchi nodded grimly as he stared at her in shock.

"Dawson thinks—or claimed she did while she was shouting at whoever was on the other end of her comm—that Murphy's lying about the numbers. He was already in deep trouble—you know how sensitive they all are to the possibility of Fringe systems going 'out of compliance'!—so Dawson's theory is that he's inventing the entire thing, or at least exaggerating it hugely, to cover his ass."

"That doesn't sound like everything we've heard about Murphy going into this," Osiecki said slowly.

"No, but aside from his family name, he wasn't exactly front and center on our radar before he got handed New Dublin, either, now was he?" Kawaguchi shrugged. "He's married into the Thakore family, so he's got pretty good connections in the Five Hundred, but he's still an outsider in a lot of ways. And it looks like he's been systematically pissing them off ever since that business at Inverness."

Osiecki grimaced. Inverness left a bad taste in his mouth every time he thought about it.

Like his cover name, the blue eyes and fair coloration that had caused him so much grief as a child—and which served him so well as a spy—were the legacy of his mother's family. And the only reason Faustyna Osiecka had ended up in the Terran League and married to Huang ShenKang instead of living in the Terran Federation was that the League had rescued her parents' family from the Godlewski System in 2350, long before the war against the Federation had begun. Janosik, Godlewski's sole habitable planet, had always been tectonically active, but no one had been prepared for the yearslong cycle of earthquakes, tsunamis, and volcanic outgassing that had destroyed that habitability. The casualty totals had been horrific, and Godlewski had lain on the very fringe of the Federation, far closer to Anyang, the League's capital system, than to Sol. And so a huge infusion of *baakgwai* genetic material had been abruptly injected into the nearby Wutai System.

Including the Osiecki family, which had embraced its new home with the patriotic fervor of refugees who knew exactly who'd saved them all from death.

That was the legacy of the League Leopold Osiecki liked to recall, the difference between the League and the Five Hundred, who would cheerfully have written off any of the Federation's Fringe Worlds the same way they'd ignored Janosik all those years ago. What that butcher Xing had done to Inverness…that was what the *Federation* did, not his star nation!

"Of course he's pissing them off," he said now. "The last thing the Five Hundred can afford is for someone to demonstrate the legitimacy of the Fringe's resentment. And I wonder how many of them are thinking about his family name while they're being so pissed? I tend to doubt old Henrik would have had much patience with their policies in the Fringe."

"Doesn't look like his grandson does, either." Kawaguchi's voice was a little indistinct as she chewed salad, and she swallowed, then sipped tea. "From the looks of things, he actually thinks a system governor is supposed to defend the system he's governing."

"You think there's anything to the Five Hundred's warlord suspicions?"

"Our other sources on that are probably as good as anything O'Casey's turning up, but, on balance, I genuinely don't think so."

Kawaguchi shook her head. "I think he really is Don Quixote, to be honest."

Osiecki snorted.

"If he is, the Five Hundred's a hell of a lot more likely to kill him than *we* are," he said. "Especially if he really did defeat that many of our carriers!"

"I'm inclined to doubt he did," Kawaguchi replied. "Oh, I think he probably did win an engagement, and if Dawson's end of the conversation O'Casey overheard is accurate, I'm pretty sure Second Admiral Xing was in command when he did it. Frankly, just between you and me, that wouldn't exactly break my heart. What she did at Inverness is only going to justify the next Federation K-strike. And then we'll retaliate for that. And they'll retaliate for the retaliation. And before you know it, we'll be killing the odd million civilians at the drop of a hat all over again."

She would not, Osiecki reflected, have said anything remotely like that to one of their joint superiors. On the other hand, their nearest joint superior was in the Cairo System, almost 360 light-years from Sol, and it was a sign of how much she trusted him—and how well she understood the way his own mind worked—that she was willing to say it to him.

"So why do you think he exaggerated the numbers?"

"Do you mean why do I think the numbers had to be exaggerated, or why do I think he chose to exaggerate them?"

"Both."

"Leopold, we both know how tight things are along the Beta Cygni Line. Do you really think the Rénzú Liánméng Hǎijūn's in a position to cut a *dozen* FTLCs loose to hit a secondary—at best—system like New Dublin?" Kawaguchi shook her head again. "I just don't see any way that many of our carriers could've been swanning around out in Concordia. We know Xing had at least a couple of them when she hit Inverness, and she could have picked up two or three more, but there's no way Navy Command would've committed more than four or five to a target like New Dublin."

She paused, head cocked, and he nodded slowly.

"Well," she continued, "even four or five of them would have been a nasty handful for a typical Fed system picket, so Murphy has plenty of justification for patting himself on the back if he held his ground in the face of an attack like that. But unless I miss my guess, he's probably pretty well aware of what the Five Hundred's been cooking up for him ever since he started looking like a 'non-compliance' poster boy. So, since he controls all the sensor records and tac data from the battle, why not pump the numbers up a little bit to try and get some of the heat turned down a notch or two?"

"Makes sense," Osiecki conceded. "I wish we had some way to confirm that, though."

"I'm checking all of my other sources—discreetly, of course," she said. "But the best we're likely to manage is to confirm what he reported, not whether or not what he reported is accurate."

"I know."

Osiecki looked down into his beer stein, turning it on the table, then looked back up at her.

"See what you can turn up in the next couple of days," he said. "Don't push too hard! I know you, and you can get carried away by your own enthusiasm. Like you say, the best we can do is to confirm what he's reported, and it's not worth risking losing you—or even just one of your sources—for something that . . . indeterminate. But I've got a courier headed out for Uromachi day after tomorrow. I'd like to send along anything we've been able to confirm—or not—when he goes."

"Understood."

Kawaguchi nodded and addressed herself to her salad once more.

The most frustrating thing about her otherwise satisfactory assignment was how long it took for anything they reported to reach home. Any spy—for that matter, anyone involved in interstellar commerce of any sort—had to factor voyage time into every equation and decision, but that didn't mean she had to like it. Especially when it came to something like this.

She didn't know what Murphy was up to any more than the Five Hundred did, but unlike the Five Hundred, she expected whatever it was to hurt the Terran League more than it would the Federation. God only knew what a truly competent Fed task force commander might do if he was prepared to ignore the Fokaides Directive and actually do his damned job. But while God might be the only one who *knew*, Kawaguchi Kurumi—and Ryom Jung-Soo—strongly suspected she wouldn't like it. In fact, she didn't much like even contemplating the possibilities.

And it was almost eight months from Sol to Uromachi by way of the Cairo System. One hell of a lot of those unpalatable possibilities could happen while their message was in transit.

CHAPTER SEVEN

Jalal System
Terran Federation
October 27, 2552

"SUBLIGHT...NOW," COMMANDER AUGUSTUS CREUZBURG ANNOUNCED, and TFNS *Ishtar* and her consorts blinked back into existence in normal space.

As always, Creuzburg's astrogation had been perfect. Murphy's flagship was just over 151.6 light-minutes from the Jalal System's primary, decelerating at 1,800 KPS^2 as she and her consorts hurtled towards it at 297,000 KPS. Even at that prodigious deceleration rate, it would take them almost six hours to decelerate to rest relative to the star at the point Murphy had christened Point Rubicon, 6.2 LM from the primary and two light-minutes outside the orbit of Jalal Beta, the habitable planet Jalal Station orbited. The station's light-speed sensors wouldn't even see *Ishtar*'s transponder code for more than two and a half hours, although that would be less than twenty-two minutes for *Ishtar*, at her current velocity. By that time, however, she would have decelerated to 131,777 KPS—"only" forty-four percent of light speed—and the relativistic time dilation would have dropped to only about nine percent. At the moment, what her light speed sensors saw was a two-hour peek into the past, and Murphy watched data fill in across the quadrants of the master display.

"No ship IDs, Sir," O'Hanraghty murmured. "Got all the standard nav beacons and general 'information to shipping' transmissions, but not a single Navy beacon. Seems a bit...odd for a place like Jalal, wouldn't you say?"

"Why would you even think that, Harry?" Murphy smiled. "It's not like they didn't know we were coming."

O'Hanraghty grunted something that was a cross between a chuckle and a laugh. They hadn't sent Jalal any ship movement information, but they knew the base's gravitic arrays had spotted their incoming FTL footprint while they were still at least twenty-four light-weeks out. That had given Jalal over four and a half hours to decide what to do when they arrived. And one of the first things *Terrence Murphy* would have done with four and a half hours in hand was to make damned sure any of his mobile assets were as hard to detect as possible.

"No challenges, either, though," Murphy continued, and O'Hanraghty nodded. Just as there'd been ample time for Jalal to shut down its ships' ID beacons, there'd been plenty of time for the station to transmit a light speed challenge they would have received the instant they arrived.

"Gotta wonder about that, Sir," the captain said.

"Why?" the tall, one-eyed lieutenant on the other side of Murphy's command chair asked. "Oh, there's a bunch of things I'm wondering about, Sir," he added when O'Hanraghty raised both eyebrows at him. "The fact that they aren't talking to us isn't as high on my priorities list as some of the other 'wonders' in question, though."

"There are a lot of things they could be saying, Callum," O'Hanraghty said. "Coming in on this heading, they have to have a damned good idea who we are. And the size of our footprint will have told them we've got a lot more carriers than we left with. So I'm not really all that surprised they aren't saying 'Welcome home! Glad to see you!' But they're also not telling us we *aren't* welcome. So the question is why they aren't. Add that to all of the ship beacons we're not seeing, and a naturally suspicious fellow—which, of course, we all know *I'm* not—would have to wonder if they aren't lying low to entice us into some sort of trap."

"I can't believe you just said that without attracting a lightning bolt," Murphy said dryly.

"What? That it's something to wonder about?" his chief of staff asked in slightly hurt tones.

"No, that bit about not being a naturally suspicious fellow."

"Ah!" O'Hanraghty touched the side of his nose with an index finger. "Just a professional intelligence geek's natural dissimula-tion." He shrugged. "Sorry. Can't seem to shake the habit."

"Which doesn't mean he doesn't have a point, Callum," Mur-phy continued, glancing up at his son. "They'd have to think we were pretty stupid if they could actually fool us that way, but it's not like it costs them anything to try."

"Which is why we went ahead and deployed the first-wave Heimdallars as soon as we dropped sublight," O'Hanraghty added, and Callum nodded.

The long range, Hauptman-coil-powered recon drones had a maximum acceleration rate of only 800 gravities, half the 17.7 KPS^2 an FTLC like *Ishtar* could produce, at least outside the primary's twenty-three light-minute Powell Limit. Their lower deceleration meant they'd be unable to decelerate to rest before they overflew the inner system—in fact, they'd still be traveling at 14,568 KPS when their Hauptman coils exhausted their ten-hour endurance. For now, however, the gap between them and the carriers was opening steadily at a rate of 25.5 KPS^2. They would overfly Point Rubicon at 214,112 KPS over an hour before *Ishtar* reached it, then streak clear across the inner system and back out into interstellar space at a velocity that would make intercepting them effectively impossible. In the process, however, their sophisticated active and passive sensors would give them a very close look at what awaited Murphy's ships, hopefully in plenty of time for him to do something about whatever surprises that might entail.

"And in the meantime, let's start analyzing that 'information to shipping' comm traffic," Murphy said.

"Analyzing it, Sir?" Callum asked.

"Of course." Murphy smiled almost serenely. "You never know what might have been...inadvertently included in a broadcast like that."

"It's confirmed, Ma'am," Captain Farkas Tibor said. "That's *Ishtar*'s transponder code."

Vice Admiral Géraldine Portier grimaced without ever look-ing away from the holo display. There'd never been much doubt who their visitors had to be, coming in on that heading. And the size and strength of the incoming Fasset signatures had warned them hours ago that whoever it was had to have more than the five to seven FTLCs Terrence Murphy was known to possess. But *twelve* of them?

Only one was showing a transponder, which was why she didn't have a clue who the extras might be. She doubted that was just coincidental, but still—

"Where the *hell* did he get all those carriers?" She kept her voice low, pitched solely for Tibor's ears, and looked away from the display to meet his eyes at last.

"Ma'am, let's be realistic," her chief of staff replied, equally quietly. "Right or wrong, a hell of a lot of people, especially out here in the Fringe, agree with him. Or at least want to hear him out." He inhaled deeply. "I'm afraid what we're seeing here is proof of that, actually. If he's got that many carriers it means other Navy units—a *lot* of other Navy units—not just Fringe Worlds, are going 'out of compliance' to support him."

"God*damn* those traitors!" Portier hissed, eyes going back to the display. "How can they not see what he's really doing?!"

Tibor shrugged, ever so slightly. He and the Jalal Station CO had served together for over four years. He respected her ability, and he liked her a great deal. But this was a conversation they'd had—or danced around, at least—often enough since word of the Battle of New Dublin reached Jalal. There was no point continuing it now, although he suspected that deep inside somewhere, even Portier had to know the answer to her question.

Tibor was as much a Heart Worlder as she was, although he lacked her ties to the Five Hundred. The Oval wouldn't have handed command of a base as important as Jalal to someone it didn't trust on multiple levels, so of course it had to be one of the Five Hundred's own. Tibor understood that, and as recently as a year ago, he would have agreed that lunatics spouting theories of secret Rishathan involvement in the endless war against the League should be locked up someplace where they couldn't hurt themselves or anyone else. But he'd seen Terrence Murphy's reports, and especially the summary report on the League shipyards at Diyu. Murphy might still be wrong, but the evidence seemed compelling. Worse, unlike Portier, Tibor completely understood why angry, exhausted Fringers would buy into it. Why they would rally behind someone as charismatic and decisive as Terrence Murphy had proved himself to be.

They'd already seen that in New Dublin's reaction to his

successful stand there. They didn't have any news of what had happened *since* Murphy's dispatch about the Leaguies' shipyards. But if he was here now, with that many carriers, it was painfully obvious the plans to arrest him on what were clearly trumped-up charges had been...less than successful. The question was how *much* less than that they'd been, and the answer would seem to be a *lot* less.

He wouldn't be here at all, much less with that many carriers, if the whole damned sector wasn't going up in flames behind him, Tibor thought grimly. *And I can't blame them, God help me. I've never met Murphy, but all I have to do is look at what he's done over the last seven months.* Of course *they trust him!*

And if there'd been even a handful of other Federation flag officers willing to do what their oaths actually required like he had, that wouldn't be a problem. But there hadn't been, and now, whether he wanted it that way or not, Murphy had become the living avatar of the Five Hundred's worst nightmares.

From his own reading of Murphy's reports, Tibor was almost certain he *hadn't* wanted to. That all he'd really wanted was to do his duty, honor his oath to protect the Federation's citizens—*all* of its citizens, not just the ones fortunate enough to live on Heart Worlds. But what he'd wanted in the beginning didn't really matter now, because there was no way in the universe Portier and the others like her would ever recognize him—or admit that they did, at any rate—as anything other than a self-serving, ambitious warlord and would-be dictator.

"Whatever his people may be thinking, they're here now," he said instead. "How do we want to respond?"

"I think we'll just have to go with Fenris and hope it works," Portier replied after a moment. "And at least we know the threat axis now. Go ahead and start deploying the Kavachas."

"Yes, Ma'am," he said, and the vice admiral looked over her shoulder at the communications officer.

"Standard challenge," she said.

"I've found something just a little...odd, Admiral," Callum Murphy said.

"No! Really?" Murphy replied, and Callum turned from his flag deck display to bestow a suspicious look upon his father.

"Yes," he said. "There appears to be an embedded data packet in the standard information transmissions. It popped out as soon as it hit *Ishtar*'s ID firewall. You and Captain O'Hanraghty wouldn't happen to know anything about that, would you?"

"As a matter of fact, we do." O'Hanraghty moved to Callum's shoulder and looked down at the same display. "We weren't positive Silas and friends would be able to pull it off, but they're very inventive."

"And a damned good thing, if this is accurate," Callum replied.

"You think?" O'Hanraghty's tone was dry, and he looked over his shoulder at Murphy. "According to this, they must've started ferrying parasites in from Sol as soon as they heard about what happened to Xing at New Dublin. There are only three carriers in-system—*Selene*, *Dictys*, and *Hylonome*—but they've reinforced the Jalal sublight picket heavily."

"How heavily?" Murphy asked. Given Jalal's strategic importance, the station had always been heavily defended—for a Fringe system—by a permanent sublight task force that included six full-strength battleship squadrons, plus screening and support units.

"They've more than *tripled* it," O'Hanraghty said grimly. "According to this," he twitched his head at Callum's display, "there are over three hundred sublight units covering the station. That's in addition to the carriers' groups. Call it three hundred sixty, with the carrier groups added to the pot."

"Ouch."

Murphy's tone was remarkably mild, and Callum looked at him sharply. The admiral noticed and pushed up out of his own command chair. A toe thrust against its back sent him across to his son's station.

"The number of sublight units they have doesn't really matter all that much, Callum," he said quietly. "We're not planning on going anywhere near Jalal Station if we have to shoot our way in. And if we don't go to them, they can't possibly come to *us*."

He quirked an eyebrow until Callum nodded in understanding.

"But what if it turns out we *do* have to 'shoot our way in'?" the younger Murphy asked. "*Ishtar*'s been squawking her transponder from the moment we went sublight. They have to know who we are. The fact that they haven't said anything to us suggests to my powerful intellect that they aren't just happy as hell to see us. So what happens if *they* start the shooting and we have to shoot back?"

"That's the last thing we want to do, which is why Rubicon is two light-minutes short of the station," O'Hanraghty replied. "At that range, anything they send our way will be ballistic long before it reaches us, so nobody but an idiot would launch in the first place. Of course, they may *be* idiots and do it anyway, but if it happens, that's why we brought along the Casúrs."

"Exactly," Murphy agreed somberly.

The drone-carried attack missiles Murphy had devised for the defense of New Dublin had been dubbed *Casúr Cogaidhs*—War Hammers—by the citizens of Crann Bethadh, and the name was only too apt. Three of Murphy's FTLCs carried cargo pods stuffed with the drones on their parasite racks instead of warships, and he'd commandeered two massive FTL freighters to haul the next tranche forward from New Dublin as soon as the industrial platforms finished building them.

If he needed it, he'd have all the firepower anyone could possibly need to take out half a dozen targets as tough as Jalal.

"God knows I don't want to use them," he said now, "but if we have to—"

He broke off with a shrug, and Callum nodded.

"Admiral, we have an incoming transmission from Jalal Station," Lieutenant Cointa Mastroianni, *Ishtar*'s communications officer, announced from the holo display of the enormous carrier's command deck.

"Well, speak of the devil," O'Hanraghty said dryly. "Took their own sweet time, didn't they?"

"I expect there was a bit of dithering at their end," Murphy replied. "It does seem a little tardy of them, though, doesn't it?"

They'd dropped sublight just under two and a half hours earlier. Their velocity had fallen to a "mere" 138,132 KPS, less than half the speed of light; they'd traveled 108.8 LM towards Point Rubicon; and the range to Jalal Station was down to 43.2 LM.

"Excuse me, Admiral," Commander Riley Mirwani, Murphy's operations officer, said.

"Yes?" Murphy looked at him.

"We're picking up Hauptman signatures, Sir. A lot of them."

A fresh sparkle of icons frosted the plot, drifting towards one another to cluster on the direct line between *Ishtar* and Jalal Station.

"My, they are untrusting souls, aren't they? You'd almost think they expect us to *shoot* at them or something," O'Hanraghty said, and Murphy snorted.

The range was far too great for detailed sensor resolution, but those had to be Kavacha platforms. The platforms came in two varieties—the Shankhas and Sharangas—but their shared function was to defend against long-range kinetic attack. Both of them were enormous, almost the size of the Casúr Cogaidhs, which made them impractical for shipboard use. On the other hand, ships could dodge, which space stations—and planets—couldn't. And targets that couldn't dodge were dead meat for kinetic attack at almost any range. It might take hours or even days for a KEW to reach its target, but it would get there eventually, and when it did, the consequences would be ugly. Unless something like a Kavacha intervened, at any rate.

Of course, he thought, his momentary amusement at O'Hanraghty's comment fading, they weren't used to defend *all* space stations and planets, were they? Providing them to systems in the Fringe was another one of those things federal governors weren't supposed to do. There'd been none in New Dublin when he arrived, which he'd thought was particularly stupid, given the way New Dublin's deep-space industry had been ungraded to support the Navy. That decision had been made in Olympia long before he ever departed for the Fringe, however, and once he'd decided to go out of compliance, he'd had to choose between Kavachas and Casúr Cogaidhs. Thank God Third Admiral Than had used only missiles in his attack on Crann Bethadh's orbital platforms!

The Shankha's function was to launch clouds of relatively small, superdense pellets—they were called kankads, from the Hindi for "pebble"—into the path of incoming kinetic projectiles. A solid slug of super collapsed material from a capital ship's K-gun massed over 750 kilograms, so even a direct collision with a kankad was unlikely to actually destroy one. *Multiple* collisions could be a different matter, but they were also unlikely as hell. The energy release of even a single impact at those velocities would deflect it significantly from its original trajectory, however. That was one reason Shankhas were deployed as far out as possible, where even a relatively small deflection could cause an incoming KEW to miss its target completely.

The Sharanga was a more capable version of the TFN's Phalanx "escort missile," fitted with multiple Alysída systems. Unlike the

Shankha's kankads, which were deployed at the lowest possible velocity in order to provide the greatest dwell time before they dispersed, the Alysída batteries of fighter-sized K-guns targeted the incoming KEW with KEWs of their own, and they were actually quite good at it. Their greater size gave them the volume not only for much better sensor suites and fire control than the standard Phalanx could boast, but also for eight times the K-guns and much deeper magazines, and their KEWs packed well over two hundred times a kankad's kinetic energy.

Unfortunately, neither Kavacha platform was as effective against missiles, mostly because, in order to be effective against KEWs, they had to be deployed so far from the station or planet they were defending. That meant an attacker usually knew where the defense had placed its Kavachas, and even after a shipkiller like the TFN's Bijalee had exhausted its Hauptman coil and gone ballistic, its fusion-powered final stage was capable of generating a pop-up evasion that was usually sufficient to clear the Kavachas' defensive zone on the way in.

"Well, untrusting or not, it's hardly a surprise," the admiral said after a moment, and shrugged. Then he looked at Mastroianni once more.

"Go ahead and put up that message now, please," he said.

"Yes, Sir."

Mastroianni disappeared from the master display, replaced by another woman—this one with dark hair, dark brown eyes, a strong Roman nose, and the uniform of a TFN vice admiral.

"This is Vice Admiral Portier," she said. "State your identity and intentions and be aware that you are forbidden to enter weapons range of Jalal Station. Portier, clear."

"Succinct and to the point," O'Hanraghty observed. "And mighty strong talk from someone who's only got sixty odd sublight ships to fend off our vicious onslaught."

"Despite that 'state your identity' business, she knows perfectly well who we are," Murphy replied, rubbing one eyebrow with a thoughtful index finger. "Well, she may not know precisely who the *other* carriers are, but she damned well knows which one is *Ishtar*, given how long we've been squawking our transponder. So I imagine she plans on showing us the others if we just keep coming. For that matter, she has to know we would have deployed Heimdallars, so she can't hope to hide them from us a whole lot longer."

In point of fact, the first-wave Heimdallars would cross Point Rubicon on their one-way voyage to infinity in just under twenty minutes.

"No, and she should sure as hell have deployed those carriers somewhere besides Jalal Beta orbit," O'Hanraghty said in the sour tone of a craftsman offended by inferior workmanship.

"I'd tend to agree, Harry. On the other hand, that's a pretty distant orbit. They may be inside the stellar Powel Limit, but at least they're outside the *planetary* limit."

"So their acceleration will match ours once we cross the limit inbound," O'Hanraghty conceded. "They're still dead meat for anyone who opts for a high-speed firing run. If we just wanted to kill them, we could carry enough velocity across the limit to run them down anytime we wanted to."

"That may be why they're where they are," Murphy said. "And what other option did they have? It's unlikely they'd be able to hide somewhere out-system and then outmaneuver us to sneak into attack range. And even if they'd thought they might get away with that, they only have three, whereas they figured we had five of our own, at minimum. Given those odds, they may have figured it made more sense to keep them inside the sublight defensive envelope just in case we were crazy enough to attack them. *I* wouldn't have done it this way." He shrugged. "If I'd been deploying them, I'd have put them at least half a light-hour from the Station, well outside the limit, with every active system locked down to make them impossible to detect. At least that way, they'd be able to run for home if we attacked. But I can more or less understand their thinking."

"Sure you can, Sir."

"Be nice," Murphy said almost absently. Then his nostrils flared. "Lieutenant Mastroianni, please get me Commodore Tremblay."

"Yes, Sir."

A moment later, Commodore Esteban Tremblay appeared on Murphy's display. The flag bridge of TFNS *Kishar*, his FTLC flagship, was visible behind him, and his expression was less than delighted, but Murphy saw no hesitation in those steady eyes.

"Yes, Admiral?"

"I'm afraid they sound just about as unreasonable as we thought they would, Steve," Murphy said somberly. "I'm not ready to throw in the towel and say we can't bring Vice Admiral Portier around, but I don't think anyone would offer very good odds."

Tremblay's jaw tightened ever so slightly, but he nodded.

"It looks like we may need Pre-Spot after all," Murphy continued. "Hopefully, we won't, but better to have them and not need them than need them and not have them." His lips twitched in a humorless smile. "At the moment, it looks like all we'll need is the Alpha deployment. I certainly *hope* that's all we'll need, anyway, but go ahead and prep for Baker, as well."

"Yes, Sir."

The commodore nodded again, crisply, and Murphy nodded back. In many ways, Tremblay and other TFN officers like him offered the best—indeed, probably the only—hope for the success of his mission. Esteban Tremblay was about as Heart World as anyone outside the Five Hundred came, and he'd also been one of the solid majority of Heart Worlders who scoffed at the very notion of Rishathan complicity, ridiculed the "tinfoil-hat" brigade of "conspiracy theorists" who were prepared to entertain even the remote possibility of the Sphere's involvement.

He no longer was. He'd seen proof that while Murphy and O'Hanraghty might be mistaken about the Rish, their intelligence of the impending League attack on New Dublin had been spot on. More than that, he'd found himself completely supporting Murphy's decision to stand and fight in New Dublin, even against the Oval's direct orders. And after New Dublin, the evidence of Rishathan involvement from the Diyu shipyards had completed his conversion from skepticism to solid support for Murphy's analysis. But it had been Lipshen's effort to arrest Murphy for the unforgivable crime of doing his duty and restoring the TFN's honor—and the murder of President Alan Tolmach—that had turned that support for Terrence Murphy's "crackpot theories" about the Rish into unflinching support for Terrence Murphy the *man*.

"Thank you, Steve," Murphy said now, hoping that Tremblay heard his deeply felt sincerity. Then he looked over his shoulder. "Lieutenant Mastroianni?"

"Yes, Admiral?"

"Be kind enough to record for transmission, please."

"Recording now, Sir."

Murphy folded his hands behind him and looked into the pickup.

"Admiral Portier, I believe you know exactly who I am, since *Ishtar's* been showing her transponder for well over two hours. As for my intentions, they are precisely what I've stated in my earlier reports to Olympia and the Oval. I intend to establish communications with the Oval and the Prime Minister and present to them the evidence that supports the analysis I've already transmitted to them. I further intend to make Jalal my communications nexus. It is not my intent to approach Sol or *any* Heart World star system with this much firepower in tow, but I have a . . . less than lively faith in the willingness of the Powers That Be to listen to me—and, especially, to make my information part of the public record—*without* this firepower at my back. Under the circumstances, Jalal strikes me as the most reasonable point from which to establish contact with our superiors on Earth. Other factors have come into play since my last report, many of them political in nature, which make it even more urgent that I establish that contact as promptly as possible. It is not my intention to engage in combat with anyone except enemies of the Terran Federation, which is exactly what I've been saying ever since the Battle of New Dublin. My force will decelerate to rest two light-minutes clear of Jalal Station—outside your Kavachas—and remain there. Murphy, clear."

✧   ✧   ✧

"And how much of that bullshit do we want to believe?" Vice Admiral Portier demanded harshly forty-three minutes later, glaring at Murphy's frozen image on the master display.

"I can't speak to his ultimate intentions, Ma'am," Tibor replied. "But his current deceleration profile tracks exactly with where he says he plans to stop."

"Sure it does . . . for now. And what about *those*?" Portier jutted her chin at a shoal of Hauptmann signatures burning in the master plot. They'd streaked past Jalal Beta seventeen minutes ago at 212,788 KPS, still decelerating at 800 gravities. To get there that soon—and at that velocity—Murphy must have dropped them as soon as he'd gone sublight.

As for Murphy himself, his carriers were down to 88,353 KPS and 30.3 LM from the system primary. Which put them a little over seven light-minutes outside the Jalal Powell Limit . . . and less than 26.3 LM from Jalal Station.

"Heimdallars." Tibor shrugged. "Anybody but an idiot—and whatever else he may be, Murphy's clearly no idiot—would have deployed recon drones. But they burned right past the Station—hell, they're already eleven light-minutes downrange!—so they didn't give him any dwell time at all." He shrugged again. "Sure, he'll have a pretty good snapshot of what we've got, but we always knew that was going to happen, Ma'am," he added almost gently.

"Doesn't mean I have to like it when it does happen," Portier growled. She frowned in intense thought, then nodded to her communications officer. "Record for transmission."

"Recording, Ma'am."

"Rear Admiral Murphy," Jalal Station's CO said coldly into the camera, "your presence here is unauthorized. In fact, given what I know your actual orders were, it constitutes an act of mutiny. Moreover, I am aware of the federal government's orders for your arrest, which you have obviously defied... in addition to all your other crimes.

"Given the number of vessels in company with you, it's clear to me that the decision to take you into custody and return you to Earth for trial were only too wise. In light of that, you are instructed and ordered to surrender yourself and your senior officers to the legitimate authorities. To be perfectly clear, in this instance, the 'legitimate authority' is *me*. Moreover, it is the lawful duty of every uniformed man and woman aboard the ships of your illegally assembled force to take you and those senior officers into custody, immediately, by whatever means are necessary. Failure to comply with the legal, binding orders I have just given you will constitute a further act of mutiny and will be met with lethal force. I advise you to consider the cost to the personnel who have followed you this far into what can only be construed as an act of treason very carefully, indeed. Portier, clear."

She paused, considering what she'd said, wondering if she should review it, possibly edit its stark severity. But then her lips firmed into a thin line.

"Send it," she said flatly. "And append an all-ships header to it. I want all of those bastards to know exactly what the real stakes are."

"Well, *that* wasn't very promising," Callum observed, rubbing the patch over his right eye socket thoughtfully.

"Could've been worse," O'Hanraghty replied.

"Really? How?"

"Well, she could have said... well, let me see here... She could've said—"

O'Hanraghty paused, then gave Callum a lopsided grin.

"Actually, considering the fact that we're too far out of range for her to actively shoot at us already, that probably *couldn't* have been any worse, now that I think about it."

"I prefer to think of it as simply her opening negotiation gambit," Murphy said calmly, contemplating the master tactical display.

Ishtar and her consorts were only 2,880,000 kilometers outside the Powell Limit now. On their current profile, they'd cross it in less than two minutes. Their velocity would have decreased to 73,500 KPS, but their maximum deceleration rate would drop to only 900 gravities once they crossed the limit. That meant they were still over two hours from Point Rubicon, and the plot didn't look promising. The initial flight of Heimdallars were long gone, but they'd pointed their motherships' sensors in the right direction, and the display was thickly populated with the icons of the hundreds of sublight warships they'd spotted, despite their rigid emissions control, on the way through.

"Opening gambit, Sir?" Commander Mirwani sounded dubious.

"Oh, she may not *realize* it's her opening gambit, Riley," Murphy replied. "But that's because she's...misreading the balance of power, let's say. And she may not realize yet that we know how much firepower she has in Jalal Beta orbit. The Heimdallars might not have picked them all up, for that matter, if Silas hadn't already warned us they were there to look for. So she's probably still thinking ambush-ish thoughts at the moment. Once she begins figuring out the truth, she's also going to realize just how unlikely anyone on our side is to do any surrendering."

He frowned, rubbing his chin thoughtfully. Then he shrugged.

"Harry, please comm Tremblay. Tell him to deploy Pre-Spot Alpha on the mark."

The incoming FTLCs continued to decelerate steadily and smoothly towards Point Rubicon. Five hours and twenty-five minutes after they'd gone sublight, with their velocity down to 47,283 KPS, one of the cargo pods riding TFNS *Kishar*'s parasite racks opened its Number Two hatch and deployed fifty Casúr Cogaidhs. Each Casúr was essentially a large, highly modified cargo drone made of EM-absorbent materials, armed with three Bijalee shipkiller missiles, and capable of up to ten hours of acceleration at 7.8 KPS^2 even here, well inside the system's Powell Limit. Now they coasted ballistically—and the next best thing to undetectably—closer to Jalal Beta as their mothership continued to decelerate behind them.

"Alpha Casúrs deployed, Sir," Commodore Trembley said from Murphy's comm screen. "Baker deploying in twelve minutes."

"Thank you, Steve," Murphy replied quietly. "I hope we don't need them. *Either* of them."

✧   ✧   ✧

"They'll be down to zero in five minutes," Captain Tibor reported. "Range two light-minutes. Exactly where Murphy said he'd stop and hold."

"And we should expect him to stay there exactly why?" Vice Admiral Portier said. She glared into the plot, rubbing her upper lip. "I don't see any—"

"Incoming transmission from *Ishtar*, Admiral," the comm officer of the watch announced. Like most of Portier's subordinates, the lieutenant commander used the FTLC's name rather than the sender's to avoid any awkward questions about traitors and their ranks.

"Put it up," Portier half-snapped, and Terrence Murphy appeared on her display once more.

"Admiral Portier, my carriers will have decelerated to zero five minutes after you receive this transmission," he said. "At that time, I will be deploying the sublight parasites from two of them. At two light-minutes, they will constitute no threat to any unit under your command, but they will provide me with additional sensor platforms and an expanded missile defense zone, should *I* need one." He smiled humorlessly. "I genuinely don't think you or anyone over there is stupid enough to waste missiles at such an extended range, but there's no harm in playing safe. I will contact you again once we reach two light-minutes. Murphy, clear."

"Deploying his parasites, is he?" Portier growled.

"Like he says, Ma'am, at two light-minutes, they don't constitute any more danger to the Station than his carriers already do," Tibor pointed out.

"No?" Portier scowled at him. "Every single one of our ships—not to mention the Station itself—is a sitting duck. None of them can maneuver against incoming fire, and his fire control knows exactly where to find all of them!"

Tibor managed not to blink. Portier was right that none of their units could dodge incoming fire, but that was why the Kavacha platforms hovered between Jalal Station and Murphy's ships. His base velocity was already down to 2,650 KPS, which gave his K-guns a maximum velocity of under 2,700 KPS. At that speed any KEWs would take almost four hours just to reach Jalal Station, which *would* give even sublight ships plenty of time to evade them. More to the point, they'd be relatively easy targets for the Kavachas, and it was unlikely as hell that he'd get one—or more than a tiny handful of them, at any rate—past the platforms. And once he'd decelerated to rest, their maximum velocity would be only 16.75 KPS. *No* KEW coming in at *that* velocity was getting through. Not from a two light-minute range.

As for missiles, even from Murphy's current velocity, a Bijalee's maximum powered engagement range was well under two hundred thousand kilometers. After that, they'd be ballistic targets with a closing velocity of barely 3,880 KPS, which would give the defenses over 35,000,000 kilometers—and better than two and a half hours—to track them. The odds of anything getting through under those circumstances was . . . minute, to say the least.

"Ma'am," he said in a careful tone, "assuming he continues his current profile, he'll be exactly on the other side of the Kavacha platforms. Given that, a kinetic attack seems unlikely to get through."

"Oh?" Portier's scowl deepened. "And what if instead of going directly after the Station, he decides to spend some time blowing the Kavachas out of his path? What then?"

This time, Tibor did blink. Not because Murphy *couldn't* do exactly that, but because Farkas Tibor couldn't conceive of any reason he'd want to. Every single thing Terrence Murphy had done since opening communications with Jalal Station tracked perfectly with his announced intentions. If one thing was obvious to Tibor, it was that Murphy didn't want a fight. The *reasons* he didn't might be debatable, but the man had done everything he possibly could to demonstrate his currently peaceful intentions. And whatever else he might be, someone who could accomplish everything Murphy had wasn't stupid. Certainly not stupid enough to believe that even a dozen FTLCs could possibly survive against the massed fury of the entire Federation Navy.

Or to think for one moment that launching an unprovoked attack on Jalal Station wouldn't produce exactly that.

He started to point that out, but he didn't.

Portier's tension had wound tighter and tighter as Murphy decelerated towards her command, and Tibor knew she was castigating herself for holding Clarence Maddox's carriers so close to the planet. He also knew better than to mention it, especially since he'd argued against that close deployment from the outset, but it was clear to anyone who knew Portier as well as he did that it was an added coal in the furnace of her unhappiness.

What worried him most, though, was the possibility that she was thinking with her frustration and anger rather than reasoned judgment. And if she was able to genuinely convince herself that missile fire from two light-minutes out represented a significant threat to her command...

"Point Rubicon, Sir," Commander Creuzburg announced.

"Thank you, Augustus." Murphy leaned back in his command chair, watching the display as TFNS *Chthonius* and TFNS *Ninshubur* deployed their sublight parasites.

Behind them, four more cargo pods detached themselves from TFN *Kishar*'s parasite racks and quietly deployed six hundred more Casúr Cogaidhs. Ahead of them, twelve minutes behind the fifty Alpha-launch Casúrs, the two hundred and sixty-four additional Baker drones continued onward.

"The Alpha pods will begin decelerating in sixteen minutes, Sir," O'Hanraghty reminded him, and he nodded again.

"I know. I'm trying not to cram things at Portier too quickly. Let's give her a few minutes to get used to seeing all of this—" he waved at the display "—before I tell her about them."

"Most likely she'll assume they're just more Heimdallars," O'Hanraghty pointed out, and Murphy snorted.

"Unless she—oh, I don't know... decides to check one of them out on her optical systems."

"Well, for her to do that, she would've had to *not* assume they were just more Heimdallars, so my point stands."

Murphy gave him a hard look, and the chief of staff shrugged.

Géraldine Portier straightened her shoulders.

"It's time," she said. "Pass the word to Admiral Maddox. Tell him to execute Case Orange."

"Admiral, I still think that's a risky idea," Tibor said urgently, keeping his voice down. "At the moment, no one's doing any shooting. There's no need to destabil—"

"Those fucking mutineers are the ones doing all the 'destabilizing' around here," Portier snapped back. "If they don't like what I'm doing, that's just too bad."

"But—"

"They've got a zero relative velocity," Portier interrupted again, "and their acceleration rate's no better than his now that they're inside the Powell Limit." She bared her teeth at her chief of staff. "And it just so happens that at this moment Maddox is on the far side of Jalal Beta, and two hundred thousand kilometers out. Even if they had a Heimdallar right on top of him, they wouldn't even know he'd started bringing his fans up for another two minutes, and that gives him a minimum three-minute head start."

"I understand that, Ma'am. It's just that we haven't even really talked to Murphy yet. All the advantages you're talking about right now will still be there thirty minutes or an hour from now—hell, a *week* from now, given Maddox's orbital period. I just think it would be a good idea to let things settle a little bit before we kick the fire that way."

"The only reason there's a fire to worry about kicking is Murphy and his mutineers," Portier grated, "and I think it's about time he got to chew on the fact that we're not just his puppets."

Tibor started to speak again, then closed his mouth tightly when she glared at him. It was a mistake. He *knew* it was a mistake. But there wasn't one damned thing he could do about it.

"You heard me," Portier said flatly to the comm officer. "Send the order."

Murphy looked up at the time display. Ten minutes had elapsed since his carriers had reached Point Rubicon.

"I think it's probably time to warn Vice Admiral Portier about the Casúrs," he told O'Hanraghty. "Or, at least, that we're sending in additional platforms to keep an eye on things." He grimaced. "I don't expect her to like it, but we can at least keep it from being a total surprise."

"I'm sure she'll appreciate your thoughtfulness, Sir," O'Hanraghty said with a deadpan expression.

"No doubt." Murphy shook his head and looked at Lieutenant Mastroianni. "Record for transmission."

"Recording, Sir."

"Vice Admiral Portier, please be advised that you will shortly detect incoming Hauptmann signatures. Those platforms will decelerate to rest relative to Jalal Station at a range of two light-seconds. They will not approach any more closely than that without prior warning to you. Murphy, clear."

"What the hell *are* those things?" Vice Admiral Portier demanded as the fresh cluster of icons appeared in the master display thirty seconds after Murphy's message reached Jalal Station.

"Hauptman coils, Ma'am," her tactical officer said. "They look like more Heimdallars." Portier glared at him. "Sort of," he added in a sheepish tone.

"Why should Murphy be sending in more Heimdallars now?" The vice admiral shook her head. "Maybe a few of them, to give him a closer look, but *fifty*?"

"I...don't think they are Heimdallars." Tibor looked up from CIC's analysis of the Hauptman signatures. "They're too big. But they're not missile drives, either. Looks like some kind of cargo pod, actually."

"Cargo pod?" Portier frowned at Tibor, and her tense-faced XO shrugged.

"I don't like it, Ma'am," he said. "Like you say, there has to be a reason for Murphy to be sending them in, and from the numbers, they're going to stop exactly where he told us they would."

Which, he did not add aloud, would put them 140,000 kilometers outside the defenders' powered missile range...and well on the Station's side of the Kavachas' defensive zone. Oh, anything Jalal might fire at them would still have its fusion-powered reaction stages, but those were good for only 150 gravities and three minutes. The drones, or whatever the hell they were, could pull *800* gravities...and dodge any incoming missiles with ludicrous ease.

"You think they're missile carriers," Portier said.

"Well, that might explain what happened at New Dublin."

Portier looked at her chief of staff, then shrugged.

"Obviously, he *wants* us to see them," she grated. "I'm sure the threat to *use* them will be along shortly." She smiled with no humor at all. "Probably as soon as he sees Maddox's carriers starting to move!"

"Twelve minutes, Sir," Lieutenant Commander Pegram announced.

"Thank you, Louise," Captain Emilios Galanatos acknowledged.

The captain stood with one toe hooked through a floor loop and his hands clasped behind him, gazing into TFNS *Selene*'s main holo display. Galanatos was tall and slender. Thirty years in the Federation Navy had put quite a lot of muscle onto that slender frame, but he'd grown up on Kavala (otherwise known as Samothrace III) in the Fringe system of Samothrace, and Kavala's gravity was only eighty-two percent that of Earth. Unlike some of his personnel, Galanatos was delighted that his command deck was at the core of his vast command's hull, where the non-spinning citadel was in permanent microgravity.

There was very little "delight" in his expression as he acknowledged his astrogator's report, however, and his eyes were bleak.

He frowned as the seconds ticked away and *Selene*'s Fasset drive powered steadily. The *Titan*-class carrier was the flagship of Task Force 1712, and as Rear Admiral Clarence Maddox's flag captain, Galanatos was much better informed than most of the task force's personnel about Vice Admiral Portier's contingency planning. There'd never been any likelihood that TF 1712's three FTLCs could go toe-to-toe even with the seven carriers they'd known Terrence Murphy had commanded as of the Battle of New Dublin. The fact that he'd turned up with almost twice the hulls of the vice admiral's worst-case projection could only have made any contest between them even more suicidal. He knew Maddox had questioned—even protested—the orders that had tethered his carriers to Jalal Beta, but Portier had been adamant about the need to protect such valuable strategic assets behind the shield of her hugely reinforced sublight defense force.

She'd been especially insistent because no one in the Jalal System knew exactly when additional combat power would be deployed to confront Murphy. It was a given that that combat power had to turn up soon, however, since Jalal Station was the logical—indeed, the inevitable—staging point for any operations against New Dublin. As Portier had seen it, that meant that in the event Murphy appeared in Jalal, her primary responsibility was to hold Jalal Station and conserve her mobile units—especially her FTLCs—until the relief force arrived.

Galanatos had no better idea than anyone else when that

would happen, but everyone knew the Oval had been ordered to assemble a fleet to deal with Murphy. As of the last dispatches from the Oval, that was still a work in progress, however, and no one back on Earth had possessed any better appreciation for his actual carrier strength than Portier had. For that matter, details on exactly what Murphy had done to win the Battle of New Dublin remained sketchy. The bits and pieces available to Galanatos, however, suggested he'd used missiles—*lots* of missiles—in a mobile engagement, not simply fighting from fixed positions. That suggested he'd probably brought as many of those same missiles with him as he could, which meant he could do the same thing again here. And what they *did* know about New Dublin indicated that they would be a significant force multiplier, making the numbers no one in the Sol System knew about even worse.

That was the real reason Portier had ordered Maddox's carriers to break orbit. It was eight weeks to Sol, so it was entirely possible the relief force would be well on its way to Jalal by the time Maddox reached it. But it was equally possible it wouldn't be, given interstellar distances and the time it took to assemble task forces and fleets. And if Maddox got there in time, Fleet Admiral Fokaides and the Oval would undoubtedly hold the relief still longer in order to assemble an overwhelming force, one strong enough to deal even with the unanticipated increase in Murphy's order of battle. Depending on how much of the Reserve they chose to commit and how many FTLCs they'd diverted from the Beta Cygni Line, they could reinforce their response force to at least twice Murphy's actual strength. Concentrating that many carriers would take time they'd hate to burn, but they could do it if they wanted to.

It was unlikely that whatever he'd done to his missiles could offset that sort of odds, especially when the incoming CO would be on the alert for exactly that. Which meant that if Maddox reached Sol in time, Terrence Murphy was doomed.

"Ten minutes, Sir," Pegram said, and Galanatos nodded.

"About time," another voice said.

It was harder, darker, then Pegram's, and Galanatos's lips tightened for a moment before he turned to face Commander Higgins, his XO. Unlike him, Higgins was a Heart Worlder. She was also a full eleven centimeters shorter than he, with the sturdy build of someone who'd grown up on Old Earth itself.

"You do realize that if Murphy's really a mutinous traitor, he'll be perfectly willing to open fire before we wormhole out, right?" Galanatos asked quietly, voice pitched to avoid other ears.

"He can't catch us, not from a cold start of his own," she scoffed.

"But if he's really as far gone as the newsies are saying, he can always threaten to open fire on Jalal Station unless Vice Admiral Portier orders us to stand down."

"If he has the balls to," Higgins acknowledged. "If he does that, though, he's openly crossed the Rubicon. Be a bit hard to keep selling his 'Rishathan conspiracy' snake oil if he opens fire on a major Federation base to stop Navy carriers from simply departing the system. A part of me almost wishes he'd try it. I know how badly *we'd* get hurt, but he'd cut his own throat as far as anyone back home is concerned. Not that anyone with a working brain's going to believe his bullshit cover story, anyway."

Her expression was scornful, and Galanatos's nostrils flared slightly. This was a conversation they'd had, in one variant or another, more than once, and he was far from certain Terrence Murphy was a snake oil salesman. Higgins wasn't a bit uncertain about that, however. In her opinion, Murphy was a proven mutineer and quite possibly the greatest traitor in the Federation's history. A narcissistic, opportunistic, would-be warlord driven by sheer, raw ambition and perfectly ready to shatter the Federation while it remained locked in mortal combat with the League.

There'd obviously been no point debating it with her then, and there was even less point now that Murphy had turned up with so many ships, he supposed.

"I'd rather not be the decisive factor in discrediting him," he said instead.

"Status change!" Commander Mirwani snapped suddenly, and the plot updated as the icons of Portier's three carriers begin to strobe amber.

"They're bringing up their fans, Sir," the ops officer continued grimly, and Murphy grimaced.

"I thought Portier was smarter than this," he said.

"It does seem a bit stupid," O'Hanraghty agreed. "On the other hand, she got caught with cold fans on all three of them.

If she'd tried to run any earlier, they'd have had an even worse chance of getting away with it."

"Precisely how much worse than 'zero' can their chances be?" Murphy demanded, and O'Hanraghty shrugged.

"Depends a lot on how willing she thinks you really are to pull the trigger," he pointed out. "And that datum's over two minutes old. For them to be this far along, they must have started before you warned her the Casúrs were inbound. For that matter, she still doesn't know what the Casúrs *are*. She does know they're Hauptman birds, though. And that means she'll probably figure her carriers still have the acceleration advantage. Which," he conceded, "they will. She couldn't have planned it this way, but they'll have decelerated all the way to zero before we could tell them different at this range."

"But it's still stupid to do it now." Murphy shook his head in disgust. "What would it have cost her to at least *talk* to us, first?"

He scowled at the plot, then looked at Mirwani.

"How far into startup are they?" he asked.

"They were already moving from Standby towards Readiness when we picked them up, Sir," Mirwani replied. "I can't say exactly how far into the cycle they were at that point, but they had to be at least a couple of minutes in. Then allow for the two-minute light-speed lag, and they can't be more than eight or nine minutes from activation."

"We're inside their loop," O'Hanraghty observed, and Murphy nodded. His carriers' Fasset drives were already at Readiness. They could be accelerating again in only five minutes, which would give *them* the crucial head start in the acceleration race. But—

"What do you want to do, Sir?" O'Hanraghty asked, and Murphy frowned, then shrugged.

"Doesn't really change anything," he said, watching the strobing icons' color darken as their drives powered steadily upward. "We always knew we'd have to send someone to Sol to tell them we were here and wanted to talk. Might as well let them take the message. It's certainly not worth charging after them to try and prevent it. The last thing we need is to start escalating! On the other hand..."

He swung his chair gently from side to side for a few more seconds, then looked at Lieutenant Mastroianni.

"Cointa, please record for transmission to Jalal Station, repeated to the carriers in orbit."

"Recording, Sir."

"Vice Admiral Portier, we've detected your carriers bringing up their drives. Be advised that I have no intention of interfering with their movements in any way. Obviously, word of my presence here—and why I've come—has to reach Earth at some point, so we might as well use your vessels to carry it. Murphy, clear."

"Good recording, Sir," Mastroianni said.

"Then send it, please. And attach an all-ships heading. Let's defuse as much tension over there as we can."

"Six minutes, Sir," Lieutenant Commander Pegram said.

Captain Galanatos nodded at the update, then glanced over his shoulder at Lieutenant Maxim Lindquist. *Selene's* comm officer was young, barely half Galanatos's age, and his expression was more anxious than his captain's.

"Max?" Galanatos said, and Lindquist's eyes darted to him.

"Yes, Sir!"

"Feeling a little antsy?"

It was a sign of Galanatos's rapport with the men and women under his command that he could ask that question without a trace of condescension...and have it taken the same way.

"Maybe just a bit, Sir," Lindquist replied with a fleeting grin.

"Well, let me show you something that might make you feel a bit more confident."

Commander Higgins snorted in amusement as the captain smiled encouragingly and unsealed the breast of his shipboard utilities. He reached into the opening, his eyes still on Lindquist.

"This is for Inverness," he said, and his voice was suddenly hard.

His hand came out of his utilities as he turned back to face Higgins, and the pistol in his hand rose.

"Stay very still, Beth," he said.

Higgins's eyes flared as she found herself confronting that pistol.

"What the hell do you—?!" she began, then chopped herself off she realized two thirds of the command deck crew, including Lindquist, had just produced weapons of their own. The handful of officers and ratings who hadn't found themselves holding just as still as the XO in the face of all those weapons.

"Max?" Galanatos said again, never looking away from Higgins.
"Yes, Sir!"
"Send it."

"Ensign Sung?"

Lieutenant SG Emmett Marconi couldn't have said why he looked over his shoulder when he heard Chief Nahrong's voice. Not really. There was just something a little...off about the chief petty officer's tone.

Which was a stupid damn thing to be thinking. If anyone had ever had an excuse for their tone to be "off," the personnel of Jalal Station did today! What with the mutinous Murphy's sudden appearance, and the rumors spreading like lightning over personal comm channels about the number of ships he'd brought with him, every person aboard the enormous station was strung tighter than a tuning fork. And as the watch officer in Fusion One, one of Jalal's three fusion rooms, Emmett Marconi had a hell of a lot better things to be wasting attention on.

Despite which—

"Yes, Chief?" Sung Hua replied. "What can I do for you?"

Sung was a bright young officer who'd signed on for Preference when her draft number came up. She'd had the aptitude to breeze through the Federation's power engineering school, and her skills would be in high demand on the civilian side once her time was up.

"Something over here you should see, Ma'am," Nahrong said, pointing at his workstation display.

"Oh?" Sung grabbed a handhold and pushed off towards Nahrong, and Marconi frowned slightly.

Nahrong wasn't in her duty section, so why—?

He unsnapped himself from his own command chair, pushing up in Fusion One's microgravity. If whatever Nahrong had turned up was important enough to show Sung, he should probably take a look at it, too.

He turned towards Nahrong just as Sung stopped beside the chief petty officer and looked down at the display. Her back was to Marconi, and her right arm moved, as if she were tapping something on Nahrong's touchscreen.

"Interesting," she said, then turned around, and Marconi's eyes flew wide.

She hadn't been tapping Nahrong's screen, he realized. She'd been unsealing the front of her shipsuit to get at the gun concealed inside it.

The gun that matched the one Nahrong had produced while her body shielded him from anyone's eyes.

"*Inverness!*" Sung barked.

She grabbed a handhold with her free hand and pulled hard, spinning aside to clear Nahrong's field of fire, and lightning bolt comprehension flashed through Marconi. He didn't try to reason it out; he only reacted.

His own right hand still gripped the back of his command chair. Now he heaved with all his strength, and the force of his pull sent him flashing across the forty-meter-wide compartment. His command station was near its center, but his trajectory took him within arm's reach of Petty Officer Loomis's station, and he kicked the back of Loomis's command chair as he went by, changing his trajectory sharply.

Loomis was just beginning to turn towards Sung and Nahrong when a chattering burst from Nahrong's pistol tore through his torso.

Marconi heard the start of Loomis's bubbling scream, but the deafening thunder of more pistols drowned it almost instantly as the entire compartment went insane. Guns seemed to be everywhere; it wasn't until later that he realized only Sung, Nahrong, and Chief Benson were actually armed. But even though they were outnumbered by three-to-one by the *unarmed* members of Marconi's watch personnel, they used the advantage of surprise ruthlessly, and their fire swept Fusion One.

"Nahrong! Get that Heart bastard!" Sung shouted through the cacophony.

Marconi heard the ensign, but recoil, even from a handgun, was far harder to deal with in microgravity than most people realized before they'd actually tried it. The murderers slaughtering his personnel weren't very accurate, and the lieutenant was a moving target, arrowing straight towards the compartment's open hatch. Bullets snapped past him, ricocheting from the bulkhead, tearing into command consoles, but unlike the conveniently stationary victims still strapped to their seats, he was a target in motion.

Fucking idiots! The thought cut through him, despite his panic. If the killers hit the wrong thing, they might throw the entire plant into emergency shutdown—if they didn't manage something even worse!

Another burst of bullets sizzled past him, missing by centimeters—if that much—and screamed off the hatch frame as he sailed into it. The heel of his left hand hit the CLOSE button, and he shoved himself hard to one side as a final handful of bullets followed him through the hatch before it slammed shut.

He grabbed a handhold, stopping himself at the bulkhead touchpad. He flipped up the touchpad cover and allowed himself a brief, triumphant smile as he tapped in a five-digit code. It wasn't much, but the test cycle he'd just initiated in the hatch locking mechanism would buy him at least three minutes.

Now what the hell did he do with them?

✧ ✧ ✧

"Admiral?"

"Yes, Cointa?"

Murphy turned to face the master display as the comm officer appeared in it once more. He stood behind Callum's chair at O'Hanraghty's tactical station, watching the Heimdallars update their sensor reports as TF 1712's FTLCs began accelerating at last.

"We just received something . . . weird, Sir."

"Weird?" Murphy repeated. "In what way?"

"It's a one-word transmission from *Selene*, Sir. With an 'all-ships' tag."

Murphy's expression tightened and he looked quickly at O'Hanraghty, then back up at Mastroianni's holo image.

"What word?" he asked.

"'Inverness,' Sir."

"Oh, *shit*," O'Hanraghty breathed, and tapped a touchscreen to plug into Mastroianni's communications feed as Murphy wheeled back to the tactical display.

"Admiral, network traffic has increased substantially," Mastroianni said from the master holo display. Text scrolled through multiple windows at the same time. "There's a lot of direct ship-to-ship popping up, and the central net's going berserk."

O'Hanraghty had one hand cupped over his earbud, listening intently. Now he looked up, his expression grim.

"She's right." His voice was as grim as his expression. "It's going to hell, Terry."

"How bad?" Murphy demanded.

"Bad. Damn! Why didn't Silas's people warn us about *this* in their data dump?!"

"About what?" Callum asked.

"That transmission from *Selene* had to be an execution code," his father told him in a flat tone.

"Execution code for *what*?"

"Mutiny, Callum," O'Hanraghty said harshly. "That's what all this comm chatter is about. And from the traffic volume, it's widespread. In fact—"

"Weapons fire!" Mirwani announced. "Weapons fire in Jalal Beta orbit!"

"God*damn* it!" O'Hanraghty snarled. "Why the hell *now*?!"

"Because Portier decided to send Maddox home." Murphy's voice was unnaturally calm.

"But we were letting them *go*!" Callum protested.

"And they didn't know that," Murphy said. "Eighty-five seconds." He jerked a hand at the time chop on *Selene's* transmission. *"Eighty-five seconds!"* He slammed the same, fisted hand into Callum's console. "They sent the execute code eighty-five *seconds* before they could have copied our transmission to Portier!"

Callum's expression was sick.

"Display Tactical in the main tank," Murphy said.

Mastroianni disappeared from the master display, replaced by a tactical plot of the volume around Jalal Station. Every bit of data on it was at least two minutes old by the time they saw it, but the explosions and the sudden eruption of atmosphere from breached hulls were horrifyingly clear. There were only a handful of them at the moment, but the carnage spread even as they watched.

"Whoever pushed the button must have been planning it for a while, Callum," Murphy continued, "and given how many Fleet and Marine personnel are Fringers, it's going to be as ugly as it gets if even a small percentage of them decide to mutiny. And they didn't know I was perfectly happy to let Maddox go. What *they* knew was that he'd arrive in Sol with detailed numbers on our order of battle." He shook his head. "That's what they're trying to stop. They don't want the Oval to realize how strong we are."

"But . . . whatever the Oval's sending is probably already on its way," Callum objected.

"Probably." His father nodded. "But we don't know that for certain any more than they do. For that matter, they probably know the Oval's deployment plans a lot better than *we* do. None of which matters, because there's no road back from this for any of them."

Increasing numbers of the sublight warships on the tactical display had begun firing, and at ranges that short, with weapons that powerful, the carnage—already terrible—was about to turn horrific. Murphy knew that, and his jaw tightened, his eyes bleak, as the first explosion sparked on the outer skin of Jalal Station's middle habitat ring.

"There's no way in hell the Oval will believe—or admit, anyway—that *you* didn't orchestrate this, Terry," O'Hanraghty said softly, and Murphy nodded.

"I know."

He watched the display for another second, then squared his shoulders.

"Harry, tell Tremblay to expedite the Baker pods. I want them in attack range ASAP. Then tell Atkins it's going to be Lepanto, after all."

A chill wind seemed to whisper around the flag bridge. Brigadier Scott Atkins was the New Dublin ex-colonel who commanded the mutinous Marines and Fringe system defense force personnel who'd been folded together into the newly organized Free Worlds Alliance Marines to provide Murphy a larger ground force component than his own task force had included, and Lepanto was the plan for that force to stage an opposed boarding action against Jalal Station. No one had wanted that escalation, and no one wanted to contemplate where it would lead when the Federation learned it had happened anyway, but O'Hanraghty only nodded.

"Yes, Sir," he said quietly.

"Commander Mirwani."

"Yes, Sir?"

"I want the Alpha pods in motion now. And use Alpha's Phalanxes to plow the road for Baker; I want the Kavacha platforms cleared."

Callum's stomach tightened. The Phalanx "escort missiles" aboard ten percent of the Alpha Casúrs mounted fewer installations of the TFN's Alysída system than the Sharanga platforms did, but their high-velocity slugs were even better at interdicting incoming counter-missiles than standard KEWs. Shipkillers were equipped with only a single Alysída each, capable of killing no more than three or four counter-missiles even under optimum conditions. A Phalanx mounted eight of them apiece...and they were inside the Kavachas, the one place none of their sensors or auto-defense programming would look for threats. That made Jalal Station's anti-KEW defenses sitting ducks, and once *they* were blown out of the way...

"Portier will see that as an escalation," O'Hanraghty warned.

"Escalation, hell!" Murphy grated, jabbing an angry hand at the plot. "People are *killing* each other out there, Harry! I can live with Portier's hurt feelings just fine!"

"Point," the chief of staff acknowledged, and Murphy looked back at Mirwani.

"CIC will identify the parasites actively shooting. I want the three largest of them designated as targets."

"Aye, aye, Sir."

That chill wind blew colder, and Murphy looked at his comm officer.

"Lieutenant Mastroianni."

"Yes, Sir?" The comm officer's always crisp voice was soft.

"General transmission to all units in-system." If Mastroianni's voice was soft, Murphy's was hammered iron.

"Recording, Sir."

"To all units in the Jalal System. This is Admiral Murphy. Stand down immediately. I repeat, stand down *now*." His eyes were harder even than his voice. "I didn't come here for men and women of the Federation Navy to kill each other. It stops now. I don't care whose 'side' any of you are on. Cease fire, cut acceleration, and *stand down*. We can sort out who did what first later, but the killing *stops*. And be advised that I have weapons deployed in range of Jalal Beta orbit. I don't want to use them, but I will. You have five minutes from the receipt of this message to cease fire. Any ship which continues to fire at the end of that time *will* be destroyed."

He stared into the pickup for two more breaths, then showed his teeth.

"I advise you to take this warning very, *very* seriously. Murphy, clear."

✧　　　✧　　　✧

Lieutenant Marconi bounded down the narrow catwalk in long, leaping strides. Thick pipes, electrical cables, and plasma conduits lined the catwalk, and his feet clanked on its bare metal grating each time he touched down. The thin air was icy, and beneath the catwalk, the inner core of Jalal Station's central spindle stretched into the abyss. Long highways of blinking lights marked logistics rails that shuttled personnel and material up and down the length of the station.

The station's fusion reactors and main environmental plants were located in its spindle to take advantage of the microgravity there. Gravity was only a little heavier along the outer bulkhead of the innermost habitat ring where the catwalk was mounted, which let him cover distance quickly, but unlike Fusion One, there was no artificially maintained overpressure here. And, along with the lower atmospheric pressure, oxygen levels were lower, as well. Normally, that was no problem, but "normally" didn't include a man running for his life, and stars twinkled across his vision as his blood oxygen levels lowered with each panting breath.

"Get back here, Heart!" Chief Nahrong called from behind him, and Marconi swore with bitter, silent venom.

There'd always been a certain tension between him and Nahrong, who obviously resented the "Hearts" he blamed for every single one of his homeworld's woes, but the CPO had never let it grow to anything that would have been called outright disrespect. Marconi would never have pegged the chief as a potential traitor, and he wondered how many other people he'd misjudged the same way.

A lot, apparently.

He'd tried frantically to use his personal comm to find someone—*anyone!*—he could alert to the massacre in Fusion One. But there'd been no response from Station Security or the command deck, and after the fourth time he'd almost been shot, he'd realized his pursuers were tracking his comm signal. When he did, he'd tossed it into the core's vast emptiness.

That sort of littering was a major breach of station protocols. An officer could lose his command over a serious Foreign Object Damage to Equipment report. At the moment, that was the least of his worries.

Another bullet snapped past his head and punched a hole in the casing of a mag regulator. Mechanical groans ran up the entire stack as safety protocols locked down more and more of the enormous platform's inner workings.

Marconi slid behind a power relay with substantially better armor plating and tried to catch his breath.

"Give it up!"

This time, it was Ensign Sung's voice, and boots clattered against other catwalks, echoing amongst the alarm Klaxons.

"Goddamn it, don't shoot me!" Marconi shouted. "If-if I'm dead... I can't repair any of this mess!"

"We don't need you!" Nahrong shouted back. "Stupid fucking Heart! You think just because we're a bunch of dumbass Fringers, we can't do anything without you lording it over us?!"

More boots echoed on catwalks above and below him, and he knew Nahrong was trying to buy time, keep him talking while mutineers got into position around him.

Marconi looked around desperately. The P-37 junction was only a couple of dozen meters away... across an open gap. If he could reach it, he could cut the power to this entire sector of the core. That would shut down all the lights and all of the logistics rails, and if they shut down, if he could use the darkness for cover and get inside one of the stacks without being crushed by moving lifters...

It wasn't much of a chance, but "not much" was a hell of a lot better than "no hope at all."

"What did I ever do to you, Sung?" he shouted, crouching as he readied for his dash.

"How many decades have you Heart bastards fucked over—"

Marconi launched himself, his eyes locked on the control panel. He'd have to cross the open gap to get there, but once he did, he'd have pretty damned good cover, at least until they could maneuver into fresh positions. That would take time, and he'd need only a few seconds to kill the power, then yank out the control module and toss it down the core after his comm.

Good luck getting it back online before I'm long gone, traitors, he thought. *And once I'm out of—*

He'd gotten three long strides across the gap when pain flared in his left calf. He was moving too quickly to react, and his left foot hit the catwalk and promptly gave out on him. A simple fall might not have been that bad, but his momentum provided more than enough inertia to make up for the low gravity, and light flashed across his vision as his head slammed into the

workstation full tilt. Then he face-planted into the catwalk grating and skittered across it, as well.

Boots pounded towards him, and he tried to at least roll over.
He didn't make it before hard, brutal hands closed upon him.

He was dazed, limp, unable to fight, but the pain of his broken
nose and the bullet wound in his leg were twin beacons. They
kept him from losing consciousness, and his heart pounded in
his ears as he was dragged away.

"You fucking well watch your ass in there, Sir," Sergeant Major
Logan's voice growled in Callum Murphy's earbud over the dedicated command circuit. "God knows what kinda shit's going on,
and I better not see you getting between the detail and any bad
guys. Hell, between the detail and *anybody*! You got that . . . Sir?"

"I got it, Smaj," Callum replied. "Trust me, I got it!"

"And I'll damn well have Eira shoot you in the leg if you forget."

Logan's growl was at least marginally less intense, and Cal-
lum's lips twitched in a smile. There wasn't much humor in it.
Not when his assault shuttle was only twelve minutes out from
Jalal Station.

The visual display was littered with broken and wounded
ships. With debris, life pods, wreckage, and drifting bodies. Callum Murphy looked at the display, and his brown eye was grim
and hard, and not just because of what he could see.

In the sixteen months since he'd first visited Jalal Station, he'd
learned a lot about himself. And in some ways, he'd learned even
more about his father, because first he'd had to *unlearn* so many
things about Terrence Murphy. He'd had to learn how much of
the man he'd always thought he knew—the man he'd loved—was
only the outer shell, the protective filter, between his father and
the world. Oh, the parent who'd loved him, the father who'd at
least tried—with, Callum had to admit, limited success—to help
his son realize how much more there was to being a man than
just the privileged life of one of the Five Hundred's wealthiest
scions, had been real. The father who'd lectured him about responsibility, when he'd wanted to be out clubbing. The father whose
quaint ambition was to return to Survey Command and explore
new star systems. The father who was about as apolitical as it
was possible to be. Who acquiesced in his father-in-law's political ambitions and plans only because it pleased Callum's mom.

That man had been real, but he'd also been a mask. Over the last two years Callum had seen behind the mask to the man who believed in honor. Believed in the Terran Federation's responsibility to protect all of its citizens. Believed in the Fringe's rights. Believed it was wrong for the Five Hundred to pay the price of an unending war in the blood of Fringers while the profits poured in from the bottomless military contracts.

Believed it was his job, his duty—his *responsibility*—to do something about the abomination the Five Hundred and the Federation it controlled had become.

Along the way, Callum Murphy had discovered that although he'd always loved his father, it hadn't been the way he loved and admired and so deeply respected the man inside Terrence Murphy's mask. The man he would follow through the gates of Hell themselves. Who he hoped *he* might someday, somehow, find the depth to become, himself.

And that man had watched as mutiny wrapped Jalal Station in a halo of fire, wreckage, and vented atmosphere. Seen it, known it was the result of his actions, although not because he'd ordered or wanted it. And not because he'd created the tensions, the hatred, that had spawned it. But he was here, he and his ships and the men and women who crewed them. That was what had touched the spark to the tinder and turned that hatred loose.

And because Callum had come to know him, he knew how soul-deep his father's pain was.

But another thing he'd learned about Terrence Murphy: he would never do a centimeter less than his duty. As explosions speckled the outer skin of the enormous station like tiny incandescent pinpricks and sublight warships savaged one another at ranges as short as a hundred kilometers, he'd done—as he always did—what had to be done.

The people killing each other either hadn't heard or hadn't believed his initial warning as the Casúr Cogaidhs accelerated once again. The Alpha drones were already well inside the Kavacha platforms. For that matter, they were inside the station's point defense perimeter. When they'd fired, there'd been no time for even cybernetically controlled defenses to react before the missiles struck, and the battleships *Sentinel, Liberator,* and *Champion* disintegrated into mangled, debris-shedding wreckage. It had been a single, finally coordinated, savage hammer blow, not the spreading chaos of the mutiny, and it had almost certainly killed over two thousand human beings.

Both sides had noticed that.

And they'd also noticed the Phalanxes as they blew the Kavacha platforms out of the way, clearing the way for the suddenly accelerating Baker Casúrs to close on the station and the warships orbiting with it. But while the ship-to-ship fighting might have faltered, it hadn't stopped.

And because it hadn't, half the Baker drones had fired six minutes later... and killed the battleship *Paladin* and the battlecruisers *Algeria* and *Nigeria*.

The other half had decelerated hard, holding position outside any effective shipboard interdiction range, and a *third* wave of Casúrs had headed in behind them. Not two hundred and sixty-four of them, this time, but over *six* hundred. That third wave was a good thirty minutes from launch range, but there was no longer anything to keep them from getting there, and they'd realized he meant it. He didn't care who'd started it; he didn't care whether they supported or opposed him. If they continued firing, he would kill them all.

Over two dozen ships had been destroyed—three quarters in mutual combat—before they absorbed that message, and three times that many were damaged, many of them heavily, but the survivors had finally stopped shooting each other. At least the *ships* had; Callum didn't even want to think about what might be happening—what almost certainly *was* happening—in the passages and compartments of some of those surviving vessels.

Even at an FTLC's 900 gravities, it had taken an hour for TFNS *Ereshkigal* and TFNS *Ninshubur* to get close enough to Jalal Station to drop their parasites and Marine assault shuttles. His father had wanted to take *Ishtar* in, but O'Hanraghty had shot that notion down quickly.

"If there's one ship out here that could convince some die-hard loyalist it was worth dying to take out, it's *Ishtar*," the captain had said flatly. "Kill you, and this whole thing falls apart, and they know it. So *Ishtar* isn't going... and neither are *you*, Terry."

"I've got to go! This is *my* mess. Even if it wasn't, I need to be there, on the ground, when decisions have to be made. I can't be at the other end of a four-minute comm lag!"

"Yes, you can." O'Hanraghty had held Murphy's eyes unblinkingly, and Callum had felt the silent agreement of every other man and woman on the flag bridge. Not because they were afraid of being shot at themselves, but because they were frankly terrified at the thought of losing *him*.

"I'll go," O'Hanraghty had continued. "I'll transfer to *Ereshkigal* before Captain Jurgens heads in. We both know Atkins will be calling the shots if it comes to actual fighting aboard the station, so you sure as hell don't need to be there for that. Anything else comes up, I can act as your deputy, and four minutes isn't that huge a lag for most of the decisions you'll have to make, anyway."

"They'll be just as eager to kill you as to kill me," Murphy had pointed out.

"And they'll be a hell of a lot less likely to actually try if they know you're still out here to kick their asses!"

"But if they think I'm hanging back, they'll all say it's part of my 'warlord' act. I'm willing to spend *other* people's blood—just like any other member of the Five Hundred—but when it comes to putting my own ass on the line, I've got better things to do. I can't hand that line to the Five Hundred . . . and we can afford it even less if it starts coming from the Fringe."

"Send me," someone had said, and Callum had realized it was him.

His father and O'Hanraghty had both wheeled to face him, and he'd shrugged.

"Captain O'Hanraghty's right, Dad. You can't go. I know you've got the guts to take point—I *know* it, Dad—but he's right. We can't afford to lose you. But I'm a Murphy, too. And I've learned a few things over the last year or so. Send me with one of the boarding parties. I know better than to think I could make the decisions he can make for you, but I can at least, oh *show the flag* for you." He'd made himself smile. "You're right. We need to put *a* Murphy on the deck plates over there, Dad. He just doesn't have to be *you*."

And that was how he found himself sitting aboard this assault shuttle as it decelerated towards Jalal Station and trying hard not to think about what he was likely to find aboard it. If the fighting between warships had been bad, then what—

"Callum, I need you to divert to the Juliet-One-Niner freight bay," his father's iron-hard voice said in his earbud. "We still don't have any clear picture of what's happening aboard the Station, and we haven't heard anything from Vice Admiral Portier since the shooting started. But we've got Heimdallars in tight enough to keep a close eye on things, and one of them just picked up some short-range comm chatter. Atkins'll have his hands full dealing with the planned Lepanto objectives. We can't divert any of his people to this. Besides I need you—you, specifically—and Logan in there as quickly as possible."

✧   ✧   ✧

The pinch of a stim patch against Emmett Marconi's neck snapped him out of his stupor.

He lay on a stretcher, his injured leg bound up and the bullet wound pulsing around a first aid clot patch. His supine position meant he couldn't see much, thanks to the crowd of station crew, all with the Terran Federation patch ripped off their coveralls, who surrounded him. But he could tell he was in one of the station's main cargo-handling boat bay galleries, because he could see the upper edges of the outsized airlocks that marched down its outer bulkhead.

His captors might have skimped on the painkillers, but not on the tightness of the flex cuffs binding his wrists. A pair of prisoners sat on either side of him, both beaten up and dejected. One was a contractor from Vargas Interstellar, one of the Heart World's major freight lines, the other a shuttle squadron commander who'd attended regular Tuesday-night poker sessions with Marconi.

"Guilty!" Chief Nahrong's pronouncement came through the crowd and was met with cheers.

"No! Wait, please!" someone wailed, and more cheers greeted the distinctive audio alert of a closing airlock door.

"Who's next on the docket?" Nahrong asked.

Ensign Sung pushed through the throng around the prisoners. She looked the trio over with a smug smile, then snapped her fingers and pointed at Marconi. A pair of mutineers grabbed him under his arms and lifted him off the stretcher. One at least had the courtesy to prop him up so he didn't have to walk on his injured leg.

"Why patch me up if you're just going to space me?" Marconi asked through thick lips. Dried blood flaked off his chin and nose.

"Justice," the ensign said. "More than your kind ever gave us."

"This 'cause I didn't sign your leave paperwork two months ago?" Marconi asked. "I'm just an engineer, Sung."

"He's awake!" Nahrong sat on a makeshift throne of cargo containers. Rank pins and epaulets were piled in front of him. Sung snapped a small blade out of a pocketknife and flicked it under Marconi's double silver bar rank. She ripped the patch away and tossed it into the pile.

"Marconi." Nahrong leaned back. "You stand accused of being part of the ruling oligarchy that's spent Fringe blood in the war against the League. A war your kind never sacrificed for. A war your kind was happy to spend Fringe blood to fight."

Marconi licked dried blood from his mouth and spat.

"I fought at Formite," he said. "I lost three fingers to a power surge keeping the *Hiroba*'s mag bottles from going critical. I don't know where you're getting all this from, but I've done my part in this war. Didn't matter who my parents were or what planet I came from."

The crowd died down.

"Well then," Nahrong leaned forward. "If you're really on the side of the fight, why don't you renounce the Federation and join the Free Worlds Alliance?"

Sung pressed the flat of her blade against the Federation flag on his right shoulder and began to cut.

Pain from his injuries started to sting. He glanced through the nearest airlock's armorplast bulkhead and saw a half dozen men and women pounding at the door.

"What about them?" he asked Nahrong as the flag came free and Sung tossed it onto the pile in front of Nahrong.

"I gave them the same chance you're getting, but all of 'em were more loyal to a corrupt institution than our cause for freedom and self-determination," Nahrong said. "You cross over to us and you get a pass. Oh, we'll keep you on a short leash until we're sure you're with us, but at least you'll have the chance to prove you mean it."

"He was trying to sabotage power to the entire core before he went down, and he knows the station's power net like the back of his hand," Sung said. "There's no place on it where he won't be a threat to us."

Nahrong held up a hand.

"Then he can space this batch." Nahrong guffawed and slapped his knee. "Damn, why didn't I think of that sooner? Why trust some Heart's words when we can judge his actions, am I right?"

The crowd cheered.

"I'll make it real easy." Nahrong pointed to the airlock controls. "You either jettison that trash or we'll make sure you're not on this station to be a pain in our ass anymore. Sound fair? Get him over there."

Sung shoved Marconi forward. One of the guards had to keep him from falling as he hopped over to the controls on his good leg. He looked down at them, told himself all those other people were going to die anyway, whatever he did. Told himself it wouldn't matter to them in the end, anyway.

And then he looked through the armorplast into the lock again.

A woman in pajamas was at the armorplast. She was a junior hydroponics tech who'd arrived two weeks ago from a Preference call-up. She'd left a little boy—a two-year-old named Prinav—back home, and there were pictures of him all over her workstation.

She mouthed "please" to him.

Marconi's index finger touched the button that would open the outer lock door. He closed his eyes, and his hand began to shake. He stood there for a long, frozen moment, his jaw aching from the pressure of clenched muscles. Then he lifted his index finger.

The crowd snarled like some vast, furious beast, and a wild, strange elation went through him as he heard it.

He switched his raised digit to his middle finger and held it over his head for all to see.

The blow to his kidneys pitched him forward, smashed his face into the bulkhead. Someone kicked him as he went down. Then someone else. He heard Sung laughing wildly, got a glimpse of Nahrong's contorted face, and then it was his turn to be chucked into the airlock. Clubs and boots beat back any of the condemned trying to escape, and the inner door closed behind him.

"Thank you. Thank you so much!" The young mother propped Marconi up against the airlock wall. She dabbed at fresh scrapes on his face with the cuff of her pajamas.

"Can't win for losing, can I?" Marconi mumbled. "I...I didn't accomplish much. Dying with a clean conscience is kind of selfish, when you think about it."

"They're just messing with us," a thin man said from the far corner. "They won't murder us for nothing."

"We're Heart Worlders," Marconi said. "Soon as that Murphy turned up, it was open season on all of us. Don't suppose anyone in here's a priest? I'd like to confess some sins before it's too late."

"I just want to see my baby again," the woman said. "I didn't *do* anything to anyone!"

A vibration began in the deck plating and the condemned froze. Marconi knew the sound airlock doors made when they opened. They must have just spaced another lock full of loyalists, he realized. No doubt they were next, and he closed his eyes. Would the mutineers pull the air from the lock first, slowly enough to make a show out of them suffocating to death, or would they override the safety controls and have a laugh as they were all blasted into space like confetti?

"Everyone exhale, unless you want to die from a lung embolism," Marconi said. "Remember, it's only nine to twelve seconds to unconsciousness in a vacuum. So just pass out and pass on from lack of oxygen."

"You shut up!" the man in the corner wailed.

Marconi let his breath out and thought of his parents. He'd promised he wouldn't get killed doing anything stupid, that last time he saw them. Getting spaced during a mutiny seemed borderline, but at least word would get to them eventually. He wouldn't be "missing in action" for seven years until he was declared dead, like his older brother or—

A hammer hit the armorplast hard enough to star even its steel-hard surface with cracks. Then an entire line of sudden divots tracked across the bulkhead, across the airlock door, into the solid alloy on its other side.

Marconi opened an eye.

"Now they're *shooting* Hearts?" the woman asked. "Anyone else get the choice between getting spaced or getting a bullet?"

"No...I think the equation's changed." Marconi rubbed a sleeve across his still bleeding nose and grimaced at the red smear.

The airlock door slid open and the muzzle of a gun barrel thrust into the chamber. It belonged to a massive battle rifle in the powered gauntlets of a Hoplon suit of battle armor. Several broken and cracked marshal's badges were fixed to the suit's breastplate, and a black shield, mounted above the trophies, with the ancient, traditional balance scale of justice, superimposed across a stylized silver tree, glittered as it caught the light.

"No one move," a deep male voice said through the battle armor's external speakers. Behind him, several mutineers lay dead. Nahrong was slumped over one side of his throne, soaked in blood from the large bullet wounds through his chest. "No one do anything stupid."

Marconi raised his cuffed hands up to his chin.

"Get corpsmen up here. Then shut down every airlock on this station until we've got this place under control," a crisp voice said from behind the Hoplon. "Eira, get in there and see if anyone needs immediate treatment."

A young blond woman in an armored vac suit with the same symbol on her chest stepped around the Hoplon. She held a sidearm that she kept pointed to the ceiling in a two-hand grip as she looked over the prisoners.

"That one," she pointed her chin at Marconi and stepped into the airlock.

"No," snapped from the Hoplon. "What's the protocol when treating potential hostiles?"

"We're no hostiles! We're super friendly. We promise!" the mother exclaimed.

She waved at the blonde. The battle rifle nudged slightly towards her and she shrank away.

"You've scanned them for weapons," the blonde said with a frown. "No uncovered sight lines to the principal...Oh right." She holstered her sidearm and clicked a biometric lock on its side. The holster tightened around the weapon, making it impossible for anyone with the wrong gauntlet code or the wrong DNA to draw it again.

"Next protocol?" the Hoplon growled.

"If attacked I—"

"Not out loud!" The Hoplon shifted its weight and Marconi tried to smile, but his lips hurt too much. "Treat him already."

The blonde tugged off her vac suit's gauntlets and mag-sealed them to her sleeves, then held her empty hands up to Marconi and knelt beside him.

"Rest of you to the back," the Hoplon said. "Don't be stupid and you won't get hurt."

The blonde touched the bandages on Marconi's calf and pressed around the edges.

"Ow," he deadpanned.

"My name's Eira." She looked at him squarely and he noticed the slaver's gene brand over one eye. "I'm going to give you medical attention to keep you stable until we can get you to a proper treatment facility."

"The guy in the tin can makes you read off a script?" Marconi asked.

"There's only one way to do things, and that's the right way," she said. She turned a palm to his face and a screen mounted on her forearm cast pale light over her face. "Deep contusions. Blood pressure elevated. Adrenaline levels are falling, which means the pain will get worse. Any known allergies to Federation standard angleasics? No, anal-gessicks. An-anal—" She looked over her shoulder to the Hoplon.

"Eyes on the patient!"

"I'll take all the painkillers you got," Marconi told her.

"Stupid big words," she muttered. But she also opened and closed her other hand quickly. An injection module snapped forward over her wrist, and she plugged a fingertip into the apparatus and touched Marconi's neck.

There was a hiss and Marconi sighed in relief as the painkiller hit.

"Whoever treated your bullet wound did a poor job," she said. "I need to redo everything or you're likely to bust your synth clots and bleed to death. Hold still."

She pulled a thin black strap from her belt and wrapped it around his leg just below the knee. The tourniquet pulled into place and the pressure would have been painful if the anesthetics hadn't already been working their magic.

Marconi sat back, his eyes on the ceiling. He'd never liked watching medics work, and he certainly didn't care for the show when he was the star.

"Sorry we couldn't get here sooner." A black-haired young man with an eyepatch stepped around the Hoplon and leaned over Marconi, blocking the light. He wore an armored vac suit with the helmet racked on his chest, and the engineer recognized the voice that had ordered the airlocks shut down. "Rough business out there."

"Who're you?" Marconi narrowed his eyes.

"Name's Murphy."

"Can't be," the engineer objected. "You're not old enough."

"I didn't say I was *that* Murphy," the other man said. "Name's Callum—Lieutenant Callum Murphy. Dad's a little busy right now, so he sent me instead." He shook his head, his single eye somber. "None of this lynch mob stuff was by my dad's order. Trust me, he's the due process type."

"Oh, so after she's done patching me up we'll all have proper trials before we get to taste vacuum," Marconi chuckled, and that still managed to hurt, despite the painkillers.

"He's also not the sort to hang you for something someone else did." Lieutenant Murphy smiled. "And the way he sees it, just being on the wrong side—excuse me, on the *other* side—doesn't necessarily make you guilty of anything. We'll get you home soon as the situation allows."

"And until then?" Marconi asked.

"We should send them all to Inverness," the young woman—Eira—said. "Kinda cold this time of the year, but it'd do them good to see it."

She tossed bloody bandages and red wadding to one side, then took a small canister off her belt and pressed the nozzle into the open wound on his leg.

"You have nothing to fear from our people," Lieutenant Murphy said. "I'm no murderer, and neither is my dad."

"How 'bout—" Marconi's vision swam from the painkillers and he was aware that he was about to ask a very stupid question, but being drugged up had removed much of his verbal filter. "How 'bout all them ships he just blew to hell?"

"I said he's no murderer. He *is* a killer, when he has to be. So am I, for that matter." Lieutenant Murphy gave Marconi a tight smile. "Guess you might say it runs in the family."

Marconi looked at him for a moment. Then his eyes dropped, and the lieutenant looked at the blonde.

"Eira, the next wave of Marines are docking soon. Pass him on to them if he's stable, then catch up to me."

"Aye, aye," she said.

Lieutenant Murphy gave her a pat on the shoulder and left the airlock.

"Is he for real?" Marconi asked. "He doesn't seem like the vids make his father out to be."

"I need you to be quiet and keep still for a minute." Eira sucked in her lips and tugged at the bandages on his leg. "This was a terrible patch job. Whoever did it was more interested in keeping you from bleeding all over the place than saving your leg. Minor perforation to the soleal vein... Do you have any sensation in the bottom of that foot?"

"It hurt like a mother flocker before. Things are all floaty now," Marconi said. "Why're you patching me up? Ain't we all going to another airlock?"

"Callu—Lieutenant Murphy meant what he said. You're lucky we docked in the same bay as you. Some of the Fringers didn't think he was serious when he ordered them to not murder you all, but—Ooh! The quick-clot compound's massing in your medial gastroc—gastro—the big blue one on my screen. Hold on."

Eira jammed a thumb under Marconi's knee and he groaned in pain.

"There. Couple hundred cc's of O negative and you'll be almost normal," she said. "Prosthetics are hard to come by these days."

"Just jam a peg in the hole and I'll join Murphy's merry band of pirates. Son's taller'n I expceded he'd be. No horns, though. Least not on him. Dunno 'bout his dad yet."

"I don't care what anyone else says about Admiral Murphy." She spritzed some blue foam onto a fingertip and swiped it across his split lips. "He saved my life and he saved millions more on Crann Bethadh."

She unsnapped the tourniquet from his leg and wrapped bio film around his fresh bandage.

"You're... super pretty," Marconi slurred.

"I gave you weight-appropriate painkillers. Are you normally this forward?"

"Nope! Near death 'speriences... make me... make me... What're we talking about?"

"Okay, you're green across all the checklists. Why don't you lean back and relax?" Eira touched his face and pushed the back of his head gently against the airlock wall.

"You tell that Murphy guy we all jus'... jus' wanna go home. If he'll let us." Marconi drifted away.

Callum Murphy stood over a corpse.

Most of the cranium was gone, smeared across the bulkhead and workstations of Jalal Station's command center. The smell of drying blood and brain matter had become unfortunately familiar to him, and he knew he'd forgo any sugar in his coffee for the next few weeks.

Two more bodies lay crumpled in pools of blood that had turned dark and tacky, and there were other blood trails, not adorned by the bodies of those who'd made them. He knelt, cautious on his prosthetic knee, and turned the mostly headless body on its side.

"This is Captain Tibor," he said.

"You're sure?" his father asked over his earbud sixty seconds later. He'd insisted on moving *Ishtar* ninety light-seconds closer to the station after the shooting had stopped. O'Hanraghty had made his opinion of that decision abundantly clear, but to no avail. Although they'd at least managed to keep him aboard the big carrier.

Callum knew his father could see the feed from his own vac suit's camera, but he couldn't see the admiral in return.

"I'm sure," he said grimly, double-checking the name tape. Then he shoved awkwardly back to his feet, covering his mouth and nose against the stench.

"And this one's Portier," Harrison O'Hanraghty said, prodding another of the bodies with his boot.

"Damn," Murphy muttered, and Callum heard him over the comm as he inhaled, pictured the characteristic shake of his father's head. "So they're both dead. Wonderful. And the rest of the command crew?"

O'Hanraghty scowled. He scraped a fingernail over a blood-smeared display, clearing away a few red flakes. Then he rapped a knuckle against a blinking cursor and sighed.

"Harder to say," he said. "We've got three of them in custody, and they're all Fringers and they all have fairly consistent stories. Tibor must've known what was in the wind. I don't know if he was actively involved in the planning, but when Galanatos transmitted the execute, he produced a sidearm from inside his shipsuit, and a couple of the junior watch officers backed his play. Apparently he thought—hoped, prayed, maybe, for all I know!— that they could talk Portier into standing down. He was wrong."

The chief of staff shook his head and used his forearm to scrub blood from another display as he continued speaking.

"He might've pulled it off if Portier'd been one bit less stubborn. Or if *he*'d been readier to pull the trigger. She hadn't brought a gun of her own, but she managed to grab one of the armed JOs. Got control of his gun, used him as a human shield, hit the panic button..."

O'Hanraghty shrugged.

"If Tibor'd just gone ahead and fired, he'd probably still be alive. But he hesitated—probably couldn't bring himself to shoot through his own man to get her—and she opened fire when one of the other JOs moved. And then Station security came busting in through the hatch on her override, and the entire situation went straight into the shitter. Thirty-three people in the compartment when it started: five of them dead, six with the medics, three in custody, and God only knows where the others are. It's a shit sandwich in here, Terrence."

"Can we at least please get the air vents functioning?" Callum asked, still covering his mouth and nose with his hand.

"I'd love to." O'Hanraghty shrugged again. "But some of the loyalists—excuse me, the Feds—had free access to the Station's systems for several minutes. Over half an hour, in at least a couple of cases, before they were taken out. They've sabotaged a lot of systems, but they didn't have control here in Command Central after the shootout, and the mutineers managed to shut down AuxCom and Engineering One. Which at least meant some frigging lunatic with a death wish couldn't blow the entire station to kingdom come."

He scowled at the displays he'd been trying to clear, then straightened and looked at Callum as the younger man moved closer to the pair of Hoplons standing on either side of Command Central's open hatch. The air on the other side of that hatch was no prize, but at least it was better than the abattoir stench of the command center itself.

"Leaving aside Callum's query about air vents, how long until we can restore full functionality?" Murphy asked.

"Hours." O'Hanraghty sighed. "For the equipment and systems, that is. Personnel matters are a bit more...complicated. I couldn't give you even an educated guess on that end."

"Can we hook me into a station-wide address?" Murphy asked after the inevitable light-speed delay.

"Soon as the central stack recompiles," O'Hanraghty said. "Half an hour at least, though."

"Another half hour of mayhem," Murphy said bleakly. "Sergeant Major Logan. What's the status on our boarding parties?"

"Better question for the Brigadier, Sir," Logan replied.

"I'm sure it is," Murphy said dryly, "but he's a little occupied right now. Besides, I want a frontline grunt's take."

"Well, if you put it that way, Sir, I'd say our people are in pretty good shape," Logan said, after a moment. "We've got enough Hoplons aboard that nobody but another Hoplon wants to mess with us. And looks like somewhere around half the Station personnel are on our side. Or not on the Feds' side, anyway. But it's messy, Sir. Be lying if I said different. Brigadier Atkins's got maybe enough warm bodies over here to lock down the control nodes, but no way enough to secure the entire station. 'Specially not with all the parasite crews. Not till we thin the herd some more."

"I knew that was going to make problems." Murphy sighed, and O'Hanraghty scowled.

"Still the best of your options, though," he said sternly, and Callum nodded.

Logan was right, of course—ordering the personnel of every parasite orbiting with the station to evacuate *to* the station—or to Jalal Beta—on pain of their ships' destruction had at least shut down the last of the fighting. It had also pulled the parasites' teeth, which was the only reason O'Hanraghty—and Callum, to be honest—hadn't pitched ten different kinds of fit when Murphy insisted on bringing *Ishtar* in closer. But it also meant that even after they'd used every available lifeboat and escape pod to evacuate direct from their ships to the planetary surface, the next best thing to 81,000 spacers and Marines had funneled aboard Jalal Station itself, instead.

The enormous station had the life support to handle the additional load, at least temporarily, and roundtrip shuttles were already delivering the rest of the refugees to Jalal Beta's surface. It wasn't the most pleasant planetary environment in the entire Federation, but it was better than being packed like sardines aboard the station. Besides, until they could "thin the herd," as the sergeant major had so eloquently put it, by getting the majority of them dirtside, Brigadier Atkins simply lacked anything like the numbers needed to effectively lock down the station.

"How bad is it, Logan?" Murphy asked now.

"Fair amount of looting through the Promenade, Sir. And I think there's a lot of score-settling going on." The sergeant major grimaced inside the bubble of his turret-like helmet. "Don't know that all of it's Fringe-versus-Heart, either. Some of it's just plain personal, looks like. But whatever it is, it's gonna leave a lot of bodies before it's done. A lot of armed Feds've gone to ground in Logistics and Hydroponics Five, and they've got control of one of the heavy-lift freight boat bays. Per your orders, the Brigadier's keeping them isolated but not looking for a fight. Right now, we've got all of the priority targets under our control."

"But you don't think we can push out from the priority targets?"

"No, Sir," Logan said firmly. "Not unless you can find the Brigadier another five, six thousand Marines, we can't. Not till we get more people out of this can and down to the planet."

"I don't want to jinx anything," Callum said, "but even allowing for what the Smaj just said, it seems like everything's gone pretty smoothly. Or a lot more smoothly than it *could* have, anyway. All things considered."

"Why did you say that?" O'Hanraghty shook his head. "Crann Bethadh should have taught you not to say that."

"What? Given the casualties we could've taken—*would've* taken, if we hadn't been able to shut down the ship-to-ship fighting and get our boarding parties aboard the Station so quickly—we actually got off lightly. And not *everything's* broken." He removed his hand from his nose and raised it, palm up. "I know a lot of people got killed, and we won't even know how many of them for a while, but we could be standing around knee-deep in blood and bodies, and we aren't."

O'Hanraghty gave him a skeptical look, and he shrugged.

"Callum," Murphy said. "Look over the munitions logs and tell me what you find. Harrison, we have a problem."

"Only one?" O'Hanraghty chuckled. "Things must be going better than I thought."

"The kangaroo court Callum interrupted wasn't the only one," Murphy said grimly.

"I know." O'Hanraghty's smile faded into a grimace. "And I wouldn't be a bit surprised if some of those 'justice-loving' Fringe bastards aren't still butchering as many Hearts as they can get away with before we catch up with them."

"Exactly," Murphy agreed. "And this isn't the last time we'll come across sudden allies with blood on their hands."

"I know," O'Hanraghty repeated. He exhaled a long breath. "But we can't hold an inquiry every time Fringers mutiny and seize a ship or remove Heart officers. If a ship comes over with eighty percent of her full complement, it'll be fair to assume most of her people agreed and came over peacefully. But it won't help our case one bit if we bring out-and-out war criminals into the fold."

"Even leaving that aside—you're right, but even leaving the pragmatic considerations aside—we're not out here to turn a blind eye to score-settling or pure vengeance. Barbarity serves no one," Murphy said. "This is a revolt. I don't want it to turn into a civil war."

"The Free Worlds Alliance would say it's a revolution, not a revolt," O'Hanraghty replied.

"What's the difference?" Callum asked, looking up from a computer workstation whose displays were thankfully free of blood spatter.

"A revolt is a forceful and often violent objection to the status quo," Murphy said. "A revolution's the *end* of the status quo. The introduction of a new order. And that's what we need to head off. The Federation's *sound*—fundamentally sound. It's governed Earth and most of her colonies—outside the League, anyway—for over three hundred years. Ushered in scientific advances and prosperity for billions. Surveyed hundreds of star systems, regulated interstellar trade, and instituted and enforced interstellar law and courts. We can't let all of that just be thrown away."

"Would those be the same Federation courts that sent marshals to arrest you on trumped-up charges and got President Tolmach killed in the process?" Callum asked.

The silence over the comm lasted longer than the light-speed lag could account for, this time.

"Bad actors," Murphy said then. "We can't hold the entire Federation responsible for the actions of an inner clique. That's why this is a revolt and not a revolution."

And that, Callum realized, was also why his father willingly recognized the Free Worlds Alliance as an organized group of star systems protesting their treatment but had always stopped short of recognizing the validity of the FWA's declaration of secession. Of course, how long he could keep that up—

"Callum has a point, Sir," O'Hanraghty said in an unwontedly formal tone. "That arrest warrant came from the highest court in the Federation. The Prime Minister and her cabinet wanted you in cuffs and humiliated in front of the entire human race, and the court issued the warrant exactly as ordered, without even a pro forma objection, as far as we can tell. And from what Lipshen said, the Oval and the IG signed off on it without so much as a protest. Then there's the Alliance's grievances—its entirely justified grievances—and the Federation's policy—its *longstanding* policy—of sacrificing Fringe worlds to protect Heart money."

"I'm aware of that," Murphy said quietly. "But the underlying cause of all this—what created the preconditions for it—is the war against the League. That's what distorted and twisted the entire system."

"Maybe it created the preconditions," O'Hanraghty conceded. "But that's not the problem anymore, is it? Preconditions or no preconditions, it's the people invested in maintaining the status quo that are the problem now."

"Back to the bloodbath out here," Murphy said.

O'Hanraghty opened his mouth, then closed it again at the admiral's abrupt change of topics and looked across the reeking command deck at Callum. Their eyes met in a moment of shared understanding, and something almost like pity, then the chief of staff's nostrils flared.

"Of course, Sir," he said.

"Every death will be investigated," Murphy said, "and unless Commodore Taylor refuses to cooperate with 'mutineers,' his people will take lead with Prajita riding shotgun."

O'Hanraghty looked dubious for a moment, but then he nodded, instead.

Commodore Aaron Taylor was—had been—Portier's JAG officer, Jalal Station's senior cop. He had a reputation as a relentless investigator and an equally relentless prosecutor, and rumor had it he'd been exiled to Jalal because he'd refused to turn a blind eye just because the object of his investigation sprang from one of the Five Hundred's premier families. Lieutenant Prajita Tripathi, Murphy's JAG, was little more than half his age and astronomically junior to him, but they were actually very much alike under the skin. And if Murphy could get someone with Taylor's well-earned reputation to endorse any investigation's integrity...

"The more egregious cases will be easy to identify and prosecute under the Uniform Code of Justice," Murphy continued. "That case law's sound...most of the time. And a few prominent prosecutions of murders will put out the word that the Alliance doesn't consist of barbarians out to loot and kill for the sake of looting and killing."

"Good policy, Sir," O'Hanraghty said. "I'll see it gets done."

"How's this going to play out back in the Heart?" Callum asked, looking back down at a lit screen and tapping in commands. "Are we the Huns or Fringe Jihadists or—That's funny."

He frowned at the data scrolling across his workstation.

"I'm not worried about the Heart's opinion," O'Hanraghty said. "We're not getting off that naughty list whatever we do."

"This can still end at the negotiating table and not at the muzzle of a gun," Murphy said. "Revolt, not revolu—Wait. What's 'funny,' Callum?"

"I just compiled the magazine inventory for the outer hull cargo rails, and there are thousands of missiles in transfer containers," Callum said. "Must've moved them out of the magazines at least three or four weeks ago, from the inventory. That's convenient. It'll shave days off how long it would take to steal what we need if we had to dig them out of the magazines ourselves."

"We don't 'steal.' We ... what did you call it, Harry?"

"Dynamically acquire, Sir." O'Hanraghty's tone was a bit absent as he woke up a nearby terminal. He pulled Callum's screen view to him and simultaneously shared it to Murphy's display aboard *Ishtar*.

"One coming in," Private Steiner said from his post beside the hatch through his Hoplon armor's external speakers. "Cleared."

Eira stepped past him onto the bridge. Her nostrils crinkled at the smell. She gave O'Hanraghty a nod and crossed to Callum.

"Did you take your peptide supplement?" she asked.

"Huh? No," he said. "Been too busy trying to stop the galaxy from burning down."

"Damn it!" Murphy snarled over the comm. "How long do you think we have, Harry?"

"Wait." Callum frowned. "What did I just miss?"

"Why would Jalal Station move missiles and warheads out of deep storage into transfer containers on the outer hull ranks?" O'Hanraghty asked in response.

"Because ... the mutineers knew we were coming and wanted to help us out?"

O'Hanraghty glanced at him, shook his head, and went back to typing queries into the workstation.

"No?" Callum frowned. "Why else would the Station pre-position all that equipment if they weren't expecting to—Oh. Oh, no."

Callum rubbed his eyepatch, and Eira pursed her lips and looked a silent question at him.

"I should've seen it on my own," he told her. "The Federation's coming here in force. That's why the out-hull cargo stations are full of weapons. They're coming here from..."

"Has to be detachments from First Fleet," O'Hanraghty said.

"First Fleet?" Callum frowned at him, because First Fleet was the primary combat component of the Beta Cygni front.

"Has to be," O'Hanraghty repeated. "Oh, they could draw some strength from the Reserve, but they won't want to cut too deeply into that. And there hasn't been enough time to assemble detachments from the Heart fleet stations. This is good news and bad news."

"Good news? If they send the entire Beta Cygni Fleet, we'll be outmanned and outgunned by—"

Callum's remaining eye looked up and to the left as he did the mental math.

"*Detachments*, I said." O'Hanraghty glanced up at him for a moment. "They won't send the entire fleet, Callum. They can't. The front would collapse."

"And they haven't had time to recall it, anyway," Murphy said over the comm. "They'll send enough of Harry's 'detachments' to convince me I can't win a standup fight, leave me no choice but to run for the Blue Line or surrender. That's Harry's bad news. The good news is that this fight was inevitable, and at least we've got time to set conditions in our favor."

"We *want* to have a pitched battle here?" Callum frowned. "I thought we didn't want to get into a fight at all. I thought the idea was to continue to Sol!"

"And what happens to Crann Bethadh and the rest of the FWA if we make for Sol now we know they're coming? You think a fleet the size they're probably sending to meet us will just turn around and go home when it gets here and finds out about the Free Worlds?" Callum could almost hear his father's headshake. "No. If we're not here to stop it, the Federation'll turn its wrath on the systems in revolt, and then it'll be Gobelins all over again. Or they'll simply invoke Standing Order Fifteen to justify the orbital bombardment of every planet in the Alliance."

"They wouldn't..." Callum went pale.

"I was on Gobelins," Logan said from his post by the hatch. "I've seen what happens when they send in the Army to deal with revolts or worlds 'out of compliance.' It ain't pretty."

"I didn't realize you'd been on Gobelins, Anniston," O'Hanraghty said, turning to face him fully. "I should've wondered."

"Why?" Callum asked, and O'Hanraghty shrugged.

"I've been through the jackets on all of your dad's security detail. There's a redacted section in Logan's from about the time Gobelins went down."

"I was there," Logan confirmed, and the voice over his armor's speaker was harsher even than usual. Harsher than the speaker alone could explain.

"I hadn't realized that, either," Murphy said over the comm, and Callum heard him draw a deep breath. "Was it really as bad as I think it was?" he asked almost gently.

"Pretty sure it was worse, Sir, if you don't mind my saying it," Logan replied. "Known you a while now. Your brain's not sick enough to imagine what it was like."

"Tell us," Murphy said. "Please."

Callum's eyes were on the sergeant major, but those eyes narrowed as he heard his father's tone. It wasn't an order. It was genuinely the request it sounded like. And as he realized that, Callum realized something else. His father wasn't asking for his own benefit; he was asking for *Callum's* benefit.

Logan was silent for a long moment, then—

"Drop didn't go bad," he said, "but none of the Marines were happy about the duty. You serve long enough, you do some shitty things. Some things you don't want to face or remember. But we spend most of our time with the Fleet. We get sent down to shoot somebody, it's usually Leaguies, not our own. That's what the fucking Army's for, Sir. Five Hundred's wrecking crew. Its leg breakers. Only time it ever gets deployed to the Fringe is when there's a 'problem' that needs ironing out, and it irons it. Fucking right, it irons it."

He paused for a moment, jaw tight enough for the muscles to ridge.

"Anyway," he resumed after a moment, "you know how it is between us and the Army pukes, Admiral. Lot of it's just the usual horseshit between branches, sure. But not all of it. Not when it comes to putting desperate folks back into compliance. So, yeah, we weren't any too happy when we got picked to back up the Army. And Alaimo knew it. Called my battalion CO a 'crayon-eating coward' to his face before the drop, and my platoon got sent to secure a mountain pass leading out of the planetary capital. Didn't want us leading the assault. Didn't trust us to be the tip of the spear, even though that's what Marines are for. What we do. We drop hard, and we kill Leaguies until the Army's ready to waltz in for the victory parade and take the credit. Way it always works. But not this time. Nah, *this* time he didn't trust us to kill everybody he wanted killed."

He paused again, and O'Hanraghty nodded, his own expression grim.

"My LT did everything by The Book. Checkpoint around a natural obstacle. LP/OPs on every likely avenue of approach. Drone and drop sensor coverage ten klicks out. Rebels weren't going to fart without us knowing about it. I was a team leader, and I was on the checkpoint when a ground car pulled up. We were supposed to turn civilians back, keep them penned in around the capital while Alaimo...did what he was sent there to do."

"Who was in the car?" O'Hanraghty asked quietly.

"A woman and three children." Logan's voice cracked for a second. "We had biometrics and photos of every high-value target. They weren't on any kill/capture list, but they were the wife and the children of one of the system assembly's delegates. Nothing in our files said he'd been part of Butler's clique, had anything to do with the decision to secede. Didn't much matter. By that time, everyone on the frigging planet knew what was happening to *all* the delegates. 'S why she was running with her kids. And I was in my Hoplon armor....God, those kids were *so* scared of me. You ever had a kid look at you in terror, Sir?"

"Can't say I have," O'Hanraghty said.

"I tried to calm them down, but that's not what the suit's voice box is built for. It carries a four-cycle-per-second frequency. It's *designed* to scare people, as if the suit's not enough by itself. The kids were begging their mother to leave, she's begging me to let them through, and I couldn't just *do* that. No matter how much I wanted to. Orders, no exceptions. Everybody had to be cleared by Central. But they were women and children. They weren't combatants, hadn't had a damned thing to do with the decision to go out of compliance. But...no exceptions.

"So the LT calls it in, just like we're supposed to. Talking to Central. Then *General* Alaimo cuts through all the channels, and he says two words: 'Eliminate them.'" Logan's voice cracked again. "The mom, she had cash and a contact that could get her and the kids off-world. And they didn't mean *squat* to the mission. Not the mission the way we'd been briefed. Not the *official* mission."

"But you weren't in command," O'Hanraghty said quietly.

"Nope. LT was. But LT, he was a good Marine. Fresh out of OCS. True believer. He'd never seen the elephant, either. First combat deployment. So he calls up our chain of command for clarification, but Alaimo pulls him into a one-on-one channel for a bit. General got his point across, and then the LT, he pulled them all out of the car—"

Callum's stomach tightened as he heard the unshed tears hovering in the sergeant major's voice. As he waited for Logan to tell the rest.

"LT, he . . . he couldn't do it. Hell, he hadn't even killed a Leaguie yet! Can't expect someone to start with women and children. He couldn't. So he breaks his wideband antenna, so Alaimo can't drop in again, and tries to get company or battalion on the horn. But we're being jammed, for some reason."

"Alaimo didn't want witnesses," O'Hanraghty said.

"Can see why you did so well in Intelligence, Sir," Logan said harshly. "Anyway, LT keeps trying to call for help. And then Alaimo's command shuttle sets down and the man himself gets out with half a dozen Army Hoplon pukes. Doesn't say a word. Just looks at us like we're worse than dog shit, and then he takes the mom and kids away in the shuttle. Thing is, it doesn't head back to the capital. No, it heads out towards the ocean. We watched it on the IFF trackers. Shuttle goes out a klick or two, does a U-turn over the water, and heads back to the city.

"Never saw or heard of those civilians again."

Callum swallowed hard, but Logan wasn't done yet. It was as if some inner dam had broken, and the words came out hard, with whetted-steel edges.

"LT, he about loses his shit. We finally get taken off the checkpoint, and he goes straight to the company commander, and Captain Arriga, she goes to our battalion commander, and they all go to confront Alaimo. Never came back. Air car accident, officially. And then Alaimo puts his Army pukes in charge of us Marines and sends us first into every fight he can find. And whatever you may've heard, they fought back hard on Gobelins, after they figured out what Alaimo had in store for 'em even if they surrendered. Casualties were . . . high. Where I took my first bullet."

"And that justified the K-strikes on Altamont and Ballston," Murphy said over the comm from *Ishtar.*

"Yep." Logan's voice was quieter now, almost washed out. "Oh, he'd've been just as happy as a pig in shit to get more Marines killed trying to break the perimeter. But he was making a point. Making a *statement.* Every civilian on the damned planet was a hostage, and he'd kill every fucking one of them if the 'rebels' didn't lie down and die for him."

"And after Gobelins was pacified, Alaimo got off clean," O'Hanraghty said, this time looking at Callum, not Logan. "Helps to be the attack dog for certain Five Hundred members whose financial interests seem to coincide with everywhere he's sent."

"I heard the Société Auchan stepped in, bought up every local corporation that didn't seem to have owners anymore, somehow," Logan said. "Hadn't seen how it worked—not up close and personal—until then. Too many years into being a Marine, I realized that even I'd been the Five Hundred's mercenary."

"Why did you stay in, Anniston?" Murphy asked quietly, and, again, Callum knew who his father was really asking that question for. "You cleared your mandatory service term years ago. So why not put in your papers?"

"Can't, Sir. I love my Marines. No one else's gonna take care of them the way I can. And they goddamn well deserve somebody who will."

Callum looked past the sergeant major's armor, saw Eira's expression—the fierce affection, the love, burning in her eyes like blue fire—and knew she hadn't been surprised by the sergeant major's answer.

"Anyway, like I say,—" Logan turned his head in his armor's domed helmet and looked directly at Callum "—it ain't pretty any time the Army moves in. And Standing Order Fifteen's even worse when it gets invoked."

"And if they'd do it to Gobelins, Callum—do it when only a single star system was involved—what do you think they'll be willing to do when they find out they're looking at over a *dozen* star systems going 'out of compliance'?"

"Of course, they don't know yet that they are," O'Hanraghty pointed out, and sixty seconds later Murphy barked a harsh laugh over the comm.

"They don't know yet, Harry, but they will. And President

Tolmach spent his dying breath begging me to protect Crann Bethadh," Murphy said. "I can't leave them vulnerable. And I can't leave a percentage of our force behind to cover every system that's pledged support to the Alliance, either. If I do that, I'll show up in Sol hitching a ride with some tramp freighter, and we have to make *that* trip with enough force to make the thought of a pitched battle over the Earth itself too costly for the Oval to contemplate. Then we can talk."

"So what do we do?" Callum asked.

"O'Hanraghty comes back to *Ishtar*," Murphy said. "I'll send Tremblay and Jurgens over to replace him on the Navy side. Until they get there, I need you to hold the fort for me, Callum. Don't joggle Atkins's elbow. That's not your job. But you're my eyes and ears—and voice—over there."

Callum's expression was unhappy, but his father continued before he could speak.

"Go ahead and start getting the Station's defenses back online, too. I doubt any Fed commander would want to destroy this installation unless he thought he had absolutely no other choice, but I want options to protect it beyond charging face-first into a missile barrage."

"So I'll just . . . stay here?" Callum said, and O'Hanraghty gave him an oddly sympathetic look as he headed for the hatch.

"Get a data feed to *Ishtar* and flag any data you find 'funny,'" he said. "And, trust me, we'll be handing you plenty of headaches of your own."

Callum looked skeptical, and O'Hanraghty waved an index finger at him.

"Stay put," he said firmly. "I know you think you should be out there sorting stuff out. But that's not your job. Let Atkins's people handle the head-knocking. That's *their* job. You stay here and do yours. Last thing we need is you going sightseeing and getting into God knows what!" He glanced at Logan. "I trust you got that, too, Sergeant Major?"

"Got it, Sir," Logan rumbled, and O'Hanraghty disappeared through the hatch.

Callum stared at the opening for a moment, then put his hands on his hips.

"They left me behind," he said.

"They gave you a job," Eira said.

"Yeah? So why did they lock me up in here instead of out there? 'Fraid I'll stub my damned toe or something?"

"They gave you a job," Eira repeated. "A pretty important one, from what I heard."

"Maybe." Callum scowled, then looked down at her. "What took you so long getting here? I was a little worried."

"I was delayed at the bars on the Promenade." Eira grimaced. "The prostitutes there are very excited to welcome anyone and everyone into their establishments. They didn't seem to understand I needed to be somewhere else."

"Yeah, well... good for them," Callum said. "At least we've got those hearts and minds on our side."

"They're whores," Logan said. "They're on everyone's side. Captain's point is that there's still a lot of people out there who *ain't* on our side. And most of 'em'd just love to put a bullet or three in anybody named Murphy."

Eira nodded quickly, and Callum shrugged.

"Fine," he said. "I'll just sit and spin here, then."

"Your father trusts you," Eira said. "If he didn't, he wouldn't have sent you in his place in the first place. And now he needs you here."

"Here in Command Central, you mean? With Hoplons at the door to keep me nice and safe?"

"He trusted you enough to send you to break up that mob," Eira pointed out a bit more waspishly. "That wasn't exactly 'nice and safe.' And if he has to risk you again, he will. You know that. But, yes, he worries about you, too. You've already lost a leg and an eye. Are you really surprised he worries about your well-being?"

"I almost had my well-being blown off in New Dublin, and *that* came out all right. Mostly," Callum growled. Then he sighed. "Okay. Okay! Guess I'll just plunder these data archives until the Feds get here, and—"

He paused and scratched his chin thoughtfully.

"What?" Eira asked.

"I was just thinking. I wonder if they'll send Uncle Rajenda with their fleet?" Callum's mouth worked from side to side.

"Admiral Murphy has a brother?" she asked.

"In-law. My mom's brother. And let me tell you something; Uncle Raj wasn't what you'd call a big fan of my dad even before this mess. I can guarantee his opinion's even worse now."

CHAPTER EIGHT

Tara City
Planet of Crann Bethadh
New Dublin System
Free Worlds Alliance
November 10, 2552

"VICE PRESIDENT KARALAKI."

The bearded man stood to offer Aikaterini Karalaki his hand as she entered his office. He was a tall, stocky fellow, with brown-blond hair going to gray, and steady brown eyes.

"President Dewar."

Karalaki gripped his hand firmly, meeting those brown eyes, and hoped this meeting was about to go better than she was afraid it might.

"I believe you've met Vice President McFarland," Dewar continued, nodding to the brown-haired woman sitting to his right, and Karalaki shook McFarland's hand in turn. "And this—" he indicated another woman, a centimeter or two shorter than McFarland, in embroidered robes and a porcelain facemask "—is Yukimori Aiko, Ryukyu's delegate to the Free Worlds Alliance. I asked Aiko to join us because she's effectively our Minister of War."

"From Ryukyu?" Karalaki smiled slightly. "I imagine she's a good choice. We've heard about Ryukyan special forces back home on Odysseus."

"So have the Hearts." Yukimori's voice was sweet, but that sweetness was ribbed with iron as it flowed through the mask's mouth opening. "They've spilled enough of our blood instead of their own, at any rate. And I don't think they'll like what they'll be hearing about us shortly."

"Aiko's husband, Saneatsu, is the CO of the Ryukyu System Defense Force. A post *I* held here in New Dublin until the Hearts murdered President Tolmach."

Dewar's voice was both deeper and harsher than Yukimori's, and Karalaki nodded soberly. Until she'd reached Crann Bethadh, she hadn't known Dewar wasn't simply Tolmach's successor as president of New Dublin. He was also Tolmach's son-in-law.

"And these—" Dewar continued in a less-harsh tone, waving at the two Terran Federation Navy officers who rounded out the people waiting for Karalaki "—are Commodore Cerminar and Captain Carson. They're our senior naval officers in-system, and the Commodore is Governor Murphy's in-space commander."

"Commodore. Captain." Karalaki shook their hands in turn. Both officers wore standard TFN uniform, although she noticed a nonregulation flash on their right shoulders. It showed a balance scale superimposed across a silver tree.

"Please, sit down," Dewar said, waving at the empty chair at the foot of the conference table, and Karalaki settled into it while he resumed his own place at the table's head. She ordered her expression to remain calm and politely attentive, although she was less than confident she'd succeeded in that.

"I promised you we'd get back to you as quickly as we could," the president said, tipping back his chair. "Obviously, there's no way we can send dispatches to all of the FWA's systems to consult with them, but that's why we have the Council of Delegates here in Tara, and I've talked to them. In fact, I put a proposal before them, and they voted to approve it."

Karalaki blinked behind her calm expression. She'd reached Tara, the capital of Crann Bethadh, only the day before, and Dewar's astonished surprise had been obvious when she walked into his office. If he'd put together a "proposal" this quickly, then what—?

"As I told you Tuesday," he continued, "no one here in New Dublin anticipated this little bonfire spreading as rapidly as your arrival suggests it may. Governor Murphy certainly didn't, although—" he smiled a trifle sadly "—that may be because he genuinely hopes that somehow this can all be 'worked out' over the conference table somewhere."

Despite herself, Karalaki frowned, and Dewar let his chair tip back forward again.

"Don't misunderstand me, Ms. Karalaki. Governor Murphy will take this wherever it goes, as far as he has to. He doesn't *want* to kill the Federation, and he'll do almost anything to avoid that...except to betray or abandon anyone he's given his word to. We've seen a lot of Hearts here in New Dublin, and we've our own vets who've seen the elephant up close and ugly, and there's not a lot of trust left in us where the Heart and the Five Hundred are concerned. In fact, most of us would sooner see the Five Hundred burning in hell than across any conference tables.

"But we've seen Murphy, too, and we've no fear at all of what *that* man means when he gives his word. And he's given his word to us—and to Alan Tolmach, when he lay dying in Murphy's arms—that he'll not betray New Dublin. He may fail, but only because he's died trying. And that leaves us some pretty big boots to fill in his absence."

"We don't know much about Governor Murphy in Bellerophon," Karalaki said into the silence, after a moment. "Only what Captain Anthellis could tell us when he got home with word of the Free Worlds Alliance. In all honesty, I have to tell you that at least some of President Xeneas's advisors back home in Kórinthos are a little...uneasy over the notion that he might be another Butler ready to run out on another Gobelins if the fire gets too hot."

Every other visible expression in the office stiffened, and Yukimori Aiko snapped upright in her chair.

"I think you can put your mind at ease about that, Ms. Vice President." There was an edge of ice in Dewar's tone. "In fact, I'm sure you can."

"What I was going to say, Mr. President," Karalaki in a level voice, "is that it's already obvious to me that those advisors were mistaken. I don't think anyone could possibly *blame* them for their fear that he might. All of us know what the Heart will do to any Fringe World that stands up for its people, so of course they were afraid. They *are* afraid. I think it would take an extraordinarily stupid or at least unimaginative person to *not* be afraid."

"You're right about that," Dewar acknowledged, and Yukimori sat back in her chair with a slight nod of her own. "Don't think anyone in this office isn't afraid—terrified—of where this could end. But we've seen enough of our blood, our kids, pissed away by the Hearts, and there comes a time you have to decide what you're ready to do to put a stop to that. It sounds like President Xeneas has reached the same conclusion. And let's be honest here. Adding all our populations together, the FWA's got less than half a billion people all told, but Bellerophon's got over a billion all by itself. Even with Bellerophon—hell, even if the entire Cyclops Sector came over to us!—we'd have fewer warm bodies than a single Heart system like Sol. So anybody we can get to join us has to be welcome, and President Xeneas's analysis of what's going to happen when the rest of the Fringe hears about all of this is probably accurate as hell."

"I wish I didn't agree with you," Karalaki said sadly. "Because even assuming we win in the end, it's going to be bloody."

"Perhaps even bloodier than you already think it could," Yukimori Aiko told her quietly. "The Hearts aren't the only threat we have to worry about, and no one knows what the Leaguies are likely to do about all of this. There's no way they can fail to see the possible opening any sort of Federation civil war would present."

"And if they somehow do, the Lizards won't," Dewar said grimly, and snorted as Karalaki's eyebrows rose.

"Yes, Ms. Karalaki, we believe the Governor about that, too. We've seen the evidence—some of our people have actually been to the Diyu System and walked the shipyards. Without that, I probably wouldn't have believed it, either, but it's true. And that means we have to be worrying about the damned Rish on top of everything else. The only good news there is how long it'll take the Sphere to find out what happened to their little pet project.

"But that's an entirely separate matter. What matters right this minute is that President Xeneas sent you to us with an offer to join the FWA and a request for assistance.

"The bad news from your perspective is that Governor Murphy isn't here, which means we have to decide what to do in his absence. And the corollary of that bad news is that he took his entire carrier strength with him when he pulled out for Jalal. We do have a single FTLC in-system, though. *Aurora* turned up just three days before you got here, and Captain Errezola's placed her under FWA command."

Karalaki nodded, trying to keep her dismay from showing.

Assuming every single carrier in the Cyclops Sector mutinied to support Bellerophon, *Aurora* would represent a twelve percent increase in the sector's naval strength. Which, if the Oval responded in strength, would mean only that the spit on the griddle might last a few seconds longer. And that was assuming Dewar and the FWA were willing to send her into such a hopeless confrontation in the first place.

"I realize a single carrier isn't a lot," Dewar continued, as if he'd read her mind. "We've got...a bit of an equalizer to send along, but I'd be lying if I said anyone in the FWA thinks Bellerophon would have a chance in hell of standing off the sort of heavy attack the Heart's likely to send your way as soon as they find out what's happened. Hopefully, President Xeneas will be able to keep word of that from getting out. Bad things happen to good people, though, so we're not planning to depend on that. Which brings me to the proposal the Council of Delegates has approved.

"Yesterday," he went on levelly, "immediately after the vote, I sent a courier to Governor Murphy at Jalal, telling him the Free Worlds Alliance has agreed to support Bellerophon and anyone else in the Cyclops Sector who chooses to join us. I realize none of us knows at this point what's happened at Jalal, but there's no doubt in my own mind that our courier will find Governor Murphy in possession. It's virtually certain that he got there before anything the Five Hundred and the Oval might have chosen to send, and, trust me, Ms. Karalaki, Terrence Murphy will pin back the ears of any Heart admiral they send to 'deal with him.' So I'm confident he'll receive our message and, knowing him, he'll respond quickly—and strongly. Most likely, he'll slice off a detachment of his own carriers and send them directly to Bellerophon to reinforce your defenses. And given the geometry, he can reach Bellerophon a lot more quickly than anything from the Heart could. If he has any head start at all, his detachment will be there before any attack from the Heart, in which case—" his smile was icy cold and razor thin "—that attack will find out *exactly* what happened to Admiral Xing when she decided to K-strike Crann Bethadh."

Karalaki's heart rose. Dewar actually knew Murphy, and if he truly believed—

"I understand it's easy to talk a good fight," the FWA president continued, "but we believe in putting our money where our mouths are. So, within twelve hours, *Aurora* will depart for Bellerophon, followed by *Charlotte* and *Andiron*, the only two FTL freighters we have in-system. They're a little slower than a carrier, so it'll take them a few days longer to make the passage. Commodore Cerminar would prefer to move his flag to *Aurora* and command the detachment himself, but he can't. There are still three FTLCs unaccounted for in Acera, and somebody has to stay home to mind the store until we know if they're going to turn up here in New Dublin. And what they'll turn up in New Dublin to *do*, of course. So we'll be sending Captain Carson—although I suppose she's *Commodore* Carson, now—instead."

"Mr. President, I deeply appreciate what you're saying," Karalaki said, "but can you really risk sending away the only carrier you've got under those circumstances?"

"Oh, trust me!" Dewar actually *grinned.* "All of us are just *hoping* some arrogant prick of a Heart flag officer will turn up and decide he can take New Dublin back with two or three carriers."

Karalaki's eyes widened as the other Fringers sitting around that table smiled in agreement with the president.

"Well, I'm certainly not going to object to anything you think you can spare for us," she said frankly.

"It's not as much as we wish we could send directly." Dewar's expression and voice alike were sober now. "It's only all we can—all we have the lift for. But hopefully, it'll help hold things together until the Governor gets there. And, trust me, Ms. Karalaki, he *will* get there."

CHAPTER NINE

Uromachi System
Di Jun Sector
Tè Lā Lián Méng
November 20, 2552

"WELL, EVERYTHING SEEMS NORMAL ENOUGH," CAPTAIN SU MUR-mured from beside Than Qiang's command chair while the continual loop of routine notices to shipping and traffic control transmissions murmured quietly in the background.

"Of course it does." Than's eyes were on the master display and the green icon of Jinan, otherwise known as Uromachi IV, gleaming before them as RHLNS *Cai Shen* and *Li Shiji* decelerated towards the G6 star's 43.7 LM Powell Limit. "As far as anyone in Uromachi knows, everything *is* normal."

They'd gone sublight 153.98 LM from the system primary seventy-two minutes ago, and their velocity had fallen to 220,743 KPS. They were still 48.7 LM from the Powell Limit, however, and Jinan—which lay 13 LM from the central star—was 30.7 LM *inside* the limit. That was far too long a distance for any sort of coherent conversation. Although they'd transmitted their transponder codes the instant they left wormhole space, those codes wouldn't even reach the massive fleet base in Jinan orbit for another thirty-eight minutes. For that matter, even at their current prodigious velocity and deceleration rate, Than's ships were still the next best thing to three hours out of Jinan orbit, and impatience simmered in his blood.

It simmered there, yet the truth was that despite his crawling sense of urgency, he would very much have preferred to stay far,

121

far away from this star system. But he couldn't, and if he had to report in, he would just as soon get it over with.

"I expect we'll be hearing from them in about—" he glanced at the time display "—seventy minutes or so. At which point, they're going to demand to know just what we're doing here." He grimaced. "I don't think Governor Zheng will be very happy when she finds out."

"I can't imagine why she wouldn't be, Sir," Su said dryly, and Than snorted.

They were still much too far out for active sensors, but *Cai Shen's* passive sensors had populated the main plot with a schematic of the inner system—or, at least, of the inner system as it had been just under an hour ago—and a dense spray of icons swarmed about the space immediately around Jinan. Navigation beacons, ships in orbit, inbound and outbound freighters, the blue diamonds that marked industrial platforms, the green stars of freight transfer points, the amber beads of power satellites...

The industrial and economic might that display represented was impressive. But only until Than thought about all that had been lost in Diyu.

Uromachi was the Di Jun Sector's administrative center. It was also home to one of the Tè Lā Lián Méng's major shipyard complexes, although the Jinan yards' tempo had been hugely reduced for the last eight standard years. That had created a lot of resentment among Uromachi's industrial magnates, who'd seen profits plunge as the demand for their orbital refineries' and extraction platforms' output plummeted. Unfortunately for them, the *guǎtóu*, the equivalent of the Federation's Five Hundred, lacked the degree of control over government policy that their Federation counterparts enjoyed. They'd been forced to swallow that resentment more or less in silence—which they'd done only sullenly—because no one in the Eternal Forward-dominated Accord that governed the League had dared tell even their closest cronies about Diyu and the Dragon Fleet.

Well, they'll find out about it soon enough, Than thought grimly. *And no doubt Uromachi's economy will take on a certain urgency now. The replacement ships will have to come from* somewhere, *after all!*

His personal comm pinged, and he glanced down at the displayed text, then snorted, unbuckled, and pushed up out of his command chair.

"Cayha says lunch is about to be served and I'd better be

there for it," he said wryly. "I should have plenty of time for that before Jinan gets back to us."

"Of course, Sir," Su murmured, and watched the third admiral push off for the flag bridge hatch.

Somehow, the chief of staff doubted Than Cayha had just happened to summon her husband to lunch at this particular moment. She knew as well as Than how thin the thread from which all of them hung truly was. Which meant she also knew it was entirely possible this would be the last meal the third admiral would ever share with his family.

Than Qiang laid down his chopsticks with a sigh of pleasure. The *char sui* had been delicious, served with the white rice he preferred to noodles, and the *xiaolongbao*, filled with crab, were the perfect side.

"That was even better than usual," he told his wife, smiling at her across the table.

"Well, one thing about being snatched away from home, your shipboard commissary is far better stocked than the arcology's shops ever were," she replied with an answering smile.

Than hid an internal wince as he saw the tension so imperfectly hidden behind that smile. The two of them had done their best to keep their son, Idrak, from realizing exactly why they'd been "snatched away from home," but he suspected their efforts had failed. For that matter, he'd never shared everything that worried him even with Cayha, although after thirty standard years of marriage, she had to know what was really going on.

And then there was—

"What's for dessert?" Kristina Moritz-Than asked, as if merely thinking of her had summoned the question.

"Yeah," Than Rao, Than's uncle, seconded.

"Don't be so impatient!" Cayha scolded.

"What's not to be impatient about?" Kristina retorted. "You know we have to get dessert in quick, because Qiang's going to run right out that door"—she pointed at the hatch to Than's dining cabin—"and back to the bridge the instant Commander Vang pages him." She snorted. "It's what he does, Cayha."

"True." Cayha's everything-is-normal tone wavered just a bit, and Than gave his sister a quelling glance. It rolled right off her like water.

"I could do with a little dessert, too," Idrak put in. "Want me to go get it, Mom?"

"That would be good, actually," Cayha said.

He pushed back his chair, got up, headed for what had been Than's steward's pantry until Cayha evicted him as soon as she came aboard, and Cayha's smile followed him through the hatch.

"He's a good kid," she said quietly, looking back at her husband.

"Always has been," Than replied with an even warmer smile of his own. "A few rough spots here and there that still need hammering down, of course. Can't imagine where they came from."

"Passed any mirrors lately?" Kristina asked.

"I don't remember soliciting any smartass remarks," Than said, and she snorted again.

"*Hǔ fù wú quǎn zǐ,*" she said sweetly, and it was Than's turn to snort. The traditional axiom—a tiger father has no canine sons—should have sounded odd coming from someone as *gwàipò* as his sister, but she had a point. Idrak truly was a chip off the old block. He *was* a good kid . . . and also stubborn, hard-headed, and determined to learn every possible lesson the hard way, exactly like Than had been at his age.

And still am, really, he thought wryly. *I suppose some things don't change all that much just because we get older.*

He smiled at the thought, but the smile faded quickly. Because Idrak was being none of those things at the moment. He was still the good kid, still the helpful son, but the stubborn determination to go his own way—and to suffer as visibly as possible in abject misery when he didn't get it—had vanished. Which was the best possible proof that their efforts to shelter him from the truth had failed.

"I'm sure I don't have any idea what you're talking about," he told Kristina, and she rolled her round, gray eyes at him. "He's just—"

Than cut off as Idrak returned with a covered platter.

"I'm just what?" the boy asked.

"And what makes you so sure we're talking about you?" Than asked.

"You said 'he,' but I'm pretty sure you weren't talking about Captain Su, and you were talking to *Shūshu* Rao. Which"—he grinned—"just leaves me."

"Boy children who're too clever come to bad ends," his father observed.

"So do boy children who're too dim," Idrak replied. "Or at least, that's what you always tell me when you chew me out for doing something less than brilliant."

"True," Than acknowledged, and waved for Idrak to set the platter on the table. "And I was simply about to observe to *Āyí* Kristina that you never got your stubbornness from me, since all the universe knows what a reasonable and flexible soul I am."

Kristina made a rude sound, and Idrak chuckled. But he also set the platter on the table, and Cayha reached out. She didn't look down at the cover—her eyes were on Than's face—and his heart tightened as she lifted it.

"Lou po beng!" Idrak said. "I love your *lou po beng*, Mom!"

"It's one of your father's favorites, too," Cayha told him, still looking into her husband's eyes.

"Yes." Than had to pause, clear his throat. "Yes, it is. Thank you, *Qīn'ài de.*"

"I thought it was . . . appropriate," she said, and he nodded. The legend behind *lou po beng*—flat, flaky cakes filled with winter melon and sesame seed—had traveled to the stars with the Tè Lā Lián Méng. Actually, there were several different legends about how they'd come to be, but he knew which one Cayha had grown up with. She'd told him her version of it the first time she'd baked them for him.

A couple in ancient China lived in a small village. They were very poor, but they loved one another dearly, and they were happy. Until the husband's father fell ill with a disease no one could cure. They spent all they had on medicines and doctors, sold all they owned for it, but it wasn't enough. Yet they had nothing left to sell, and so, without telling her husband, the wife sold *herself* into slavery for the money to save her father-in-law's life.

When the husband discovered what she'd done, that he'd lost her forever, he baked the very first *lou po beng*, filled with candied winter melon, and dedicated it to her. He'd sold it on the street, telling her story to all he met, and it became so popular he was able to earn enough money to buy his wife back again.

"I don't plan on selling myself into slavery, Xīn'ài," she'd said to her new husband as they sat across the first dining table they'd been able to call their own in the married quarters assigned to a very junior Navy lieutenant, *"but I know if we are ever separated that no power in the universe will keep you from finding me again*

and bringing me home. And no power in the universe will keep me from coming home to you, my love."

"I remember the first time I made this for you," she said now, softly, and he nodded.

"So do I," he told her. "So do I."

"Let's eat!" Idrak said.

✧   ✧   ✧

"That really was delicious," Than Rao said after the table had been cleared and Idrak had reported—only a *little* rebelliously—to the tutor his parents had refused to allow him to escape.

"It was," Than said, smiling warmly at Cayha.

"And you actually had time to eat it before Commander Vang came after you." Kristina shook her head. "I'm surprised."

"I'm not," Cayha said, and Than raised an eyebrow at her.

"And why would that be?" he asked.

"Because I told Zhihao I'd hurt him if he interrupted for anything short of a dire emergency."

"You did?" Than straightened in his chair, and she nodded serenely.

"Most of the time, I'm prepared to put up with what the Navy demands out of you. I knew when I married you that at best I'd be allowed to share you with your other mistress, Qiang. But there are times I won't do that. And this is one of them."

He looked at her for a moment, then sighed and nodded.

"I'll have to have a word with him about exactly whose orders come first," he said wryly. "On the other hand, Zhihao's a smart fellow. So he's probably a lot more scared of you than of a mere admiral."

"And well he should be," she said with a faint smile. The smile didn't last long.

"Are you sure about all this?" she asked him after moment. "*Really* sure?"

"I am." He met her gaze squarely. "We all know how badly this could go. I need you and Idrak—all of you—" he swept his eyes over his uncle and his sister "—safely out of harm's way if it does."

"You know they're going to scapegoat you, don't you?" Kristina said harshly.

"I don't *know* that's how it will play out," Than said firmly. "A lot will depend on how Governor Zheng decides to respond. I'm pretty sure Admiral Deng will authorize the troop lift to recover our people from Diyu. Looking at the take from our passive sensors, there's probably enough FTL lift in the system to collect at least two thirds of them in a single operation, and I'm sure she can impress more. If she does that—if the Accord and, especially, Liu know all those people will be coming home again—they'll have a lot less motive to sweep me under the rug, because shutting me up won't keep the story from coming out. And if Zheng signs off on my report and my agreement with Murphy—if she gives her imprimatur to the operation to recover our personnel because they represent such a vital industrial resource—it'll be harder for Liu and his cronies to lay Xing's failures off on me."

"And if pigs had wings they could fly," Kristina said, and Than saw the worry—the fear—in her eyes.

"No doubt they could," he replied. "But all I can do is the best I can do, Kristina. And this is it."

"But if you send us—"

"Cayha, I love you. I even love Kristina!" Than rolled his eyes at his sister. "But I'm not discussing this. I can't risk it—I *won't* risk it."

Kristina glowered at him, and he met those hot, angry eyes levelly while he remembered the day his father had brought home the three-year-old *gwáimūi* who'd just become his sister. He'd been thirteen standard years old, and he'd been horrified at the thought, but Than Jianhong had been a man of honor. A man Than Qiang had tried hard to be worthy of. It was one of Jianhong's boarders who'd killed half the crew of the Federation freighter Jianhong's raid on the Metaxa System had surprised in planetary orbit. And he'd done it after Jianhong had promised its captain his people's lives would be spared.

The high political connections of the officer who'd defied him, violated his commanding officer's sworn word, hadn't protected him from Captain Than. He'd been tried, condemned, and executed—for disobedience to orders, not murder; even then, it would have been difficult to convict a League officer simply for slaughtering Feds—within a week. Which was why a man of Than Jianhong's abilities had retired as a captain... and the reason his son had done his damnedest to completely eschew any political involvement.

But Jianhong had brought home the small, terrified orphan his officer had created, and despite the near universal disapproval of his decision, he and his wife, Xiuying, had legally adopted her and raised her—and *loved* her—as their own. The only stipulation Jianhong had made was that Kristina Moritz keep her birth name to commemorate her parents.

It hadn't been easy for Kristina to grow up in the League. There were probably billions of *baakgwai* in the *Tè Lā Lián Méng*, but in a population the size of the League's, they were a tiny percentage of the whole, and they tended to be concentrated in only a handful of star systems. And as the war's bitterness had intensified, the prejudice against them had intensified right along with it. Which was ironic, since from Than's observation, most of those "white people" were even more patriotic than their ethnically "pure" co-citizens.

Of course, he thought now, looking at Kristina, sometimes that wasn't a good thing, since it was *her* patriotism, her devotion to the star nation and cause of the family who had given her a home and love, that had turned her into an investigative reporter. And it was the stories she'd filed—and, even more, the exposés her editors had spiked—that had ultimately gotten her deplatformed and left her unemployed.

"If there were, in fact, such a thing as justice—which, I know perfectly well, there isn't," she said now, "they'd give you the second Flying Dragon you deserve!"

Despite himself, Than's lips twitched in a smile. The *Mínzú Yīngxióng Xūnzhāng*—known more or less affectionately as the Flying Dragon because of the magnificent winged dragon engraved into the teacup-sized golden medal—was the Terran League's highest award for valor. They'd given it to him after the Battle of Callao, which was probably the reason he'd been tapped as Dragon Fleet's original CO. Even at the time he'd received it, though, he'd been aware of the degree of political calculation behind the award.

"They don't give the Flying Dragon to the CO of the *losing* fleet, *Shǎguā!*"

"That wasn't you; that was Xing!" she shot back.

"Kristina, I love you, but the truth is that if I'd been in command in New Dublin, I would have taken Murphy's bait exactly the way Xing did. The difference is that I would've sailed straight into his ambush with our entire fleet, not just three quarters of it. In which case, he would've done to me exactly what he did to her."

She glared at him, and he shrugged.

"She was an arrogant, amoral, narcissistic, murderous, calculating, dishonorable bitch with a severely overinflated opinion of her own capabilities," he said dispassionately. "In that particular instance, though, I read the tactical situation as poorly as she did."

"But you—"

"But I *didn't* K-strike Crann Bethadh," Than interrupted. "I think that was the right decision. Xing and people like her—and anyone looking for a scapegoat—are likely to disagree, once they find out. Which, hopefully, they won't for a while. And then, after that, I pulled out of Diyu and abandoned the shipyard to the Feds."

"They had *seven* carriers, and you had two, both already damaged! You couldn't have prevented that!"

"No, but do you really expect people—especially the sort of people who're currently in the Accord—to admit that when they start looking for someone to pin their disaster on? And, to be honest, all I did was decline to get still more of our people killed. Well, that and convince Murphy to spare our yard workers' lives." He shook his head. "No. I agree with you that the universe isn't exactly running over with justice, but there's no point pretending that as the senior surviving officer involved with this debacle I'm not the one the politicians and the *xīxuèguǐ* are going to lay the blame on. And *that*—" he turned his gaze back to Cayha "—is why we're going to do this my way."

"But—"

"*Qīn'ài de*, this one will have every senior politician in the League running for his or her life. Even people who didn't know a thing about Diyu or the Dragon Fleet will be tarred with the brush of failure, and you know damned well that the politicians who were actually responsible for it will spread the blame onto as many of their colleagues as possible in an effort to save their own necks. Moderation . . . is not going to be in great demand from our political lords and masters."

"No, it's not," Kristina said, and her tone was flat, defeated. "He's right, Cayha. He may be able to dodge the bullet, especially if Governor Zheng backs him. She's not just the Uromachi System Governor, she's also the Governor for the entire Sector, so her approval will carry weight not even Liu can ignore. But if they do ignore it, or if she declines to paste a big target onto her own back just because it's the right thing to do, these bastards will trot *zuzhu* back out if only to warn the rest of the Navy's senior officers they'd better not even consider supporting Qiang."

Than nodded soberly. Officially, the League had never embraced the ancient Chinese penalty of "family execution." That was a point its propagandists had always hammered away at in their vehement denouncement of the *Federation*'s propagandists' claim that it did. And, to be honest, the League had never actually *executed* an offender's entire immediate family.

Yet, at least.

But the reason the Federation claimed the Tè Lā Lián Méng's penal code did enshrine *zuzhu* was that over the last twenty-odd standard years, the League *had* embraced a policy of collective responsibility. As the odds turned ever more heavily against the League, the consequences for those who failed their political masters had grown ever more drastic. After a failure as colossal as the Dragon Fleet fiasco, there'd be no hope of mercy for whoever the politicians could fasten the blame upon. And that meant—at best—that Than Qiang's wife, son, uncle, and sister could expect to spend the rest of their lives in miserable poverty. More likely, they'd find themselves imprisoned in one of the "rehabilitation camps," where they would serve as horrible examples for the recidivists who might learn from their experience.

And quite possibly, in this case, they *would* be executed.

"I need you to be safe if I'm going to do this," he said softly. "And—"

His comm chimed with Su Zhihao's priority override attention signal. He looked down at it and frowned. It wasn't Van Raksmei, his comm officer; it was Su. He hesitated a moment, then tapped the tiny screen.

"Yes, Zhihao?"

"Sir, we've received a burst transmission from Jinan. It's... not from Governor Zheng."

"Oh?" Than was surprised his own voice sounded so calm. "Who *is* it from, then?"

"It's signed by Governor Shen," Su said flatly. "Shen Hanying. Apparently, Governor Zheng died two months ago."

"I see," Than said, and looked up to see his sister staring at him in horror.

CHAPTER TEN

Zhìgāo Bǎozuò Station
Jinan Planetary Orbit
Uromachi System
Tè Lā Lián Méng
November 22, 2552

THE DELAY WAS A BAD SIGN, THAN THOUGHT.

Cai Shen and *Li Shiji* had been in Jinan orbit for almost thirty-six hours, and Governor Shen Hanying had had Than's full report for thirty of them. Than hadn't wanted to transmit it until he had the opportunity to make it himself, face-to-face, but Shen had insisted. And Than could think of only one possible reason for his delay in dragging the third admiral into his office.

Just as he could think of only one reason he'd been specifically instructed to report alone for this interview, without Su Zhihao. And without Fourth Admiral Deng's presence.

Damage control. The son-of-a-bitch is already thinking about damage control and how to pull it off with the least possible witnesses. Especially Navy *witnesses. If all he wanted was to do his damned job, the transports would already be on their way back to Diyu.*

Than's mouth tightened as he stood, square-shouldered, hands clasped behind him, gazing out the floor-to-ceiling crystoplast bulkhead at the gorgeous gem of Jinan, moving steadily across his field of view with Zhìgāo Bǎozuò Station's rotation. He made himself maintain a calm, semi-relaxed posture, but it wasn't easy. Because if he was right, then Shen wasn't going—

"The Governor will see you now, Third Admiral."

Than reminded himself to turn slowly to face Shen's aide. The younger man's expression was bland, the sort of mask someone aspiring to a political career developed early, but his eyes gave him away. He wasn't looking at a naval officer. No, he was looking at a scapegoat.

"Thank you," Than said, and followed him from the waiting area down the passage towards Shen's office.

He'd visited that office before, when it had belonged to Zheng Nuan, and now his memory replayed those earlier visits. He hadn't really expected to like Zheng before they first met, given that she'd been a career politician since before the war against the Federation even began. Nobody survived in politics in the Tè Lā Lián Méng for six standard decades without becoming a full-blown captive of the system.

But Zheng had surprised him. Yes, she was a politician, and even a member of Eternal Forward. But she'd also been rational and as much a patriot as Than himself. Not only that, she'd had a sense of humor! The diminutive governor had worn her hair in a short-cut, silver helmet that made her look like a mischievous, misplaced elf, and her brown eyes had twinkled each time she dropped one of her atrocious punchlines on him. She hadn't been part of Eternal Forward because she bought the party line. She'd joined it because Party membership was the only way she could have retained her position, done her job in the service of the League, and her faction of Eternal Forward had fought Liu Gengxin's steady ascension to power tooth and nail.

They'd lost that struggle. Or they'd been in the process of losing it, at any rate, and everyone who'd known about Dragon Fleet had recognized it as the deathblow to Liu's opposition. But her stature and seniority had still made her a force to be reckoned with, especially in light of her governorship in the Di Jun Sector. If anyone had been in a position to face Liu down, it would have been her and her remaining allies in the Party leadership.

Shen Hanying was a very different story.

One of Liu's toadies and an ambitious, unprincipled political hack who'd hitched his own future to Liu's success, he could have been the dictionary illustration of exactly what citizens of the League meant when they used the term *xīxuèguǐ*—bloodsucker—to describe their political leaders. And that was precisely what made Than Qiang so unhappy about the way this interview had been delayed.

His guide reached the open door to Shen's office and rapped lightly on the frame.

"Third Admiral Than is here, Governor."

"Ah, splendid! Show him in, Qigang!"

"Of course, Sir."

The aide turned, bowing to Than and waving him through the door, and Than gave him a nod whose courtesy was as false as the aide's own bow as he stepped past him.

"Third Admiral!"

Shen stood behind his desk, reaching across it to offer Than his hand. He was a tall man—seventy centimeters taller than the petite Zheng Nuan had been, almost as tall as Than himself—and he squeezed the third admiral's hand firmly. In fact, he squeezed it *very* firmly, and Than smiled blandly at the governor as his knuckle-crushing attempt came to nothing.

Eventually, Shen gave it up and waved at one of the armchairs in front of his desk.

Than settled into the indicated chair and Shen resumed his own seat behind the desk, leaned forward slightly, propped his elbows on the blotter, and steepled his fingers under his chin as he regarded the naval officer. Silence stretched out, and Than let it. He only gazed back at the governor with polite attentiveness.

"I've viewed your report, of course, Third Admiral," Shen said, finally, and his expression turned grave. "Obviously, I found it ... disturbing. In many ways, actually. I hardly need to tell you how catastrophic the Dragon Fleet's destruction is likely to prove."

He paused, eyebrows raised, obviously inviting a response, and Than nodded somberly.

"Believe me, Governor, I understand fully. Dragon Fleet was my life's work for the last six standard years. To see it just ... thrown away like this ..." He shook his head. "'Catastrophic' is likely to prove far too weak a word for what's happened."

"Agreed." Shen nodded and straightened, leaning back in his chair and laying his forearms along its rests. "And, as a naval officer, I'm sure you understand that Minister of War Liu and the entire Accord will want to hear what happened from your own lips. I'm afraid," his expression turned graver than ever, "that some significant errors of judgment led us to this disastrous pass."

"I doubt any reasonable person could disagree with that," Than replied. "In Second Admiral Xing's defense, however," he continued calmly, ignoring the flash in Shen's eyes as he brought Liu's protégé into the conversation, "from the moment the Feds intercepted the final shipment of singularity manifolds, the situation changed drastically from what had been originally envisioned. She had no way of knowing what other information they might have obtained, but the potential of a direct attack on Diyu clearly existed. Under those circumstances, the decision to launch a preemptive attack of our own with all of our available strength certainly seemed justified."

"But an attack in that strength wasn't—couldn't have been— the overwhelming assault Dragon Fleet had been built to carry out," Shen said sharply.

"No," Than agreed. "It was simply her view—and, despite my own unhappiness with the situation, I completely concurred with her—that the heaviest attack we could mount then, immediately, would at the very least force the Feds to withdraw strength from Beta Cygni. And we could easily—*should* easily—have penetrated deep into the Heart before they could stop us. At the very least, it ought to have bought time for our ... allies to fabricate and deliver replacement manifolds."

"But instead, it failed miserably." Shen's voice was flat now, and Than regarded him imperturbably.

"It did, because the Fed Governor—Admiral Murphy—had clearly devised a new, unanticipated weapon Second Admiral Xing had no reason to suspect existed. In addition, he possessed three times the strength in FTLCs she'd anticipated. To be brutally honest, Governor, the only reason two of my own carriers survived was because Second Admiral Xing detached them from her main force while she went in pursuit of the two FTLCs we had then detected. In retrospect, I think it's evident that had my squadron been in company with the rest of Dragon Fleet when Murphy sprang his trap, it would have been destroyed, as well. And, again in the Second Admiral's defense, had I been in overall command, I *wouldn't* have detached one of my squadrons. I would have maintained concentration of force ... and almost certainly suffered the same defeat she did. A defeat which would have included the destruction of *all* of her carriers."

Shen glowered at him wordlessly for a moment, then inhaled deeply.

"It seems to me that it's ... most unfortunate this Murphy was subsequently able to locate Diyu. Would you care to comment on that aspect of the operation, Third Admiral?"

"It's remotely possible that the same intelligence source that led him to intercept the *Val Idrak* also revealed the fact that Diyu and Yuxi were the same star system," Than said in measured tones. "I don't believe that's what happened, however. If he'd already known Diyu's location, he would have arrived there far more promptly than he actually did. Moreover, he wouldn't have checked Hefei first; he'd have come directly to Diyu, especially since he knew Second Admiral Xing's carriers had sustained significant Fasset drive damage, which would have limited her wormhole velocity. He might well have beaten her to Diyu—indeed, he almost did beat her, despite the detour to Hefei—had he known its location. Given those facts, and the additional fact that my own ships executed a radical evasive track to avoid giving him a possible bearing to our base, I can only assume that he projected Second Admiral Xing's heading with sufficient accuracy to define the volume in which Diyu must lie."

"So you're blaming Second Admiral Xing for what happened?" Shen asked a bit sharply.

"It's a Navy axiom that the commanding officer is always responsible for the consequences of actions he—or she—orders, Governor. As I say, no one can fault the Second Admiral's decision to launch the attack. Nor, I think, can she be blamed for failing to anticipate that Murphy had deployed some radically new weapon. However, it's unfortunately likely that her lack of ... battlefield experience led to a significant—indeed, fatal—misjudgment after her command was so severely damaged."

And if that idiot Liu hadn't jumped her over my head to command Dragon Fleet, it wouldn't have happened, he very carefully did *not* say out loud.

"I see." Shen looked at him, as if he'd heard what Than hadn't said, then waved one hand. "And your own decision against standing and fighting to defend Diyu?"

"I considered doing just that, Governor." Than made his expression remain calm, his voice level. "I was, however, outnumbered by better than three-to-one by an opponent who'd already demonstrated that he possessed a novel weapon that was a significant force multiplier. All my two surviving carriers could realistically have accomplished would have been to die in Diyu's defense. And had that happened, Governor, the Tè Lā Lián Méng wouldn't know a thing about what had happened to Dragon Fleet. My ships were the only FTL-capable units in-system, aside from Second Admiral Xing's badly damaged carriers and...our ally's transport, and the geometry of Murphy's approach made it impossible for her ships to evade him or avoid action in isolation from my own carriers."

He paused, looking levelly across Shen's desk at him, and then shrugged.

"My primary responsibility—as, indeed, Second Admiral Xing emphasized in the single omnidirectional transmission from her which I received—was to report what had happened to Uromachi and Anyang. That was crucial. And it's exactly what my squadron and I have done."

"So I see."

Shen swung his chair from side to side, gazing thoughtfully at Than.

"You must be aware, Third Admiral, that the Accord will be...most distressed by what's happened. For many reasons."

"Of course I am, Governor."

"Yes, well, I think it's imperative that you move directly to Anyang to report this." Shen smiled coldly. "In person."

"I had already planned on doing precisely that, Governor," Than replied calmly. "It was necessary to divert to Uromachi to warn Governor Zheng—and now, you, of course—and Fourth Admiral Deng about what had happened. I don't know precisely what Murphy and the Feds are likely to do, and it's entirely possible they won't push into the Di Jun Sector. It's equally possible they will, however, so warning Uromachi was obviously one of my first responsibilities. Moreover, Uromachi was the nearest system along my route to Anyang where I could hope to find the personnel lift to retrieve our shipyard workers from Diyu."

"Retrieve them?" Shen repeated, arching both eyebrows.

"Of course, Governor. Especially now that we've lost the physical plant from Diyu, those workers will be a critical asset for our building capacity."

"And you honestly believe this Murphy will let us have that 'critical asset' back again?" Shen shook his head. "Ridiculous. All of the personnel you left behind are dead by now, Third Admiral.

Either that or parked in some POW camp hellhole somewhere in the Federation!"

"Governor," Than said carefully, "whatever else Murphy may have had, he didn't have the troop lift to pull those thousands of workers out of Diyu. And he gave me his word that he would allow them to evacuate to the sublight ships in-system before he destroyed the yard and withdrew."

"And you *believed* him," Shen said almost pityingly.

"I had no reason *not* to believe him, after he allowed Fourth Admiral Xie and all of his personnel to surrender at New Dublin. That was, as I'm sure you're aware, highly unusual after all these years of mutual bloodletting. Whatever else he may be, it would appear Murphy is not a typical Fed butcher."

"And the only actual *evidence* you have that the Fourth Admiral was allowed to surrender is the fact that Murphy knew his name," Shen pointed out in a rather nasty tone. "Moreover, unless I'm sadly mistaken in my reading of your report, what he was actually doing was threatening to *not* allow Xei to surrender if you K-struck Crann Bethadh."

"That may be true," Than conceded, blessing Su Zhihao's foresight in "losing" the portion of the comm record in which Xing had directly ordered him to do precisely that.

"And," he continued, "I won't deny that worrying about our captured personnel was a factor in my decision to settle for destroying New Dublin's industrial base rather than bombarding the planet. Either way, however, New Dublin's been neutralized as a major fleet base, at least until the Federation can rebuild. And that assumes Murphy's actions haven't caused the federal government to declare him and New Dublin 'out of compliance.' In which case, the Feds are probably looking at a civil war, Governor."

It was unfortunate, he thought sardonically, that he'd been unable to include a definitive damage estimate after his alpha strike on Crann Bethadh's orbital infrastructure. But that omission would at least keep Governor Shen from panicking—further panicking—over the unhappy fact that the orbital infrastructure in question had almost certainly emerged substantially intact.

And it might also help one Than Qiang and Su Zhihao avoid a firing squad. It might not, too, given everything else, but it was at least possible...however unlikely.

"It would be nice if something like that were to happen to them," Shen said now. "Given that, according to his Intelligence dossier, this Murphy is a member in good standing of their Five Hundred, that outcome strikes me as . . . unlikely, shall we say. No, he'll go home to bask in the glory of his victory, and they'll fall all over themselves loading him down with medals and promotions. None of which has anything at all to do with whether or not he was stupid enough to leave all of those yard workers just hanging around for us to reacquire their services. Only a fool would do that, Third Admiral, and I'm afraid our friend Murphy has demonstrated that a fool is the one thing he *isn't*."

"That may be true, Governor. In fact, it's quite probable that it is. But it's also possible he honored his promise to me. And if he did, there are seventy-five thousand of our people waiting to be picked up. If Murphy did as thorough a job of wrecking the yard and the facilities as I'm sure he did, they don't have the resources to survive indefinitely, either. I believe we must at least send someone to find out, and under the circumstances, I think it would only make sense when we do to send sufficient personnel lift to retrieve them if Murphy did keep his word."

"No," Shen said flatly.

Than stiffened in his chair, and the governor glared at him.

"*You* may believe in miracles and Fed admirals who actually keep promises, but I don't," he said. "And I don't believe in Feds stupid enough to give us back the next best thing to eighty thousand trained workers, either. Nor do I intend to further compromise security on Diyu by giving its coordinates to *anyone* who doesn't already have them. And I'm certainly not going to permit a fleet of transports to wander into Diyu and gawk at the wreckage of what was supposed to win the damned war!"

Than started to speak, then forced himself to keep his mouth tightly shut.

This wasn't about military security. It wasn't even really about whether or not Shen believed Murphy had kept his word. For that matter, if Than hadn't personally spoken to Murphy, *he* might not have believed the Federation admiral's sense of honor went deep enough for him to keep it. But that didn't matter to Shen. What mattered was slapping a lid on the entire fiasco. Making sure it didn't leak out and embarrass his political masters.

And, after all, what would it cost him, even if he was wrong?

Only the lives of seventy or eighty thousand League citizens. A trifling price to protect the Accord and, especially, Liu Gengxin and Eternal Forward.

"With all respect, Governor, I think that's the wrong decision," he said, after a long moment spent making sure he could control his tone. "It's also your decision to make, of course. I would like the record to note that I . . . did not concur in it, however."

"That's your option, Third Admiral," Shen replied in a voice that added the unspoken *and it's your funeral, too.*

"Thank you, Governor."

Shen grunted, then shoved himself up out of his chair.

"Very well, Third Admiral. I won't pretend I've enjoyed viewing your report or hearing anything you had to say here today. It's not your fault, of course," his voice oozed insincerity, "but that doesn't make it any more palatable. I really shouldn't have held you here as long as I have, but I wanted time to consider what your report had already told me. Nothing in our conversation today has changed the decision I made last night, however. I want you back into wormhole space on your way to Anyang as soon as possible. And I'll be sending Fan Qigang—the young man who greeted you for me this morning—along with you as my personal representative and the courier transmitting my own report and dispatches to Minister of War Liu."

"Of course, Governor. My ships can break orbit within the hour, if Mr. Fan can be ready by then. Otherwise, we'll await his convenience."

"Very good." Shen held out his hand again. "In that case, I won't keep you from your own preparations. Good day, Third Admiral."

CHAPTER ELEVEN

RHLNS **Cai Shen**
Uromachi System
Tè Lā Lián Méng
November 23, 2552

"GOOD MORNING, SIR," SU ZHIHAO SAID AS THAN QIANG DRIFTED through flag bridge hatch.

Some of the Rénzú Liánméng Hǎijūn's flag officers would have expected their staffs to spring to attention when they graced the flag deck with their presence. Than preferred for them to get on with their jobs, unless there was "company" present that needed impressing.

And it didn't hurt one bit when it came to building his people's loyalty.

"Good morning," he replied, sailing across to his command chair, then fastening the lap belt loosely. "How long to translation?"

"Thirteen minutes, Sir," Lieutenant Commander Kong Tai replied from Astrogation.

"You hit it pretty closely, as usual," Captain Su observed, settling beside Than's chair.

"Because I never get tired of watching." Than shook his head with a smile. "I know some people do, but I hope I never will."

"It is pretty spectacular," Su acknowledged.

The master display was configured to visual mode, looking ahead as *Cai Shen* approached the threshold of wormhole space. The blueshifted stars ahead of her—those visible around the blind spot created by her Fasset drive—blazed blue white and furious while, contracting into a smaller and smaller disc. It was like looking into an incandescent jewel box, waiting for the enormous ship, beckoning her into the vastness of interstellar space.

"And how is *Zhùshŏu* Fan settling in?" Than asked casually.

"Well, I think," Su replied. "Lieutenant Zhang moved in with Lieutenant Pan to free a cabin for him. I'm afraid—" the chief of staff's lips twitched "—that *Zhùshŏu* Fan expected rather more luxurious accommodations. Of course, he understood when I explained to him that as a ship of war, *Cai Shen* isn't equipped with passenger suites."

"I'm glad he was so understanding." Than's tone was admirably grave, but there was an undeniable twinkle in his eyes. Fan Qigang had proved just as insufferable as he'd feared.

Fan was obviously well aware of his status as Shen Hanying's representative...and spy. The fact that he clearly shared Shen's machine-politician contempt for the military only made him even more insufferable, and much as Than would have loved to slap him down, his position as Shen's aide gave him a certain insulation. Su, on the other hand, could find all manner of reasons it was "regretfully" impossible to comply with his desires.

"I don't think he was delighted, but I'm sure he'll make the best of it, Sir. I hope so, anyway. It's a long trip."

It was, indeed, a long trip from Uromachi to Anyang, Than reflected. Two hundred and seventy-five light-years was over three months' travel for the universe at large. Thankfully, that would be only a bit more than two weeks in *Cai Shen's* pocket universe, although he was certain Fan's presence would make it seem far longer. He'd already realized he'd have no choice but to invite the *xīxuèguĭ* to dine with him each evening. That would be fun.

"Oh, by the way, Sir, Commander Quan got that personnel matter cleared up, and Commander Yu asked me to tell you that she had a word with Captain Teng about that small matter you wanted her to discuss with him. She says that he doesn't see any problem."

"Really?" Than looked up at the chief of staff. "That's good to hear," he said.

"I thought so, too," Su agreed, and Than turned back to the visual display.

Teng Huang was Fourth Admiral Deng's logistics officer, the man who knew where every hull in Uromachi was at any given moment. And he also just happened to have been a midshipman under then Commander Than Qiang far too many years ago. They remained close, and while Than had hated to involve him, he'd known how hurt Teng would have been by the very notion of *not* involving him. Than expected that Deng would be more than willing to turn a blind eye to any favors Teng might do for his old CO. He was far less confident of that where Shen Hanying was concerned, but he hoped—devoutly prayed, actually—that his and Su's security would hold.

Commander Quan Kun, his staff personnel officer, was central to that security. He was the one who'd manufactured civilian travel authorizations for two women, a teenaged boy, and a disabled veteran. And Commander Yu Yawen was his logistics officer, the one who'd asked Captain Teng to find berths for those civilians aboard any Navy transport that might happen to be headed in the right direction.

Despite everything, Than had been far less certain than he'd admitted even to his wife that Teng would be able to pull it off, but now he treasured his vast sense of relief. There were entirely too many ways his arrival in Anyang could end badly, but at least he had his family out of the line of fire.

Probably.

He shook his head, watching the display's gems blaze still hotter before him, and reflected upon the perversity of a universe in which he had more faith in an enemy to whom he'd spoken exactly once than he did in his own duly constituted government.

CHAPTER TWELVE

The Oval
City of Olympia
Old Terra
Sol System
Terran Federation
November 23, 2552

AMEDEO BOYLE SWIRLED SMALL ICE CUBES AROUND HIS GLASS. Melting ice had watered the whiskey down and he thought about refreshing it. But tempting as that might have been, blunting his wits was contraindicated just now

The conference room—a bunker, actually, hundreds of meters beneath the Oval—had excellent air-conditioning and environmental systems, and its smart-screen walls gave the impression he could look out into the French countryside, instead of at the bedrock that actually surrounded it. Yet despite the lying smart walls, what Boyle was uncomfortably aware of at the moment was all that invisible bedrock's weight. Or perhaps what he actually felt was a quite different weight pressing down upon him, because the pressure in that bunker was... significant.

Yes, that was a good word for it, he decided. Significant.

The conference table was full of officers, politicians, and prominent members of the Five Hundred, none of whom seemed any more enthusiastic about being there than Boyle was.

Verena Schleibaum, the Prime Minister of the entire (nominally) Terran Federation, sat at the head of the table, three places up from Boyle. She'd neither touched her water nor sent anyone to the snack table for her since the meeting began, two hours ago.

"Next on the agenda is the Admiral Henrik Murphy memorials on Earth and across the Federation." A harried-looking aide tapped a stylus to the screen before him, and the statue of a more loyal and less troublesome Murphy popped up from the holo projectors above the table. Terrence Murphy's grandfather had been taller than he was. He'd also been handsomer, and he'd earned a chest full of awards during his service to the Federation.

"Public sentiment across monitored networks remains highly positive for Murphy's grandfather," the aide continued. "Our analysis suggests that that positivity may attach, at least to some extent, to Murphy himself when he's brought to trial. In light of that, Admiral Fokaides has proposed removing any and all positive references to the Murphy name. Shall we have a quick consensus vote?"

"It should be discussed, first."

Vice Admiral Yang Xiaolan stood from her chair in the cluster of military officers at the far end of the table from the Prime Minister. One or two faces frowned, but she ignored them and looked directly at Schleibaum.

"Every naval officer receives a block of instruction on Admiral Murphy's contributions to the modern Navy and his initial victories over the League," she said. "He's a vital part of our sense of continuity, of purpose. At the Academy, there's a tradition that midshipmen will approach the statue on the Academy grounds in full uniform at midnight before a test. They believe it's lucky to touch the statue's shoe. Which is why that part of it is always polished."

"Why are you wasting breath on this?" Jugoslav Darković, the leader of the Conservative Coalition and arguably the most powerful single political leader present, leaned forward from his own seat. "Murphy needs to be crushed. Anywhere and everywhere. We can't allow any positive public sentiment for him or his family."

"Navy traditions are important." Yang's tone was respectful but stubborn. "Spacers can be a superstitious lot, and Murphy's long-dead grandfather isn't—"

"Henrik Murphy has already done too much to help his bastard of a grandson," Fleet Admiral Arkadios Fokaides interrupted, and tapped his data slate against the table's edge for emphasis. "Murphy never would've married into the Five Hundred without his surname. And his pitiful excuse for a military career—he spent most of it in *Survey*, for God's sake—would never have qualified him as the governor of any system without it, either."

Yang's eyes narrowed slightly, and Boyle used his glass to hide his smile. Federation military officers did not disagree with one another in formal settings. Professional courtesy demanded that disagreements be settled—or rejected by the superior officer—before they interacted with civilian authorities. But Fokaides had been scheduled for retirement, before Murphy's defiance threw everything into disarray, and Yang had been his designated successor. It would seem she was a bit chafed at being held back.

And, in fairness, it could be argued either way, he thought. Instead of erasing the Murphy name, they could actually burnish old Henrik's halo and point out how much more despicable that made the current Murphy's betrayal of all the old man had stood for, fought for, and bled for. Of course, there'd be the minor problem that if Boyle's reading of Henrik Murphy's history was accurate, his ghost must be enthusiastically egging his grandson on.

Probably best not to mention that at this particular meeting, though.

"Sir," Yang said now, "Admiral Murphy began most of the traditions that form the bedrock of the Navy's culture. Are we going to throw all of that away, as well?"

"Keeping it is more trouble than it's worth," Fokaides replied curtly. Boyle suspected they'd already had this conversation and that Fokaides resented repeating himself. "We cut Murphy off from his lineage, and it weakens his stature in the eyes of the military. We can replace the statue with someone else once this is over." He shrugged irritably. "It's not like we can't find a more 'respectable' candidate for the honor. Ten years, and no one will even remember Henrik's statue never existed."

"Treason must have consequences," Schleibaum said. "We're not going as far as the League and their *zuzhu* family extermination policies, but we need to hurt Murphy now and nip future rebels in the bud. That's all that matters. No legacy for traitors."

Boyle raised an eyebrow as the prime minister spoke for the first time since the meeting had begun. Actually, nothing Murphy had done—or, at least, nothing they *knew* he'd done—came close to meeting the definition of treason. He'd been well within the letter of his authority as a system governor, at least until he rejected the Oval's order to abandon New Dublin. It was hardly surprising that the *Five Hundred* saw that as treason, of course. Especially given how the Fringe was likely to react when it found out. *That* didn't surprise Boyle at all, but—

The prime minister leaned back slightly as one of her aides whispered in her ear, and Boyle hid another, broader smile, as she looked up to give the unfortunate young woman a scowl. He wouldn't have wanted to be the one to correct Verena Schleibaum about the fact that the League's use of *zuzhu* had no basis in reality. That less-than-factual allegation had been a long-standing part of Federation propaganda for so long that everyone just assumed it was true.

"Any opposition?" the original aide asked a bit nervously. The prime minister was the titular head of the Federation, but it was still an oligarchy controlled by the Five Hundred.

No one spoke.

"The motion passes," the aide said.

"I'll take the lead on removing *all* Murphys from the Navy," Fokaides said.

Boyle set his drink down and turned it slowly on the coaster as he considered Fokaides's profile. The old admiral was either afraid he hadn't done enough to call the current Murphy to heel, or else he wanted to push himself into prominence, once he toppled the departed Murphy's statue. Which was fine with Boyle. In fact, conflict between Fokaides and Yang was fine with *everyone* else in the room. It made the Navy easier to manipulate.

"There's more than just that Murphy." Madison Dawson, the CEO of Astro Engineering, slapped a palm against the table. "There are his in-laws. We're all aware of why Kanada Thakore isn't in here."

"And what do you want, Dawson? A civil asset forfeiture of everything Venus Futures has?"

The question rumbled from a grossly fat man seated in a chair against the wall. Gerard Perrin had pendulous jowls and deep-set, darkly ringed eyes, but he was also the Director and CEO of Société Auchan, the largest single corporation in the entire Five Hundred. He might not be *seated* at the table because of his girth, but that certainly didn't mean he had no place at it.

"I thought you'd be a bit subtler in your quest for a larger market share, Madison," he added now, and Dawson scowled.

"Thakore's building a significant percentage of our warships," she said. "Do we want to trust he'll deliver *functional* ships if his precious son-in-law goes warlord on us? We can either take over his holdings now, or else we can wait until the first time those ships go into battle to find out if they blow up at the first scratch because of a 'design flaw.'"

"We've sent Admiral Thakore to deal with Murphy," Fokaides said. "Rajenda Thakore received the orders with great enthusiasm. And there were no protests from Kanada that I'm aware of."

Boyle raised his glass for another sip.

"Thakore's been quiet—publicly," Darković acknowledged. "But as for what's really going on in private? That could be something else entirely." He shrugged. "Boyle's closest to him."

Boyle nearly spat out his whiskey, then shook his head emphatically.

"Don't lump me in with him. I'm here with the inner council. Thakore isn't. On the other hand, I did happen to have lunch with him yesterday—by coincidence, not plan—and from his conversation, he's worried about his son. That's all. He didn't say one positive word about his son-in-*law*."

"I don't trust him," Dawson said. "The Federation hasn't had a crisis like this since the League broke through the Dyson front at the beginning of the war. It's time for extraordinary measures."

"We don't use the Executive branch against each other." Perrin leaned forward and folded meaty fingers over a cane handle made of wrought gold and platinum. "You know we have rules, Dawson."

"We have *traditions*," Dawson said softly, stubbornly, but she also sat farther back in her chair. Her eyes were stubborn, yet it was clear she had no intention of challenging Perrin any more strongly than that.

Not surprisingly. Gerard Perrin had a knack for intimidation that Boyle, for one, *never* wanted to challenge. Being corpulent in the modern age was a choice, and Perrin liked to use his bulk to impose on all of those around him. But that was the smallest part of his daunting presence, because he was also reputed to be the Chairman of the Commission, the shadowy organization that arbitrated disputes within the Five Hundred. No one had ever officially admitted the Commission existed, although everyone knew it did, just as everyone was always *very* careful to avoid confirming the rumors that the Commission's actions were often quite a bit more...proactive than mere arbitration. And because the Commission's membership—if it actually existed, of course—was kept secret no one ever dared criticize it.

"I'm not so inclined to destroy the arrangement that's worked so well for all of us over the centuries," Perrin said now. "A man's first loyalty will be to his blood, not to those who married into his line. If we seize all of Thakore's assets, we could have *two* fleet commanders not so happy with us. Admiral Thakore likes his leash? Fine. Then we're not going to kick a good dog. Instead, let's have Kanada and his daughter make public statements denouncing Murphy, yes? Some fodder for the paparazzi and our messaging campaigns."

"I think that's an outstanding idea." Boyle nodded quickly, and Perrin grunted.

"Then you tell him," he said. "No...suggest it. See how he reacts. If he's less than eager, then let him know the rules might change this one time."

"Certainly." Boyle licked his lips. "I'll go talk to him immediately after this meeting."

"Good." Perrin scratched two days' worth of stubble on his round chin. "Be a shame if we had to send the Hand after him," he added.

"Not here," Dawson hissed, then looked at the prime minister and smiled.

A stab of cold went through Boyle. Every senior member of the Five Hundred knew about the Hand, the off-the-books enforcers who dealt with...issues...that those in power didn't want made public or known to the Federation's official organs. Officially, the Hand was only one more security firm whose client list happened to include an extraordinary number of the Five Hundred's most powerful members but was beholden to no one. One that was never sent to deal with one of their own. After all, the Five Hundred vied amongst themselves for money and power as a game, something to keep them amused amid the leisure of incalculable wealth. That was the way it was, the foundation of their universe. Unleashing the Hand on their fellows might lead to its being loosed on *them*, and none of them wanted to go there.

But *unofficially*, the Hand was a creature of the Commission that did whatever the Commission decided needed doing. All of them knew *that*, too, just as they knew Perrin was a stickler for the status quo. Which meant his hint that the Hand might be employed this time was a warning to Boyle that he'd better succeed in his task.

Boyle was still digesting that unpleasant thought when a series of high-pitched chirps sounded from Prime Minister Schleibaum's and Admiral Fokaides's emergency comms. The room went still as the two of them held up their comms to project mono-directional holograms into their eyes.

"It's too soon to have heard anything back from Jalal or the Fringe..." Dawson said while the prime minister and the admiral looked at the images only they could see.

Boyle doubted she realized she'd spoken aloud, but his attention was on Fokaides as he watched the CNO glance back and forth between his holo and Schleibaum several times. Then the prime minister inhaled and killed her own display.

"A freighter just arrived in-system and burst-transmitted a message directly to the Oval," she told the table flatly. "According to its captain, the Bellerophon System's declared its independence."

A man cursed and slammed a fist against the table.

"I just closed escrow on the samarium mines in the Achilles Belt!" he snarled.

"Is that confirmed?" Darković asked sharply, and Schleibaum grimaced.

"All we have is what the captain could give us, and he's a civilian. But he included the message the system president—Xeneas—broadcast just before his ship wormholed out. He didn't get all of it; he went into supralight only ten minutes or so into Xeneas's broadcast. But according to what he did get, every carrier we had in the system's mutinied."

Someone swore in a soft, stunned voice.

"Oh, it's worse than that," Schleibaum said harshly. One or two people looked incredulous, as if unable to believe it *could* be worse, and she bared her teeth. "Also according to Xeneas's little broadcast, Bellerophon has decided to join something called 'the Free Worlds Alliance.'"

"The what?" Darković asked blankly.

"We don't have anything but the name," Schleibaum said. "Xeneas was still talking about it when the freighter wormholed. But according to the part its captain did hear, it's an alliance of multiple Fringe Systems which have *all* chosen to go out of compliance. Which—" she stabbed a look at Boyle "—lends extra credence to whatever's going on in New Dublin and the Concordia Sector."

This time no one said a word. No one could.

"And Murphy?" Darković asked into the ringing silence after a long, frozen moment.

"The freighter captain didn't report anything directly about Murphy, and Xeneas didn't mention any names in the broadcast the freighter brought with it." Schleibaum's voice was, if anything, harsher than it had been before. "But if this 'Free World's Alliance' *is* coming out of Concordia, it certainly looks like Murphy didn't do anything to *stop* it, now doesn't it?"

"But how could anyone in Bellerophon even know about something happening in Concordia?" another voice asked. "They're—what? Eighty light-years from New Dublin?"

"Seventy-five," Fokaides replied. "And I don't have any idea how they found out so quickly. Assuming this Alliance abortion is coming out of Concordia, that is. It may not be, in which case it could be located a lot closer to Bellerophon than that."

"Just how many plague spots do we *have* out in the Fringe?" someone asked.

No one answered for a moment. Then Vice Admiral Yang straightened her shoulders.

"Quite a few . . . at least potentially," she said, and looked around the conference table almost defiantly, then turned to Schleibaum. "It's been building for years, Madam Prime Minister. We've always known that, but ONI's seen a significant uptick in it since Inverness. And not just in Concordia or Acera. Word's spread widely around the entire Southern Lobe and to at least some of the Northern Lobe systems. So I'm afraid Admiral Fokaides is right. This could have come from almost anywhere and not necessarily out of New Dublin at all."

"Except that it was Murphy's diversion to Scotia and his 'heroic' rescue of the Inverness survivors that gave the entire story such legs in the Heart World media," Fokaides added harshly. "And the same thing in the Fringe, for that matter. He may not've had a single thing to do—directly—with Bellerophon, but he sure as hell lit the fuse!"

A rumble of agreement growled its way around the table.

Oddly, no one saw fit to mention Yance Drebin's role in the Inverness atrocity.

"Well, even if 'Governor Murphy' was nowhere near it when it all went into the crapper, what the hell was the *Bellerophon* system governor doing while all this was happening?" Darković demanded.

"That's a very interesting question," Schleibaum said coldly. "And I'm beginning to wonder just how 'spontaneous' all of Murphy's rogue actions truly are."

"Why?" Darković asked, eyes narrowed.

"Because he doesn't seem to be the only system governor we have going off the reservation. Governor Ramsay appeared side by side with Xeneas when he made his announcement. She's signed off on it."

"What?!"

Darković stared at her in shock, and she shook her head slowly, grimly.

"This invalidates too much of our messaging," she said. "We've put out that Murphy's a lone lunatic. A corrupt, bribe-taking criminal. We wanted him disgraced and taken down without ever even talking about treason. And if we *had* to go there, he was a Fringe warlord, a self-seeking usurper with only a single ragged-assed system behind him. His supporters were nothing but a bunch of opportunists and traitors on the far edge of the Federation. That's been our position from the start. And now this." She shook her head. "Bad enough if he *has* gone warlord in Concordia, but it may be even worse if he didn't have a damned thing to do with Bellerophon!" She shook her head again. "If the rot's spreading into Cyclops, if the Fringe *in general* is headed in the same direction—"

She drew a deep breath. "This is a problem," she said flatly.

"A problem we've had before," Perrin snorted. "Who else remembers all the doom and gloom when Gobelins tried to secede? We dealt with that without pissing ourselves. The same solution will yield the same results this time...if not better."

"No." Fokaides shook his head. "Not him. We can't cover-up another bloodbath."

"We did last time...well enough," Perrin replied. "And let's be honest here. A certain amount of, ah...notoriety can be a useful commodity. General Alaimo earned his reputation on Gobelins, and every system governor and local potentate across the Fringe knows the truth, whatever the 'official record' says. We let him loose in the Cyclops Sector, and we'll send a message to every other traitor out there."

"I'm not sure that's the way we want to go about this," Heghineh Suzmeian said, and Boyle's eyes narrowed as he considered her.

Frankly, her presence for this meeting had come as something of a surprise when he first saw her. Suzmeian Pharmaceutical was the Federation's third largest biomedical conglomerate, which certainly justified Heghineh's place at this table, but she'd always struck Boyle as a bit weak-kneed when it came to practical realities. She could be as ruthless as anyone else when it was purely business, yet it often seemed her heart wasn't in the larger game.

"Why not?" Perrin asked, and Heghineh swallowed. But she also met his gaze levelly.

"From a purely selfish and pragmatic perspective, Suzmeian has a very substantial financial interest in the Cyclops Sector," she said. "Our Bellerophon Biorepair Center is the fourth largest cloning facility in the entire Federation, and we probably provide replacement limbs and prostheses for at least twenty-five percent of our war wounded. I'd hate to see that get caught up in the sort of general destruction Gobelins saw.

"That's my personal, economic concern in what you're proposing, Gerard. But I also have to wonder if we need to be kicking that particular fire when we still haven't definitively dealt with Murphy. Cyclops is closer to Sol, it's wealthier, and it has a lot more people. Do we really want to send all of it up in flames? Which doesn't even consider that creating additional 'martyrs' Fringe apologists can point to as proof of how horrible we are is only too likely to provide the lunatics in this Free Worlds Alliance with additional propaganda points."

"Propaganda points are moot at this point, Heghineh," Perrin said coolly. "New Dublin's bad enough, but as you just pointed out, Bellerophon has ten times the population and at least eighty times the system gross product. Hell, the Cyclops Sector has at least six or seven times the total population of Concordia *and* Acera! And if Xeneas and his bastards did take all the carriers in-system that gives him—how many?"

Perrin looked the question at Fokaides, who shrugged unhappily.

"There were four assigned to the system."

"And in the rest of the sector?" Perrin pressed.

"Two at Cyclops itself and one each in Achilles and Minotaur."

"The farthest of which are only sixty light-years from Bellerophon, while we're *ninety-three* light-years away. That gives Xeneas potentially *eight* carriers, one more than Murphy has, with a hell of a lot more industrial support for them, and he can concentrate all of them before anything from Sol gets to Bellerophon." He shook his head. "Verena's right. With that kind of firepower, *and* the population and industry of Cyclops to back it, he's a worse threat than Murphy could ever be. And it completely undercuts our position that all the bad news coming out of the Fringe is the result of just one more man who would be king. We can't afford that."

"Yes, but—" Heghineh began, but he cut her off.

"The line's already been drawn where Murphy's concerned, and this 'Free Worlds' bullshit only proves the problem's even worse—and deeper—than we'd been afraid it was. We've been too frigging easy on the Fringers, put up with too much crap from them, and this is the result. Well, that old axiom about sparing the rod and spoiling the child comes pretty strongly to mind at the moment. Only in this case, we don't need a rod—we need an iron boot right up the Fringe's ass to remind it of its place. And if we show we're willing to hammer even a system with as much invested in it as Bellerophon, that reminder will pack a lot more emphasis."

"I didn't say I disagreed with the need to show strength," Heghineh replied. "I'm just—"

"I will remind all of you that Standing Order Fifteen applies to *any* planet not under Federation control," Prime Minister Schleibaum said coldly, and Heghineh closed her mouth. The prime minister glared at her for a moment, until her eyes dropped to the tabletop. Then Schleibaum swept the conference room with an icy stare.

"Any such planet is subject to orbital reduction if it declines to surrender. I don't want to invoke that on worlds that have been part of the Federation for centuries, but if they want to claim they aren't part of it anymore, I'm not going to sit here kvetching over military necessity like an old woman. We need strong, overt action, and we need it now. Fokaides?"

Fokaides's jaw clenched, and he glanced at Yang, who sat very straight in her chair, her expression unreadable.

"I'll...I'll process General Alaimo's reinstatement paperwork immediately," he said. "We've just finished standing Ninth Fleet back up. We were holding it here in Sol to backstop Admiral Thakore, but I'll send it to Cyclops, instead, along with the Thirteenth Army Corps. That'll reduce the Sol System's mobile defenses to just Home Fleet, and I'm afraid it'll take some time to backfill the combat power from other Heart sectors. But it should give him almost twice the worst-case firepower Xeneas could have."

"This revolt needs to end. Now." Schleibaum stood, and the rest of the room—except Perrin—followed suit. "We shielded the public from the full truth of what happened on Gobelins. Perhaps that was a mistake. It would appear the Fringe, at least, interpreted it as weakness on our part. No more. I'll sign a writ for Alaimo. Preemptive pardons for any and all actions carried out in the course of his duties in the Cyclops Sector...and wherever else he might be needed."

She gave all of them a curt nod, then turned and strode out of the bunker.

A heavy, sweaty hand landed on Boyle's shoulder.

"Good luck with Thakore, son," Perrin said. "It's good we know you're on the side of the right."

"Certainly."

Boyle downed the last of his whiskey and held his smile as it burned down into his chest.

CHAPTER THIRTEEN

Venus Futures Corporate HQ
City of Olympia
Old Terra
Sol System
Terran Federation
November 27, 2552

SIMRON AND REAGAN MURPHY TOOK THE EXTERNAL LIFT UP THE South Tower towards Kanada Thakore's office. The view from the crystoplast-walled lift at sunset made this Simron's favorite time to visit Venus Futures' enormous headquarters complex. The golden hour before twilight, glinting off the endless vista of skyscrapers stretching away into the Federation's capital, had always given her a sense of calm.

But not today.

"What does Grandpa want?" Reagan asked. "Do you think he's heard something about Dad and Callum?"

The sixteen-year-old wore all black. Simron wasn't sure if she was mourning anything in particular or if she was going through a phase amidst the family and Federation-wide crisis in which they found themselves.

Now Reagan scratched at the security band wrapped around her upper arm. The device, which camouflaged itself to be virtually invisible when worn, carried transmitters that broadcast health, location, and stress levels to the Venus Futures proprietary network tapped into electronic and communications systems all over the planet. All over the Sol System, actually. It could be programmed for any megacorp's network, really, which explained why it was the top seller for those who needed another security layer to safeguard themselves and loved ones.

"It's...too soon for any word to've come back from the Fringe," Simron said. "But that doesn't mean he hasn't heard something else. It could be good news."

"If it was good news, he'd have just told us over the link." Reagan rolled her eyes. "He wants us in his office because that way, no one else knows what he has to say to us."

"You're reading too much into this." Simron adjusted the drape of her sari over her left arm.

"You just don't want it to be *bad* news," Reagan replied.

"Is that what *you* want?" Simron snapped as the lift came to a smooth stop and the doors opened soundlessly behind them.

"I just want them to come home," Reagan said. "Dad and Callum were supposed to babysit some Fringe planet full of barbarians for two years. Not become warlords."

"They're not warlords," Simron said as they stepped into an enclosed foyer. Security lasers scanned them both.

"That's what the news is calling them. And all my friends at school," Reagan pouted.

"Maybe we should switch to private tutors for the rest of the semester," Simron said, giving her daughter a quick hug.

"I guess so. No one's even asked me to the junior prom...."

"Well, no one at that place is good enough to *take* you."

Simron linked arms with Reagan as the foyer's security doors opened to give access to her father's office.

Kanada Thakore stood behind the desk of Midden wood to greet them as they stepped into the office. The wood grain's fractal patterns glinted with embedded flecks of golden resin. Just how those flecks had been embedded had mystified Simron ever since she was a little girl, but it had been passed down through generations of Thakores.

Kanada wasn't alone. Amedeo Boyle sat across the desk from him and Simron stiffened as he gave her a nervous smile, then dabbed sweat from his forehead with a silk handkerchief.

The hair on the back of her neck prickled as she saw him, and the prickle grew stronger as she looked behind her and saw a pair of men in simple business suits standing against the wall to either side of the portrait of Sudharma Thakore, Venus Futures' founder. She'd never seen either of them before, and something tightened in her stomach as they gazed back at her, as calmly emotionless as predators.

"Father, Mr. Boyle," she said. "What's the occasion? And—" she waved her free hand at the two men against the wall "—who's this?"

"More security for me," Boyle said nervously. "My underwriting department insisted on some enhanced measures while things are so...uncertain. I'm sure you understand."

"They can leave," Simron said flatly, but Kanada shook his head.

"I'm afraid not," he said. "It's not just Amedeo's underwriters. There are quite a few members of the Five Hundred with augmented security at the moment." He grimaced. "And these two bodyguards come from a highly recommended agency. One that's worked with the Oval and the Prime Minister's office quite often. In fact, they've done so much...sensitive work that they've all been conditioned against discussing any of their clients' proprietary information. Isn't that right?" he said, looking over her head, and one of the bodyguards nodded.

"Our psychological profiles have been altered to prevent unauthorized disclosures," he said. "And we put up a significant bond with each employment contract," he added with a smile.

Simron regarded the two bodyguards. Each stood with a degree of confidence that was at odds with the protective details that had been part of her own life ever since she was a little girl. Security details—*good* security details—were constantly on edge, alert for danger to their charges. But the air around these two was more relaxed, as if they were certain there *was* no danger. Not for them.

"Just think of them as more furniture," Kanada said, interrupting Simron's thoughts. There was no protest from the bodyguards, and he gestured to an empty chair next to Boyle. "And, please, have a seat. We have some matters to discuss."

"Is there news from Terrence? Or from Callum?" Simron stayed where she was and gripped her sari tighter. "If there is, just say it."

"Nothing." Kanada shrugged. "It takes time for word to come back from the Fringe. We've had some...minor news from other sectors, but nothing more from New Dublin or Terr—your husband. The message lag is a fact of life."

"I'm well aware of how long it takes to send news back and

forth," Simron snapped. "But if it's not that, then what *is* it? Why did you summon me here with Boyle...and those two?"

Kanada looked at Boyle. The other man gazed back for a moment, then shook his head slightly, and Kanada looked back at his daughter.

"Simmy, your husband's actions have had an extremely negative impact on Venus Futures," he said.

"Along with the rest of the Federation," Boyle added, just loud enough for the two bodyguards to hear, and Simron's fear flashed over into simmering anger.

"Terrence is no traitor! He crushed the League's fleet at New Dublin, then ran them to ground and destroyed their hidden shipyard. He should be as honored and appreciated as his grandfather!"

Boyle grimaced and looked away.

"Some of those points are...in doubt." Kanada held up a hand. "Terrence's actions as governor were erratic. Leading missions beyond the Blue Line without orders from the Oval would've been enough to—"

"Why are we here?" Simron hissed.

"Nothing good is coming from this." Thakore raised both hands. "The best we can do now is mitigate the destruction before more people are killed and it does even more damage to the Federation."

"Then perhaps the Five Hundred should have considered that before they decided to arrest my husband for succeeding at his job," Simron said. "Was that because someone in the Oval had some victory in a minor skirmish to announce and Terrence stole their thunder? It certainly wasn't because he'd done what he was *accused* of, and you know it!"

"It's not—" Kanada put his hands on his hips and turned away, looking out his office's windows rather than at his daughter. "We have to do what's right for the Federation now, Simmy. Venus Futures needs to take a stand—publicly—on the matter. He's my son-in-law, after all, and that puts the entire family in one hell of an awkward position. We can't have one foot on Earth and the other in the Fringe."

"What did you threaten him with?" Simron demanded, wheeling on Boyle. "Cancellation of the new carrier program? Audits from the Taxation Bureau?"

"There was no need for threats," Boyle said. "Kanada's loyalty is to the Federation, and that's never been in question among those who know him."

Simron's eyes narrowed.

"But?" she said.

"But the entire Federation doesn't know him—or you—the way I or the rest of the Five Hundred do," Boyle said. "We need you all to make a statement. A public statement denouncing Murphy's treason for violating his orders, and—"

"He's no traitor!" Simron snapped so sharply Boyle shrank back as if she'd slapped him. He looked at her for a moment, then he raised his palms almost placatingly.

"Then a public statement against any violence and a plea for peace. Is that too much? Because that sounds very reasonable to me."

Boyle looked at Kanada, then back at Simron, and one of the bodyguards cleared his throat.

"We can't be lukewarm about this," Kanada said, very carefully not looking at the bodyguard. "Not when Rajenda's deployment to Jalal Station will hit the nets in the next day or two."

"Wait. Rajenda's already been *sent*? I thought he was bringing back units of First Fleet from Beta Cygni?"

"That was the original plan," Kanada said. "It turns out he was already in transit back from Beta Cygni before his new orders even reached him. Fleet Admiral LeBron had sent him home to report to the Oval after First Fleet took Kellerman. The good news was that he got home earlier than anyone expected; the bad news was that, aside from three damaged FTLCs that need massive amounts of yard work, he didn't bring any carriers with him. So they gave him a task force from the Reserve, instead, and sent him directly out to secure Jalal."

"Jalal, not New Dublin?" Simron asked sharply.

"Only to Jalal," Boyle replied before Kanada could, and Simron glared at him. She wouldn't have trusted him if he'd told her water was wet.

"When?" she demanded, turning back to her father. His eyes evaded hers for a moment, then he inhaled deeply.

"Two months ago."

Simron stared at him, her eyes wide. For a handful of breaths, she literally couldn't move. Then she shook her head as if her father had just punched her.

"Two months ago," she repeated. "You knew he'd been sent *two months ago*, and you never told me?!"

"There was nothing you could have done, Simmy! I didn't see any reason to... distress you any more than you already were."

"*Distress* me?" Simron's eyes blazed.

"Not his worst decision," Boyle muttered and got an angry look from Kanada.

She opened her mouth, then remembered the bodyguards and closed it again. Silence hovered for a long, tense moment, and then she inhaled.

"What did the Oval send *my brother* to the Fringe to do? Exactly?"

"To bring Murphy to his senses before his actions sparks some sort of revolt—I'm not saying that's what he *wants*, Simmy, but you know it could happen!—that kills even more people than the war with the League," Kanada said. "The Federation simply can't tear itself apart over this, Simron. We have to think of what's at stake here. It's larger than me. Larger than even Venus Futures."

"He's my husband, and the father of my children," Simron said coldly. She stepped over to Reagan, who sat on a small couch with her head bowed, and touched her shoulder. "And the Five Hundred sent my own brother to kill or capture my husband? How 'rational' am I supposed to be about something like that?"

"You're actually taking it better than I expected, if that helps," Boyle said with a chuckle.

Matching daggered glares from two sets of Thakore eyes cut his humor short, and then Kanada looked back at Simron.

"Yes, the Oval sent your brother. Do you think I wanted that? Do you think I wanted to put my only son into harm's way, along with one of my grandsons? I lose, no matter what happens, Simmy. Again, no good is coming from this. I'm willing to concede that Terrence didn't set out to commit treason—even that that's not what he *thinks* he's doing, even now—but that's beside the point by now. The Federation's on the verge of *civil war*—a civil war that could dwarf the casualty rates from the war against the League and give the League the military victory it could never achieve any other way. That's where we are, that's the reality of the situation. At this point, we have to do whatever we can to limit the harm."

"They sent Rajenda to punish us." Simron's face was dark with anger. "He's never cared for Terrence, and if one—or both—of them..."

She sank onto the couch beside Reagan and put her arm around her daughter.

"They're both smart men," Kanada said. "Smart enough to figure out how to—" he waved a hand "—come to some sort of arrangement without killing anyone. I pray for that. But the orders have been sent. That's beyond our influence or control now, and we have a duty right here at home to mitigate any further harm."

"And what does the Five Hundred have in mind?" Simron glowered at Boyle. "This isn't your idea, Amedeo. You're too much of a yes-man to be bold enough to suggest all this on your own."

Boyle hovered on the brink of protest for a moment, then let it go.

"A news conference," Kanada said. "We read prepared statements, and then you and the children retire from public view until this is over. For your and their protection."

"Protection from what?" Simron demanded.

"Do you think you can walk through the galleries here in Olympus, or the red carpet at the Las Vegas Fashion Gala, and not be recognized?" Boyle asked. "Of course you can't. And not everyone's going to be...happy to see you. There's what you believe about your husband, and then there's what everyone else *knows* about him."

"They only know it because of what the Five Hundred's put out on the nets. Why isn't news of Terrence's victory at New Dublin on the feeds? Or his capture of the League's shipyard? All I see or hear from those marionettes on the feeds are stories about his supposed corruption and the federal marshals sent to kidnap him!"

Kanada winced at her choice of verbs, but her glare never wavered from Boyle's face.

"Any discussion of intelligence derived from the purported raid on the purported shipyard is classified," one of the bodyguards said. "You're not read in on any of that information. I strongly encourage you to not disseminate it any farther."

"What are you going to do? Cut out my tongue?" Simron snapped.

The man smiled at her.

"Simmy," Kanada tapped his desk, "the truth will out. But at this moment, none of us can be positive what the truth really is. Eventually, it will all come out, I'm sure, but not anytime soon, it seems. And at the moment, we have to deal with what's already out there. Like I said, Rajenda and Terrence are both smart men, and I'm positive neither of them wants to get anybody killed unless they absolutely have to. It's entirely possible they'll arrive at a sort of . . . standoff. A stalemate, while they negotiate with one another out in the Fringe. And if the two of them are facing off out there, and Terrence sees your statement, it may just tip the balance in favor of his seeing reason and backing off the ledge."

Simron looked at him, stunned that anyone as smart as her father could believe anything of the sort might happen. But then she realized he wasn't actually explaining that theoretical logic for *her* sake. It was for Boyle's and the Five Hundred's.

"Either way, we have to make our public statement *before* any dispatches from Rajenda make it back to Earth," Kanada continued. "We have to get ahead of whatever report comes in from Jalal and New Dublin, good or bad. If we're reactive, we'll look like we're trying to play both sides."

"Not once have you—" she pointed a finger at her father "—or you—" the finger moved to Boyle, and then she snapped her hand at the bodyguards "—or *anyone* from the Five Hundred been the least concerned about the truth. Or about justice. You don't care about that. You're all just afraid of losing control."

"And if we do lose control?" Kanada demanded. "What happens then, Simron? I'll tell you—anarchy! Chaos! A civil war worse than anything in human history! We have to set aside our pride for the sake of peace and think of the good karma we'll earn."

"And so now you expect me to sacrifice my integrity, as well as my husband, is that it?" Simron said. "You want me to denounce my own husband, when I know everything that's being said about him is a lie. How can I do that?"

Kanada's head drooped and the room was silent. Then she heard a noise from behind her. The sound of a throat being quietly cleared.

She turned her head and looked behind her, and the bodyguard who'd spoken earlier smiled at her.

And in that moment, Simron Thakore realized who Amedeo Boyle's "bodyguards" truly were. Agents of the Five Hundred.

Fixers.

She'd grown up with the rumors of the *Bauk*, boogeymen, that were always watching the Five Hundred, although she hadn't *really* believed them, as a child. After all, who could possibly threaten *her*? Her father wasn't simply the most handsome, strongest, smartest man in her world, he was also *Kanada Thakore*, one of the dozen or so most powerful men in the entire Federation!

But then, in her final year of high school, Angela Cole, the rather pretty daughter of another conglomerate's scion and one of her friends from the year before, had . . . disappeared. She'd spent the previous summer as an intern for the CEO of Zaibatsu Industries, and there'd been some sort of data breach at Zaibatsu. No one in Simron's circle had known what sort of data had been hacked, but they'd known it had been serious, and she'd looked forward to pumping Angela for the details. But Angela hadn't returned to school after all. No one knew where she'd gone instead, but when she finally did come home again, eight months later, she'd been a sadder, quieter ghost of the mischievous Angela Simron had known.

And she'd refused to answer a single question about where she'd been.

When Simron mentioned Angela to her mother, Dušanka Thakore had grabbed her by the shoulders and told her to never speak of it again, or the Fixers would pay the Thakores a visit.

Dušanka's obvious fear had astonished high-school-aged Simron, but she'd learned more about the Hand—and the Fixers who served it—as she maneuvered through the Five Hundred and assumed an ever larger role in Venus Futures' management. In fact, she'd learned more than enough to understand her mother's fear—far more than she wished she'd ever learned. The Fixers were always for hire, willing to tie off any loose end, tidy any problem, for a fee. But they never came cheaply, and despite their official assertions, she was convinced their fundamental loyalty was seldom to their "clients."

It was to the Commission, and the Commission was as dedicated to keeping the rest of the Five Hundred in line as it was to dictating the policies the Federation's government "spontaneously" adopted. The organs of government's obedience could be insured through corruption and blackmail, but the Five Hundred was more . . . amorphous. Its members sometimes forgot they, too, were part of the system that regimented the Federation and thus subject to the will of those who controlled that system. Yet the more those members relied upon the Fixers, the deeper into their lives and businesses the Fixers—and the Commission—sank their claws, because whatever the *rest* of the Federation might know or suspect, the Fixers knew *precisely* what they'd done for those who engaged their services. And if any of the Five Hundred caused enough problems for the rest, or threatened the Commission's control, damning evidence would emerge for either the federal prosecutors, most of whom answered directly or indirectly to the Five Hundred themselves, or into the media, most of which was controlled and owned outright *by* the Five Hundred.

All of that was true, and so was the fact that anyone who engaged the Fixers exposed themselves to the danger of retaliation from their fellows if the fact that they'd hired the Fixers ever came out. And the odds that it *would* come out were...nontrivial. Their claim of being psychologically blocked from disclosing anything was hard to believe in its own right—anything that could be done to a mind could be un-done—but even that was the least of it. Because the Fixers would use any weapon someone had been foolish enough to leave in their hands—including evidence of the things the Fixers had done for *them*—against previous employers if a new one, or the Commission, made it expedient.

There was a reason—there were a *lot* of reasons—her father had always categorically refused their services and Simron was happy to keep that policy in place.

Reagan gripped her hand hard. Simron doubted very much that the girl had any true idea of just who it was that stood behind them, but she obviously sensed enough to be frightened. And as Simron recognized her daughter's fear, a fiery corona of rage wrapped itself about her own fear. She'd wondered why her father had insisted on Reagan's coming. Now she knew. *He* hadn't insisted at all, really. It had been Boyle. Boyle, who'd wanted Reagan there to make the threat from the Hand that much worse.

Boyle...who'd had the temerity to threaten *her* daughter.

Fury boiled up within her, but she knew the danger now.

Carefully, she thought. *Carefully, Simron!*

"My integrity matters to me," she said evenly, "and so does my belief in my husband. But you're right, Father. This situation is cascading from bad to worse. I can't—and don't—believe Terry is a traitor, but I can issue a statement in the interest of peace.

But let me write my own. You may be right about a statement from me influencing him to see reason, but, as you say, he's a smart man. He might suspect I'm being coerced to speak out, or that I'm being held hostage, if I read something prepared."

"I brought a draft statement for you all," Boyle said. "But it *is* a draft. So long as you hit the high points, I'm sure everything will be fine. I'm certainly satisfied."

He stood and looked at the Fixers. For approval, Simron realized.

"In that case, Sir," the Fixer who'd spoken said, exactly as if Boyle were actually in charge, "I suppose we should be on our way."

Boyle's shoulders relaxed ever so slightly, and he nodded, but the Fixer wasn't quite finished. He moved smoothly towards the coffee table in front of Simron and Reagan's couch. He stopped a step or two away and snapped a plastic card against the glass tabletop, and Simron glimpsed the edge of a holstered pistol inside his jacket as he bent over.

"Send your statement for approval to this address, please, Ma'am," he said.

His tone was calm, courteous, but his eyes held hers for a heartbeat. Then he, his companion, and Boyle stepped out of the office, and the security doors slid shut behind them.

"Grandpa!" Reagan sobbed. "How could you—?"

"Wait."

Kanada opened a desk drawer and removed a slate. He tapped a ten-digit code against the screen, and a pair of small drones lifted from the top of a bookcase. They flitted about the room, then slowed into a hover before the painting near which the Hand agents had stood. Something like thimble-sized lightning bolts flashed from the drones, and a smoldering disc fell from the underside of the frame.

"Is that the only listening device?" Simron asked.

"It's the only one the best detectors money can buy could find, anyway," her father replied. "And then there's this. I had it developed in-house."

He tapped another code, and Simron felt a dull ringing sensation in her ears.

"It's uncomfortable, I know." Kanada's words were muted and he stuck the tip of a pinky into his own ear and shook it. "But the multipath fading keeps our conversation localized to a few yards around me. Nowhere near where those two were."

Simron pointed to Boyle's seat and raised an eyebrow, and Kanada snorted.

"Would *you* trust him to plant a bug?"

"No." It was her turn to snort, yet any temptation towards levity was short-lived. "But, Father, we can't—"

"We must!" Kanada covered his mouth for a heartbeat. "Everything's at stake, Simron—everything. Venus Futures, everything our family's built over generations, could just vanish if we give the Five Hundred reason to destroy it."

"And Rajenda really has been sent out already? Or was that just some sort of test?"

"He has." Kanada nodded heavily. "And, no, I didn't tell you about it before he left the system—for which, I apologize." He met her angry, frightened gaze levelly. "But I'd do the same thing again, Simmy, because there was nothing you could have done about it—nothing *I* could do about it, given the timing—and I knew how . . . painful any scene between the two of you would have been."

"*Painful*," she repeated bitterly, and he nodded.

"I love you both, and I *know* you both. You would have done your best to stop him or make him promise you Terrence won't get hurt, and he wouldn't have done it. All that conversation could have done would be to make it hurt worse. And, to be honest, I truly do think sending him is the best option available to us. Partly because of how it helps protect the family, of course, but also because even though you're absolutely right about how much he and Terrence dislike each other, he's probably the only Heart flag officer with a single chance in hell of talking Terrence into surrendering peacefully. And, frankly, Simmy, that's the only hope he has of getting out of this alive, and again, to be honest—" Kanada's shoulders slumped "—even that's not a good one. I don't know exactly what new information's been added to the mix, but *something* has. And the only thing I can think of is that they think the Fringe is going out of compliance."

He met his daughter's eyes levelly, and she felt herself pale. Unlike Reagan, she knew what that meant. But surely they were wrong! Terry believed in duty, in honor, and he was *Henrik Murphy's* grandson. He'd *die* to preserve the Federation!

Yes, he would, a tiny voice said in the back of her brain, *but if doing his duty leads him into* conflict *with the Federation...*

No. Not with the Federation; with the Five Hundred.

"He's terrified too many people too badly," her father said, speaking her own fear out loud, "and the Five Hundred is out for blood this time."

"This is that O'Hanraghty's fault, isn't it?" Reagan demanded. "Dad was so happy as a Survey officer. Then he met that red-headed asshole, and—"

"Your father's a Murphy." Simron patted her daughter's hand. "Yes, he loved Survey, and he was happy there. But over the last few months I've begun figuring a few things out. Things he didn't share even with me, probably—" she looked defiantly at her father "—because he was protecting the family."

Kanada looked as if he were about to reply, but then he shook his head and sat back in his chair while Simron returned her gaze to Reagan.

"The reason he'd chosen a Survey career to begin with was because he knew how the Five Hundred would react to the possibility of a Murphy they didn't feel confident they could control in command of a war fleet. They knew a thing or two about Murphys, the Five Hundred. Things I'm ashamed to say I didn't think about. Not as deeply as I should have, at any rate."

Reagan looked puzzled, and Simron grimaced as she reminded herself that her daughter was only sixteen. She considered her next words carefully.

"Your father," she said, "embraced a Survey career partly because he truly loved survey duty, partly because he knew how... hesitant some of the Five Hundred would be to give him a combat command, and partly because he knew it would convince them he only wanted a governorship to get his ticket punched before he went into politics or back to Survey."

She locked eyes with her own father again and saw the recognition—and chagrin—in Kanada's eyes as he realized, possibly for the first time, just how completely his son-in-law had played him to get what he wanted.

"They wanted a Murphy they could control?" Reagan said slowly, then barked out a harsh laugh. "How's that working out for them?"

"Not well," Simron acknowledged with a wry smile that—somewhat to her own surprise—held quite a lot of pride.

"We could pin this all on O'Hanraghty," Kanada said thoughtfully. "Make him out to be someone like that Iago character from that play you starred in all those years ago."

"You really think that would work?" Simron said, and, after a moment, her father shook his head regretfully.

"Not at this point. No, they want their kilo of flesh, Simmy. And if we don't give it to them, then all the rest of the family goes down right beside Terrence."

"I can't do this, Father," Simron said. "Not against my own husband. Not against *Terry!*"

"I should've raised you to be more flexible. Rajenda knows how the game is played. You, though—you never learned how to compromise those principles of yours, did you?"

She looked at him, one arm around her daughter, and he sighed.

"No, you didn't. But we've bought some time, at least. The earliest Rajenda can reach Jalal is two weeks from today. Assuming he spends a week or so integrating the Jalal System picket into his fleet before he moves on, the soonest he's likely to reach New Dublin would be sometime around January tenth. That means the soonest we could hear back from him, even if he and Terrence get this thing settled the very day he arrives, would be February twenty-fifth. We've got one day less than that."

"We can run." Reagan perked up. "We'll...we'll meet up with Dad someplace. Then at least we'll all be together!"

"No." Simron shook her head. "We don't know he's still in New Dublin. Even if he is right this instant, there's no guarantee he'd still be there by the time we got there."

"Then we can—"

"Stop this." Kanada looked around the room. "If we try to run, it makes us look like we support your father, and we can't risk that, *Priy*. Not now. That's why Earth is the best place for us right now...as long as we cooperate, we're safe. If we give the others a reason, they'll drop the hammer on us."

"Well, I'm not saying *anything* against Daddy."

Reagan crossed her arms and glared at her grandfather. In that moment, she looked a great deal like her mother.

"No, you don't have to," Kanada said. "You're a child. Just your mother and me. And Vyom. Who's out past the Snow Line, shaking down the latest FTLC to come out of the yard.

I couldn't get him back here in time for our little meeting. I'll set you both up in my private quarters here. Then I'll send for your things, and—"

"I will *not* imprison myself or my children." Simron stood. "We have our own home. We'll stay there while I...think of something. Anything."

Kanada considered arguing, but he recognized futility when he saw it.

"I'll send over a security detail," he said instead. "Milunka Savic and some other old hands I trust."

"You think they can stop the Five Hundred if they come for us?" Simron asked.

"No, but they *will* dissuade any paparazzi that come snooping around. The media firestorm's just beginning, Simmy, and Milunka can help a lot with that. Remember what she did to that reporter who tried to follow you into the bathroom while you were pregnant with Vyom?"

"Didn't she break every bone in that scumbag's hand?"

"Up to the elbow." Her father nodded. "And she rather enjoyed it. She'll keep you both from being bothered."

"And what about Vyom?" Simron asked, and her face darkened. "He was so looking forward to all the wedding planning...."

"I'll speak to him when he returns to Earth," Kanada said. "I won't send him back to hide behind his mother's sari, though." He snorted. "He'd probably refuse to go, anyway."

"Is the wedding still on?" Reagan asked. "Are Vyom and Ingrid still engaged?"

"Her mother hasn't sent me a text message since the word broke." Simron shook her head. "Not a good sign, honey."

"I'll take no news as good news for the time being," Kanada said, and tapped a slate on his desk. "Here's the draft statement Boyle brought. Take it with you and—"

"No, I'm reading it now."

Simron snatched it up and began scrolling. Her face tightened, then lost color as she continued reading.

"They're insane." She looked up, wiped a tear from her eye. "I can't say this...I can't say *any* of this!"

"Let me push back—see where we can compromise. Give me some time," Kanada said. "I have a lot of favors I can call in."

"Did you know they want me to get a divorce?"

Simron slapped the slate down on his desk.

"*Hai raam.*" Kanada ran a hand through his hair. "I'll read it later. Please, go home. And don't do anything rash. We need a plan, not just reactions. Just give me some time to think, okay?"

"Mommy, no! You can't divorce Daddy!"

Reagan began sobbing, and Simron stroked her hair.

"Never, sweetheart! They're mad. Let's get home before the traffic gets too bad." She gave her father a dagger-sharp look. "And don't you 'forget' to tell me when Vyom gets here, Father. He's the one we have to worry about."

"Yes, yes!" Kanada waved his hand at her, then activated the holo projectors that cast screens around his desk. "Simmy...I love you. All of you. Don't ever doubt that."

"I never have," Simron said.

She went to the card the Fixer had left behind and hesitated before she picked it up. Somehow, it radiated an actual foul aura, and she refused to carry it with her. Instead, she memorized the only text on the card—a simple comm combination—and then helped Reagan stand and guided her to the lift.

CHAPTER FOURTEEN

TFNS Lelantos
Wormhole Space
November 29, 2552

"FOUR," CAPTAIN OZBEY SAID.

"*Oooh.*" Commander Alioto looked at his cards dubiously. "I was gonna bid nil."

"Sure you were." Vice Admiral Rajenda Thakore looked at his own hand. "And if I believed that, I might be worried." He rubbed the tip of his nose with his right index finger. "Three," he said finally, and looked at Alioto. "And your nil bid?"

"Five," the commander said with a grin, and Thakore shook his head.

"One of these days you may actually learn to bluff," he said dryly, then cocked an eyebrow across the table.

"Well," Commodore Christina Zebić said, "since Saffiro isn't going nil after all, I suppose I should." She shrugged. "Or are we playing 'no ace, no face, no Spades' and I get to throw it in?"

"Talk about people who can't bluff," Captain Ozbey observed to no one in particular, and Zebić chuckled.

"Okay, skeptic. Wait and see for yourself," she said. "Go ahead, lead something."

Ozbey glanced at his cards, then played the three of Hearts. Thakore dropped the Jack on it, Alioto followed with the Queen, and Zebić played the ten.

"One away," she said, and Alioto led the five of Clubs. She dropped the six on it, Ozbey played the Ace, and Thakore took the opportunity to get rid of the three.

"And that's two," he said.

The hand proceeded, but the truth was that Thakore was on autopilot. He supposed he should be paying more attention, but he was an excellent Spades player, so his "autopilot mode" was pretty damned good. And despite the much-needed relaxation, he had other things to worry about.

Lelantos had departed the Sol System on October twelfth, and by the rest of the galaxy's clocks, it was November twenty-ninth. But while forty days had been passing by those other clocks, only about five and a half had passed aboard *Lelantos* as she hurtled through wormhole space at 99.9 percent of light speed.

He wished the voyage had gone equally quickly for the galaxy at large.

Too long, he thought, playing the Queen of Diamonds to take another trick. *God only knows what Terry's been up to with that much time.*

A dull burn of rage went through him, although no sign of it showed in his expression. His family didn't show its emotions, although Simron had always been something of an exception in that regard. Of course, Simron's judgment wasn't always the best, as Rajenda's current mission demonstrated. He'd told her to turn down Terrence Murphy's proposal. He'd *told* her. Warned her Murphy would never be a comfortable fit in the universe of the Five Hundred. But had she listened? Hell, no! And now there was hell to pay, because she hadn't. Bad enough for the rest of the Federation, but potentially disastrous on so many levels for the Thakore family.

Alioto played the six of Hearts, and Zebić grimaced as she dropped the nine on it. Ozbey chuckled and sluffed a diamond, then grimaced in turn as Thakore played the two of Spades.

"Nice try," he told *Lelantos*'s commanding officer, and led the Ace of Spades. Zebić played the Ace of Hearts and grinned at the flag captain.

"Well, I may have fibbed a little bit about not having any face cards, but I wasn't lying about the Spades."

"So I see, Ma'am. Well, we'll just have to work a little harder. Or possibly set the Admiral."

"Who already has two of his three tricks," Rajenda pointed out. "I've got a feeling *I* may not be the one getting set around here."

Ozbey chuckled and led the seven of Spades. Rajenda played the Jack and sat back in his chair.

This would be their last Spades game before Jalal, he thought. After which, they'd have a rather more serious game to play. And that could get tricky. Especially after this much delay. It had taken entirely too long to put together his task force, but at least they'd given him plenty of power when they finally sent him off.

It irked him that his command was designated Task Force 804. Twenty-four FTLCs—twenty-five, counting *Lelantos*—with their embarked sublight parasites should have been designated a *fleet*, in his opinion. Especially, he acknowledged, if it was under *his* command. In fact, they *had* been designated a fleet until they'd actually been concentrated and sent off to Jalal. But the Prime Minister and the Oval had been adamant. They couldn't call the force sent off to deal with a single ragtag would-be warlord a "fleet" without alarming the public. And it would never do to alarm the public, now would it? So instead of sending Eighth Fleet, the Federation Navy's strategic reserve, they'd sent only a single task force *from* it, instead.

Apparently they actually believed—hoped, anyway—that no one would notice that the "task force" in question contained every single one of the "fleet" in question's FTLCs.

In Rajenda's opinion, anyone with two functioning neurons was already "alarmed" by his brother-in-law's antics, and fiddling around with "reassuring" unit designations was unlikely to change that. On the other hand, he wasn't in the best position to go pushing demands right now. Terrence Murphy might be only his brother-in-law, not a Thakore by blood, but his antics threatened to splash all over the entire family. Rajenda was more than sufficiently pissed off with Murphy to do what needed to be done, even if Simron would never forgive him for it, simply because of the threat he posed for the *Federation*. But he never knowingly lied to himself, so he couldn't pretend that the need to protect the family didn't add significantly to his determination.

He and his staff had considered their options carefully, and Zebić wasn't simply an excellent chief of staff, she was also a first cousin on his mother's side. In fact, aside from her fairer complexion, she looked a great deal like his sister, complete to her blue eyes, although hers were the ice blue of a Norwegian fjord, a lighter shade than Simmy's. They were very much the same height, however, and Christina's brain was every bit as sharp as Simmy's. Maybe even sharper, given his sister's taste in husbands.

Rajenda was confident they were as prepared as they could be, but that wasn't remotely the same as being as prepared as he would have *preferred* to be. They simply couldn't know what Terry had been up to since his last report to Olympia. If the marshals sent to arrest him had succeeded, then the problem was under control. If they'd *failed*, somehow, it could be... bad. And unlike some members of the Five Hundred, Rajenda was less than confident of the marshals' success. He wouldn't know for certain until he reached Jalal, of course. There'd been time for Captain Lipshen, or at least dispatches from him, to get that far. But his orders in the event that Lipshen wasn't waiting for him there with Murphy in custody were clear. And if that happened...

The Oval insisted Murphy couldn't possibly have more than the seven FTLCs he'd short-stopped before the League attack on New Dublin. Rajenda wasn't so sure. There was too much unrest in the Fringe, and much as he detested Terrence Murphy, he'd come to the conclusion that he'd badly underestimated his brother-in-law's personal charisma, at least with Fringers. He would never have expected the second-rate officer he'd always known, the man who'd yearned for survey duty in the middle of humanity's bloodiest war, to get away with appropriating even four additional carriers. He would have been wrong about that, and he wasn't prepared to compound the error by assuming he might not have added another handful to them. But even if he'd somehow managed to secure command of every Navy picket within seventy light-years of New Dublin, TF 804 would still hold a seventy-plus percent edge in hulls. And that didn't include Clarence Maddox's carrier division, waiting for him at Jalal Station, either. With them added to his task force, he'd have the next best thing to a two-to-one advantage even if Terry had picked up every FTLC in the vicinity. It wouldn't be as good as the *four*-to-one advantage the Oval had promised him he'd have, but it would be more than enough.

I'd feel even better if I knew what the hell he'd used against the Leaguies in New Dublin, though, he acknowledged. That was another place he found himself in less than complete agreement with the Oval's assessments.

Officially, Admiral Fokaides had assured him that all available intelligence indicated that Terry had significantly exaggerated the odds he'd faced at New Dublin. He'd undoubtedly inflated them in order to bolster his claims that he'd had no choice but to violate his very specific orders from Olympia. After all, the CNO had pointed out, he hadn't said a word about exactly *how* he'd managed to defeat twelve League FTLCs with only seven of his own. Under the circumstances, that had to suggest there hadn't actually *been* twelve of them to begin with. Indeed, given the historical League deployment patterns in the region, ONI was convinced TF 1705 had actually had at least parity with—and more likely the numerical edge over—Second Admiral's Xing's raiding squadron. In which case, there was no reason to assume Terry had devised some new, super-powerful wonder weapon or tactics no one else had ever thought of. Certainly Rajenda should be wary, but the last thing they could afford was to let Terry bluff them into weakness with a secret weapon that probably didn't even exist.

Rajenda had nodded, but inside he'd wanted to smack Fokaides across the top of the head.

He didn't like Terrence Murphy, and he never had, but one thing Murphy had never been was stupid enough to be caught in a blatant lie. His claims about Rishathan involvement were clearly ludicrous, but, then, Terry had always had a few loose screws about the Rish. He'd even confided to Rajenda once, when they'd both had a bit too much to drink, that his analysis of the Brin Gap action suggested the possibility of Rish tech transfers, and everyone knew his buddy O'Hanraghty was a card-carrying member of the tinfoil-hat brigade. But Rajenda very much doubted that he'd have falsified his after-action reports, especially given how carefully he knew the sensor data from them would eventually be reviewed. Nor did Rajenda think he was lying when he said he really had found and destroyed a major League shipyard the Federation hadn't known thing about.

For that matter, the New Dublin numbers had been signed off on by Commodore Esteban Tremblay, and Tremblay was—or had been, at least—as loyal a Federation officer (and Heart Worlder) as Rajenda had ever known.

True, he'd allowed himself to be co-opted for Terry's defense of New Dublin, but Rajenda could understand that, in many ways. There *had* been a hundred million Federation citizens on Crann Bethadh. Fringers, perhaps, but still citizens. And Tremblay had always chafed over the way FTLCs' strategic value made it impractical for the Navy to defend every pissant system in the Fringe. So, no, his willingness to stand with Terry in New Dublin's defense was no great surprise. And he'd also appended his own report to Terry's report on the battle they'd fought there. No doubt it had been censored by Terry—or, more probably, by that asshole O'Hanraghty—since *it* didn't mention exactly what Terry had done to take down no less than eight FTLCs, either. But it supported Terry's op force analysis, and one thing Esteban Tremblay would never have done was falsify a report like that.

That was why Rajenda was pretty certain Tremblay was no longer in command of his carrier division. Not if Terry had successfully defied arrest. He sure as hell hadn't done that without somebody—probably quite a few somebodies, given the Army Hoplons sent to back Lipshen and the marshals—getting killed along the way, and that would have been a bridge too far for someone like Tremblay.

None of which told him what rabbit Terry had pulled out of his hat in New Dublin, and assuming *Tremblay's* report was remotely accurate, it was obvious his brother-in-law had come up with *some* edge Second Admiral Xing had never seen coming. That was why, Fokaides and ONI intelligence appreciations notwithstanding, he intended to approach that system with extraordinary caution after he picked up Maddox's carriers at Jalal.

And whatever the hell it was, at least I know to be watching for something, don't I? That's more than the idiot League admiral who sailed right into whatever it was managed. For that matter, it's even possible Terry will just throw in the towel when he sees how much firepower I've got. Simmy would probably prefer that. That's because she doesn't want to admit that, one way or the other, unless he's already in custody, he's a dead man. The rest of the Five Hundred can't let it end any other way. If they managed to arrest him, then they may *settle for breaking him out of the Navy and sending him to prison for a decade or two for corruption.*

A corner—a *tiny* corner—of Rajenda's brain winced at that. No one who knew Terrence Murphy, not even—or perhaps especially—Rajenda Thakore, would believe the charges of corruption and embezzlement for a heartbeat. But Murphy had better hope to hell the *rest* of the Federation did, because if the Five Hundred decided it couldn't sell that narrative—

They have *to bring him down, and if they can't railroad him into prison, what other option do they have? New Dublin has to have made him a hero to the Fringe. A Heart World admiral who defied orders to protect a Fringe system? Of course it has! And the Federation can't afford to give the lunatics in the Fringe someone to rally around. So if he's defied arrest, and he—and whoever may have helped—aren't turned into examples pretty damn quick, we'll be looking at whole star systems going out of compliance, and probably sooner rather than later. That's why I hope he isn't smart enough to cave, if it comes down to it.*

He told himself that firmly, and it was true. But there was another reason he hoped Terrence Murphy didn't surrender as soon he came face-to-face with the Federation's hammer, as well. After his actions, suspicion must always linger where the Thakore family was concerned. After all, *Terry* was a Thakore, even if only by marriage, wasn't he?

That sort of suspicion could be fatal for a family's position in the Five Hundred. Unless, of course, the family in question demonstrated its reliability by dealing with the threat itself. If Terrence Murphy was a dead man anyway, there was no reason at all Rajenda Thakore shouldn't personally deliver his head to Olympia to prove his own and his family's loyalty.

The Pinnacle Health and Fitness Center
City of Olympus
Old Terra
Sol System
Terran Federation
December 4, 2552

KANADA THAKORE STEPPED OFF THE TREADMILL, PICKED UP HIS towel, and wiped his sweat from the machine. Then he wrapped the towel around his neck, braced both hands in the small of his back, and stretched hard.

He always felt better in the endorphin rush after a workout, but the health club's cardio section was oddly empty today. He felt the stillness around him, and the quiet was almost unnerving. It certainly wasn't *typical* for an early Tuesday evening. Not for the Pinnacle.

The Pinnacle was the most expensive fitness center on Earth, with annual dues several times higher than the salary Venus Futures paid its junior managers. Members didn't pay just for the exercise opportunity, either. The cost of admission was its own...filtration device. Members paid it for the opportunity to network with equally wealthy members of the Five Hundred as often as possible.

Which was why there ought to have been at least a dozen other people on the floor, so why...?

A man in a well-cut charcoal-black suit came around a corner. Ceiling lights reflected off his slimline sunglasses, and Thakore's stomach tightened. Bodyguards in business suits were no rarity among The Pinnacle's members, but somehow he knew that wasn't what this man was.

This man regarded Thakore as a target, not as someone to protect. And not as one of the most powerful members of the Five Hundred, either. Another Fixer. They usually weren't this visible, but they were living in interesting times.

The newcomer carried a fluffy bathrobe, held in front of him on his palms, like a serving platter, and he smiled as Thakore saw him.

"Ah. Makes sense, now." Thakore waved one hand at the empty space around them, then walked across to the Fixer. "Where?"

"Mr. Perrin will see you in the sauna," the Fixer said. "He appreciates the opportunity to speak with you off-the-record."

"No doubt."

Thakore snatched the robe from him and went into the locker room. He dumped his sweaty clothes and slipped into the robe, then followed his guide to the sauna.

Two more Fixers stood guard on either side of the sauna entrance. One opened the door for him, and Thakore went inside. The dry heat kept his workout sweat going, and his first breath felt like something out of an oven.

Perrin sat on one of the benches. His upper body was bare, his flab drooping down, and a pair of towels protected his modesty.

Thakore decided he'd seldom seen a more disgusting sight and looked away, to the man sitting across from Perrin. *His* body was bulky with muscle, a physique built for combat and strength, not for aesthetics. A young, effeminate man and a woman with a body sculpted as if she lived in the gym were busy giving the bruiser a pedicure. Both had towels wrapped around their waists and nothing else.

Thakore was well aware that etiquette proscribed eye contact in the sauna, but the sight of the other man froze him in place. When the Fixer closed the door behind him, he felt as if he'd just been locked into a cage with a tiger.

"Ah, Kanada!" Perrin raised a faux-cigar and puffed. "How kind of you to join us."

"Perrin. Haven't seen you here in a while." Thakore shifted his weight from foot to foot as the temperature gradient worked on him. "What's the occasion?"

"Why...*you* are." Perrin chuckled. "Take a seat, please. Our tea boy will fetch anything you ask. We don't pay Pinnacle prices for anything less than the best, now do we?"

"Don't you own this place?" Thakore asked, sitting on Perrin's bench but well beyond arm's length from him.

"Hmmmm, do I?" Perrin smirked. "So many assets to manage, so little time."

Thakore was well aware that Perrin was the health club's owner. And there'd been so many rumors of listening devices planted throughout the facility—and of Perrin swooping in to snatch opportunities from other club members—that Thakore made it a point to never discuss business on site.

Actually, the truth was that he would have canceled his membership outright, if he hadn't needed to make appearances here for the sake of the Five Hundred. And if the juice bar hadn't been so incredible.

"You know General Alaimo, don't you?" Perrin waggled his cigar at the other man.

"By reputation." Thakore nodded courteously to the general.

"Pleasure," Alaimo said with a smile. "Venus Futures warships have taken me to and from many a battle. I appreciate the care and workmanship you put into them."

One of the pedicurists wobbled. A dollop of sweat fell from his forehead and landed on Alaimo's ankle and he froze for an instant, then immediately dabbed it off with a cloth.

"Thank you," Thakore said to Alaimo without much sincerity.

"The situation's deteriorated to a point where the Oval had to 'break glass in event of war,'" Perrin said. "General Alaimo's been recalled to active duty to deal with one of our more... troublesome sectors."

The general smiled again, a bit more broadly, and a sliver of cold grew in Thakore's chest, despite the heat.

"Who authorized this?" he asked.

"Admiral Fokaides, naturally." Perrin smiled, then shrugged in a monstrous billow of obesity. "Once the report of sedition and treason came in from the Cyclops Sector, we decided to let Alaimo off his leash. He's the only commander we have with a perfect track record when it comes to turning restive populations into compliant ones."

"You have—" Thakore wiped sweat from his forehead and flicked it at the hot-rock coals of the sauna stove "—roughly twelve percent of your total holdings in Cyclops."

"Ha!" Perrin slapped his buttermilk-colored thigh. "I told you he was well-informed, didn't I, Taskin?"

"Yes, Sir, you did." Alaimo leaned back, interlaced his fingers behind his head, and contemplated Thakore as if he were something to be eaten.

"I keep our good general here comfortable between assignments," Perrin told Thakore. "He's had some bad press he didn't deserve, and it's wrong for the Federation to not take care of our veterans, don't you agree, Kanada? Taskin lives at my estate in the Canary Islands. And have I ever neglected any of your needs, General?"

"Never, Sir. Much appreciated," Alaimo said, leering at the woman taking care of his left foot. He bumped his leg against her exposed chest. She looked up at him and gave him a forced smile.

"'Bad press'?" Thakore arched an eyebrow. "Forgive me, but I heard he enjoyed every minute of it."

He watched Alaimo as he spoke, and the general winked at him.

Thakore felt his skin crawl.

"Well, my boy here does what needs to be done to win what must be won," Perrin said. "That's been the Federation's attitude ever since the Aggamar strike. And that being the case, Taskin and I are going over which assets need to be preserved once he moves on Bellerophon and the rest of the sector. He's taking Ninth Fleet and the Thirteenth Army Corps with him."

"And are Federation citizens among those assets?" Thakore asked, and Perrin chuckled.

"If they're not in compliance, they've decided for themselves that they aren't our citizens. Not too bright of them, admittedly, but that's why Standing Order Fifteen applies." He shrugged again. "They're peasants, Kanada. I've got almost all of them toiling their little lives away to escape the debt traps they entered voluntarily. Once upon a time, people like them were called serfs. Slaves. The names change, but the truth doesn't: they work, and they do what they're told by the people they work *for*. Economists and historians can debate where true wealth comes from, but you and I know the answer to that, don't we?"

Perrin rapped a knuckle against his bench twice, and the female pedicurist instantly pulled a bottle of water from a small refrigerator near the door. She picked it up in a clean cloth, so as to avoid getting her own sweat onto it, and handed it to Perrin.

"*Labor* is the source of all wealth, and the fuel of all economies," Thakore said. "Nothing happens unless there's someone there to make it happen."

"Of course *you* know that," Perrin said. "You wouldn't have become relatively wealthy if you didn't."

Thakore let the slight against his own net worth pass.

"What good is an asteroid full of gold and platinum, if there's no one to mine it out?" Perrin continued. "No one to run the refineries and smelters? If there's no one to manage the shipping, or the fabrication centers? If there's no market demand from people to make it valuable?" He puffed his cigar. "How can a government function, if there are no citizens to pay taxes through their labor?"

"That's why I treat my employees well and deliver quality ships to the market," Thakore said. "The free market—"

"Doesn't exist," Perrin interrupted. He gulped down water, much of it spilling from the sides of his mouth, then lowered the bottle. "We at the top command everything. Tax brackets here, government budgets there, suppressing competition, and patent sniping, from time to time. The only thing that matters is that we keep the population working. All the rest is just window dressing." He waved the water bottle dismissively. "The peasants can have the illusion of freedom, and we don't care, as long as they're working the mines or running numbers for actuaries. They make a pittance and we skim off the rest. We used to give them *nothing,* but then we realized it's easier for the proles to convince themselves they're not slaves so long as we give them a sliver of freedom. It's amazing how much easier that makes it to keep them in line, isn't it?"

"And the consequences of that attitude are what's coming back to haunt us, aren't they?" Thakore asked with a levelness that surprised him just a bit.

"Bah! From time to time we have to crush skulls to keep the rabble in line. Other times, we can just give a little on the tax rate, and then raise fees elsewhere to make up the difference. How we do it matters less than the fact that we'll always be in charge, Thakore. But we can't permit our wealth to leave us." Perrin slapped his fat belly. "We've squeezed the Fringe since this war began, and they've minded their manners and stayed in their place. But now, the curs are growling in their kennel, so we have to reconstitute our authority. That's where General Alaimo comes in. He and Ninth Fleet wormhole out for Bellerophon on Tuesday."

Shock hit Thakore in the chest. He'd heard rumors—but *only* rumors—about Alaimo's return to duty. Which meant the rest of the Five Hundred had made sure rumors were all he'd hear. But Ninth Fleet had been organized by scraping up every available unit to cover Sol when Rajenda took the entire Reserve to the Fringe. They were diverting *that* to Cyclops, as well? And when Alaimo got there...

"Is he—is *that* really necessary?" He felt sweat ooze from his entire body. "My son will reach Jalal day after tomorrow. Even if Murphy's actually endorsed this 'Free Worlds' madness, Rajenda will deal with it. One battle to end New Dublin's rebellion is all we need to convince the other Fringe systems to see reason. Adding General Alaimo is likely to...compound the problem."

"I have full confidence your boy will do his best," Perrin said, "but whether he wins or loses—wins, preferably—the Fringe still needs a lesson. One it won't soon forget."

"And just how many planets will need to learn that lesson?" Thakore asked. "One like the one Gobelins learned, I presume?"

"I had my hands tied on that one," Alaimo said.

The young man polishing his toenails faltered. He drooped forward, as if he were on the brink of heat exhaustion, until his forehead bumped the bench. Alaimo looked down, then put his foot against the man's face and pushed him towards the door. The pedicurist muttered apologies and crawled out of the sauna. Alaimo patted the wood next to him, and the mostly nude woman sat on the bench. He examined his fingernails, then set the hand on her lap, brushing the towel away to touch her skin.

She took a small file from an open pouch on the bench and began making his pinky nail more perfect.

"Why are we having this discussion?" Thakore asked.

"Because there've been some doubts about you, Kanada." Perrin leaned forward over the dome of his belly, spreading his arms wide enough he could prop his elbows on his knees. "You pushed for Murphy to be governor out in New Dublin. Nothing wrong with that. There's no point being in the Five Hundred if you can't use a little nepotism to shore up your legacy! But you did get Murphy into that position, and now it's become a problem for all of us."

"I didn't—"

"No, no! You didn't. And your daughter's playing ball. Your boy's playing ball. None of you are the problem; your *son-in-law's* the issue. See, I rather like you, Kanada. Shrewd. Honest," Perrin said the word as if it were made of salt. "You're popular in the Five Hundred, too. But in trying times like these, we get to see everyone's true colors."

Thakore glanced at Alaimo, then back to Perrin.

"Not everyone in the Five Hundred stays in the Five Hundred, my friend." Perrin heaved himself back into an upright position and scratched his triple chin. "And in times like this, we need to be sure where everyone stands. That means we're going to shake out everyone who's not playing the game. You understand?"

"Of course." Thakore smiled. "Just out of curiosity, has anyone expressed any concerns over the General's upcoming deployment?"

"That twerp Vice Admiral Yang," Perrin grunted. "Which is fine. Like I said, we need to know where everyone stands, and we're looking for a new replacement for Fokaides now. Your son's in the running, just so you know . . . provided he can deliver on the orders we sent him to kill Murphy."

"Kill . . . or capture," Thakore said.

"Huh? Oh, yes. Of course."

Perrin nodded with enormous insincerity.

Silence fell. Perrin let it linger for almost a full minute, then took a long drag from his faux-cigar.

"This conversation was a professional courtesy to you, Kanada," he said then. "I hope you appreciate it."

"I do." Thakore stepped down from the bench. "Since I'm pretty sure you're well aware of my loyalty to the Five Hundred, though, I'd appreciate it if some of the bottlenecks and price gouging Venus Futures is dealing with would go away. The Navy still needs those ships, and we're all on the same side, aren't we?"

"I'll have a word with my subsidiaries." Perrin waggled a hand at him. "Once the Murphy situation's been handled, I'm sure things will go back to normal."

"Thank you," Thakore said as pleasantly as if Perrin hadn't just confirmed that the Five Hundred would keep the pressure on and the knife of economic ruin at his throat but wouldn't drive it home...for now. "If you'll excuse me, then?"

"Toodles!" Alaimo said with a wave as Thakore reached for the sauna door's inside handle.

"Send your girl over here," Perrin said to the general as the door opened. "Just because I can't see my toes doesn't mean they can't look good."

The two of them were still laughing when the door closed.

Thakore stood for a moment, aware of the Fixers on either side of him, then turned and headed straight to his private locker room.

He walked as quickly as he could without running.

CHAPTER SIXTEEN

Jalal System
Terran Federation
December 7, 2552

"CAN WE TURN OFF THAT ALARM, PLEASE?"

Terrence Murphy's tone was a bit testy as he strode into Jalal Station's Command Central. The strident alarm—admittedly, it hadn't been all that loud, but it was carefully engineered to be impossible to ignore—died suddenly, and he nodded.

"Better."

He still sounded less than delighted, and Harrison O'Hanraghty hid a smile as Murphy walked across the command deck to him. Both of them knew Jalal Station was the last place Terrence Murphy wanted to be just now. The fact that both of them also knew it was the one place he *had* to be didn't make Murphy one bit happier, however.

Murphy crossed to the enormous holo display. It was configured in astrography mode, and he gazed for several seconds at the lurid crimson icon pulsing in its depths. That icon marked a projected wormhole emergence, ninety light-minutes beyond Jalal Zeta, the system's outermost ice planet, and he pursed his lips thoughtfully.

"I suppose that pretty much has to be the Oval's reinforcements," he observed after a moment.

"On that bearing?" O'Hanraghty nodded. "And from the size of the signature, it looks like they've done us proud."

Someone chuckled, albeit a bit nervously, at the chief of staff's dry tone, but Murphy only nodded back.

The gravitic signature of the incoming task force—and that was what it had to be—was exactly where he'd expected to see it. Where it almost had to be on a least-time trip from Sol to Jalal, which was undoubtedly what its commander had been ordered to make. There was every reason for the Oval to get its reaction force to Jalal as quickly as possible, and no reason it should try for any sort of stealthiness when it arrived. Personally, he would have sent something—*anything*—a hell of a lot sooner than this, on the assumption that even half a dozen additional FTLCs at Jalal would have cramped his own style when he arrived. But now that Sol finally had gotten the reaction force here, there was no point in subtlety, given that it was impossible for a starship in wormhole space to "sneak up" on a normal-space target with decent gravitic arrays. Knowing exactly where to point Jalal Station's arrays *had* increased detection range by about ten percent, though, and they'd picked up the incoming visitors at just over twenty-six light-weeks, which gave him about five hours' warning before they could drop sublight.

Of course, that wasn't the only thing his accurate prediction had allowed him to do, either.

"I'm assuming you would have told me if Dormouse has sprung a leak?" he said now, cocking his head at O'Hanraghty.

"As of this moment, nobody outside Command Central and Gravitic One knows a thing about this," the captain said, twitching his head at the icon. "The Station is solid, and Galanatos has his carriers' gravitic arrays completely offline."

"Good. Let's keep it that way." Murphy shook his head, his expression showing more worry than he would have displayed under other circumstances...or to other people. "There are still too many potential loose ends flopping around the system to make me happy, Harry."

"You think?" O'Hanraghty shook his head. "All we can do is all we can do, Terry."

"I know. Just humor me." Murphy flashed a brief, tight smile. "Even the unflappable Admiral Murphy gets to worry about stuff sometimes."

"And I get to help you worry," O'Hanraghty said. "Part of the job description. But, as far as I know, Bryant and I are on top of this."

"Good," Murphy repeated, and touched O'Hanraghty lightly on the shoulder.

O'Hanraghty had doubled as Task Force 1705's intelligence officer from the outset—inevitably, given that he was essentially a "spook" at heart...and the only spook Terrence Murphy had fully trusted. Since taking Jalal Station, however, his primary job as Murphy's XO had eaten up too much of his time for him to continue as Murphy's SO2 as well. That was why he'd recruited Commander Bryant MacTavish to replace him. He and MacTavish had known one another for years, and the commander was as smart as they came. In fact, he'd been smart enough to keep anyone from suspecting he was a member in good standing of the tinfoil-hat brigade.

Between them, he, O'Hanraghty, the rest of Murphy's staff, Esteban Tremblay, and Joseph Lowe, *Ishtar*'s CO, had labored like Trojans to prepare Jalal Station against this moment. They'd had a bit over a month to work with, and they'd accomplished more, frankly, than Murphy had expected.

Which wasn't to say that they'd accomplished remotely enough for his peace of mind.

Operation Dormouse had put Jalal's gravitic arrays under complete lockdown, manned only by personnel who'd accompanied Murphy from New Dublin, and the same draconian staffing restrictions had been applied to Command Central. No one outside that trusted coterie had any access at all to Gravitic One's output, and as O'Hanraghty had just observed, the only *off*-station arrays in the inner system, the ones aboard Emilios Galanatos's carriers, were completely shut down. That, hopefully, meant that no one outside Murphy's immediate circle was aware of the impending arrival of Olympia's long-awaited response.

They intended to keep it that way as long as they possibly could, because it was impossible to guarantee that no Federation loyalist had access to a long-range transmitter. The last thing they needed was someone alerting the incoming Federation commander to Jalal's change in management one moment sooner than they could help, but if they didn't know there was anyone to alert...

In addition to Dormouse, they'd also done their best to clean up the debris from the thankfully brief but bitter fighting among the system's sublight parasites. The bigger pieces of wreckage, including over a dozen complete but brutally damaged hulls, had been accelerated along a vector that had dumped them into the system primary. The smaller pieces—of which there had been many—had simply been deorbited on trajectories that took them down over Jalal Beta's Cronkite Ocean. That left gaps in the ships that should have been there, and they had to assume any incoming TFN force would have been provided with a complete order of battle for Jalal. So they'd deployed matching units from Murphy's parasite strength, with suitably modified transponders, to fill the holes.

Things were a little trickier where Admiral Maddox's FTLCs were concerned.

Maddox had been a Heart Worlder and a member in good standing of the Five Hundred. In fact, he'd been Madison Dawson's third cousin. He'd also been absolutely furious with Murphy for launching a "Fringe rebellion" that was likely to tear the Federation apart, and as a complete Rish-denier, he'd regarded Murphy's claims as no more than a pretext to justify his rebellion and raw ambition.

It was perhaps fortunate Maddox hadn't survived the mutiny aboard TFNS *Selene*, but before he went down, he and the other loyalists in TF 1712 had fought back hard. In fact, *Selene*'s company had suffered over three hundred casualties. It had been equally bad aboard the other carriers, and the loyalists aboard one of them—*Hylonome*—had secured control of her bridge and primary engineering spaces. They'd done their damnedest to carry out Admiral Portier's orders to head home with news of Murphy's arrival... until, at least, their FTLC consorts' point-defense lasers, firing with pinpoint accuracy at less than two hundred kilometers' range, had crippled the control runs to her Fasset drive.

The control runs themselves, fortunately, had been repairable by Jalal's Engineering staff, but she'd taken other damage that would be obvious in any close visual examination. It didn't render the *Marduk*-class carrier combat ineffective, but the hull breaches would tell any observer she'd been in a fight. So Murphy had pulled her out of the provisional squadron he'd put together under Captain Galanatos and replaced her with her sister ship, *Ereshkigal*, from TF 1705's original strength. The two ships had swapped transponder codes, as well, so—hopefully—even a terminally suspicious TFN CO wouldn't suspect the switch.

And that wasn't all they'd done, either, Murphy reflected, gazing at the icons of the pair of freighters that had arrived from New Dublin only days before.

"I suppose we'd better warm-up Admiral Portier, then," he said now.

"She's already stirring," O'Hanraghty told him with a small, tight smile.

⬧   ⬧   ⬧

"Confirmed, Sir," Captain Rashida Kerbouche said from the comm display in Commodore Esteban Tremblay's sleeping cabin aboard RHLNS *Kishar*. "ETA one hundred and forty-seven minutes. Right on Admiral Murphy's prediction."

"The Admiral," Tremblay observed with a cheerfulness he would once never have believed he might feel, "has a remarkable habit of making accurate predictions."

"He does that, Sir," Kerbouche agreed.

"Very well." Tremblay ran a hand over his close-cropped brown hair. "I'm confident you've already notified Commander Beaudouin, efficient soul that you are. Tell Commander Soria to send the alert to Jalal Station—I'm sure the Admiral will be glad to know we're on our toes out here—then get the entire task force moving ASAP. I'll get back to you as soon as I throw some clothes on and make it to Flag Bridge."

"Yes, Sir. I've already passed the word to prep the fans."

"I knew there was a reason you make such a good flag captain. Let me go get dressed."

⬧   ⬧   ⬧

"Incoming message," Callum Murphy said, and his father turned from a three-way conversation with O'Hanraghty and Captain Galanatos.

Like his father, Callum would have vastly preferred to be on one of the FTLCs holding station with Esteban Tremblay, a light-hour and a half from the system primary. But, also like his father, he couldn't be. And not just because a one-legged, one-eyed lieutenant might be a dubious tactical asset.

"From Tremblay, I assume?" Murphy said.

"One word, Sir: 'Inbound.'"

"Steve's come a long way," O'Hanraghty observed, and Murphy nodded.

"Yes," he said in a tone of intense satisfaction. "Yes, he has."

"Do you really think this is going to work, Sir?" Galanatos asked from Murphy's comm.

"Oh, I'm sure it's going to work at least partially. I'd love for it to come off without a hitch, but this, unfortunately, is the real world, Captain. What I can say is that I'm totally confident of Commodore Tremblay's ability to play his part. Whether or not we manage to pull Spider off completely is another matter."

"Well, I'm not going to bet against you at this point," Galanatos said, and Murphy snorted.

"Sooner or later, I *am* going to stub a toe, you know, Captain."

"But not today, Sir." Galanatos smiled from the comm screen. "And, with your permission, I'll just go and get ready for my own bit of Spider."

"Of course." Murphy nodded and walked across to stand beside Callum.

"I have to agree with Harry, Dad," Callum said very quietly, voice pitched solely for his father's ears. "I never would've seen Tremblay as a 'Murphy partisan' that first day when you stole his task group."

"There's nothing at all wrong with Esteban Tremblay's brain," Murphy returned, equally quietly. "And there's nothing wrong with his moral compass, either. It just needed a tap or two to get unlocked from the Heart World perspective. And I wouldn't say he was a 'Murphy partisan,' either. What he is, is a patriot. The kind of patriot who understands that the people running a star nation may not always be worthy of that trust."

Callum nodded, although he suspected Murphy might be underestimating the degree of Tremblay's "partisanship." Much as he'd come to respect his father, and especially his father's judgment, he'd also realized Terrence Murphy did have his own blind spots. Including the one that prevented him from recognizing the degree of personal devotion he'd won from his personnel.

Or the one that kept him from admitting to himself how broken the Federation and its Constitution truly were. It was odd, really. He'd opened his *son's* eyes to that unhappy awareness, but he refused to acknowledge it himself. Or to confront—*really* confront—the true depth of what that might require of him in the end.

Callum put that thought carefully away. It wasn't one his father would be happy to entertain, he suspected. Besides, there were other things to think about, including Operation Spider.

He'd thought it was an odd name for an ops plan, until O'Hanraghty quoted an ancient poem about a spider and a fly.

Then he'd understood it perfectly, and he hoped like hell it was going to work.

Tremblay's shorter-ranged shipboard gravitic arrays had detected the incoming wormhole signature a good two hours after Jalal Station had. That had been a given, as had the fact that if Tremblay had waited for light-speed orders from the station to begin executing his part of the ops plan, it would have been far too late. For that matter, it had taken an hour and a half for his own message to reach Jalal Station.

Fortunately, professional spacers were used to allowing for that sort of communications lag. And what mattered was that "Incoming" meant the twelve FTLCs of Tremblay's "Hammer Force" were currently accelerating towards Jalal Station—or, rather, towards the point in space Jalal Station would occupy in about nine hours—at 1,900 gravities. They'd actually started as soon as they'd detected the incoming wormhole signature, and they'd be shutting down their fans once more within the next fifteen or twenty minutes. That meant they would have gone ballistic and disappeared into silent running, under strict emissions control, by the time the incoming TFN task force dropped sublight. They should be within about four light-minutes of the newcomers' emergence point, but they'd be the next best thing to completely undetectable. Of course, their velocity would be little better than half that of the new arrivals when they went sublight at 297,000 KPS, which meant those newcomers would be running away from Hammer Force at very nearly twice Tremblay's base velocity. But they'd also be decelerating hard towards an eventual rendezvous with Jalal Station. So, eventually, if all went according to plan, their velocities would equalize and Hammer Force's overtake velocity would begin to increase steadily.

If everything went *perfectly* according to plan, Hammer Force would bring up its Fasset drives and begin decelerating just about the time the incoming task force crossed the stellar Powell Limit and its maximum acceleration rate dropped to 900 gravities. At which point, it would become impossible for the newcomers to avoid Hammer Force if Tremblay wanted to force action upon them.

And that, he reminded himself, was supposed to convince the newcomers to adopt a peaceable attitude. He hoped it would.

And he wished he was as confident of that as Captain Galanatos appeared to be.

✧   ✧   ✧

"Sublight in one minute, Sir," Lieutenant Massengale, RHLNS *Lelantos's* astrogator, announced. That announcement was directed to Captain Ozbey, but Rajenda Thakore was tied into the big carrier's command deck from Flag Bridge, and he nodded in approval.

"Thirty...fifteen...ten," Massengale droned. Then, "Sublight!"

Task Force 804 dropped back into sync with the rest of the universe, and the visual displays were suddenly speckled with pinprick stars and not the eye-bewildering blur of wormhole space. An instant later, the master tactical plot came online, the icons of standard navigation beacons and scores of ship transponder codes glowed to life in its depths, and the routine, looped "information to shipping" transmissions began to spool up.

Obviously no one in Jalal Beta orbit was worried about keeping a low profile.

"Well, that's reassuring," Christina Zebić observed at Rajenda's elbow, and he nodded. It was not only reassuring, it was—probably—a vast relief. Of course, it remained to be seen if—

"Incoming message, Admiral!" Commander Ntombikayise Abercrombie, TF 804's communications officer called out, and Rajenda glanced at her. Whoever had sent the message in question had predicted their emergence time almost perfectly when he decided to send it. Not that there was really much rush at these sorts of distances.

"It's addressed to 'Commanding Officer, Relief Force,'" Abercrombie added.

"Really?" Rajenda shook his head with a dry chuckle. "Portier must be feeling even more nervous than I expected, if she decided to hang that ID on us."

"Oh, I don't know," Zebić said. "If I'd been holding the fort out here this long, I'd be feeling a bit 'relieved' right now, myself."

"Fair enough, I suppose." Rajenda shrugged. "With that much firepower, though"—he waved at the hundreds of sublight parasite transponders—"I'd have felt pretty confident about handling a half dozen or so FTLCs if I had to."

His cousin nodded, and he turned his attention back to Abercrombie.

"Put it up on the main display, please, Ntombikayise."

"Yes, Sir."

An instant later, the tactical data disappeared and a woman's image replaced it. Rajenda recognized her immediately. He scarcely

knew Geraldine Portier well, but they'd met more than once...
and as Zebić had predicted, she looked distinctly relieved at the
moment.

"Welcome to Jalal," she said. "I won't pretend for a minute
we're not hugely relieved to see you people. Whoever you are."
Her lips quirked a smile. "We were starting to feel a little lonely
out here. From the size of your footprint, my people are guessing
you are at somewhere around twenty to twenty-five carriers. I
believe we can probably find a place to put you. If you have any
special requirements, go ahead and transmit them, and I'll start
putting arrangements in train. Portier, clear."

"Do we have any 'special requirements'?" Zebić asked with
a smile.

"No, not really. But go ahead and thank her for her welcome,
Ntombikayise." He smiled rather more broadly than Zebić had.
"Inform her I intend to make my best speed to Jalal Orbit and
that I'll contact her again when the time dilation's equalized a
bit and the comm lag's shorter. I'm sure it will make her feel
more appreciated."

✧　　✧　　✧

"Well, so far, it's looking pretty good," Commander Nathanaël
Beaudouin observed. He floated beside Commodore Tremblay's
command chair, one toe hooked through a floor loop to keep
him there, and looked thoughtfully at the plot.

"If you persist in tempting Murphy—the demon, not the
Admiral—that way, you and I are going to have words, Nate,"
Tremblay said.

"Sorry about that, Sir." Beaudouin smiled crookedly. "I really
have to work on how I pass these little operational reports and
observations along to you."

Tremblay snorted. He was still a bit surprised by how well
he and Beaudouin got along and worked with one another. The
commander, a native of Gregor II, was as much a Fringer as
Tremblay himself was a Heart Worlder, and there'd been a certain tension between him and the rest of Tremblay's staff when
he stepped in to replace Linda Harrison, the task group's original
XO. Tremblay deeply regretted that he'd had to replace Harrison,
but the Free Worlds Alliance had been one step too far for Linda.
She'd been more than willing to defend New Dublin, and what
they'd discovered at Diyu had convinced her Murphy was no

lunatic. She didn't even think he was a warlord seeking personal power. But she was horrified by the threatened dissolution of the Federation, no matter what the justification, and she'd drawn the line at "treason."

She'd also been right up front about that, though. She'd requested relief, and Tremblay's already deep respect for her had grown only deeper. She might not have been able to support the FWA, but she hadn't pretended she could, either. He wished he could be certain none of his other officers and spacers had pretended *they* could until they got the opportunity to betray the "traitors" at a critical moment. In fact, he wished he *wasn't* certain at least some of them had done just that.

He'd approved her request for relief—regretfully—and he was delighted by how well Cormag Dewar's recommendation of Beaudouin as her replacement had worked out. The fact that Dewar had become President of New Dublin after Alan Tolmach's murder had made him President of the Free Worlds Alliance, as well, and no one could doubt his fiery commitment to the Fringe's revolt. But however deep his anger at the Heart Worlds might run, he'd also been a Marine, and a damned good one, in his time, and it showed. That was another advantage the FWA had in its confrontation with the Federation. It might not have remotely the same industrial muscle, but its leadership included an enormous percentage of veterans, most of whom knew their asses from their elbows when military decisions had to be made. And its citizens included an equally huge percentage of veterans. In fact, given how inequitably the burden of actual combat had been spread, it was probable the Fringe, despite its far smaller total population, had at least half again as many trained, experienced combat personnel as the entire Heart.

One of whom was named Nathanaël Beaudouin. And the number of Fringers with matching experience—and the sheer competence people like him carried around in their spacebags—should make the Oval and Olympia very, very nervous, Tremblay thought.

In the eight months since the Concordia Sector had announced its secession, Beaudouin had fitted smoothly into Tremblay's team. He'd been well aware that its other members had to regard him as an intruder, at least initially, and he'd avoided stepping on any toes, but he'd also made it clear that he was now the chief of staff and that if they were wise, they would accept that and move on. Which all of them had done.

Of course, I have to wonder if one reason Dewar recommended Nate was to be sure there was someone he *trusted inside my staff to keep an eye on all of us,* Tremblay thought now. He'd wondered that at the time, and he still didn't know. Neither did he care. If he was going to be party to treason—and it was hard to think of a better word for his current activities, however he might justify them—he preferred for the leaders of that treason to be smart and to take precautions.

Besides, even if Nate is—or was—Dewar's spy, he's also a damned good officer. I trust his judgment, and I trust him. *And even if he is tempting fate, he's right about how good things are looking, too.*

So far, at least.

At the moment, Hammer Force was coasting ballistically in-system towards the stellar Powell Limit, following along behind the incoming Task Force 804—they'd been able to read the intruders' omnidirectional light-speed transponders for the last eleven minutes—at 155,690 KPS. They'd been 3.52 LM behind the newcomers when the relief task force dropped sublight. Now, fifteen minutes later, the interval was up to over 13.6 LM, and continuing to widen at 125,423 KPS, and he was delighted it was. There'd been a distinct possibility Hammer Force might have been picked up by visual observation if the Feds had looked behind them immediately after they'd arrived. Tremblay's ships had dialed up their "smart" hull surfaces to maximum light and EM absorption, but that wouldn't have helped if they'd occluded a star and anyone had noticed. By now, however, the chance of detection was effectively nil. And it would stay that way until Hammer Force had to bring up its own Fasset drives.

Perhaps even more to the point, there was nothing TF 804 could have done about Hammer Force even if it had detected it, since they couldn't possibly have engaged one another, given their relative velocities. None of Hammer Force's weapons—not even the Casúr Cogaidhs—had the acceleration rate and endurance to overtake the task force, and none of TF 804's weapons had the acceleration rate and endurance to overcome their current velocity to engage a target anywhere astern of it. Which was good, since Hammer Force was outnumbered by two-to-one. He doubted even the Casúr Cogaidhs riding his parasite racks could have equalized those odds in a standup fight.

Which was why he was just delighted Terrence Murphy had no intention of engaging in any standup fights.

"Well," he said after a moment, "in about three and a half hours they'll know we're here, won't they?"

"Oh, I think we can take that pretty much for granted, Sir," Beaudouin agreed, and Tremblay could have shaved with his smile.

✧   ✧   ✧

A musical tone sounded, and Callum looked up from his command station as Commander Mirwani tapped a screen to shut down the timer.

"Systems check!" he announced.

"Initiating systems check," Lieutenant Tyler O'Gormley acknowledged.

O'Gormley was a Crann Bethadhan who'd been home on leave when the Battle of New Dublin rolled through his home star system. He was also an excellent tactical officer, who'd been a welcome addition to Murphy's command crew.

Now he tapped a series of commands and watched his displays carefully.

"Confirm green board on the Kavachas, Sir," he said. "And... green board on the Casúrs."

"Good." Mirwani nodded and looked over his shoulder at Murphy and O'Hanraghty.

"Green boards, Admiral," he said formally.

"Thank you, Riley," Murphy said just as gravely as if he hadn't already heard O'Gormley's report, and Callum smiled down at his own displays.

There'd been a time when he would have found that entire exchange silly, but that had been before the Battle of New Dublin. Now he understood that the reason for it was anything but silly. It was Mirwani's responsibility to be *certain* his CO had all the critical information, and it was Murphy's responsibility to confirm that he *did*.

Especially now.

Callum shook his head as he admitted that his father had been three steps ahead of him yet again when he deployed the station's Kavacha platforms a full month ago. From where Callum had sat, there'd still been plenty of time to set their defenses, and keeping the anti-KEW platforms active and on station for extended periods put time on their clocks that increased the possibility of systems failures at the critical moment. And, given the accuracy with which Murphy had been able to predict their visitors' probable approach vector, there'd been more than enough time to get them into position before any intruder got close enough to detect their Hauptman signatures.

But then Callum had realized the real reason his father had deployed them early. Because he'd pre-positioned them and set up a regular schedule for checking their systems, he didn't have to move them now. Nor did he have to initiate any *unscheduled* systems checks now that the moment had arrived. Either of those things might have alerted some loyalist aboard Jalal Station that the long-awaited relief force was finally incoming. And if the loyalist in question didn't know it was here, then he wouldn't be trying to find a way to warn it about the true state of affairs.

Callum glanced back at the master plot. An icon blinked there, tracking the newcomers' projected position, but they'd been in-system for only about an hour and a half. There hadn't been time for the station's light-speed sensors to detect them, so that position was *only* a projection. So far, at least.

Be interesting to see how they respond to "Admiral Portier," though, he thought, with a broader smile. *I always thought I was pretty good with computers, but Bryant takes it to a whole 'nother level!*

They'd found literally months' worth of comm traffic and electronic memos from Vice Admiral Portier in the station's databanks. Armed with that, Bryant MacTavish had created a computer-generated Portier avatar. He'd done the same thing for Captain Tibor and half a dozen other senior officers, as well as all six of Jalal Station's senior communications watchstanders, but they had far more data on Portier, and McTavish and O'Hanraghty had strongly recommended putting "her" on point for any communications with the relief force. Not only was her avatar the best developed and most convincing, but the real Portier almost certainly would have done exactly that, anyway.

Of course, good as we all think we are, it's still possible—

"Status change!" Mirwani announced, and the single strobing icon of the newcomers' projected position suddenly resolved into an entire cluster of icons. Icons tagged with transponder ship IDs.

A *lot* of ship IDs, Callum thought with a certain undeniable dryness of mouth.

"CIC makes it twenty-five FTLCs, Admiral," Mirwani continued, studying his own display. "Transponder codes identify them as Task Force Eight-Oh-Four."

"*Eight*-oh-four?" O'Hanraghty repeated.

"Yes, Sir."

"Well, I'll be damned," the chief of staff said. "Sounds like they did slice these people off the Reserve." He shook his head. "I didn't think even Fokaides was *that* stupid."

Callum frowned, trying to follow O'Hanraghty's logic. Part of it was clear enough. If this task force had been diverted from First Fleet, the primary formation assigned to the Beta Cygni Line, then the first digit of its designation would have been a "1." The fact that it was TF 804 indicated that, as O'Hanraghty had said, its units had been taken from *Eighth* Fleet, the Federation's strategic reserve, instead.

That made total sense to Callum, since the Reserve's units were all stationed within thirty light-years of the Sol System, which meant they could be called in and dispatched to Jalal far more rapidly than anything could be diverted from the Beta Cygni front. So why—?

"Now, now, Harry," his father said. "There's still Home Fleet. They haven't left Sol *completely* uncovered."

"This is at least at least ninety percent—probably more like *all*—of Eighth Fleet's available carrier strength," O'Hanraghty replied. "And Home Fleet is—what? Two squadrons?"

"Three, actually," Commander MacTavish offered. "Three squadrons of FTLCs, that is. They've also got something like—I don't know. Fifteen hundred or so parasite capital ships? Not to mention the fixed defenses."

"All of which would be dead meat against a properly executed attack in force, even without the Casúrs," O'Hanraghty retorted. "Without a decent carrier force as a maneuver element, *any* system would be."

"And if I had any intention of attacking Sol, that would probably get me all excited," Murphy said dryly. "As it is, though—"

"Excuse me, Admiral," the comm officer of the watch said, "but we have an incoming message from the task force."

"Put it up, then, please, Lieutenant Thurman," Murphy told

her, turning towards the master display. "I'm curious to see just who they picked to come visit us."

A very dark-skinned commander appeared in the display. A data tag identified her as ABERCROMBIE, NTOMBIKAYISE.

"Jalal Station, this is Task Force Eight-Oh-Four," she said. "We've received your initial message. Vice Admiral Thakore has asked me to inform you that we have no immediately pressing requirements, and he will open personal communications with you when the time dilation factor and range permit. Abercrombie, clear."

Callum suddenly discovered he'd come to his feet, and he darted a look at his father.

"Well, there's a thing," Terrence Murphy said mildly.

"Velocities equalizing...now," Commander Dai Zheng, *Kishar*'s astrogator, announced.

"Thank you, Zheng," Captain Kerbouche acknowledged, and glanced at the time display. After just over two hours of deceleration, TF 804's—by now, the task force CO had probably identified herself to Jalal Station, but Kerbouche had no idea who it might be yet—velocity had finally decreased to match Hammer Force's. The gap between them had opened to over thirty-three light-minutes first, but from this point on, Hammer Force's overtake velocity would climb steadily.

She looked down into the screen tied to Tremblay's flag bridge and raised an eyebrow, and Tremblay shrugged.

"To quote my sometimes overly optimistic chief of staff, looking good so far," the commodore said.

"I admire a good, sneaky ops plan as much as the next woman, Sir," Kerbouche said. "This feels a little like mugging a baby for candy, though."

"Oh, indeed it does!" Tremblay agreed with a smile. "I wish I could remember who it was that first told me if you aren't cheating, you're not trying hard enough." He shook his head. "Admiral Murphy definitely is, though. Trying hard enough, I mean."

"And a damned good thing, too," Kerbouche said in a rather more serious tone. "Two-to-one odds would suck in a fair fight."

"Well, hopefully there won't *be* a fight. But if there is one," Tremblay smiled coldly, "I want it to be as *unfair* as possible."

"You're sure?" Adan Zamorano's voice was as nervous as his eyes. "I haven't heard a damned thing!"

"Keep your voice down!" Lieutenant Albert Vítek hissed. He glared at his fellow lieutenant for a moment, then glanced around the big, almost deserted mess compartment. There were only two other occupants, both engrossed in a chessboard mag-sealed to a corner table to keep it anchored in the microgravity. Neither of them was paying any attention to him and Zamorano, and he made himself inhale deeply.

"Sorry—sorry, Adan!" He shook his head. "Didn't mean to jump down your throat. It's just...I guess I'm just a little antsy."

"Antsy," Zamorano repeated, and despite his own obvious nervousness, his lips twitched on the edge of a smile. "Can't imagine why that might be!"

"Just a natural worrier, I guess," Vítek said. "But, yeah, I'm sure. Deng passed the word to Bourcier eight minutes ago."

"Shit."

Zamorano felt his stomach clench in a reaction that owed nothing at all to the lack of gravity.

Like most crewmen serving in a sublight warship, he was accustomed to spending time in microgravity. They were too small for the spin sections FTLCs incorporated, so whenever possible, their personnel spent all the time they could aboard their carriers, luxuriating in the sense of gravity nature had evolved them to expect. But when they were independently deployed in defense of point targets like Jalal Station, they *had* no handy mothership. Most parasite skippers were pretty good about allowing off-watch personnel to spend time on one of the rotating habitat rings of the station they guarded, but even that had been in short supply since Murphy's arrival in Jalal, because—little though anyone was prepared to admit it—no one could be absolutely positive about where any given spacer's true loyalties lay. Under the circumstances, it only made sense to restrict their freedom of movement, he supposed.

He would have preferred to hold this conversation somewhere else, though. Somewhere they wouldn't have to worry about who might overhear. But at least they had an established cover for it. Although he was an engineer while Vítek was in TFNS *Champlain*'s Communications Department, they'd been friends since the Academy. They'd frequently gone on liberty together, back when they'd been allowed off the ship, so no one was surprised when they met here to share a cup of coffee when they were both off watch. They'd been careful to maintain that routine ever since that lunatic Murphy and his murderous butchers arrived. Just as they'd been careful to keep their heads down once they realized their sublight battlecruiser was going over to the mutiny, whatever they did.

That had been Vítek's idea. Left to his own devices, Zamorano probably would've gotten himself killed right along with Captain Stano. Not because he was so brave, but because he wouldn't have realized until too late how futile resistance was. Especially with Commander Moghadam, *Champlain*'s executive officer, actually *leading* the mutiny. It was fortunate Vítek had gotten to him before he'd done something stupid, and since the mutiny, the two of them had very quietly reached out to a handful of others in preparation for this very moment.

And now we're all probably going to get killed, anyway, he thought. *But at least we may actually accomplish a little something first. I'd like that.*

"How do we play it?" he asked now.

"I wish we knew more," Vítek said. He picked up his bulb of coffee, made himself sip, then lowered it to the magnetic plate in the mess table with a smile that looked almost natural. "All Deng was able to tell Jasmin was that the relief force is inbound. She couldn't push her hack deep enough to get more than that."

He cocked an eyebrow, and Zamorano nodded in understanding. Senior Chief Petty Officer Jasmin Bourcier was Vítek's senior noncom in Communications, but Deng Yazhu was only a third-class petty officer, an electronics tech assigned to the tactical department. Her official reach into the systems was restricted, especially since the mutiny, but she'd managed to create a few backdoors.

"She's not sure how long they've been decelerating, but she estimates it's been at least a couple of hours. Which means they're walking right into whatever the hell Murphy plans to do to them."

"They've *got* to be at least a little suspicious," Zamorano objected, but he heard the self-convincing edge in his own voice, and Vítek shook his head.

"Why?" he asked. He kept his expression bland, but his lowered voice was bitter. "I'll guarantee you the bastards are saying exactly the right things to them. That's what I do for a living, right? They know all the SOP comm procedures as well as I do, and trust me, they got total access to the Station's data files when they took it over. They got all the authentication codes, all the background info. Hell, they've probably built CGI versions of Admiral Portier and her entire fricking staff! How is somebody hearing all the right things from all the right people supposed to figure out something's wrong before Murphy opens fire and blows his ass right out of space?"

"We don't know Murphy's going to do that," Zamorano pointed out.

"The hell we don't!" Vítek leaned a bit closer. "You think he just *happened* to have those goddamned missiles of his parked close enough to start killing ships when he first got here? If the traitorous sons-of-bitches like Moghadam hadn't just handed him the keys, he would've killed however many of us he had to before we surrendered to him. Look what he did to those marshals and Hoplons in New Dublin!"

Zamorano's face tightened, but he had to nod. The story of what had happened to Captain Lipshen and the marshals sent with him had spread throughout Jalal Station, although he doubted there was a single word of truth in the version Murphy's people had allowed to "leak" out. Even if there had been, even if Lipshen *had* started the shooting, that didn't change the fact that it was all Murphy's fault. They wouldn't even have been there if he hadn't stepped so far over the line.

"Well," Vítek shrugged, "whoever the Oval sent out here has to've come loaded for bear. And I'll bet there hasn't been time for anybody to organize any goddamned mutinies in *their* ships companies. So what do you think Murphy's going to do when whoever's in command tells him to pound sand?"

"All right," Zamorano sighed. "All right. You're right. So what do we do about it?"

His tone said he already knew, and Vítek reached across the table to squeeze his friend's forearm almost gently.

✧   ✧   ✧

I wish we'd had time to set this up better, Zamorano thought, ten minutes later. *Not that it's going to matter a lot in the end.*

He felt as if there were a flashing sign on his back as he and Vítek drifted as nonchalantly as possible along the passage, yet he knew no one else in the ship's company felt the terrible, stomach-churning anxiety he did. In fact, he'd wanted to scream at the people they'd passed on the way here for being so damned calm. Not that it was their fault. Murphy couldn't wait too much longer before he started prepping his units for battle, but he hadn't said a word about it yet, and despite his burning hatred for the man, Zamorano had to admire his coolness. He was pretty certain that if he'd been in Murphy's shoes he would have already begun doing just that, even if it would have told all of the other Albert Víteks and Adan Zamoranos what was happening.

Which might have at least meant Albert and I wouldn't be ones who had to do this, he reflected grimly, feeling the heavy weight in his shipsuit pocket. *Damn it, why does it have to be us? Why can't some—*

"...and then I told him I bet him fifty credits the Coheteros took the Cup this year," Vítek said easily, for the ears of anyone they passed. "'Course, it's gonna be—what? Six, seven months before we know who won? But when we do know, he's gonna have to pay up, right?

"Hockey's not my thing," Zamorano said, trying gamely to hold up his end of the conversation. "I'm more into soccer and null-gee basketball."

"I don't know how you can say that," Vítek said as they passed through the last passage blast door before the bridge. "How could anybody prefer floating around to getting out on the *ice*, man? It's just—"

He caught the bulkhead rail to stop himself outside the open command deck hatch. A Marine sergeant in a master-at-arms brassard stood post just outside it—a new addition, since the mutinies—and Vítek nodded to him, still holding the bulkhead rail with his left hand while the other hand reached casually into his shipsuit. Then it came back out, and the pistol in it barked spiteful death.

The Marine flew back into the bulkhead. Crimson bubbles of blood and splinters of bone spiraled away in the microgravity, and Vítek pulled hard on the rail, sending himself through the command deck hatch.

"What the fu—?!" someone began, and Vítek fired again.

Zamorano hurled himself through the hatch behind his friend, his own handgun ready, and the two of them swept the bridge with their fire.

It was a massacre, and he wanted to vomit as he saw men and women—men and women he'd known, in some cases, for years—raising their hands in futile surrender. But Albert was right. They couldn't risk trying to hold people at gunpoint along with everything else, and he made himself fire again and again.

No one else on the bridge was armed. Commander Moghadam had confiscated all personal weapons and locked them down in the armory after seizing control of the ship. That had applied to Vítek and Zamorano, as well, until Sergeant Gleeson, *Champlain's* assistant armorer, had smuggled half a dozen sidearms back out for them.

Now Lieutenant Carmichael, the officer of the watch, flung himself desperately at Zamorano, arms spread, and the engineer shot him squarely in the face. Someone else screamed, and the scream went on and on until Vítek fired again and it stopped abruptly.

Then he and Zamorano were the only living humans in the entire compartment, surrounded by drifting bodies and ribbands of blood.

"Take the hatch!" Vítek snapped, shoving his gun into his belt, and Zamorano nodded choppily. He sent himself scooting back to the hatch and hit the button that closed it. It wouldn't hold anybody on the other side long—not once they got hold of Moghadam or whoever had the watch in Engineering and over-rode Zamorano's locking code—but every second counted.

Behind him, Vítek shoved the body of one of his own communications ratings out of the way and started tapping commands into the dead woman's console.

"Attention, incoming task force!" he barked into the microphone. "Attention! You are sailing into a trap! Jalal Station is in mutinous hands! I repeat, Jalal Station has been taken by mutineers! They have a total of *fifteen* FTLCs!"

"Eight minutes till they hit the Powell Limit, Admiral," Commander Mirwani reported.

"Good." Murphy nodded. "I'll be happier when Rajenda—I mean, Vice Admiral Thakore—crosses the line."

"Doesn't really make much difference at this point, Sir," O'Hanraghty pointed out. "He's pretty much committed, no matter what."

"I know. But there's a psychological element to it. He'll *feel* it more once his max acceleration drops. And—"

"Oh, *shit*," Callum Murphy said.

His father's head turned towards him, and Callum tapped his screen, throwing the audio from his earbug onto the command deck's external speakers.

"—repeat, Jalal Station has been taken by mutineers!" a taut, strain-flattened voice said. "They have a total of *fifteen* FTLCs! All mobile units in the system are under the traitor Murphy's command. I repeat, Jalal Station has been taken by mutineers!"

"Where's that coming from?" Murphy asked sharply.

"I don't know," Callum replied, turning down the volume so his father could hear him. "There's no identifier, and it's omnidirectional, not a comm laser."

"On it," Bryant MacTavish threw in, entering rapid-fire commands at his own station. "It's got to be one of the parasites somewhere in the outer shell. Looks like one of the battlecruisers, maybe."

"But it's omnidirectional?"

"Yes, Sir," Callum confirmed.

"Makes sense," O'Hanraghty said. "Probably, anyway. Whoever it is must've figured out what's going on but doesn't have access to the actual tracking data. He can't know exactly where Thakore is, so he's shotgunning."

"Got it!" McTavish announced. "It's coming from *Champlain*. Commodore Bartowski's squadron."

"—don't know how much longer I've got," the voice in Callum's earbud continued. "Murphy has some kind of extended range missile system. Don't know how it works, but he used it to—"

A sudden thunder of gunfire came through the earbud, and the voice died with its owner.

"Well, since the cat is out of the bag," Murphy said into the ringing silence, "I suppose I should go ahead and say a few words of my own."

"Five minutes till they cross the limit, Sir," Commander Beaudouin said, and Tremblay nodded with an undeniable edge of satisfaction.

The range to TF 804 had fallen to under twenty-seven light-minutes as it continued to decelerate. Its velocity was now little more than half of Hammer Force's and it was only about 20.5 LM short of Jalal Station.

"All right," Tremblay said, and looked at the main holo display. Captain Kerbouche looked back at him from it, and he nodded to her.

"Bring the fans up, Rashida," he said. "It's time we started doing a little decelerating of our own."

"Yes, Sir!" Kerbouche replied with a huge grin, and Tremblay looked back at the tactical plot.

Now that they'd reached this point, he admitted to himself that he hadn't really expected things to go quite this perfectly, but damned if it hadn't worked out exactly as Murphy intended. By the time TF 804's light-speed sensors detected Hammer Force's Fasset signatures, it would be a good seven light-minutes across the limit and into the Powell sphere, its acceleration reduced to only nine hundred gravities. And *Hammer Force*'s deceleration would bring Tremblay's FTLCs to rest relative to the primary while it was still 200,000 kilometers outside the limit, capable of a full 1,800 gravities. For all intents and purposes, TF 804 would be a fish in a barrel, unable to escape the inner system without being intercepted, no matter what it did.

Of course, this particular "fish" is something of a great white shark, he reflected. *But I'll be in a hell of a position to hammer it with Casúrs, and that doesn't even count what the Admiral will be doing!*

"Admiral Thakore!"

Rajenda Thakore turned towards Commander Abercrombie. It wasn't like her to blurt out his name that way. That was his first thought. But even as it crossed his mind, he realized he'd never before heard that note in the comm officer's voice, either, and his eyebrows rose.

He opened his mouth, but she went on before he could speak.

"Sir, we've just picked up a transmission from Jalal," she said. "It's not from Admiral Portier. In fact—"

She broke off—which was also very unlike her—and the sheer shock and confusion in her normally composed expression sent a chill through Rajenda.

"Who *is* it from?" he demanded.

"It's— Sir, I don't *know* who it's from! There's no header, it just—"

Abercrombie paused, inhaled deeply, and shook her head.

"You'd better hear it for yourself, Sir."

"All right, put it up," he said, but the comm officer shook her head.

"I think *you'd* better hear it first, Sir," she said.

He looked at her for another moment, then nodded impatiently. She tapped her screen, and a harsh, staccato voice came suddenly through his earbud.

"Attention, incoming task force!" it said. "Attention! You are sailing into a trap! Jalal Station is in mutinous hands! I repeat, Jalal Station has been taken by mutineers! They have a total of *fifteen* FTLCs! All mobile units in the system are under the traitor Murphy's command. I repeat, Jalal Station—"

Rajenda stiffened, his own eyes suddenly wide, listening as the desperate man at the other end of that comm link blurted out his message.

"—range missile system. Don't know how it works, but he used it to—"

A deafening crackle of gunfire cut the voice abruptly short, and Rajenda Thakore's face was a mask of iron.

He felt Commodore Zebić staring at him, and he shook his head, like a man shaking off a punch to the jaw.

"It would appear," he said to his cousin, and his voice was insanely calm in his own ears, "that we've been hoodwinked."

"Sir?" Zebić sounded confused, and he barked a hard, harsh laugh.

"I don't think that's Admiral Portier we've been talking to," he said. "In fact—"

"Sir," Abercrombie interrupted in a very careful tone. "We have another incoming transmission. This one—" She cleared her throat. "This one *is* from Jalal Station, Sir, but—"

"Isn't from Portier," Rajenda interrupted. "I know." His nostrils flared and he squared his shoulders. "Go ahead and put it up, Ntombikayise."

"Yes, Sir."

Abercrombie tapped her screen, and Rajenda heard someone gasp as a face he knew entirely too well appeared on the master display.

"Hello, Rajenda," Terrence Murphy said. "I don't imagine you expected to be hearing from me today." He shrugged, ever so slightly. "I suppose that's fair enough, since I didn't expect to be speaking with you under these circumstances. But here we are, aren't we?"

Murphy paused, and Rajenda Thakore's eyes blazed as he glared at his brother-in-law. Somehow, he thought, Murphy should've changed. Should have become another man than the one who'd departed for New Dublin fifteen months ago. He should have sounded different, looked different. But he didn't, aside from the glittering silver leaf he wore now above the ribbons on his uniform's breast.

"I realize you probably won't believe this any more than Admiral Portier did," Murphy resumed, "but I truly don't want a fight. There's already been one here—one I never wanted, and that I did my best to terminate as quickly as possible. I was willing to allow Admiral Maddox's carriers to leave for Sol, but some of the Fringers in his ships companies—and aboard the system defense parasites—didn't know that. They mutinied before they received my comm message telling Portier I had no objection to their departure." His expression turned grim. "A lot of people died who didn't have to. People wearing the same uniform you and I are wearing. I never wanted that. I don't want any more of it. But somehow, I have to get Olympia and Prime Minister Schleibaum to listen to me, and you and I both know the Five Hundred won't let that happen unless I find a way to *make* them listen. That's the only reason I'm here."

Rajenda felt the frozen, stunned silence of *Lelantos*'s flag bridge all around him, but he couldn't look away from the display.

"This situation has gone a lot of places I never intended for it to go," Murphy continued, "and we've got to get a handle on it before it goes even further. In fact, it's gone further than you could know yet. The Concordia Sector has gone 'out of compliance' and declared its independence as the Free Worlds Alliance."

Rajenda flinched, and someone else on the flag bridge gasped audibly.

"I didn't want that to happen," Murphy continued. "It was never what I wanted, and I truly think I could have prevented it—convinced them to give me a chance to speak for them, at least—if Andy Lipshen hadn't managed to murder the New Dublin system president in front of hundreds of witnesses. That was too much for them, Rajenda, and the only way I could have stopped it was by going to Standing Order Fifteen, and there was no way in hell I was doing that. Not when they were right to be so enraged."

His lips tightened and he paused, his eyes grim.

"You may not want to admit it, Rajenda, but you know as well as I do why the Fringe is as angry as it is. The FWA trusts me enough to be willing—for now, at least—to let me try to speak for them, try to find a way to put the Federation back together on some sort of equitable basis. And I hope to hell we can, because if those issues aren't dealt with, the situation is unsustainable. There's only so much the iron fist can achieve, even if the Five Hundred doesn't want to hear that. The fact that there were 'mutineers' aboard every single ship deployed to Jalal—that they were the *majority* on almost all of them—should demonstrate that to anybody with a working brain.

"But that's a separate issue, really. The *main* issue is that, whether or not you—or the Five Hundred—want to admit it, I have *proof* the Rish have been supporting the League. Helping them build warships. I can't think the Sphere would be doing that unless it had an endgame planned, and I very much doubt that anyone in the Federation *or* the League would like whatever that endgame is.

"I don't have answers to way too many questions about their intentions, how long they've been helping the League, what they plan to do when they find out we know they have been, or a *lot* of other things. But I do know the Federation has to find those answers, and the first step in finding them is listening to me and looking at my evidence. And that means I have no choice but to *make people listen.* That's why I'm here at Jalal, and I will happily *stay* here at Jalal, far, far away from Sol, if Schleibaum and the Oval are willing to send someone out here to look at the evidence."

He paused again, then grimaced.

"I don't expect you to be happy to hear any of that, and I don't expect you to be happy about what I'm going to say next, but I'm afraid I'll have to insist you listen anyway. One thing's been made abundantly clear to me, starting with the decision to send Andy Lipshen to New Dublin to drag me home in chains, and that is that no one's going to listen to a word I say unless I make them. And, unfortunately, that means I need the firepower to force them to at least negotiate. It also means I can't let you drag me home the way Lipshen was supposed to.

"So in order to avoid any further...unpleasantness, you are instructed to divert from Jalal Station. You will assume a stellar orbit, three light-minutes inside the Powell Limit, and all but one of your FTLCs will stay there. Your flagship may approach within one light-minute of Jalal Station, so that you and I can talk to each other without an enormous comm lag. And after we've talked, you and your flagship will depart for Sol to report what I've told you to Olympia.

"I'll be honest, Rajenda. I wish they'd sent almost anyone besides you, for a lot of reasons. Including, whether you believe it or not, the fact that this is about to put you, your father, Simmy— *all* of us—in one hell of a deep hole where the Five Hundred are concerned. I regret that, but I don't have much choice."

His recorded image looked out of the display for a handful of seconds in silence, then he shrugged.

"Your informant was correct, by the way. I do control all of the ships in Jalal orbit, and I do command fifteen FTLCs. I realize that still gives you the edge in firepower—or that you *think* it does, at any rate. Unfortunately, you're wrong. Admiral Xing thought she had the edge in New Dublin, and she was wrong, too. Please—*please*, Rajenda—don't force me to prove that to you. Too many Federation personnel have already died. Let's not make the casualty list even longer.

"Murphy, clear."

The display blanked, and Rajenda turned away from it to face his staff.

They stared back at him, expressions shocked, and he wondered what they saw in his own face.

Nothing good, he suspected.

"That was...unexpected," he said finally.

"Do you believe him?" Zebić asked, and Rajenda coughed out a laugh.

"What part of it?" he demanded. "All that bullshit about his noble intent? Or all about the 'proof' that his tinfoil-hat lunatic friends have been right all along? Or that he has *fifteen* carriers?" He shook himself. "I don't have a single goddamned idea how much of it I should believe, except that there's no way in hell we're going to just roll over and let a single rogue admiral rip the guts out of the Federation!"

"So what do you want to do, Sir?" she asked.

"First—" He looked at Abercrombie. "Record for transmission," he said.

"Recording."

"Admiral Murphy," he said, and his liquid-helium tone was warmer than his eyes, "I don't care about anything you've said. What I care about is that you are in a state of mutiny. That, by your own admission, you've violated your standing orders, refused to return to Old Terra when so ordered, and are now in the position of a traitor waging rebellious warfare against the Constitution and the duly constituted government of the Terran Federation. You've betrayed every oath you ever swore as an officer of the Terran Federation Navy, and so have any other personnel who have followed you into this damnable treason.

"You *will* stand down, Admiral. You will surrender yourself and every vessel under your control to me, and you will return to the Sol System as my prisoner, there to stand trial for your crimes. Should you refuse to do so, I will *compel* you to, and I have the firepower to do just that. I advise you to take what I've just said very, very seriously. The consequences for those you've seduced into supporting you will already be extraordinarily grave. Do not make it worse.

"Thakore, clear."

He stood for a moment longer, then nodded to himself, once.

"Send it," he said. "And then set up the conference circuit. I want all squadron commanders on the line immediately."

"Yes, Sir!"

"If he's got all those damned carriers, where the hell are they?" Rear Admiral Jonas Baumgartner demanded from his quadrant of the flag bridge display.

"I don't know," Rajenda replied a bit testily. "No doubt he'll tell us—in about another twenty-five or thirty minutes. Of course, whether or not we *believe* him will be something else."

"So you don't think he really has that many, Sir?" Rear Admiral Nakanishi asked. His tone was very careful, Rajenda noted with bitter amusement.

"I don't know," he said frankly. "That's the thing, isn't it? We *can't* know. From the sensor data we've got, it certainly looks like he got Maddox's carriers, but they're in orbit with the Station, so assuming he's telling the truth, he must have another dozen of them tucked away somewhere. But that would mean he had virtually every picket on Concordia's side of the Fringe. Every single one of them." He shook his head. "As 'worst-case' scenarios go, that one would take some beating. I don't think *all* of them could have successfully mutinied against their legal orders and commanders and gone over to him. If they have, then the situation's gotten a lot worse than anyone back home was prepared to believe it could. Which makes it even more imperative that we deal with this now."

Several heads nodded, and Rajenda showed his teeth in a tight smile.

Every one of his squadron commanders had been chosen for loyalty. For having amply demonstrated that loyalty in the past. Of course, that should be true of any flag officer, which was the main reason so few Fringers ever broke into the rarefied heights of senior flag rank. But until Murphy went so completely off the rails, no one—not even Rajenda Thakore—would ever have questioned his fundamental loyalty to the Federation. In the light of *his* treason, the loyalty of every other flag officer had to be looked at very, very carefully, because the Federation Navy couldn't afford to discover another Murphy hiding in its senior echelons. That was why Rear Admiral Kashyap had been transferred in to command FTLC Squadron 15 when Rear Admiral Stimson was quietly promoted out of that slot because of his Fringer daughter-in-law.

Overall, Rajenda was confident of their loyalty, but some of them—Nakanishi was one—looked more than a little uneasy about the thought of a pitched battle.

"I've given him his options," he said now. "Once upon a time, I would have expected him to be smart enough to accept the inevitable. Now...?" He shrugged. "Now, I'm not so sure. But if it comes down to it, we still have twenty-five carriers. Even if he has fifteen, that's still a sixty percent edge, as long as we stay far enough out from Jalal. Hell, if Maddox's carriers really are still in orbit with the Station, then the odds out here are two-to-one in our favor, even assuming he's got twelve more stashed away. And then—"

"Status change," Commander Alioto interrupted, and Rajenda wheeled from the comm with an irritated expression.

An expression that smoothed into blankness almost instantly

when he saw the twelve Fasset signatures that had suddenly appeared on the master plot, decelerating steadily towards Jalal... and Task Force 804.

"They should be picking up Tremblay about now," O'Hanraghty said.

"What do you think Uncle Rajenda's going to do?" Callum asked softly. His father stood beside him now, hands clasped behind him as he gazed calmly at the master plot.

"I wish I knew," he said, turning his head to look at Callum. "We should have some clue in the next couple of minutes, given the message turnaround time. But I don't expect it to be good." He shook his head, his eyes shadowed. "I was always afraid they might send Rajenda. I hoped they wouldn't, but from the Five Hundred's perspective, he was the perfect choice, really, if he was available."

Callum looked back at him, and in that moment, he wished he could see inside his father's head. Not because he thought Murphy would lie to him. That had never been his father's style. But that wasn't the same as saying that he'd share his darker thoughts with the son who, aside from his far greater height, had always been a dead ringer for the man commanding Task Force 804.

"He never liked you, did he?" Callum said now, and Murphy frowned ever so slightly.

"Picked up on that early, didn't you?" he said after a moment.

"Honestly, Dad. He never really tried all that hard to hide it."

"No. To tell the truth, that's one of the things I've always rather admired about him. Whatever else he may be, he's no dissembler. Although, to be fair, he did try to avoid rows over the family dinner table."

"Why?" Callum asked. His father raised an eyebrow, and he shrugged. "Why did he always dislike you so much? It's not like you don't brush or mouthwash."

"Son, your uncle—and your grandfather—are perfect examples of both the good and the bad sides of the Five Hundred." There was an edge of sorrow in Murphy's voice. "They're both highly intelligent, hardworking, gifted in their own fields, and determined to succeed. They're both very good at their jobs, and both of them have made tremendous contributions to the things they believe in. Your grandfather's always treated his employees decently, pays fair wages, and respects their value. Neither of them ever just 'coasted' on their status in the Five Hundred the way far too many of its other members have, and your grandfather did his damnedest to make sure you and Vyom didn't grow up to do that, either. Because the truth is that they're good, decent fathers and sons who do their damnedest to take care of the important people in their lives. There's a tremendous amount to respect in that.

"But, at the same time, they've been completely—and, in your uncle's case, at least, willfully—blind to where the Five Hundred's excesses ultimately *have* to lead. They see the Federation as a snapshot, an old-fashioned still photograph, not the video of a human society that—like all societies—is in a constant state of change. Changes may be excruciatingly slow, or they may be catastrophically fast, but social matrices *always* change, sooner or later. And for someone in the Five Hundred's position, change is a threat. The keys to the kingdom are already in their pocket, aren't they? It's hard to imagine the kind of change that could *improve* their position, so they aren't interested in *any* change.

"There's nothing at all wrong with your uncle's brain, Callum. And by his lights, he's a good man. He loves his family, loves his father, and he's completely loyal to the Federation. Or, at least, to the Federation as he understands it. And that's the rub."

"So it's all about your wanting to change things?" Callum asked just a bit skeptically. "That's why he's always detested you?"

"Oh, that's not how it started!" Murphy surprised Callum with a chuckle. "It *started* because he thought I wasn't good enough for your mother."

"What?" Callum blinked, and Murphy snorted.

"To be honest, I agreed with him about that," he said. "Not for quite the same reasons, maybe, but I did agree. Your mother—" He paused, shook his head, his gray eyes suddenly softer. "Your mother is an extraordinary woman, Callum. In *so* many ways. She's got a lot of the same blind spots your grandfather and your uncle do, but there's never been a cruel or malevolent bone in her entire body, and she's flat-out brilliant. I think she's actually quite a lot smarter than I am, really, and—all false modesty aside—I'm not exactly a dummy, myself. And she's just as beautiful as I am homely, *and* she comes from one of the wealthiest, most powerful families in human history, whereas *my* family was barely respectable, by the Five Hundred's standards. Of *course* she was out of my league!" He twitched a grin. "So I knew when I proposed that Rajenda was going to oppose any engagement. And, to be completely honest, I knew it was a mistake when I did propose, too. I just...couldn't help myself."

"A mistake? Proposing to Mom was a *mistake*?" Callum frowned, and Murphy shook his head quickly and laid one hand on his forearm.

"Oh, it was the *best* mistake I ever made, trust me! But it *was* a mistake. I was already headed down the path that's brought us all here." He took his hand from Callum's arm to point at the decksole under their feet. "I hadn't worked it all out yet, but I did know it was likely to end badly, and I didn't have any business dragging her into that with me. For that matter, while there might be some tactical advantages to having a toehold in the Five Hundred myself, I already had a pretty good notion as to how the rest of the Five Hundred would react if I ever truly kicked the traces over. I should've thought about that. I should've kept your mom clear of the mess. But the problem was that I loved her."

He looked at his son, and something deep and warm welled up in Callum's chest as he saw the softness, the glow, in his father's eyes. The vulnerability he'd never shown so clearly before.

"I loved her so much, Callum. I still do." Murphy blinked. "I always will. I couldn't imagine living my life without her. Didn't *want* to imagine it. And because I was too selfish to walk away, I've brought all of this down on her, just as much as I've brought it down on you and Vyom and Reagan. I can't tell you how deeply I regret that. But somebody had to do it, and no one else was stepping up. So—"

He shrugged, and it was Callum's turn to grip his father's shoulder and squeeze hard. Murphy looked down, then reached up and put his own hand over Callum's.

"Anyway," he said more briskly, "Rajenda never thought I was good enough for your mom. For his entire family, really, but especially for his baby sister. I think a part of him realized I'd never be a good fit for the Five Hundred, no matter how much she and your grandad cleaned me up and polished me." He smiled briefly. "I doubt he had any idea where I was really headed, but he may have...sensed something. Anyway, he was against it. Your mom, on the other hand, was all in. Can't imagine what she saw in me, but she was pretty fierce when he opened his mouth to object! Cut him right off at the ankles in the middle of La Cuillère d'Argent one day, between the salad and the main course, with half the waitstaff watching her perform a double orchidectomy without ever raising her voice once. It was beautiful to see!" He smiled again, much more broadly. "And she *is* a Thakore, you know, right down to her toenails. When your grandfather seemed a bit dubious, *she* was the one who trotted out how valuable the connection to Henrik Murphy might be for someone doing so much business with the Navy!"

"That does sound like Mom," Callum agreed with a chuckle.

"It does, indeed," Murphy acknowledged, but then his smile faded and he shook his head, turning back to the plot.

"But your uncle has a lot more reasons to hate me now," he said softly. "By his lights, I'm a traitor, and not just to the Constitution. Oh, I'm sure he thinks I've betrayed that, too, and I'm not trying to make light of how furious he'd be over that by itself. But I've also betrayed your mom, you—the entire Thakore family. And for all its collegial veneer, the Five Hundred is about as voraciously competitive as social organisms come. They'll turn on your grandfather—and your mom—in a heartbeat if they think either of them is even remotely likely to support what we're doing out here. And even if that weren't the case, your grandfather's competitors, people like Madison Dawson, have to taste the blood in the water. They'll use me against Venus Futures and the family any way they can, and Rajenda knows that, too.

"Which is why I'm very much afraid he's *not* going to do the smart thing here. I hope he does. I hope that brain of his realizes I wouldn't have gone this far if I wasn't prepared—and able—to make it stand up. And that making it do that has to include the military capacity to handle even his task force. I hope he'll realize he *has* to talk to me . . . but I don't think all those other factors will let him."

"You don't hate *him*, do you?" Callum said slowly after a moment, and Murphy looked back, cocking his head. "I mean, I know you two never liked each other. I've known that since I was a kid, even if I didn't know why, but I can tell. You don't."

"No." Murphy shook his head. "It took me a while to realize I don't, but you're right. And if he weren't so deeply committed to the Five Hundred—and if I weren't so completely committed to smashing what the Five Hundred stands for—I think we'd actually be friends. But he is, and I am, so we aren't. And the Five Hundred couldn't possibly have picked someone who'd be more motivated for more reasons to smash everything I'm trying to do, instead. I'm not just an existential threat to the Federation, or to the Five Hundred at large, I'm also an existential threat to his family. And one of the central girders of your uncle's strength is his commitment to and his love for his family. In fact, that probably makes him even more furious with me, because he can't understand how someone who loves his family could put you all at risk the way I have. And I have, Callum. Trust me, if anyone knows that, I do. And that's why I understand Rajenda will do *anything* to protect the things he loves. Just like I would."

"Dad," Callum looked deep into his father's eyes, "I love you. And I think I must have the same Murphy 'stupid gene' that you do, because right this minute?" He smiled crookedly. "Right this minute, I think I love you more than I ever have before."

Murphy's eyes widened. Then he reached across, cupped the side of Callum's face in his hand, and shook him gently.

"From one 'stupid-gene' Murphy to another," his voice was ever so slightly frayed around the edges, "that means a lot."

"Yeah. Well, let's not get too mushy, right?" Callum made his own voice deliberately brisk. "Kinda doubt this is the best moment for it."

"No." Murphy nodded in agreement. "No, probably not. And I doubt your uncle's feeling especially 'mushy' just now, either."

"Uncle Rajenda? *Mushy?* The mind boggles, Dad—it just . . . *boggles.*"

Terrence Murphy laughed out loud, and never noticed the way eyes turned towards him and his son from all around Command Central.

"In that case—" he began.

"Excuse me, Admiral," Lieutenant Thurman interrupted from Communications. "We have an incoming transmission from Task Force Eight-Oh-Four."

"Oh, joy," O'Hanraghty said, and Murphy snorted.

"Might as well see what he has to say, Harry."

"Just as long as you don't get your hopes up too high," O'Hanraghty replied dryly.

"I'll try not to." Murphy looked back at Thurman. "Put it up, Lieutenant."

"Yes, Sir."

A window opened in the master plot, and a steely-eyed Rajenda Thakore looked out of it. His expression, Callum thought, was... less than promising.

"Admiral Murphy," he began in an ice-cold voice, "I don't care about anything you've said. What I care about is that you are in a state of mutiny. That by your own admission..."

✧   ✧   ✧

Rajenda Thakore tried to throttle his rage as he glared at the plot's proof Murphy really did have fifteen carriers... and realized what that meant for the true scale of the disaster the Federation faced. Only two carriers—*two,* out of all the pickets deployed to Concordia and the neighboring sectors—*weren't* in Murphy's order of battle.

But it all comes down to Terry, really, doesn't it? he thought grimly. *He's the one who brought all this to a head! And he's the figurehead, the focus. If he goes down, his precious Free Worlds will disintegrate into a rabble we can deal with one system at a time, if we have to. And whatever he may have done—or not done—at New Dublin, he's a frigging Survey nerd who doesn't know his ass from his elbow up against an experienced, competent CO.*

He made himself sit on his fury. Made himself think as coldly as he could, reminded himself that only a fool let anger shape his tactical perceptions. He felt the eyes of his staff and his squadron commanders on him as he folded his arms across his chest, frowning down at the decksole while he considered all the moving parts. Then he inhaled deeply and looked up again.

"All right," he said harshly. "I'd hoped we could settle this without killing anybody else, but it's obvious they aren't interesting in cooperating. Either that, or they expect us to cave in the face of their bluff."

One or two sets of eyes cut ever so briefly away from him towards the plot and the glowing icons of those incoming FTLCs, and he smiled thinly.

"I realize all these Fringe bastards think my esteemed brother-in-law can walk on water," he told them bitingly. "But he can't, and he's screwed the pooch on this one. It looks like he expected us to fold when his carriers turned up outside the Powell Sphere, but if he did, then he must have underestimated how much of the Reserve the Oval was willing to send out to swat him. He always wanted to be a Survey officer." He snorted. "Well, from the looks of things, he should've stayed there."

"Sir," Nakanishi said, "I agree we have the edge against his carriers, but they *are* outside us. With that accel advantage, they can intercept us when we try to break back out across the limit, whatever we do."

"Of course they can, but they're also isolated. His forces are divided, and we're between them, with the 'interior line.'"

Rajenda looked at the plot himself for a moment, then at the comm display tied into *Lelantos*'s command deck.

"Lieutenant Massengale!" he said.

"Yes, Admiral?" *Lelantos*'s astrogator was outside the comm camera's field of view, but his voice came through clearly.

"We're done decelerating," Rajenda said. "Plot a least-time course to take us past Jalal Station, range two light-seconds, and go to maximum *accel*."

"Yes, Sir!"

Rajenda turned back to his senior officers.

"At our crossing velocity, we'll be well inside missile range of the Station as we pass." His tone was flat and iron-hard. "We'll cut accel and deploy the parasites ten minutes before we launch. And then, if Murphy refuses to see reason, we'll blow the hell out of these mutinous bastards as we go by. There won't be squat their carriers can do to stop us, and if they want to intercept us at the limit on our way out, I'm totally willing to take them on at two-to-one odds."

Someone inhaled audibly.

"I agree that their carriers won't be able to interfere, Sir," Zebić said after a moment. "They've still got over three hundred sublight units, plus the station's orbital batteries. That's a lot of fire."

"They may have a lot of fire, but we've got a lot of point defense," Rajenda replied. "And we've got two hundred and fifty parasites of our own on the racks, including two hundred and five capital ships. That's a lot *more* point defense. And between them and the carriers, we can lay down over four thousand missiles in a single launch." He shook his head. "Their base velocity will be zero, our passing velocity will be right on a hundred thousand KPS, and none of that orbital infrastructure out there can dodge. So we'll be able to hammer it with our K-guns, as well." He shook his head. "If he insists on being stupid, we can turn this entire base into rubble in a single firing pass."

Zebić opened her mouth. Then she stopped, visibly reconsidering what she'd been about to say, and closed it.

"I don't want to kill a couple of hundred thousand people, even mutineers and traitors, any more than you do, Christina," Rajenda said in a marginally gentler tone. "For that matter, if we are forced to fire, we'll be killing a lot of people who probably *aren't* traitors, and I like that thought even less. But if we don't get on top of this, if we don't stop it right here and right now, a hell of a lot more people are going to die. And if this goes on and the entire Fringe goes up in flames, we'll probably lose the frigging war, as well! And in that case, every single person who's ever died fighting for the Federation will have died for *nothing.*"

He shook his head, nostrils flared, but his eyes were level and his voice had hardened into iron once more.

"I'm not letting that happen. If Murphy forces my hand on this, I'll just have to live with it."

There was silence for a moment, and then his cousin nodded.

"Yes, Sir," she said quietly.

"Incoming message, Admiral," Lieutenant Thurston said.

"Bets on what he's going to say?" O'Hanraghty asked quietly, and Murphy gave a grunting cough of a laugh.

"No." He shook his head, eyes hard but also said. "I've known what he's going to say since he started accelerating again. Damn, I *hate* this."

"Not a lot you can do about it at this point," O'Hanraghty said. "Only way out is through."

"I know. I know!"

Murphy shook his head and looked at Thurston.

"Put it up, Lieutenant."

Rajenda Thakore appeared on the master display once more, his eyes harder than flint, and the battle boards of the FTLC flag bridge visible beyond him glared a uniform crimson.

"All right, Admiral," he said, "you've had your say. And, yes, I see the damned carriers coming up behind me. But they're behind me, and you're *in front* of me. So this is how it's going to be. You'll stand down, Jalal Station will stand down, and those carriers will cross the hyper limit and go into that stellar orbit you wanted me in, well away from the Station. I will see every one of your sublight ships accelerating away from the Station at six gravities, and they will continue to accelerate away from it until they've exhausted seventy-five percent of their reaction mass. My carriers will collect them later, but they will *not* be in support range of Jalal Station.

"Once you've agreed to my terms and the sublight ships are underway, I'll decelerate to rest at a range of one hundred thousand kilometers from the Station. From there, my shuttles and the Army troops aboard my transports will take possession of Jalal Station, and be forewarned that they will employ lethal force at the first sign of resistance. You and your senior officers will surrender yourselves to me, to be transported to Old Terra, there to face court-martial and trial for treason and for mutiny under the relevant Uniform Code of Justice and the Articles of War.

"You may choose not to accept my terms. That's your option. Be aware, however, that if you do *not* accept my terms, and if the mutinous units under your command do not comply with my instructions, I will have no option but to open fire on Jalal Station. I do not desire to do so. I do not desire to kill thousands of Federation personnel, nor do I desire to reduce one of the Federation's premier naval stations to wreckage, but cancers must be cut out to save the rest of the body, and I am prepared to cut you out, whatever the cost in lives, to save the Federation and the Constitution. I will *destroy* Jalal Station as I pass, and then I will recover my parasites, and your twelve carriers are welcome to intercept my *twenty-five* at the Powell Limit.

"At my current acceleration, I will enter my attack range forty-seven minutes after you receive this transmission. If I haven't seen your sublight units accelerating away from the Station within five minutes of your receipt of this message, I'll consider that a declaration that you don't intend to comply, and the blood which will be shed and the lives which will be lost will be on your head."

He glared out of the plot for ten ice-cold seconds. Then—

"Thakore, clear."

His image disappeared, and Callum reminded himself to breathe again. He'd never before seen his uncle that coldly, viciously furious, and he didn't doubt for one moment that he'd meant every word he'd said.

"That's what I was afraid he was going to say," Murphy said sadly.

"I don't think it really matters who they sent at this point, Terry," O'Hanraghty said almost gently. "Anybody Schleibaum and the Five Hundred trusted enough to send out here would probably have said exactly the same thing, and you know it. That's why you set Spider up the way you did."

"I know." Murphy turned from the display to look at his friend. "And it's not like either of us didn't see this coming. But I don't want to kill thousands of Federation people any more than he does. And, on a personal level, if I kill Rajenda, it'll break Simron's heart."

"You think it won't break her heart if *he* kills *you*?" O'Hanraghty asked quizzically.

"Of course it will. That doesn't mean I want to be the one to hurt her that way, though."

Murphy touched the silver leaf on the breast of his tunic, then inhaled.

"Lieutenant Thurston, please send the Execute Alpha Seven signal to Commodore Tremblay."

"Yes, Sir."

"By this time," Murphy continued, looking back at O'Hanraghty and including Commander Mirwani in his conversation, "Tremblay's probably already gone to Alpha Seven, since there's only one reason Rajenda would be accelerating deeper into the Powell Sphere. Never hurts to make sure, though."

O'Hanraghty nodded, and Murphy turned directly to Mirwani.

"Our deployment looks pretty close to perfect," he said. "I imagine he'll drop his parasites to thicken his defenses and clear their launchers at least ten or twelve minutes before he enters his chosen attack range. I want the initial launch to target them."

"The parasites, Sir? Not the carriers?"

"Not in the initial launch." Murphy's expression was grim. "Given what's about to go down, there's no path back from here that doesn't include more bloodshed farther down the road. We'll probably need all the FTLCs we can get our hands on, and I don't want to destroy any more of his carriers than we absolutely have to. I know we'll have to hit them anyway, probably with the second wave, to convince him we're serious, but let's at least give him a chance to rediscover sanity."

"Yes, Sir."

"No sign they're going to be reasonable," Christina Zebić said quietly, and Rajenda nodded grimly.

If Murphy had been inclined to accept his terms, those sublight parasites would have begun moving just under thirty minutes ago, and even with their light-speed limitations, TF 804's sensors would have detected it ten minutes ago. Now the range to the station was down to barely seven and a half light-minutes, and TF 804's closing velocity was back up to 89,000 KPS.

Which meant that in about twenty-five minutes, Rajenda Thakore was going to kill the better part of a hundred and fifty thousand Federation Navy personnel.

No, I'm going to kill the better part of a hundred and fifty thousand mutineers, *dammit!*

He told himself that, very firmly.

It didn't help.

"Oh, those poor bastards," Nathanaël Beaudouin said softly from beside Esteban Tremblay's command chair.

Hammer Force had detected the change in TF 804's acceleration rate twenty-two minutes ago, and Esteban hadn't needed Murphy's orders to know what he was supposed to do if the task force committed to an attack run. Personally, he'd always thought that was the most likely outcome, and he'd come to terms with it. Or he'd thought he had, at any rate. Now it was coming to pass, and he realized Beaudouin had just spoken for him, as well.

At the moment, Hammer Force had gone back to full acceleration on an adjusted vector that would just skim across the top of the Jalal System Powell Sphere. It would bring Tremblay's carriers back down to intercept TF 804 if it continued directly across the system, and the combination of his higher starting base velocity and vastly higher acceleration rate meant the task force couldn't evade him whatever it did.

No doubt the Federation commander thought it would be a case of a hunting hound "catching" a sabretooth, but then, the Federation CO didn't know what Murphy had waiting for him. Tremblay knew he didn't, because if he had, he'd never have adopted the approach he'd obviously chosen.

"It's not like the Admiral didn't give them a chance to back down, Nate," he said now.

"No, but he also didn't tell them what would happen—or

how it would, anyway—if they didn't," Beaudouin replied. "He couldn't, if Spider's going to work."

"War isn't about giving the other side fair warning." Tremblay's voice was harsher than it had been, and he shook his head. "I never wanted to be a mutineer, and I never wanted to commit treason, and I still don't. But the Admiral's right. We have *got* to make these people *listen*, and they obviously aren't going to until we've killed enough other people that they have to. And it makes me want to puke, but it's not going to make me stop."

He turned in his chair, facing his chief of staff squarely, and his eyes were dark.

"It won't make me stop, and I'll tell you something, Nate. There's nothing in this universe that will make the *Admiral* stop, either. Not until they *do* listen."

"And after that, Sir? *After* they've listened? What then?"

"Then we all have some hard decisions to make," Tremblay said. "I know you and the rest of the Free Worlds Alliance want your independence, and I understand that—better than I ever did before. But there are other people—I'm one of them, and so is Admiral, I think—who want to heal the breach, somehow. Find a way to keep the Federation from tearing itself apart in the face of both the League and the Rish."

"You really think that's possible at this point?" Beaudouin asked very quietly, and Tremblay shrugged.

"I have to believe it's *possible*," he said. "Which is a completely different thing from 'likely.' But I never would have believed the Admiral could get *this* far, so I'm not ruling out the chance that he has another miracle or two tucked away in that spacebag of his. *I* don't know what they might be, but I'm willing to back his play long enough to find out."

Beaudouin considered that for several seconds, then nodded.

"Works for me, Sir."

"Admiral Thakore, I've got something over here you should take a look at," Saffiro Alioto said.

"What?"

Rajenda kicked off from his command chair, floating across Flag Bridge to the ops officer's console, and Alioto tapped in a command.

"I'm trying to figure out what *this* is, Sir," he said, as a diamond dust coating of icons illuminated. They represented a vast cloud of Hauptman signatures.

"Repositioning the Kavachas, most likely." Rajenda shrugged. "He knew the most probable threat axis all along, but he couldn't predict exactly what our vector and velocity would be until we actually arrived. Not surprised he's doing a little adjusting."

"That's what I thought, too, Sir." Alioto nodded. "But there are an awful lot of them. And, to be honest, they're farther out from the Station than I would have expected."

"Um."

Rajenda rubbed his chin thoughtfully, then leaned across the ops officer's shoulder and tapped a query of his own into the display. Numerical data scrolled up one side of the screen, and he watched it for a second, then tapped again, freezing it.

"He's buying more depth," he said. "Look here. He's basically sending out three waves of platforms." He shook his head. "God only knows how much that deployment of his is costing the taxpayer, but *he's* not paying for them. He probably wants to be able to attrit our K-gun fire as much as possible, and it'll make problems for the missiles, too, if he can get it wide enough we can't maneuver around it. And I wouldn't be surprised if he's pushing some more Heimdallars out right along with them. He'll want the best look he can get at us. For all the good it'll do him."

"Makes sense," Alioto said thoughtfully, after a moment. "I guess I'm just surprised Jalal had that many Kavachas in stores!"

"Well," Rajenda shrugged, "it *is* one of our primary bases out this way. We always knew that if the Leaguies got this deep, they'd do their damnedest to take it out. I don't see any reason to be surprised our good friend Murphy is pulling out all the stops, too."

"With that many platforms, Sir, he probably is going to knock back the effectiveness of our fire pretty significantly. More significantly than *I* anticipated, anyway."

"Best-case scenario, from his perspective, he's only stretching out the agony," Rajenda replied. "At our attack range, his K-guns will be completely ineffective against evading targets. That only leaves missiles, and he can't fire enough of them to hurt us all that badly in the time he'll have and at the crossing velocity we're generating. So even if he survives one firing run, we'll have plenty of time to decelerate—still inside the Powell Sphere—and come back to do it all over again. And the only way his carriers could do anything about it would be to come into the sphere after us." He showed his teeth. "I don't think they'd like that very much."

"Coming up on Snapcount, Admiral," Commander Mirwani said quietly. "And they are deploying parasites."

"Proceed," Terrence Murphy replied. "And may God forgive us all."

"Proceeding. Snapcount in thirty seconds from ... now."

"Parasite deployment complete, Sir," Zebić said. "Target designations accepted and locked. Tactical says the Kavachas are so thick the K-guns' effectiveness is 'doubtful.'"

"Doubtful." Rajenda snorted. "I'll say this for Terry, I've never seen a Kavacha deployment that heavy even in a simulation! Of course, it's got to play hell with his own targeting and return fire, don't you think?"

"Probably." Zebić nodded. "And you're right. We can come back and do it over again, if we have to. It's not like he's got an unlimited supply of the things!"

"No, he doesn't. But—"

"Admiral Thakore!"

Rajenda whirled towards Alioto, eyes narrow as the ops officer's tone registered.

"What?" he demanded.

"The Kavachas!"

Alioto pointed at the plot, and Rajenda's narrowed eyes flared wide. What the hell did Terry think he was doing? It made absolutely no—

Four thousand Casúr Cogaidhs, delivered from New Dublin aboard the freighters Murphy had commandeered and left behind to collect them from the Crann Bethadh industrial platforms, went to 800 gravities of acceleration and lunged directly at TF 804.

The task force was still one hundred and seventy light-seconds—and ten minutes' flight time—short of its launch point. The Casúr Cogaidhs were 400,000 kilometers out from Jalal Station, which put them roughly 168 LS short of TF 804, and they accelerated towards it at 800 gravities for sixty seconds. TF 804 had gone ballistic, but the Casúrs' acceleration still increased the closing velocity to 97,900 KPS... and reduced their range to target to only 45,342,000 kilometers.

And then they released twelve thousand Bijalees straight into TF 804's teeth.

Rajenda Thakore stared at the plot in horror as the missiles blossomed upon it. They had to be missiles, although there was no sign of any Hauptman signatures. Not from the missiles, at any rate.

Not yet.

That's what he did to the Leaguies in New Dublin, an icy corner of Rajenda's brain said. *Those weren't Kavachas. Or most of them weren't, anyway. They're some kind of fucking missile pod, and I walked straight into them.*

Their closing velocity at launch would carry those missiles all the way to TF 804, which meant they'd have every second of their Hauptman coils' endurance to burn on terminal evasive maneuvers when they hit his missile defense perimeter. That *never* happened in ship-to-ship missile combat, and even his highly disciplined brain quailed as he thought about what that meant for intercept probabilities. A horrendous percentage of those birds were getting through, whatever he did.

He heard the urgent, disciplined chatter of reports around him as his tactical officers reacted to the sudden, totally unanticipated threat. Despite the massive closing velocity, they had six or seven minutes to respond, he thought, but even as he thought that, a second, equally large wave of Casúr Cogaidhs accelerated out of the concealing clutter of the Kavacha platforms.

And there was no way in the universe TF 804 could avoid that oncoming missile storm. The FTLCs were anchored to their sublight parasites, and the reaction-drive parasites lacked the acceleration to maneuver effectively against missiles coming in at that velocity.

"Launch now," he heard himself say.

"But, Sir—"

"I know our birds will be ballistic by the time they enter the bastards' defense zone," Rajenda grated. "But some of them may get through anyway. Launch!"

"Yes, Sir. Launching now."

Missiles roared out from TF 804, but less than a third of the number coming at it. And unlike the Bijalees streaking towards it, TF 804's missiles couldn't reach their targets purely ballistically. The Casúr Cogaidhs had accelerated their cargo onto an intercept vector before they released it; Jalal Station would be beyond the cone of TF 804's fire for another ten minutes. That meant *its* birds needed their drives to reach the point in space Jalal Station would occupy when they arrived. And *that* meant they'd be coming in inert, which would make them easy meat for the station's missile defenses.

The outgoing waves of TF 804's missiles stippled the plot, but the glaring red icons of Terrence Murphy's missiles charged onward, coasting for 6.7 minutes. And then, at 5,926,950 kilometers, they engaged their own drives and came shrieking in at a final closing velocity of 100,000 KPS.

Counter-missiles streamed to meet them, but the solutions were late and hurried, because no one had anticipated the threat, and the attack wave was liberally seeded with Fallax EW missiles and Phalanx escort missiles. They cut through the froth of counter-missiles, drove into the teeth of the point defense lasers and autocannon. At that closing velocity, with the full endurance of their Hauptman coils for terminal attack maneuvers, the close-in defenses had time for only a single shot each, and well over eight thousand Bijalees broke through everything the task force could throw at it.

A shroud of nuclear detonations wrapped itself around TF 804 as 8,265 laser heads spawned 49,590 bomb-pumped lasers.

Not one of them targeted an FTLC. *All* of them targeted Rajenda Thakore's two hundred sublight battleships and battlecruisers. It was like some huge, obscene pre-space flash gun, glaring in space, hurling lances of coherent radiation like demented harpoons that ripped deep, deep into hulls that simply could not be armored on the same scale as an FTLC. Plating shattered, atmosphere belched into space, and eleven seconds after the first laser head detonated, only nine of TF 804's battleships survived.

Rajenda watched sickly, his face like iron, as his parasites died. And then, on the heels of their deaths, a second wave of Casúr Cogaidh-launched Bijalees came roaring in. He clung to the armrests of his command chair, watching them come, and TF 804's defensive fire was only a pale shadow of what it had been.

The missiles streaked closer, reached attack range, and fresh clusters of lasers ripped out from them.

But this time their targets were FTLCs, with vastly heavier armor. Unlike any sublight ship, Fasset-drive starships didn't care about things like mass. They carried up to ten meters of SCM armor, half again as dense as osmium, over their most critical systems, and their outer hulls were intricately subdivided into damage-absorbing compartments. They shot the rapids of the second laser-head holocaust, shuddering and bucking as transfer energy blasted into them, ripped holes in that massive armor.

Despite their armor, despite every protective system incorporated into them, RHLNS *Eurynome* and RHLNS *Poseidon* were unequal to the storm. *Eurynome* survived as a recognizable hull, but her drive fan was a shattered ruin, her hull threshed and broken. Intact though she might nominally be, her catastrophic damage was far beyond anything any navy might consider repairable.

Poseidon simply broke up.

Her consorts *Aphrodite* and *Freya* were almost as battered as *Eurynome*, although at least their drive fans survived, which meant they were—probably—repairable, but TF 804 emerged from the missile storm a broken force. Rajenda Thakore had gone into the attack with twenty-five FTLCs. He came out of it with twenty-one, all of them damaged. *Aphrodite* and *Freya* were the worst, but *Braggi, Artemis, Heimdallar, Saga,* and *Styx* were almost as badly hurt. All of the others were at least nominally still combat-capable, but their parasite groups had been gutted, and without their parasites...

Flag Bridge was awash with damage reports, casualty reports, requests for orders, and Rajenda shook himself as he realized there was no *third* wave of missile drones. Maybe—

"Incoming message, Admiral."

Ntombikayise Abercrombie's voice was raised enough to cut through the background of reports and orders, but he heard the shock—the horror—in it as he turned towards her.

"It's...Admiral Murphy, Sir."

Of course it is, Rajenda thought almost numbly.

"Put it up," someone said with his voice.

"Yes, Sir."

Terrence Murphy appeared on the master display. His expression was somber, his eyes dark, as he looked out of it at the brother-in-law he couldn't see from his end.

"I'm sorry, Rajenda," he said. "I didn't want to do that, but I had no choice. You and your people did your duty, I understand that, but—*God*, I wish you'd taken my offer to talk first. We've just killed way too many people between us, and it has to *stop*. Olympia, the Oval—the Five Hundred—they *have* to listen to me. You've known me for almost forty years. Do you really think I'm some kind of warlord out for personal power who doesn't give a single solitary damn how many people he kills to get it?! Use your *brain*, Rajenda! We don't need to—"

He broke off, drew a deep, visible breath, and shook his head.

"You and your people are screwed," he said then, flatly. "It's not twenty-five carriers versus twelve anymore. It's maybe nineteen carriers, with no parasites, against *fifteen*, with full parasite loadouts, because there's no way you're getting out of the Powell Sphere with Tremblay out there waiting for you, and there's no way you can survive against the missile fire Jalal can hand out if you try to attack the Station again. You can stooge around the inner system for a while, but sooner or later we can bring you to action and destroy every one of your units, and you know it.

"So *this* time, you're going to listen to me. You and I are going to sit down, face-to-face, and talk. And then you're going to do exactly what I was willing to let Clarence Maddox do— what I *would* have let him do, if the Fringers here in Jalal hadn't taken the decision out of my hands—and take my message and my data back to Sol.

"I have no intention of attacking the Sol System or any other Heart World system. I never did. But I do intend to do whatever I have to do to make you people *listen* to me. And, yes, there's going to have to be some redress of the Fringe's grievances. That has to be on the table, too. But that can be dealt with later. What matters now is the fact that the war we've been fighting against the League for sixty damned years isn't what we thought it was.

"You may think I'm a lunatic, and that's fine with me. But I need you to take my message back home, and we need to get this settled, one way or another, before even more of the Navy's ships and people kill each other. And if you're not willing to do that, then I will, by God, hunt down and kill every one of your remaining ships." His face was stone. "I don't want to, but if that's the only way to get through to you people, then as God is my witness, I'll *do* it.

"So you make up your mind, Rajenda. You decide what it's going to be. I'll be waiting for your call."

CHAPTER SEVENTEEN

Jalal Station
Jalal System
Terran Federation
December 9, 2552

"SO, THOSE ARE THE FIGURES," HARRISON O'HANRAGHTY SAID, tipping back in his chair in Terrence Murphy's comfortable suite, one deck up from Jalal Station's Central Command. "I wish to hell your brother-in-law had been even a bit more reasonable, but it could've been worse."

"It was plenty bad enough for me," Murphy said grimly. "There were over a hundred and fifty *thousand* Federation personnel aboard his battleships and battlecruisers, Harry. And another thirty-five hundred aboard just the FTLCs we destroyed outright. We killed somewhere over a hundred thousand of them. I don't see how it could have been a *lot* worse."

"We could have lost," O'Hanraghty said flatly. "In which case, the death toll would have been just as bad—if not worse—and your precious brother-in-law would have moved on to K-strike Crann Bethadh."

He held Murphy's eyes steadily, unflinchingly. Silence hovered between them for a long, tense moment, and then, unhappily, Murphy nodded.

"I know, Harry. I know!" He leaned back, his expression inexpressibly weary. "I hoped—prayed—it wouldn't come to this. But deep inside, I was always afraid it would. I think a coward part of me had to pretend I might be able to avoid it or I could never have even started this."

O'Hanraghty started a quick reply, then made himself stop. He suspected no one else in the entire galaxy knew Terrence Murphy as well as he did...including Terrence Murphy himself. There were things Murphy wasn't comfortable admitting about himself *to* himself, like the unflinching integrity, the absolute inability to evade his duty, that was the wellspring of his personality. The one thing Harrison O'Hanraghty had never seen anywhere in Terrence Murphy's makeup was a scrap of cowardice.

But, of course, that wasn't something he could say. Especially not at a moment like this.

"Well," he said instead, "it did happen, and pissed as I am at dear Rajenda, I doubt anybody else they sent would have been any more reasonable. And it does say some interesting things about the current balance of power, doesn't it?"

Murphy snorted, but he had to nod.

He'd arrived at Jalal Station with twelve FTLCs. He'd added Clarence Maddox's three carriers to his force, and two more carriers—all but one of the uncounted-for pickets in the Concordia and Acera sectors—had arrived to join him less than thirty-six hours after the battle.

And then there was TF 804.

Rajenda's parasites had been virtually annihilated, and four of his carriers had been destroyed or so brutally damaged there was zero chance they might be repairable. Of the remaining twenty-one, six had surrendered virtually undamaged, seven had taken damage but remained combat effective, and eight had been at least half wrecked. All of that last group were still FTL-capable (or could be made that way out of Jalal's resources), although their speed in wormhole space would be on the low side, but no one could conceivably consider them fit for action. They'd need the services of a fully equipped shipyard for that.

Effectively, however, Murphy now commanded thirty-three FTLCs, counting Harriet Granger's detached command. And the Terran Federation Navy's carrier strength—or at least the portion of it still immediately answerable to the Oval—had been reduced by thirty-*seven* units.

That was thirteen percent of its total carrier strength. And since twenty-five percent or so of the TFN carrier force was down for overhaul at any given moment, that meant Murphy's FTLCs were equal to fifteen percent of the Oval's available strength.

Only it was even worse than that, because a hundred and thirty of the Oval's remaining carriers were in First Fleet, deployed to the Beta Cygni Line. Which meant it had only fifty or so, total, that it could deploy against Murphy and the Free Worlds Alliance without gutting Beta Cygni. And *that* meant Murphy's carrier force was sixty-six percent as strong as the Oval's total currently available carriers.

No doubt the Oval was straining every sinew to get more FTLCs out of yard hands, but that would take time. And transferring additional strength from First Fleet to confront Murphy would risk catastrophic defeat by the Terran *League* Navy.

"At the moment," O'Hanraghty said in a carefully neutral tone, "nothing the Heart has could keep you from walking straight into the Sol System, Terry. Oh, we'd have to send the newly caught carriers back to New Dublin to pick up fresh parasites from the ones we captured from Xing, and the crews would have to adjust to League designs. For that matter, we'd be light on trained personnel—especially personnel we can trust. But with that many carriers and a shitload of Casúr Cogaidhs, you could be in Earth orbit dictating terms within . . . five months, outside."

"And the bloodbath on Old Terra would make the casualties out here look like a flea bite." Murphy shook his head. "If there's any hope of settling this without a body count that makes historians sick for the next two hundred years, we can't get it at the point of a gun, Harry. I've never had any intention of attacking the Heart, and you know it. Hell, we told Fokaides and Schleibaum that when we sent in our original report on Diyu! I can't change tack on that, for a lot of reasons. Including the way it would up the stakes where the Free Worlds Alliance is concerned. The minute I use *force majeure* to compel the federal government to accept some sort of surrender terms, I shoot any hope for the Federation's survival right in the head."

O'Hanraghty nodded, although in the quiet space behind his eyes, he wondered how long it would take Murphy to realize they'd already done that. That the Federation as it had originally been constituted was already dead . . . and had been, ever since the Five Hundred and the Heart Worlds turned the Fringers into serfs and cannon fodder. He couldn't begin to predict—yet—what would inevitably replace the moribund, shuffling zombie Terrence Murphy was determined to save, but he'd begun to suspect it would require an even greater sacrifice from Murphy than his friend had yet imagined.

"All right," he said out loud. "I knew that was a nonstarter before I brought it up, but it needed to be said. Because whether you're planning on doing it or not, you know damned well that as soon as Fokaides finds out what happened to Task Force Eight-Oh-Four, that's going to become the Heart's worst-case scenario. It's what they'd do in your place, so I guarantee they'll assume it's what *you'll* do. And that means they'll pull out all the stops to crush us and the entire Free Worlds Alliance as far away from Sol as they can do it."

"Of course they will."

Murphy closed his eyes and pinched the bridge of his nose. He sat that way for a moment, then inhaled sharply and lowered his hand.

"We have to try talking to them—again, Harry. Maybe they'll finally be scared enough, thinking about that worst-case scenario of yours, to actually listen for a change. More probably, they won't. But if there's any hope at all of a negotiated conclusion to this mess, I need to stay as far away from the Heart as I can. So, Jalal has to remain our contact point. We'll send dispatches to Sol, repeating our demands—including that they frigging well *talk* to us!—and reemphasizing that we are *not* taking advantage of our temporary ascendancy in combat strength to move against the Heart."

"And if they still won't talk to us?"

"In that case, I turn warlord," Murphy said harshly. O'Hanraghty's eyes popped wide, and Murphy chuckled. "Oh, I don't mean it the way the Five Hundred is throwing the accusation around! But if the Heart won't listen, then we start using some of this naval strength of ours to go calling on other Fringe sectors to extend an invitation on behalf of the Free Worlds Alliance. I've tried like hell to avoid encouraging this revolt to spread into a genuine revolution, but if they won't talk to us, I don't see any other choice."

"Terry, the Heart has seventy-five percent of the Federation's industry and two thirds of its total population. *And* it would have the interior position." O'Hanraghty shook his head, his expression somber. "Those are pretty heavy odds."

"Agreed." Murphy nodded. "And that's one reason I want, more than almost anything else in the universe, to avoid it. But, first, you know as well as I do that a lot of other Navy units would mutiny to come over to the Fringe at the drop of a hat if they only had the chance. What we've already seen is proof enough of that! And there's not a hell of a lot the Heart can do in the short term about replacing the Fringers in their crews, because there aren't nearly enough Heart Worlders in uniform. So the immediate, current military balance would shift steadily in our favor, at least until the Oval decides to uncover Beta Cygni, and you know how unlikely that is.

"But, secondly, and more importantly, a genuinely Fringe-wide rebellion would terrify the Five Hundred, and not just because of the Fringe." He shook his head. "Not every Heart Worlder belongs to the Five Hundred, you know. In fact, it represents at most two or three—certainly less than four at the absolute outside—percent of the total Heart World population. The wealthiest, most powerful less-than-four percent, true. The ones who effectively control all the federal levers of power, as well as the Federation's economy . . . at the moment. The thing is, though, Harry, that quite a lot of the Federation's citizens resent the hell out of the Five Hundred, whenever they think about it. And that sort of distribution is always subject to change if the other *ninety-six-plus* percent of the population is sufficiently motivated."

"That's true," O'Hanraghty said slowly. "But given the inequities you're talking about, and given how infuriated the Fringe is, a full-scale rebellion or civil war of the kind you're talking about would be an incredible bloodbath. Worse than anything in Old Terra's history, including the Russian and Chinese revolutions! *Any* of the Chinese revolutions."

"If it comes to that, yes." Murphy nodded. "But the thing is, the Five Hundred is driven by its desire for wealth and power and keeping that wealth and power for itself. By its vision of itself as the keepers of the keys for the entire Federation. And if the entire Federation goes up in flames, the Five Hundred goes up in flames right with it. So if I can't make them listen to reason, then I'll by God terrify them into listening to self-interest and self-preservation."

"All right," O'Hanraghty said again. "I think that strategy would be risky as hell, but as an ultimate, it's-all-gone-to-hell fallback, I could see it. In the meantime, though, I think we need to operate on the theory that it's at least possible they *will* be willing to talk to you. And the more likely corollary that we'll have to kick their asses again at least a time or two before they will."

"As soon as we send someone home, the Oval will know about our 'secret weapon,'" Murphy pointed out. "And as you just mentioned, the Heart has seventy-five percent of the Federation's industry. I have the strangest suspicion that they can outproduce us in Casúr Cogaidhs if they put their minds to it."

"Of course they can. But they won't come as a surprise to *us*, and you and I have been working on tactics to reflect that capability from the get-go. Yes, they'll have a significant impact on how battles are fought, but if both sides have them, it still comes down to concentration of force and competence of command, and at the moment, we have the edge in both of those."

"That's true." Murphy grimaced. "I wish we didn't have to think in those terms, but it *is* true."

"Then let me throw this out," O'Hanraghty said. "Diyu."

Murphy frowned.

"What about Diyu?" he asked after a moment.

"There's been plenty of time for the League to organize the withdrawal of its personnel from Diyu," O'Hanraghty said, and Murphy's frown deepened at the apparent side excursion.

"And?" he said.

"And I haven't seen Harriet Granger dropping sublight, have you?"

"No," Murphy said slowly.

"Well, if the Leaguies had turned up to collect their personnel, she would have blown the yard to keep them from putting it back online, and then hauled ass to New Dublin—or to here—to join us. The only reason we didn't *already* blow it was that we wanted it to rub in the Five Hundred's faces, so she damned well would have gotten it done before she pulled out. And we both know she's too smart and too competent to have let them mousetrap her division, which is the only way the League could have prevented that from happening. So, it would appear that, for reasons best known to the League, it isn't *going* to collect its personnel."

"What?" Murphy cocked his head. "Why wouldn't they? That's a lot of trained yard workers, Harry! And they're going to need working shipyards worse than ever after what we took away from them."

"Sure it is, but what happened to Diyu was a disaster, not just militarily, but politically. As a general rule, Terry, you do a pretty fair job as a political analyst, so think about this. The Eternal Forward Party was the driving force behind Diyu. We know that from the records we captured there, and, frankly, because they're the only ones who could have arranged it. And if we—you—hadn't come along and screwed their plans completely, those carriers would have cut loose in the Federation's rear areas, and the League would almost certainly have won the war. Huge kudos for Eternal Forward, new lock on power, and everybody's happy.

"But now what was supposed to be Eternal Forward's overwhelming, culminating triumph has turned into the greatest military disaster in League history. The physical plant in Diyu's lost to the League, no matter what, because Than knows perfectly well that, at the very least, you'll have left a caretaker force to destroy the yard the instant the League turns up to retake possession. So the only resource they could really recover would be the *workers*. And as an intel weenie who's studied the League for several decades—I wasn't *solely* a Rish nutcase, you know—I think it's entirely possible Eternal Forward would choose to let them rot rather than bring that kind of proof of failure home again."

"You really think they'd believe they could *hide* it?" Murphy asked skeptically.

"Wouldn't be all that hard, actually." O'Hanraghty shrugged. "They built the place under security that was so good nobody ever got even a *sniff* of it. The records we've already examined make it clear that once someone transferred into Diyu they didn't transfer back *out* again. And we just happen to have eliminated virtually every mobile unit, aside from Than's carriers, that ever based out of Diyu. So where, exactly, would the leak to the League news media—assuming there *was* any League news media that wasn't completely controlled by Eternal Forward—come from?

"As long as they don't bring any of those shipyard workers home, that is."

"What about Than?" Murphy asked, but his tone said he already knew how O'Hanraghty would answer.

"Than and his people are probably just as much dead men walking, as far as Eternal Forward is concerned, as you and I are where the Five Hundred are concerned, Terry. The Five Hundred can't let our report go public, not with any kind of official imprimatur. Than is in exactly the same position, and, frankly, I'll be amazed if he's not already dead."

"Damn." Murphy shook his head. "I'd hate that. The man's entirely too competent for my peace of mind, but he deserves better than that."

"Far be it from me to point out that that's true of quite a few people I could think of," O'Hanraghty said dryly. "Including two people sitting here in your office at the moment."

"Point taken," Murphy acknowledged with a chuckle. But then he cocked his head. "Where, exactly, have you been headed with all of this?"

"I'm headed to the possibility that Diyu could be the Free Worlds Alliance's hole card from hell," O'Hanraghty said flatly. "There's an entire highly trained workforce sitting there, abandoned by their own government. The yard itself is bigger than any single yard in the entire Federation. Hell, its capacity's at least as big as Venus Futures' entire Sol System operation, and it's even more heavily automated. It doesn't have the capacity to fabricate Fasset drives, but it can certainly *repair* them, and it has the foundries and the extraction industry to have built the hulls of every single one of the FTLCs the Rish were providing drive fans for. All we have to do is figure out how to convince that highly trained workforce to come over to our side."

"A nontrivial challenge, I would suspect." Murphy's tone was even drier than O'Hanraghty's had been a moment earlier.

"If it were easy, *anyone* could do it," O'Hanraghty shot back. "But I don't think it would be quite as hard as you may be thinking. First, by now they have to realize their ride home isn't coming. They've been abandoned, written off, and they'll never see their families again. That's got to affect their loyalty—to Eternal Forward, at least, if not to the concept of the Tè Lā Lián Méng itself.

"Second, they know you're essentially in rebellion against the federal government. I tend to doubt they'd be willing to accept that you're trying to *save* the Federation, even if we told them that. People judge other people's motives on the basis of previous experience, and their experience with Eternal Forward isn't likely to encourage a belief in selflessness on the part of anyone's political leadership. But even if they were to decide that was what you were trying to do, consider this. The more powerful we become, the greater the strength the Heart will ultimately be forced to divert if it ever hopes to defeat us. And every carrier diverted from Beta Cygni is one less for their own navy to face out along the line. So from that perspective, they'd actually be doing their patriotic duty by helping support the fragmentation of the Federation. And either way, we'd be the only hope they'd ever have of going home, whether because we somehow beat the League and *let* them go home, or because we help the League beat the Federation and it *takes* them home after it kicks the TFN's ass."

"Damn, Harry," Murphy said after a moment, his eyes a bit distant. "You make a fine snake oil salesman." He shook his head, and his eyes refocused. "But the really scary thing is I think you might be right. We might actually be able to pull that off. Of course, we've been inviting—*imploring*—the Oval to send an inspection team out to Diyu, so its existence isn't exactly a secret."

"And we've also been telling them Granger's under orders to blow the yard when the League transport force finally turns up," O'Hanraghty countered, then shrugged. "We've got the most detailed photographic records imaginable. We've got complete clones of most of their cyber systems. We've got captured examples of both League and Rish hardware, along with the holo record of our removing those examples from the warships we captured in Diyu. There's nothing an actual, physical examination of the yard could provide that that evidence doesn't already provide, Terry. Face it, anybody who'd believe us under any circumstances would have to be convinced by that mountain of evidence.

"So, in your next message to Olympia, you tell them that, regretfully, it will no longer be possible for them to examine the actual yard, since we were forced to destroy it rather than allow it to fall back into League hands. And then we send our damaged carriers off to Diyu, and when they get there, we lay the proposition before Captain Sunwar and his senior officers and see how they react.

"The worst that can happen is that they say 'no.' But if it should happen that they say 'yes'…"

He raised both hands, shoulder high, and smiled thinly.

CHAPTER EIGHTEEN

Jalal Station
Jalal System
Terran Federation
December 11, 2552

RAJENDA THAKORE LOOKED UP AS THE ADMITTANCE SIGNAL CHIMED.

It chimed again, and his mouth twisted in a sour smile.

I wonder what they'd do if I just ignored them? he wondered. *Somehow I doubt the polite fiction that I have a choice would last very long.*

It chimed a third time, and he grimaced and tapped the lock icon on the suite's control panel.

The door slid open, and his grimace disappeared into iron-faced immobility as his brother-in-law stepped through it. Looking past Murphy, he saw an armed Marine against the far bulkhead and snorted in bitter amusement. His palatial quarters were located in the flag officers' section of Jalal Station's transient quarters and were about as pleasant as a cage came. But they were still a cage. He could open their door only when someone asked for admittance from the outside, and that Marine in the passage didn't just happen to be standing there.

Murphy walked into the comfortably furnished day cabin and looked around, then turned his gaze back to Rajenda.

"Good morning," he said.

Rajenda gazed back in stony silence, and Murphy's lips twitched.

"Not talking to me won't accomplish much, Rajenda," he observed in an affable tone. "Except, I suppose, to give you some sort of obscure satisfaction. Besides"—the lip twitch turned into something that could only be called a smile—"think of all the really *cutting* things you want to say to me now that the opportunity's fallen in your way, as it were."

"There are quite a few things I'd like to say to you, now that you mention it," Rajenda replied after a moment. "I don't see much point, though. I'd only be wasting my breath on a dead man."

"Oh? You really think so?" Murphy strolled across the compartment and settled into an armchair that faced Rajenda's across a crystoplast coffee table that supported an ornate tea set. "And here I thought you were the POW and I was the admiral who'd kicked your sorry ass up one side and down the other."

Rajenda's upper lip curled back in a snarl before he could stop it, and his eyes blazed.

"You've just killed over a hundred thousand Federation military personnel," he said in a voice of frozen lava. "You're a mutineer, a traitor, and a mass murderer, and you've led all these other poor bastards into treason with you, which is going to end with them on gallows or breathing vacuum and their planets slagged by K-strikes! I don't really think you've got much in the way of accomplishments to brag about, Terry."

"Maybe all those things will happen...someday," Murphy said calmly. "But they aren't happening today. And the reason those thousands of Federation spacers and Marines are dead is because *you* were too fucking stupid to take me at my word. If I'd had my druthers, no one would've been killed. Hell, no one would even have stubbed his toe! But you couldn't let it happen that way, could you? You couldn't stand down even temporarily, long enough to talk. No, you had to make your attack run." His calm voice turned to iron. "How'd that work out for you, Rajenda? Refresh my memory."

Rajenda came halfway to his feet with a snarl, and Murphy looked at him with cold gray eyes.

"Sit...down," he said with icy, measured precision.

"Why?" Rajenda demanded. "Because you'll whistle up your Marine attack dog if I don't?"

"No, because I will take immense pleasure—believe me, at this moment you have no frigging *idea* how much pleasure—in personally ripping off both your arms and shoving them up your ass," Murphy told him, and Rajenda abruptly realized just how much fury truly blazed behind those level gray eyes.

For a moment—briefly—he thought about pushing it. But only *very* briefly. Rajenda Thakore was no coward, but he *was* a realist… and, like his sister, he had not inherited his father's height. He was well-muscled and fit, but so was Murphy—who was also twenty-two centimeters taller than he and outmassed him by over thirty percent. And whereas Rajenda had gone out for track and tennis at the Academy, Terrence Murphy had been captain of the unarmed combat team in both his junior and senior years.

Stillness hovered for a moment, and then he settled stiffly back into his chair and glared at his brother-in-law.

"Better," Murphy said, then pinched his nose and drew a deep breath.

"Actually, I'm sorry I said that," he continued. "Not because it's untrue, and not because there haven't been plenty of times before today when I *wanted* to say it. But because it's unproductive. And because as deeply and utterly as you have pissed me off on more occasions than I can count, I know you have a pretty damned good brain. The only challenge—and it's a big one—is getting you to use it."

"Funny, I was just thinking the same about you."

"Oh, I'm sure you were."

"So why are you wasting time talking to me? Where's the firing squad?"

"There isn't one." Rajenda widened his eyes, and Murphy snorted. "Trust me, there are plenty of people who'd pay good money to be included in your firing squad. For that matter, I've already shot half a dozen people who were 'executing' Heart Worlders after kangaroo courts, and I've got a dozen more under arrest awaiting trial. I'm pretty damned sure I still haven't caught up with all of the ones who'd *like* to've done that, either. So if I were interested in that sort of thing, I could find plenty of volunteers to wax your arrogant ass. Fortunately—for you, anyway—I'm not."

"So all of a sudden you're worried about blood on your hands? What about all of my spacers you murdered a few days ago?"

"I tried my damnedest to convince you to stand down," Murphy reminded him. "And after the battle, we recovered every single life pod and shuttle."

"Oh, really? In that case I guess you're not—technically—a war criminal; only a murderer. That's lots better!"

He sneered at Murphy, then shrugged brusquely.

"So, if you're not going to shoot me, what'll it be? A show trial, and then your Fringer lackeys get to hang me the way I understand they hanged Lipshen? That'd keep my blood off your hands, wouldn't it? Technically, at least. Or do you plan on holding me and all my surviving people for ransom?"

"Your 'surviving people' will be treated exactly as the Articles of War say we're supposed to treat POWs. Mind you, the Federation's record in that regard is almost as execrable as the League's. My 'Fringer lackeys' have had a little more practice with it than most of our personnel, though, since Crann Bethadh's currently babysitting over sixty thousand League spacers who surrendered to me in New Dublin. We've seen to it that the Articles of War were actually honored in their case, and we'll do the same for your people until this... unpleasantness can be cleared up and they can be repatriated."

Rajenda stared at him. Over *sixty thousand* Leaguie POWs? He was lying. He *had* to be lying! Even if there'd really been as many enemy carriers at New Dublin as he'd claimed, he'd have had to capture the League's entire parasite force effectively *intact* to have that many prisoners, and that was ridiculous! It had never happened *anywhere*! Those numbers had to be inflated. Besides...

"And me?" he demanded, shaking free of his thoughts.

"And you I'm sending home, Rajenda. Safe and whole. No conditions, except that I want you to take a message back to Fokaides and Schleibaum. One I want them to see, and the Oval to see, and the Cabinet to see, and everyone else in the Heart to see."

"Really?" Rajenda eyed him narrowly. "All right. You have my attention."

"I've had *Lelantos's* magazines emptied, and I'll be putting you aboard her. And when I do, you'll go back to Sol with the evidence of Rishathan lethal aid to the League and—"

"Please." Rajenda shook his head. "Don't insult my intelligence, Terrence. This isn't about the Rish, and it never was. This is entirely about the ego of a Survey officer at the ass-end of his relevance. Your governorship was the pinnacle of your mediocre career, and when you realized you'd return to whatever bottom-of-the-totem-pole position my father was willing—"

Murphy slammed a palm against the coffee table. One of the

tea set's cups leapt into the air, then crashed to the floor, and Murphy shook pain from his hand as he glared at his brother-in-law.

"Raj, you've been an asshole since the first day I met you. I've always wanted to tell you just how *big* an asshole you are, but I've been married to your sister long enough to know how much hell she'd've given me for telling you off. And that juice wasn't worth the squeeze. Now? Now the equation's different.

"It must be incredibly difficult for someone as smart as I know Simmy's brother has to be to turn himself into such an invincibly asinine idiot, although I suppose arrogance helps. God knows you've got plenty of *that*! But do you seriously think I chased down Rishathan smugglers out past the Blue Line just for the hell of it?" He barked a laugh. "I reported what we found aboard the *Val Idrak*—or did they send you out without bothering to share that with you?"

"Oh, please!" Rajenda rolled his eyes. "One tramp freighter, from which you *claim* to have recovered *one* singularity manifold which you *claim* 'someone' was supplying to the League out of the goodness of their hearts and that *might* have been manufactured by someone besides the League. And on the basis of that you took an entire goddamn sector out of compliance, Terrence!"

"And *because* of that, the League attacked New Dublin prematurely with the largest task force the TLN had committed to a single operation anywhere outside the Beta Cygni front in over forty years," Murphy replied. "And my people and I destroyed that fleet. Then we hunted down its lair and seized the shipyard that built it—and that was building another *fifty* FTLCs. That would have given them *sixty-two* carriers before New Dublin, Rajenda, and Eighth Fleet had exactly twenty-six. Even if Fokaides had called in everything else within fifty light-years of Sol, he could only have gotten it up to forty. So what do you think would have happened if a fleet fifty percent bigger than anything we could throw at it had gotten loose in the Federation's rear?" He glared at his brother-in-law. "I'll tell you what would have happened— they'd have killed *billions* of Federation citizens, Rajenda, and they'd have cut their way clear to Sol before anyone could have stopped them!

"And you think I did all of that, *prevented* that, just for the hell of it? Just because 'a Survey officer at the ass-end of his relevance' didn't have anything better to do? I did it because it was about frigging time at least one governor actually did his job and protected the people he was *supposed* to be protecting. And because I was willing to do the work to prove the Rish have been pulling strings in the background, probably since this entire war started."

Rajenda rolled his eyes.

"You're a smart man, Terrence. How you can possibly buy into all these lunatic conspiracy theories is beyond me, but—"

"Mostly because it's the truth," Murphy snapped, cutting him off sharply, then drew a deep breath.

"As I say, I'm sending you home," he said in a calmer tone, "and the trip's long enough that even someone like you may have time to recognize the truth when it bites you on the ass. You'll have plenty of time to review all the data logs and the scans, anyway. And all the yottabytes of data we pulled off the Diyu servers. And I'm sending Rish-designed components we recovered from the Diyu yard along with you."

"Oh, goody. Homework!" Rajenda shook his head. "Excuse my skepticism. When I received orders from the Oval to wormhole out and put down your little rebellion, they somehow neglected to give me any details about Rish or League superweapons. How odd. I would have thought that if there'd *been* any evidence, they'd have shared it with the fleet commander sent out to deal with you. Oh, wait—I used that 'evidence' word, didn't I? And I didn't put the word 'manufactured' in front of it."

"So all of this is a fabrication?"

"Catching on, are you?" Rajenda's tone oozed sarcasm. "But if they didn't tell me all about your...let's be polite and call them 'fantasies' instead of 'out-and-out fucking lies,' they did tell me about how you'd abandoned your oaths to the Federation. And that was true even before you murdered Federation officers and marshals when they tried to arrest you for it."

"Schleibaum and the Oval tried to arrest me on false charges, and the attempt left several good men dead, including the President of New Dublin."

"Mm-hmm." Rajenda cocked his head. "I could swear I've heard something like that before. Taking notes from Governor Butler, are you?"

"Jerome Butler was at best a fool and at worst really *was* a traitor," Murphy said. "Gobelins didn't deserve what it got, but whatever their motives, he and his supporters really were trying to secede from the Federation and he really was trying to set up as a warlord. That's not what I want, Rajenda. I want the truth about the Rish to come out, and after that—"

"Will you *please* stop blathering idiotic conspiracy theories at me! At least respect my intelligence enough to admit what you're really after!"

"It's not a 'theory' where the Rish are concerned," Murphy said flatly. "Not anymore, anyway. It took them and the League at least—*at least*, Rajenda—ten years to build the shipyards we took out. And that means the Rish have been helping to prop the League up for a minimum of ten years, and probably a hell of a lot longer, and the Federation's bled every day for it."

"You say that like it should matter to me." Rajenda leaned back. "I didn't come home from the Beta Cygni front because of the Rish. Hell, I didn't come home because of *you*! Your insanity was only the welcome home prize waiting for me when I got there to tell the Oval that Admiral LeBron and First Fleet had broken through to Kellerman. *Kellerman*, Terrence! We haven't been that deep into League territory since the first three years of the war. LeBron sent me home for reinforcements to exploit the opening, to drive all the way to Kaoshing. We were *that* close—and now it's all gone! Thanks to *you*!"

"And taking out Diyu and the fleet they were building there's hurt *them* even worse than your idiocy *here* has hurt the Federation!" Murphy snapped. "We've cut the main conduit for Rishathan support for the League, and one look at the size of the Diyu yards is proof of how close to the bone they have to've cut their forces out in Beta Cygni. They couldn't have freed up the resources any other way. Hell, that's probably the reason LeBron was *able* to break through to Kellerman! And we can *end* the war with the League when we expose the Rish. Anyang won't have any choice but to come to the table when we point out how their logistical support's been—"

"Stop with the 'we'!" Rajenda snarled. "There *is* no 'we.' There's the Federation, and there's your rebellion. You think the Oval or the Five Hundred will give two shits about the League when they find out you've carved away more sectors and more planets in four months than the League's taken in *fifty years*? And let's not forget the domino effect, Terrence! I'd bet my rank the Five Hundred would let the League have everything from Kellerman to Bellerophon if it meant keeping the Fringe under control. They'll call home however much firepower it takes, and the hell with Beta Cygni, and when they do, the Leaguies will smash right through the front. That's what you've done, Terrence. You've lost the entire war with the League. Decades of sacrifice, all flushed away because of your ego."

"This isn't just about me, Rajenda." Murphy's voice was calm now, almost dispassionate. "The Free Worlds Alliance didn't secede from the Federation because I asked them to follow me. They did it because they're sick of sacrificing their lives, their futures, and—especially—their *children* to the Five Hundred. If I'd surrendered to Lipshen, New Dublin and the rest of Concordia would still have done *exactly* what it's done. And if I'd surrendered to you here in Jalal, when you demanded it, nothing would be different. Except that the Five Hundred would have to contend with the fact that it had given the Fringe a martyr instead of a living, fallible man like me."

"Oh, it *is* about you. Don't shield yourself behind those traitors. There's a warrant for your arrest for malfeasance, corruption, and theft. You were looking at decades in prison when you finally had to face the music! But now this rebellion you've whipped up gives you an excuse to avoid the consequences of your own actions, doesn't it?" Rajenda shook his head again, his expression disgusted. "I told Simron not to marry you."

"You really are a one-trick pony, aren't you, Rajenda?" Murphy asked wearily. "Still *that* pissed off because she told you to pound sand?"

"I told her not to marry you because there was nothing remarkable about you, Terrence. Your sole claim to fame was your grandfather's legacy. Survey? Seriously? *My* sister married a Survey Corps *bevakoof*? Not even a *Battle Fleet* officer? I told her it was demeaning—humiliating! But you! Father gave you a path to actual relevance. To a spot in the Five Hundred—towards the bottom, even married into my family, to be honest, but still a spot—which was more than you'd ever have achieved on your own. And that wasn't enough for you?"

"You've been a Battle Fleet officer since you were a midshipman," Murphy said. "Remind me which one of us just won the second or third largest fleet engagement the Federation's fought in the last forty years?"

"You—You miserable—" Rajenda cut himself off. His jaw clenched and his nostrils flared. "There were variables I couldn't allow for," he bit out, finally.

"It was my impression that a *competent* officer did his damnedest to make sure there'd be 'variables' his opponent couldn't allow for. And to assume his opponent was doing the same thing to him."

Rajenda glared at him, and Murphy sighed.

"Look, one more time, this isn't about my ego, Raj. We can stop the Federation from tearing itself apart—*and* end the war with the League—if we just keep our minds open and commit to an honest dialogue that tries to reach some sort of compromise."

"'Compromise'?" Rajenda repeated incredulously.

"Compromise," Murphy repeated. "Passions within the FWA are...elevated, right now. Their star systems have tried for decades to get some sort of redress from the federal government and from the Five Hundred. And every time they've tried, the *best* that happened was that they got ignored. Most of the time, they got another kick in the teeth, or another Gobelins. So, finally, they'd had enough. It wasn't the Battle of New Dublin that kicked this off, Rajenda—it was *Inverness*. It was another inhabited Fringe planet abandoned to die by the Navy that was supposed to defend it. What the Battle of New Dublin did was to put me in a position to at least try to be a restraining influence, but the secession Olympia is looking at right now would have happened whether I'd been sent to New Dublin or not."

"Oh, of course it would have."

"If you'll stop and use the brain that—Jalal Station aside—is normally capable of analyzing tactical data, you'll realize exactly why that's true," Murphy said. "And you'd also realize the Free Worlds Alliance can still be brought back into the fold if Olympia—and the Five Hundred—are willing to change."

"Are you telling me this as the Alliance's warlord?" Rajenda asked.

"I'm telling you this as the voice of sanity. Look, the Fringers—the Alliance—aren't fools. Even if every Fringe sector united to form a single star nation, its economy would be a train wreck compared to the Heart, given the way the Five Hundred's kept most of the Federation's heavy industry deep in the Heart. Amazing how that just happened to deprive the Fringe of the industrial muscle that might have let it break away."

"You mean it 'just happened' to keep critically valuable assets out of range of League attacks, don't you?" Rajenda shrugged. "Seems like a sensible policy to me."

"That made a nice, tight rationalization, at least in the beginning, didn't it? But over the last thirty years?" Murphy snorted contemptuously. "The Five Hundred haven't been protecting their assets from the League, Rajenda—they've been putting them out of range to be seized and nationalized by Fringe System governments!"

Rajenda started to reply, then sat back with another shrug, and Murphy leaned forward, resting his forearms on his thighs.

"What the Free Worlds Alliance really wants are peace talks with the League," he said. "They want amendments to the Constitution to protect the Fringe, keep its citizens—its sons and daughters—from paying the blood price of the Five Hundred's war. Yes, the Five Hundred would have to make economic concessions, as well, some that might cost them as much as—oh, ten, even fifteen, percent of what they've squeezed out of the Fringe. But if there's any hope at all of healing this breach, then the Federation has to be willing to make those concessions."

"Which would undoubtedly include amnesties all around?" Rajenda smiled thinly. "Do you want a crown, too? A laurel wreath?"

"I want the dying to stop, Rajenda. Trust me, I've seen way too much of it already.

"I walked the streets of Inverness. I *smelled* the bodies of *ninety-six* percent of a Federation planet's population, rotting despite the cold. The body bags were stacked up like cordwood, in piles taller than *I* am, and when there were too few left alive to stack them, they just rotted where they fell. *That's* what I saw on Inverness, and I saw it because a frigging coward used the cover of his standing orders to run for it instead of defending them.

"And then I saw...I saw my own son taken off a broken cruiser on the edge of death, when the same murderous bitch came after Crann Bethadh. And now I've fought a pitched battle with you, and between us we've killed another hundred thousand people. I won't lie and say I've never disliked you, Rajenda—you've been way too arrogant an asshole ever since I've known you for me to pretend I haven't. But I've never *hated* you, and I sure as hell never wanted to be firing the odd thousand missiles at your flagship. I'd just as soon not repeat the experience."

"The consequences are starting to compound, are they?" Rajenda smile turned even thinner. "You ever think what your actions have done to my family? Your wife?"

"Of course I have. But whatever I may think of you—or vice versa—I know your father will do everything in his power to protect her and our children."

"What? Is this your attempt to rope Father into your madness? Set him up as up some sort of back channel for communications?" Rajenda's eyes narrowed. "We're much too prominent for that, Terrence, and there's no way in hell I'm going there for you. Have O'Hanraghty or whatever cabal of conspirators is running at your heels try that."

"I'm not asking you—or Kanada—to be a back channel," Murphy said. "I'm sending you back to the Oval openly, with my evidence. And, frankly, if Schleibaum or Fokaides—or the Five Hundred—have the brainpower of a gnat between them, they'll realize the Rish connection is the key to settling this. It's the rallying point they can throw out for the Heart and the Fringe, the common threat—besides war against the League—that can refocus their animosities and hatreds. It'll have to be approached side by side with those concessions, but it can provide a unifying focus, one with none of the sideband issues of the League War, if they'll only take advantage of it."

"You're an idiot." Rajenda shook his head. "No one will believe any of this. You think the Five Hundred will give up one iota of what they control because of *your* claims about the Rish?"

"What part of it don't you believe?"

"*Any* of it!" Rajenda waved both hands in frustration. "Even assuming the odds at New Dublin were remotely as heavy as you're claiming—which I doubt—it still could've been a Hail Mary from the League because it knew the Beta Cygni front was beginning to crumble. *Which—*" he added pointedly "—LeBron's breakthrough to Kellerman demonstrates it is—or was, before your . . . minor diversion of combat power."

"The hulls we destroyed at New Dublin were all new construction," Murphy replied. "You don't have to take my word for it; the evidence is right there in the orbital breakers over Crann Bethadh. And at the moment I occupy the League's shipyard at Diyu." He shrugged. "I don't know how much longer that'll be true, because it's too close to the League. My picket doesn't begin to have the firepower to stand off a serious League effort to retake it, and one of those just about has to be in the offing. When it comes, my people are under orders to destroy the yard before they pull out, because that's the best we can do. For that matter, that could already have happened and we just don't know about it yet. But if it hasn't, what if you could see it all with your own eyes before I send you back to Earth?"

"You could have a Rishathan matriarch lay an egg in front of me and then hatch out the League President and have him admit everything, and it wouldn't make a bit of difference. The Fringe is in revolt, Terrence. The lizards don't matter."

"They matter a hell of a lot more than you seem to realize."

"You're entitled to your opinion," Rajenda said sardonically.

They sat in silence for over a minute, and then Rajenda raised an eyebrow.

"So, you'll send me home in *Lelantos*," he said. "Then what?"

"I thought I'd made that clear. I'd rather negotiate an end to this madness than see a new war that lasts decades and accomplishes only more bitterness and death. So, obviously, I want you to tell them to send somebody back out here to do the negotiating. I realize they aren't going to fall all over themselves to do that. Not after they've pushed themselves so far into the corner. I imagine the panic when they find out what happened to you will throw a little grit into the works. So you can tell them I'll give them a thirty-day window before I assume they're unwilling to do that."

"And when your time window runs out and they tell you to piss up a rope, instead?"

"That would be just about par for the course for them, wouldn't it?" Murphy grimaced. "Let's just say I'm prepared to take this to the next level if I have to."

"Which would be...what?" Rajenda asked, and Murphy snorted.

"If I told you what my next move will be, would you believe me?"

"You're an idiot, but you're not a big enough idiot to tell me that. For that matter, I'm not a big enough idiot to believe anything you did tell me. Not sure why I bothered to ask," Rajenda said, and, for the first time, they actually smiled at one another.

"You said Callum was hurt," Rajenda said after a moment. "How's he doing?"

"Nothing a trip to a cloning clinic can't fix once we get him home, but at the moment, he's still in a lot of discomfort." Murphy grimaced. "Even the prostheses out here aren't as good as those in the Heart, and he's refused the more expensive augmentations that *are* available until every vet can have the same opportunity. Just tell Simron he's well. The more details she hears, the more she'll worry."

Rajenda sniffed and leaned back, resting his right ankle on his left knee.

"Simron," he said. "You ever consider what all this is doing to my little sister?"

Murphy looked away and his mouth tightened.

"I only ask because this—" Rajenda waved a hand over his head "—is the end of her life, Terrence. She's a pariah now, thanks to you. She'll never have a career in any business connected to the Five Hundred, or anywhere else in the Federation, again. Not when her husband's a traitor."

"You don't know that," Murphy said, and Rajenda laughed.

"The hell I don't! I've been neck-deep in the Five Hundred's backstabbing and whisper campaigns for my entire life. She's *done*, Terrence. You flushed her life away for this. So what's she going to do now? Her only hope is that my father can convince her to publicly denounce you and get a speedy divorce. And don't think you'll get anything in the settlement, in case you're hoping."

"You'd like that, wouldn't you?" Murphy's voice was icy again.

"Of course I would! She never should've married someone outside the Five Hundred in the first place. Your grandfather's family name sure as hell isn't worth the suffering you're putting *my* family through!"

"You probably won't believe it, but I'd prefer not putting even *you* through this wringer," Murphy said. "I definitely regret what it's doing to your father. And I'd give my right arm not to have done it to Simmy." He looked into Rajenda's eyes. "But some things are bigger than me. They're even bigger than my love for her. I've had Simron's support for our entire married life, and unlike you, she'll understand—and admit—the truth when she hears it."

"You go on and convince yourself of that," Rajenda growled. "Deep inside, you know better. But at least Father can probably shield her from any direct repercussions, as long as she shows even a modicum of good sense. Vyom, too, probably."

"Have you heard anything from them?"

"Nothing dated after your mutiny." Rajenda shrugged.

"Well, when you do, you'll find out it's not *all* bad news," Murphy said. "Vyom's engaged."

"What? To whom? The Kirchner Dynamics girl he brought to that launch celebration at the yards?" Rajenda snapped his fingers several times. *"Ingrid,"* he said as he came up with the name.

"To her, yes." Murphy nodded.

"Well, I didn't know. But I *do* know it's over now," Rajenda shook his head. "The Kirchners haven't married for love since the first Fasset drive went online. And then you went and did all this?" He waved a hand in a sweeping gesture. "Didn't consider *that,* did you?"

"I was kind of preoccupied trying to save the odd billion or so human lives," Murphy said. "To be honest, I didn't know about the engagement until after we hit Diyu, but even if I had, I couldn't have put my son's happiness ahead of my responsibility to save lives and try to finally *end* this bloodbath. You keep talking about my ambition and my ego, but you've known me for more than thirty years. You *know* this hasn't been an easy decision for me, Rajenda, and you know Simmy is the reason it hasn't. It sure as hell wasn't any sense of loyalty to the *Five Hundred*! So don't pretend you don't know I thought long and hard about it—and her—before I made it. You, though . . . Did you pause for even a moment to consider what would happen to *your* relationship with her before you accepted the order to come out here and blow me out of space?"

"What I considered was that it was an opportunity for her to save face and a way for me to protect my family and Venus Futures," Rajenda said. "A man shoots his own dog."

"I was never your responsibility, Rajenda. But now you're mine."

"Obviously." Rajenda shrugged. "So do with me as you will."

"I've already told you what I'm doing with you. And I've told you what I want you to do once you get home." It was Murphy's turn to shrug. "What's so mysterious about that?"

"That's it? No parole? No gentleman's agreement that I won't return to the battlefield?"

"Why would I want that? I know how to beat you, after all," Murphy said with a smile. Then the smile faded. "No gentleman's agreement. And I'm not sending back any messages for Simron or the kids with you. It'd be too easy for the Five Hundred to manipulate my words for their own purposes. But tell them I love them . . . if you're willing."

"I'll do that," Rajenda said. "For them, more than for you."

"Thank you," Murphy said with quiet sincerity, and Rajenda grimaced.

"This could go easier—for them, at least—if you don't come any closer to the Heart Worlds," he pointed out.

"I already told you I don't intend to do anything of the sort . . . as long as the Five Hundred's willing to send someone out here with the power to look at my evidence and negotiate with me."

"And after they refuse to do that, which you and I both know they inevitably will?"

"In that case, you—and they—will find out what I'll do next when I *do* it, won't you?" Murphy showed his teeth for a moment, then stood.

"Take care, Rajenda," he said. "Godspeed."

Then he turned and walked back out the door.

CHAPTER NINETEEN

Jalal Station
Jalal System
Terran Federation
December 13, 2552

"I HAVE TO SAY, I DIDN'T EXPECT THIS TO TURN UP QUITE THIS soon," Harrison O'Hanraghty said.

"This *soon*?" Callum repeated.

"Oh, it was inevitable," O'Hanraghty said. "Maybe not from Bellerophon, but from *somewhere*, Callum. Assuming Prime Minister Schleibaum—and the rest of the Five Hundred, of course—were as frigging stupid as usual, that is. The one way they could have *possibly* headed it off was to show even a trace of willingness to admit the Fringe's grievances and get the word out that they had. Which, of course, was the one thing in the universe they could be absolutely counted upon not to do."

"Harry's right, I'm afraid, son," Murphy said sadly. "I never wanted this to spread beyond Concordia, but from the moment New Dublin went 'out of compliance,' other Fringe Worlds were bound to follow suit. But, like Harry says, I thought we'd have more time. Probably months more time. I certainly never anticipated someone as far away as Bellerophon might find out about it this quickly."

"So what do we do about it now that they have?" Callum asked after a moment.

"Admiral, with all due respect, I don't see any choice but to back President Dewar," Esteban Tremblay said from the far end of the briefing room table.

Murphy raised an eyebrow at him, and Tremblay snorted harshly.

261

"Trust me, Sir, I know exactly how surprised you must be to hear me saying that. And a few months ago, you *wouldn't* have heard me saying it. But you were right, that first day in New Dublin. The last thing the Federation needs is a civil war brought about by the way the Fringe's been used and abused, and that was exactly what would've happened sooner or later—probably sooner—even if you'd never been sent out to Concordia. I knew that even before you rubbed my nose in it, whether I wanted to admit it or not. Now?" He shrugged. "I don't know if the Federation can be saved. Frankly, there are nights I'm pretty sure it can't, and that someday the history books will look at you and the rest of us and decide we're the ones who flushed it down the tubes. But it's headed that way anyhow. You rubbed my nose in *that*, too. And if there's anyone in the entire rotten system who might be able to stop that, you're that man."

O'Hanraghty's eyebrows rose far higher than Murphy's had, and Tremblay barked a laugh.

"Don't think for a moment that I enjoy agreeing with you about *anything*, Harry! You have been *such* a prick for so damned long that it comes really, really hard to admit you might have had even a scintilla of accuracy on your side. Unfortunately, that doesn't change anything. And I'm not saying I think the Admiral has a *good* chance of pulling this off. I'm just saying that I know for certain no one *else* does, and I can't just sit by and watch the shipwreck without at least trying."

"Commodore—Steve, that means a lot," Murphy said quietly. "Not listening to you polish up my halo, because God knows if there are any halos around here, they're not mine! But because that's why all of us"—a wave of his hand took in the starships beyond *Ishtar*'s hull—"are out here. To at least try to stop the shipwreck. And there's nothing I can ever say or do to thank all of you for helping me try."

"Believe me, Sir, if I thought there was any other option, any other way to do it, I wouldn't be here," Tremblay said frankly. "As it is...?"

He raised both hands, palm uppermost, and shrugged, and Murphy nodded back to him, then looked at Callum.

"As the Commodore's just pointed out, I don't see any option but to back Dewar and the Council, either," he told his son. "And the good news is that with your uncle headed back to Sol, it will be a while—probably a pretty *long* while—before Fokaides and

Schleibaum send any new task forces off to retake Jalal. Especially after Rajenda tells Fokaides about the Casúrs."

"In some ways, I hate that we had to let that little surprise out of the bag, Terry," O'Hanraghty said. "Oh, it's not like we had any choice, and no 'secret weapon' stays secret forever. Not if it's going to do you any good, anyway! But the next time, they'll have a clue it's coming."

"Worse than that, they're not idiots," Callum pointed out. "Well, maybe *politically*, but not in most other ways. And it's not like figuring out how the Casúrs work will take a bunch of geniuses."

"Exactly," his father said with a grimly approving nod. "That's been part of my thinking all along, and, frankly, that's the worst part of Bellerophon's timing. It would be so much better from our perspective if we could force the pace on Schleibaum, make her negotiate with us *now*. I didn't have any choice but to send Rajenda back with a *request* that she send representatives out here to meet with us—not if there's going to be any chance of convincing Heart World public opinion that I'm truly not some crazed, megalomaniac warlord. We have no choice but to look as much like the voice of reason as a batch of mutinous rebels possibly can. And that means *being* the voice of reason. Of approaching this without bloodthirsty threats and promises of retribution in hopes they'll read the writing on the wall and meet us at least part way. Show at least a scrap of willingness to listen and *do* something to repair the damage."

"And how much chance of that was there ever, really?" O'Hanraghty asked gently.

"Not much," Murphy conceded. "And that's why my thinking was that if we hadn't heard back from them by the deadline I gave Rajenda, we'd move on Sol itself."

The other people around the briefing room table stiffened, and he shook his head.

"I have no more intention of attacking Sol than I've ever had. But if they reject every offer to actually sit down and talk, our only option is to take it to the next level, and they gave us an opening when they pulled Rajenda's units out of the Reserve. They can't have much left to back up Home Fleet. In fact, unless they've got a lot more in the pipeline coming back from Beta Cygni than anything in Rajenda's databases indicated, we've got at least parity with Home Fleet *and* anything of the Reserve they may have called in to help cover Sol. So if we turn up—especially with the Casúr Cogaidhs, before they have time to 'figure out' how they work and put their own version into production—it'll come as an enormous shock to the public's system. I'm sure the Five Hundred's pet news channels have painted all of us as bloodthirsty, barbarous, mutinous monsters, but there's a downside to that, because if we turn up at Sol, there's no way they could possibly jam or block our own transmissions without completely shutting down the system datanet. Once we're in near-Sol space and they can't drive us out of broadcast range of the planets, we can *hammer* the news channels. We've got enough power to burn through anything they could put up to stop us, and for all their wealth and power, the Five Hundred is only a minute slice of the total population, and most Heart Worlders are already cynical as hell about the accuracy and honesty of the news they receive. If we saturate the news channels, 24-7, with the truth against that background, the Five Hundred's credibility will nosedive. And if that happens, their ability to control events will erode in a hurry. I don't really want to do that, either, because the truth is that the Fringers aren't the only people the Five Hundred's been abusing for so long, and if it goes as ugly as it has the potential to turn—as ugly, frankly, as the Five Hundred *deserves* for it to go—then it's likely to be messy—and bloody—as hell."

He shook his head sadly.

"That's another reason I hoped so hard that Schleibaum would listen to us before it reached this point. On the basis of everything we've seen so far, though, that's not going to happen. Or, at least, neither she nor the rest of them are going to listen until they realize we really can get the word directly out to all those proles they've been controlling for so long *and they can't stop us from doing it.* Maybe, I figured, if I put it to them in those terms, they'd finally recognize the Sword of Damocles hanging over them and grow a working IQ. I didn't *expect* it, but I figured it was our last shot short of that.

"So, what I was planning to do, was to leave by mid-May with a big enough detachment to make that point to them. But I can't do that now. Not with this." He tapped the slate lying on the table with Dewar's messages.

"In fairness," O'Hanraghty began, "Bellerophon isn't—"

"Yes, it is, Harry." Murphy's tone was quiet, but firm. "If everything went the way Xeneas hoped, then he's got all of the Cyclops pickets and nobody in the Heart knows a thing about it yet. But when was the last time anyone's plans worked out exactly the way he'd hoped? Or did you and I *expect* to be sitting here at Jalal with a mutinous fleet going eyeball-to-eyeball with the entire rest of the Federation?"

"Point," O'Hanraghty conceded.

"The odds are that Xeneas didn't get away with it clean," Murphy went on, letting his eyes circle the table. "Maybe one of the FTLCs got away. Maybe he succeeded in taking every unit of the Bellerophon picket but there was a courier boat or a passenger liner or a freighter in the wrong place at the wrong time when 'his' carriers went to call on the other pickets. I can't *know* that's happened, but I'm as certain as I'm sitting here that *something's* happened, and there are a billion people in the Bellerophon System, alone. If I couldn't let Xing K-strike Crann Bethadh, how in God's name can I let the Federation carry out Standing Order Fifteen against Odysseus? And completely leaving aside the moral implications, if I let that happen, how could I possibly expect anyone in the Fringe to believe me when I tell them I'm an honest broker they can trust to at least try to convince the Five Hundred to treat them like human beings again?"

There was silence for a moment, then he inhaled deeply.

"Esteban, I hate to do this to you, but I'm leaving you and your division here at Jalal. With all the sublight parasites and Casúr Cogaidhs to back you, you should be able to handle anything the Oval has left to throw at you, at least in the short term."

"Does that mean what I think it means?" O'Hanraghty asked.

"If it means you think I'm taking everything else to Bellerophon, yes," Murphy said flatly.

"That might be just a bit of overkill," the chief of staff pointed out. Not in the tone of someone disagreeing, so much as in the tone of a chief of staff making certain his CO had considered all the implications.

"It almost certainly will be," Murphy replied. "And everyone in Bellerophon—and all the rest of the Cyclops sector—will realize that just as well as you do, Harry. Which means they'll know the Free Worlds Alliance responded just as quickly as it could and just as heavily as it could, even with zero warning we might be needed. Trust me, when word of that spreads through the rest of the Fringe, it'll be like applying a spark to a jet of hydrogen."

"But—"

"But I've been focused on keeping as tight a handle on this as I could. On trying to prevent it from turning into such an obviously existential threat to the Five Hundred that they automatically reached for the biggest hammer they could find," Murphy said unflinchingly.

"Pretty much, yes," O'Hanraghty agreed with a nod.

"Well, old friend, that's because you and I—or I, at least— were hopelessly overoptimistic when we set out." Murphy pinched the bridge of his nose. "Maybe if things had gone the way we'd originally hoped, it wouldn't be *quite* this bad, but it probably would've ended up someplace close to here, anyway. Maybe— *maybe*—we could've still kept it under control if Rajenda had been willing to talk instead of attacking. But the truth is, we probably never had a chance once the Fringers snatched the ball out of our hands exactly the way they had every damned right to do. And Xeneas's seen that sooner and more clearly than you and I did. Or, maybe not sooner and more clearly than *you* did."

He lowered his hand and smiled crookedly at his friend.

"I know you've been pushing harder and faster than I wanted to go, Harry. Maybe it was idealism, maybe it was cowardice, an unwillingness to look the truth in the eye, but Xeneas won't let me do that any longer. He's right. The Fringe *is* going up in flames, and there's no way in the universe anyone—not Schleibaum, not Fokaides, not the Five Hundred, and not you and I—can stop that from happening now.

"So the way I see it, the only option we have now is to stop trying to prevent it from happening and get behind it and push, instead. It's New Dublin all over again on a bigger scale. The only way we can exert *any* control over where this goes and how well—or badly—it turns out is to prove to the Fringe that we have its back and prove to the Heart that neither the Fringe nor this fleet is going anywhere until the Fringe's grievances are addressed . . . one way or the other.

"I can't move directly on Sol the way I'd planned, not with Bellerophon and Cyclops at risk behind us. So instead, my only option is to move to Bellerophon's rescue, instead, and convince Cyclops and all the rest of the Fringe to *trust* me. Because if I do that, and if I can prove to Schleibaum and Fokaides and the rest that I have, then maybe—just maybe—a big enough hint of sanity will peek through to stop this from turning into an actual civil war that completely destroys the Terran Federation."

CHAPTER TWENTY

Ithaca House
City of Kórinthos
Planet Odysseus
Bellerophon System
Terran Federation
December 14, 2552

KONSTANTINOS XENEAS LOOKED UP FROM HIS QUIET CONVERSA-
tion with Justine Von Undingen as Menelaos Tolallis and the trio
of Navy officers followed Erasmia Samarili into the secure bunker
buried deep under Ithaca House. The other civilians seated around
the long, polished table in the palatial, subterranean conference
room turned their heads, following his gaze, and all conversation came to a halt—and the tension level ratcheted upward—as
he rose in greeting.

"Mr. President," Tolallis said in his best formal tone as Xeneas
extended a hand.

"General," Xeneas replied, then turned to the Navy officers.

"Commodore Carson." He held out his hand to the dark-
skinned, blond-haired FWA officer, then looked past her at Captain
Mariaxuri Errezola and Achilleas Rodoulis. "Captain Errezola,
Captain Rodoulis."

"Mr. President," Lauren Carson replied for all of them, and
he waved at the empty chairs awaiting them.

He settled back into his own seat as they found their places,
then circled the table with his gaze before he returned his attention to Tolallis and Carson.

"Obviously, we're glad all of you could make it down from your ships," he said then. "I know you won't be able to do that once we get closer to Naxos—" he saw Carson's lips quirk; he'd been surprised she'd already known the name of the island where the invading Persian army had landed on its way to the Battle of Thermopylae in 492 BC "—and I certainly don't want to take you away from training time between then and now. But face-to-face discussions and briefings are still better than even the best comm conference."

"That's certainly true from a morale perspective, Mr. President," Carson said with a small smile. "And—" her smile grew broader "—anything that boosts morale is a decided plus just now."

Several of those present chuckled, and if those chuckles were just a bit strained, Xeneas couldn't blame them. On the other hand, they were far less strained than they'd been before Aikaterini Karalaki's return from New Dublin aboard Errezola's FTLC.

The Cyclops Sector's other star systems' response to Bellerophon's defiance had been more favorable than Xeneas had dared to hope. There still hadn't been time to bring the sector's smaller, more distant systems up to speed, because they simply had too few FTL hulls for that, but they'd contacted the major systems: Cyclops, Achilles, Cerberus, Dordogne, Espeadas, Loire, Minotaur, and Mulhacén.

Xeneas had scarcely been surprised when Cyclops rejected any possibility of joining Bellerophon. Sector Governor Utada was a Heart Worlder who'd been chosen for his position on the basis of his unswerving loyalty, and Steropes, the system's habitable planet, had a far higher concentration of federal enforcement agencies and their armed personnel than any of the sector's other systems. The fact that System President Hastings had married into the Five Hundred had probably played at least a small part in the system's decision, as well.

Espeadas had declined to send a delegate to Bellerophon. Xeneas suspected System President Borobia *would* have signed on with the secessionists if not for his lively fear of what the Heart would do to Bellerophon, and he expected Espeadas to be along shortly...if the secession stood up.

All of the others had at least sent plenipotentiary delegations to Bellerophon's Secession Convention, although so far only Minotaur, Mulhacén, and Loire had actually signed the Declaration of Secession. Assuming they all survived the next month or so, he anticipated that the other delegations would sign on, especially once their system governments discovered that the Free Worlds Alliance had offered the entire sector both admission to the Alliance and military assistance.

Of course, first they had to do that surviving, he thought grimly.

"If everyone's agreeable, I thought we'd ask General Tolallis and Commodore Carson to bring us up to speed on their side of the shop," he said. "There are a lot of civil and political issues we still need to iron out, but those will be relevant only if our military personnel can keep us alive."

He bestowed a wintry smile upon his fellows, then nodded to Tolallis.

"General?"

"With your permission, Mr. President," the general said, "I'd prefer to let Commodore Carson and Captain Rodoulis lay out the Navy side of our position before we get into the planetary side."

"That sounds more than reasonable," Xeneas said, and cocked his head at Carson. "Commodore?"

"Actually, Mr. President, I think it would be best to let Captain Rodoulis cover the basic naval position before I offer my credit's worth. As we say back home on Adenauer, he's from around these parts, and I'm not."

Several people surprised themselves with another round of chuckles, and Carson smiled tightly, green eyes touched with what looked like genuine amusement of her own. But then the smile faded.

"The truth is, Mr. President, that even though I may be the senior Free Worlds Alliance officer present, and even though you've placed your defensive units under Alliance command, this is *your* fight. Aside from *Aurora* and Captain Errezola's people, everyone involved in this situation is from Bellerophon or one of the other Cyclops systems, or at least a Fringer who made her own decision to support you before *we* came along. That means there's a lot more at stake here for your people than for the Alliance at large. So I'd really prefer for you to hear an Odyssian's evaluation before I start flinging around opinions or projections."

"I appreciate that, Commodore," Xeneas said, and he meant it. He looked at Rodoulis. "Captain?"

"Of course, Mr. President," Rodoulis replied. He paused for a sip of ice water, then looked around the table.

"In general terms, we're far better off than we were afraid we might be," he said then. "Largely, that's because of President Dewar's response. None of us anticipated that he'd have another carrier in-system or that he could—and would—send it to help us out. And no one in Cyclops had any clue about the... 'Casúr Cogaidhs'—" he pronounced the Gaelic words a bit carefully "—or what that might mean for our defenses.

"I'm not trying to suggest we don't still face a very, very serious threat, but I'm completely positive that no one in the Oval can have the least idea just how dangerous those defenses of ours have become. I wish we'd been able to bring *Saga* over to our side as well, but *Aurora* and the Casúr Cogaidhs are one hell of a replacement!"

Heads nodded soberly.

The truth was that they'd done extraordinarily well where the Cyclops Sector picket forces were concerned. All four of the carriers stationed in Bellerophon itself had come over to the mutiny, along with virtually their entire sublight parasite complements. Half a dozen of the parasites—including two battleships—had been destroyed or gutted in the process, but they represented only a relatively minor loss in combat power. TFNS *Hermes*, the single carrier in the *Achilles* picket, had joined the mutiny the instant *Ninurta* dropped out of wormhole space and Captain Rudnicka received the burst-transmitted personal message from her old Academy friend, Khairi al-Massoud.

The situation in Minotaur had been a bit more ticklish, since Captain Gyatso, TFNS *Bienor*'s CO, had been a Heart Worlder to the core. Unfortunately for him, seventy-plus percent of his crew hadn't. Once they found out why Commander Marchant and *Khandoba* had come calling, the situation aboard *Bienor* had turned nasty very, very quickly. Gyatso had survived, although not without a certain amount of damage, and been replaced by Captain Jakab Dorottya, the senior squadron CO from *Bienor*'s parasite group.

And then there'd been Cyclops.

Rodoulis and his fellows had known Rear Admiral Källström would never join them willingly. That was why they'd called on Cyclops first—and taken all four of the Bellerophon FTLCs with them—before they'd dispatched envoys to the other systems. They'd arrived with twice Källström's combat power, hoping he'd see reason, but they hadn't really expected him to, and their expectations had proved only too well grounded when fierce fighting broke out aboard both FTLCs.

No one would ever know what had actually happened aboard TFNS *Saga*, Källström's flagship, but the scraps of comm traffic they'd picked up suggested that most of the big ship's senior officers had backed the rebellion. They did know Källström himself had been killed in the fighting that took his flag bridge, but that hadn't been enough. From the sensor data, Rodoulis suspected that a Heart loyalist in *Saga's* engineering department had gotten to one of the carrier's fusion plants. That was certainly one explanation for the explosion that had destroyed her with all hands.

Her consort *Enlil* had been more fortunate. Rafal Makowski, her captain, had been badly wounded, but his XO had carried the ship for the mutiny, which had given Bellerophon seven of the sector's eight FTLCs, and they'd been concentrated in Bellerophon by the time *Aurora* arrived from New Dublin with the FWA's response.

"If I were Fokaides," Rodoulis continued, "I'd plan my deployments based on a worst-case assumption, which would be that we'd taken all eight of the sector's carriers. It would be nice if we had, in which case *Aurora* would constitute an even nastier surprise for the Hearts, but that would still be his worst-case estimate for the numbers he might face. Unfortunately for his calculations, there's no way he or any of his planners can have allowed for the existence of the Casúr Cogaidhs. In addition, it's unlikely as hell that anyone in the Sol System has any inkling of the buzz saw waiting for them at Jalal Station. We know from Commodore Carson that Governor Murphy hoped to resolve any confrontation at Jalal without violence, but we've had several days now to look at just what the Casúr Cogaidhs mean tactically." He shook his head. "If there *was* any violence, I'll guarantee it didn't end the way the Heart expected it to."

He took another sip of water.

"We can't know what they're going to send our way," he said then, his expression somber. "But I think we can all assume Fokaides will send every ship he can scrape up. For that matter, he won't send *anything* unless he figures he can take down the biggest force he believes we can put up against him. The last thing any of those Heart World bastards is about to do is commit a force they think could lose, because they absolutely can't afford any more failures in the Fringe. So we can probably assume we'll be looking at a minimum of twelve-plus carriers and probably as many as sixteen, if they can dig up that many. Personally, I don't think they can—not if they're also sending a force after Murphy—but even our minimum number is one hell of a lot of firepower."

He looked around the table, his eyes level.

"If they managed to put together a force they think is big enough and got it into wormhole space within a week or so of the *Lucille Anderman*'s arrival in Sol, they could be here by January eighth. Which means we've got about a month—worst-case—before they arrive. Assuming Murphy is in a position to send reinforcements our way from Jalal as soon as President Dewar's courier reaches him, *they* could be here by the fifteenth or sixteenth. So we're essentially looking at a one-week window between his and the Hearts' earliest possible arrival dates. I don't see any way Murphy could better that, but if we're lucky, it'll take the Oval longer than that to scrape up the naval and planetary combat forces they expect to need."

"And if we're not lucky, Captain?" Xeneas asked quietly, when Rodoulis paused.

"And if we're not lucky, Mr. President," the captain said flatly, "our task group hits them head-on and does as much damage as we possibly can, buys as much time as we can. If I were Murphy, I'd slice off maybe half a dozen of my carriers. I don't see how he could possibly justify reducing his own strength below that level, when he only has twelve. That means we need to chop the Hearts back to something he can handle with that many ships. Given the fact that he'll come in heavy with Casúr Cogaidhs, he could probably hack superior numbers, but we've still got to prune them back as hard as we can."

"Forgive me, Captain, but may I ask a question?" Justine Von Undingen said.

The Minotaur System's chief executive was the only elected system head of state to come sign the Declaration in person. At barely 157 centimeters, she was the smallest of the Secession Convention's delegates, but she was also the most fiery.

"Of course, Ma'am."

"If the object is to 'buy time' until Governor Murphy's reinforcements arrive, then might this not to be the time for what

I believe you Navy officers call a 'fleet in being' approach? Is it really necessary for you to lock yourselves into a headlong battle against superior numbers?"

Rodoulis began to answer, but Commodore Carson raised her hand before he could.

"Believe me, Ma'am, if we thought we could avoid that, we would," she said with a bittersweet smile. "And against another opponent, under other circumstances, maneuvering in the outer system, threatening her rear, might deter her long enough for our purposes. But I'm afraid any CO the Oval sends out here will be under orders to move directly against Odysseus, even if that means completely ignoring any mobile elements we might have in-system. And that's especially true if they have a significant numerical edge. They don't really care about our ships as such, Ma'am. They care about the planet, the star system. And if they reach attack range of Odysseus, and if Prime Minister Schleibaum's authorized Standing Order Fifteen, they'll threaten to K-strike every city and town on the planet unless all of our warships surrender. And they can do that from well beyond the Powell Limit. Planets are very slow, very predictable targets. They aren't hard to hit, and if we try to provide some sort of close-in shield, they can just stand off and hammer us with wave after wave of KEWs and missiles. Trying to keep them off the planet will weaken our own point defenses, which will tilt the tactical equation even further in their favor, but that's not the real reason we can't do that."

Her dark green gaze circled the conference room.

"The *real* reason is that it's a statistical certainty we *couldn't* stop them all. No missile defense is perfect, even under ideal conditions. And if a single Bijalee gets past us at, say, a hundred and twenty thousand KPS, you're looking at a seventy-megaton impact. That's a fireball with a seven-kilometer radius. Blast will flatten even ceramacrete buildings over a zone eighteen kilometers in diameter. The thermal pulse will inflict third-degree burns at almost *sixty* kilometers. Admittedly, a planet can absorb a lot of damage. Ocean strikes will be pretty bad, but survivable, and hits in the back of beyond won't kill a bunch of people. But they won't target the back of beyond. They'll target *cities*. And if even one hit gets though to, say, Kórinthos..."

She let her voice trail off, and silence fell. It lingered for several seconds, then—

"Do you really think they'd go that far, Commodore?" Mathis Levasseur asked. At forty-six, the Loire System's assistant prime minister was the youngest of the Convention's delegates, and his brown eyes were worried.

"Of course they would!" Rajeev Sonarkar said before Carson could reply. He was barely seven years older than Levasseur, with a very pale complexion, a depilated scalp, and a neatly trimmed brown beard. He was thirty-seven centimeters taller than Justine Von Undingen, but his commitment burned almost equally hot.

"If there's ever been a dictionary example of a system—hell, an entire sector!—going 'out of compliance,' we're it," he continued harshly. "We all know what they did to Gobelins, despite the effort to hush it up, and that was a single system. A whole sector? Added to what's already happened in Concordia and Acera?" He shook his head, his expression grim. "They won't give a damn how many eggs they smash here as long as they get their frigging omelette made."

"I'm afraid Rajeev and the Commodore are right, Mathis," Xeneas said heavily. "That's part of what drove this whole thing from my perspective from the outset. Whatever happened in New Dublin, however it began, the entire Fringe has just been set on fire. Frankly, I don't think it's physically possible for the federal government and the Heart to stop it—not this time. But that doesn't mean they won't try, and one thing they've already demonstrated is that they're perfectly willing to slaughter however many civilians it takes. So we have to assume from the outset that Gobelins will be their *starting* point for what happens to Odysseus and the rest of the sector...unless we stop them."

A cold, chill silence fell over the conference room. It lingered until Carson cleared her throat.

"I think the President's right, Mr. Levasseur," she said then, softly. "The Heart Worlds don't give a single solitary damn about Fringer deaths. If anyone at this table knows that, *I* do." She swept the civilians with bitter green eyes. "I watched a Heart system CO refuse action against an *inferior* League attack force and then leave an entire planetary population to die on Inverness, and if it hadn't been for Admiral Murphy, every single one of those people *would* have died. Even after everything he could do, ninety-plus percent of them did. And I have to live with that. It wasn't my decision, wasn't my choice, but it was *my* ship. My captain. And not one single politician or flag officer in the Heart would've said a single damned word about it ... if not for Murphy. If they're willing to stand for that, Fokaides and Schleibaum and the Five Hundred have to figure the voters will stand for whatever they do 'to suppress rebellion and mutiny.' And this system is where they'll start."

Levasseur looked at her for a long, still moment, then nodded.

"In light of that," Carson continued, "we don't have any option but to fight. In fact, we really need to fight and *win* before they even know we're here. Before they think there's any reason to stand off and use the threat of Standing Order Fifteen to make us lie down for them. And the nature of the engagement—the probable balance of firepower and the geometry of their approach and our defense—limits our options badly. We've come up with what we believe is the best available tactical plan. There's no guarantee it will work, and even if it goes perfectly we may take heavy losses among our own units. We hope we won't. We hope sheer surprise and the Casúrs will let us get in and gut them before they even know we're here. We may not, in which case we'll probably get hammered hard ourselves. But we still believe it's our best chance of 'pruning them back' for Governor Murphy. And I'll tell all of you this, too. I *won't* see another, bigger Inverness. Whatever it costs, whatever it takes, that is *not* happening on my watch."

She paused again, let the silence linger, and then her nostrils flared and her shoulders squared themselves.

"Understand me, please." Those steady green eyes swept the gathered civilians yet again. "We don't *want* to fight that sort of battle. No sane naval commander would. And all of us are hoping—praying—Governor Murphy's reinforcements get here first, so we don't have to. If those reinforcements *don't* get here first, though, then this is almost certainly our best—our *only*—shot at plowing the road for him. But after we take it, unless our intercept plan goes perfectly, there won't be anything else we can do from outside atmosphere. So if worse comes to worst and our ops plan falls apart, it'll be up to General Tolallis and you ladies and gentlemen to buy the rest of the time the Governor will need."

Silence fell again, because every individual in that conference room understood why there wouldn't "be anything else" their defensive task force could do from outside atmosphere. It would be because the naval officers seated at that table with them would almost certainly be among those "heavy losses" Carson had just described.

"If that happens, Commodore, we'll do our very best," Xeneas said, and it was an oath—a promise to the woman who'd come all the way from New Dublin to die in his star system's defense.

"I know you will, Mr. President," she replied. "I'm counting on it."

"In that case," Xeneas said in a deliberately brisker tone, "where are we on the groundside planning, General Tolallis?"

"Actually, we're doing better than I'd hoped," Tolallis said. "Which isn't to say we're in any position to hold off a major assault force indefinitely, but I think we'll represent a lot harder bite to chew than anyone in the Oval might anticipate. The System Defense Force has called up all the reserves, and we're raising additional volunteer battalions for rear area security out of our local pool of veterans. And Commissioner Ganatos has taken over Civil Defense from the SDF, since that's mostly a police function, anyway, which frees us up to focus on the shooters' responsibilities.

"We've actually had enough time to spin up small arms and ammunition production, so we ought to have more than enough personal weapons to go around. We're shorter on heavy and crew-served weapons, and I very much wish we had more air and drone support, but we're better off even there than I'd really expected, and at least everyone who's willing to stand up and fight will have *something* to do the fighting with. And we're preparing dug-in positions to cover critical targets like the power grid, while teams of engineers have prepared facilities and locations we've identified as operationally critical to an invader for command demolition.

"We've also prepared several dispersed, fortified command-and-control centers, with secure landline and laser connections to remote communications nodes. Hopefully that will prevent orbital recon from pinpointing them for K-strikes or assault landings. Every one of my upper-tier HQs has been tasked with preparing multiple fallback command posts, as well. And we've established links to all government and commercial security systems. We won't be able to match their ability to look down from orbit, but we'll have a much better ground-level recon ability than they will, at least in our urban areas, and we're in the process of creating decoy communications and command sites to help keep them guessing.

"We've already begun moving as many civilians as possible out of immediate threat zones, but there's a limit to how much of that Commissioner Ganatos can do without disrupting critical industries and services. Besides, we don't really have places to put millions of civilians. We've commandeered most of the civilian construction printers on the planet, and we've got them cranking out bare-bones prefab housing, but there are limits on how much we can produce in the time we have. Same thing with stockpiling food outside the towns and cities. We're doing our best, and Commissioner Ganatos has prepared evacuation plans for all of the major cities. Our deep-space sensor arrays should give us a minimum of four hours warning before any attack force drops out of wormhole space, and at maximum deceleration rates, it'll take them another six and a half or seven hours to decelerate into planetary orbit. Commissioner Ganatos's current objective is to have everyone out of our major urban areas—or at least into the deep shelters—in six hours, and it looks to me and my staff like he'll pull that off.

"Now, in addition to protecting our population to the best of our ability, we have to be concerned about maintaining continuity of the *government*."

The general looked at the civilians at the table.

"I've already had to deal with some of my own officers'... unhappiness over 'going bush' in the face of a possible attack. They know better, but some of them still appear to feel as if that's an act of cowardice, as if they're running out and abandoning the civilians they're supposed to defend. It isn't. It's an act of sanity, and a recognition of their responsibilities. And the same thing is true for our *civilian* leadership. Everyone out there who's given his or her support to the Declaration—or who's just keeping his or her head down and trying to survive—is your responsibility, and you can't discharge that responsibility if you're caught in a K-strike or taken into custody by the same sort of people who massacred every political leader they could get their hands on in Gobelins. Accordingly, I've prepared evacuation plans for all of you, as well as secure, concealed sites from which the government can continue to function. And I've taken the added precaution of compartmentalizing the site locations. Obviously, we can't keep their coordinates completely secret if they're going to function, but I *am* restricting the knowledge of those locations to the greatest extent possible."

"Is all of that really necessary?" Xeneas asked.

"Mr. President, the one thing I can tell you with absolute certainty is that not everyone on Odysseus agrees with the Declaration." Tolallis's eyes were bleak. "Some of them because they're ex-pat Hearts; some because despite everything the Heart's done to the Fringe, they're still 'patriots,' God help them; and others because they're terrified of where it's going to end for them and their families. It can't be any other way. And that means that when the pressure comes on, any security I may've been able to set up will still spring leaks. I just don't know how many leaks or where they'll be, so humor me on this."

He looked around the table.

"Every one of us is praying Governor Murphy gets here before the Heart. I think we've got a far better shot at that than I ever would've anticipated before the Vice President got back from New Dublin. But if it doesn't work that way, if someone like that butcher Alaimo gets here before the Governor, it's going to be bad. It's going to be *very* bad. And if that happens, it's my job to keep you—all of you—alive so you can keep doing *your* jobs while we try to survive until the Governor *does* get here."

CHAPTER TWENTY-ONE

Dyatlov Station
Nova Khahkova Orbit
Timmerman System
Rhodes Sector
Terran Federation
January 3, 2553

SILAS WATCHED THE MAINTENANCE BOT SCAN THE CARGO CONtainer.

Despite the enviro systems, the bowels of Dyatlov Station, orbiting Nova Khahkova, smelled of must and decay from abandoned or sequestered cargo that had been pushed to the cargo bay's back corner.

The bot in question was running standard safety and serviceability checks on a large container stuffed with cryo-stabilized hemp seeds bound for an agricultural collective farther into the Rhodes Sector. That "standard" had been considerably upgraded after the transplanted chestnut forests of Apalachee III were devastated by blight from an agricultural shipment that hadn't gone through the proper customs checks. Since then, anything organic transiting through Timmerman had picked up a number of additional inspections.

The cost of which was passed on to the consumers. Naturally.

Silas had been aboard the station for almost thirty-six hours, since shortly after the tramp freighter *Reynaldo* entered planetary orbit. He hated being out in the open for that long, but his cover as *Reynaldo*'s assistant purser was solid. And it was what gave him an excuse to be here in this particular cargo bay on this particular day to watch this particular bot carry out its totally uninteresting scan.

He looked around the cargo bay, then glanced at the lower left corner of the holo screen on his left forearm. What looked like a simple projection artifact of amber flickers told him his ECM hadn't picked up any surveillance, and he tapped a four-digit code.

The bot froze, and he knelt beside it to open its power access hatch. He flexed his forearm, the glow on his screen changed hues, and a brief line of alphanumeric characters appeared on the underside of the hatch: 37/B/NEV.

He looked at it for a moment, then clenched his left fist. His forearm screen emitted a weak laser that erased the words in a puff of smoke, and he stood with a sense of satisfaction. What had looked like normal station scrawl from maintenance workers had actually been a message from his contact. She was waiting for him at their normal spot, no distress.

"As long as a damned Rish doesn't jump out at me," he muttered, and shivered at the memory from Port Montclair so many years ago. The trauma of fighting a three-meter matriarch armed with nothing more than a sidearm had plagued his nightmares and given him a permanent aversion to lonely maintenance bays.

He closed the hatch and punched the bot's power switch. It chirped several times, then floated up into a ceiling docking station, and its report on the container dropped onto his forearm PDA.

Silas pretended to read it as he made for a lift on the far side of the bay. He stepped through its open doors and hit a button for an upper level, but the doors didn't close immediately. His mouth went dry, and his hand moved to a multitool hanging from his belt. His thumb found the activation button for the vibroblade it concealed as memory replayed the sound of heavy footfalls and the scrape of claws across a deck. He started to press the button, but then the doors finally closed. His tight shoulders relaxed—some—and he shook away the fear and made himself take his hand away from the vibroblade.

As the lift rose, he sent a quick text to Hendrix, his backup, to pass on his next stop and waited until he reached his destination.

The lift opened again onto a promenade that circled the inner edge of the habitat hub. Gravity was light here, and Silas slipped easily into the crowd of spacers on shore leave and longshoremen coming off-shift. This part of the station was normally a nonstop party of working-class men and women, blowing off steam and backpay at the overpriced bars and fast-food stalls scattered across the promenade. The current crowd was more subdued, though. In fact, the pulse of nightclub music was louder than the conversations at the open-air tables and kiosks.

Fear did that to people, Silas mused. The Rhodes Sector was actually closer to the League's central worlds than New Dublin, and while the war had never directly threatened its star systems—or not in the last forty years, at any rate—the Rhodes Sector was most definitely Fringe space. Its more affluent residents insisted—strenuously—that it was Heart territory; those of lesser means disagreed with them. Based on the casualty totals its people had paid over the decades to support the Heart Worlds' war, Silas thought they had a point.

He climbed a wire-tread spiral stair to the promenade's second level and crossed to a rundown storefront. It was an eatery—of sorts—although a holo sign in its less than pristine window advertised lockboxes and lockers, as well. The quick-fried food stand that hadn't seen a health inspector in years was flanked by crystoplast-faced refrigerated display cases offering bottled beer and other beverages. The crystoplast was no cleaner than the rest of the food stand, and an elderly woman tended a vat of boiling grease behind the counter.

"Pickup for Josh Gray," Silas said, tapping the side of his hand against the pay plate. The woman looked up from her vat, then dropped a dozen spring rolls into it and wiped her hand on a none-too-clean apron.

"It's a big one. Go on to the back to get it," she said, scooping up French fries from a different trough and squeezing out red and white sauces onto them.

"Thanks."

Silas rested his hand casually on the disguised vibroblade as he stepped around the food stand towards the rear of the establishment. He shouldered through a bead curtain and into a small storage room. The woman seated on a largish crate in one corner came to her feet as soon as she saw him.

"Picking up?"

She reached behind a pile of boxes, and Silas's lips quirked. He didn't need to see the weapon hidden behind the pile to know it was there.

She was middle-aged, with a few strands of gray in the dark hair of a mixed heritage that could have blended in on any world from one end of the Federation to the other end of the League. That anonymity was highly useful to someone in her line of work, he thought.

"I need the data wafers heading to Rhodes Prime," he said.

Her expression eased ever so slightly—only a trained eye could have detected it—at his coded challenge.

"I didn't think they wanted Quarn dramas," she replied with the phrase that indicated they weren't under any surveillance or threat, and Silas nodded and took his hand from the vibroblade.

"Good to see you again, Tara," he said.

"Sweet merciful Cai Shen, Silas, what the hell's been going on out there?" She sat back down on the box as an enormous weight seemed to shift off her shoulders. "I've never been happier to have a gutter accent. Anyone sounds the slightest bit posh and they get their asses kicked for being a Heart."

"Seems some things have been boiling over." Silas leaned against a wall and crossed his arms. "Inevitable, when you think about it. But let's not waste time. Mama-san runs this spot for us because we don't draw attention to her, and the longer I'm back here, the more likely it is to raise questions. What news from the Rish?"

"The news is that there's no news." Tara tossed her hands up. "The lizards stopped all trade through their outposts as soon as the word about how Murphy trounced the League at Crann Bethadh made its way out here. The Quarn had to dump an entire shipment of live *krishal* shrimp at customs two days ago because their Rish customer had disappeared, and they're pissed. *So* pissed. My source with them didn't have anything else meaningful to report."

"So the Rish are buttoning up. Mmm..."

Silas's jaw worked from side to side while he pondered that. The inability to glean any information on the Rishathan Sphere made his job as an intelligence collector difficult. But every action an enemy took betrayed him in one way or another, if one only knew how to read behind it, and...

"Why?" he asked after a moment. Tara cocked her head, and he shrugged. "Why are they buttoning up? How did they justify it?"

"They didn't. No reason given. Which upset the Quarn even more. You know what sticklers they are for contracts. But it's not bloody likely the timing of Murphy's mutiny and the Rish going dark is a *coincidence*." She shrugged. "Rumble from the common folk—" she pointed her chin at the door "—is that they're worried about the conflict spilling over, so they're cutting trade so they don't look like they're playing favorites to anyone. Lying bastards. Is it true about what Murphy found? Some hidden League shipyard built by the Rish?"

"Not exactly, but close." Silas drew a small data wafer from a breast pocket. "Here's the truth, straight from Murphy and O'Hanraghty. Raw feed from his ships at the Battle of Crann Bethadh and his raid on Diyu."

"Diyu?"

"What the Leaguies called their shipyard." It was Silas's turn to shrug. "It's in the astro catalogs as Yuxi."

"So we finally got the smoking gun against the Rish? We can prove they've been—"

"Close enough to it for anyone with functioning brain cells." Silas handed the wafer to her. "But our directives have changed since Murphy got back from League space."

"What?" She frowned. "Why?"

"Because the Hearts sent a batch of federal marshals and a backup of Army Hoplons to arrest Murphy on some trumped-up bullshit charges. They really wanted his ass for defying orders and defending New Dublin, of course, and Crann Bethadh wasn't having it.

"Murphy tried to keep it under control. Had his own Hoplons there for cover. Even offered to return to Sol voluntarily, aboard his own flagship. But the frigging idiot they'd sent to manage their clusterfuck wasn't having it. He actually started shooting... and managed to murder the planetary president in front of four hundred or so witnesses."

Tara's eyes had grown steadily larger as she listened to him. Now they flared wide in mingled shock and disbelief.

"That was the final fucking straw," Silas told her grimly. "Most of the marshals and Army bastards were killed on the spot, the planet went 'out of compliance,' the system government tried and *hanged* the idiot Hearts who didn't manage to get killed in the initial fighting... and the whole damned Concordia Sector's decided to follow New Dublin's lead."

"*What?!?*" She stared at him, and he grimaced.

"Yep. They're calling themselves the 'Free Worlds Alliance.'

And unless I miss my guess, their 'Alliance' is going to spread clear across the Fringe, at least the Southern Lobe, as soon as word gets out." He smiled thinly. "I'm betting you can at least guess how completely into the crapper *that*'s likely to throw all our plans. Mind you, it's not necessarily a bad thing from our perspective, but it *does* mean we need to do some...rethinking."

"Holy shit." Tara rolled her eyes. "Still have a gift for understatement, I see! I didn't know about Concordia, but I do know the *Rhodes* Sector's about to blow up, Silas. My Quarn contact asked me how he can reengineer starfish weapons for human hands." She snorted. "They can always smell new market opportunities, can't they? What worries me is that they're probably right about that one."

"I know. That's where you come in." Silas turned to gently open a peephole in the beaded curtain behind him. "I need you to get all this information on the gray net," he said, gazing through the opening. "Upload it to every Alliance-friendly space you can find. Get it close to mainstream media, and it'll bleed over. The more the Heart tries to suppress it, the more people will believe it."

Tara regarded the data wafer dubiously, then slipped it into her bra.

"I thought we were doing this to expose the Rish," she said.

"We were. We succeeded. And now there's a new problem for the Federation. Murphy's on the side of the light, Tara. He's not leading the revolt for his own sake. He's trying to preserve the Federation and end the war with the League."

"And how's he doing that by killing Hearts?" Tara demanded skeptically. "I'm not that fond of federal marshals, but *hanging* them?"

"They shot first. And New Dublin hanged them for murdering its president; he just didn't stop it. The thing is, this either ends quickly, with Murphy negotiating with the Heart from a position of strength, so we can keep the Federation together, or the Federation shatters when the Five Hundred and their thugs try to force their Fringe wage slaves back onto the plantation. We help Murphy, and it's less dying. Less suffering. And what do you think the Rish will do if there's no Federation anymore? Dozens of sectors and stars fending for themsel—"

"I'm sold," Tara interrupted. "I'm sold! I never cared for the Hearts anyway. I could have been raised by my father, but he went Preferences instead of Needs and got called back up when I was a baby. He never came home."

"Spoken like a true Fringer." Silas gave her a slap on the shoulder. "When can you get that data out?"

"Today, if need be. I've got sources and embeds all through Nova Khahkova and prospects on ships embarking for Rhodes Prime and out to Zolist by the next night-cycle. Where are you heading next?"

Silas canted his head at her, and she grimaced.

"Shit. Sorry I asked. I don't know, I can't spill. I got it." She rolled her eyes. "So, that question not asked, what next from my end?"

"There's contact codes on the wafer to link up with Alliance forces if or when they arrive here. Do what you can to support the people when they decide it's time to rebel. Agitate. Rabble-rouse. Make life hell for the Five Hundred here, and Murphy's job will be that much easier."

"I'm no terrorist, Silas." Tara looked away.

"No, and that's what the newsies will call us, however careful we are," he agreed. "But it's coming anyway, and somebody needs to steer—if we can—to keep it from all going straight to hell. Keep the violence away from the civilians as best you can. There's going to be plenty of people who want plain old revenge killings, and we need to step on that as hard as we can. Butler screwed up there. Gobelins was practically begging for the Army to come in and restore order. They got more than they bargained for when that monster Alaimo showed up."

"What'll it be like with Murphy in charge?" she asked.

"All I can say is he's a good man. When the Hearts gave him power, he used it to save lives. Not everyone passes that test. Hell, for that matter most of the real Hearts could give less than a rat's ass about Fringe lives. He does."

He shrugged, and after a moment, Tara nodded.

"Don't follow me right away," he said. "Don't go through the promenade. Get that information out, but do it safely."

"Come on, Silas. I know no one's coming to my rescue if I screw up. That's one of the first things you taught me. Godspeed."

She waggled her fingers at him.

"I'll leave a little extra to Cai Shen for you," Silas said, and ducked through the beads. He set a large-denomination credit chip on the cooktop for the woman running the stall and it vanished into her apron as soon he stepped outside.

As he walked away from the storefront, Silas texted Hendrix to warn him he was on his way to their shuttle and telling him to ready it to unmoor from the station and alert the *Reynaldo's* skipper to clear their departure from the system.

He walked through a throng of people who stood up at a news crawl across the bottom of one of the central holo displays. He heard a lot of grumbles about the news that Vice Admiral Thakore had been dispatched to crush Murphy's revolt. Of course, given the timing on Thakore's departure, if there'd been a fight at Jalal Station, it was already over. The news just hadn't reached the Rhodes Sector yet. When it did—

A flash of golden light caught his eye, and he turned to look at the source. An elderly man in a suit that was too nice for this part of the promenade raised a glass at him from a small table outside a bar. Then the old man slipped a laser pointer into his cuff and sat patiently.

Silas slowed to a stop. He hadn't encountered that bit of field craft in many years, an iris light tuned to the individual rods and cones of a single person's eye. The hair on the back of his neck stood up and he felt the station close in around him as he realized the man who'd taught him that signal was at the bar. He swallowed hard and rubbed his wrist, and his thumbnail tripped a switch built into the side of his forearm PDA and sent an alert to Hendrix that something was about to go very, very wrong. Then he turned sharply and went up a short staircase. A barfly with too much makeup and not enough clothing sauntered over to him.

"I'm thirsty. You buying?" she asked.

"Let me eat first."

He winked at her and went to sit down across from the well-dressed man. A trio of empty glasses clustered together on one side of the table.

"Silas." The man waggled a fourth, nearly empty, beer glass at him. "I'm glad you finally showed up. The girls keep calling me a 'Cheap Charlie,' but I tip the bartender a bit extra."

"Robinson...You retired."

Silas sat close to the edge of his chair and his eyes darted around the bar, trying to identify who was paying too much attention to them.

"I did!" Robinson worked a sip from one side of his mouth to the other. "This is watered down. I expected that, but this is almost egregious. And you're right. I did retire, so you should appreciate how much of an inconvenience this is for me. One day I'm fly-fishing on my land in Montana, and the next I'm reactivated. Seems retirement isn't the end of one's service to the Federation."

"I don't think you're here to defect," Silas said, looking thoughtfully at a man with wide shoulders and a too-new shipsuit a dozen yards away, taking his time deciding which Quarn silk scarf he was going to buy.

"Certainly not." Robinson set his glass down and pushed it aside. "You had so much promise, Silas. Then you went down the Rishathan conspiracy rabbit hole....Look where you are now."

"I was right," Silas huffed. "The only people who still think it's conspiracy paranoia have their heads buried in the sand."

A small drone zipped overhead, and Silas rested one hand on the disguised vibroblade.

"I'm not here to kill you, my boy," Robinson said. "Professional courtesy and all that. It was my one demand before I came out of retirement."

"How'd you find me?"

"Tsk-tsk-tsk." Robinson wagged a finger at him. "I taught you a lot. I didn't teach you everything. And if I do tell you—"

"I have to assume you're lying. And when I try to figure out where my seals went bad this time, it'll just open me up to your next surveillance target."

The scarf-examiner turned away from the display and Silas tensed slightly.

"Again, I'm not here to kill you." Robinson ran a fingertip around the rim of his glass. "I'm here to talk, on behalf of the Five Hundred and the loyal intelligence community. You're our best direct line back to Murphy that isn't a missile."

Silas laid his hands on the edge of the table.

"Do you remember what I taught you about those in power?" Robinson asked "Back when you were embedded in that pirate clan past the Blue Line?"

"'To lose power is to die.'" Silas nodded. "Then you rambled on about class struggle and long-dead ideologies."

"You don't think there's a class struggle now? The Fringe is breaking from the Heart. Six decades of war, and it was some nowhere colony eating a K-strike that finally broke the camel's back." Robinson shook his head. "Took everyone back home by surprise, actually."

"It was the Heart abandoning people on Inverness to be murdered by the League that did it," Silas said. "Then they wanted Murphy to do the same thing in Crann Bethadh. Enough was finally enough. All it took was a little unvarnished truth. But, much as I enjoy the chance to catch up … what's your message to Murphy?"

"Ship waiting for you?" Robinson smiled and raised his drink to his mouth. "All right. We'll let Murphy live. He gets an FTLC with its parasites crewed by all the seditious scum he can carry and takes himself out beyond the Blue Line. We won't come for him. And when he sends for his family on Earth … they'll come to him. Unharmed."

"Rather generous of the Five Hundred." Silas caught the bartender staring at them. The man reached under the bar and moved something into easy reach. "What about the Alliance and all the Fringers with them?"

"Do you really think the Five Hundred will give *them* up?" Robinson chuckled. "Tell Murphy to set up his own little rabble paradise beyond the Blue Line. Give the Fringe someplace to run to."

"And then a fleet will show up on his doorstep and apply Standing Order Fifteen. The Alliance may be made up of Fringers, but they're not stupid."

"I've been told that won't happen." Robinson sipped.

"And if Murphy refuses?"

"Kanada Thakore can't protect Simron or Vyom or the girl …"

"Reagan." Silas's face went hard. "They're not involved. They're civilians. *Children!*" he hissed.

"I never threatened them," Robinson said mildly. "On the other hand, sometimes bad things happen even to good people."

He set his glass aside.

"We're in uncharted territory here, Silas. The League has never had—and will never have—the strength to threaten the Heart Worlds. Xing? Even if she'd had every ship Murphy allegedly destroyed at Crann Bethadh—or in the shipyards he supposedly took out—she'd never have reached Earth or the worlds that really matter. The Five Hundred were spooked by her, but they're *terrified* of Murphy, son. He's done more damage to their control than all those years of war with the League combined."

"The Five Hundred did this to themselves," Silas shot back.

"They can't demand generations of blood from people and get rich off their sacrifices forever. Sooner or later the wheels come off. The Alliance is the monster *they* made."

"I'm aware." Robinson nodded. "Some old hands saw this coming years ago...but hindsight isn't all that useful in the midst of a crisis. I'm no part of the Five Hundred, Silas. I'm a useful tool of theirs that earned the right to die comfortably out in a pasture. But I *know* the Five Hundred, and they aren't going to let the Fringe go, son. They'll scorch every last world from New Dublin to the League if they have to. Murphy can't win this."

"He's proven he can beat the odds," Silas replied. "This won't be like Gobelins where the Army and the Five Hundred managed to cover up what they did. If the Five Hundred act like tyrants, the entire Federation will see it."

"And you think that will matter to the Five Hundred? The Federation is their fiefdom, Silas. They play their games amongst each other, and we're the pawns. They'll upend the table before they lose the game."

"I'll pass that on to Murphy." Silas hooked a thumb under his forearm PDA and depressed a small trigger as he removed a magnetic button. He set the button down in the middle of the table.

"Do you know what that is?" he asked.

Robinson raised an eyebrow and shook his head.

"It's Quarn tech. Amazing what you can pick up if you know the right people. I send the activation code, and a cloud of *gomi* poison will annihilate everyone on this promenade in minutes. The Five Hundred don't care about your life. Or mine. Or anyone else's out here. But you *do* care about yours, don't you, Robinson?"

Robinson stared at the button.

"My first great-grandchild will be born in a month," he said.

"Then when I walk away from here, I'd better be able to keep walking. There's a motion sensor and a rangefinder in the base. It's keyed onto you. You move the button? Poof of gas. You get up and try to walk away? Poof of gas. Either way, you die. And a lot of other people, too. Including your backup looking at the scarves, the bartender, and the spotters milling around the holo show."

"Are those the only ones you've picked out?" Robinson half smiled at him.

"*Gomi* will get them all. I'll send the self-destruct codes soon as I'm clear. Don't go anywhere."

Silas stood.

"Silas! I wish it didn't have to be this way. You were always my favorite," Robinson said.

"And you were my best teacher," Silas said. Then he squeezed his forearm PDA and raised it to his lips.

"Drop it," he said. "Drop it all, now!"

His partner, Hendrix, touched the macro tapped into the station's control grid.

Power cut out across the promenade. Yells and shouts rose as opportunists swiped merchandise and the already paranoid crowd panicked. Silas shoved his way through a knot of spacers and vanished behind a massage parlor. He stabbed a small screwdriver into the frozen handle of a maintenance hatch, and the tiny battery in its handle powered the lock long enough for him to open the hatch and slip away into the pitch-dark passage.

An hour after the chaos began, Robinson still sat waiting at the table while the station's bomb squad examined the tiny button in full gear. They took their time. But, finally, a technician—who looked more like a bear than a man in his protective suit—twisted off his helmet.

"There's nothing in it," he said. "It's a lump of plastic."

"Son-of-a-bitch!" Robinson grimaced as he shoved up out of his chair and waddled towards the back of the bar. "Where's the pisser?!"

"Not here!" The bartender waved his arms. "You go next-door!"

Robinson stopped, slapped a palm against the back of the bar, and bent forward slightly at the waist.

"Too late," he grumbled and unzipped his pants.

"Five different ships have shoved off since the power outage," a voice said in Robinson's ear. *"Port Authority can still stop and board two of them before they're out of range. Which—"*

"Don't bother," Robinson snapped as he relieved himself. "I want him to get away and send a message to Murphy. That's the plan."

"Then why'd he cause all this trouble?"

"Professional courtesy.... And it was his own way of telling me I'm too old for this shit."

CHAPTER TWENTY-TWO

TFNS Ishtar
Wormhole Space
January 2, 2553

"WHY AREN'T WE USING THE TRANSIT SHAFT...SIR?" EIRA ASKED.

Callum caught a handhold, halting himself, and rolled in the microgravity to look back at her. She gave him one of her best "what silliness are you up to now?" looks, and he grinned.

"I needed the exercise?" he suggested.

"No, you didn't," she replied. "And if you did, there's always the officers' gym two decks down from your quarters."

"Eira, don't you *ever* do things just because it might be fun to try something different?"

"I do lots of things for fun, Sir. When," she added pointedly, "I'm not on duty."

"I'll have to take your word for that, I guess." Callum's grin turned into a grimace. "Since I never see much of you when you're not on duty. Not like when your room was right across the hall like it was on Crann Bethadh, anyway."

"That was different," she said. "Different from shipboard duty, I mean. You're an officer; I'm enlisted. You're in officers' country, and I'm down on Berthing Deck Seven." She shrugged. "Probably just as well. I never liked what some people thought on Crann Bethadh."

"Thought about what?" Callum asked, and a hint of color might have touched her cheekbones as she looked away.

"About us. About why my room was next to yours. They thought we were...well, they thought exactly what the Sergeant Major wanted them to think."

"What he—?"

Callum paused and his good eye narrowed.

"Why in the world would he have wanted people to think *that*?" he asked.

"Because . . . because if they thought that we were . . . you know . . . then they wouldn't realize I was really your bodyguard, so they might underestimate me. Not realize you had someone watching your back. Sir."

"Why that sneaky old bastard," Callum said softly, then snorted. "I should have figured that out for myself, shouldn't I? Not that I'd ever have tried to do anything of the sort, of course." She shot him a quick glance, and he grimaced again. "I mean, best estimate, you're four years younger than me, just for a start. And I know you were a slave. I even know what kind of slave you were supposed to be. And you don't have any family, no one to look out for you. And I was the Governor's son—just like I'm the Admiral's son, now. Of course I wouldn't have put that kind of pressure on you! What kind of man *would*?"

"Oh, a lot of them," she said, with an edge of bitterness. "They see this—" she tapped the genetic slave brand above her left eye "—and they think 'why not?'"

"What?" Callum frowned. "Who? When? I'll—"

"Don't worry about it, Sir." She shook her head. "I had to put up with a lot of the same kind of stuff on Inverness. And at least nobody pushes it now, the way some of 'em did there." She flashed him a smile. "Smaj told me that as long as Faeran can put them back together again, it's all fine with him."

Callum gazed at her for a long moment, then chuckled.

"And how many has she had to put back together again?" he asked.

"Only a few." Her smile grew broader. "I think word got around."

"Well, good for you!"

"But you still haven't answered my question, Sir," she pointed out. "Why are we going the long way instead of using the transit shaft?"

"Mostly because I wanted to take the scenic route," he said. "Most people just automatically hop into the intra-ship car and never think about the scenery they're passing up."

"Scenery," she repeated in a dubious tone and looked around.

At the moment, they were at just about the midpoint of the manual access way that served PR-2, *Ishtar*'s Number Two parasite rack, and the well-lit passage narrowed to pinprick size both ahead and behind. Not surprisingly, since it was sixteen hundred meters long and only five meters in diameter. The rounded outer edge of the transit shaft cut a half-moon-shaped slice out of that five meters, which meant the actual passage width was no more than three and a half meters, and as Eira had just suggested, very few people used it. The transit shaft was much faster and easier, even in microgravity.

"Yeah, scenery," he said, checking the frame number stenciled on a bulkhead. "We're almost there. Come on."

She regarded him skeptically, but pushed off behind him as he started along the passage once more. They traveled another fifty meters or so before he caught another handhold and stopped. Eira settled beside him, after her usual spinal-reflex look both ways along the deserted, brightly lit bore. He looked down at her with a grin, and she gave him the sort of exasperated look governesses and tutors had bestowed upon their wayward charges since at least Hammurabi's day.

"You don't see it?" he asked.

"See *what*?"

"Oops. Wait a sec!"

His grin grew broader, and then he tapped the control pad she hadn't noticed and the surface of the passageway's outboard bulkhead slid aside to reveal a six-meter-long, overhead-to-decksole viewport.

Eira's eyes went wide as she found herself staring out into wormhole space through the water-clear crystoplast.

Very few people cared to look at the emptiness around an FTLC when it went supralight. It was such a *complete* emptiness. It wasn't black, wasn't light or dark, offered no pinprick stars, no moons. Just nothingness. An absence of visual stimuli to which the human eye and brain were ill adapted.

But that wasn't what Eira saw now. Not this time.

The flank of TFNS *Gallant*, the sublight battleship riding the lead position on PR-2, loomed out above their viewpoint as far as she could see in either direction. She'd never seen a parasite warship from such a short range, and she saw two of *Gallant*'s running lights, burning the steady green of a docked vessel, before her. The edge of a laser point defense station's emitter heads were just visible, protruding beyond the battleship's curved flank, and knife-sharp sensor arrays projected even farther, looming against the featureless blur. And beyond that—so far away even its stupendous bulk appeared no larger than a child's toy—was *Ishtar*'s sister ship, *Ereshkigal*. The black hole of *Ereshkigal*'s Fasset drive was far too tiny for anyone to have seen, even if the artificial black hole hadn't drunk in any light that hit it, but the huge ship's drive fan was almost four hundred and thirty meters in diameter, and its thirteen-hundred-meter circumference was a corona of lambent flame. It was vanishingly rare for ships in wormhole space to be close enough to pick out with the naked eye, but TF 1705 was a fleet in everything but name. And as Eira stared at *Ereshkigal*, she saw the glitter of yet another, more distant drive fan that must belong to *Gilgamesh*, the third unit of FTLC Squadron 19.

That was more than startling enough, but a flickering nimbus seemed to crawl along *Gallant*'s armored flank, as well. It was an eerie blue glow that was oddly, serenely gorgeous and seemed almost...liquid. She knew it wasn't—that it couldn't be—but that was what it looked like. In fact, she almost thought she could see...droplets of it splashing astern from the sensor array's aerials.

"I never knew the carriers looked like *that*," she said, after a moment. "And what's that...glow on the battleship?"

"*That's* what I brought you to see," Colin replied. "Or, rather, to *think* you're seeing."

"What?" She looked away from the viewport, peering at him with the expression of someone who knew she'd just missed the punch line to a joke.

"No one really knows what you're seeing." Callum's tone was more serious than it had been. "As far as we've ever been able to document, it's an optical illusion. But the funny thing is that only the human eye actually sees it."

"What do you mean?"

"I mean that there are megabytes—hell, exabytes—of recorded imagery of exactly what you're looking at right this minute... that doesn't show any of that blue glow. None. And nobody's ever been able to measure any energy flow, any emissions, any radiation, or anything *else* that could produce it. Every instrument we have insists it's not there, but anyone who actually looks at it with his or her own eyes sees it. And the really funny thing is that nobody's ever sure they're seeing exactly what someone else sees. Because we can't record it. We can't copy it for reference so we can both say, yup, that's what it looks like to me, too." He grinned at her. "Pretty cool, huh?"

"That doesn't seem possible," she said.

"Lots of stuff we still haven't explained, Eira," he said, turning back to the viewport, his single eye darkly thoughtful. "Not too surprising, I guess. I mean, the universe's a big place, and whatever most people think, we've only seen a tiny little piece of it so far, really. But the working spacers call that 'Barend's Candle,' after some historical sailor named Barend Fokke, from way back in the seventeenth century on Earth."

"Why?" Eira asked, looking back with a fascinated expression at the nonexistent glow her eyes insisted she saw.

"I don't know all the details, but my grandfather told me a lot of people think he was the model for something called the Flying Dutchman—a ghost ship that can never make port." Callum's expression was almost dreamy. "Makes sense, I guess. You can only see it—if you really *do* see it, of course—in wormhole space, and you can't measure it, can't record it, can't even *detect* it even here. But there it is. If that's not 'ghostly,' I don't know what is."

"It's...beautiful, Sir," she said.

"Don't call me that," he said, turning his head to look at her.

"Call you what?"

She looked back at him, her expression confused.

"Sir." He shook his head. "Don't call me that when we're alone. I don't like it."

"You're an officer. I'm a lance corporal. That's what I'm supposed to call you, Sir," she said.

"In public, maybe."

"Everywhere!"

"Eira, you've been there when Captain O'Hanraghty calls my dad Terry, and everybody knows an admiral comes *maybe* a half step behind God. If he can do that in front of the entire flag bridge, then you can call me Callum when it's just the two of us."

"But—"

He held up an index finger, and she stopped in midsentence.

"Callum," he said.

"But—"

He waggled the finger.

"Cal-lum. Two syllables. It's not hard."

She frowned at him, and he tapped the tip of her nose gently with his finger.

"Callum," she said finally.

"There! Was that so hard?"

"Yes, actually," she said.

It was his turn to frown at her, and she shook her head.

"Structure . . . structure is important," she said. "It's the place I stand. Sam and I never had anything in our lives that was real, that might last. Not when the slavers had us, not on Inverness— nowhere, until you and the Admiral rescued me. I don't think you can understand what that meant. You were born in the Five Hundred. You always knew who you were, who the people around you were, that your world—or your brother's world—wasn't going to just . . . end tomorrow. There was *order* in your life."

He gazed into her blue eyes, saw the darkness behind them, and felt a stir of something like guilt. It wasn't guilt—not exactly. But it *was* the awareness, the realization, of just how completely Eira's universe had tried to chew her up and spit her out.

"When you got your father to let me enlist instead of sending me back with Drebin to face trial for attacking him, you did more than just save my life . . . Callum. You *gave* me a life. You gave me Smaj, and the team, and a place to stand. A place I know is *mine*. Sure, I'm only a lance corporal, the most junior noncom there is. But that's mine, too. I know who I am today, and I know who I'll be tomorrow, and that's why structure and procedure and doing it right the first time is *so* important. I'm not . . . I'm not fighting some kind of holding action against the entire universe anymore. I'm *me*, and for the first time in my entire life, I'm *proud* of who I am.

"That's what you gave me when you talked your father into letting me enlist." Those blue eyes gleamed now, with what could have been unshed tears, and she shook her head again, slowly. "You and the Admiral saved my life on Inverness; you *gave* me my life here in *Ishtar*."

"I never thought of it that way," he said slowly.

"I know." It was unlike her to initiate physical contact with him, but she reached out, patted him on the forearm. "It's not your fault," she said almost gently. "We just...come from really different places."

"But I should've thought about it." He frowned, touched her cheek gently. "I mean, I knew things were bad on Inverness and...before. And I guess that's one reason I want to give you things, to make up for it."

"Like that Silver Tree sculpture you bought me that first day in Tara?" She smiled at him. "I'd never even dreamed of having something that nice, that beautiful! It was wonderful."

"But it was so small compared to everything else."

"Not to me," she said simply. "But that's why getting things done the right way first is so important to me."

"All right, I can see that. But I'm not the most military of officers, in case you haven't noticed. I'm planning on going back to civvies as soon as this gigantic mess is over with, and I guess that colors my thinking. Because I don't—maybe I *should*, but I don't—think of you as a subordinate. I know you're my official bodyguard. But I'm not supposed to need bodyguards. And there's a part of me—a pretty big part—that thinks I should be the one protecting you. And, no," he smiled almost naturally, "not because you're such an itty-bitty thing you need taking care of. It's just—"

He paused for a moment, then shrugged.

"Remember when you were in that field hospital on Inverness and I was feeding you ice chips?" She nodded, and he shrugged again. "That reminded me of this time my sister Reagan and I were playing in the family garage and I dared her to trip the maglev safeties on Mom's antique Tesla Model 37. She got knocked off her feet—not hurt, but scared to death—and I felt so bad..."

"So I'm like your sister?"

"No. No! You're a lot prettier than she is. I meant—Wait." Callum pressed the back of his hand against his eyepatch and grimaced. "Damned thing's itching again."

"Let me see."

She raised a hand to his face, but he caught her wrist gently.

"It's not pretty under there." He pushed her arm down slowly. "I'd rather you keep the same high opinion you had of my face when we first met."

"Si—Callum, I had to drag you into the life pod while the *Kolyma* finished coming apart around us, and then I had to patch your helmet visor and put a tourniquet on your leg. Had to cut your vac suit off to get at it, for that matter, and you were bleeding bad. Your blood was all over the place—including all over *me*—and I even saw the marrow of your leg bone leaking out. So—"

She slapped a hand over her mouth.

"I shouldn't have said that," she said, turning away.

"Why? It happened. That bone's gone, anyway." He rapped on his prosthesis. "It'll get replaced eventually."

"Maybe." She lowered her hand. "But my point is the way your eye looks now can't possibly be any worse than it looked then."

"Point," he acknowledged. "But I don't remember you seeing me that way. So it's like it never really happened, right?"

"That has to be the silliest thing I've ever heard, even out of you."

"No, it's perfectly logical." He raised his nose with an audible sniff. "It's not my fault if you are incapable of following my own scintillating powers of reasoning."

"I'm a backwoods Fringe girl from Scotia, so I'm not sure what 'scintillating' is, but I'm pretty sure it's not the way *your* 'powers of reasoning' work," she said severely. "Now move your hand and let me look!"

He looked at her for another moment, then moved his hand.

"Yes, Ma'am," he said, and leaned down closer to her as she gently lifted the patch and examined the empty, badly scarred socket.

"I see a little irritation," she said, peering at it carefully, and he bent still closer. "It doesn't look too bad, though. We might want to stop by sick bay and see about getting some—"

Her voice stopped in mid-word as his lips suddenly touched hers.

Her eyes flared wide and her entire body stiffened in astonishment. For an instant, the universe seemed to stop, and then her hands cupped his head and her lips were hot and welcoming under his, pressing back into the kiss until—

"Oh, God!" Callum pulled back. "Oh, my God, Eira! I never meant to do that! I *didn't*! You don't need me doing...doing things like that! I'm so—"

"Sir—*Callum*!" She grabbed the front of his shipsuit and shook him. "Shut up!"

"I promise I'll never do— Wait." He stopped, looked at her sharply. "Did you just tell me to shut up?"

"Uh, yes. I guess so." She gazed back up at him, and her fair complexion showed a rosy edge of blush. "It's not the first time anybody ever kissed me, you know," she added.

"It's not?"

"No, of course not! It's just...the first time I *liked* it." The blush grew stronger. "A lot, actually."

"Oh, lordy." Callum shook his head. "Dad is so gonna kill me dead for this! He's got these ironclad principles, and I think I just sort of stepped all over them."

Eira smiled.

"I think he'll probably forgive—"

She broke off, looking up the passage beyond Callum, and slapped a hand against her holster.

He turned to look in the same direction and saw another crewman swimming rapidly down the microgravity passage towards them.

"I can explain," he began. "We were just—"

The newcomer's head snapped up at the sound of Callum's voice. Something about his expression poked at Callum, but before he could put a finger on what it was, the other man had grabbed a handhold, stopped himself in midair, and reached into the front of his shipsuit.

His hand came out with a pistol.

Eira's left hand struck like a viper. It locked on Callum's shoulder even as her right hand drew her weapon. She yanked him down and to the side, flinging him out of the line of fire, while her right foot wedged itself into the viewport's recess to stabilize her as her own pistol rose.

Callum felt his face hit the decksole even as gunfire shredded the quiet. His right hand reached for a holster that wasn't there as the rapid shots deafened one of his ears, and then he twisted around, eyes searching frantically for Eira.

The newcomer floated in the microgravity. The back of his skull had disappeared, and dark red chunks laced with gray and white drifted in a cloud. His limbs jerked and twitched as his nervous system faded away.

Callum couldn't have cared less. His entire world was focused on Eira, and his belly knotted. She was curled into a ball, her left arm—its sleeve already crimson—crushed against her side, and blood trickled from the corner of her mouth. Her eyes were unfocused, but her gunhand was still up, the muzzle still tracking towards the man who'd shot her.

"Cal—" she got out.

"Eira!"

He hurled himself through the air towards her, slapped a hand against the wound in her side, felt bits of shattered rib.

"Don't—don't move. I'll get you out of here!" Callum tried to maintain the same steady bearing his father and O'Hanraghty always seemed to have.

Eira coughed out a globule of blood and her eyes rolled up.

"Oh, Jesus," Callum Murphy whispered. Then he wrapped both arms around her, gathered his legs against the bulkhead, and straightened them explosively to send them streaking down-passage to the nearest transit shaft access point.

Terrence Murphy looked down at a display screen in his flag briefing room.

Callum sat next to Eira's sick bay bed. Three different IVs ran into her arms, the synthaflesh dressing on her side was pinker than it ought to have been, and her eyes were closed as she lay very, very still.

Callum's shoulders were hunched, and he rocked slightly.

"Dr. Barbeau says she'll recover pretty quickly, all things considered," O'Hanraghty said from behind him. Murphy looked up, over his shoulder, and the chief of staff shrugged. His tunic hung half open and a lick of his red hair was out of place, exposing a growing bald spot. "It's a good thing he got her to a corpsman as quickly as he did, though. Took one round right through her left lung. Doc says it did a *lot* of damage."

"What the hell were they *doing* there?" Murphy demanded, and O'Hanraghty chuckled.

"Callum was supposed to join me, Mirawani, Commodore Hinson, and the parasite group skippers aboard *Trebuchet* for that in-person brief on our deployment options if the alpha plan goes belly-up when we hit Bellerophon. I figured it'd be good experience for him, and God knows he needs as much of that as we can give him. Boy's smarter than hell, Terry, and he's working his ass off, however hard he tries to pretend he's not. But there are still too many blind spots the Academy would have taken care of."

He arched an eyebrow at Murphy, and the admiral nodded.

"Anyway," O'Hanraghty resumed, "he decided to leave early and swim the passage so he could show her Barend's Candle. Apparently she'd never even heard of it." He shook his head with a tiny smile. "Sometimes I forget how damned young she is and how little she's actually seen. I'll bet it really knocked her socks off. But—" his small smile disappeared, and his eyes hardened as he, too, gazed at the wounded Marine in the bed "—it didn't lessen her situational awareness one bit, Terry. She's the only reason Callum's still alive."

"Again." Murphy ran both sets of fingers through his hair and exhaled explosively. "Again," he repeated more softly.

"I'd say stopping off at Inverness has paid off several times now," O'Hanraghty agreed, and Murphy nodded.

"It has that, Harry. Indeed, it has. But—" he waved O'Hanraghty into one of the briefing room chairs "—who the hell was that guy and what the hell happened?"

"First part's easy enough," O'Hanraghty said, dropping into the indicated chair. "Petty Officer (Engineering) Second-Class Augusto Cortaberri, from Caledonia Secunda. Assigned to *Gallant*'s Electronics Department. Pretty good cyber tech, from his efficiency reports."

"Caledonia Secunda…that's Fringe," Murphy murmured.

"Yep. But it's Northern Lobe, not Southern. Don't know how much difference—if any—that makes, but there it is."

Murphy nodded and tipped back in his chair.

"Okay, that's the who. At least tentatively. What about the what?"

"That's where it gets interesting," O'Hanraghty said. "*Gallant*'s one of the ships we picked up at Jalal. Came over with basically her entire crew, including her CO—Cecilia Porro, good skipper, from her record—but according to his crewmates, Cortaberri pretty much sat the mutiny out. He didn't rush to join Captain Porro when she declared for the mutiny, but he didn't try to oppose it, either. Maybe just because he wasn't in any position to.

"Anyway, since the mutiny, his behavior's been exemplary. In fact, the only thing Commander Trossingen—he's Porro's XO—could tell me about any changes in it is that he hasn't been spending his free time with other members of *Gallant*'s company when they come aboard to use *Ishtar*'s visiting crew's rec compartment and gymnasium. Apparently, he's been taking the opportunity to get to know the parasite group's other personnel, instead, since *Gallant's* new to the task force. Captain Lowe's looking into the security cam imagery from the times he's been aboard, but so far nothing especially suspicious about that.

"On the other hand," O'Hanraghty's expression turned grimmer, "if we don't find anything, it's only going to be because we aren't looking in the right place. Or else because our deceased friend was a lot more careful than most of the professional spooks I know, because he was definitely dirty, Terry."

"How dirty? And how do you know, if Joe hasn't found anything in the security imagery?"

"I could begin by pointing out that he tried to shoot Callum and Eira," O'Hanraghty said dryly. "I don't think he had a clue who Callum was when he went for his gun—I could be wrong about that, but it happened awful quickly—so I doubt he was some kind of assassin. I think he was headed to meet someone aboard *Ishtar* as secretly as possible and took the scenic route to avoid being seen in one of the intra-ship cars or turning up on its security cam video. He never expected to see anyone rubbernecking in wormhole space, and I think he just panicked when he realized he'd been spotted and that Callum and Eira might remember seeing him and be able to describe him. If he'd just kept his head down and kept going, he'd probably still be alive, Eira wouldn't be in sick bay, and we might've found ourselves pretty much screwed when we get to Bellerophon."

"Why?" Murphy's eyes narrowed.

"Because he had a flash chip in his pocket. Very interesting flash chip, with a clutch of really cute Trojans. Bryant's looking at them right now—and keeping them the hell away from the main servers while he does it—and there's at least one program he hasn't been able to crack yet. Got a pretty good idea about three of the others, though."

"And those three are . . . ?" Murphy asked.

"One of them would have used *Ishtar's* tac net to shut down all of our parasite group's point-defense stations at the moment her own were ordered to engage. Another one would have locked the parasite racks when we tried to deploy. That one we could've gotten around pretty quickly, which is probably why number two was waiting to shut down their point defense just as the missiles came in. My favorite was number three, though. That's the one that would have used *Ishtar*'s main dish to burst-transmit our ID, our order of battle, and a summary report of the Battle of Jalal to Odysseus the moment we dropped sublight in the Bellerophon System."

"And MacTavish says there's a fourth one?"

"Yep. May never figure out what that one was supposed to be, though. He doesn't think he's gonna break it by the time we hit Bellerophon, anyway."

Murphy nodded. By the universe at large's calendar, *Ishtar* and her consorts were still thirteen days out of Bellerophon. By her own, she was only about forty-three hours from arrival. That didn't give his intelligence officer a lot of time to work the problem.

"On the other hand," O'Hanraghty continued, "the fact that Bryant can't even get into it is another indication Cortaberri wasn't working alone. According to Bryant, the holdout's fingerprints indicate that it was created by somebody a lot sneakier than Cortaberri. For that matter, Cortaberri couldn't have uploaded his chip to *Ishtar*'s servers. He didn't have access. So what it *looks* like was happening here was that he was on his way to hand deliver the chip to someone aboard *Ishtar*—or someone assigned to one of our other parasites—who *does* have access." He shook his head. "Either way, we've got rats in the woodwork, Terry."

"That was always a given." Murphy sighed. "We had proof enough of that with Vitek and Zamorano in Jalal. And hard to blame them, in some ways. But I want all of Cortaberri's movements and contacts under a microscope, Harry. We need to find out who he was talking to."

"Joe and I are both on it, and Bryant's taking another real hard look at our cybersecurity. At least we know what the threat is now. Thanks to Callum and Eira."

"Yeah." Murphy turned back to the display, watching as Callum reached out and touched Eira's limp hand very gently. "Thanks to them." He shook his head. "I almost got both of them killed in New Dublin when *Kolyma* got hit. Now this." He shook his head again. "It's costing too much, Harry. They can't keep dodging forever."

"The one thing we're all promised is that nobody gets out of life alive." O'Hanraghty's eyes were sad as he, too, looked at the sick bay feed. "So far, they've both done pretty good. It's up to you and me to keep it that way, I guess."

"I know," Murphy said quietly. "Believe me, I know."

✧   ✧   ✧

Eira's eyes fluttered open.

For a long moment, she had no idea where she was. But then those eyes moved to the blurry figure beside her bed and sharpened.

"Callum?" She blinked. "Callum, are you okay?"

"You're awake!" Callum reached out, grabbed her hand. "How's your pain level? Are you hungry? Thirsty?"

"Are you okay?" she repeated more sharply.

"I didn't get shot. You did. You saved my life." He smiled and squeezed her hand. "Again."

"How bad is it?" she asked, sweeping her free hand in a gesture that encompassed the sick bay cubicle.

"Could be better." His smile faded. "You took three hits. The bad one was your left lung, but Doc Barbeau says you're gonna be fine. It'll be a while before Logan gets to start running you ragged again, though."

Eira winced at the mention of the sergeant major.

"He's going to be *so* angry at me for letting you get shot at," she said.

"It wasn't your fault!"

"Doesn't matter whose 'fault' it is. What matters is that it happened."

"What *matters* is that you kept me alive, which should be enough to keep even Logan satisfied. And if it isn't, he'll hear about it from me!"

She looked at him dubiously, then shook her head on the pillow.

"The killer?" she asked, pulling her hand out of his grip and trying to push herself more upright.

"You nailed him." Callum tapped the bed controls, raising the end of the bed behind her shoulders. "I don't have all the juicy details—I've been hanging around here waiting for some-body to wake up—but O'Hanraghty and MacTavish say he was a saboteur. Had a bunch of Trojans for the central computer net. I dunno exactly what they would've done, but I'm pretty sure it would've been bad. Except you were in the right place to stop him. You're a hero!"

He patted her shin through the sheets.

"Is it supposed to hurt this much?" she asked.

"If you need more painkillers, don't be stupid enough to not ask for them. Trust me, I speak from a certain level of personal experience on that one."

"Am I in trouble?" she asked, and his eyebrows rose in surprise. "For almost letting you be killed," she clarified.

"Trouble with who?" Callum shrugged. "Logan's been a frigging whirlwind looking for more spies, and O'Hanraghty and MacTavish have been taking the bad guy's Trojans apart. Far as I know, the only person who seems to be pissed with you is you."

"But—"

"We need to stop doing this," Callum interrupted.

"Sir, I'm sorry if—"

"The whole dying thing, I mean."

"I don't think either of us *chooses* to get blown up or shot," she said. "Don't send me away. I'll do better next time, I promise!"

"No, no, no." Callum put a hand on her shoulder. "That's not what I mean. I mean let's not do this whole bleeding on each other thing again. I don't want you to go anywhere. I just want you to...be more careful. Seeing you like this...hurts me."

She looked at him for a long, silent moment, then smiled. It was oddly fragile, that smile, but real.

"I hate to say this," she said, "but I'm a little hungry."

"Doc says you can eat...assuming you can handle sick bay food." He rolled his eyes. "Trust me, it really sucks."

"People keep saying how bad the food is," she said. "They should try eating what Sam and I had to eat on Inverness."

"Well, I guess given a bar that low even hospital chow isn't *too* terrible," he acknowledged. "I'll get you something."

He stood and turned towards the cubicle door, then paused. He stayed that way a moment, then turned around and slid an arm behind her shoulders. He hugged her—hard—and she closed her eyes, ducked her head, and nuzzled her cheek against his chest.

CHAPTER TWENTY-THREE

Venus Futures Corporate HQ
City of Olympia
Old Terra
Sol System
Terran Federation
January 11, 2553

"I HATE THIS," SIMRON MURPHY SAID QUIETLY, LOOKING OUT THE aircar's side window.

"I know," her father replied. "It's not like we have a lot of options, though."

She turned her head to look at him, and despite her own residual anger at him, a pang went through her as she saw the worry in his eyes. He wouldn't have let anyone else see it, but there were fresh lines around his eyes, and she reached across to pat his knee.

"He really has put you in an awful position, hasn't he?" she asked with a crooked smile.

"I think you might say that, assuming you were given to massive understatement." Kanada's smile was considerably tarter than hers. "And I'm not going to pretend I'm not thoroughly pissed off with him, Simmy!"

"Of course not." She squeezed his knee, then sat back. "But *I'm* not going to pretend—not when it's just us, anyway—that I'm not proud of him."

"*Proud* of him?" Kanada looked at her. "Everything our family's built over the centuries is about to come down in ruins, Simmy! And that may be the least of it, given the mess in the

Cyclops Sector. If the rest of the Five Hundred decides to blame him for that, too—!"

"You know as well as I do that all the charges against him were trumped up out of whole cloth," Simron said rather more sharply.

She held his eyes with her own, and, after a moment, he grimaced and looked away.

"Maybe you've got a point," he half muttered. "But why did he have to bring the storm down on all of us? On Venus Futures? On our entire family?"

"Because—" she said levelly "—the Five Hundred is just as corrupt as all of its critics have ever said it was. And that includes us."

"Corrupt?" Her father's head whipped back around. "You think I'm *corrupt*, Simmy?"

"I think we both are." Her tone never wavered, but her blue eyes were somber. "I think the entire Five Hundred is. I think the entire *Federation* is, and we—you and I and Venus Futures—are part of the same system. We didn't ask to be. But the truth is, Father, until Terry rubbed everyone's nose in it, I was just as oblivious to the corruption around me as anyone else."

"Simmy, I never—"

"Father, Father!" She shook her head and reached up to touch his cheek. "On a personal level, you're one of the most honest men I know, but you *are* part of the system. You were born into it. It's the only universe you've ever known, and you accept its ground rules because they're the only ones you've ever been able to play by. And, to be honest, you're very, very good at gaming the system, making it work for you. So am I, because you're also a wonderful teacher, which means *I* know how to make the system work, too. But that doesn't mean it isn't corrupt. And that doesn't mean that all those Fringe Worlds who resent the hell out of what happens to *their* families and *their* kids don't have a point. Of course they do! That's the real reason the Five Hundred has to destroy Terry, and you know it!"

Kanada stared at her. For a moment, neither spoke. Then he inhaled deeply.

"Obviously I'm not a wonderful enough teacher," he said. "If I were, you wouldn't be as crazy as your husband!" He shook his head. "Even assuming you're right—and, to be honest, you probably are—that doesn't change what we're up against right now. The only way we're going to survive is to throw Terry out of the aircar. You know that. Even if Rajenda talks him into coming home peacefully, the rest of the Five Hundred can't let his example stand—especially after Bellerophon—no matter what."

"It can't let his example stand unless ... something changes the equation," Simron said, and his eyes widened.

"Simmy—"

"Father, you're the one who told me the Five Hundred—excuse me, *Prime Minister Schleibaum's Government*—was sending Alaimo out to 'deal with' Bellerophon. No matter what happens with Terry and New Dublin, Cyclops has already turned into a disaster zone, and letting Alaimo turn Bellerophon into another Gobelins will only make the disaster even worse! In fact, it's the stupidest thing we could have done!"

"I admit the thought of 'another Gobelins' turns my stomach," Kanada said, "but I don't know that there was another solution, another answer that was any better!"

"There couldn't possibly have been one that was any *worse*," she said flatly. "Think about it, Father. I know how smart you are, so *think* about it! We already know at least some of the Cyclops system pickets have mutinied, and I've been thinking back to all those boring conversations of Terry's. All the times he wanted to talk to me about the Navy and the Fringe but I had something else to think about. And one of the things he told me that stuck in my mind is that two thirds—*at least* two thirds—of the Navy's personnel are Fringers. I remembered that when you told me about Alaimo, and I did a little additional research, and I found out he was right. And I also found out that the percentage is even higher for the Marines. Not the Army, but then you and I both know the Army's real job, don't we?"

Her eyes challenged him, and he nodded slowly, as if against his will.

"So how do you think that two thirds of our armed forces are going to react if they find out Alaimo's been sent to 'Gobelins' Bellerophon? If this time it's open and aboveboard? Nobody tries to sweep it under the carpet or deny it really happened?" It was her turn to shake her head. "The genie's not going back into the bottle this time, Father, and if the Fringe really does go up in flames, it will burn the Federation to the ground. Unless someone prevents that from happening. And that means that at the end of the day, the best the Five Hundred can hope for—what the Five Hundred had damned well better *pray* for—is that Terry, *my husband*, can somehow keep a handle on what's coming out of the Fringe. I'll be honest—I don't know if even Terry can pull that one off. But I'll tell you this. If he can't, no one can, and in that case the Federation itself is coming apart."

"You really think it's...that bad? And that if it is, *Terry* has a chance to turn it around?"

"I remember something else Terry said to me once." Simron looked away, gazing out the front windows as Venus Futures' HQ complex appeared on the horizon. "He told me that the vast majority of human beings always assume that the way things are is the way they've always been and always will be. It's the only world they know, because they never look beyond it. And that, he said, is the real reason for every disastrous political and social shipwreck in human history. The people in positions of power never saw it coming, because none of them were interested in looking for it.

"I thought that was just another example of his...romantic disconnect from the real world. The fact that he loved history more than the present. But I should have been listening, because he's right. I was no more interested than the rest of the Five Hundred in looking for possible shipwrecks because everything seemed so wonderful on the promenade deck and in the owner's suite. But he and that incredibly irritating O'Hanraghty were up in the crow's nest, looking for icebergs, and I think you and I had damned well better hope they and their friends can do something to prevent—or at least...ameliorate—*this* shipwreck. And that means the last thing we can afford to do is to demonize him. If we back him and any Fringer 'moderates' who might be willing to listen to him into a corner, any soft landing for the Federation—and even the Five Hundred—gets a lot less likely. That's one reason—a *big* reason—I've been fighting so hard to keep this 'spontaneous statement' from squirting any more hydrogen into the fire."

Kanada frowned as the aircar dipped towards the landing pad atop the South Tower. That might have been *a* reason for her resistance, he thought, but it wasn't truly *the* reason. No, the true reason was far simpler: she loved him. That didn't mean her analysis was wrong, of course, although the possibility that she might be right terrified him, but that wasn't the reason she was willing to listen to Murphy in the first place.

She loved him.

Well, Kanada loved *her*. That was the reason he'd supported her version of the statement the Five Hundred demanded of her. What she was willing to say fell far short of what they wanted, but she'd dug in her heels, stubbornly refused to be the obedient daughter of the Five Hundred they wanted her to be. And because he recognized that stubbornness's invincibility—and because he loved her—he'd fought hard behind the scenes to support her. He'd told himself he had to broker the compromise to protect Venus Futures, and there was a huge, terrifying element of truth in that, but the real reason was that he loved his daughter.

He'd burned a lot of IOUs along the way, and only the fact that the rest of the Five Hundred knew how determined Rajenda was to bring Murphy back dead or alive had let him protect her from the demands of Perrin and the rest of the Commission this long. And that was the most frightening thing of all, he thought, as the aircar touched down on the landing pad, because she was right about the Five Hundred's probable reaction if Rajenda failed to bring Murphy home in abject surrender and disgrace. And how did he protect her if full panic mode set in among the Five Hundred's leadership?

And if she was right about the peril the Five Hundred already faced, did Gerard Perrin or Jugoslav Darković have even the faintest idea of how much worse they could make it? Of how Terrence Murphy would react if something...untoward happened to Simron or their children? If *anything* happened to them, he would become the Five Hundred's worst nightmare.

And so, Kanada Thakore realized, would he.

The producer looked up with a nervous expression as Simron and Kanada walked into the twenty-third-floor studio. Taraneh Mehrian had produced hundreds of video clips and full-length programs for Venus Futures over the years, but never one like this. Never one with Amedeo Boyle and two expressionless security agents standing against the wall, watching her work.

The only person in the entire studio who looked calm was Simron Thakore. She glanced coolly at Boyle and his "security" as she entered, then ignored them completely as she walked past them to the set's comfortable "casual conversation nook" and paused beside the polished coffee table.

"The couch or the armchair, Taraneh?" she asked in a voice as cool as her eyes.

"The couch, I think, Ma'am," Mehrian said. "I've got the lighting adjusted for that, so if you don't—"

"The couch will be fine!" Simron assured her.

She settled onto the couch, adjusting the drape of her sari, and waited patiently while Mehrian fussed with her camera and lighting drones. There was really no reason Simron couldn't have recorded the same statement on her personal data pad, but this particular video clip had to be perfect.

And, of course, Perrin's lackey has to be here to make sure it is, doesn't he? she thought, glancing coldly at Boyle.

It took a while, but finally Mehrian nodded in satisfaction— from a technical perspective, at least.

"We're ready, Ma'am," she said. "Just begin whenever you're comfortable."

"Fine," Simron said, and leaned back slightly on the couch, looking into the center of the five drones hovering around her.

"Good evening," she said then. "For those of you who don't recognize me, I am Simron Murphy, Admiral Terrence Murphy's wife. As I'm sure the vast majority of the Federation's citizens know by now, there are all manner of allegations swirling about where my husband is concerned. Given the realities of interstellar flight and how long it takes for information to get from star to star, it will be some time still before we here in the Sol System can know what's actually happening someplace as distant as New Dublin. I certainly don't know any more than any of you view-ing this video know. That's why I'm recording this statement. Because I think it's important that we not allow our ignorance and uncertainty to get...out of hand.

"Obviously, the conflicting stories about my husband and his possible actions are extremely distressing to me, not simply as his wife but as a loyal citizen of the Federation. I very much want—even need—for there to be an explanation that exonerates him of all the allegations leveled against him. At the same time, I'm aware that the Government has no option but to proceed cautiously and on the basis of a worst-case scenario. So at this present moment, I join with everyone, I'm sure, in hoping and praying for a peaceful resolution to the entire situation. And until we know more, until I've had the opportunity to hear my husband's side of the story, my children and I will continue to pray for his safe return and—if God is good—exoneration.

"I realize it will be months before Prime Minister Schleibaum's government can know with certainty what's transpired in New Dublin and the rest of the Concordia Sector. Until that time— until we do know, with certainty—the Government has, of course, my and my family's full support. My own brother, Rajenda, has been sent to get to the bottom of the conflicting versions, and I promise all of you that no one could be more determined than he to do precisely that. If it should turn out that Terrence has unintentionally—or even intentionally—violated Federation law or his own oath as an officer in the Federation Navy, he will be held fully to account for his actions, and I will—however regretfully— abide by the decisions of the Navy and the civilian courts.

"In the meantime, I ask only that we not rush to judgment until we know what those actions truly were. Thank you."

She paused long enough for a decent fade, then looked at Boyle with one raised, contemptuous eyebrow.

"I trust that was sufficient?" she said coldly.

From his expression, he clearly wanted to tell her it wasn't, but his eyes fidgeted away from hers, and he shrugged.

"I think it will do, thank you. For now, anyway."

"Good. Then I believe we're done."

Simron Thakore was the smallest person in that studio, but she strode from it like a Titan.

CHAPTER TWENTY-FOUR

Bellerophon System
Free Worlds Alliance
January 12, 2553

THE BEDSIDE COMM CHIMED.

The soft, musical tone wasn't all that loud in the silent sleeping cabin, but Lauren Carson's eyes popped open almost instantly, with the spinal reflex of eighteen years of naval service, and her hand reached out to the touchscreen even as she sat upright in bed.

"Yes," she said, accepting the call voice-only.

"They're here, Ma'am," Commander Michael Fleischmann, her chief of staff, said tersely from the display's wallpaper.

"On profile for Horatius?" Carson's voice was sharper.

"It looks that way," Fleischmann replied. "At least we just picked up a hellacious Fasset footprint coming in on a least-time bearing from Sol." Carson could almost hear his teeth-baring grin. "And from its strength and how far out we saw it, they're loaded for bear."

"We knew they would be," Carson pointed out, much more calmly than she actually felt, then inhaled deeply. "Get us moving, Mike. I'll be on Flag Bridge in five."

"Aye, aye, Ma'am."

✧ ✧ ✧

"Well, Alessandro?"

Admiral Regis Hathaway turned his command chair to face his chief of staff on TFNS *Dione*'s flag bridge and raised an eyebrow over one blue eye.

"Final readiness reports coming in now, Sir," Commodore

315

Covino replied, watching his own displays. He waited another heartbeat or two, then looked up and met Hathaway's gaze. "All units report ready," he said.

"Good!"

Hathaway nodded crisply, then turned back to his own console, wishing he felt remotely as confident as he sounded. Although, he conceded, "confidence" might not be the very best word for what he lacked. He wasn't certain what the best word was, though. Although perhaps "hope" would have been a better one.

There wasn't very much of *that* around, either, after all.

How had it come to this, he wondered. How had everything gone so totally off the rails? So completely into the crapper? Hadn't *anyone* out here in the Fringe realized how it had to end? How the Federation had no choice but to *make* it end?

He thought again about the intelligence briefings. For all the good they were likely to do any of the people charged to deal with this mess. In fairness, he supposed, there hadn't been a hell of a lot of hard intel for the briefers to share...and what there was had been preposterous.

Hathaway had never met Terrence Murphy. For that matter, as far as he could tell, not a single one of Ninth Fleet's senior officers had ever served with Murphy. Not surprising in something the size of the TFN, if he'd spent his entire career in Survey. But according to the intel weenies, the man had never even seen combat...until that business at Steelman, anyway. And yet he was supposed to have kicked the Leaguies' ass not just once, but twice? To have taken out a *dozen* League carriers and captured every single one of their parasites intact? Won the biggest engagement the TFN had fought in *decades* and then backtracked them to some secret shipyard on the back-ass side of nowhere...where they'd been building another *forty* damned carriers? And that didn't even mention his lunatic ravings about the Rish!

At best, and being as charitable as Hathaway possibly could, the man had to be insane. But whether or not that was true in any clinical sense didn't really matter, because whatever the reason for his delusions, what he certainly was was the spark that was about to plunge the Terran Federation into a spasm of bloodshed and chaos only too likely to piss away everything it had bought with sixty years of bloody warfare. It didn't really matter whether or not he truly was the would-be warlord the

Oval and Prime Minster Schleibaum's government thought he was. In fact, it didn't even matter if he'd rolled over and surrendered as soon as Task Force 804 reached New Dublin. What he'd already done—at Inverness and in the "Battle of New Dublin"—had obviously been the first shifting stones of an avalanche whose potential for disaster would be impossible to overestimate. The lunatics in Bellerophon who'd chosen to go out of compliance had to have been inspired by *something* and there was no doubt in Regis Hathaway's mind who the face of that something had been.

The need to somehow stave off that disaster was what had brought Hathaway and Ninth Fleet here, and he closed his eyes for a moment, his back safely turned to his staff, and wondered what the history books would have to say about what he was about to do. What he had no choice *but* to do.

Hathaway was a Heart Worlder, but he'd put in his time in the Fringe. He understood why so many Fringers were so bitter. And as far as that went, he was prepared to admit—off the record—that they had a right to that bitterness. But secession from the Federation wasn't "reform;" it was treason. It was tearing the system down, not fixing its flaws, and if the system went down, the *Federation* went down.

That wasn't happening on his watch.

He prayed the people of Odysseus would be smart enough to recognize the inevitable and accept it, because he was afraid of what someone like Taskin Alaimo would do to them if they didn't. For that matter, a corner of his mind, one he tried not to look at closely, was afraid of what someone like Alaimo would do to them even if they *did* surrender.

Examples, he thought bitterly. *There have to be "examples," because that bastard Murphy's let the genie out of the bottle and it's not going back in without them. But doesn't anyone back home in Olympia understand what letting someone like* Alaimo *make the examples is going to* do?!

Obviously, they didn't. Or, worse, they *did* understand ... and didn't care. And if Odysseus wasn't smart enough to stand down, if Alaimo ordered Ninth Fleet to apply Standing Order Fifteen, then it would be Regis Hathaway's finger on the button.

"Two minutes to sublight," Commander Vaníčková announced quietly from Astrogation, and Hathaway nodded.

At *Dione*'s current velocity, two minutes ship-time would be almost three hours for the clocks of the Bellerophon System.

Assuming they got the system arrays intact, they've known we're coming for at least an hour already. And the size of our footprint's going to tell them we came loaded for bear. I wonder what they've been up to for the last hour—their time—or so?

"Point Alpha in fifteen minutes, Ma'am," Lieutenant Commander Gray said, and Commodore Carson—who'd never expected to be the commodore of anything, far less of something as powerful as what had been designated the Bellerophon System Navy—nodded at the reminder.

"Thank you, Chloe," she said, and she was just a bit surprised by how level her own voice sounded.

It wasn't as if she'd really needed the reminder. Every single person on TFNS *Aurora*'s flag deck was burningly aware of the digital timer counting down in one corner of the main display. But it was Gray's job to give it to her, just as it was her job to project an aura of confidence.

The BSN had been accelerating for over two hours since picking up the incoming FTL signature of what had to be the Oval's response to Bellerophon's secession.

She'd been able to get underway so quickly because her ships had been waiting for its arrival in close company with the main gravitic sensor platforms that had detected it. She'd needed to be close to them to cut down transmission lag when the attackers' FTL footprint was detected, which was why the Calloglou Consortium's tugs had moved them to a point just outside the Bellerophon System's 58.3 LM Powell Limit on a direct line with the most probable arrival vector for anyone coming directly from Sol. And they'd actually picked up the footprint earlier than Carson had counted on... which, unfortunately, undoubtedly meant the incoming force was even larger and more powerful than she'd feared.

Her ships' initial position also had lain just outside the limit, where their full acceleration rate was available to them And while she couldn't be positive of the exact range at which the attack force would drop sublight, its track told her the exact bearing to the spot upon which it would reenter normal-space, and she'd pushed her fans to 1,900 cee, a bit above their designed acceleration rate. Now, after two hours and twenty-five minutes, the BSN's carriers were up to a velocity of 162,103 KPS relative to the system primary... and 39.2 LM out from the Powell Limit.

No way in hell anybody on the other side's going to expect this one, she thought grimly. *Mostly because it's as crazy as anything Governor Murphy ever came up with. One thing about him, watching him in action. It does teach you to think outside the box!*

And now, *because* it was so far outside the box—and if everything only worked perfectly—nobody on the other side would see it coming until it was too damned late to do anything about it.

Of course, as she'd told the civilians, that was assuming everything worked *perfectly.*

"Sublight... now," Vaníčková said, and the display configured for external view was suddenly spangled with pinprick stars. "Range to system primary is... one-niner-zero-point-five light-minutes."

"*Very* good, Aneta," Hathaway approved, and it was. The astrogator had hit almost exactly their intended emergence point, which wasn't remotely as easy as a layman might think. Not after a ninety-three-light-year voyage! "And the transport echelon?"

"We don't have them on sensors yet, Sir," Captain Naidu, Ninth Fleet's operations officer, replied. "They dropped off right on the mark, though, so we should be seeing them... shortly."

Hathaway snorted. If the transport group and its escorting task group had, in fact, gone sublight on schedule, they were five light-minutes farther out than the rest of Ninth Fleet. Given that his flagship's velocity was 297,000 KPS, any light-speed emissions from the transports had only a 2,800 KPS overtake speed. Had both forces' velocities held constant, it would have taken almost nine hours—well, only a bit over one and a half hours, shipboard time, thanks to relativity—for those emissions to catch up with *Dione* and her consorts. Of course, they weren't going to remain constant, given that *Dione* was already decelerating hard.

General Alaimo had complained about Hathaway's decision to drop him and Rear Admiral Jorgensen's Task Group 901.3 that far out, but Hathaway didn't need them underfoot while he dealt with any defending naval units.

It was remotely possible—unlikely, but possible—that he'd need Jorgensen in a worst-case situation. He had no intention of crossing the Powell Limit until he knew whether or not he would, and if he did, he'd hold off while Jorgensen and the transports caught up with him. But it wouldn't have been that hard for any defenders to estimate his emergence locus with a fair degree of accuracy, assuming he wanted a least-time course to Odysseus. Five light-minutes should be an adequate safety margin, and he had no intention of letting anyone sneak into missile range of those transports and the Expeditionary Force until he knew exactly where any defenders might be located. Speaking of which...

"Deploy Heimdallars," he said.

"Deploying now, Sir," Naidu acknowledged, and Hathaway nodded as Ninth Fleet decelerated towards the distant, tiny pinprick of the star called Bellerophon at 1,800 gravities and the survey platforms coasted ballistically onward ahead of it.

"They're sublight, Ma'am," Commander O'Flanagan announced as the FTL footprint they'd been tracking disappeared from *Aurora*'s plot. "We won't have them on light-speed sensors for a while, but it looks like they hit almost exactly on their projected emergence point."

"Good," Carson replied, and looked at the comm display. At the moment, it showed the COs of all eight of her FTLCs, including *Aurora*, and she smiled thinly at them.

"And now," she told them over the tight, whisker-thin comm lasers, "we sneak up on the bastards and shoot them in the fucking face."

"Works for us, Ma'am," Captain Rodoulis told her from TFNS *Freyr*, and the others nodded in grim agreement ... and anticipation, in a few cases.

There was a reason Lauren Carson had named her ops plan "Horatius," and all of them recognized just how all-or-nothing, go-for-broke it was. But that very audacity was what gave it a chance of success, because no TFN flag officer had ever been crazy enough to try something like this.

Except for Terrence Murphy, perhaps.

The Bellerophon System Defense Force had accelerated for 160 minutes, to a velocity of 178,873 KPS, and then, just over an hour and a half ago, shut down its Fasset drives and gone to silent running. Their velocity had carried them 47.7 LM from the Powell Limit, 84.7 LM from the point at which the incoming fleet had just gone sublight. But they had shut down 100 minutes before that, which meant their last light-speed emissions had already passed the incoming hostiles before they ever dropped out of wormhole space.

At the moment, the BSN was closing with the new arrivals on a direct reciprocal at a combined apparent velocity of 475,800 KPS, well above the speed of light, under complete EMCON, and at a range of 1,524,600,000 kilometers, over twice the distance from Earth to Jupiter, there was no way in hell their visitors could have a clue Carson and her people were there.

Now if it just stays *that way*, she thought to herself.

"Signal from Admiral Jorgensen, Sir," Commander Sundqvist said, and Regis Hathaway raised an eyebrow at his comm officer. "He confirms sublight with all units at the designated coordinates."

"Always good to know," Commodore Covino said dryly, and Hathaway chuckled.

"Be nice," he told his chief of staff quietly, and Covino snorted.

"I know," he said. "But Jorgensen's just so…so—"

"He doesn't have a lot of imagination," Hathaway acknowledged. "And you and I both know why I picked him to ride herd on the transports instead of Hendricks or Sumio. But he's solid, Alessandro."

"I know," Covino repeated, this time with an edge of contrition, and Hathaway nodded before he turned back to the main plot.

It was true that Elijah Jorgensen was a tad short on both imagination and initiative. For that matter, he was a bit of a fussbudget, a chronic, compulsive dotter of *I*s and crosser of *T*s. His transmission only underscored that. It had taken just under ten minutes for the light-speed message to catch up with *Dione*, and it hadn't been necessary in the first place. The flagship's sensors had picked up his ships' equally light-speed normal-space emissions a clear twenty seconds before his transmission had arrived.

So, yes, Hathaway understood Covino's comment. But as he'd just pointed out to the chief of staff, Jorgensen was also as solid and unflinching as a flag officer came. He might not be as… tactically nimble as Hathaway's other division commanders, and no one in his right mind would assign him to a major independent command, but give him a clear set of orders, and he would execute them faithfully and well, come hell or high water.

Hathaway shoved Jorgensen back into his mental filing cabinet and returned his full attention to the plot. It would be a while yet before even the Heimdallars racing ahead of his decelerating FTLCs could give him any kind of close look at the inner system, but at the moment that plot seemed remarkably barren of transponder codes or emission signatures. No doubt the defenders—and there would *be* defenders, he was sure, since the secessionists had taken at least the four carriers of the Bellerophon picket—had followed SOP and gone to strict emissions control the moment his own incoming Fasset signature had been detected. That had been a given from the get-go. On the other hand, if they intended to intercept him anywhere short of the inner system, they'd have to be getting a move on sometime soon. In fact, they probably had started moving already and their emissions just hadn't reached him yet. He'd only traveled 9.9 LM since going sublight, after all, which meant anything his sensors saw inside the Powell Sphere was still at least a two-hour look into the past.

He'd feel a hell of a lot more comfortable when he knew exactly where the bastards were—and, for that matter, how many of them he actually faced. Even in a worst-case scenario in which every single carrier in the Cyclops Sector had mutinied, his main striking force had a fifty percent advantage in FTL platforms, but he hoped like hell his edge was actually bigger than that.

"Point Beta."

Commander Fleischman's quiet announcement seemed to echo like a gunshot through the nerve-twisting quiet of TFNS *Aurora*'s flag bridge.

There were several reasons no one ever adopted the tactics Lauren Carson and the Bellerophon System Navy had chosen. The main reason—at least for most flag officers—was that one simply did *not* bring one's FTLCs into a close-range engagement if one could possibly avoid it. They weren't designed for that, they weren't intended for that, and they were far too strategically valuable for that. In Carson's case, the need to intercept any attackers—intercept them in a way that forced them to engage, deprived them of any option to evade her and avoid action—trumped the value of her own carriers. She *had* to strip them of the ability to simply stand off and threaten Odysseus with long-range bombardment. Like the ancient Roman for whom she'd named her ops plan, she had to bar the gate and *keep* it barred until Terrence Murphy's reinforcements could arrive.

But there was another and far more nerve-racking reason most admirals would have avoided Horatius like the plague. At their closing velocity, the attacking carriers were so close behind their light-speed emissions that she wouldn't even be able to see them until a handful of minutes before they actually engaged. Although the incoming FTLCs had presumably been decelerating for over half an hour now, their velocity was probably still close to 260,000 KPS, right on eighty-seven percent of the speed of light. Assuming that was true, their emissions signature, propagating at 300,000 KPS, was all of 2.4 LM ahead of them. So Carson still had no way to know just how heavy the odds against her command were.

Of course, the invaders were almost certainly blissfully aware of her silent-running task force. While it was true that any of her emissions would reach them far sooner than theirs reached her, there were damn-all emissions for their passive sensors to see, under full emissions control and with her own Fasset drives down. About the only thing that could give away her presence was an optical scan directly ahead of them, and no one bothered with optical scans, given all the other, far more sophisticated systems available. For that matter, every one of her ships had its smart paint dialed up to maximum absorbency, turning them into little more than dark blotches in space. Unless someone was looking in exactly the right instant one of her ships occluded a star, they should be virtually invisible. Which should mean there was no way the invaders could know she and *her* carriers were barely twenty-five minutes short of that head-on intercept...assuming her estimate that her foes were on a least-time heading for Odysseus was correct.

Not that either side actually had twenty-five minutes, given the relativistic effect of their velocities. At the BSN's current velocity, what was twenty-five minutes for the rest of the universe would be only twenty minutes aboard its ships, and it was even worse for the attackers. For them, it would be less than thirteen minutes, and The Book set *thirty* minutes as the time requirement for an FTLC to deploy her sublight parasites. They could *launch* in less—the absolute minimum for a crash launch, assuming her parasites were fully prepped and manned, was about five minutes—but it would still take them another fifteen to reach their assigned positions in their carriers' missile defense formations. And *unless* they were fully prepped and manned, they couldn't even get them launched in less than fifteen.

And what are the odds the Oval could find an admiral stupid enough to not have her birds prepped? Carson thought. *Hell, Yance Drebin would be smart enough to man all stations at the start of an attack run!*

Her lips twitched ever so slightly at the thought.

"Deploy," she said.

"Deploying," Dominic O'Flanagan acknowledged, and Carson watched the status boards as the BSN's parasites—and cargo pods of Casúr Cogaidhs—detached from the FTLCs' racks.

There were fewer of those parasites than there might have been, partly because close to twelve percent of the Cyclops Sector's sublight units had been significantly damaged when their crews mutinied in Bellerophon's support. But there was another reason she'd embarked fewer than she might have, because each of her eight carriers had embarked four cargo pods stuffed with a hundred and thirty-two Casúr Cogaidhs apiece in the space the same number of battlecruisers might have occupied. In theory, that had cost her thirty-two sublight platforms, but Lauren Carson was fine with that, because it gave her 4,224 Casúrs in their place.

Now the missile pods spread out, using only their reaction docking thrusters and not their Hauptman coils. They settled into attack position, taking station well ahead of her carriers while her parasites formed up behind them.

"Still no sign of the bastards, Sir," Alessandro Covino murmured, floating in Flag Bridge's microgravity beside Regis Hathaway's command chair.

"Well, we've only been sublight for thirty-five minutes," Hathaway pointed out. In fact, by *Dione*'s clocks, they'd been sublight for less than *eighteen* minutes, but professional spacers learned to allow for time dilation.

"Agreed, but they had four hours' notice we were coming," Covino countered, "and we're still over a light-hour and a half from the Powell Limit. If they're out there and coming out to meet us, we should've seen *something* by now. Fasset drives aren't exactly the stealthiest things in the universe."

"That's true," Hathaway acknowledged. "But we don't know what kind of flight profile they may have decided on, either. For that matter, they may *not* have decided on their profile ahead of time. It's entirely possible they're waiting until they get an actual count on what we've brought to the party. It'd make sense for them to be somewhere outside the limit with us, probably somewhere off to the side in a position that would let them generate an intercept, assuming we came in on a least-time vector. That would give them their best opportunity to assess the odds and decide whether or not they can afford to engage us before they actually do."

"Maybe." Covino nodded. "On the other hand, whether they like the odds or not, they've still got the planet to defend. Be pretty ballsy of them to risk letting us blow right past them if they guessed wrong or if we decided to just ignore them."

Hathaway rubbed an eyebrow thoughtfully. On the one hand, a CO who knew he'd be outnumbered but couldn't be positive by how much probably would be looking for a position that would allow him to generate an intercept but wouldn't allow his numerically stronger opponent to force a sustained engagement. On the other hand, Covino had a point. A defending admiral who guessed right about his opponent's approach vector could generate a crossing engagement, and if he came in at the right angle, the attacker would be unable to generate sufficient Delta V to bend his own base course enough to force any sort of *sustained* engagement. That sort of high-speed, hit-and-run engagement was far less likely to end in the weaker force's destruction. But it also meant the *defender* couldn't force the kind of sustained engagement that might actually stop the attacker short of the planet that was his true objective.

And Covino was also right that Fasset drives weren't exactly hard to spot on passives.

"I imagine we'll see some sign of them shortly," the admiral said. "Because you're right, they do have to stand and fight somewhere."

He grimaced unhappily.

"I'm not looking forward to it when they do, frankly," he said in an even quieter tone, for Covino's ears alone. "I know they're mutineers, and I know we've got it to do, Alessandro, but this is going to be ugly." He shook his head. "God knows I never thought I'd be killing Federation starships, but—"

The sudden, shrill whoop of an alarm slashed across the flag deck's quiet, and Hathaway's eyes snapped back to the main plot as an icon blazed suddenly upon it. It strobed the rapid, crimson of an unidentified contact, and—

"Unknown contact!" *Dione*'s tactical officer announced sharply over the intra-ship comm from the big carrier's CIC. "Single-point source, bearing zero-zero-one, zero-zero-four. Estimated range two-eight-point-six light-minutes!"

Hathaway stared at the plot in disbelief, then looked at Captain Naidu as the ops officer bent over his console, flying fingers working to refine the data.

"Whatever it is, it's not radiating," Naidu said.

"Then what the hell *is* it doing?" Covino demanded. "If it's not radiating, how do we know there's really something there in the first place?"

"May be just a glitch in the system, Sir," Naidu replied, never looking up from his display. "May not be, too, though. Whatever it is, CIC picked it up optically."

Hathaway frowned. Optically? At that range?

"Optically?" Covino repeated out loud, as if he'd heard his admiral's thoughts, and his tone was skeptical.

"I think somebody in Combat Information was searching visually for our Heimdallars," Naidu said.

"What?!"

Hathaway stared at him. Isabella Whitworth, *Dione*'s tactical officer, was fond of unscheduled training exercises at the most unexpected moments possible. It was one reason her department was so good. But the recon platforms were incredibly stealthy, and they'd drawn almost two and a half light-minutes ahead of Ninth Fleet as they continued ballistically at 297,000 KPS while the carriers decelerated at 1,800 gravities. Expecting her people to visually locate Heimdallars at 41,400,000 kilometers was a bit... demanding even for her. Oh, it wasn't an *impossible* challenge—not quite—when they already knew where the Heimdallars in question were supposed to be, but it still came pretty damned close.

That was his first thought. Then he frowned. Whatever the hell CIC thought it had found, it was one hell of a lot farther out than the Heimdallars could possibly be.

"Sounds like a ghost to me," Covino said.

"Yes, but on an *optical* search?" Hathaway shook his head. "That's not your usual sensor ghost, and—"

He stiffened as another flashing icon popped onto the display. Then another. Then *dozens* of them!

"Bogies!" Commander Whitworth's voice snapped from CIC. "Multiple bogies closing at four-three-six thousand KPS!"

Even as Hathaway stared in disbelief, icons began to stop blinking, and he inhaled sharply as CIC tagged them with identifiers. At least—at *least*—seven FTLCs' icons glared at him, with dozens of deployed parasites riding shotgun.

"Jesus!" Covino muttered harshly from beside him, and Hathaway sucked in a deep breath.

He knew he was actually looking into the past, but he also knew CIC had allowed for that in the range information glaring in the plot. And according to that, the "bogies" were less than twenty-nine light-minutes from Ninth Fleet, closing at better than 436,000 KPS on a direct reciprocal. That meant their courses would intersect in barely twenty minutes—less than *eleven* minutes, by *Dione's* clocks. And *that* meant—

"Alpha launch—now!" he barked.

"Alpha launch, aye!" Naidu replied almost instantly, and another alarm howled as every FTLC in Hathaway's force launched its own parasites.

"They must be out of their goddamned minds!" Covino said. Even in his shock, he kept his voice down, but Hathaway heard the sheer consternation rattling around in its depths. "This is fucking suicide!"

"Not if Whitworth hadn't decided to conduct her little training exercise," Hathaway grated, watching the plot as the first of his parasites accelerated furiously clear of the carriers at ten gravities. "They've got all of their parasites spotted. If we hadn't picked them up—if they'd hit us head-on this way, without warning and with all our birds still on the racks—they'd have ripped the ever-loving shit out of us. In fact, they're still going to. The only difference is—" he bared his teeth "—that now we're going to rip the shit out of *them*, too."

The Oval hadn't given Ninth Fleet anywhere near as much working up time as Arkadios Fokaides would have preferred or as Regis Hathaway could have wished for. But Hathaway had known that would be the case going in. That was why he'd drilled his personnel mercilessly on the month-long voyage from the Sol

System to Bellerophon, and the consequences of that drill showed as his sublight units spread out around his carriers in far less time than The Book required.

The brains of the men and women crewing those parasites fought to catch up with the situation as they launched from an absolute cold start at maximum acceleration. They'd gone to their stations even before Ninth Fleet dropped sublight, but no one had anticipated launching this far out. They were still four hours' flight short of the Powell Limit, much less the planet, for God's sake!

As the acceleration crushed them back into their couches, they found themselves very much in agreement with Commodore Covino. This was insane! Navies didn't fight this kind of battle. FTLCs had no business in point-blank combat with anybody, far less *other* FTLCs! But the only way Lauren Carson could get her parasites—and the Casúr Cogaidhs about which not a single soul in Ninth Fleet knew a single thing—into range of Regis Hathaway's FTLCs was to carry them there aboard *her* FTLCs. Without those carriers' lift and the acceleration of their Fasset drives, Hathaway's starships could have evaded them with ludicrous ease, especially outside the Powell Limit. Indeed, if Whitworth's "exercise" had spotted them even a few minutes earlier, he could still have evaded them. But only by holding his own parasites on the racks, where their point defense would be virtually useless, and he needed that defensive depth to protect his carriers against the parasites he knew she'd already deployed.

Unfortunately for Ninth Fleet, he didn't know what *else* she'd deployed.

Not that knowing would have done him any good.

✧   ✧   ✧

"Shit!" Commander O'Flanagan snarled. He turned towards Carson. "Ma'am—"

"I see it, Dominic," the commodore said as the plot updated suddenly. She had more time, subjectively, than Hathaway to watch it at the BSN's lower velocity, but that didn't make it one bit better.

"I wonder what the hell they spotted." Fleischman sounded far calmer than he had any right to sound.

"No EMCON is perfect," Carson replied almost absently. "They could even have picked us up on optics. They'd've had to be looking in exactly the right direction, but if we occluded the primary, that might've been enough. Not that it matters."

"We'll still catch them before they're fully deployed," Fleischman said, watching the battleships and cruisers accelerating away from Ninth Fleet's carriers. "Their defensive basket's going to be a lot shallower than ours."

"Oh, I'm confident we're about to rip the absolute hell out of them," Carson said. "They don't have any clue what's about to happen to them. Unfortunately, with all those additional platforms out there, they're going to rip hell out of us, too."

She looked at the plot a moment longer, then back at O'Flanagan.

"Fire plan Alamo," she said.

"What the hell is all that little shit?" Hathaway demanded irritably.

The plot continued to change as CIC refined its data, and hundreds of far smaller Hauptman drive point sources had just appeared on it, frothing ahead of the mutinous carriers like some sort of bow wave.

"We don't know, Sir," Naidu replied, still working at his console. "They look like some kind of outsized drone."

"Bastets?" Cosimo asked in a dubious tone, and Hathaway grunted. It would make a lot of sense for whoever was in command over there to get his anti-missile defensive platforms deployed well ahead of time, but nobody carried *that* many Bastet drones. Besides—

"Too big for that," Naidu said. "Maybe even bigger than Heimdallars."

"What the hell are these people playing at now?" Hathaway growled.

"Launch," Lauren Carson said.

Three quarters of the Bellerophon Defense Force's Casúr Cogaidhs were loaded with Bijalee shipkillers, each of them fitted with the Alysída self-defense system. Half of the remaining Casúrs carried Fallax missiles, EW platforms fitted with decoys and jammers, while the other half were loaded with Phalanx "escort" missiles to "plow the road" for their shipkiller sisters.

Now they launched, and 12,672 missiles erupted into Ninth Fleet's face.

Oh, Christ. *I guess* that's *how the bastard did it.*

The thought flashed through Regis Hathaway's mind almost calmly as the plot exploded with an utterly impossible tsunami of missile signatures and he realized, almost instantly, exactly how Terrence Murphy really had defeated twice his own number of League carriers in a system named New Dublin.

And that his own carriers were doomed.

"Retarget," he heard his own voice say. "Put everything on their carriers."

"Retargeting," Naidu replied a heartbeat later, and the admiral smiled bitterly. He knew what had waked the ops officer's tiny pause.

"You're sure about that, Sir?" Cosimo asked softly, and Hathaway looked up over his shoulder at the chief of staff.

Targeting only the mutineers' FTLCs would leave their sublight units unscathed to deal with his own ships, but that wouldn't make much difference to Ninth Fleet's fate. That many missiles, closing at 437,000 KPS—almost half again light-speed—were going to get through. Even under the circumstances, his defenses might stop a lot of them; they couldn't possibly stop enough to save his carriers. And despite his greater numbers, his total weight of fire would be only a fraction of what was coming at him.

"I'm sure," he said, equally softly, and actually managed a crooked smile. "We take out their carriers, and any of their parasites that get away don't mean squat. Not out here."

Cosimo looked at him for a moment, then nodded. No sublight warship ever built carried enough reaction mass to decelerate from the mutineers' current velocity. Without carriers of their own, they could only continue helplessly into the depths of interstellar space.

"They've fired," O'Flanagan announced, and Carson nodded in acknowledgment.

Of course they'd fired, she thought bitterly. And they'd gotten all those damned parasites off the racks before they did. Their targeting solutions would be rushed, without the tracking time her own ships had used to refine *their* solutions, but they'd get at least two salvos off before her own missiles hit them, even at these velocities.

And she was grimly certain what they'd chosen to target.

Rival hurricanes of destruction screamed through space.

Ninth Fleet could bring 1,300 missile tubes to bear on Lauren Carson's ships, while she had only 520. But she had the Casúr Cogaidhs, as well. That meant Regis Hathaway could put 2,600 missiles into space in the time he had... but Carson could fire almost *six times* that many at Ninth Fleet.

There'd been a term for it, back on pre-space Earth. Mutually Assured Destruction, they'd called it.

Unlike Regis Hathaway, Carson and her captains had known from the beginning what they might encounter. Had they been detected even a handful of minutes later, the slaughter would have been as one-sided as the one Murphy had wreaked upon Xing Xuefeng in New Dublin. But they *had* been detected, and along with its missiles, Ninth Fleet's deployed parasites could bring almost a thousand K-guns to bear, with three times a missile tube's rate of fire, and no counter-missile or point-defense laser could stop a K-gun's solid SCM slugs.

They had almost six minutes, by the rest of the universe's clocks, to shoot at each other before they interpenetrated—not passed each other, but *interpenetrated*—and ran out of range of one another again.

Six minutes.

Six minutes in which 16,276 missiles and over 7,600 KEWs ripped and tore and gouged. Six minutes of mutual, point-blank slaughter such as no Federation Navy flag officer had contemplated in over fifty years.

There were just over 102,000 men and women aboard Regis Hathaway's ships, almost ninety percent of them aboard his sublight ships; there were "only" 60,080 in Lauren Carson's.

Six minutes after the first missile fired, 132,586 of those 169,000 human beings were dead.

None of Ninth Fleet's FTLCs, and only twelve of its parasites, survived, still coasting onward at 0.86 cee. Six of Lauren Carson's carriers were destroyed outright. Only *Freyr* and *Aurora* survived, and *Aurora*'s Fasset drive was a shattered, broken ruin. Almost three quarters of *her* parasites were actually still combat capable, but as Hathaway had said, without carriers, they were useless for the system's defense.

CHAPTER TWENTY-FIVE

TFNS **Somaskanda**
Bellerophon System
Free Worlds Alliance
January 12, 2553

ADMIRAL ELIJAH JORGENSEN STARED AT THE PLOT IN DISBELIEF.

About him, TFNS *Somaskanda*'s flag bridge was a silent, stunned mirror of the shock rolling through his own brain. His task group flagship and the Bellerophon Expeditionary Force's transports had been five light-minutes astern of the fleet flagship, so there'd been no point deploying Heimdallars of his own, since he was receiving the take from Admiral Hathaway's platforms. He wished now that he had deployed them. Wished he had a better picture of just what the hell had happened in that savage, brutally short engagement. Wished he had a closer look at what was left of the rest of Ninth Fleet and—even more—of the mutineers.

Not that he really *wanted* "a closer look" at what was probably the worst disaster in the Terran Federation Navy's history. Still—

"Force estimate?" he made himself ask into the singing silence.

"It—" Commander Linda Zalewska, his Operations Officer, had to stop, clear her throat.

"It looks like all of Admiral Hathaway's carriers are gone, Sir," she said then. "We're reading active transponders on twelve of his parasites, but nine of them are Code Omega. Three of his battleships and battlecruisers...may be combat capable. It's just impossible to tell from here."

Jorgensen winced. Hathaway's FTLCs had entered the system

with a hundred and twenty sublight warships, and now *three* of them *might* be fit for combat?! That was...that was...

He couldn't come up with a word for what it was.

"And the mutineers?" His voice was harder and harsher.

"Admiral Hathaway took out six of their carriers," Zalewska replied. "Hard kills. At least one of the survivors still has her drive fan, but from her emission signature, she got hit hard. The other one looks to have even more damage and there's no sign of her Fasset drive. I think she has to be counted a complete mission-kill at this point."

Six enemy FTLCs—seven, if he counted the mission-kill—were a piss-poor exchange for twelve of their own, Jorgensen thought, but he sensed the ripple of savage satisfaction blowing through the flag bridge personnel.

"And *their* parasites?"

"Admiral Hathaway concentrated his fire on their carriers," Zalewska said. "It looks like at least three quarters of their sublight platforms are still there. Based on the last tac upload from *Dione*, CIC is estimating twenty-five to thirty *Canadas* and six to ten *Oceans* are probably still combat capable."

Jorgensen's jaw tightened. All three of TG 901.3's FTLCs were *Vishnu*-class ships with 1,700-foot parasite racks. Ninth Fleet hadn't wasted any rack space stowing cruisers or destroyers, so that gave him thirty capital ships of his own: fifteen *Conqueror*-class battleships and fifteen *Ocean*-class battlecruisers. That was a lot of firepower, but even CIC's most optimistic estimate gave the mutineers' parity in total platform numbers. Even though the *Canadas* were an older, slightly smaller design than his own *Conquerors*, they were just as heavily armed...and the enemy had twice as many of them. Assuming they were undamaged—which, admittedly, they probably weren't—he'd be screwed if he went in against them. And even if they *were* damaged, it was highly unlikely his nine-ship advantage in battlecruisers would even the odds.

Jorgensen glared at the plot, then looked at his astrogator.

"Side vector, Hamish," he said. "Keep us clear of the bastards."

"Yes, Sir," Commander Whitworth acknowledged, and the line indicating TG 901.3's vector began to bend away from Lauren Carson's survivors.

Jorgensen watched it for a moment, then swiveled his chair to face his staff.

"Do we have any better idea what the hell they did to us?" he demanded.

"Nothing definite, Sir," Captain Jesus Romero, TG 901.3's chief of staff, said grimly. "Best we can do at this point is guess."

"If you've got *anything*, don't keep it to yourself," Jorgensen half snapped.

Romero had been replaying the brutal, point-blank massacre while Zalewska worked on the numbers. Now he turned, anchoring his toe to one of the tactical rating's bridge chairs in the microgravity, and faced Jorgensen squarely.

"It was obviously missiles," he said. "All those frigging Hauptman signatures make that much clear. But nobody's ever thrown that many missiles into someone's face that way before. Hell, nobody's ever even *tried* to, Sir! No way in hell we could've expected it or Admiral Hathaway could've seen it coming, even if the bastards hadn't gone for that intercept profile, because nobody ever had that many missiles *to* throw! But it must've been from those 'drones' his sensors picked up just before they engaged. That suggests they deployed some sort of missile carrier. The numbers were down on their parasites, so I'm guessing—but it's *only* a guess, Sir—that they must've loaded the missile drones in cargo pods that displaced some of their sublight platforms."

"But where did the frigging drones come from, Sir?" Zalewska asked. She shook her head. "I think you nailed *what* they did. I just can't see where they got the pods—and all those damned missiles—to do it *with*."

"I think it's pretty obvious ONI's analysis of what the hell is going on our here was just a bit off," Jorgensen said bitingly. They looked at him, and he shrugged. "We knew from what that Devinger Lines freighter picked up that Bellerophon planned on joining something called the 'Free Worlds Alliance,' but no one had any idea what the hell that was. What it consisted of. Well, I think we just found out."

"Sir?" Zalewska looked puzzled, and he barked a laugh.

"There's only one place it *could* have been, Linda. This has to've come out of Concordia. Assuming there's any truth at all to what 'Governor Murphy's' supposed to've done to the Leaguies in New Dublin, those missiles have to be the way he did it, and the only way he could've had the pods was if he'd *built* the damned things in-system. Which means New Dublin has the production lines in place to build still more of them." He saw Zalewska's eyes flicker at the thought of what weapons like that meant for systems that went out of compliance. "But the important point right now is that if they're *here* now, then Bellerophon's 'Free Worlds Alliance' has to've started out in Concordia."

"Does that mean *Murphy* is behind this whole thing, Sir?" Romero asked. "Do you think he's *that* far gone?"

"I have no idea," Jurgensen said grimly. "The fact that they're here already, that they actually beat us here from Sol, suggests Bellerophon must have been in contact with *somebody* in Concordia before they decided to secede. I wouldn't have believed any flag officer could have been so far gone as to throw in with a bunch of outright rebels, but we certainly have to consider the possibility, don't we? And even if he tried to suppress the 'Free Worlds' instead of joining them, he sure as hell didn't succeed! Those frigging pods woouldn't be here if he had."

There was silence for a moment and Romero nodded thoughtfully. Then his eyes narrowed.

"Do you think he came in person, Sir? Because if he did—"

"If he did, we may well have just killed him." Jorgensen nodded. "I'd like to hope *something* good came out of it, anyway. But whether we did or not, the question now is what kind of hard number we have on how many of the damned things there were. And whether or not they used all they had."

"*Dione* never got a hard count on the drones," Romero replied. "And we don't have any idea how many birds each drone might have carried. Best estimate from CIC is that they hit us with over ten thousand missiles, though, and at that range and velocity with those numbers, they might as well have been K-guns. They blew right through Admiral Hathaway's intercept zone, especially with his parasites still in that close."

Jorgensen nodded again. It was a miracle Hathaway had gotten his parasites away at all, but they'd been given far too little time to provide any proper depth for missile defense.

"Without knowing how many drones they had or even how many missiles each drone carried, there's no way to realistically estimate whether or not they flushed them all," Romero continued grimly. "In their place, I'd have been inclined to do just that, especially if they didn't know we'd come in divided. On the other hand, they probably figured ten thousand missiles at that range would do the job, so if they had still *more* of the damned things, they might have decided to hang on to them, instead."

"Agreed. But I don't have any intention of letting them prove that to us the hard way," Jorgensen said with a thin smile.

"Excuse me, Sir," Lieutenant Commander Nandy said, "but—"

"Let me guess, Girish." Jorgensen interrupted his comm officer bleakly. "General Alaimo wants to talk to me."

"Yes, Sir."

Of course he does, Jorgensen thought. *Not like I have anything else I should be dealing with right this minute, is it?*

He'd never met Taskin Alaimo. Their paths had never crossed—for which Jorgensen was grateful—before Ninth Fleet got rushed off to Bellerophon, and he'd been completely happy to let Admiral Hathaway deal with him. Jorgensen knew he wasn't an especially imaginative man, and some things, like the stories that had come out of Gobelins, made him grateful for that. Unfortunately, he wasn't *totally* without imagination, and that meant he already felt sick to his stomach thinking about Bellerophon and the fact that he'd just inherited command of the naval side of what was about to happen.

He was a Heart Worlder, of course. The Oval—and the Five Hundred—wouldn't have tolerated a flag officer who wasn't, under the circumstances. And he understood why Bellerophon's treason couldn't be allowed to stand. That didn't mean he had to like what it would take to crush that treason, though. And he knew now that a part of him had been hiding behind Hathaway, hiding behind the fact that he'd only be "following orders" when the time came. The fact that he wasn't the one who'd be making the decisions the history books would never forget.

But now he was, and he inhaled deeply.

"Put him through, Girish. My number three display."

"Yes, Sir."

Jorgensen looked back down as the display by his right knee lit with Taskin Alaimo's image. He was obviously in one of his transport's spin sections, since Colonel Rayko Hepner, his slender, fair-haired chief of staff, stood at the far more massive general's shoulder with what was clearly a comfortable sense of up and down.

Despite which, neither of them looked happy.

"General," Jorgensen said as calmly and courteously as he could under the circumstances.

"What the hell happened?" Alaimo asked without preamble.

"We're still trying to put that together," Jorgensen replied. "We haven't had much time to look at the data yet," he added a bit pointedly.

"Captain Saggio says we're changing course." Alaimo's hadn't raised his voice, and his tone was almost lazy, but something glittered deep in his eyes. "Why are we diverting from Odysseus?"

"We're not." Jorgensen looked at him levelly.

"According to Captain Saggio, we are," Alaimo said almost softly.

Jorgensen considered how to respond to that, and discarded the first two responses that came to mind.

Ernestine Saggio, the senior transport commander, was an experienced, levelheaded officer, who'd suffered the misfortune of having Alaimo for a passenger aboard TFNS *Gregor Willmott*. She was also a woman of few words, but he was positive she'd never said that they were "diverting from Bellerophon." Which suggested Alaimo knew even less about naval operations than Jorgensen had feared. And that he wasn't about to allow ignorance to provoke him into asking the questions that might have enlightened him.

"If that's what Captain Saggio told you, General, she was mistaken," he said.

"Are you saying we're not changing course?" Alaimo demanded in that same soft, lazy tone. "Because if we are, I'm afraid that's . . . unacceptable."

"I didn't say we weren't changing course," Jorgensen replied. "I said we aren't diverting from Odysseus. And we aren't. We *are* changing our approach vector, but under the circumstances, it would be . . . imprudent not to."

"Why?"

"Because, General," Jorgensen said, a bit more sharply than he'd intended to, "I'm pretty sure we just lost somewhere around a hundred thousand Navy men and women and I don't intend to lose any more."

"A hundred thousand?" Alaimo repeated, and there was something repellent about his matter-of-fact tone.

"I told you we're still trying to sort out exactly what happened. But we do know Admiral Hathaway's entire carrier force has been destroyed. Only a handful of his sublight parasites are still intact. Which means my task group now represents the Navy's total combat power in the Cyclops Sector."

"Well, what happened to the traitors?"

"As nearly as we can tell, two of their carriers survived the engagement, but one of them's lost her Fasset drive. They're still on their intercept vector, which is why I've changed ours. If we'd maintained our original heading and deceleration, we'd have run headlong into them, exactly the way Admiral Hathaway did."

"Excuse me for asking this, Admiral, but if you have *three* carriers and they only have two, at least one of which is too badly damaged to maneuver, why aren't you *closing* with them, instead?"

The question came out almost idly, and Jorgensen allowed himself to snort.

"Because, General," he allowed a little deliberate patience to color his own tone, "their carriers may have been hammered—I strongly suspect that Admiral Hathaway concentrated on them deliberately—but something like eighty percent of their sublight warships appear to be combat-capable. That's twice the effective fighting strength of my own parasite group. I have no intention of engaging against that sort of odds and risking the chance of their getting a shot at the transports."

"I realize I'm only an Army officer, not an expert on naval tactics, but won't leaving an intact hostile force in your rear do just that?"

"No, it won't," Jorgensen said flatly. Alaimo arched one eyebrow, and the admiral shook his head.

"At the moment, every one of their sublight units is headed for the local Oort Cloud at almost sixty percent of the speed of light, and without Fasset drives of their own, they'll never be able to kill even a fraction of that velocity. They're as totally out of the fight here in Bellerophon as if they'd been blown apart with their carriers. So what we're doing is sidestepping them. General, I don't *care* where they go . . . as long as we don't run our nose into them. That's the reason Admiral Hathaway concentrated on killing their carriers."

"I see." Alaimo folded his arms and cocked his head, and some of the glitter in his eyes faded. "So you're not worried about the one carrier they still have operating in your rear?"

"Even assuming that carrier still has all five of her parasite racks—and given the hammering she took, it's unlikely she does—she can put only ten parasites onto them. We have thirty." Jorgensen bared his teeth. "I wish they *would* be stupid enough to engage us at one-to-three odds. But they won't."

"I see." Alaimo cocked his head, his expression thoughtful. "That makes sense. I wish Captain Saggio had bothered to explain it as clearly."

She probably would *have if you'd bothered to* ask *her about it,* Jorgensen thought acidly from behind a calmly attentive expression.

"But I'm still a bit concerned," the general continued. "I understand the odds you just described are unfavorable, but what happens if another mutinous unit turns up? Joins forces with this batch? Wouldn't it be better to risk some losses now in order to neutralize the threat we know about?"

"There aren't any other units to mutiny in Cyclops," Jorgensen said grimly. "There were only eight carriers deployed to the sector. Apparently, every damn one of them went over to the rebels. And Admiral Hathaway just killed all but two of them." He shook his head again. "They've hurt us worse than I ever thought they could, General, but Admiral Hathaway gutted them in return. There's nobody else to come sneaking up behind us, and even if there were, we'd pick up their Fasset signatures long before they dropped sublight."

"I see." Alaimo considered that for a moment, then smiled. It was a cheerful but somehow ugly smile, and his eyes were bright now.

"I see, indeed," he repeated. "And I'm sorry to hear about how badly the traitors hurt us. I suppose I'll just have to make the point of how . . . *unwise* that was of them, won't I?"

CHAPTER TWENTY-SIX

TFNS **Aurora**
Bellerophon System
Free Worlds Alliance
January 12, 2553

"I'M AFRAID THE REPAIR DRONES CONFIRM JOSEPHINE'S ESTIMATE,
Ma'am." Captain Mariaxuri Errezola's expression was grim on
Lauren Carson's display. "The fan's completely shot. Nothing left
to repair, really."

"I wish that was a surprise," Carson said bleakly.

She'd wanted to hope Commander Josephine DuPont, *Aurora*'s
chief engineer, had been overly pessimistic in her initial estimate,
but she'd known better. Which didn't make the confirmation one
bit better now that it was here.

She was as shaken by the carnage as anyone else, although
at least she and her people had had more warning of what was
coming than the poor bastards on the other side could have had.
And she already knew what kind of nightmare fodder the deaths
of so many people had laid up for her. And how much more
fodder was waiting to happen on Odysseus as a consequence of
her failure.

She only had to remember Inverness to know that. But it was
still her job to decide what to do next.

God help her.

One thing she didn't have to decide was what to do with
Aurora. At this velocity, with her fan destroyed, she was just
as much a write-off as *Enlil*, *Perseus*, *Hermes*, *Khandoba*, or
Ninurta. She'd taken substantially less hull damage than any of

them had—Pascual Aguayo's *Khandoba* had actually blown up with all hands, and *Enlil* had broken her back and shattered into three separate, jagged chunks of wreckage—but that didn't matter, because she was too enormous to dock on anyone's parasite racks, and not even one of the TFN's huge FTL repair ships was capable of a complete fan replacement. So there was no way to recover her to a dockyard, and no way to repair her without one. She still had power—and probably enough life support to keep all of Carson's surviving people alive—but she could never take them home again. Ultimately, the only option would be to pull her people off and abandon ship.

But that presupposed there was somewhere to pull them off *to*, didn't it?

"All right, Mariaxuri," she said. "Go take care of your people." She smiled thinly. "Looks like we'll be waiting a while for a ride."

"Yes, Ma'am."

The display blanked, and Carson looked at her comm officer. "Captain Rodoulis, Gaston," she said.

"Yes, Ma'am," Lieutenant Pasteur replied, and Carson scrubbed her face with both hands while she waited.

You blew it, a merciless voice said in the depths of her brain. *You fucked up by the numbers. Idiot!*

She lowered her hands and glanced at the master plot.

Despite the damage *Aurora* had taken, her deeply buried, massively protected flag deck, bridge, and combat information center were as untouched and quiet as they'd ever been, and the air circulating about Carson was as fresh as it ever was. The stink of terror and despair wasn't a physical thing, after all.

The carrier's sensor arrays had been brutally hammered, and most of them were down, but she still had her datalinks to her surviving parasites, and their sensors—and the Heimdallars she'd deployed—still drove her displays.

The displays that showed the *second* federal task force. The one busily shifting vector to avoid what was left of the Bellerophon System Navy.

And there wasn't one damned thing she could do about it.

"Captain Rodoulis, Ma'am," Pasteur said, and she turned back to the comm as Achilleas Rodoulis appeared upon it.

"Commodore," he said. His expression was as grim as Carson felt, but his voice sounded almost—*almost*—normal.

"Achilleas," she replied. "How bad is it over there?"

"Not good, and that's a fact." His voice had gone deeper, harder. "Unlike *Aurora*, our fan's in good shape. Didn't take a hit. But we're down to Number Two and Number Four racks."

Carson grimaced. That was even worse than she'd feared. With only two racks, *Freyr* could embark a grand and glorious total of four parasites, and even four battleships would be spit on a griddle against the task force still headed for Odysseus.

"Mariaxuri says we still have three over here," she said. "Michael's coordinating search and rescue, and we're pretty sure we have enough life support to handle everyone. Everyone who's *left*, anyway." Her lips twisted, but she made herself go on levelly. "He's prioritizing to get the ships with the most WIA into a docking queue that gets their worst-hurt people into our sick bay."

"Good," Rodoulis said. "That's good."

"For certain pretty piss-poor definitions of 'good,' maybe," Carson said bitterly. "And it's the only damned 'good' thing we've got. I blew it, Achilleas." She shook her head and looked away, eyes burning. "I *blew* it!"

"Bullshit!"

The snapped word jerked her back to the comm, and Rodoulis glared at her.

"Every single one of us agreed with you, Lauren," he said then, flatly. "Every. Single. One. And we kicked the ever-living hell out of the bastards! If they hadn't seen us coming—and it's obvious they *didn't* see us until the very last minute—we'd have caught them with their parasites on the racks and they'd have been dead meat. Hell, they *were* dead meat! These other bastards—" he jerked his head to the side, obviously indicating his own tactical plot "—wouldn't have had a prayer against us after that!"

"I should've remembered Murphy's law," she said. "What could go wrong damned well *did* go wrong. I should've remembered it could and not put everything on one roll of the dice!"

"Without knowing how big a fleet they were sending?" Rodoulis shook his head. "You had one shot, Lauren—*one*. And to make it count, you had to get them into range of the Casúrs. Sure, you could have deployed them from farther out, but how the hell were you going to hide that many thousands of Hauptman signatures from them? Keep them from deploying all their parasites? Or just changing vector and out-accelerating the best the pods could do?

You had to get in close, and you did, and it worked. Even with whatever went wrong, whatever fluke let them spot us, however badly we got hurt, it *worked*."

"Not against their trailers," Carson said harshly.

"You couldn't know they were going to do that."

"But I should have anticipated they *might*. And when I realized there were only twelve carriers coming at us, I should've held back some of the Casúrs. If I'd held just four cargo pods, *Freyr* could still—"

"Oh, stop it!" Rodoulis shook his head again, harder. "I know you're looking for clubs to beat yourself with—don't think I'm not doing the same thing! But just what sort of godlike power of precognition was supposed to tell you that? And if it did, was it also going to tell you which of forty parasite racks to put them on so they wouldn't get destroyed? It's *done*, Lauren, and you did the best anyone could possibly have done under the circumstances."

"But they're getting through, Achilleas," she half whispered. "They're getting *through* to Odysseus, and there's nothing— *nothing*—we can do about it."

"Nothing except pray whoever Governor Murphy sends gets here quickly," Rodoulis said.

It was odd, she thought. It was his star system she'd failed to defend, but he was actually trying to comfort her. And as he looked out of her comm display, his brown eyes hardened and he bared his teeth.

"Trust me," he said flatly. "It's going to be ugly—I know that, and I know I can't begin to imagine *how* ugly, however hard I try—but my homeworld is tough. It'll survive until Murphy's detachment gets here. And after what we did—what *you* did—to these bastards' main force, they are *toast* when it does."

CHAPTER TWENTY-SEVEN

Parnassus Tower
City of Kórinthos
Planet Odysseus
Bellerophon System
Free Worlds Alliance
January 12, 2553

MOLLIE RAMSAY TAPPED THE SMART SCREEN AGAIN, AND BIT HER lip as the error codes continued to flash.

They shouldn't have been there. She was the system governor, for God's sake. But it didn't seem to matter.

"Still nothing?"

She looked away from the screen and shook her head at the man seated in one of her office's comfortable powered chairs.

"No," she said. "I'm afraid not."

"Somehow, that doesn't strike me as a good sign." Eric Humbolt tried to inject a note of humor into his voice.

He failed.

"There's a lot of uncertainty out there," she said. "I could wish there was less in here. Or that they'd at least talk to me!"

She smacked the smart screen as she spoke, and Humbolt managed a weak chuckle. His suit was tailored from a fire-wire weave popular among the Five Hundred. The genetically engineered hemp fibers were permeated with actual gold and reflected the light differently every time he moved, with a flickering fire guaranteed to catch the eye. That single suit had probably cost half as much as Ramsay's luxurious office's furnishings, which was why the Five Hundred were so fond of it. Now he dabbed a silk handkerchief along his unnaturally perfect hairline and shook his head at her.

"I'm sure they'll talk to you as soon as they realize they can, Madame Governor," he said. "That's why we're both here, after all."

"I hope you're—we're—right about that," she sighed. "I'd feel more confident if they'd at least acknowledged my initial transmission, but I still hope you're right. To be honest, the main reason I disassociated myself so strongly from the system government after they issued their declaration was to be available to broker some sort of... rapprochement when the moment came. Even if the break really is irreparable, there's no benefit for the Federation in harming civilians or wrecking the system's infrastructure out of some misplaced sense of vengeance. Either way, go or stay, someone has to serve as the interface between Odysseus and whoever Olympia's sent out here, and I doubt whoever they've sent will be very interested in talking to President Xeneas. But if they won't even—"

She shook her head, then climbed out of her own chair and walked to the floor-to-ceiling window wall of her fortieth-floor office. That window looked out across the capital of Odysseus, and her mouth tightened as smoke and flame billowed before her. The thud of muffled explosions reached her even at her elevation, and she saw flashes in the smoke where KEWs and old-fashioned chemical explosives added to the canopy as the Federation assault troops continued their attack.

Konstantinos Xeneas had declared Kórinthos an open city and withdrawn all military personnel from it at the same time the civilian government evacuated to its preselected dispersal sites. Unfortunately, whoever commanded the forces the federal government had dispatched didn't seem to care about that.

It was quite possible some of the city's civilian population hadn't heard the president's proclamation... or just didn't care. Any Fringe World population had more than sufficient reason to hate Heart Worlders, and unlike most Heart Worlds, Odysseus had a robust tradition of armed civilians, especially among the veterans who'd survived their military service. So yes, it was entirely possible some of those armed civilians had decided to resist, whatever their system president might have declared.

But it was equally possible the Federation commander—whoever he was—had simply chosen to ignore Xeneas's declaration and come in guns blazing, without giving much of a damn whether anyone offered active resistance or not. In fact, Ramsay was very much afraid he'd done just that, given the way he'd completely ignored her own transmissions. No, that wasn't really accurate. He hadn't *ignored* her transmissions; he'd jammed them, just as he had all other civilian and military channels and frequencies.

He wasn't supposed to do that. Not on the priority frequencies. And she didn't want to think about the reasons he might have done it anyway.

She bit her lip harder, looking directly down at the beautifully landscaped grounds around the foot of Parnassus Tower. The tower had been built by the people of Odysseus decades before the endless war with the League. Built when they'd been proud of their membership in the Federation, proud of their home system's growth and prosperity—of the Heart World investment helping them build better lives for themselves and their children. Parnassus Tower had been the expression of that pride, a monument to the Federation and all for which it stood.

It hadn't been any of those things for a long time now, and Mollie Ramsay had understood that. She'd wept for it, inside, but she'd understood, and there'd been times she'd deeply envied Konstantinos Xeneas, and not just because he hadn't been hated the way too many Odyssians hated her simply because she was their system governor. She'd done her best to mitigate the sources of Odysseus's anger and hatred, yet there'd been all too little she could do about the policy directives coming out of the Heart. She'd known that, too, and so she'd been less surprised in many ways than she probably ought to have been by the system's decision to secede in the wake of Inverness and the creation of the Free Worlds Alliance.

That didn't mean she hadn't recognized the enormous potential for disaster in that decision. If she could have talked Xeneas and his people back off the ledge, she would have done it in a heartbeat. For that matter, if she'd thought she could have stopped them by force, she'd have done that, too. But neither of those things had ever been a realistic possibility, and so she'd done the best she could by ordering all federal agencies in Bellerophon to stand down. They couldn't have stopped what was happening anyway. All they could have done was to produce a bloodbath, and she'd been determined to avoid at least that much.

She was still determined to avoid it. That was why she and Humbolt were here, in this office. Why she'd been trying to get someone to answer or at least acknowledge her transmissions. Somebody had to talk to the people the Federation had sent out here to restore federal control before Odysseus turned into another Gobelins, and it was her job as system governor to start that conversation.

For all the good it looked like doing in the end.

A trio of assault shuttles howled low over the city, fuselage racks heavy with external ordnance as they swept towards Parnassus. One of them peeled off, dropping its nose, and Ramsay stepped back from the window as the bow-mounted cannon poured fire into one of the streets. She had no idea what it was shooting at, and she had little time to worry about it as the other two flared, riding the howling thunder of their vectored thrust down into those landscaped grounds. Shrubbery, flowerbeds, ornamental trees were torn apart by the hurricane, crushed by landing skids as the armored craft slammed down, and hatches opened. They spilled heavily armed troops into the desecrated gardens, and she saw them storming towards the ground level entrance.

Gunfire thumped and crackled, and she bit her lip again, this time hard enough to draw blood. Despite Bellerophon's secession, the system government had made no effort to seize control of Parnassus Tower. Just as Ramsay had realized resistance couldn't have prevented the system's secession, Xeneas and his fellows had recognized that even in a best-case scenario, there would have to be some sort of resolution with the Federation in the fullness of time. They'd been careful to maintain their channels of communication with Ramsay and to respect the "extraterritorial integrity" of the federal government's enclave in the heart of Kórinthos.

The troops pouring out of those shuttles seemed unaware of that, and Ramsay's heart froze as she heard weapons fire inside the tower. She'd ordered her staff, and especially the personal security team Xeneas and General Tolallis had insisted she retain, *not* to resist! There was no reason—

The sound of gunfire swept closer, louder and more savage, and Humbolt stood and crossed to join her.

"This isn't going the way I'd envisioned," he said, brushing his hands down his jacket, trying to smile.

"Not the way I had, either," she said as the cacophony grew louder. She turned, putting her back to the windows as she faced the office door, and held her hands out from her sides, fingers spread. "Best that they see we're unarmed when they arrive," she said. "Trigger fingers can get itchy."

Something banged against the office door, and Humbolt twitched. Then he nodded convulsively and his hands went high.

Ramsay gave him a quick, nervous smile, then tried to focus her thoughts on what she would say when the moment arrived. The Federation commander's refusal to accept her call didn't fill her with confidence, but—

Something *snapped* against the door, and her eyes widened as a tiny camera lens bored through the doorframe. Nothing happened for an instant, and then the doors flew wide and a team of Federation soldiers in light powered armor with Army markings poured through them.

Ramsay held very still as she and Humbolt found themselves looking into a dozen carbine muzzles. Her gaze flickered across the intruders, looking for one of them with obvious rank. Their armor bore scrapes and divots from bullet strikes. Several of them had bloodstains on their boots and gauntlets. She couldn't see faces or expressions through their full-face helmets, but one of those helmets nodded quickly, as if its wearer was speaking to someone.

Then feet crunched behind them and another soldier strode into the room. He was taller than most of the others, with wider shoulders and a pearl-handled pistol in a chest holster. His armor bore the paired golden stars of a major general, and she turned to face him.

"I'm System Governor Ramsay, General," she said briskly. "I'm relieved to see that Prime Minister Schleibaum's responded so quickly to the situation here. I was afraid that—"

The general tapped the side of his helmet. The visor slid up and over his head, he arched an eyebrow at her, and she clamped her jaws shut. Blood drained from her face, and Humbolt collapsed into a chair beside the window as his knees failed.

"Ah, then I don't need to introduce myself." Taskin Alaimo pulled his helmet completely off and held it in the crook of one arm. "It's convenient when one's reputation precedes one. Cuts down on all the chitchat."

He walked into the office, put his free hand on Humbolt's head, and tousled the other man's hair playfully.

"And since we're dispensing with chitchat," he said, "let's get right to it. Where is Xeneas?"

He turned from Humbolt to face Ramsay. Unlike the troopers behind him, his armor was pristine. In fact, he smiled faintly of cologne as he frowned at her.

"I don't know."

She kept her voice firm and met his eyes levelly. It was one of the hardest things she'd ever done.

"Really?" Alaimo cocked his head, his eyes bright. "That seems... unlikely. I mean, you are—or were, at least—the system governor, after all."

"It's true," she said. "I wasn't privy to any of the system government's plans or actions after Bellerophon declared its independence."

"Really?" he said again. He set his helmet on her desk and ran one hand over sweat-damp hair. "They didn't confide in you after you aided and abetted their treason?"

"I didn't 'aid and abet' anyone, General!" she said sharply.

"Ah! So it was someone *impersonating* you who surrendered the federal authority in Bellerophon to them?"

"I instructed the federal agencies in Bellerophon not to resist," Ramsay said. "It would have been pointless. By the time anyone realized what was happening, it was too late to organize any *effective* resistance. Trying to prevent the secession at that point would only have gotten hundreds, possibly thousands, of people killed without affecting the outcome at all."

"Is that how you see it?" Alaimo said in an interested tone. "I can understand why you might prefer that interpretation of your actions. But you seriously expect me to believe you truly don't know where I might find President Xeneas to discuss his decisions with him?"

"I can only tell you the truth, which is that I don't know where he is. There's no reason anyone should have told me that. I told President Xeneas at the time that, as the Federation's governor for Bellerophon, I couldn't possibly concede the legality of his actions. I couldn't prevent them, given the fashion in which they'd been planned and executed, but I refused to—and he never asked me to—approve their decisions or cooperate with them in any way. So I'm sure I'd be the last person on Odysseus to whom they'd have given classified information like that."

"Reasonable, I suppose." Alaimo pursed his lips. "But I'm afraid I'm not the trusting type," he said. "So we'll talk more about that later. In the meantime, I assume your little friend in the bespoke suit isn't here for simple moral support."

"Eric Humbolt, General." Humbolt snapped up out of the chair. "Chief executive officer for Epoch Industries' operations in Bellerophon."

He extended his hand to Alaimo. Alaimo didn't take it.

"I—I, uh, I'm here to specify which economic assets are critical to sustaining the civilian economy and separate from potential military targets. As you know, Bellerophon is a Beta tier system, and—"

"You're already boring me." Alaimo held up a finger, then snapped it towards the chair, and Humbolt sat back down immediately.

"I *was* asked by President Xeneas to convey a message to you," Ramsay said, and Alaimo cocked his head at her again. "He communicated with me shortly after your fleet was detected," she continued. "He asked me to inform whoever commands the Federation forces that he's declared every refugee center an open city which will provide no material support for him or the troops under his command. He also—"

Alaimo held up a hand.

"This . . . is not what I want to hear," he said and drew his pistol.

"Shooting me won't give you information I don't have in the first place."

Ramsay managed to keep her voice level despite the icy fear spreading through her chest, and Humbolt began praying out loud.

"Hmmm?" Alaimo looked over his shoulder at the CEO. "I suppose my reputation truly does precede me. Everyone knows what had to happen on Gobelins to return that world to compliance. Most necessary, I'm afraid. Too many bad apples in the barrel for too long. Everything was rotten."

He strolled across the office to examine a hundred-year-old painting of the first landing on Odysseus, then turned back to face Ramsay.

"I'm curious, Governor. If you'd known the Oval was going to send me . . . would you still have supported the traitors when they went out of compliance?" He glanced at the empty chair behind her desk, then back at her. "You really should sit down. You don't look comfortable at all."

"I didn't support them. I only tried to prevent bloodshed."

"Semantics," Alaimo chided. "I'm hearing semantics here, Governor."

"I did what I had to do." Ramsay laid a hand on the edge of her desk to steady herself. "It wasn't what I *wanted* to do, just—"

"My question was whether or not you would have done it if you'd known the Oval was going to send *me*." He waved his left index finger gently. "It's a simple question. I mean, you have heard of Gobelins, haven't you?"

"Of course I know what you did on Gobelins. Everyone knows. But I had to decide what to do *here*, on Odysseus, and—"

"Not an answer." Alaimo wagged his index finger a bit harder. "I don't like repeating myself, Governor. Slimy politicians have a habit of couching every single thing they say so that they can claim they were on the right side of an issue when the wind blows the other way. Now..."

He laid his free hand on the corner of the desk, bouncing his pistol gently against his thigh, and Ramsay froze as he gazed across her own blotter at her. His face seemed to harden and something almost...jovial built behind his eyes. And then—

"Sit!" he shouted.

Ramsay obeyed instantly, nearly tipping over her chair the process.

"I try to be nice." He shook his head sadly, then inhaled deeply.

"Back to the question," he said. "And if you make me repeat it again, I'm going to assume the prisoners we've taken from your staff here weren't simply following orders and aren't due for a bit of mercy—"

"Yes, I would've done it! I would've done exactly what I did anyway," Ramsay snapped.

"Well, that's certainly forthright," Alaimo said brightly. Then he shook his head again. "But, you know, Governor, you really shouldn't have betrayed your oath of office that way." He made a tsking sound. "That wasn't a very...helpful thing to do."

She looked at him expressionlessly and he sat on the corner of her desk.

"The Federation has a problem, Governor. Part of the problem is people like these traitors here in Bellerophon who don't want to be part of the grand system we've established over the last four hundred years. But another part is people like you, who don't stop them when they rock the boat. All of you are clearly doing well for yourselves. Your children have excellent careers, and the Fringe population as a whole has a standard of living anyone in the League would just...die for. So why put all of that at risk? Explain that to me, Governor. Why would someone like Xeneas throw that all away? And why would someone like you stand on the sidelines and cheer while he does?"

Ramsay felt as if she were shrinking in her chair, but something else was happening as well. She couldn't have explained what it was. Perhaps it was fatalism, the awareness that she had no control. Or perhaps it was a moment of self-clarity she'd tried to avoid for too long.

"They did it for freedom," she said quietly, and somehow she was speaking as much to herself as to Alaimo. "They want freedom from the Heart Worlds. From the Five Hundred. They don't want to give up their children to a war they're sick of fighting. They're tired of giving up their wealth to fund a war that never ends. And they're tired of knowing that if they object, if they refuse, the Federation will set a monster upon them."

She met his gaze, and he looked back for a moment, then nodded.

"Yeah, that's...I've heard that before." He patted his palm against the desk and stood. "Heard it on Gobelins. Heard it aboard the *Scharnhorst*, when the crew mutinied and had to be brought back into the fold. I've heard it all before, and I've got to tell you, Governor...it doesn't matter. Doesn't matter one bit, because the Five Hundred simply adore the status quo. They're filthy rich, and they don't care how hard the peasants toil and suffer to *keep* them filthy rich and away from the war that's *made* them so rich. What the Five Hundred don't like is change. No, no, no. If the proles start getting ideas, then it's the Thirteen Colonies in 1776. It's France in 1789. Russia in 1917. China in 1949. The list goes on and on, and that's not acceptable. That's why they sent me. I'm here to stop it."

"It's too late for that," Ramsay said. "If you try to stop it, you'll only make it worse. If you massacre the people here on Odysseus, it will only motivate the Free Worlds Alliance to fight back even harder. Other systems will—"

Alaimo raised his pistol. She found herself looking into the muzzle, and he put his finger on the trigger and snapped the safety off.

"We don't say that." He waggled the pistol gently. "Although your observation does have at least a bit of merit." He took his finger off the trigger. "After I brought Gobelins back into compliance, I had the opportunity, during the time I spent sequestered from the rest of the Federation, to reflect on my impact. While everything I did was certainly justified, it seems my methods were a bit polarizing. Oooh. Did you know people on Gobelins won't even use *Hansa*-pattern shuttles anymore? So many 'disappeared' after taking a flight that the fear ingrained itself into the planetary zeitgeist. Sorry. Sidebar. Where was I?"

Ramsay fought the urge to vomit.

"Ah, yes. Second- and third-order effects from Gobelins." He nodded. "When the peasants think it's the big, bad Five Hundred's iron boot coming down on their throat, they point their grubby little fingers at the Five Hundred, and then their betters get all the blame for everything. Can't have that anymore—look how counterproductive it gets."

Alaimo raised his free hand in a waving-away gesture, then tapped his index finger across his lips with an almost conspiratorial smile.

"But that only matters if they think they have any voice in what happens to them. It only matters if they believe there's even the remotest possibility they can do anything about it. And I'll let you in on a little secret, Governor. The *good* slave keeps his head down and stays far away from *anything* that might piss his betters off because he realizes that there *isn't* anything he can do about it. Not a single, solitary thing. And that's what I'm going to teach this planet."

"Spare the civilians," Ramsay said. "Xeneas won't endanger them, but he's not going to surrender the planet to you. Never."

Alaimo holstered his weapon, clasped his palms together, fingertips just below his lips, and gave her a look of concern.

"Governor . . . the traitors running this planet after you meekly handed it over to them have sent as many civilians as possible to evacuation centers," he said. "And here you are, with a corporate representative to whimper about what not to blow up. Do you think I'm the League?"

She looked at him, wondering where his non sequitur was headed, and he shook his head.

"Oh, come now, Governor. You know how it works! The Fringe Worlds—ours and the League's—have this sort of informal understanding. One where populations are moved away from key planetary targets in some sort of appeal to the conquering commander's humanity. 'Oh, please, blow up the industry, but spare our people!' That sort of thing. It's adorable, really."

He bent forward, bringing his face uncomfortably close to hers.

"Do I look like a League officer?"

"N-no," she said softly.

"Really? I thought I must, if you and Xeneas believe I'll leave the peasants to their own devices, safe in their camps, eating ration bars while I fight him and his militia in collateral-damage-free streets. Does that summarize his thinking, in a general sort of way?"

"President Xeneas won't endanger the civilian populace during your occupa—*urk!*"

Alaimo clamped his free hand around her throat and squeezed.

Humbolt made a meek protest, but went silent at a glance from Alaimo. The general's arm shook as he applied more force to the vise around Ramsay's neck. Her vision grayed as he tilted her chin up with his forearm and looked straight into her eyes. She expected to see malice or anger...instead, he seemed almost amused.

He squeezed still harder, until the room began to darken. And then, as suddenly as he'd seized her, he let her go.

She collapsed over the desk, fighting to breathe, and he stood back.

"You think I'm going to fight on his terms? On *yours*?" He clicked his tongue. "You think you and he have...any power here? I'm afraid it's time for a reality check. Come with me. It's time for a little lesson in loyalty."

The armored personnel carrier stopped, and rough hands hauled Ramsay and Humbolt out of its dark interior. The governor blinked in the late afternoon sunlight, then inhaled—in dismay, not really surprise—as she found herself in Ochi Square. The magnificent façade of Ithaca House looked down from Acropolis Hill at the teeming activity in the enormous square. Federation landers dotted it, and troops were already unloading point defense turrets and heavy weapons from them. Small drones buzzed overhead, firing single shots into the evacuation zone around the square.

Alaimo led the way up the grand steps from the square to Ithaca House. A pile of dead Odyssian soldiers had been stacked at the stairs' base. Red drag streaks across the stone paving pointed to their final moments.

There was a spring in Alaimo's step as he stepped from the stairs' top step out onto the wide terrace from which Odyssian presidents had traditionally addressed the entire star system.

"Volkov?" Alaimo held up his helmet, looking at his reflection in the visor. "Volkov, I need the angle for our demonstration. And make sure the auto filters do something about the bags under my eyes. Can't look puffy."

A soldier with wide features and a bald head hurried up the stairs. A trio of camera drones hovered just behind him, at shoulder level.

"Sir, the demonstration is at niner-niner-four mils from magnetic north." Volkov pointed a knife hand to the southwest. "I'm afraid the time window's going to be tight, especially with the clouds."

Ramsay's heart skipped a beat.

"Wait. What are you doing? That's— There's a civilian evacuation center in that direction. There's nearly a quarter million people in it. You can't—"

Alaimo sucked air through his teeth and shook his head slowly.

"Can't I?" He furrowed his brow at her. "Volkov, what's the splash time? We can edit it all together in post if we have to, but I don't want to lose this light."

"Time on target is... eighty-four seconds," Volkov read from the screen on his forearm.

"Cutting it tight, but if we can get it in camera, all the better." Alaimo grabbed Ramsay by the arm and spun her around. He kept her next to him as the camera drones flitted around them, projecting different light levels. "Just stand still, my dear. Smiling is optional."

He scrunched his face from side to side, warming up his mouth.

"He thrusts his fists against the posts and still insists he sees the ghosts," he enunciated carefully, peering into the distance.

"Why are you doing this?" Ramsay's voice was raspy and strained from the damage his choking hand had inflicted.

"Peanut nostril happy clams." Alaimo winked at her. "Carrots and sticks. Volkov, make sure we get a composite for HD release to the nets."

"Got it, boss." Volkov gave him a thumbs-up. "And *Sentry* confirms launch."

"You can't!" Ramsay reached for Alaimo, but the heel of his open hand slammed into her sternum and sent her backpedaling. "Why? They're not even fighting you!"

"I'm afraid the near future is in the hands of physics," Alaimo said. "The Federation incurred significant expense to secure the system. Now I'm passing those costs on to those responsible. Volkov, I need to concentrate."

Volkov wrapped a hand around Ramsay's mouth and stuck a pistol against her back. Alaimo ignored her and turned slightly towards Ochi Square. He set his face firmly and gazed into a camera drone.

"Attention, citizens of Odysseus," he said evenly. "I am General Taskin Alaimo, and by special order of the federal government, I am now the Bellerophon System Governor. The illegal rebellion instigated by President Xeneas and former Governor Ramsay is over. It is my duty to transition this system back to effective local self-governance under the Constitution and to minimize further damage to the greater Federation. As such, I now instruct all individuals currently in so-called 'open city' evacuation centers to return to your homes. Anyone in those evacuation centers past midnight Kórinthos time will be considered party to the insurrection.

"Unfortunately, I have traced several of the rebellion's ring-leaders to the Lake Orestiada encampment. I have called upon them to surrender themselves to me in order to avoid needless bloodshed. They have refused. It's regrettable that President Xeneas and his conspirators have chosen to shield themselves behind noncombatants, but my mission here is quite clear and their intransigence leaves me no option."

Behind him, three pencils of intolerable brilliance tore suddenly through the overhead cloud cover. At 33.5 KPS they were less projectiles than eye-tearing beams of light that blazed overhead until, as suddenly as they had come, they disappeared over the near horizon. And as they did, a terrible flash of light burst upward, etching Alaimo's profile against the sunset. Each of those KEWs struck with the power of well over one hundred tons of old-fashioned TNT, in an equilateral triangle centered on the Lake Orestiada evacuation center. They weren't nuclear, but the savage explosions swept the encampment like a brimstone broom.

Ramsay fought Volkov's grip as the horizon blazed, but he was far stronger than she would ever be. He held her with ease and pressed the muzzle of his pistol hard against her spine.

"Further rebellion will not be tolerated," Alaimo continued. She could barely see him through her tears, but the obscene calm of his tone burned into her like a curse. "Further damage to the Federation's economy will not be tolerated. All citizens will return to their homes immediately, and all workers will return to their normal places of employment tomorrow morning. Any and all who refuse to obey my lawful orders will be treated as insurgents."

He shook his head sadly, his expression grave.

"I deeply regret the fashion in which I have been forced to these stern measures, but there is no need for any further loss of life or hardship. I now order President Xeneas and any and all who fomented Bellerophon's rebellion and enlistment in the illegal 'Free Worlds Alliance'—a treasonous organization whose avowed purpose is the complete destruction of the Federation—to surrender to justice. There is no negotiation on this point, but there will be mercy for those who surrender themselves and their coconspirators quickly. This means that any further suffering your world may experience will be a direct result of your own decision to continue to defy my lawful orders and authority. I advise you to decide wisely."

He gazed into the camera for a handful of seconds, until a small red light blinked off. Then his sad expression segued into an almost impish smile. He drew his pistol once again, and Ramsay stopped fighting Volkov. Her eyes locked to the weapon, but he wasn't looking at her. He was looking at Humbolt, and she turned her head, following his gaze.

The CEO stood staring at the evil, mushroom-headed clouds rising above the horizon, and face was white.

"My... my parents were in that evacuation center." He took a halting step towards the destruction. "My wife—*my kids!*"

"Really?" Alaimo looked at him, then down at the data screen on the forearm of his armor. "I didn't realize. How horrible. On the other hand..."

A soft tone sounded, and the data scrolling up the display stopped abruptly.

"Ah, *there* you are, Mr. Humbolt! I see you truly are with Epoch Industries. Which, as it happens, is, a wholly-owned subsidiary of the Société Auchan." He shook his head. "This treason you've helped support has had a significant effect on Auchan's bottom line," he said chidingly. "I'm afraid that puts you on the list of Mr. Perrin's problems."

He raised the pistol, aligning it with Humbolt's forehead at a range of perhaps a meter. He held it there until the man's stunned eyes tracked from those mushroom clouds to the weapon's muzzle and began to widen.

Then he squeezed the trigger.

Humbolt's head snapped back as if it were on a hinge. A red and gray cloud burst from the back of his skull, and his body tilted away from Alaimo. He collapsed, falling backward onto the grand stair, and his corpse flopped halfway down them, trailing spatters of blood and reddish-gray lumps every few steps.

"And there's one issue resolved," Alaimo sighed. "So many still to deal with." He looked at Ramsay. "Somehow, there are never enough hours in the day, Governor. Or, rather, ex-Governor."

He smiled at her, then looked across her head at her captor.

"Keep her tucked away for later, Volkov. But no records in the system."

"Got it, Boss."

Volkov twisted Ramsay around and pushed her towards the grand stair. She tried not to look down as they walked through the splatter pattern of brain matter. She stumbled as she stepped across Humbolt's sprawled body, but Volkov kept her from falling and pushed her onward towards a waiting lander.

CHAPTER TWENTY-EIGHT

Command Post
Third Regiment
Bellerophon System Defense Force
Planet Odysseus
Bellerophon System
January 12, 2553

"AND I WANT A BETTER UPDATE ON OUR RECON ASSETS." COLONEL Minos Palides looked around the faces of his regimental staff. "We're going to start losing drones as soon as anyone picks up their transmissions, so make sure the uplinks are secure. These bastards have the orbitals. That gives them the high ground, and that makes our air-breathing platforms even more critical. I don't want to lose my eyes any sooner than I have to!"

"Understood, Sir." Lieutenant Michail Tolallis nodded. "I think Captain Vallakos has enough on his plate at the moment, though. I'll take it."

Technically, Zaharias Vallakos, as Third Regiment's S5, in charge of its communications, was responsible for the security of their platforms' uplinks, not Tolallis's. But Vallakos would have his hands full maintaining the regiment's comm net, and as Palides's S2, in charge of the Third's intelligence assets, Tolallis was the logical person for him to hand off to.

"Good man," Palides said with a quick smile.

That smile didn't do much to lighten the tension in his expression, and he moved his attention to where Captain Demetra Fotidi, his operations officer, sat with her attention glued to the maps on her tactical display. She looked up as if she'd felt his gaze, and he arched an eyebrow at her.

"Not much new yet, Sir," she said. "It looks like not everybody in Kórinthos got the word about standing down. And the Feds came in hot." She shook her head, her expression angry. "We're getting the feed directly from the Alpha One bird right now. I don't know long she'll last—the Feds have to spot her pretty quickly, I'd think—but from the imagery, the bastards bypassed Ithaca House and went for Parnassus, instead."

"Parnassus?" Palides frowned. "Not Ithaca House?"

"Actually, that's not entirely correct," Tolallis said. He tapped his own number two display, throwing the imagery into the main holo at the center of the buried CP. "They're all over Ochi Square," he continued, nodding his head at the holo. "The President evacced as soon as we got word these people were coming. Wasn't even a caretaker staff in the mansion. I'd say the Feds probably put a squad or so into it and then moved on to what looked like bigger fish to fry."

"Michail's right." Fotidi nodded. "I should've said their *assault elements* bypassed Ithaca House. But they put three *Perseus*-class shuttles down in the Parnassus Gardens."

"Probably to 'rescue' Governor Ramsay," Major Toccou, Palides's XO said. "Recovering the 'legitimate' system governor has to be pretty high on their list for reestablishing Fed authority."

"Don't think so, Sir," Tolallis said grimly. "They came in mighty hot even there. This is about thirty minutes old."

He flipped more recon imagery to the main holo. As long as the Alpha One satellite stayed online, they had as good a look-down capability on the capital as the orbiting TFN warships. They probably wouldn't have it for long, of course, but while it lasted—

"Shit," someone muttered as they watched Federation Army assault teams storm into the tower.

"I thought you said Ramsay had ordered her people to stand down," Palides said sharply, and Tolallis nodded.

"She did. Apparently, either they weren't listening or they just didn't care."

"That's not good," Toccou said quietly, and Palides snorted.

"That's one way to put it," he agreed.

The CP was silent, aside from the unending background matter of comm traffic, as they watched the imagery. Then the colonel shook himself and inhaled sharply.

"This is going to get ugly fast, people," he said. "I'm willing to bet we've got a hell of a lot more bodies than they do, but *they've* got the orbitals. That gives them a hell of a lot more KEW capability than we've got, and I guarantee they'll use it. In fact—"

"Flash traffic incoming!" Vallakos's sharp interruption cut Palides off. "Priority One from Delphi."

"Put it up!" Palides said, and Tolallis's satellite imagery disappeared from the main holo, replaced by what looked like an older clone of the lieutenant.

A clone with a tight, angry expression.

"I want this message relayed to every man and woman in BSDF uniform," he said curtly. "*Everyone* sees it."

He paused for a moment, letting that sink in, and then his nostrils flared.

"This is General Tolallis," he said. "I know a lot of you—a lot of us—have questioned whether or not our secession from the Federation was really necessary. Whether or not it was justified. It was. Five minutes ago, we learned who the Schleibaum Government sent to drive us back into our kennel."

He disappeared from the holo for a moment, replaced by file footage of an immaculately groomed Army officer. There was something familiar about him. . . .

"This," Tolallis continued, "is Taskin Alaimo." Someone swore softly and viciously behind Palides. "The Federation's sent the Butcher of Gobelins to Bellerophon. According to our best current information—which is still fragmentary—he's arrested Governor Ramsay. We can't confirm that yet, but we can confirm that he's announced that *he* is now our governor in the Federation's name. And if there's any remaining question in anyone's mind about how the Federation—or its representative here, at least—intends to address our 'treason,' allow me to resolve it.

"He announced his 'legal authority' with a K-strike on the Lake Orestiada evacuation center. Current estimates are that there were very few—if any—survivors."

The command post was deathly quiet with the still, stunned silence of disbelief. That was—

"There were a quarter of a million Odyssians—Odyssian *civilians*—in that evacuation center." General Tolallis's voice was frozen battle steel. "He killed them all. *That's* what the Federation's sent to our star system, our planet, to destroy our homes and murder our people. That's the twisted, corrupt Federation we seceded from. *That's* what we're fighting . . . and Alaimo obviously doesn't give a single good goddamn about open cities or collateral damage."

He paused again, letting his words settle into them.

"This is going to be even uglier than we'd feared," he said then, very quietly. "God only knows how many more people this murderous son-of-a-bitch will slaughter out of hand just to make a point. But if he's willing to murder a quarter million civilian men, women, and children just to announce his arrival, I think we can assume he plans on murdering a lot more of them before he's done. He has a point to make. The point that as far as the Heart Worlds are concerned, we don't matter. We already knew they didn't consider us full citizens; now we know they're willing to massacre our women and our children if we don't fall down and lick their boots the instant we see them. And now that the gloves are off, we know they'll do that to *anyone* who doesn't acknowledge them as the rightful gods of creation.

"Laying down our weapons, surrendering, won't stop this. He'll go right on, and the only thing standing between our civilians and him is *us*. You and me, the men and women of the System Defense Force. We're it until and unless someone from the Free Worlds gets here. And the way we protect our people is to take the fight to Alaimo and his butchers. We hit them hard, wherever and whenever we can. We make them concentrate on us instead of our civilians.

"A lot of us will die doing that. But that's our job. That's why we're here.

"I want all of you to fight smart. Remember they own the skies. Get in, hit hard, get out fast. That's the way it has to be. I never wanted to fight Federation troops. I never wanted to fight *anyone* right here on Odysseus. But they're here now, and they brought this to us, so I want every one of you to remember Lake Orestiada. Remember every single civilian who died there. The order is: God defend Bellerophon . . . and *damnation* to the Feds!"

CHAPTER TWENTY-NINE

Parnassus Tower
City of Kórinthos
Planet Odysseus
Bellerophon System
January 12, 2553

"GENERAL DUDINA'S HQ IS DOWN AND SETTING UP IN AGRINO," Major Anthony Bisgaard said. "She's about an hour ahead of schedule."

"Because the damned Odyssians completely evacuated the damned town," Colonel Rayko Hepner growled. "Fucking bastards. I'd hoped Kamisa would have the chance to make the point to them."

Thirteenth Corps's fair-haired, slender chief of staff probably weighed no more than two thirds as much as Taskin Alaimo, but under the skin, and allowing for a certain lack of polish on Hepner's part, they were very much alike. And he'd been with Alaimo for a long time...including the time they'd spent beached after doing what had to be done in Gobelins.

At the moment, he and the rest of Alaimo's staff were in the process of settling into what had been Mollie Ramsay's comm center. It was a little cramped for their needs, but both its surface-to-space capability and its links to the planetary datanet were excellent.

And there was a certain symbolism to putting Alaimo's HQ there.

"Now, now, Rayko." Alaimo waved a chiding finger. He'd shed his armor in favor of fresh, crisp fatigues, and he smiled gently.

"I expect Lake Orestiada's made the point. Once it percolates through their brains, anyway. I'm sure Kamisa would have preferred to decorate a few streetlights with traitors, but she'll have her opportunity later. After all—" his smile sharpened "—they'll all be coming home to her shortly. She'll know what to do when they do, and in the meantime, there's no one underfoot to get in her way while she settles in."

He smiled. He'd assigned General Kamisa Dudina's First Division as his lead ground component because he trusted her mettle more than he did General Filenkov's. Filenkov, who commanded the Third Division, sprang from a powerful Five Hundred family, or he wouldn't have been here, but he was obviously less . . . committed than Dudina to what had to be done. He'd be fine as a combat commander—probably—if the traitors were stupid enough to fight after Alaimo's modest object lesson, but he didn't have enough fire in the belly to command Alaimo's lead echelon.

"I know she will, Sir." Hepner grimaced. "I guess I'm just naturally impatient. And these goddamned traitors have run up a pretty steep bar tab after what they did to Admiral Hathaway." His jaw tightened and he shook his head. "This never would've happened if the Government hadn't run so scared after Gobelins."

"We don't know that for sure," Alaimo replied. His tone was almost serene, although that fooled none of his staffers. "And at least they've decided to let us take the gloves off this time. But don't be so impatient! A good baker knows it takes time to bake the perfect cake."

"Of course, but—"

"Excuse me, General."

Hepner broke off as Captain Yerlikaya, Alaimo's comm officer, raised his voice. The chief of staff looked irritated by the interruption, but Alaimo only smiled. Despite his reputation with the Federation at large, he was almost always patient and pleasant to his personal staff.

Of course, he chose . . . compatible people *for* that staff.

"Yes, Arsal?" he said.

"You have an incoming communications request, Sir."

"Really?" Alaimo's smile broadened. "Odd. I don't remember giving anyone on Odysseus my comm combination. Who is it?"

"I don't know, Sir," Yerlikaya said. "The sender's ID is blocked. And when I tried to put a trace on it, we came up cold."

"Excuse me?" Hepner asked sharply, and the captain shook his head.

"I've traced it back to the point at which it enters the datanet, Sir. It's a processing node in a little town north of here—Vyronas, I think it's named. But it looks like the feed's coming from an Agni drone, and I can't trace back beyond that point."

Alaimo raised an eyebrow at Hepner. The chief of staff looked back for a moment, then shrugged.

The Agni was the Federation Army's standard battlefield communications drone. It was small, fast, and very stealthy, yet provided an enormous bandwidth. In this instance, however, it clearly wasn't one of *their* Agnis... which underscored the point that Bellerophon enjoyed the next best thing to Heart World levels of wealth and technology. Unlike the raggedy-assed, piss-poor Fringers in Gobelins, the Bellerophon System Defense Force was equipped with first-line military hardware, just as good as the Federation Army's own. That was a sobering thought, since the BSDF outnumbered Thirteenth Corps by a considerable margin. On the other hand, its atmospheric component was largely a dead letter—manned air-breathing aircraft simply couldn't live in the air if someone else controlled the space around a planet—and it had never had any heavy armored vehicles. Still, if they were foolish enough to fight, it could get nasty.

That might just be the point Alaimo's mysterious caller wanted to make.

"Put it through, Arsal," the general said.

"Coming up on your Number Four display, Sir."

Alaimo looked down and a black-haired man in the green tunic and brown trousers of the System Defense Force appeared on it. His collar bore the same pair of stars Alaimo's did, and a data crawl blinked across the bottom of the display as the computers compared his features to the database. It stopped blinking almost immediately, and Alaimo cocked his head.

"General Tolallis," he said. The name came out liltingly, almost caressingly, and he smiled. "I assume you got my message about the evacuation centers." His smile broadened. "Is this your surrender call?"

"No," Tolallis replied.

"Then to what do I owe the somewhat dubious pleasure?"

"You sent a message with Lake Orestiada," Tolallis said coldly. "I thought it would be only courteous to send you a reply."

"Really?"

"Yes, really." It was Tolallis's turn to smile thinly. "I suppose we shouldn't be surprised that a butcher like you thinks in terms of mass casualties. However, you should be aware of two things. First, we're not going to roll over for you. We'll be perfectly happy to give up enough dirt to bury every Fed butcher you brought with you, but if you want the rest of our world, you'll goddamned well have to fight for it. And, second, we're aware you have ships in orbit around Odysseus—a hell of a lot *less* of them than you expected to have, I'm sure, but still there—and you've just demonstrated what you're willing to use them to do. What *you* may not be aware of is that we have more than a dozen Telum systems deployed in hides across this continent. For that matter, we deployed twenty-plus Fulmen platforms before you got here."

The muscles around Alaimo's eyes tightened. That was the only sign he gave, but it was more than enough for those who knew him as well as his staff did.

The Telum was a ground-based KEW platform. It was mobile, for certain values of the term, and although its 25 KPS launch velocity was little more than two thirds of a Navy K-gun's, its projectiles were far larger. First, to make up for their lower velocity—they were almost twice as massive, which gave them almost as much destructive power, despite their lower velocity— but also because, unlike the naval weapon, they incorporated airfoil control surfaces. They could change flight profiles after launch, which allowed for indirect fire and ground-skimming flight paths. The launch platforms were easy to find and kill from orbit... but not until they unmasked and fired, and they were remote-commanded systems. Killing the launchers wouldn't do a damned thing to the people who'd just fired them.

The Fulmen was even worse.

Alaimo had brought along a couple of hundred Fulmens of his own, although he hadn't bothered to deploy them yet. A capital ship's K-guns were more than adequate for anything he might need. But the Fulmen was an extremely stealthy drone that fired a 2.5-tonne slug of SCM—over three times the mass of a capital ship's K-gun slug—wrapped around a Hauptman coil capable of

3,000 gravities of acceleration. From a launch altitude of three hundred kilometers, it produced 5.2 kilotonnes of kinetic energy.

"I'm sure your Navy officers—the surviving ones, anyway—will tell you even something as stealthy as a Fulmen isn't that hard to find in a close planetary orbit," Tolallis continued. "That's why we didn't put them there. They're much farther out, but that just gives the KEWs more time to build velocity. The coils are only good for about four minutes, which means we had to put them within less than nine hundred thousand kilometers of the planet, so it's not *impossible* for you to find them. Eventually, at least. On the other hand, they'll be megaton-range weapons, coming in from that far out."

Tolallis paused, letting that sink in, then shrugged.

"I'm sure someone like you is already thinking about using our civilian population for cover. It's the sort of thing you *would* think of. And I won't lie, Alaimo—we don't want to kill hundreds of thousands or even millions of our own people, so forcing them back into the cities will give you a certain amount of cover. But there's a curve. A point where what you do may just convince us to go ahead and pull the trigger anyway. And if you start throwing around city-killers of your own, we'll reach that point in a hurry. If you want to come after us on the ground, fine—you bring it. You start killing our cities, and we will fuck you up. I just wanted to make sure you understand that, without any ambiguity."

"That sounds very impressive," Alaimo said after a moment. "Assuming there's anything to actually back it up, of course."

"And I knew you were going to say *that*, too," Tolallis said. "It would give me great pleasure to resolve any reservations you might have about my veracity by dropping a KEW right on your head, but so far, you haven't pushed it to that point, given where you happen to be hiding your cowardly ass. So I guess I'll just have to settle for a front row seat at your firing squad and find another way to resolve those reservations, instead. I'm sure something will come to me. Goodbye, General."

The display went blank.

Alaimo sat for a moment, gazing at it almost thoughtfully, then shrugged.

"It would appear this cake's oven needs a little higher temperature than I anticipated," he said almost whimsically. "Since that's the case, perhaps we—"

An alarm howled suddenly.

"Hauptmann signature inbound!" Major Bisgaard barked as a bloodred icon flashed into existence on the master plot. "Launch point, two hundred thousand kilometers!"

Alaimo's eyes snapped to the plot, and his jaw tightened as that glaring icon's velocity spun upward.

It accelerated for just over a hundred seconds. Then, still ten thousand kilometers out from the planet, it went ballistic at a velocity of 3,343 KPS.

Three seconds after that, a 3.4 megaton explosion vaporized the heart of the city of Agrino—and half of Kamisa Dudina's First Division, Terran Federation Army—in a four-kilometer fireball.

CHAPTER THIRTY

Potamia Valley Evacuation Center
Planet Odysseus
Bellerophon System
January 12, 2553

CAPTAIN AHMET YILDIZ LEANED OUT THE SIDE DOOR OF HIS SMALL gunship, one armored hand clutching a handgrip to keep him from plummeting two hundred meters to the evacuation center below. His visor overlay picked out the locations of his soldiers forming a cordon around the rows of temporary shelters and warehouses. Civilians milled about, most clustering outside the tents.

He checked the time display on his visor.

"Bulldog Six," he said over his company command channel. "Green Six, there's no one exiting the facility."

"Bulldog Six, this is Green Five," the platoon sergeant for Baker Company's lead ground element came up on the channel. "Six Actual is with the local poobah. She's not having much luck convincing him to give the evac order."

Yildiz grimaced.

"Copy. I'm going skids down and will be there ASAP. Bulldog Six, out."

Yildiz leaned back into the gunship and thumped a fist twice against the ceiling. The copilot gave him a thumbs-up, and the gunship settled towards the ground. A soldier on one of the side-mounted rotary barrels angled his weapon downwards and tensed against the stock.

"Did you positively ID a threat, Parsons?" Yildiz snapped, and the door gunner's head jerked up.

"Huh? There's a pair of Leaguies on a rooftop, Sir. I mean, not Leaguies, but—"

The soldier kept his weapon aimed at the same spot as the gunship angled slightly towards the landing zone.

"They're civilians—our civilians—until they act otherwise."

Parsons looked at him for a moment, and Yildiz knew what was going through the gunner's mind. He'd heard about what had happened to First Division's other brigade in Agrino, and the Army wasn't used to taking casualties like that. No wonder he was jumpy.

"We're trying to pacify this planet, not kill everyone on it," the captain said. "And whatever happened in Agrino, *these* people didn't have a thing to do with it."

Parsons looked at him a heartbeat longer, then nodded.

"Yes, Sir."

"Good! But that doesn't mean I don't want you to keep your head on a swivel."

Parsons grinned quickly, and Yildiz gave him a pat on the shoulder and stepped out of the gunship before the skids had touched completely down. He carried his carbine, muzzle towards the ground, as he half jogged towards a fire team guarding the refugee center's main entrance.

Most Army troopers wore the current Mark 12 powered field armor. It was too light to rival the sheer firepower and heavy protection of an all-up Hoplon, but its far lower power requirements gave it many times a Hoplon's endurance. It was also vacuum-rated and heavy enough to protect against small arms fire, and if its servos were less powerful than a Hoplon's, they still allowed its wearer to carry weapons capable of taking down League Oni battle suits. But armor or no armor, Baker Company was outfitted for crowd control and anti-insurgency, not pitched combat, with carbines and bandoliers of gas canisters. Seeing his men and women outfitted as occupiers gnawed at Yildiz's pride, but what truly worried him was that they were still *soldiers*, not cops or peacekeepers. They were trained for *combat*, not crowd control, and if their instincts and training took over—

"Sir, you need a security detail?" a soldier asked as Yildiz marched into the evac center.

"Do I need protection from a bunch of unarmed men, women, children, and elderly?" Yildiz shot back, meeting the angry gazes of Odyssian adults as they watched him move towards the HQ building. Unlike all too many Army personnel, Yildiz had put in his time at the sharp end of the stick, facing the League in combat and not sitting around in garrison in case the politicans decided he was needed someplace else. The Odyssians' faces were different from those he'd seen on the League worlds upon which he'd served, but the fear in their children's eyes was exactly the same.

"Well, Sir, they ain't been overtly hostile, but they sure ain't happy to see us," the soldier said.

"I'll take it. Back to your post," Yildiz said as he spotted the platoon sergeant. The noncom stood outside a propped open doorway, and the captain stepped past him to slip through it into what was obviously the evac center director's office.

One of his platoon leaders had her helmet off and locked to the back of her utility belt while she leaned across a desktop with a pistol under one hand. A slightly chubby man with a salt-and-pepper beard and pronounced widow's peak stood behind the desk, his arms crossed and his cheeks red, and the optics in Yildiz's helmet captured the man's features. His armor's computer pulled up the Odyssian's Federation identity file, and Yildiz did a double take at his service record.

"At what point are you going to realize I'm not *asking* you to do this?" the lieutenant barked.

"Maybe you should put your helmet back on, because your ears just don't seem to work," the Odyssian shot back. "We *can't* leave. We're perfectly safe here so long as—"

"You're not," Yildiz said over his armor speakers. "No one within a five-kilometer radius of where you're standing will be 'safe' in the next few hours." He took his helmet off, tucked it under one arm, and looked at Green Six.

"Lieutenant Reynolds, wait outside."

"Roger, Sir."

Reynolds dragged her pistol across the desk, shoved it into its holster, and marched out of the office.

"Yildiz," the captain said, tapping his chest. "And you're Masson. Major Paul Masson."

"Not in a long frigging time," the Odyssian said.

"Maybe not, but you came away with the Cross of Valor with cluster. Medicaled out when you lost a foot at Brixton."

"Already got me in your files, huh," Masson said disgustedly.

"Of course I do. And because I do, there's something you need to understand. Time is absolutely of the essence right now. I understand that these people—" a sweep of his arm took in the Odyssians outside the small office "—are angry and confused right now. They're pissed off, they're probably confused as hell, and they're not real inclined to cooperate with us. I've got that, but they're also in your charge right now. They must respect you, given your record, and you need to get them out of here before—"

"This is exactly where they should be!" Masson shouted, and Yildiz stood a bit taller, his face hard.

"At midnight—Kórinthos time—a K-strike will annihilate this facility and everything within a five-kilometer radius," he said. "That's...four hours and thirty-seven minutes from now. What are you waiting for?"

"The Federation doesn't target civilian concentrations." Masson shook his head stubbornly, and Yildiz's eyes narrowed.

"You know better than that," he said flatly.

"We're not talking about Leaguies," Masson shot back. "We're talking about *Federation* citizens on a Federation world!"

"Which has declared itself out of compliance. You know what that means."

Yildiz's voice was flatter than ever and Masson's eyes flickered. He looked away for a moment, then back at Yildiz.

"My people are here to keep them *safe*," he said. "And I don't know if you've noticed, but there's precisely zero transport out there, and we're in the middle of a valley, forty klicks from the middle of nowhere. They put this center here specifically because it's so far from any towns or any other conceivable military target, and without transport, it's impossible for me to move anyone to a safe location!"

"Walk," Yildiz said, and Masson's brows shot up.

"Beg your pardon?"

"Lead them out on foot. You're right, it's a forty-klick walk back to Politeas. I know it'll be rough for some of them. But they'll get there, and at least they'll be alive. Which they won't be if you don't lead them out. Because this facility will be subject to a K-strike whether anyone's here or not."

Masson's lips trembled for a moment, but then anger overwhelmed his other emotions.

"This isn't the Federation I fought for," he said. "We don't kill our own women and children!"

Yildiz looked at him, then nodded slowly.

"Things ... are different. You were at Hualien, right? Which continent?"

"North," Masson replied, frowning in obvious surprise at the sudden non sequitur. "I was with the Eighty-Fifth when the Leaguies hit Kilai. We pulled out of the line to evac what was left of the division across the straits. It was ..." Masson rubbed his chin. "It was—"

"The Third Spaceborne. I was with them." Yildiz scratched a phantom wound on the side of his face. The scar had faded after enough dermal treatments, but the memory remained. "I appreciate your pulling our asses out of the fire."

"That was a long time ago," Masson said, peering at Yildiz narrowly.

"I'm older than I look and it was my first deployment. I was enlisted, back then, too. And Hualien was almost my *last* deployment, on a couple of occasions. Listen to me, Masson. One evac center's already been K-struck. I don't think there were any survivors. There certainly weren't very many."

Masson's eyes went wide, and Yildiz shook his head.

"The man at the top of my chain of command here isn't ... He's not here to win hearts and minds. This is a compliance issue for him, and as long as Bellerophon is out of compliance, he's got cover to do whatever the hell he wants. There's no mercy to appeal to here."

"If we comply, then we've lost. We're fighting for—"

"It doesn't matter what you're fighting for. You accomplish nothing if you're dead. Those people out there are waiting for you to save them, and I don't want to convince them to leave by burning this place to the ground. But I sure as hell will if I have to!" Yildiz slapped a hand against the desk. "Don't make me save their lives that way, because sure as hell, some of those innocents will get killed in the process if I do."

"I don't believe you," Masson said. "Attacking a declared evacuation center would—"

Yildiz tapped commands into his forearm screen and the holo of Alaimo addressing Odysseus projected onto the desk. Masson paled as the general identified himself, and his jaw tightened as he watched silently until the mushroom clouds rose in the distance.

Yildiz cut the holo. Best not to mention Agrino just now, he thought.

"Lake Orestiada," he said instead. "And there were a lot more people in that center than there are in yours. I hope things are in a better perspective for you now."

"I can't believe even the Five Hundred sent that monster."

Masson slumped into a chair, shaking his head, and buried his face in his hands for a moment. Then he lowered them and stared daggers at Yildiz.

"This is why we were right to secede. This is exactly the reason why!"

"I don't care," Yildiz said softly. "Get your people out of here. Now."

"We don't have any buses—not even a flatbed truck to get the handicapped out!" Masson raised his hands.

"I. Don't. Care." Yildiz pointed to the door. "Walk. The lethal radius from a K-strike on a target this size is three kilometers. Five kilometers is the casualty limit. Whoever's that far away when it hits may suffer a headache from the overpressure, but at least they'll be alive. The longer you sit there whining, the more likely people will get hurt or killed. What the fuck are you waiting for?"

"Why destroy this place if we're not even here?"

"So there's no place to run to," Yildiz said. "How many non-ambulatory cases do you have? I've got four *Hecate*-class gunships I can use to move them to the hospital in Politeas."

"Don't." Masson shook his head. "I heard there's a System Defense Force battalion in Politeas. Drop them at the abandoned police station in Logotis. We'll collect them on our way back to Politeas."

"I appreciate that," Yildiz said.

"I don't want any of my older, disabled vets getting killed when your birds get shot down." Masson shrugged. "Their lives have been shitty enough already."

He opened a drawer and took out a megaphone disc.

"I have your word we'll be safe moving back to Politeas?" he asked, and Yildiz nodded slightly.

"You have my word as a Federation officer."

Masson looked at him as if he were an idiot, and Yildiz rolled his eyes.

"Fine. You have my word as one veteran of Hualien to another."

"Better."

Masson limped out from behind the desk on the prosthesis that had replaced his left calf.

"Keep moving!" Masson called through the megaphone ring. "There's only one road back home. Stay on it, and you'll be fine."

Civilians filed out of the evacuation center. Most carried bags and suitcases, and an air of shocked disbelief permeated the column. They'd rushed to get out of the city to be safe; now they were being herded back to the very place from which they'd fled.

Yildiz knew many of them would abandon their burdens long before they ever made the forty-kilometer trudge back to the city, but at least they were moving.

"Tell them where they have to be in the next four hours," he said from where he stood behind Masson at the front gate.

"We have to reach the Corinia Bridge by nightfall," Masson blasted. "If you're not past Marra Falls Park in the next two hours, you are wrong! Let go of your miniatures collection, Mr. Anastopoulos! They're not worth your life!"

An old man at the tail end of the column shook a fist at Masson as he dragged a heavy case out the gate.

"You just want my vintage Space Marines!" he yelled, and Masson pinched the bridge of his nose, then looked over his shoulder at Yildiz.

"Can I borrow a gun for a warning shot?"

Yildiz stared at him blankly.

"Worth a try," Masson said as he brought the megaphone back to his mouth.

"No, it wasn't," Yildiz said, and Masson shrugged.

"Area's clear, Sir," Lieutenant Reynolds said through Yildiz's earbud.

"No stragglers," Yildiz said to Masson. "You did good."

"Well, then." Masson powered off the megaphone and stuck it onto a belt loop. "Guess I'd best be on my way, too. Got a long limp ahead of me."

He took a step away, but Yildiz grabbed him by the wrist and slapped a cuff onto it.

"What the hell are you doing?" Masson tried to pull his arm back.

"General Alaimo's ordered the arrest of every evacuation center commander. I'm sorry."

Yildiz reached the man's arm around his back and cuffed the other wrist.

"You rotten son-of-a-bitch!" Masson kept struggling. "You knew this would happen, but you—!"

A corporal slipped a sound-dampening hood over Masson's head and activated the security band at the bottom. Masson kept yelling, but only muffled sounds made it through the fabric, and Yildiz put a hand on his shoulder.

"But your people are safe," the captain said, leaning close, his voice low. "You and I know that's all that really matters to you. You were a hell of a good officer, Masson, and at least *you've* got a clean conscience right now."

His eyes held the Odyssian's for a moment. Then he tapped the side of his neck to activate his armor microphone.

"Reynolds, call in the transports and set the incendiary charges. We're burning this place down as soon as we evac. Keep anyone from changing their minds. Yildiz, out."

CHAPTER THIRTY-ONE

Planet Odysseus
Bellerophon System
Free Worlds Alliance
January 13, 2553

THE HOOD CAME OFF MOLLIE RAMSAY'S HEAD.

Bright lights stung her eyes as Alaimo dangled the hood in front of her. They hadn't removed the sound-dampening mask over her mouth and nose, and with her wrists and ankles cuffed to a chair bolted to the floor, all she could do was glare at him.

"Glad we're all here."

Alaimo dropped the hood into her lap. He stood with her in the cone of merciless light pouring down from overhead. Its brilliance made the blackness beyond him even more impenetrable. He wore fatigue pants and boots, and a tight sleeveless shirt that wasn't standard Federation issue showed off his bulky physique as he smiled at her, then looked at someone behind her.

"Volkov, get the holos going."

"Sir," the other man acknowledged, and she heard more people shuffling in the darkness where she couldn't see.

"Good, good."

Alaimo wagged two fingers in the air in front of him and Ramsay, and dozens of holo displays appeared. Each showed a person bound to a chair, just like Ramsay, although she was the only one who was gagged. She recognized several faces as trusted and respected individuals active in Odyssian society.

She couldn't begin to identify all of them, but those she did recognize had all been appointed leaders of evacuation centers.

379

"Before we get started..." Alaimo said. He set the edge of his hand close to Ramsay's neck, and despite herself, she flinched slightly. The bruises from his earlier touch were still raw and throbbing. "I'm going to give you the choice to end this little exercise at any moment. All you have to do is—"

He pulled a silver spoon from his pocket. From the handle's intricate designs, she recognized it as part of the Ithaca House formal silver. He reached down and slipped the spoon into the fingers of her right hand.

"When you're ready to tell me where to find President Xeneas, just drop the spoon, and everything stops." Alaimo raised a finger. "But if you drop it and don't tell me where to find him immediately," he tapped the tip of her nose playfully, "you won't like what happens. After all, I have plenty of potential informants. I can afford to turn a few of them into... teaching examples for people who waste my time."

Ramsay tightened her grip on the spoon.

"Drone," Alaimo said.

He took a step away from Ramsay's chair, and a camera drone swooped in to hover a few feet in front of him. The red LED beside the lens lit, and his holo projection appeared in every prisoner's individual feed.

"Good evening," he said cheerfully. "I'm General—I'm sorry; I'm *Governor* Alaimo now, aren't I? I do tend to forget some of the details, I'm afraid! Well, no matter. What's important is that all of you have been in recent contact with President Xeneas and that I—" he put a hand on his chest "—am a humanist, fundamentally. Unfortunately, altruist though I may be, it's my responsibility to end this rebellion. And while my ships have total control of the orbitals and I can end not just the rebellion but this entire planet with a single transmission, what I'd really prefer is to keep this world producing for the good of the Federation. And yet, people are being so *unreasonable*. In fact, while I've already eliminated every evacuation center—all of them received *ample* warning to vacate, of course—to convince the populace to return to productive labor, I'm afraid there are already reports of organized attacks on my forces."

He put his hands on his hips.

"I'm afraid that's unacceptable, and that's what brings me to the point of our little meeting today. President Xeneas is directing this insurgency, which means he's responsible not just for these ongoing attacks on the Expeditionary Force, but also for the enormous casualties the Navy suffered on our arrival. I will have Xeneas, and I will end this illegal resistance. The problem, of course, is that I don't know where to find him. But I'm confident that at least one of you does. So where is he? Tell me now."

He paused, watching the holos as the prisoners reacted. There was no sound from their cells, but AI transcription recorded and displayed their responses in a text crawl across each display, and Ramsay noted a number of expletives and a few creative invitations to Alaimo to engage in impossible anatomical acts.

"Nothing?" Alaimo asked whimsically. "Fine by me. The spinner, please."

He held out a hand, and Volkov placed an object in his palm. It looked like something from a child's game: a small plastic circle with an arrow and numbers printed around its edge. Alaimo flicked one end of the arrow, and it spun several times before slowing to a stop.

"Thirty percent power," he said cheerfully, looking up at the holos, and smiled.

The prisoners screamed, jerking at their cuffed wrists and ankles as electricity slammed through them. Somehow, the inability to actually hear their screams made it even worse for Ramsay. They writhed in all those dozens of holos while the agony lashed through them, and then, abruptly, the torture stopped. They slammed back into their chairs, and a part of Ramsay's mind realized it had lasted no more than a handful of seconds. She *knew* that, but watching so many people screaming like some silent chorus of the damned made it seem like an eternity.

Alaimo smiled brightly, then looked down at her and glanced at the spoon.

"Timer," he said. "One minute."

He traced a circle over one shoulder and a countdown projected from the drone. It appeared in each of the holos, and Alaimo smiled even more brightly.

"Tell me where to find Xeneas," he said, clapping his hands in time with the words like a child reciting a nursery rhyme.

Some of the prisoners continued to curse at him, and he shrugged.

"Let me have Major Perkins up here," he said, and held out

the spinner as a man in light powered armor jogged up to him. The newcomer spun the needle, and Alaimo chuckled.

"Oooh, *fifty* percent. That's gonna sting!"

He hummed gently to himself while the time display ticked downward. The last few seconds trickled away. It reached zero... and people began screaming again.

Ramsay cried out, twisting from side to side in her chair, fighting to get loose, and one projection flashed red as the prisoner in it slumped forward in his own chair.

"Whoops! Got a cardiac arrest already." Alaimo snapped his fingers while the others continued to scream. "Get medics into room twenty-four and stabilize that one. He'll continue as soon as he's conscious again."

The shocks stopped—finally—and Alaimo tapped a foot on the floor.

"Where's Xeneas?" he asked more loudly. "All this stops as soon as you tell me where he is."

Ramsay shouted as loudly as she could—loudly enough to finally catch his attention. He waggled two fingers together and the drone stopped projecting him into the prisoners' cells.

"Something to tell me?" He cocked his head to one side. "Drop the spoon. Otherwise, this doesn't stop."

She shook her head, and he shrugged.

"Volkov, get me...Colonel Jurayev."

A woman in simple fatigues walked into the light. He held out the disc, and she spun the arrow.

"Mmmmm." Alaimo frowned at the number and shook his head. "Only ten percent. I'd hate for the subjects to think this is getting easier. As soon as some resistance builds, they—"

Jurayev grabbed the pointer and shifted it slightly.

"Now, there's the kind of gumption I like to see!" Alaimo said enthusiastically. "*Sixty-five* percent, if you please, Volkov."

Ramsay squeezed her eyes shut and lowered her head. Shutting out the images' silent shrieks. It didn't help. She still knew they were there, knew what was happening...and that the agony of so many who'd tried to save innocent lives would never leave her, no matter how little time she had left herself.

"Two more cardiac events." Alaimo tsked. "I expected better out of such hardy Fringer types. Well, onward and upward! I believe you're up next, Captain Yildiz."

He held the spinner out to his side nonchalantly, his attention on the many holo projections, and Ramsay's eyes opened, almost against her will, as a tall, broad shouldered man with bristle-cut dark blond hair and a strong nose walked up to Alaimo. He, too, wore fatigues, and he moved stiffly, his hands balled at his sides.

Alaimo rattled the spinner at him, and his nostrils flared.

"Sir, I believe—"

"Hold that thought, Captain," Alaimo interrupted as the text crawl on one holo flashed brightly. "Sound, Volkov!"

"I'll talk! I'll talk!" The voice was raw, hoarse, and Alaimo pointed at the interrogation subject. He swiped his finger towards the middle of the projection, and the image enlarged to display an elderly man. His gray hair was a wet mop and his lips were deathly pale against his dark skin.

"P-please. I'll . . . I'll tell you everything I know. Just don't shock me again," he whimpered.

Alaimo tapped the upper right corner of the man's projection and the display edge went green.

"Talk," the general said, peering closely at the screen while background data on the man scrolled across his face.

"I . . . I know where one of Xeneas's people is. She works for him—works in Ithaca House. She must know where he is! That's it. That's all I know!" Mucus and spittle blew from his mouth as he spoke.

"Yildiz, this is your target," Alaimo said without looking directly at the captain. He tapped on his forearm screen, and light broke across the prisoner a few seconds later as the door to his cell opened. "If he's leading us to a dry hole, let me know ASAP. He'll have some work to catch up on."

"Sir, there's no way we can corroborate any information he gives us," Yildiz said. "It's just as likely he'll direct my company into a trap as—"

"You'll verify it." Alaimo shooed him away. "Get armored up and get your people aboard the ready transports. We'll transmit the target packet to you before you can even get to the flight line. Happy hunting! Bring in everyone you can. Alive, since I can't make a corpse talk."

"Moving, Sir," Yildiz said through a tight jaw.

The captain jogged away, and Alaimo stuck his fingers into

the broken prisoner's holo. He flicked it to the side, and the other displays rearranged themselves to fill in the gap.

"That's enough of a break," he said. "Volkov, repeat the last motivation."

Ramsay tried screaming, rocking her chair from side to side, and Alaimo glanced at her.

"Something to add?" he said. "No? That's ... unfortunate. But never mind! *You* may not want to talk to me, but all of them know *something*, Madame Governor. So I suppose the interrogation continues until they think up something to tell me or they— Damn it, medics to cell thirty-seven."

Ramsay tightened her convulsive grip on the spoon. She knew absolutely nothing that might lead Alaimo to Xeneas, but he would never believe that. She knew that. Just as she knew that if she tried to lie, it would doom all of the prisoners to slow, violent death.

All she could do was pray the others broke before they died.

CHAPTER THIRTY-TWO

City of Nafplio
Planet Odysseus
Bellerophon System
Free Worlds Alliance
January 14, 2553

SERGEANT KORINA PRISCIDE OF THE BELLEROPHON SELF DEFENSE Force leaned against the wall of the empty apartment bedroom while sweat seeped down the seals of her body armor. The body glove under it was fresh from stores and still didn't fit right. New armor normally took a week or so of wear before it was comfortable enough for constant use and optimal performance. Just her luck to be issued a brand-new Mark 12 three days ago.

"Third Squad, you have eyes on the target?" Lieutenant Slovens asked over her earbud.

A private hurried past Priscide into the bedroom and snapped an optic onto the window frame. His well-worn armor was older than the sergeant's with a slight but noticeable bulge around the middle. Vangelis Agnellis had been called up from the reserves and plugged into Alpha Company to bring it fully up to strength, and his weight had crept a bit over regulation. Fortunately, there was a bit of play built into the Mark 12, so Agnellis's armor still fit . . . barely.

"Eyes in place," he said, and Priscide nodded. The private might be plump and twelve years her senior, but he was also good at his job.

Picture captures flipped up in the upper corner of her visor, showing her the Nafplio Federal Courthouse from multiple dispersed cameras. At least the Feds hadn't shut down the local police cameras yet, so they hadn't had to deploy camera drones to get the imagery. In a way, that almost made what Priscide was seeing even more bizarre. She'd already known what the courthouse looked like, but she'd never seen it overlaid with military graphics depicting phase lines and target reference points for mortars.

An Army fire team manned a sandbagged emplacement in front of the building, and the Federation's flag flew from both flagpoles above it, including the one that would normally have displayed the Bellerophon System's flag. A Long Eye recon drone hovered above the courthouse, and Priscide bared her teeth in a tight grin as she saw it. Bastards were looking in the wrong direction. Second Platoon had infiltrated into position using the city service tunnels, and one of the first things the SDF had done was to "adjust" the servers that managed the security and safety cameras. They'd planted multiple back doors in all of them, and not just to provide the reconnaissance imagery Priscide was looking at. There was no way to keep the Feds from using the exact same cameras...except for the carefully hidden programs that could command any given camera or group of cameras to loop up to forty minutes of imagery as SDF personnel moved past them. It was unlikely the defenders would be able to get away with that unnoticed for long, but while it lasted...

Nafplio wasn't anything Priscide would have called a city, and its courthouse wasn't anything she would have called a critical target. But Nafplio *was* a fairly large town and the troopers dug in in front of it—and the federal administrator installed inside it—certainly made it a *legitimate* target. She knew other SDF units were tasked to hit larger targets, and an air defense team from Third Brigade had taken down no less than three *Perseus* assault shuttles on their approach to the city of Livadeia on the Chalkidiki Peninsula. Beside that, Nafplio was small beer, but that was fine with Priscide.

Bastards don't have unlimited manpower, especially after Agrino. That means they'll have to spread themselves thin if they expect to hold us down. And when they do—

"Squad leaders." Lieutenant Slovens's voice came up in her earbud. "Listen to me. Most of us are veterans. We fought for a Federation that told us it cared for us, that it would protect us and our homeworlds. We found out the hard way that that was a lie...those of us who survived. Now our entire star system's finding out the same thing. The same Federation we fought for killed a quarter million of our people yesterday. What happened to Agrino may have convinced even a butcher like Alaimo to not K-strike more of our cities, but the mass arrests have already started, and we have confirmation of firing squads in Kórinthos and virtually all of the state capitals.

"Any armed combatant you see in there is our enemy. Here to kill us, to enslave us. Remember that.

"That's why we're here. We take out the Feds here in Nafplio, and they find out they need bigger detachments to cover their asses outside the major cities. The bigger the detachments, the fewer they can throw out. And if we just happen to acquire a few prisoners of our own to use as bargaining chips, that won't hurt a damned thing.

"All right, First and Second Squad will clear the holding cells while Third and Fourth—"

"Break, Break, Break."

An ID code flashed in the corner of Priscide's visor, but she didn't need it to recognize Platoon Sergeant Teresiadis's voice. It took either guts or profound stupidity to interrupt an officer at a moment like this without very good reason, and Pannikos Teresiadis had plenty of the former and very little of the latter.

"We've got hostile birds inbound," he said.

"Oh, shit. Are we compromised?" Agnellis asked over Priscide's squad channel.

Imagery of Army gunships flying a rooftop profile replaced the courthouse on Priscide's visor.

"They're coming right at us," the private hissed, and double-checked his rifle.

"No, they're not." Priscide smacked him on the back of his helmet. "Look at the coordinates. They're already past us, you idiot. Get your shit together and keep it that way, Agnellis!"

"Thanks, Sarge." Agnellis nodded slowly. "I see why you've got stripes."

"Stand by..." Lieutenant Slovens said.

An endless five seconds trickled past. Then—

"They're not vectored towards us or the courthouse. They're assaulting a house in the Thissio neighborhood."

"What's there?" Agnellis asked Priscide.

"Bunch of rich people, I think." Priscide shrugged.

"Change of mission," Slovens said. "The courthouse isn't going anywhere."

Captain Yildiz kept a hand on the back of his prisoner's neck as he directed her towards a waiting gunship. A sequestration hood covered her head and her wrists were cuffed in front of her, anchored to a heavy belt locked around her waist.

His company had assaulted the villa with textbook precision and found the target and several other individuals of interest exactly where their informant had said they'd be. They'd been in—and now they were pulling out—in less than thirty minutes. So far, everything was green, but this was still hostile territory. A Federation planet where every square meter was "hostile territory."

Yildiz still had trouble with that concept.

Their landing zones had been designed to seal off the target villa, and he'd seen only a handful of Odyssians outside the perimeter his troopers had set up. None of them had approached his people with any sort of useful information. Most had sent obscene gestures and colorful metaphors, instead, and he'd seen naked hatred on most of the faces he'd glimpsed.

That hatred was scarcely a surprise. He'd been on Odysseus for less than forty-eight hours, and he'd already seen exactly how its people thought about the Federation. It was even worse than he'd feared it would be from the mission briefs during the long voyage from Sol, and it wasn't getting any better. Anything they accomplished out here would last only as long as the Oval was prepared to maintain a massive garrison—an occupation force, on what was supposed to be Federation territory. There was no way that could last forever. It had to come down, one way or the other. He knew that. But for now, he just prayed Odysseus would realize it had to bend the knee at this moment, whatever happened later, before Alaimo decided the planet wasn't worth the effort and ended the problem with K-strikes.

What had happened in Agrino might dissuade him.

Might.

Personally, Yildiz didn't think it would. Not in the end. Not if the Odyssians continued to defy him and his ego.

A soldier grabbed the prisoner under her arms and hoisted her into the gunship's midships hatch.

"Alpha Target secured, collapse the perimeter," Yildiz announced over the comm while the door gunner swept the muzzle of his weapon slowly from side to side, showing enough alertness to keep any insurgent from considering it an easy target.

Yildiz's lieutenants acknowledged the order and he watched the transponders for all his people coalesce quickly into the other gunships. Yildiz was the last one off the landing zone, and he banged a fist twice against the gunship roof as he vaulted through the hatch.

The pilots lifted them off the ground, and he settled into the jump seat beside the prisoner's. Her ankles were cuffed to a ring in the floor, and her entire body shook with fear or adrenaline.

"Shit, Sir." The door gunner gave him a thumbs-up. "Way too easy. All it took was one rod from God to get them into compliance. Good thing the League don't know how soft these Fringies really are."

"Really?" Yildiz said. "Keep that up, and I won't need to rip you a new one, Harrelson." The door gunner's head snapped up, his eyes widening, and Yildiz snorted harshly. "You tell General Dudina and Corps HQ how easy they rolled over, because I don't think the Odyssians got that memo. They will shoot your sorry ass dead in a heartbeat, and I'd just as soon not get anyone with a *brain* killed at the same time."

Harrelson swallowed, then nodded almost convulsively and returned to his weapon.

Yildiz glowered at him a moment longer, then inhaled deeply. The private had needed kicking, but he had to wonder how much of his... vehemence stemmed from his own sense of despair.

The company's flight plan off the target came up on his visor. They were taking a different route on the way out, skimming past the Federal Courthouse Plaza.

"Green Six, what's the status on the prisoners in your bird?" he asked over the comm.

"One of the older males decided to be a hero," Lieutenant Reynolds replied. "He'll have a couple of new bruises when we get back to the—"

The gunship ahead of Yildiz's blew up.

The trajectory of its shoulder-fired hypervelocity executioner painted itself across Yildiz's visor, and the pilots automatically banked hard and dumped altitude.

Yildiz dropped to the floor and put an arm over the prisoner's shoulders as the door gunner opened fire. The captain didn't know if he had an actual target, but the chain-saw bellow of his rotary-barrel ripsawed through the gunship and triggered Yildiz's audio dampers. The comm was chaos as platoon leaders barked orders and pilots called out warnings to each other. An instant later, another SAM took down a second gunship, and then incoming fire ripped through the command gunship's troop compartment.

The gunner took rounds to his legs that punched up into his body and burst out his throat. He flopped over his weapon, and only the tether from his shoulder harness kept the sudden corpse from falling out of the bird.

"Get us out of—"

A sledgehammer smashed into Yildiz's gunship. The Federation's shoulder-fired Wasp SAM's velocity was over two thousand meters per second. At this short a range and that velocity, it was effectively an energy weapon, not a projectile, but the pilots' evasive maneuvers almost denied it a clean hit anyway.

Almost wasn't good enough. The Wasp missed the fuselage, but it punched through the starboard wing root, and the starboard fan, and two thirds of the rest of the wing, disintegrated. The gunship rolled right and into a dive that threw Yildiz against the ceiling. He tumbled towards the troop hatch, sliding helplessly until he slammed into the dead gunner. He hooked an arm around Harrelson's waist and got an excellent view of the street in the instant before the plummeting gunship smashed into the side of an apartment building.

Smoke and powdered ceramacrete blew into the compartment as the gunship broke through the wall and the third-story floor collapsed across it. Yildiz lay crumpled between the dead gunner and the bulkhead that separated the cockpit from the troop bay. He wiped grit from his visor and made out a dark figure in front of him.

The prisoner hung from the ceiling, twisting in obvious terror—and pain—as she dangled from her chained ankles, and he pushed himself to his own feet. No jabbing pain indicated broken bones, and he keyed his comm with a jab of his chin even as he wrapped one arm around the prisoner. She twisted still harder, but even her panic-fueled struggles meant little beside his armor's servo-driven strength.

"This is Bulldog Six," he said over the comm. "My bird is down. Prisoner still viable."

He reached up with his free hand as he spoke and grabbed the cuffs on her ankles. They sprang open as they synced with his armor's control codes, and he caught the rest of her weight and set her on her feet before she could hit the ground.

"Quiet," he hissed at her over his armor speakers. "I don't want to kill you. Maybe your friends don't, either."

"Bulldog Six!" Reynolds came over the comm. "I've got eyes on your location, but there's—Goddamn it! Get fire on that building!"

The rippling thunder of rotary-barrels, grenades, and pod-launched chemical warhead rockets sounded over the comm and echoed through the buildings around them. Yildiz looked for the pilots, but the cockpit had been ripped away. There wasn't even a body.

He saw light through the swirling dust and pulled the captive behind him, guiding her through the wreckage of someone's living room. He was tempted to remove her sequestration hood, but she could give away position with a single shout, and Yildiz wanted more firepower around him before that could happen.

They stumbled out into a hallway. Sparks rained down from ruined light fixtures. Smoke clung to the ceiling, swirling in a gray fog.

"Keep moving," Yildiz told the prisoner. "Just keep moving. I'll keep you safe."

A stairwell door burst open and a soldier came through it, sweeping to the right as he entered the hallway in a turn that took him away from Yildiz and the prisoner. He wore standard Mark 12 armor, identical to Yildiz's, but no transponder came up on the captain's visor and instead of the star and planet Earth of the Federation, it bore the blue shield and white cross of the Bellerophon System Defense Force.

Yildiz slammed the prisoner against the wall with one hand and fired his carbine with the other.

Bullets smashed into his target's back and shoulder, knocking the Odyssian forward. Yildiz lunged towards him, slamming the door with his right shoulder and the full weight of his body. It hammered into the weapon of the next man in the BSDF stick coming up the stairs, trapping the weapon, and Yildiz turned his carbine to one side and fired through the metal door as he charged past it after the first Odyssian trooper.

His fire had knocked divots into the insurgent's armor but

hadn't penetrated. At less than three meters' range, though, the blows had still hit like hammers, stunning the other man, and Yildiz went to one knee on his back, jammed the muzzle of his carbine under the back edge of his helmet, and squeezed the trigger twice.

The Odyssian's head flopped forward, dangling by what remained of the bodysuit.

Yildiz released his carbine and the powered sling sucked it around to his shoulder as he took a grenade from his belt. He came back to his feet as he double-clicked the activation stud, then took two long strides back to the stairwell door while the grenade ticked down. He grabbed the bullet-riddled door's edge and heard confused shouts as he yanked it open just far enough to toss the grenade through it.

He slammed it shut again without slowing, then tackled the prisoner, knocking her to the floor and protecting her with his own body as the grenade exploded. The blast hit him like a full-body punt, shoving him and the prisoner across the hallway and into the other wall.

"Up. Up!" Yildiz grabbed her by the waist-level restraining strap and hauled her to her feet. She was unsteady, probably suffering from a minor concussion, and still blind to everything around her, but she moved where he directed her.

He reached back for his carbine with his right hand as he got her to the emergency stairwell. He held her at his side as he kicked the door open and made a quick combat peek down the stairwell. Neither his eyes nor his armor sensors saw anything, and he hefted the prisoner onto his left hip and started down it.

"This is Bulldog Six. Anyone monitor?"

"Bulldog!" Lieutenant Benson's voice came back over the comm as he and the prisoner emerged from the stairwell into the apartment building's lobby. "White platoon is in—What is this place . . . a steakhouse? One street west of where your bird went down. Enemy is attacking us from—"

A blast rattled the lobby windows, and Yildiz went to his knees, pulling the prisoner with him, to get below sight level. He raised his carbine, using its optics to look out a window, and found a firefight raging from one side of the street to the other. Bullets kicked spurts of dust as they pockmarked walls. Glass rained down, twinkling in the sunlight.

"Get fire on that position before we eat another rocket!" someone shouted.

"White Six, I need smoke!" Yildiz said. "I've got the HVI, and she's unarmored!"

"Hope to hell she's worth all this," Benson replied. "Stand by, Bulldog Six."

Yildiz checked the prisoner. Her entire body shook, and the skin of her hands had a bluish tint. Shock was a risk, he thought, but she was still upright on her knees.

Plasteel canisters bounced into the street, then spewed glittering billows of blue smoke. That smoke was designed to block thermal imaging, as well as most electro-optical systems, and Yildiz cycled through his optics as it filled the space between the buildings. He couldn't see through it, which meant the enemy couldn't, either.

"Move." He snapped upright, grabbed the prisoner by the restraining strap, dragged her up beside him, and dropped his shoulder to bulldoze out the lobby's doors. He couldn't see a damn thing through the smoke, but he knew which way he was supposed to go.

A stray round from something far heavier than his own carbine smashed into his shin, and he stumbled hard, kept upright only by his armor's servos. The pain was manageable, but an icon flashed in one corner of his visor, indicating critical damage to his right greave.

The prisoner coughed hard, then began wheezing.

A wall loomed out of the smoke barely in time for Yildiz to alter trajectory and slam into a door, instead of a stone wall, and crash through into the bar area of what looked like a decent restaurant. One of his troopers swung her rifle towards him, then lifted the muzzle high when she recognized him. The captain grabbed the prisoner by her belt, pulled her farther into the restaurant, and shoved her to the floor, where the air was clearer.

"Sir!" Lieutenant Benson jogged into the room. "We've got insurgents coming out of the goddamned woodwork! They're all over the place. We need Hoplon support!"

"Just hold the perimeter for now," Yildiz replied, and punched up the company command net.

"Green Six, Blue Six, Bulldog Six," he said. "What's your status?"

"Bulldog, this is Green. I've got three urgent critical casualties and I lost one prisoner when my bird went in," Lieutenant Reynolds replied. "We've got the building to the north of you secure. Moving to higher floors for better visibility on the roads."

"Bulldog, this is Blue," Lieutenant Kelly said. "Got two dead and one ambulatory. We—"

Her transmission broke in a rapid crackle of automatic fire.

"Movement by that van!" Benson snapped.

The lieutenant was raising his weapon when the rocket-propelled grenade smashed through the center of the restaurant logo on the crystoplast front windows. It struck the back of the bar and exploded, shattering dozens of bottles and spraying the seating area with glass and metal shrapnel. Benson took most of the blast and went flying face first into a leather-lined booth. He splintered the wooden table when he hit . . . and lay ominously still.

The prisoner squealed and collapsed from her knees, wailing in pain.

"Medic! Get a medic over here!"

Yildiz turned the prisoner towards him. A hunk of the wooden bar had impaled her forearm, and a bloody splinter the size of a thick pen jutted out either side of the limb.

She squealed again as Yildiz yanked the splinter free. Blood flowed harder, and he jerked a med pack off his belt and pressed his thumb against a red button. A hypo spray popped out the side. He pushed the prisoner's head back to expose her throat and gave her a quick press from the nozzle. Another compartment opened, and he plucked a bandage from the pack and stretched the fabric around the bleeding wound. The smart bandage tightened on its own, flooding the skin and flesh with painkillers and quick clotting agents.

"Lieutenant's down!" someone shouted.

"Monitor her." Yildiz grabbed a soldier moving towards the booth where Benson had landed and redirected him towards the prisoner.

"Bulldog Six, this is Central," a nonchalant voice said in his earbud. "Are you viable for evac?"

"Central, this is Bulldog. Yes, we're viable!"

Yildiz tossed the broken table aside. Benson's right arm was a mangled mess. His visor was cracked, and blood seeped from his armor. Yildiz put a palm against the lieutenant's breastplate bio reader and far too many injury codes cascaded across his visor as the lieutenant's armor's report scrolled down it. A lacerated artery in the wounded arm pumped blood with each heartbeat, and he pulled a deltoid plate off.

"Talk to me, Benson," he said as he reached under the plate, hooked a finger into a tourniquet loop, and yanked hard. The built-in tourniquet clamped down, stemming most of the blood flow, and a strained burble came from Benson's visor.

"I know. Hold on!"

Yildiz pressed a button on Benson's helmet and the visor popped off, dropping broken shards onto his face. The impact that had broken the visor had crushed the lieutenant's right eye, as well, and its ruin leaked blood and what looked like retinal fluid down his cheek.

"Bulldog, this is Central. General Alaimo's authorized evac from your current location. Gunships will extract you from the roof in ... nine minutes."

"Nine?" Yildiz repeated. "We're still engaged with the enemy. I don't have the time to—"

A warning icon flashed on his visor. The same lurid flash and digital timer appeared on every other Baker Company visor at the same instant, but only Yildiz's showed the concentric rings spreading from their current location across most of the town.

"Central ... did you just release a K-strike on my location?" he demanded.

"Roger that, Bulldog."

"But we don't need—"

"Not my problem, Bulldog. And not much I can do about it. Release order's been locked, so you'd best have your company in place for evac at the designated location. The birds won't make a second trip. Central, out."

Yildiz's onboard computer connected to the Nafplio civil defense network as it blared sudden warning of the incoming KEW, and he swore with silent venom. Fifteen minutes. That was how long they—and the city's civilians—had.

"Alaimo's a lunatic!" he snarled, but he'd retained enough control to mute his comm. Then he shook his head quickly and opened the company's general frequency.

"Team leaders, team leaders! Stampede order to the top floor of my building. All personnel to the roof ASAP. Don't worry about gear; get everyone moving. Now!"

"Sir, did you call in a K-strike on us?" Lieutenant Kelly asked. "I didn't think we were in any danger of being over—"

"No, I goddamn didn't!" Yildiz snapped. "But there's not a thing I can do about it now."

He reached under Benson and pulled two belts out of the lieutenant's buddy-strap rig. He moved Benson's legs apart, sat between them, and locked the straps together around his own waist. He reached back, grabbed Benson's good arm, and pulled the lieutenant against him, then stood up, carrying his platoon leader like a backpack.

"Up the stairs! Now!"

Yildiz pointed to the stairwell in the back of the restaurant. Benson's platoon—all of whom knew there was a K-strike inbound—didn't need much more in the way of motivation, and the gunfire slacked off as Green and Blue rushed into the restaurant from neighboring buildings.

Yildiz grabbed one of the incoming noncoms and pointed at the prisoner with his other hand.

"Get her up there, Sergeant Connors," he snapped, and waited long enough for the sergeant to snatch the prisoner up in a fireman's carry.

Yildiz himself was the last to the stairwell, and Benson groaned and mumbled as he took the steps two at a time. Bloodstains and red smears from the other wounded marked the way to the roof.

"Bulldog, got eyes on the enemy in the open," Kelly said in his earbud. "Permission to engage?"

"What are they doing?"

Yildiz reached an arm back to get a better grip on Benson as the lieutenant squirmed.

"Uhhh...they seem to be evacuating civilians," Kelly replied.

"Negative. Say again, negative—do *not* engage," Yildiz said. It came out labored. Even with his armor's augmentation, the stairwell and the extra weight were taking a toll on him.

He got to the roof in time to see the first gunship lift away and a second touch down. Kelly knelt beside a soldier on a stretcher, yelling at the next pair of fire teams to load into the second gunship, and nameplates for the wounded popped up on Yildiz's visor.

"Why wasn't Spellman on the first bird out?" Yildiz asked, turning to let one of the platoon medics take Benson off of him and carry the wounded lieutenant to the gunship.

"He bled out," Kelly said harshly. "I pulled him for someone with a heartbeat. The HVI went out on the first bird."

Yildiz's jaw clenched as he heard the pain in her voice. Dino Spellman had been her platoon sergeant from the day she took over Third Platoon. He knew how that hurt. He'd been there and done that. But—

"That was...a good call," he agreed.

He touched her shoulder lightly, then looked over the edge of the roof and saw people running out of buildings and down streets, away from his building. BSDF troopers waded through the chaos, directing people towards safety and yelling instructions.

It was damned unlikely many of those civilians would outrun the K-strike, the captain thought grimly. On the other hand, Odysseus was a Fringe World. Unlike lower priority systems, it could probably have relied upon a defense against any light League raiding force, but it wasn't a Heart World the Navy would fight to the death to save. And because it wasn't, it still had deep shelters under most of its larger towns and all of its cities, rated to resist most tactical K-strikes. It was remotely possible Nafplio's were deep enough to ride out this strike, but from the damage projected on his visor, it was from one of Alaimo's Fulmens and well up into the megaton range. Probably as tactically "excusable" payback for Agrino.

"Move your asses!" a crew chief yelled from the side hatch of a cargo shuttle, hovering beside and just above the rooftop. "How close do you want to cut it?!"

The cargo bird wasn't part of the evac plan and Yildiz had no idea what an unarmed trash hauler was doing in the middle of this shit-fest, but he didn't really care as its cargo ramp extended across the edge of the roof. It might be unarmed, but it also had significantly more internal volume than any gunship. At this moment, that was the only thing that mattered, and his remaining soldiers poured across the ramp.

Kelly dragged Spellman's corpse to the edge of the roof, but the cargo bay was already packed and the crew chief swiped his fingertips across his neck and shook his head.

Yildiz shoved his fingers into the upper edge of Spellman's breastplate and pulled his ID tag.

"Go." He grabbed Kelly by the shoulder. "He's gone. And we need to be, too!"

Kelly set Spellman's head against the roof gently, patted his breastplate once, then jumped onto the ramp. Yildiz was the last man into the shuttle, and the ramp closed behind him with a hydraulic *thump* as it sped away from ground zero.

Yildiz checked the timer, and his jaw tightened. They'd cut it close—maybe too close.

He pulled off his helmet and looked at his surviving troopers. Many were wounded . . . all looked shocked and angry as the shuttle's engines roared at maximum power. The last city roofs were a blur, flashing past outside the viewports, and they streaked across the suburbs and over the second growth woodland that surrounded the city.

"Brace, brace, brace!" the crew chief shouted, waving his hands overhead.

The shuttle rattled hard as the shock wave from the K-strike hit. Yildiz grabbed a tie-down cleat and held on as the shuttle lost lift for a few seconds and his feet lifted from the deck.

Someone let out a string of expletives as the shuttle leveled back out, then climbed steeply to regain altitude.

"This is bullshit, Sir," Kelly said in a low, bitter voice.

"Which part?" Yildiz asked.

"All of it! What're we even *doing* out here?"

"We're taking care of our people." He passed Kelly a set of bloody dog tags. "Because nobody else will do it for us."

Kelly rubbed a wet, sticky smudge off the tags, then gripped them tightly.

ᐊ CHAPTER THIRTY-THREE ᐅ

Field Hospital
City of Tyrnavos
Planet Odysseus
Bellerophon System
Free Worlds Alliance
January 14, 2553

THE FEDERATION ARMY HAD ARGUABLY THE FINEST MEDICAL technology in the human-explored galaxy. An entire trauma center, deployed from a single cargo container, could be ready to receive patients within minutes of being offloaded. Robotic and human doctors could treat almost any wound . . . if the casualty was delivered in time. And because time was so often critical, they were designed to be located anywhere, usually in close proximity to the fighting.

This one was located over eighty kilometers from Nafplio, in the town square of the much larger city of Tyrnavos, and Ahmet Yildiz tried not to think about why that was so as he stepped out of the temporary structure into the shadows of a setting sun.

More wounded flowed past him—a few of them ambulatory; most carried on litters—from the landing zone established on a rooftop parking structure at the edge of the square. He tucked his helmet into the crook of his left arm and scrubbed dried sweat from his face with the other hand, grateful for the fresh air and the cooling temperature. He inhaled deeply, then cocked his head as he caught an unexpected scent. Field hospitals tended to smell of blood and antiseptic, but this was a smoky sort of aroma, and he looked over his shoulder, seeking the source.

Another officer leaned against the field hospital's outer wall, arms crossed over his chest and a nicotine tube between two fingers.

"Ahmet," Major Arturo Lopez, Second Battalion's S3, said. "Tough day."

"Fuckin' tell me about it." Yildiz shook his head. "I've got one brain-dead and three more that need prosthetic limbs. And Benson's gonna need nerve shunts to see out of that eye again. Once they fit his prosthetic, that is. And that doesn't count the seven who never made it out."

"Yeah, but look on the bright side. The General's happy with you."

Lopez offered his nicotine stick to Yildiz, and the captain reached for it. Then frowned as he noticed Lopez's collar insignia. It was a lieutenant colonel's.

"I thought your promotion board wasn't for another six months... Sir," Yildiz said as he took the stick and inhaled deeply before blowing the smoke out his nose.

"Funny, that," Lopez said. "Soon as you left for your mission, Alaimo called Colonel Fiori up to spin the dial for the next torture—excuse me, the next 'enhanced interrogation'—setting and Fiori balked. Alaimo had him taken away, and I got brevet rank and command of the battalion half an hour later."

"Then where's Fiori?" Yildiz asked.

"No idea." Lopez shook his head. "I cause a stink looking for him, and I'll probably find out the hard way. And that's not doing anybody any good."

"I wasn't going to play Alaimo's sick game either." Yildiz glanced around. "That asshole called in a K-strike on my position. Then Central acts like they're doing me a favor by giving me barely enough time to evac... Sir. Sorry."

"It's rare that a commander actually exceeds his reputation," Lopez said.

"I really and truly didn't think Alaimo could," Yildiz said bitterly.

"Seems to come naturally to him. You heard about Steinbolt?"

"What about her?" Yildiz asked warily.

Lieutenant Colonel Diana Steinbolt was Alaimo's JAG officer, the senior legal officer assigned to the Expeditionary Force, and the next good thing Yildiz heard about her would be the *first* good thing he'd ever heard about her.

"She set up shop in Markos Botsaris Stadium. Three tribunals, twenty-six-seven, no waiting. Firing squads've been busy since about eight A.M."

Yildiz stared at the other man. Not in disbelief, but because he wished he *could* disbelieve what he'd just heard.

"How the hell did this turn into such a clusterfuck in less than seventy-two hours?" he demanded.

"Alaimo," Lopez replied, and grimaced. "Man obviously doesn't like to let the grass grow under his feet. And you're not the only K-strike he called in today. Took out a little burg named Loutraki about thirty minutes before he hit Nafplio. Preliminary reports are that somebody with a Wasp took down one of our cargo shuttles. Probably had something to do with the fact that they'd just tossed the city's mayor out the hatch at two hundred meters. Seems like the shooter must've had friends along, too, because when the gunships closed in on his position, we lost three more birds. So now the entire town's gone. 'Course, there was a minor consequence."

"What kind of 'minor consequence'?"

"Seems the locals don't much care for the way he's been flinging KEWs around. Fourth Brigade ate another KEW of its own about twenty minutes after Nafplio. Didn't hit the HQ—that's in one of their bigger towns—but the vehicle park, the maintenance section, and the bivouac area, all gone. Best estimate is around nine hundred dead. But what the hell? Alaimo's safe and sound in Kórinthos, isn't he?"

Lopez reclaimed his nicotine stick and drew deeply on it.

"How's Alaimo going to get away with all this?" Yildiz demanded bitterly. "I'm not talking about incoming KEWs—you're right, no way these people are taking out their own capital city and everybody in it just to get his ass, however much he deserves it. But the rest of this shit. These are *war crimes*, Sir!"

"Not...technically. You didn't read Annex W in the Corps-level operations order, did you?" Lopez asked. Yildiz shook his head, and the lieutenant colonel snorted. "Not too surprising, I guess. After all, the legal provisions almost never change. They just get cut and pasted from one order to another. When we're fighting the League, at least. But there were some very interesting additions to the Law and Order Annex for this mission."

"I only read the op order for division and lower," Yildiz replied. "What got snuck into the Corps-level order?"

"It seems every Federation soldier on Bellerophon's been issued a general pardon," Lopez said. "*Preemptive* pardons."

Yildiz stared at him, and the lieutenant colonel shrugged.

"Only for infractions against the local populace, of course. Insubordination and refusal to follow lawful orders are still on the books. As Colonel Fiori probably found out."

"Hold on. Who the hell authorized that? Alaimo doesn't have that authority, not at two stars. Not at any rank!"

"Doesn't seem to bother him much. Which suggests to me that the fix must be in at a higher level. He's put it in writing, after all, and that makes it official record. You really see someone like Alaimo doing that if he didn't know for damned sure no one could hang him out to dry for it?"

Lopez looked at Yildiz until the captain shook his head, then shrugged.

"I don't think so either. Which means he's pretty damned sure the pardons will come through when he needs 'em. Of course, for that to happen, the Prime Minister herself would have to sign off on the actual pardons. And there has been one other time the PM issued blanket-pardons, although that was after the fact, not before it."

"Gobelins," Yildiz said harshly.

"Of course."

"Figures." Yildiz's jaw clamped in anger, but he paused and made himself inhale deeply.

"There a reason you brought this up, Sir? Even with permission, I'm not sending my people out to pillage and burn, and I'm sure as hell not shooting up civilians to 'send a message.'"

"Which is the reason I brought it up. You're not that type, Ahmet. I'm not that type. Problem is, Alaimo *is* that type, and Steinbolt's gonna rubber-stamp every bodybag Alaimo wants to fill, especially since her ass is covered. But I don't like killing civilians. Especially not *our* civilians, even if the Powers That Be think it's a good idea. Bringing League worlds into compliance is one thing, but this... this ain't right."

"Then what do we do?" Yildiz threw up his hands. "Alaimo's got a personal security detachment larger than most sector commanders."

"We resist where we can. Spare civilians whenever we can. Keep an eye open for opportunities. But don't try and recruit anyone else to our side. Captain Donalds from Charlie Company was nowhere near as open to the suggestion as you are. In the meantime, Alaimo wants me to process your entire company for Bronze Sol Medals. You get a Silver."

"Lose my paperwork." Yildiz scraped dried blood off his helmet with a fingernail. "I'm with you, Sir. I'll try to spare civilians where I can. Now, if you'll excuse me, I've got to go share the bad news about Tolesti and Andrews with my people."

"Today's been shit, and tomorrow ain't looking any better." Lopez flicked his nicotine stick into a trashcan and straightened. "I can give you at least eight hours off before Alaimo tasks us with another target for action."

"That's . . . Oh, fuck this war."

Yildiz walked away.

CHAPTER THIRTY-FOUR

TFNS **Somaskanda**
Bellerophon System
Free Worlds Alliance
January 15, 2553

ADMIRAL JORGENSEN HAD JUST PICKED UP HIS ICED TEA GLASS when the dining cabin's comm panel pinged. He paused, then turned his head, glass still raised, to glower at the interruption.

His glower eased—a bit—and he nodded approvingly as Lieutenant Constantinescu popped up from his own chair. The flag lieutenant crossed to the smart wall and tapped the bulkhead touchscreen.

"Admiral Jorgensen's quarters, Lieutenant Constantinescu," he said, and Commander Zalewska appeared on the smart wall.

"Hi, Dan," she said. "I know it's lunchtime, but I'm afraid I need to speak to the Admiral, if he's available."

"I'm here, Linda." Jorgensen raised his voice, pushed back his chair, and walked into the comm's visual field, still carrying his glass of tea.

"I'm sorry to disturb you at lunch, Sir," the red-haired ops officer said. "But we've just picked up an incoming Fasset footprint. A big one."

"Really?" Jorgensen managed to keep his voice a bit calmer than he actually felt, and he sipped from his tea glass to buy a little time while his mind raced. Then he lowered the glass. "I'm assuming Tracking's had time to establish their approach vector?"

"Yes, Sir." Zalewska nodded. "It's on the right bearing for a least-time approach from Jalal."

405

"Doesn't mean it's actually *coming* from Jalal, though," Jorgensen mused. He thought for another moment, then cocked his head. "Is Captain Romero with you?"

"I'm here, Sir," another voice said, and Zalewska's image split to share the smart wall with the chief of staff.

"Thoughts?" Jorgensen prompted.

"I think it almost has to be good news," Romero said promptly. Jorgensen cocked an eyebrow at him, and he shrugged. "Like Linda says, this is a big-assed footprint. Gotta be at least twenty carriers, maybe twenty-five, and it sure looks like it's coming from Jalal."

"So you think it's Vice Admiral Thakore?"

"Seems like the most reasonable hypothesis." Romero shrugged again. "It's sure as hell too many hulls for Murphy, anyway, even if it wasn't on the wrong bearing!"

Jorgensen frowned down into his glass, but he had to admit Romero had a point. Less than sixty FTLCs had been assigned to the entire Fringe when all the madness began, and fourteen of them were assigned to the Northern Lobe, the Fringe Systems close enough to the Beta Cygni Line for fear of the Terran League to keep them honest... and for Tenth Fleet to respond in force if they were needed. The Southern Lobe was a far vaster area, which meant the forty-three carriers assigned to its picket stations were far more thinly—and widely—spread, and eight of them had already been accounted for right here in Bellerophon. That set an absolute ceiling on how many of them might have mutinied to join Murphy. For that matter, there were limits to how fast information could spread over interstellar gaps. The marshals sent to arrest him couldn't have reached New Dublin until August, which was less than five months ago, and that limited how many of those other carriers could even have heard about his defiance of orders across such enormous distances, much less actually reached New Dublin to join him.

They'd finally confirmed what Jorgensen had suspected from the moment the defending task force ambushed Admiral Hathaway, yet despite Alaimo's... rigorous efforts—efforts that turned Jorgensen's stomach, even from the public reports—they still hadn't found out just how Bellerophon had learned that the entire Concordia Sector had gone out of compliance so damned quickly. That information had clearly been tightly compartmentalized, and until they got their hands on someone deep inside the Xeneas government, they were unlikely to unravel it. But it possessed a certain burning relevance, under the circumstances, since no one in *Ninth Fleet* had known a thing about the "Free Worlds Alliance"—except for Xeneas's announcement on the day of the coup that Bellerophon intended to seek membership in whatever the hell it was—until they reached Bellerophon. Admiral Hathaway's officers had known how worried the federal government had been over Murphy's... outré behavior, but they'd had no idea that his behavior might have spilled over into outright rebellion. *That* news certainly hadn't reached the Sol System until after they'd departed. For that matter, it might *still* not have reached Earth!

So how the hell had a star system seventy-three light-years from New Dublin found out so quickly? And acted so promptly? One possibility Jorgensen really didn't like to consider—but one he knew Alaimo had chosen to embrace—was that Bellerophon's rebellion hadn't been isolated from Concordia's at all. That they'd been closely coordinated as the result of some long-standing, traitorous conspiracy among the Fringe Worlds. That even though Murphy's defiance of his standing orders might have been the spark that touched it off, the kindling had been laid long ago.

Jorgensen didn't know about that. On the other hand, those missile pods Bellerophon's defenders had used on Admiral Hathaway hadn't been manufactured in-system. They had to have come from Concordia, and Murphy had to have whipped them up before his engagement with Admiral Xing. And that, unfortunately, seemed to indicate that there'd been *something* going on between New Dublin and Bellerophon well before Bellerophon's secession.

All of that raised ominous questions about what else what was left of Ninth Fleet might not know, but what mattered most right this moment was that without more information about events in Concordia, they couldn't possibly know what Murphy had done after the sector decided to rebel. Obviously, he hadn't successfully used his authority as system governor to prevent Concordia's action. Indeed, Jorgensen strongly suspected that he hadn't even tried—which probably confirmed ONI's estimate of the extent of his ambitions—but Jorgensen would dearly love to know what he'd done with the seven carriers under his command at the time. The eight that had gone "out of compliance" here in Cyclops had done more than enough damage to make anyone nervous about that. The important point just now, though, was that he'd had only seven, which, with the eight destroyed here, left only twenty-eight of the Southern Lobe FTLCs unaccounted for, and they were scattered to hell and gone. No, if this really was at least twenty carriers, they couldn't be Murphy.

On the other hand, it *shouldn't* be Vice Admiral Thakore, either. Jorgensen knew the Oval had sent an urgent courier after TF 804 the moment word of Bellerophon's secession reached Olympia, but it wouldn't even reach Jalal Station for another five days. Which meant it would be over another month before any response from Jalal—assuming Thakore hadn't moved on to New Dublin and the courier had found TF 804 there when it arrived—could reach Bellerophon.

"If this is Vice Admiral Thakore, how did he know to come calling so quickly?" he asked aloud, looking up from his glass.

"I don't know, Sir," Romero admitted. "But it's too big and it's coming in on the wrong bearing for anything out of Concordia."

"I know. I know! But . . ."

Jorgensen rubbed the tip of his nose for a moment, then nodded decisively.

"All right. Have Girish pass the word to General Alaimo. Tell him we anticipate their arrival in—what? Four hours?"

"A bit longer than that, Sir," Commander Zalewska replied. "It's a *big* footprint."

"All right, we anticipate their arrival in a little over four hours. Emphasize that we don't know who these people are yet. And emphasize to Girish that he's to decline to speculate on that point. If General Alaimo wants to do any speculating, connect him directly to me."

He couldn't quite keep an edge of distaste out of his final sentence, and Romero grimaced as he nodded in acknowledgment.

"Then pass the word to all units and recall all small craft. I want the task group underway to Point Lookout within thirty minutes."

"Yes, Sir!" Romero said crisply, and Jorgensen grimaced.

He'd held his task group, minus the three battleships he'd detached to provide Alaimo with the kinetic interdiction platforms he'd insisted he needed, twenty-one light-minutes from Odysseus. He hadn't done that to insulate himself from events on the planet. Dearly as he would have loved to be able to do that, mere distance couldn't keep him from knowing what Alaimo was doing...or make him feel less soiled by it. No, he'd done it because his carriers' acceleration inside the Powell Limit was only 900 gravities, and he'd wanted to position himself to reach the limit at a relative velocity of zero within less than four hours. There was, unfortunately, no way he could get there in time to prevent whoever the incoming ships might be from detecting his Fasset drives, but he intended to hang on to the most flexible menu of maneuver options he could. The last thing he wanted to do was find himself committed to the kind of death ride Bellerophon's defenders had embraced, especially against a force as large as this one...and without any damned missile pods of his own.

And, he acknowledged in a corner of his own mind, if it turned out somehow that this *was* Murphy, if whatever evil spirit had birthed him in the first place had brought him here with *this* many ships, Elijah Jorgensen had no intention of engaging at one-to-seven odds.

He knew what would happen to his career if he cut and ran for it. But if that was Murphy, or Leaguies, or crazed gerbils from Andromeda and they'd come to kill any more of his people, he'd see them in hell first.

CHAPTER THIRTY-FIVE

City of Kórinthos
Planet Odysseus
Bellerophon System
Free Worlds Alliance
January 15, 2553

GOVERNOR RAMSAY'S WHEELCHAIR BUMPED OVER SOMETHING, and something else brushed solidly against her shoulder. The hood over her head kept the air around her face stuffy and warm. She hadn't brushed her teeth in days and smelled their foulness on her breath.

The hood came off. Bright light stung her eyes, and her stomach tightened—in fear, not surprise—as she recognized the brilliant cone of light and the darkness beyond it.

"Hello, again, Governor."

Alaimo laid a heavy hand on her shoulder, and she shrank away while disgust surged in her throat. He only smiled and bent at the waist to look her in the face.

"Ready to tell me where Xeneas is hiding?"

"I don't know," she said softly. "I didn't know yesterday. I don't know today."

"Wrong answer." Alaimo flicked a fingertip against the tip of her nose. "But if that's your decision, we'll play the game your way."

"You're the one doing this!" She pulled against her restraints. "I can't tell you what I don't know. Don't make anyone else suffer for something I *can't* give you!"

Alaimo hooked his thumbs into his belt. He wore fatigue pants

411

and a T-shirt, and his body was sweaty, as if he'd just finished a workout. That was her first thought. Then she noticed the raw knuckles on both his hands.

"Well, considering how much trouble I went to to find someone so close to you, we can't let this opportunity go to waste, can we?" he said brightly, then raised a hand and waggled two fingers together.

A holo display appeared. At least this time it was only a single cell, not dozens of them. That was Ramsay's first thought. But then she recognized who was *in* that cell. Erasmia Samarili, President Xeneas's personal aide, was lashed down to a bodyboard. Her feet were slightly higher than her head, and a wide repair patch covered her right forearm.

Ramsay gasped, then looked quickly away. Not that it would do any good. She knew her body language had betrayed her.

"My intelligence officers did a thorough search of the planetary databases, and we found a wedding registry for a future Mr. and Mrs. Faben." Alaimo tapped an index finger against his bottom lip. "They had gifts from the whole who's who of Bellerophon, so, obviously, they were important. But we had the hardest time figuring out who these 'Fabens' were. Until we cross-referenced delivery addresses, that is. When we did, it turned out that Mr. Faben is your son Derek, and the soon to be *Mrs.* Faben is..."

He waved a graceful hand at the holo display.

"The Five Hundred do enjoy their little social games with weddings and whatnot."

"Please, she's just Xeneas's secretary!" Ramsay lied desperately. "She was only in charge of his calendar, for God's sake!"

"Oh, I think she was a bit more than that," Alaimo said with a smile.

"She was his *secretary*!" Ramsay repeated, her heart a lump of ice as terror for the future daughter-in-law she loved crashed through her. "Yes, his *personal* secretary, but she didn't have anything to do with policy decisions! That's why he left her home, to keep her out of the line of fire! She doesn't know where—"

"She'll talk," Alaimo interrupted. "Had to medicate her out of shock from her capture, but she's lucid enough for what comes next."

"But nobody told her where the planetary government's dispersal sites were, either! She wasn't going with Xeneas, so she was never cleared for that information!"

"I'm afraid you really can't expect me to take the word of a proven traitor for something like that," Alaimo chided. Then he slapped his hands together. "Same rules as our last game."

He took a spoon from his back pocket and slid it between Ramsay's fingers.

"General, please." Ramsay fought back tears. "I'm telling you, she doesn't know anything! And I don't—"

Alaimo clamped a hand over her mouth, driving fingertips into her cheeks painfully, and shook his head.

"I find serial lying extremely annoying, Governor," he said. "You may not have any plans, but *my* time's too valuable to waste on this kind of nonsense."

The tears Ramsay had fought blurred her vision, and he shook his head again.

"Have you ever watched a waterboarding?" he asked. "It's really something else."

He slid his hand off her face as he moved behind her and began massaging her neck and shoulders as two men stepped into the cell with Samarili. Each of them carried a bucket in each hand.

Samarili whimpered and wiggled against her restraints, and Alaimo raised his voice slightly.

"Microphone, Volkov," he said.

"Live now, Sir," Volkov's voice replied out of the darkness, and Alaimo smiled down at Ramsay.

"Don't worry, Governor, we won't miss hearing anything, but I'm afraid my voice is the only one coded to go through to them."

Ramsay stared up at him, her eyes filled with sick hatred, and he chuckled. Then raised his voice.

"Mr. Grant, please begin," he said.

One of the men in Samarili's cell set down his buckets and plucked a small towel from his back pocket. He shook it out, then laid it over Samarili's face and held it taut. He said something to her, and the young woman screamed as the cloth covered her entire face.

The other man lifted a bucket and poured a steady, heavy stream of water onto the towel. Chunks of ice bounced off Samarili's covered face as her scream ended in a gurgle. She bucked against her restraints, her head thrashing from side to side. It seemed to go on forever before Grant slid the soaking towel off her face and let her suck in a breath.

"Please," she gagged. "Please stop! I can't help you!"

Alaimo chuckled.

"They're always so precious when they're just starting out," he told Ramsay, then raised his voice. "More, please, Mr. Grant."

The towel went back over Samarili's face and another bucket's water flooded over it. It was poured more slowly this time, and she jerked frantically.

"It's a funny thing." Alaimo patted Ramsay's cheek. "The human body and mind react to waterboarding exactly as if they were actually drowning. Same panic. Same pain through the entire body from oxygen deprivation. You know what that's like? Being unable to breathe when your lungs still work? Sucking down that ice cold water—"

"Stop!" Ramsay screamed. "Please stop!"

Alaimo snapped his fingers and another bucket flooded down. This time, Grant stepped back, leaving the wet towel on Samarili's face. Her struggles became even more frantic, then slowed as she began to pass out from lack of oxygen.

Grant plucked the towel away and slapped Samarili across the face to wake her up. It took quite a few slaps. Finally, she coughed up the water and started sucking in deep, ragged breaths.

The other interrogator left...and returned a moment later with more buckets of water.

"This goes on as long as you want it to," Alaimo said to Ramsay. "Grant and his assistant are well-versed in this. They almost never cause lasting brain damage, although sometimes—"

"You're going to burn in hell!" Ramsay shouted.

"Ehhh...Continue, Mr. Grant."

Alaimo mussed Ramsay's filthy, unwashed hair. Grant poured cold water directly onto Samarili's face; she gagged and spat a mouthful of water at him.

"Derek!" she wailed. *"Derek!"*

Ramsay dropped the spoon.

"Hold," Alaimo said over the microphone, then picked the utensil up and waggled it beneath the lights. "Give me something actionable right now, Governor. You won't like the penalty phase of our little game if you don't."

"Xeneas...he trusts me." Ramsay's mouth went dry. "Have—have me meet with him. Just let me go, and he'll have me brought to him. Everyone on Odysseus knows me, and it'll take no more than a few hours before—"

"Oh, that's not what I'm asking for." Alaimo shook his head. "I'm afraid you've committed a foul. Pick a city."

"Put a tracker on me! Implant a *bomb* in me! I'll do anything—"

"Anything but tell the truth, it seems. Don't drop this again."

Alaimo slid the handle of the spoon back into her hand and tapped his personal comm.

"Central, K-strike authorized on... Chios, that sounds appropriate," he said. "Authorization Kilo Alpha Three-Seven-Three-Seven."

Ramsay's heart twisted. Over forty thousand Odyssians called the city of Chios home.

"Now, where were we? Where were we?" Alaimo mused. "Ah, yes! Resume, Mr. Grant."

The waterboarding began again, and Ramsay squeezed her eyes shut and forced her chin down to her chest. A moment later, cold metal touched her jawline. Alaimo pressed the edge of the knife against her skin hard enough for her to feel its razor sharpness but not—quite—hard enough to draw blood.

"You chose this," he told her. "You have to watch."

"I don't. She's not part of this. Please, I'm begging you," Ramsay pleaded.

"There's a comm net!" Samarili gasped. "I... I don't know where the President is—I swear I don't! But I know where one of the emergency comm nodes is!"

"That's progress." Alaimo pulled the knife away, nicking Ramsay's chin. "But I'm not incredibly pleased with *you*, Governor. I try and I try, and I can't quite seem to find the motivator to recall you to your sense of duty as someone who was once the official and appointed representative of the Federation here in Bellerophon."

He shook his head sadly, then smiled.

"Actually, you know," he said, "maybe there *is* someone who could supply the right motivation. Unfortunately, we don't have him in custody at the moment. But I'll bet that with that nice piece of bait right there, we can reel in young Mr. Faben with minimal effort. And once we do, I'm sure *he* can convince you to see reason."

Ramsay's heart seemed to stop. She stared at him, then dropped the spoon.

"You... you win," she said softly. "I'll tell you what you want."

Her voice was barely above a whisper, and Alaimo leaned in closer to listen.

Her mouth opened—and she lunged forward to the full scope of her bonds. Her head darted out, her teeth snapped shut on the lobe of his ear, and she bit down savagely. He jerked back, she saw his fist swing, and then the world vanished in a bright flash of light as he punched her squarely in the face. Her head snapped back, then rebounded forward, and blood ran from a broken nose over split lips.

"Rude. Very rude, Madame Governor." Alaimo pulled out a handkerchief, holding it to his bleeding earlobe while he shook the hand that had punched her, and her heart sank as she realized she'd failed. She was still alive.

"It seems I've been too merciful," he continued. "Your future daughter-in-law could have gotten through all this with no lasting physical harm. But now I'm going to let my personal security detail . . . enjoy her charms. And you get to watch before—"

"Um, Sir?" Volkov's voice interrupted. "There's been a . . . development you need to know about."

Alaimo scowled at the interruption. For just a moment, the vileness of his soul showed in his eyes, but then the genial mask snapped back into place.

"It would seem duty calls," he said, still holding the handkerchief to his mutilated ear. "But it wouldn't do to leave you unrewarded for your efforts, Governor."

"Grant?" He raised his voice, turning back towards the holo. "Get Ms. Samarili's statement and move her back to holding. Then swap in the good Governor."

Grant nodded, and Alaimo patted Ramsay's shoulder with a broad smile.

He left, and Ramsay watched as Samarili was rolled away on her bodyboard. She knew what was about to happen, and yet she smiled. At least the young woman she loved would be spared for a bit.

It was the only gift Ramsay could give her, and pathetic as it was, a sense of gratitude flowed through her.

Grant came for her a few minutes later.

CHAPTER THIRTY-SIX

TFNS **Somaskanda**
Bellerophon System
Free Worlds Alliance
January 15, 2553

"SIR, I'M AFRAID YOU HAVE A MESSAGE FROM GENERAL ALAIMO."

Elijah Jorgensen pushed with a toe, turning himself in the microgravity to look at Lieutenant Commander Nandy. He'd arrived on *Somaskanda*'s flag bridge only five minutes ago, after a somewhat truncated lunch, and there was something about Nandy's tone. Like the rest of Jorgensen's staffers, he was appalled by the reports coming up from Odysseus. And, as Jorgensen's comm officer, he was also the one tasked with monitoring the planetary data channels and news broadcasts. That gave him far too good a look at what was actually happening, including Alaimo's regular pleas for Odysseus to "see reason" and "return to its loyalty," which just happened to give him an excuse to "regretfully" report the latest atrocity to which he had been "forced." Small wonder he hated and despised the general. Even so—

"Really?" The admiral put just an edge of chiding reproof into his tone, then shrugged. "I'll take it at my station," he continued, pushing off to his command chair and beckoning for Romero to follow him.

He settled into it, fastened the seatbelt loosely to keep himself there, and nodded to Nandy.

"Ready," he said, and the surge of distaste he always felt when he was forced to speak to Taskin Alaimo was stronger even than usual when the general appeared on his display. Alaimo wore only fatigue pants and a T-shirt. He looked sweaty, and he held what appeared to be a bloody handkerchief against one ear. Given what he'd heard about Alaimo's tendency to go...hands-on, Jorgensen was only too certain of what his comm message must have interrupted.

"I've received your message, Admiral," the general said in that lazy, predator's voice, "and I understand your intent. I do, however, have a few...reservations, shall we say?" He smiled thinly. "While I would never presume to dictate naval tactics to an officer of your experience, as the System Governor of Bellerophon, I believe it would be imprudent to provide any unnecessary information to these people until we're certain of their identities. Your estimate that they're friendly units is probably correct, but we can't know that, now can we? And, frankly, I don't see any reason the Oval or the Government should have sent a 'reinforcement' this powerful to Bellerophon, even if the ships had been immediately available, given that they had no idea of the unfortunately severe losses Admiral Hathaway would suffer. So, as Governor, I'm instructing you to not challenge them immediately. Let's give them an opportunity to announce their identity before we give them any information about who we are.

"Alaimo, clear."

"Well, *that's* stupid, if you'll pardon my saying so," Jesus Romero said, just quietly enough they could both pretend no one else had heard him.

"It's not the very smartest thing I've ever heard," Jorgensen agreed. "On the other hand, he *is* the system governor." He looked up and grimaced at the chief of staff. "At least he's not telling us we can't continue to Point Lookout. That's something."

"Why do I think you're trying to make lemonade, Sir?" Romero asked dryly.

"Because you're such a clever fellow."

"Excuse me, Sir," Commander Zalewska said, fifteen minutes after General Alaimo's message had arrived. Jorgensen looked at her, and something tightened inside him as her expression registered.

"CIC's just received an informational update from Captain Sherwood," she said, and Jorgensen's stomach twisted even tighter.

Eloise Sherwood commanded TFNS *Sentry*, the senior battleship survivor of Hathaway's orphaned parasites. Jorgensen had recovered them and placed them in Odysseus orbit, and Alaimo had used his authority as system governor to detach those ships from TG 901.3's chain of command. Legally, Jorgensen no longer had any authority over them, but he'd known Sherwood a long time. He was pretty damn certain how she'd felt about the K-strikes her command had been tasked to carry out.

The fact that she'd refused to allow any of the other skippers orbiting Odysseus to execute those strikes said a great deal about her, as well. And he suspected Alaimo would be less than delighted if he discovered she'd been forwarding the details of every one of those strikes in "routine, for your information" transmissions to *Somaskanda*. It probably wouldn't matter in the end, but she clearly wanted the Navy to have a complete—and independent—record of what Alaimo had done.

"What sort of update?" he asked after a moment.

"*Sentry* just executed a K-strike on the city of Chios," Zalewska replied, and Jorgensen's jaw clenched.

Even leaving aside the hundreds of thousands of deaths Alaimo had already inflicted, any sane commander would have realized what continuing K-strikes on civilian targets would mean for the men and women under his command. Certainly the Odyssian General Tolallis had made that abundantly clear, and Jorgensen didn't blame him one bit. But Alaimo didn't care. He was safe from reprisal in their capital city, after all.

"Thank you, Linda," he said.

"Ah, there was one other thing about Captain Sherwood's message, Sir," the ops officer said. Jorgensen cocked an eyebrow at her, and she shrugged. "Apparently, some glitch in the targeting sequence delayed the strike's execution. I'm not certain what it was, but by the time they straightened it out, the strike went in almost twenty-five minutes late. Although—" there was an undeniable glint of satisfaction in her gray eyes "—*Sentry*'s fire control lidar had illuminated the target right on schedule. And it seems the point of impact was outside of usual tolerances. It landed on one of the suburbs, not downtown Chios."

Jorgensen's lips twitched and he heard Romero snort. Right off the top of his head, the admiral couldn't think of any reason lidar would have been needed to execute a kinetic strike on a nonmoving target the size of a city. On the other hand, it would have been very easy for the Odyssians to detect.

"She better hope to hell Alaimo doesn't find out she gave the Odyssians a heads-up," Romero said very quietly, and Jorgensen nodded.

"Even with twenty-five minutes they won't have gotten everyone into the shelters," he replied. "But she just saved a lot of lives, Jesus. And knowing Eloise, she'll consider that a bargain well-made even if Alaimo does find out."

"This is making me a little nervous," Romero said forty-five minutes later, floating at Jorgensen's shoulder on *Somaskanda's* flag bridge. "If they're friendlies, why haven't we heard from them yet?"

That, Jorgensen acknowledged, was an excellent question. One that was causing him more than a few qualms of his own.

The FTL signature they'd been tracking had disappeared from their sensors over two hours ago at an estimated range of 132 LM from the Powell Limit, which was just about right for a least-time profile to Odysseus orbit. But that meant there'd been time for any incoming admiral to identify himself and announce his intentions. So why hadn't whoever was in command over there done that?

"Fair's fair, Jesus," the admiral said now. "Even if they'd sent us something the instant they went sublight, it would only have gotten here a couple of minutes ago. But they've had us on their sensors from the get-go, and they haven't heard from us yet, either, now have they?"

In fact, thanks to Alaimo's orders, TG 901.3's carriers weren't even squawking their transponders. Jorgensen had considered doing just that, despite the stupidity of his "don't tell them we're here" orders, since he hadn't been *specifically* ordered not to. But in the end, he'd decided—regretfully—against it.

That hadn't done a single thing to hide their normal emissions, however, and as he'd said to Romero, whoever this was had to have detected them from the moment of his arrival.

Now he and the chief of staff looked at each other, and Jorgensen puffed his lips thoughtfully. Then he shrugged.

"The one thing we do know is that a force this size didn't just happen by for a port call," he said. "The only reason these people could be here is because they know Bellerophon's gone out of compliance. I have no more idea than you do about how they could have found that out, but the truth is, if they are friendly units, there's only one place they could've come from. The cupboard was too bare back home for them to be from Sol, so this *has* to be coming in from Jalal. But if it is, they must have left Jalal before any courier from Sol got there to tell them *we* were headed out here. They know we're here, but they don't have any better picture of the situation in Bellerophon than we do of who the hell they are. For all they know, we're a mutinous task force just waiting to attack them."

His jaw tightened as he remembered the "mutinous task force" that had done just that to Ninth Fleet, but he went on steadily.

"We should be seeing them on light-speed sensors in the next few minutes. At that point—depending on what we see—I think it becomes tactical decision-making time. And, unfortunately, we're over forty-five light-minutes from Odysseus now, so it won't be possible to consult with General Alaimo, will it?"

"Pity about that, Sir," Romero replied.

They fell silent, watching the main plot. Minutes ticked by, and then—

"Unidentified units detected," Commander Zalewska announced. "Many units. CIC estimates . . . twelve FTLCs. Range two-seven-point-eight-four light-minutes. Velocity one-four-niner-seven-two-two KPS. Deceleration rate one-seven-point-six-five KPS squared."

The incoming ships appeared on the plot while she spoke, tagged with type designations and vector information, and Jorgensen frowned.

"Only twelve?" His frown deepened. Twelve carriers weren't enough to generate the powerful Fasset signature they'd detected. "Where are the rest of them?"

"Like you said, they can't know what the situation is here in Bellerophon," Romero replied. "I'll bet they did the same thing we did. This—" he pointed at the plot with his chin "—is probably their vanguard. If it's only about half their total force, that would account for the signature's strength."

"Point," Jorgensen acknowledged. "And I think it *is* that tactical decision-making time." He looked at Lieutenant Commander Nandy. "Send it," he said.

"Transmitting now, Sir," and the prerecorded message Alaimo had prevented Jorgensen from sending sooner went speeding out to meet the strangers.

✧ ✧ ✧

"It looks like Captain Romero was right, Admiral," Zalewska said, and Jorgensen nodded.

Seven and a half minutes after TG 901.3's light-speed sensors picked up the first incoming carriers, the icons of a second wave—this one fifteen FTLCs strong—blinked into existence on *Somaskanda*'s main plot. Coming in 7.43 LM behind the first wave, their deceleration would bring them to rest relative to the system primary right on the Powell Limit.

"That's a smart CO over there, Sir," Romero said approvingly. "He's still got time for his lead task group to divert to a fly-by vector outside the Powell Sphere, if he sees something he doesn't like; he's got the *second* task group as a hammer, if he decides he needs one; and if he doesn't need the hammer, they'll make their zero-zero right on the limit, where they'll have their max accel if they need it to chase down anything trying to bug out from inside the sphere."

"Well, hopefully he'll know in about—" Jorgensen glanced at the time display "—eleven minutes that he won't be needing any hammers after all."

"I imagine that would come under the heading of a Good Thing from everybody's perspective," Romero said dryly.

❖ ❖ ❖

"Incoming transmission, Sir!" Nandy announced, and Jorgensen looked up from his slate quickly.

His own transmission had reached the newcomers just over thirty-four minutes ago, at a range of 19 LM, and he'd half expected a reply sooner than this. Still, whoever had sent it couldn't have spent more than two or three minutes thinking about it first.

"My display, Girish."

"Yes, Sir."

The wallpaper disappeared from Jorgensen's display, replaced by a compact, slender man in a vice admiral's uniform, and the admiral exhaled in relief. The man on his display was a bit taller than he was, with an even darker complexion, and the comm image was tagged "VADM R. THAKORE."

"Admiral Jorgensen, I'm Rajenda Thakore," he said. "I apologize for the delay in my response, but given how little information I had, we needed to dig through the intel files. Especially since *my* latest information had Admiral Hathaway still back home in Sol getting his command organized. Under the circumstances, I felt just a tad of caution was in order." He bared his teeth. "The good news is, we found you in the files and that Ninth Fleet beat us here. The bad news is that anyone had to come in the first place.

"I'm assuming you've picked up my second task group by now. As you can see, they'll be decelerating to rendezvous with you on the limit. I'm afraid my lead group's committed to Odysseus orbit, but that may not be a bad thing."

For just a moment, his dark eyes might have been agates, amd Jorgensen nodded to himself. There was a reason he'd included the name of the new "system governor" in his initial transmission. Obviously, Thakore had only too good an idea of what might have been happening here in Bellerophon, and he clearly didn't like it. But then he inhaled and gave himself a little shake.

"I realize you don't know anything more about what TF Eight-Oh-Four's been up to than I knew about Ninth Fleet," he continued. "To update you, Admiral Murphy—" His expression twisted ever so slightly, and Jorgensen felt a flicker of sympathy. It couldn't be pleasant to know his own brother-in-law had gone rogue. "—is in custody and en route to Sol. I'm sure he'll face charges once he gets there." Thakore inhaled again, more deeply than before. "I'm afraid he'd moved against Jalal before we got there, but that was a step too far. He'd picked up a couple of additional mutinous carriers, but when Admiral Portier refused to surrender at his demand and he moved to attack the Station, one of the officers whose carrier divisions he'd appropriated in his persona as system governor refused to obey his orders. And when Commodore Tremblay refused, three of the other carrier captains did the same thing in his support. I'm afraid it was ugly, and over half his parasites and three mutinous carriers who'd opened fire on Tremblay's division were destroyed in the fighting. But it was all over by the time Task Force Eight-Oh-Four got there. Losses are heavier than anyone could have wished but far lighter than they might have been, and at least that's over."

He paused, his eyes dark, then shook himself.

"Apparently, however, Murphy's poison is continuing to spread. A freighter—the *Tyonna Ogilvie*—came into Jalal from Dordogne with a message from System Governor Gallagher. The governor didn't have a lot of information, but according to him, Bellerophon had decided to 'secede' and wanted all the rest of the sector to go along. So since we'd already dealt with one forest fire, it seemed best to come pour water on this one. And—" he twitched a smile "—to bring plenty of buckets when I did.

"Until you identified yourself, I wasn't at all sure what we'd be dealing with here, and it seemed wiser to stay incognito until I knew. Needless to say, I'm delighted you seem to have the situation so well in hand.

"Thakore, clear."

Jorgensen felt the echo of his own vast relief sweeping around his flag bridge, but despite that, his expression tightened. The one thing he *wouldn't* call the situation in Bellerophon was "well in hand," and he wished like hell he could avoid the report he had to give Thakore. But as Ninth Fleet's senior flag officer—hell, its only *surviving* flag officer—he couldn't pass it off to anyone else.

"Relay Vice Admiral Thakore's message to General Alaimo, Girish," he said. Odysseus was outside TF 804's direct transmission path to TG 901.3, so its orbital arrays wouldn't pick up Thakore's messages directly. "And then stand by to record a reply to him."

"Yes, Sir."

Nandy's hands were busy for a few seconds, then he looked back up.

"Ready when you are, Admiral."

"I'm happier to see you than you can possibly imagine, Admiral Thakore," Jorgensen said into his pickup then. "Like you, I wish neither of us had to be here, but that wasn't our decision. And, frankly, it's a very good thing Governor Gallagher got that message to you, because I'm afraid things didn't go very well when we first arrived. Admiral Hathaway didn't realize that—"

"Message from Admiral Thakore, Sir."

Jorgensen nodded. He'd sent his reply to Thakore's initial message eighteen minutes ago, and the range to the steadily decelerating TF 804 was down to only a little over six light-minutes now, but he wasn't surprised it had taken the vice admiral a while to digest what had happened to Ninth Fleet.

"Put it up," he said.

"Yes, Sir."

The comm display lit, and Thakore looked out of it, his expression grim.

"I don't envy your having to make that report, Admiral Jorgensen," he said without preamble. "I thought what happened at Jalal was bad. This is worse. I can't fault Admiral Hathaway, given what he knew coming in, though. And you're right: those missile carriers must have come from New Dublin. Another little present from Murphy, I suppose. God, when I think—"

He chopped himself off and inhaled deeply.

"At any rate, at least the situation seems to be under control. At least for certain values of the word 'control,' given how the rest of the sector seems to have reacted. It looks like we'll have our work cut out for us convincing the rest of these people to see reason."

His eyes were flinty, and Jorgensen wondered how much of that was truly concern about the rest of the Cyclops Sector and how much of it had to do with Alaimo's reputation. Despite his naval rank, Thakore would have no legal authority to give a system governor—even an *acting* system governor—orders, which meant he couldn't call Alaimo to heel even if he wanted to. But he was senior enough that whatever Alaimo did was going to splash onto him for *not* calling him to heel.

"It won't be possible for me to rendezvous with you at your current position," Thakore continued. "However, Admiral Nakanishi, commanding my second task group, will be able to do that. In the meantime, I suppose, I should be getting in touch with Governor Alaimo."

From his expression, he wasn't looking forward to it, Jorgensen thought.

"Thakore, clear."

"Now that's a beautiful sight," Jesus Romero said.

He floated side by side with Jorgensen, watching not the tactical plot but the visual display, and his tone was one of profound satisfaction as no less than fifteen FTLCs and four FTL freighters decelerated smoothly towards rest. They were actually going to end up about two thousand kilometers short of the limit. That wasn't perfect, but it also wasn't that bad, given how tricky plotting an exact emergence from wormhole space could be. Despite the range, the visual pickups made them look as if they were merely at arm's length, and behind them, Captain Alvin Akram, Rear Admiral Nakanishi Ichibei's operations officer, looked out from the main holo display, coordinating the final approach with Linda Zalewska.

"No argument from me," the admiral replied. "And, just between you and me, Jesus, I am *totally* relieved to hand this ball of snakes over to Vice Admiral Thakore."

"Can't say I blame you for that, Sir."

Romero shook his head, then looked over his shoulder, checking for the proximity of other ears.

"The truth is, Elijah," he said, then, turning away from the visual display and using the first name he was always careful to avoid on Flag Bridge, "I hope Thakore has enough pull with the Five Hundred to sit on Alaimo. Somebody *has* to."

Jorgensen glanced at him, then allowed himself a micrometric nod. Now that he was no longer the senior naval officer present, he could admit that.

To some people, at least.

"Maybe, but—"

"Jesus Christ!"

Jorgensen never found out who the shout had come from, but it snapped his head back around to the visual display, and shock crashed through him as every one of the incoming carriers flushed its parasite racks. A hundred and fifty sublight warships—thirty of them showing Terran *League* emission signatures—erupted away from their motherships, decelerating at ten gravities on their fusion drives. Their lower decel meant they'd come to rest relative to TG 901.3 still outside the limit but a mere 1,500 KM from *Somaskanda*, and eight cargo pods deployed from the freighters' racks, as well. They spilled scores of drones that decelerated at the Hauptman drive's full 800 gravities, and as they did, the dark-complected Akram disappeared from the holo display and a blond-haired commodore with eyes of gray ice replaced him.

"My name is Pokhla Sherzai," she said in a steel-hard voice even colder than her eyes, "and I demand your surrender in the name of the Free Worlds Association. Stand down and prepare to be boarded, or we *will* destroy you."

CHAPTER THIRTY-SEVEN

City of Kórinthos
Planet Odysseus
Bellerophon System
Free Worlds Alliance
January 15, 2553

"THERE'S A PERSONAL MESSAGE TO YOU FROM VICE ADMIRAL Thakore."

Alaimo paused the recording of Governor Ramsay's introduction to the fine art of waterboarding and looked up at Rayko Hepner with an almost petulant frown.

"And just what does he want now?" he demanded.

"I don't know," Hepner replied. "It's encrypted. Your personal encryption, Sir."

Alaimo's frown segued into a scowl.

Thakore's initial comm message to Odysseus had come in only twenty minutes earlier, and it had made it abundantly clear that the vice admiral intended to be a pain. His distaste for some of what his comm sections must have picked up from the planetary datanet was obvious, and although Alaimo was completely covered by his orders and the preemptive pardon he'd been issued, Thakore's family wasn't one to trifle with. And while Gerard Perrin was far more powerful than Kanada Thakore, he was also a man who chose his battles with cold pragmatism. If it became expedient to sacrifice a tool, he wouldn't hesitate.

Hopefully, Alaimo's own reply to Thakore, subtly emphasizing his authority as System Governor of Bellerophon, had warned the naval officer that some sleeping dogs were best left

David Weber & Richard Fox

alone. Under other circumstances, he would have been confident
that it had, given the Thakore clan's vulnerability in the face
of Terrence Murphy's shenanigans. But Thakore had just more
than repaired any damage the family name might have taken.
Trouncing and capturing his own brother-in-law? Returning him
to face trial—and, no doubt, execution, after what had happened
at Jalal—would burnish the Thakore halo remarkably with the
rest of the Five Hundred.

And the fact that he'd chosen to use Alaimo's personal encryption, made sure that none of his staff would see whatever he had to
say, suggested Alaimo wouldn't enjoy hearing whatever it was, either.

"I suppose I'd better take a look," he said. "Put it through."

The imagery on his display disappeared, replaced by a standard access screen, blinking a request for his encryption code. He
glowered at it, then entered the code and offered a palm to the
DNA sniffer built into the touchscreen. The software considered
for a moment, then unlocked the message, and Rajenda Thakore
looked out of the display at him.

"General Alaimo," he said, "I expect you'll be receiving a burst
transmission from Admiral Jorgensen sometime in the next ten
minutes or so, depending on how long it took your communications people to process this message. I'm afraid that transmission
will come as something of an unpleasant surprise to you, so it
occurred to me that common courtesy suggested I should break
the news to you personally."

Alaimo frowned, wondering what in the hell the idiot was
talking about now.

And then he jerked upright in his chair as the face on his
display abruptly changed. The compact, dark-skinned vice admiral
disappeared, transformed into a far larger man with sandy hair
and gray eyes.

"Computer-generated imagery can be a very useful thing, don't
you think?" the man who'd replaced Thakore said in quite a different voice and with a thin, cold smile. "Allow me to introduce
myself. My name is Murphy. *Terrence* Murphy."

Alaimo sat frozen, unable to move.

"I would have preferred to wait until my ships were actually
in orbit around Odysseus and I could see your response to this
revelation in real time," Murphy continued, "but I can't prevent
Admiral Jorgensen from alerting you to what happened to his

task group about fifteen minutes ago. Since I'm still just over forty minutes out and I've been monitoring the situation on the planet, I thought it would be best to speak to you now, because someone like you could do a great deal of damage in that much time. And I'm sure someone like you would *want* to do a great deal of damage, because, after all, that's what sick, sadistic, murdering bastards do. However, you might want to rethink that.

"By the time you see this, the Navy units you've been using to slaughter this planet's population will already have been informed of the change in management. I don't think they'll be carrying out any more K-strikes for you, and I've ordered them to take out any Fulmens you may have in orbit. Given the firepower coming at them, I'm confident they'll do just that. But that leaves your forces dirtside. I allowed a four-minute window between this transmission and the next one, because it seemed only courteous to give you a little advance notice. But my *next* message will be a general broadcast on all civilian and military channels. One directed to all Federation personnel in this star system. And what it will tell them, General, is that they'll at least get trials for anything they've done before my arrival. If a single one of your personnel kills a single Odyssian after my message reaches them, however, there will be no trial for that person. There will be a bullet behind his or her left ear.

"And to be perfectly clear, that includes you.

"I look forward to meeting you in person—briefly, at least—very soon.

"Murphy, clear."

CHAPTER THIRTY-EIGHT

City of Kórinthos
Planet Odysseus
Bellerophon System
Free Worlds Alliance
January 15, 2553

"OH, SHIT, SIR. WE ARE *SO* SCREWED," AUDREY REYNOLDS SAID, eyes still fixed on the smart wall from which Terrence Murphy's stern-faced visage had just disappeared.

"Ya think?" Ahmet Yildiz replied. He started to add something further, then stopped and looked around the room.

Lopez's promised eight hours off had turned into twelve, but all good things came to an end, especially in a shit-fest like this one had turned into. The good news was that his surviving people had gotten at least a little rest. The mostly good news was that Brigade HQ had turned up at least some replacements for the people they'd lost in Nafplio. And the potentially not so good news was that two of those new people—Lieutenant Lyam Routhier and Staff Sergeant Loki Thrane—were parked in chairs looking at the smart wall which, until about six minutes ago, had been a briefing map for Baker Company's next op.

It wasn't that Yildiz had anything against them, but then again, he didn't really know them yet, either. Which, especially in the pressure cooker the Expeditionary Force had become, could make a too honestly expressed opinion bad for the opiner's health. He looked at First Sergeant Mueller, who'd been conducting the brief before his display was commandeered, and Mueller shrugged ever so slightly.

"I expect it's going to change our tasking order," Yildiz said.

"And a damn good thing, too," Bennath Kelly said harshly. She'd taken Spellman's death hard, and Yildiz knew what she was thinking. If Murphy had turned up eighteen hours earlier, Dino Spellman would still be alive. And so would all the other people Baker had lost along with him.

Lieutenant Routhier around the briefing room, then grimaced.

"Right after they K-struck Agrino," he said, eyes fixed on the overhead, speaking to no one in particular, "all I wanted was payback. Not so much, anymore. So, if you don't mind my half credit's worth, Captain," he brought his gaze down to Yildiz, "I think I'm onboard with Lieutenant Kelly on this one."

"Indicates you've got a working brain, Sir, if you don't mind my saying so," Mueller said. "Always a good thing to see in a lieutenant. No disrespect."

"None taken, First," Routhier replied with something more like a grin.

Yildiz cocked an eyebrow at Thrane, and the staff sergeant who'd replaced Spellman shrugged.

"Hey, I'm the new kid. Good news is that most of the people this Murphy's gonna be really pissed with are way above our pay grade."

"That's true," Yildiz said, "but—"

His earbud buzzed, and he held up a raised index finger.

"Hold that thought," he said, and tapped to open the channel.

"Lopez," a voice said in his ear. "Arm 'em up, Ahmet. We're going to Kórinthos."

"Yes, Sir. May I ask what our mission brief is?"

"You and I are taking Baker and Charlie, and we're gonna arrest that son-of-a-bitch Alaimo," Lopez said flatly. "Able is staying here to watch our backside. And what I really, really hope is that those fucking security troops of his try to get in the way."

"And Brigadier Cowan?" Yildiz inquired in a calm voice.

"I'm afraid I've relieved him and placed him under arrest at the moment. Is there a problem?"

"No, Sir," Yildiz said with a smile. "No problem at all."

"Gunships and transport birds lift in twenty minutes, Captain. Get your asses in gear!"

Ahmet Yildiz felt more cheerful than he'd felt in days as Second Battalion's aircraft entered Kórinthos airspace. The possibility that they might eat an Odyssian Wasp or two on their way in had occurred to him, and it would've been exactly the sort of bitterly ironic thing he'd come to expect here on Odysseus. But no one had shot at them, and now Parnassus Tower loomed ahead of them.

"Baker has the ball," Arturo Lopez's voice crackled over the command net. "Charlie is backstop. Iron Hand, set the bleachers. Go!"

The ground-based air defense systems had noted the First Division transponders, and Second Battalion's lead element was inside the defensive perimeter before anyone on the ground had a clue what was coming. Some of the automated gun turrets started to train out as Yildiz's command bird swept towards the raw, churned-up landing ground that had replaced the landscaped beauty of Parnassus Gardens, but the Iron Hand gunships were right ahead of him, tasked to suppress the defenses. A holocaust of rocket and cannon fire ripped down from the incoming "friendly" aircraft and tore those turrets—and every lander and shuttle parked on the landing ground—into flaming ruin.

"Go, go, go!" Yildiz barked as the transport birds went into ground hover on vectored thrust, skids a half meter from the field, and armored troopers spilled from the hatches and stormed towards the building.

The tower's ornately decorated entrance was protected by heavily sandbagged autocannon and machine guns, but the gunners' surprise was total. They wasted a handful of heartbeats gawking at the sudden assault, then flung themselves onto their weapons. But by that time, Audrey Reynolds's platoon was down and in the prone, and deadly accurate rifle fire picked them off before they got there.

And about now—Yildiz thought.

As if the thought had conjured them into existence, a Hoplon fire team burst out of the tower. They were armed not with carbines but with auto rifles that would have been called medium machine guns under other conditions, and their heavy armor scoffed at mere rifle and carbine fire. Several of Kelly's Third Platoon troopers went down, but Second Platoon had been waiting, and shoulder-fired rockets met the Hoplons head-on. Each of them took at least two direct hits from shaped-charge weapons designed to knock out heavy armored vehicles, and that was that.

"*Go!*" Yildiz barked again.

Unless Alaimo had changed his procedures in the face of Murphy's arrival, that team had been his security detail's only armored-up Hoplons. Lopez's assault plan didn't envision giving any of the others time to climb into their armor.

First Platoon was backup, leapfrogging through Third to take the doors with Second on their heels, and Yildiz went in with Routhier.

"Bulldog Six, Blue Six," Lieutenant Kelly's voice crackled in Yildiz's earbud. "We're at the objective line."

"Blue Six, hold while Green gets into position."

"Bulldog, we've got what looks like a lot of movement. Sensors are picking up a lot of foot traffic. Might be trying to rabbit."

Which, Yildiz reflected bitterly, was exactly what someone like Alaimo would do. If he could. The question was *whether* he could. Baker Company had been inside the tower for almost thirty-five minutes, and in theory—in theory—Charlie Company had sealed off all ground-level and subsurface access behind them. Resistance had been even heavier than he'd feared, though—apparently Alaimo's company-sized security detail had a pretty shrewd idea of what Murphy had in store for them—and he'd lost a lot more people than he wanted to think about.

And he wasn't about to lose any more than he could help.

"Hold," he repeated, and punched channels to First Platoon. "Green Six, Bulldog six. Say position."

"Bulldog, some bastard with a heavy machine gun's dug-in on the mezzanine on the thirty-eighth floor. We're flanking. Three minutes."

"Copy." He punched channels. "Blue Six, Bulldog. Three minutes."

"Bulldog, I don't think we have three minutes!"

"Yes, you *do*," Yildiz said flatly. "Hold position. Acknowledge!"

"Blue Six acknowledges hold position."

Kelly's voice was bitter, but Yildiz could live with that. The last thing he needed was—

The explosion shook the entire tower.

"What happened?" Lieutenant Colonel Lopez asked.

Yildiz looked up, then patted Lieutenant Kelly's shoulder, nodded to the medics to take her away, and heaved himself to his feet.

"Bastard had the entire fortieth floor wired with demo," he said bitterly. "Took out most of the two floors above when it went." His lips twisted. "Lost a quarter of Third Platoon when he blew himself the hell up. And I fucking never saw it coming."

"Would've been worse if you'd let Bennath go in when she wanted to, Sir," Reynolds said. Her armor was streaked with blood from the wounded she'd helped dig out of the rubble, and she shook her head when Yildiz glared at her. "It would've," she said stubbornly, "and you know it."

"That's probably gonna make her feel a lot better when they start fitting her with her prosthetic legs," Yildiz growled. But then he made himself draw a deep breath and nod at his one surviving original platoon commander.

"We knew going in he might do something like that," Lopez said. "That's why you *didn't* let her go in unsupported. So don't tear yourself up over it. Shit happens. And, truth to tell, I never really figured him for the suicide type. Bastard like him figures he'll always find a way out, somebody to swoop in and haul his ass out of the line of fire."

"Yeah, that's what I thought, too." Yildiz grimaced, looking after the litter bearers and his vanished lieutenant. "Guess we were both wrong."

"Guess so." Lopez pulled a nic stick out of his belt pouch, flicked it alve, and took a deep drag. Then he shrugged.

"Suppose I'd better see about accepting those surrender demands Murphy's issuing," he sighed.

CHAPTER THIRTY-NINE

TFNS **Ishtar**
Odysseus Planetary Orbit
Bellerophon System
Free Worlds Alliance
January 17, 2553

TERRENCE MURPHY SAT BACK FROM THE DISPLAY, RUBBED HIS eyes, and reached for his coffee cup. Chasing paperwork had never been his favorite sport, and it was even worse than usual right now.

Why am I always playing cleanup? he thought, sipping from the self-heating cup. *I am so frigging sick and tired of digging through the wreckage.*

At least it wasn't as bad as Inverness, he reminded himself. Not proportionately, at least. In absolute terms, the death toll was far higher than that of Inverness, but Odysseus's population was almost fourteen hundred times the size Inverness's had been. That would make the final numbers no less horrendous when they had them, but at least Alaimo and his butchers hadn't managed to kill off an entire planetary population.

It would be a while before they did have those totals, he thought grimly. Unlike Gobelins, though, this time they would. There'd be no cover-up, no "disappeared" people who were simply swept under the rug and conveniently omitted from any official inquiries. The Xeneas Administration was just beginning to sort through the rubble, come up with some sort of rough count for total casualties, but they were going to account for every damned one of them in the end, and every single name would be remembered.

It was a monumental task, and it would be a heartbreaking one, and it wouldn't be completed for far too long. On the other hand, they'd gotten a running start, at least on the executions.

In less than ninety-six hours, Alaimo's pet monster Diana Steinbolt had "conducted trials" for 146,712 men, women and children. Most of those trials had consisted solely of recording the "accused's" names and alleged offense. Every single verdict had been "guilty," and every one of the convicted "traitors" and "insurgents"—some of them as young as eight years old—had been executed. A hundred and forty-six thousand people—hell, call it a hundred and forty-*seven* thousand—slaughtered in Markos Botsaris Stadium, the planetary capital's biggest soccer stadium, alone. Ffty-six hundred *a day*. Five hundred per "firing squad." The sound of gunfire had been virtually continuous, hammering home the horror for every ear in Kórinthos.

Entire families executed—murdered—while parents held their children in their arms. And Steinbolt had recorded all of them in meticulous detail.

That was only the capital's total, of course. There'd been "tribunals" and firing squads in half a dozen other cities, although none of the others appeared to have been quite as...efficient as Steinbolt's round-the-clock operation in Kórinthos. Their files were sloppier, too, although they'd still made the mistake of recording more than enough to justify the verdicts the people behind those tribunals and firing squads would receive in turn.

Then there were the K-strikes. Xeneas's and Tolallis's decision to launch reprisal strikes had almost certainly prevented an even more ghastly death toll, even if Alaimo himself had been safely sheltered in Kórinthos and knew it. He'd obviously understood that the Odyssians weren't going to destroy their own largest city, but he hadn't brought unlimited manpower to Bellerophon with him, either. He'd lost the equivalent of two complete brigades, over a third of his total Army strength, to BSDF ground attacks and retaliatory K-strikes. That hadn't stopped him from calling more in—like the one on Chios—but there was no question in Murphy's mind that it had at least slowed him down.

Which hadn't prevented him from killing another seven million Odyssians, including the death toll from the Lake Orestiada atrocity.

And then the murderous bastard had blown himself up to

avoid capture. To deny the people of Odysseus—and Terrence Murphy—any chance to administer the consequences of his actions.

Don't dwell on it, he told himself sternly. *There's only so much you can do. Focus on that.*

He put the coffee cup back on its saucer and let his chair come fully upright. He was due at Ithaca House for a conference with President Xeneas and Mollie Ramsay—assuming the medicos let her attend—in another three hours, so—

The comm chimed, and he glanced at the caller ID, then tapped ACCEPTANCE.

"What can I do for you, Harry?" he asked as O'Hanraghty's image replaced the report.

"I think you should drop what you're doing and head for Briefing One," O'Hanraghty said. "President Xeneas, General Tolallis, and Commissioner Ganatos are inbound, and they say they need to talk to you."

"About...?" Murphy's eyebrows rose in surprise. "I'm supposed to be talking to them down there in only about three hours!"

"I know. And they didn't say a word about why they need to talk to you *now*, instead. Which I find very interesting, don't you?"

❖ ❖ ❖

"Mr. President," Murphy said, coming to his feet and holding out his hand as Konstantinos Xeneas strode into the briefing room. It was located in one of the enormous carrier's spin sections, which imparted a comfortable sense of up and down, and O'Hanraghty, Menelaus Tolallis, and Lazaros Ganatos, both of the latter in uniform, followed the president through the hatch.

"Admiral Murphy." Xeneas clasped Murphy's hand in both of his own and shook it firmly. "Thank you for seeing us on such short notice."

"It's not really a sacrifice," Murphy replied with a crooked smile. "After all, *you* were going to be seeing *me* in about—" he glanced at the time display "—two and a half hours, anyway. Under the circumstances, I had to assume what brings you here was at least moderately pressing."

"You might say that."

There was something about Xeneas's smile, Murphy thought. Something... hungry. He didn't know exactly why that adjective had occurred to him, but he knew somehow that it was the right one.

"First, though," Xeneas continued, his expression sobering, "please let me tell you how grateful everyone on Odysseus is that you've managed to recover all of Commodore Carson's surviving people. God only knows what would've happened if they hadn't inflicted so much damage when Alaimo and his killers arrived."

"I'm afraid Lauren doesn't see it that way." Murphy shook his head, his eyes dark. "The way *she* sees it, she let Alaimo past her."

"With all due respect for the Commodore, that's bullshit, Admiral," Tolallis said flatly. "I've read Captain Rodoulis's report, and I've spoken with both Madelien Hoveling and Khairi al-Massoud, as well. Nobody could have done a better job than they did. And it's obvious Hathaway didn't see them coming until the very last moment." He shook his own head. "I don't know what gave them away—we'll never know. But she came within *minutes* of taking out Hathaway's entire vanguard without a single hit in return."

"I know. I've told her the same thing. And, intellectually, she knows it, too. But what she also knows is that Jorgensen's task group got by her, and she knows what Alaimo did to Odysseus while she couldn't do one damned thing to stop him. She'll be a long time letting go of that."

"Then we'll just have to convince her she's the only one who feels that way," Xeneas said. Murphy looked at him, and the system president's smile had turned much gentler. "The Senate's already confirmed the award of the Chrysós Stavrós, Admiral. That's the Golden Cross of Courage. It's our planet's highest award for valor."

"She'll try to refuse it," Murphy warned the Odyssians.

"I'm sure she will." Xeneas nodded. "We don't know her as well as you do, of course, but we knew her well enough to figure that out. That's why we were crafty enough to write the citation to include everyone who fought and died under her command."

"That probably *will* work," Murphy acknowledged with a smile of his own.

"Yes, but that's not why we're here," Xeneas said, and that hungry edge was back.

"So I gathered," Murphy said, waving the visitors into chairs.

"Actually," Xeneas said, settling into the indicated chair, "this is really Lazaros's bailiwick."

"Ah?" Murphy looked at the tall, gray-haired police commissioner.

"I wish I could claim credit for the brilliant investigative work that led to this, Admiral," Ganatos said, "but I can't. It just sort of fell into my lap. And it only did that because I met someone a bit like you and Governor Ramsay."

"I beg your pardon?"

"A Heart Worlder with a conscience and a sense of responsibility." Ganatos shook his head. "A month or so ago, I wouldn't have believed in mythological creatures. In fact, thirty-six hours ago, I wouldn't have believed in them, after what the Heart sent out to massacre my home world. But then there's you, and the Governor—my God, what that son-of-a-bitch did to her—and to my considerable astonishment, there's Richard Cuvillier."

"Excuse me?" Murphy cocked his head.

"Richard Cuvillier. He's the Chief Financial Officer for Malik Nanotech. It's one of the Société Auchan's more profitable operations here in Bellerophon, and the Société doesn't hand assignments like that to people it doesn't expect to follow the corporate line. For that matter, he's a Heart and a member in good standing of the Five Hundred himself. Some sort of cousin of Madison Dawson's. And he's had his fingers in at least a dozen kickback schemes here in Bellerophon."

"That doesn't exactly sound like the bio of a philanthropic humanitarian," Murphy said dryly when he paused, and Ganatos snorted.

"No. No, it doesn't. But it would seem Mr. Cuvillier has at least some unsuspected depths. Which is why he walked into my office this morning and told me Alaimo is alive."

Murphy snapped upright in his chair and O'Hanraghty muttered something pungent under his breath.

"Alive?" the admiral repeated sharply.

"According to Cuvillier, Alaimo evacuated from Parnassus before that battalion went rogue on him." From Ganatos's tone he was one of the many—*very* many—Odyssians who regarded Lieutenant Colonel Lopez's attack on Alaimo's HQ as primarily an attempt to buy clemency for his own actions. "He wasn't even in Kórinthos by the time the attack went in, and he'd planned that explosion to cover his escape from the get-go. Given the way his head works, I doubt very much that he told any of his security detail what he had in mind. Hell, for that matter he may have *wanted* them all dead, just to keep them from testifying against him.

"At any rate, he contacted Cuvillier within five minutes of receiving your comm message. And it's pretty obvious he expected Cuvillier, as a loyal employee of the Société Auchan—and someone scared to death of Gerard Perrin and the Five Hundred—to cover for him. Because what he demanded was that Cuvillier smuggle him, his staff, and the dozen or so members of his detail he *didn't* blow up to Euboea Island."

"Euboea Island?" Murphy repeated, leaning forward with his elbows on his thighs, his eyes intent.

"It's a large island in the Thálassa Krasioú, Admiral," Tolallis said. "Malik's primary business is nanotech, but it controls about a third of the seafood industry here on Odysseus, as well, and a quarter of the island is devoted to the fisheries. But the rest of it's been preserved in a pristine state, aside from some very nice recreational facilities for Malik's top executives and their families."

"And Alaimo's there?"

"According to Cuvillier," Ganatos said, "and I can't conceive of a reason for him to have invented this out of whole cloth. According to him, Alaimo plans to lie low there until our inevitable defeat at the hands of the heroic Federation." The bitter hatred in those last two words would have melted asbestos. "And he also seems to have suggested that it might be possible for a truly resourceful chief financial officer who didn't want Gerard Perrin and the Hand going after his family to figure out a way to smuggle him back to the Heart even sooner than that."

"Classic sociopathic megalomaniac," O'Hanraghty said. "I'll bet you that, deep inside, he truly can't believe he won't win in the end."

"Then I suppose it's time we taught him otherwise." Murphy's smile was a razor. "A job for Logan, I think, Harry. Let's get him in here and up to speed."

CHAPTER FORTY

Euboea Island
Planet Odysseus
Bellerophon System
Free Worlds Alliance
January 17, 2553

THE ASSAULT SHUTTLE SQUATTED LOW OVER THE MOON-SILVERED waters of the Thálassa Krasioú. Eumaeus, the larger of Odysseus's two moons, was about half the size of Earth's Luna. It hung off the shuttle's starboard wing tip as it rose in the east. Arcos, Odysseus's smaller moon, was barely two thirds the size of Eumaeus and low in the west, which did interesting things to shadows. Not that shadows were particularly important to Sergeant Major Anniston Logan at this particular moment. He was far more interested in the pair of shuttles flanking his own, and he watched the optical feed on his Hoplon armor's HUD as the trio of sleek transatmospheric craft raced northward at twice the speed of sound, so close to the ocean they left visible wakes.

They probably didn't need to come in quite this low, Logan reflected. Their target was too busy lying low to screw around with radar or lidar or anything else that might be detected and give away his hidey hole. But the mission plan hadn't made any assumptions.

Logan approved of that. He *wanted* this one. Wanted it so badly he could taste it.

He felt the anticipation rising again, felt it bubbling like lava under the professional calm someone who'd been at his trade for twenty years knew to maintain going into combat.

"Comms check," he announced.

"Faeran, check," Sergeant Lorna Faeran replied. She'd been a corporal when they left New Dublin for Jalal, but she'd also been long overdue for promotion. It had taken Logan a while to find the notation in her file that explained why she hadn't been, and he was pretty sure the dipshit Heart World lieutenant she'd slugged had had it coming. He was only a sergeant major, of course, so his opinion might not have mattered under most circumstances, but when the endorsement to his memo suggesting the long-ago black mark might be set aside came from Terrence Murphy, things happened.

"Steiner, check," Private Ismael Steiner announced a heartbeat later. Steiner had also been a corporal. In fact, he'd been a corporal twice, Logan reflected. One day he might be again.

"Kavanagh, check," Corporal Philip Kavanagh, the Crann Bethadhan who'd replaced Rodrigo Chavez after Diyu, chimed in. Logan had interviewed over two dozen candidates looking for Chavez's replacement in Murphy's personal security team. It wasn't easy to find someone to fill Chavez's boots, and the team's chemistry had to work. He'd stopped looking after he interviewed Kavanagh. Unlike Steiner, who seemed to have a lot of ferret in his ancestry, Kavanagh was a bear. Almost as tall as Logan, with coarse black hair, eyes so dark they looked like coal, and the hooked nose of a fairy-tale highwayman, he looked like a blunt object, but he'd turned out to have very sharp edges indeed.

There should have been one more, Logan thought grimly. Lance Coporal Eira. No last name—just "Eira." She wouldn't have been fully geared up as a Hoplon—she needed another thirty hours or so in the simulator before he'd sign off on that—but she should have been here, sitting in her nest of displays, anchoring her teammates, monitoring their communications and their armor telemetry. Only she wasn't this time. Not physically, anyway. The docs wouldn't let her out of sickbay for a while yet, and that was fine, in some ways. It gave Logan a little longer to rethink the implications of her relationship with Lieutenant Murphy. But it wasn't fine with *her*, because she was champing at the bit to return to active duty and finish that Hoplon sim time. She didn't seem to realize—and he'd made damned sure no one told her—that she was on the brink of setting a new record for completion of Hoplon training. He'd known the half-starved waif from Inverness had the killer instinct when he first met her, but not even he had realized just how true that was. She might not be here in person, but she was damned well here in spirit. Part of his team, the way she always was.

It wasn't very big, his team, but it was *solid*, and he'd never had a more satisfying assignment in his life. He really ought to be holding down a first sergeant slot in a battalion somewhere, of course. In fact, that was where he'd been before he'd been sliced off and assigned to ramrod the bodyguard for another useless Five Hundred asshole headed for a ticket-punching stint as system governor in some podunk Fringe system. God, he'd been pissed!

Now, he thought, not so much.

"Remember," he told them. "Anybody's unarmed or doesn't resist gets taken alive. I know you'd just as soon waste them and be done, but those are the rules, and we've gotta play by 'em or the Admiral will have our asses. And don't anybody forget we want Alaimo alive. Everybody got that?"

Acknowledgments flashed on his visor, and he grunted in approval. He did, indeed, know how badly they wanted to just kill them all and let God sort them out. As a matter of fact, that last sentence was at least as much for himself as for any of the others.

"Feet dry in five mikes," the copilot's voice said in Logan's earbud.

"Copy," he replied, then turned his head in his armor's turret-like helmet dome to look at his team. "Five minutes," he said, and right fists were raised, gauntlet thumbs extended, in acknowledgment.

A *Perseus*-class shuttle's normal loadout was a hundred and fifty troopers in battle dress or a hundred in light powered armor, like the Mark 12. Logan's team had the entire troop compartment to itself for this operation, and the four Hoplons took up only about ten percent of the available volume. If everything went well, quite a bit of that space would be occupied by unwilling guests in an hour or so, he thought, and called up the real-time overhead imagery of Euboea Island as the shuttles howled towards it.

The fisheries along the long, narrow island's southern tip worked twenty-six hours a day, seven days a week, and the docks and processing sheds were a brilliant sea of light. He wasn't interested in those, and the display's filters prevented the light glow from overwhelming the details he *was* interested in.

The buildings of their objective looked incredibly out of place in Euboea's lush, semitropical vegetation. They would've been more at home in a ski resort somewhere, in Logan's opinion, but he wasn't there to worry about the aesthetics. What mattered was that the target chalets were a blaze of power sources, and there seemed to be an extraordinary number of air cars on their landing apron.

He zoomed in. The atmospheric drone driving his display circled lazily at five thousand meters, but the night air was crystal clear. Despite its altitude, Logan could have counted the leaves on the trees if he'd really wanted to, and his eyes narrowed as he spotted the sentries spotted around the compound. The rifle-armed, unarmored guards were unlikely to make a difference, and he wondered what genius on Alaimo's staff had decided putting them out there had been a good idea in the first place. Nothing could have been better designed to scream "Hey! Here we are!"

"Two minutes," the flight deck announced.

"Dismount in two!" he told the team, and magnetic restraining clamps *thunk*ed open. All four Hoplons lumbered to their feet, and Logan's eye ran one last check of his armor's telltales. Then he banished them from his visor display and stepped closer to the hatch as the *Perseus* deployed its spoilers and its turbines shrieked as the pilots reversed their vectored thrust to kill airspeed.

It wasn't the stealthiest arrival in the history of warfare, Logan reflected, but he'd been on the receiving end of that sort of sudden banshee scream. He knew how even elite troops reacted when the hell howl of an incoming assault announced itself out of a calm, still night, and he bared his teeth as he reflected upon how *these* sorry bastards would react.

The light above the hatch flashed once and the door hissed sideways into its recess. The spoilers deployed around its leading edge created a pocket of stillness, despite the fact that the *Perseus*'s speed was still somewhere north of two hundred fifty kilometers per hour. Logan watched the digital timer spin downward on his visor.

It reached zero, and he stepped out into the night.

Major Tony Bisgaard sat in his comfortable bedroom, glaring at the document on his display. He wasn't remotely as confident as his general that he'd ever have the opportunity to file it, but he had to do something while they hid out on this miserable, pissant excuse for a planet, and as Alaimo's ops officer, the rough draft was his to write. Of course, the report in question wasn't going to say what he'd expected it to say when they shipped out.

His scowl deepened.

Like most of Alaimo's staff, Bisgaard had been on Gobelins with the General. And he'd spent the years since effectively in limbo, shuffled aside, hidden and ignored like some sort of unsightly excrescence. They'd done what needed doing, shown the uppity Fringers the error of their ways. And as soon as they'd finished, their reward was to be banished. Bisgaard's little corner of limbo had been pleasant enough, in many ways. Not as luxurious as the General's, perhaps, but he couldn't honestly say any of his wants had gone unprovided for. Yet it had burned, that exile. That unspoken but abundantly clear contempt for the men and women who'd made the hard choices. The ones who hadn't been afraid to get down in the mud and the blood if that was what the job required.

And like Alaimo, Bisgaard had known—*known*—Bellerophon would be their vindication. The operation that would "rehabilitate" them and prove they'd been right all along in Gobelins. If the gooey-hearted idiots who ran the Five Hundred had listened to them then, made Gobelins the clearly enunciated consequence of Fringe rebelliousness, none of this shit would have happened. But had they done that? No, of course they hadn't! They'd actually tried to sweep it under the rug, keep it under wraps. And now that Bellerophon had gone south on the General through no fault of his own, Bisgaard knew exactly who'd end up carrying the can.

Again.

He read back through the last section and tweaked a few words, then nodded. Not so much in satisfaction as in the awareness that it wasn't going to get any better if he kept poking at it. The entire thing would be disassembled and picked to pieces by Hepner and the General himself before he got to compose the final draft, anyway, and—

His head snapped up as something shrieked in the night. It took him only an instant to recognize that earsplitting howl, and he swore with suddenly panicked savagery as he came to his feet.

He snatched his sidearm from the holster hanging from his desk chair, for all the good it was likely to do, and reached for his comm with his free hand even as he turned towards the door.

"Incoming!" he shouted into the comm. "We've got incom—"

Thunder bellowed, lightning struck, and Tony Bisgaard staggered back as the massive, hulking Hoplon crashed through the chalet roof and the ceiling of his room.

The Hoplon's impact shook the bedroom floor like an earthquake. Its breastplate bore a pair of broken marshal's badges and a black shield with a silver tree and a balance scale, and through the domed helmet he could just see the operator's tattooed face and the dark prosthetic orb in her right eye socket.

His gun hand rose without conscious thought and he squeezed the trigger again and again while she just looked at him through that dome of armorplast. It was pointless, of course. The bullets simply bounced, screaming as they ricocheted around the room. One of them gashed his own cheek, but he went on squeezing the trigger until the magazine emptied and the slide locked back. Then he stood there, the useless weapon in his hand, staring at her...and she smiled.

"Thank you," she said over her external speakers.

His eyes widened in confusion. Even through his panic a corner of his mind knew that was the stupidest thing anyone could possibly say at a moment like this. What the hell did she think—

Lorna Faeran squeezed the trigger and a three-round burst of hollow-nosed expanders tore Bisgaard's torso apart. The butchered corpse hit the bedroom's expensive wooden floor with a sodden *thump*, and she keyed the comm with her chin.

"Ratcatcher Two," she said. "Confirm Tango Three, but he didn't want to come easy. One armed target neutralized."

Ismael Steiner heard Faeran's report and tried not to feel jealous. They wanted any of Alaimo's troops they could lay hands on, but his staffers were primary targets. Just like Faeran to land right on top of one of them! And for the stupid bastard to give her an excuse. Some people had all the luck.

He thudded up the staircase, his suit's heavy feet shaking the chalet while small-arms fire whined and skipped from his armor. It was noisy, even with the sound-deadening earbuds, but he'd heard it before. He pivoted his carbine and a quick burst took down the idiot with the rifle on the landing above him. Then he topped the stairs and charged straight through the door at the top. It was locked, which meant exactly nothing to a Hoplon moving at the next best thing to twenty-six kilometers per hour.

He crashed through the rain of splinters into a palatial sitting room just as a naked, fair-haired man charged out of the bathroom with a towel wrapped around his waist. A corner window in Steiner's visor flashed as his armor's computer IDed the newcomer.

"Ratcatcher Three has eyes on Tango Two!" he announced jubilantly, and thumped forward with one enormous armored "hand" spread wide. "Come to Papa, you bastard!" he said over his external speakers.

The naked man dropped his towel, squirming frantically as he tried to avoid the Hoplon, then squealed in anguish as that armored hand closed on the calf of his right leg. Steiner yanked, and the squeal segued several octaves higher as the captive found himself hanging upside down from one leg while his arms flailed uselessly.

"In case you hadn't already noticed," he said, "you're under arrest."

Anniston Logan heard both reports and smiled. He had a pretty fair notion of what had happened to Bisgaard, but if the idiot really had been armed, Faeran was covered. And Steiner might just get to be a corporal again—for a while at least—if he really did have Rayko Hepner. But Logan himself was after bigger fish. There was a reason he'd assigned himself the largest and most luxurious chalet of all.

Now he stormed across the entry foyer, armor shrugging aside the hurricane of small arms fire while his carbine blazed back. The incoming fire died abruptly, and he jogged across a pair of bodies as he headed for the stairs.

"Ratcatcher Six, Sweeper Six," his earbud told him. "Getting some leakers out here, Smaj!"

"If they're packing, shoot the bastards," he said. "If they wanna roll over and make nice, we gotta let 'em, but I'm fine either way, long as they're not on the priority list."

Officially, "Sweeper Six," Major Tarasoff, who commanded the Marines from the other two shuttles, who formed the perimeter around the chalets, outranked Logan significantly. But the Admiral had made it clear this was Logan's op, and Tarasoff was far too wise to get between Logan and his prey.

"That's affirmative, Ratcatcher," he said.

There were two doors at the head of Logan's stairs, and Cuvillier had had no idea how the chalets had been divvied up by Alaimo and the other fugitives. The door to the right would have a better view of the ocean; the one to the left would have a better view of the island's mountainous spine.

Logan flipped a mental coin and went right.

He crashed through the door and slid to a stop.

Taskin Alaimo's dress uniform was perfect. He looked like someone headed for a formal dinner, not someone surprised in his bedroom in a chalet hideout, and he looked at Logan with almost casual indifference.

A bodyguard came charging in behind Logan, carbine firing on full auto. The sergeant major's visor popped up a view from the camera mounted between his shoulder blades, and he swung his left arm almost casually. The massive limb crunched through the doorframe—and a meter and a half of the wall beyond it—and scythed into the unarmored bodyguard like the hammer of Thor.

The shattered body flew back off the landing and crashed brokenly to the floor below, but Logan never looked away from Alaimo, and the general cocked his head quizzically.

"Please." Logan's voice was soft, almost caressing, over his armor's speaker. "Please. Try to run."

"I doubt I'd get far against a Hoplon," Alaimo replied, seating himself in one of the luxury suite's sinfully comfortable armchairs.

"You might. Then again, you might not."

"How did you find me?" Alaimo asked.

"You may find that out at your trial. Probably not." Logan bared his teeth. "I expect it to be too short for a lot of information to be exchanged."

"You don't sound like one of the local peasants," Alaimo said thoughtfully.

"I'm not."

"I thought not." Alaimo crossed his legs. "Look, do you have any idea who I work for?"

"I don't care."

"Gerard Perrin. *Perrin!* The richest single guy in the entire Five Hundred. When he says jump, the only thing the rest of them ask is 'how high?' And the Five Hundred run the Federation. Do you understand what I'm worth to him?"

"What part of 'I don't care' failed to register?" Logan asked quietly.

He thudded across the floor, reached down one massive powered gauntlet, and closed his armor's hand around Alaimo's neck. Not tight enough to strangle him, but tightly enough to be uncomfortable.

"No! Wait, wait, wait, wait! You look away, forget what happened to me, and I can get you anything. Anything! Perrin— Perrin he set me up in paradise, with all the drugs and booze and ass and—"

Logan tightened his grip slightly.

"—any...thing!"

Logan keyed his helmet and the visor slid up. His slate-gray eyes were granite hard, boring into Alaimo's.

"Did she beg?" he asked softly. "The mother with three children you personally picked up at Checkpoint Bravo outside Capital City on Gobelins? The one who'd surrendered to the Marines to save her kids from your butchers? One of them was three years old. Tell me, did she *beg*, General?"

Alaimo's face hardened.

"I don't have the slightest idea who you're talking about. I don't remember her—whoever she was—and I don't remember *you*, either. Is that what this is all about for you? Some Fringer bitch and her worthless kids? Is that—*urrrrk!*"

His eyes widened, his face darkened, and Anniston Logan looked down at him with a basilisk glare of death. Alaimo arched backward over the chairback, both hands clutching uselessly at the Hoplon's mechanical arm. But then Logan's nostrils flared, and the servo-mech vise around the general's throat relaxed...slightly.

"I don't remember her." Alaimo's voice was hoarser, his hands still clung to the Hoplon's arm, but there was a strange light in his eyes. "But she probably begged. They always beg, and it never matters. Tell you the truth...I like it. All that control. All that power. That's how you're feeling right now, isn't it? All you have to do is close your hand, and I'm dead, and that...that's a high nothing else comes close to, isn't it?

"But the thing is, I never did it. Not on my own! I always followed orders from the Five Hundred. Perrin wanted Gobelins back under control. So did the Zaibatsu and the O'Carroll families. It was them! They told me what they wanted, and I gave it to them. Just following orders. You do what they want, and they'll always take care of you. That's how it works for men like us. You see?"

"I—" Logan released his grip on Alaimo's neck "—am nothing like you."

"Then take me into custody." Alaimo shrugged. "Perrin will pay a fortune to get me back. A prisoner exchange, even a—"

Logan reached out with both hands, gripped Alaimo's upper arms, and raised him effortlessly until his toes dangled six centimeters from the floor and the pain of the Hoplon's merciless gauntlets flared through him.

"I could rip you apart right now," Logan told him. "All I have to do is twist. Your arms would come right out of the sockets. I bet I could rip your head off before you bled out, too. Should I? What would *you* do, General?"

Alaimo clamped his jaw against a pain sound, and Logan smiled a thin, cold smile.

"I want to," he said. "God, how I want to hear you scream all the way to hell. But Admiral Murphy's got other plans. And justice won't grind quite as slowly out here as it usually does. So I can wait just a little bit longer. Meanwhile, I'm not giving you the chance to ruin what he has in mind."

A small port opened in Logan's breastplate. A flexible arm extended itself and a jet of gas from the dispenser at its end squirted into Alaimo's face. The general's eyes rolled back, and he went limp.

"Ratcatcher Six," Sergeant Major Anniston Logan said over the comm. "Jackpot on Tango One. Repeat, jackpot on Tango One."

CHAPTER FORTY-ONE

Tara City
Planet Crann Bethadh
New Dublin System
Free Worlds Alliance
January 18, 2553

"WHAT DO YOU THINK THIS IS ALL ABOUT, SIR?" COMMANDER YE asked quietly as the air car descended towards Halla Tionóil, the New Dublin System's capitol building.

Since Concordia's declaration of secession, it had become the home of the Free Worlds Alliance's governing Council, as well as the New Dublin legislative branch, which, Fourth Admiral Xie Peng thought, added a certain point to Ye's question. Almost exactly one standard year had passed since Xie had surrendered his sublight parasites to Terrence Murphy in direct defiance of Second Admiral Xing's orders. His presence had been "requested" in Tara City a handful of times during that year, but his destination had always been the Ceannasaíocht, the New Dublin System Defense Force's HQ building, not Halla Tionóil.

And he'd always known why he was visiting the Ceannasaíocht ahead of time. Usually, it had been to discuss the administration of the POW camps in which his people were housed, but this time, no one had told him a thing about the reason for the trip.

"I assume we'll find out before much longer, ZhenKang," he said calmly.

Ye looked at him just a bit skeptically, and Xie hid a smile.

Physically, he and his chief of staff might have been designed as a study in contrasts. Ye was a couple of centimeters taller than he was, but Xie was a stocky, burly sort with bristly black hair. He outmassed Ye by a good ten kilos, and he knew he always looked a bit...unfinished, however immaculate his uniform might be. Ye, on the other hand, was built on the slender, greyhound model, with sleek seal-brown hair and a pencil mustache, and he'd always been something of a clothes horse. Despite that, though, they understood one another well and they'd been an effective command team until that unfortunate afternoon here in New Dublin. Which meant Commander Ye was perfectly aware that Xie was somewhat less blasé about the unexpected summons than he chose to appear.

On the other hand, for all his own curiosity, Xie truly was almost as calm as he sounded.

Terrence Murphy had promised his people honorable treatment if he surrendered them, not that Xie had believed him for a moment. Things like that didn't happen between the Tè Lā Lián Méng and the Federation after sixty years of bitter, bloody war. Given that Xie's only other option would have been to carry out Xing's lunatic orders and engage Murphy's carriers, however, he hadn't had much choice. His sublight parasites could almost certainly have destroyed the pair of Federation FTLCs immediately in front of them, but without carriers of their own, they would have been doomed to continue onward into interstellar space until their reactors ran out of fuel mass and every single one of Xie's people died.

Even the brutality they could expect in a *gwáilóu* prison camp was better than that. And the fact that Xing had clearly written all of them off as disposable assets she expected to expend themselves in obedience to her orders while she got her own precious ass safely out of harm's way had made the choice even easier. Xie Peng had been damned if he'd do *anything* to cover up that bitch's monumental clusterfuck.

But it hadn't worked out he way he'd expected. Instead, it turned out, preposterous though it clearly was, that Murphy had meant it. He and the Crann Bethadhans had recovered not just all of Xie's people but every survivor from the crippled ships Admiral Than had been forced to leave behind, as well. They'd transported their wounded prisoners to the best hospitals they had and the unwounded ones to the McDermott Archipelago, a group of fairly large, sparsely inhabited islands thirty degrees or so above Crann Bethadh's equator. The local inhabitants—of whom there'd been no more than a couple of thousand—had been moved out, and the POWs had been moved in.

At first, there'd been only tents, and precious few of them to go around, which had appeared to justify Xie's doubts about Murphy's promises. On the other hand, he'd told himself, no one in New Dublin could reasonably have anticipated the sudden arrival of sixty-four thousand prisoners of war. Under the circumstances, a certain shortage of housing had probably been inevitable, and at least it had been summer in the McDermotts.

Indeed, it had been, and if roofs had been in short supply, his people had been well fed and the Crann Bethadhans had treated his wounded as well as their own. More than that, prefab housing units had arrived as quickly as the planetary infrastructure could print them out. Within two months, Crann Bethadhan construction crews had put in a power net, along with enough roadways, foundations, sewerage, and water lines for a small city, and their captors had provided Xie's people with the tools they needed to assemble their own housing.

There'd been no brutality, no unnecessary hardship at all, and General Dewar—before he'd become *President* Dewar—had treated Xie with a degree of courtesy he was unaccustomed to receiving from far too many of his own superiors. Murphy's orders undoubtedly accounted for much of that, but not all of it, and Xie had wondered more than once what that said about the Federation's citizens—out here in the Fringe, at least. It certainly didn't jibe with the Tè Lā Lián Méng propagandists' official line.

He was thinking about that as the air car grounded on the Halla Tionóil parking apron and the squad of SDF troopers awaiting it formed into an honor guard. At least that was what everyone was polite enough to pretend it was, Xie thought with a hidden smile.

He preceded Ye out of the hatch, and the SDF lieutenant commanding the "honor guard" saluted sharply. Xie returned the courtesy gravely, and the lieutenant turned and gestured at a walkway leading to the Halla Tionóil's graceful portico.

"If you'd come with me, please, Fourth Admiral?"

"Of course, Lieutenant," Xie replied, exactly as if he'd had a choice. "Please, lead the way."

✧   ✧   ✧

David Weber & Richard Fox

It was a fifteen-minute walk from the parking apron, into the building, and then up to the wooden-paneled, comfortably furnished conference room on its third floor. The lieutenant opened the door for his League "guests."

"Fourth Admiral Xie and Commander Ye, Mr. President," he announced, and stepped aside for Xie and his chief of staff.

Xie stepped into the room, then paused. He'd expected only Dewar and possibly one or two aides, in line with his previous visits to the system capital. There were rather more people than that present, however, and none of them looked like aides or secretaries.

"Fourth Admiral," Cormag Dewar said, standing at the head of the conference table to hold out his hand.

Xie crossed to him and shook the proffered hand, and Dewar nodded to Ye, then waved both of them into waiting chairs.

Xie took inventory as he sat.

He recognized Vice President McFarland, and he'd met Yukimori Aiko twice, although he still had no idea what she looked like behind that formal ceramic mask. The auburn-haired woman at Yukimori's elbow was General Chloe O'Kieran, who'd replaced Dewar as the New Dublin SDF's CO, but he didn't know the tallish, brown-haired man on the far side of the table from her or the shorter bald fellow beside him.

He did, however, recognize Captain Jordan Penski. Penski had commanded the sublight parasites that had defended the New Dublin orbital infrastructure against Admiral Than's missile strike. And he'd also commanded the SAR teams who'd worked around the clock until they were positive they'd recovered every living survivor from Than's cripples. He'd taken personal responsibility for getting all of those people safely dirtside, and his medical teams had fought for every League life as tenaciously as for any of their own.

Xie extended his hand across the table.

"Captain—no, I see it's *Commodore* Penski now," he said with a slight smile, noting the other man's new rank insignia. "It's good to see you again."

"And to see you, too, Sir," Penski replied as they shook hands. "I trust everything's gone smoothly out there in the islands?"

"For castaways thrown ashore on barren, desert isles it hasn't been *too* bad, I suppose," Xie said with an absolutely straight face, and Penski chuckled. One thing no one would ever call the heavily forested, well-watered McDermotts was a barren desert. "In fact," Xie continued, this time with a slight smile, "Colonel Keefe delivered the first surfboards about a month after you and Admiral Murphy departed. For which my people were suitably grateful."

"Admiral Murphy promised you'd be treated well," Dewar said, and shrugged. "We tend to take the Admiral at his word around here."

"I will undoubtedly deny this if it's ever reported to my superiors," Xie replied, "but so do I."

"I'm glad," Dewar said simply. But then he tipped back in his own chair and cocked his head. "In fact, I'm glad for several reasons. But, first, let me introduce you to the two people I'm sure you've never met. This—" he gestured to the taller of the men Xie hadn't already recognized "—is Dylan O'Kirwan, the New Dublin Secretary of Industry. And this—" he indicated the shorter man with the depilated scalp "—is Myles MacRannall, Dylan's Director of Construction."

Xie nodded courteously to each of them in turn, then cocked his head at Dewar.

"I must confess, Mr. President, that while I appreciate any opportunity to leave my barren, desert-island prison camp, however pleasant it may actually be, I'm somewhat at a loss for the reasons for this particular trip."

"I've no doubt of that," Dewar said, "but there's a reason—and a good one—I assure you. The same reason Dylan and Myles are present. Admiral Murphy's sent Commodore Penski as his personal representative to this meeting, but before he tells you what it's all about, I want you to know two things. First, the Free Worlds Alliance would very, very much like you to accept Admiral Murphy's offer. But, second, if you decide that you can't, there'll be no negative repercussions here in New Dublin. I can honestly say there wouldn't have been, anyway, but Admiral Murphy made that a specific condition in the dispatches he sent home with the Commodore."

Xie's eyes narrowed for a moment. Then they moved back to Penski, and the dark-haired commodore looked back at him levelly.

"Precisely what sort of 'offer' does Admiral Murphy wish to make to me?" Xie asked slowly.

"Before I get to that, let me preface it by pointing out a few things, if I may," Penski replied, and Xie nodded.

"First, the Admiral asked me to point out to you that there's been ample time for your own naval authorities to send transports to collect the personnel waiting for them in Diyu. They haven't. If they had, Commodore Granger would have destroyed the yard facilities and withdrawn her carriers from the system as soon as she was certain they'd be safely recovered by your navy."

He looked into Xie's eyes.

"They aren't coming, Fourth Admiral," he said quietly, almost compassionately. "If they were, they'd have done it by now."

Xie's nostrils flared, but he said nothing, only gestured for Penski to continue.

"There could be several reasons for that," the *gwáilóu* commodore continued, "but you and I both know the most likely one is that Eternal Forward's chosen to write off all of those men and women. To abandon them. And they've almost certainly done it out of political calculation. Their return to the League—and yours—would be a political disaster for Liu and his . . . associates, so they prefer to let you rot as Federation prisoners. Or worse."

"If you wish me to acknowledge that my star nation's political leaders are almost as capable of corrupt decisions as those of the Federation, I'm prepared to do so," Xie said after a long, still moment. "The question that occurs to me is why you might wish me to make that acknowledgment. And I should point out to you in return that, as with your own military, the officers of the Rénzú Liánméng Hǎijūn take their oaths much more seriously than our political leadership deserves."

"Believe me, the Admiral knows that. Both parts of that." Penski shook his head. "Everyone in this room has had ample experience of exactly what betrayal in the name of political expediency and self-serving calculation means. And at this moment, Admiral Murphy's trying to do something about that. Obviously, his most powerful motive is to reform the Federation, to put an end to the sort of abuses which led to the creation of the Free Worlds Alliance in the first place. But almost equally strongly, he wants the war between the Federation and the League to end. It's gone on for sixty years, Fourth Admiral, longer than any person in this room at this moment has been alive. I don't think most people on either side really think it ever *can* end, and it's thrown up officers on your side like Xing and on our side like Yance Drebin and political leadership like our Five Hundred and your Eternal Forward. And given what was going on at Diyu, you know the Rish have been involved in it from the outset. I doubt very much that you believe in Rishathan altruism any more than I do, and you know as well as I do that they wouldn't have been there unless they've got an endgame planned. One I'm pretty sure neither the Federation nor the League will like very much.

"I believe Admiral Murphy represents the best chance either of our star nations has for an end to the war. He certainly represents the best—the only—chance the Federation has of reform, and without reform, the Five Hundred will have zero interest in ending a war that's worked so very well for them. It's the source of their enormous wealth and the reason they've been able to seize effective control of what used to be a functioning star nation, when you come down to it. What possible interest could *they* have in ending it? So I submit to you that it would be in the true best interests of the League, as well as the Federation, for the Admiral to succeed."

Penski paused, watching Xie's face, and the fourth admiral puffed his lips slightly. He sat that way for a handful of heartbeats, then shrugged.

"That may all be true. In fact, I'm prepared to stipulate that it is. I'm still not certain why you're telling me all this, however."

"Because it's become evident to the Admiral that he won't be able to accomplish that without fighting after all," Penski said. "He'd hoped—however realistically or unrealistically—that Prime Minister Schleibaum and, more importantly, the Five Hundred, would at least talk to him. He's discovered differently. And the wave of defiance in the Fringe is spreading. You may not be aware the Cyclops Sector has gone out of compliance and joined the FWA. And I'm certain you weren't aware that Admiral Murphy will be taking a substantial portion of his fleet—which is considerably larger than it was, after he defeated the fleet sent to drag him home in chains even more decisively than he defeated Second Admiral Xing—to defend the Bellerophon System against the punitive expedition the Heart will definitely send to crush Cyclops. I left Jalal before President Dewar's dispatch to him about Bellerophon reached him, but I know—I *know*, Fourth Admiral—what that man decided when he got it.

"What matters right this minute, though—the reason I'm here—is that whatever he may have wanted or hoped for in the beginning, it's come to open fighting. His forces killed over a hundred thousand TFN personnel in the Battle of Jalal, and it's only going to get worse, until either he wins or the Heart manages to crush him after all. There's no other way home now—not for him, not for the Free Worlds Alliance, and not for any hope of peace between the Federation and the League."

"Then despite my great admiration for Admiral Murphy as both an officer and a tactician, I'm afraid those hopes are... dim," Xie said quietly.

"Admiral Murphy has a knack for accomplishing impossible tasks," Cormag Dewar put in. "He might as well be a Crann Bethadhan, for he's as stubborn and as unwilling to admit *anything's* impossible as ever we were."

Heads nodded around the table, and Xie was a bit surprised to realize that one of those heads belonged to him.

"The Admiral himself would agree the odds against him are formidable," Penski said. "On the other hand, the Five Hundred has a few challenges of its own. Including the fact that two thirds or three quarters of its military personnel are Fringers who won't take kindly to killing their own in the Five Hundred's service. But however true that may be, the Admiral needs every advantage he can find or create. Which is what brings me to you... and Diyu."

Xie felt Ye stiffen beside him, and his own eyes narrowed. Surely Penski wasn't about to suggest—

"The Admiral's sent me to ask you to accompany me to Diyu," the commodore continued levelly. "He'd like you to tell the League personnel marooned in Diyu about the way you and your people have been treated here. To tell them that there's at least one Federation flag officer who damned well means it when he gives his word of honor. *One* Federation flag officer who will die before he breaks it."

"And why should I do that?" Xie asked softly.

"Because Mr. O'Kirwan and Mr. MacRannall will also be accompanying me, and because I'm going there as the Admiral's personal representative to make them an offer."

"What sort of offer?" Xie's voice was even softer than before.

"The Admiral intends to ask them to put the Diyu yard fully back online to support the Free Worlds Alliance and his warships,"

Penski said flatly. "As his spokesman, I'll point out all the things I just pointed out to you about his intentions and about what his success could mean for bringing this endless, bloody war to an end. And—" his lips twitched ever so slightly "—I'll also appeal to their patriotism, by pointing out that every ship the Five Hundred and the Heart Worlds are forced to divert to fighting *him* is one less ship the Federation can throw at the League out in Beta Cygni. Trust me, even if he fails, before he goes down the Admiral will be the biggest, most effective military diversion the League could ever hope to find. And he's authorized me to give all those League citizens marooned in Diyu his personal word of honor that if he succeeds, he *will* bring the Federation to a conference table with the League to negotiate a cease-fire and an end to the war. Obviously, he can't control how the League responds to his offer, but he will absolutely give your star nation the opportunity to end this slaughter.

"If he survives, if he can manage all of that, Fourth Admiral, then you and all your people here in New Dublin, and all your people in Diyu, will be able to go home again after all. And your homes will still be there, without worrying about Federation K-strikes, or which of their sons and daughters will die next week, or the week after."

"And if he survives but my own government refuses to negotiate?" Xie said. "What then? All of us will have become traitors in Eternal Forward's eyes." He shook his head slowly. "There will be no 'going home' if that happens."

"And will there be one if he doesn't—if *we* don't—survive?" Dewar asked softly.

Xie's eyes darted to him, and the president shook his own head.

"If Admiral Murphy goes down, so does the Free Worlds Alliance," he said unflinchingly. "And what do you think will happen to your people here in New Dublin when the Heart moves in? At best, you'll find yourself in a *Heart World* prison camp, and that's not so very good a place to be. At worst, your camps will be hit 'accidentally' when they start K-striking our people. But either way, you'll not be going home, and neither will any of your people trapped in Diyu.

"On the other hand, he might actually pull it off, here in the Federation. I'll be honest with you, Fourth Admiral, I'm not so very sure even Terrence Murphy can come up with a solution that lets the Fringe and the Heart stay married to one another. That's not a simple challenge like, oh, walking on water or raising the dead, after all! But it's possible. I'm thinking it's more probable we'll see the Federation split asunder, though, which might just give the League the opportunity it needs for victory. More likely, the Hearts will decide they've no choice but to spend their own children's blood instead of ours and go right on fighting rather than give back all they've gobbled up, and they've the bulk of the Federation's industrial power to do the fighting with. But this I'll tell you—if they do, they'll not have the Fringe at their side, because the Free Worlds Alliance is tired of losing our own and killing yours in the service of two corrupt star nations that deserve neither of us. *We'll* follow Murphy to make peace with the League, whatever the Federation does, and maybe even Eternal Forward will be smart enough to see the advantage in doing just that.

"Yet either way, I'll promise you this as President of the Free Worlds Alliance. You'll have a home here, whatever happens back in the League." He looked into Xie's eyes, and his voice was forged of iron. "We in the Fringe, Fourth Admiral—we know our friends. We've precious few of them, but we treasure the ones we have, and we'll no more abandon you and yours, should you stand with us now, than we'd abandon our own."

Silence hovered in the conference room for what seemed an eternity. Then Penski cleared his throat.

"I know this possibility never occurred to you, Sir," he said. "It never would have occurred to me, either. But this offer is from Terrence Murphy. Not a politician, not a member of the Five Hundred, not a flunky of Eternal Forward. It's coming from *Terrence Murphy*, and there's no one and nothing in this galaxy that could convince him to break his word to you.

"So the question you have to answer is whether or not you believe that the way I do."

CHAPTER FORTY-TWO

City of Kórinthos
Planet Odysseus
Bellerophon System
Free Worlds Alliance
January 20, 2553

GENERAL ALAIMO PACED FROM ONE SIDE OF HIS CELL TO THE other, executing neat about-face movements whenever the front edge of his sandal touched the wall, and his orange jumpsuit was fresh from the printers. The drones had delivered it...a while ago. With no watch, no datalink, no clock, it was hard to keep track of time.

Part of the plan, he knew. This wasn't the way he would've done it, but he recognized the technique. The isolation, the sensory deprivation. They figured that by the time another human being finally deigned to speak to him again, he'd be babbling like a brook. Tell them anything they wanted to know.

They were good, though. He had to give them that. He'd already been in his first jumpsuit, already locked in this cell, before he ever regained consciousness. And he hadn't been allowed out of it. No exercise excursions, not any visitors. Nothing, aside from endless, gray monotony, the silence, and the drones that delivered and collected his tray of bread and water at what were *probably* regular intervals.

His cell was inside a larger confinement area. The bars were electrified—he'd found that out the hard way, when the shock knocked him on his backside. He didn't know if the lighting was on a timer or if they just turned it off or turned it on whenever

463

it struck their fancy. The main door was like a bank vault's, and it had never opened since he'd woken up. The drones came and went through a smaller door, too tiny for anyone bigger than a six-year-old to squeeze through.

Formidable. He had to admit, it was formidable. But—

Something clacked loudly, and he wheeled towards the sound as the never-opened door swung wide. A very tall, sandy-haired man in naval uniform with an admiral's insignia walked through it, carrying a metal tube. Another man—darker and twelve centimeters shorter—followed him. Both of them had gray eyes, Alaimo noticed. Just like the Hoplon who'd captured him. The second man's eyes glowed like gray lava with the fire of his hatred, but the admiral's...the admiral's were almost—almost—cool.

As they crossed the vault, Alaimo noticed two nonregulation elements of the admiral's uniform. The first was the silver leaf worn across his left breast, above the normal medal rack. That was minor, but the other...the other not so much. The Federation shoulder flash every serving member of the Terran Federation Navy wore had been replaced with the same black shield and silver tree he'd seen on the Hoplon's breastplate.

"Ah, Admiral Murphy." Alaimo approached the bars. "I suppose congratulations are in order. You've captured the big, bad me. And President Xeneas! We meet at last. Admittedly, not in quite the way I'd intended, but better late than never. I thought you'd be taller, though."

"Governor Ramsay never knew where to find me," Xeneas said in a voice of flat, hammered iron. "You tortured her—and all those other people—for *nothing!*"

Alaimo leaned close to the bars and smiled.

"You're welcome," he said.

"You son-of-a-bitch!" Xeneas drew back a fist, but Murphy caught his wrist gently.

"The electricity would hurt," he said.

"I understand you're upset," Alaimo said. "But you really should think this through, because the truth is, I *saved* all the other people on this planet through my actions." He held out his hands. "This world—this entire star system—is out of compliance. That means Standing Order Fifteen is in effect, which means it was my duty to launch a kinetic bombardment that continued until whoever was left surrendered. My duty was clear...yet I chose magnanimity."

"We know about Standing Order Fifteen," Murphy said, "but we also know that wasn't what you were actually sent out here to do."

"Really?" Alaimo stepped back to his cot, sat on it, crossed his legs and clasped his right knee in both hands. "That's a fascinating thought. Why else would they have sent me?"

"To make a statement," Murphy said. "To replicate Gobelins on a far bigger scale and this time record every bit of it. I'd wondered why Steinbolt recorded every one of those judicial farces of hers, every execution. And I wondered why there was so much video, why you'd gotten every bit of it down on chip. But then it came to me: psywar. This whole atrocity was supposed to be one huge psyop. When the rest of the Fringe saw what you'd done here on Odysseus—realized it could happen to their families, their children—they'd be too terrified to ever again raise their hand against the might and majesty of the Five Hundred's Federation. That's what it was about, wasn't it?"

"Well, you have to admit, the notion would have a certain appeal," Alaimo said.

"For people with sufficiently depraved minds, I suppose," Murphy agreed with a nod. "I really don't think it's going to work out the way you and Gerard Perrin had in mind, though."

"Oh, be serious, Admiral?" Alaimo snorted. "It *always* works out the way the Five Hundred has in mind! It may take a while, there may be a bump or two in the road, but it's inevitable. You're a *member* of the Five Hundred, at least by marriage. By now, you have to understand how it works."

"You're right. I am a member of the Five Hundred, and until I reached Bellerophon, saw what you've done on this planet, I did think I understood how it worked. Now I realize I really didn't. But knowledge that comes late is better than knowledge that never comes."

"Bravo!" Alaimo raised his hands to clap the fingers of his right hand against the heel of his left rapidly and politely, like someone applauding an excellent golf putt. "And now that we've established we both know how the galaxy works, let's show each other the respect of laying our cards on the table. You've got something in your hand there, I see. From my quarters in Parnassus Tower." He quirked a smile. "That security vault I borrowed from Governor Ramsay must've been tougher than I thought."

"You're right, it was. And in addition to this—" Murphy held up the tube "—we recovered the security copy of your orders to Thirteenth Corps. I found them very interesting reading, especially Annex W. A blanket pardon for anyone assigned to your command for crimes committed against any populace that's out of compliance anywhere in the Cyclops Sector." He shook his head. "I wish I could say I had to wonder about the mentality of anyone who'd hand out an unlimited hunting license like that."

Alaimo shrugged with a smile, and Murphy cocked his head.

"But the thing is, General, that I had a long talk with Lieutenant Commander Tripathi—you haven't met; she's my JAG. And then the two of us had an even longer conversation with Commander Anisimov, Admiral Jorgensen's JAG."

He paused, one eyebrow quirked, and Alaimo shrugged again.

"I'm afraid I've never met him, either."

"Well, the interesting thing about our conversation, General, is that both of them agree you didn't have the authority to write that into Thirteenth Corps orders. Which brings us to..."

Murphy waved the tube gently, and Alaimo shook his head.

"Well played, Admiral." He leaned back on the cot. "And, in answer to your next question, I'm willing to testify to everything. After all, I'm aware that the strength of my bargaining position is...dubious."

"I'm sure you are." Murphy lowered the tube. "But let's consider how that would play out. An infamous Army officer, in rebel custody, probably under duress, detailing how senior members of the Federation authorized the wholesale murder of Federation citizens. It would be rather easy for the Federation to disavow your actions, label you a rogue actor.

"But—" Murphy tapped the tube gently against his palm "—you're not an idiot, Alaimo. Ever since Machiavelli, 'princes' have known it's expedient to lay all the blame on a subordinate for committing the atrocities they want. Send him out convinced you have his back, and then punish him for the 'excesses' he committed without any orders from you. And then there was your experience after Gobelins. Right after it happened, there was that debate in the Five Hundred. Should they cover it up or broadcast it? And if they went public with it, did they condemn the 'excesses' or sneer at the Fringers and dare them to do anything about it? Went on for quite a while, didn't it? That must have given you a lot of time to think about how tempting it would have been for them to hang you out to dry if the fire got too hot. And this one was going to be a lot more blatant. You knew going in no one would even try to hide this one the way they had Gobelins. So you wouldn't have accepted this job without tucking an ace up your sleeve to keep the Federation from throwing all the blame on you as soon as that became convenient. Before you issued any blanket pardons to Thirteenth Corps, you already had a preemptive pardon of your own in your pocket, didn't you?"

"There are no 'crimes' against out-of-compliance planets," Alaimo said. "I just made sure no one was going to change the rules on me if I had to get a little...draconian."

"Open this for me." Murphy held up the tube. "O'Hanraghty tells me it's a onetime-use data cylinder. The data in this cylinder can't be altered, and any attempt to break into it will also delete everything."

"Quite correct." Alaimo nodded. "But...why would I do that?"

"You're useless to me as a witness against the Federation... on your own. It's too easy for the Hearts to brush aside anything you say. But if I had access to the data on this cylinder then you might just be worth taking with me to Sol. This is evidence. If I took you with me, you'd provide context and corroboration."

"Or you can stay here on Odysseus," Xeneas said coldly. "I think you know how *that* would work out."

"Well, that's quite an offer," Alaimo said. "All right. I'll be your bloody shirt. The code is One-Seven-Alpha-Niner-Six-One-One-Delta-Kilo-Niner."

Murphy looked down at his data pad, where the code had been captured as Alaimo spoke. And then, very carefully, he entered it into the tube's keypad. A green light blinked on its cap and a tone sounded.

"Galaxy. Chaos. Hash Tag-Delta-Charlie-One-Four-Three-Charlie. Destiny," Alaimo said, and the cap unscrewed itself.

Murphy pulled out a smaller rod and tugged a small tab at its midpoint. A sheet of holo paper stretched from the rod, and he looked at it.

"It's all here," he said softly, and his hands trembled ever so slightly. "Prime Minister Schleibaum. Admiral Fokaides. Every member of Schleibaum's Cabinet. And Chief Justice Claremont. *All* of them signed this."

He handed it to Xeneas.

"You seem surprised." Alaimo leaned forward and put his hands on his knees. "It wasn't too big a stretch to get it preemptively instead of after the fact." He shrugged. "It's pretty much the same pardon I got after Gobelins. Just a little earlier in the process."

"The Federation excused the slaughter of its own people before you ever arrived here." Murphy crossed his arms. "Every branch of government—the Executive, the Legislative, and the Judiciary... *and* the Military. Every single one of them."

"Of course they did," Alaimo said. "The Five Hundred needs control. That's how the Federation works, Murphy. What? You thought it was supposed to be about justice and freedom?" He shook his head, his expression almost pitying. "I was sent to bring Odysseus back into compliance so it can continue producing for the Five Hundred. And a few extra deaths here and there on Odysseus would probably have meant fewer deaths in the rest of the Cyclops Sector. Eventually, I would've been reinforced and gone on to the sector's other systems, and they would've come back into compliance without a fight. Sure, the ringleaders would've had to die, but everyone else would've survived, and Cyclops would be back to its proper place."

"We should've left the Federation after Gobelins," Xeneas said, and handed the data rod back to Murphy.

"The Free Worlds Alliance has adopted an expedited legal system for war crimes," Murphy said, "so let's go ahead and get this out of the way, shall we? General Alaimo, you stand accused of nearly eight million homicides, of torture, of—"

"I did it all." Alaimo waved his hand at Murphy. "No need for the complete catalog. Yes, I did it. But I committed no crimes. See the document in your hand."

"I'm not the Federation," Murphy slipped the inner rod into his uniform pocket, "and neither is Bellerophon." He looked at Xeneas. "Guilty?"

"By his own admission," Xeneas said, and smiled at Alaimo.

"Hold on." Something like genuine alarm flashed in Alaimo's eyes for the first time. "You just said you need me to validate the evidence!"

"No, I said you *might* be worth taking along to do that, not that I had any intention of doing so." Murphy smiled thinly. "Sorry if you misinterpreted a mere hypothetical observation on my part. Thank you for opening the rod for me, though." He tapped his comm. "Sergeant Major Logan?"

The vault door opened again, and Anniston Logan stepped through it in light powered armor.

"Take the condemned to the field and carry out sentence," Murphy said as he turned towards the door.

"Wait, let Odysseus have its due," Xeneas said. "I can arrange a firing squad in a heartbeat."

"He's in my custody. He's my problem," Murphy said.

Alaimo shot to his feet, his body tense.

"Wait. Wait!" He reached for the bars only to snatch his hands back as the electricity hit them with a sharp, clear *snap*. "We had a deal!"

"No," Murphy said. "You *thought* we had a deal."

He and Xeneas left the cell, and Logan approached the bars, holding up a pair of cuffs.

"Turn around and be restrained," he said.

"Is this…This is all some sort of game, isn't it?" Alaimo smiled. "Fake executions are part of good detainee interrogations, yes? Ha! You think you're being clever, don't you? Thought I wouldn't see through your little ruse. Come on, then. Let's be about it."

Alaimo turned and put his hands behind his back. Logan deactivated the electric bars, reached past them and cuffed his wrists together. Then he opened the door and Alaimo stepped through it.

"I know why they picked you after that little drama of yours in the chalet," he said.

They walked out the vault door and down a bare ceramacrete hallway.

"Of course Murphy wants me to think he'll have me killed by the bleeding heart who didn't want to spare me at the point of capture," Alaimo sneered. "It must irk you to know this is all show for my benefit. To know I'm not going to be executed for anything. That's always the way things are when you work for the right people."

He looked over his shoulder at Logan and winked.

"And I *do* work for the right people. So, what's the script? How does this 'Free Worlds Alliance' of yours execute people? Hanging? Spacing? Seems like a bit of wasted time and effort to take me all the way up to orbit to convince me you really, truly intend to kill me."

Logan held up a hand and bolts unlocked in a heavy door. He opened it for Alaimo, who kept his head high and his chin raised as he stepped into a small exercise yard. A dozen long boxes were stacked against the back wall, and there were several dark blotches on the dirt.

A pair of Marines with holstered pistols flanked the doorway.

"Those all sound a bit fancy for the Free Worlds Alliance," Logan said. "We use lethal injection."

"Really? What injection is that? Berinium flesh decay? Something dull, like Pancuronium bromide?" Alaimo chuckled, looking around the yard. "Something to keep my face pristine for pictures?"

Logan accepted a pistol from one of the Marines and leveled it at the base of Alaimo's skull.

"Tungsten," he said, and squeezed the trigger.

CHAPTER FORTY-THREE

City of Kórinthos
Planet Odysseus
Bellerophon System
Free Worlds Alliance
January 25, 2553

AT LEAST THEY HADN'T SHOT HIM YET, HE THOUGHT AS HE FOL-
lowed the major who'd come to collect him from the barracks
in which Baker Company's surviving officers and senior enlisted
had been confined.

That had to be a good sign, given the coverage the Odyssians
had been careful to make available to all their prisoners. From the
drumhead court-martials he'd seen broadcast, Terrence Murphy
and his associates—and, for that matter, the government of the
Cyclops Sector—had chosen to pay a lot more attention to the
letter of the law than Alaimo ever had. But if the Free Worlds
Alliance showed more concern for actual justice than Alaimo and
his butchers, they weren't mucking around with the guilty, either.
And thanks to the fact that idiots like Steinbolt had recorded
their own criminal acts in loving detail, there was no shortage
of evidence against them.

The firing squads had been busy, and Ahmet Yildiz expected
they'd stay that way for a while. God knew there were enough
bastards who needed shooting, anyway. He was totally prepared
to acknowledge that, although he'd really, really prefer not finding himself among the ones being shot.

He and his people had been subjected to less brutality than
he'd anticipated, given what they and their fellows had inflicted

471

upon Odysseus. Their captors hadn't been precisely *gentle* with them, but they'd been treated in accordance with the Articles of War's stipulations for POWs. Precious few League prisoners got that sort of treatment from the Federation, which was why he wouldn't have expected his people to get it from the Odyssians, either, especially after everything that had gone down here. They'd been denied comms, but they'd been allowed download access to the system datanet, which was how he knew about the tribunals Terrence Murphy and Konstantinos Xeneas had impaneled. And they'd been allowed showers and the dignity of their uniforms, rather than the orange prison coveralls people like Steinbolt had modeled during their brief appearances before the aforesaid tribunals. At the moment, Yildiz was not only un-manacled—which he really wouldn't have expected even now—but wore fresh, crisp fatigues, with all of his ribbons, and somehow as a prisoner he felt far cleaner than he had as a fearless defender of the Federation against the vile treason of the Free Worlds Alliance.

That probably said something unfortunate about his internal loyalty meter. On the other hand, that meter had taken a beating over the last week or so.

His guide—or his guard, depending on how one chose to look at it—led him down a hallway, then paused outside a large, old-fashioned, unpowered set of double doors. He knocked.

"Enter," a female voice called, and the major opened one door panel and nodded for Yildiz to step through it.

The captain obeyed the nod, and the door closed quietly behind him.

He found himself in a moderately spacious office. To his right, wide, latticed windows looked out over Ochi Square. From the angle, they were on the far side of the enormous square from Ithaca House, in one of the older sections of Kórinthos. Sunlight poured into the office through those windows, pooling on a mosaic floor patterned with the white-on-blue emblem of the BSDF. Old-fashioned oil portraits of uniformed men and women hung on the walls, and another pair of double doors were set into the wall opposite the doors through which he'd entered.

A woman in the uniform of a Marine colonel sat behind a desk that faced the windows, and he marched across to her, cap clasped under his left arm, made a sharp left face, and braced to attention.

She regarded him thoughtfully for several long seconds, and he looked back levelly. Her uniform was immaculate, textbook perfect ... aside from the silver-tree-and-balance-scale patch that had replaced the Federation's shoulder flash, and there was nothing particularly remarkable about her brown hair and eyes. But something dark and still looked back at him from the depths of those eyes, and the fruit salad on the left breast of her uniform was headed by a red-white-red ribbon he'd seen exactly five times in his career. He might not have any idea who she was, but that ribbon told him a lot about *what* she was, because the Federation Marines didn't leave too many Lions of Lucerne lying about in used ration tins. The Lion was second only to the Grand Solarian Cross among the Federation's medals of valor.

After a long, still moment, something seemed to warm slightly in those brown eyes.

"Captain Yildiz, I presume," she said.

"Yes, Ma'am!" he responded crisply.

"My name is Barr," she said. "I imagine you're curious about the reason you're here?"

"I believe the Colonel may correctly assume that, Ma'am."

"Well, the truth is that you present something of a problem, Captain," she told him. "Frankly, it hasn't been too difficult to decide what to do with most of the Army pukes—I hope you'll forgive me my parochial loyalty to my own service branch—the Five Hundred sent out here. I won't use terms like 'scum of the earth,' however fitting they may be, but I suspect you saw quite enough of the sort of people I'm talking about. The kind who'll be guests of honor for firing squads sometime soon."

Discretion, Yildiz decided, was the better part of valor in this instance, and he simply looked back steadily.

"Some of Thirteenth Corps's personnel, however, comported themselves with at least a modicum of honor and discipline," she continued after a moment. "According to at least some reports, you may have been one of them. Would you care to comment on that?"

"Ma'am," Yildiz said after a moment, "that's what we call a leading question back home on Izmir. No matter how I answer it, I'm potentially screwed."

"Really?" She cocked her head. "Why?"

"Because if I tell you that, hell yeah, I was one of the good guys, then I'm setting myself up as one of those lying bastards who'll say anything to get their asses out of the crack they damned well deserve to be in. And if I say that I *don't* think I was one of the good guys, it may be all you need to flush me right down the crapper."

"Interesting." Barr frowned thoughtfully. "I had a bet with my boss that you'd answer that question. He thought you wouldn't. Damn."

Despite himself, Yildiz felt his eyebrows quirk, and Barr chuckled.

"The reason you present something of a problem—or may, at any rate—is that the Odyssians aren't very fond of any of you at the moment. Absent some pretty significant extenuating circumstances, they regard all of you as one shallow step—at best—above war criminals. I'm sure you've been watching the HD broadcasts about how the FWA is dealing with war criminals, but the Bellerophon System undoubtedly plans on confining even the non-war criminals amongst Thirteenth Corps's personnel under rather . . . stringent conditions until such time as there's a prisoner exchange with the Heart. I'm sure," the colonel continued in a desert-dry tone, "that you can appreciate that that's likely to take some time to arrange."

Yildiz nodded, trying to keep his sinking sensation out of his expression, and she stood.

"Come with me, Captain," she said, and led him through the other set of double doors.

The office beyond them was larger than the one they'd just left, and a black-haired, mustached man, also in Marine uniform with the same shoulder flash, turned from his own set of windows to face them. At 185 centimeters, Yildiz wasn't exactly short, but this fellow was a good eight centimeters taller and built on the lines of a Terran bear. He also wore brigadier's insignia, and he raised an eyebrow at Colonel Barr.

"You won," she told him wryly. "He didn't waffle, but he didn't go around blowing his own horn, either."

"Told you he wouldn't," the brigadier said, then looked directly at Yildiz.

"My name's Atkins," he said. "I'm the senior officer in Admiral Murphy's ground combat component. As such, he's tasked me with deciding what to do with you, Captain Yildiz, and I don't have a lot of time to do that deciding in, because the Admiral's pulling out of Bellerophon within the next few local days. And that's a problem, because I've got two contradictory narratives about you."

He clasped his hands behind him, gazing at Yildiz thoughtfully, then shrugged.

"One set of reports says you personally arrested the head of the Potamia Valley Evacuation Center and handed him over to be systematically tortured by General Alaimo. And, not content with that, you personally captured Erasmia Samarili, President Xeneas's personal aide, dragged her through the middle of a firefight, and then handed her over to Alaimo to be water boarded...just before he did exactly the same thing to Governor Ramsay. And those same reports say that you and your Battalion CO—a Lieutenant Colonel...Lopez, I believe—were so desperate to save your asses that you tried to shoot your way through Alaimo's personal security detachment to grab him as a token you could trade to get those asses out of the 'war criminal' crack you'd wedged them into."

He contemplated Yildiz, obviously waiting for him to respond, but the captain only looked back steadily.

"Now, that's *one* set of reports," Atkins resumed after a moment. "There's *another* set which paints a somewhat different picture. For example, it suggests that what you were really trying to do in Potamia Valley was to get the people in that evacuation center the hell out of the way before Alaimo could murder them, too. Interestingly, a fellow by the name of Masson, who otherwise isn't incredibly fond of you for some reason, thinks that's what you were doing. And then there's the fact that you were directly ordered by the acting system governor to bring in Ms. Samarili and given a damned narrow time window to do it in. That didn't leave you a lot of wiggle room, but you managed to mount the operation in the time you had—and to avoid killing everyone else in her uncle's house when you executed it. And at least some of the Odyssians I've spoken to are of the opinion that what you were really trying to do in Alaimo's case was to grab him before he could disappear and evade us.

"As you can see, the information available to me is...conflicted."

He strolled across the office to the large desk at the far end, sank into the chair behind it, and pointed at the one in front of it.

"Sit, Captain," he said.

Yildiz obeyed the order and sat with his cap in his lap, facing the brigadier.

"I decided the best way to approach this was to lay it in April's lap," Atkins said, nodding at Colonel Barr. "She's been around the block a time or two, and she's hard to bullshit. So she sat down with Masson, walked him through that entire operation, and found out that even though Masson does carry a thoroughly understandable grudge, he also admires you...a little. 'A tough, no-bullshit bastard,' I believe he said."

Yildiz felt his lips try to twitch and strangled the incipient smile stillborn.

"Given what he had to say about you, the Colonel had the tac records pulled from your armor's computers," Atkins continued in a more serious tone. "Not the after-action reports written to cover your ass with your superiors—which, by the way, would have buried your ass with me, if I'd taken them at face value—but the raw records. And she says—and I believe her—that you're the only reason Ms. Samarili is still alive. In fact, she told me she doesn't know many Marines who could've gotten her through that firefight in one piece. And she also went through the tactical data—and the recorded comm traffic—from your raid on Parnassus Tower. She says there's nothing in any of that data, or any of that traffic, that suggests you were simply trying to cover your ass."

He tipped back in his chair, and his expression was somber.

"We've always known there are decent human beings in Federation uniform," he said. "Hell, all of *us* once wore the same uniform! And there are sick Fringer sons-of-bitches just looking for the opportunity to commit atrocities of their own. I shot more than a few of 'em in Jalal, and the Admiral executed even more of them after we secured the Station. Problem is that sometimes good people find themselves doing shitty things because that's the job and those are the orders. It takes a special kind of 'good people' to do even shitty things with as much humanity, as much decency, as they can manage. People who haven't had the opportunity to examine your record the way Colonel Barr has may not think you're one of them, Captain. But she does—and so do I."

"Brigadier—Sir," Yildiz said after a moment, "I've got a lot of blood on my hands. And I've always thought 'I was just following orders' is a piss-poor way to excuse what you've done. Yeah, I tried not to kill anyone I didn't have to, but I killed plenty of Odyssians anyway in firefights, in the drone strikes I called in to support my people. And I knew—nobody'd told me, but I goddamn *knew*—what someone like Alaimo was going to do to

Masson and Ms. Samarili. I can't pretend I didn't, but I handed them over anyway." His jaw clenched. "God help me, I thought long and hard about just letting her go after the BSDF brought down my bird. About telling higher command she'd been killed when we went down. I *thought* about it...but I didn't do it."

"If you had, and assuming she hadn't been killed in the firefight—which she probably would've been—she still would've been killed when Alaimo dropped the K-strike in the middle of town," Atkins pointed out. "And you had to make your decisions then, Captain—right then, in the middle of the shit-fest. Been there, done that." He shook his head. "All you can do is the best you can, and that's what I think you did."

"But—" Yildiz began, his expression troubled.

"You say you killed a lot of Odyssians," Atkins interrupted. "I imagine most of them were soldiers, or at least shooting at you at the moment?"

"Well, yes, but—"

"When someone's shooting at you or your people, you shoot back. Wasn't your decision to come to Odysseus in the first place. Wasn't your call about putting Alaimo in command. And one thing every Soldier or Marine learns early is that the shit *always* flows downhill."

Yildiz fell silent, looking back at the brigadier. Then, finally, he nodded.

"All right, here's the deal," Atkins said. "The truth is that moral integrity is sadly lacking in far too much of the Army's officer corps. You know that as well as I do. Sure, I was a Marine, so a certain degree of intramural hostility is inevitable, but you know the Five Hundred and the Oval have always seen the Army as the club to beat down the Fringe. And because they do, that's how they recruit it, staff it, and train it. So when someone in Army uniform does display integrity, especially in a rolling clusterfuck like this one, it's worth taking note of. Admiral Murphy's aware of that, and he's going to need good people. People who've demonstrated that kind of integrity. So he's authorized me to offer you a choice. You can spend the rest of the Alliance's war against the Federation in a prisoner of war camp, or you can join the fight."

Yildiz stared at him, yet deep inside, he'd wondered if—hoped, feared—that this was where the entire interview had been headed.

"I'd think it over carefully," Atkins continued. "First, because if this goes south on us, or if you end up in Federation hands for any reason, they'll shoot your ass as a traitor in a skinny instant. And, second, because if evidence ever comes to light that you *were* involved in the extrajudicial killing of civilians or intentionally harmed noncombatants, you'll be shipped back here on a slow boat to face an Odyssian court."

"I've done no such thing," Yildiz said flatly, then furrowed his brow. "But what about my company? What happens to my people?"

Atkins smiled slightly.

"Are you in or not?" he asked.

"What's next, Sir? Tell me what the Admiral's planning so I know I'm not signing up as a foot soldier for the next Alaimo."

"I don't have the full skinny this instant myself," Atkins said. "I know the Admiral's been adamant about *reforming* the Federation, but that was before Bellerophon. Before he found Alaimo's orders. I don't know how that's going to affect his thinking, but I do know he's no Alaimo. He does what needs doing, and sometimes he hates it, but that won't stop him from doing it. And at the end of the day, however it happens, he'll see to it that another 'Bellerophon Expeditionary Force' is *never* sent out in the Federation's name again. If I didn't believe that—if I didn't *know* that—I wouldn't be wearing this uniform."

He thumped the breast of his crisp fatigues.

"No blanket get-out-of-jail-free amnesties for his people?"

"The Free Worlds Alliance is still teething, but the Admiral's made it *damned* clear that its soldiers and Marines are required to act like decent human beings, and the Uniform Code and Articles of War all apply. *Really* apply, in our case."

"Then I'm in," Yildiz said. "But my people, Sir. My company. They're—"

"You go to them and offer the same deal," Atkins said. "Sit out the war in a POW camp or join the fight. The Admiral's not leaving any of Alaimo's people here—not the innocent ones, at least. Odysseus is out for blood, and they deserve to get every drop of it, at least from the guilty."

"Can't disagree there, Sir," Yildiz said grimly. "But Lieutenant Colonel Lopez, Brigadier. He's good people, too."

"He's waiting for you downstairs," Atkins said, smiling broadly at last. "Already switched jerseys. In fact, I thought the two of you might go have a word with his entire battalion."

CHAPTER FORTY-FOUR

City of Kórinthos
Planet Odysseus
Bellerophon System
Free Worlds Alliance
February 6, 2553

THE CONFERENCE ROOM WAS FILLED WITH SUNLIGHT. THE THICK, yellow honey poured down through the skylight that both roofed the room and provided just enough polarization to moderate that brilliant tide's heat and kill any glare. The contrast between that bright warmth, that sense of light and life, and what Odysseus had endured at Taskin Alaimo's hands could not have been more profound.

Nor was it accidental, Terrence Murphy thought, as he strode into the conference room, flanked by Harrison O'Hanraghty and Joseph Lowe, while Callum followed at his back. Konstantinos Xeneas had chosen the venue for this meeting, and he'd wanted one that would let everyone step back at least a pace or two from the hatred, fury, and despair that had been so much a part of their lives.

He and his officers were the last to arrive, and all the other attendees rose as he walked to the place waiting for him at the head of the enormous conference table. A part of him wanted to wave them back into their chairs, but he suppressed the urge until he reached his own chair. Then he seated himself, and movement rustled around the table as the others all followed suit.

He looked around, then down the table's length at Xeneas. Their eyes met, and the system president rapped his knuckles

479

gently on the tabletop. The sound wasn't loud, but it carried clearly in the sunlit silence, and all eyes turned attentively to him.

"Thank you for coming, Admiral," he said. "I know you're scheduled to depart in four hours, and I think all of us appreciate this opportunity to express our enormous gratitude at least once more before you go. On the other hand, I'm reasonably certain you didn't request this meeting just so we could polish up your halo for you. So, with no further ado—"

He raised his right hand, palm-up in an invitation to Murphy, and the admiral allowed himself a brief, harsh chuckle.

"Thank you, Mr. President. I don't think there are too many halos in this room, and if there are, mine doesn't deserve any more polish than anyone else's. But there are some things I think it's important to say before we depart for Jalal."

He looked around the table again, letting his eyes linger on Mollie Ramsay, who sat at Xeneas's right shoulder. There were shadows in her eyes, but she looked immensely better than she had when Brigadier Atkins's Marines pulled her out of the cell in which she'd been tortured, and she returned his gaze levelly, her chin high.

"Some of the people in this room," he continued, never looking away from Ramsay, "have had their attitudes . . . clarified over the last couple of weeks.

"I'm one of them."

He paused again, letting that settle in, then leaned forward and folded his hands on the tabletop in front of him.

"I believe in the Terran Federation," he said quietly. "I believe in its Constitution, its institutions, its laws. I believe in the ideals, the rights, it was designed and built to protect. When the Concordia Sector went out of compliance, when its member star systems formed the Free Worlds Alliance, I recognized it as a legitimate protest group. As a legitimate association of individual star systems with every right to petition as a group for redress and to defend its people. But even though I recognized that, I was an officer of the Terran Federation Navy. I'd sworn an oath to the Constitution—and to God—to protect and defend the Federation against all enemies, domestic or foreign. So I was willing speak for the FWA, to represent it, even to defend it, but I couldn't *join* it."

He paused once more, then took one hand from the table to touch O'Hanraghty's shoulder.

"When Captain O'Hanraghty and I deployed to New Dublin, it was never my intent to provoke or enable a rebellion against the Federation. We suspected certain things, hoped to find evidence to prove or disprove those suspicions, and I fully intended to do my damnedest to actually protect the star system I was assigned to govern. We never anticipated what's actually happened, and, to be honest, in a lot of ways I've just been trying to stay on the back of the tiger. To at least steer things towards some sort of resolution that we could reach at something besides gunpoint. When I headed to Jalal, all I wanted to do was establish communications with Sol, *make* them listen to the proof of the things Captain O'Hanraghty and I had suspected for so long. I never intended to take over Jalal Station, and to be honest, I *wouldn't* have if the Fringers who mutinied against Admiral Portier's orders hadn't forced my hand. But they did, and I did... and I still hoped to make the Federation listen.

"But then the Oval, and the Schleibaum Government—and the Five Hundred—sent my own brother-in-law to kill or capture me and crush any potential 'rebellion' in the Fringe. And when he refused to stand down, I opened fire in self-defense, and killed over a hundred thousand *other* members of the same Navy I'd joined straight out of the Academy. And then I got the word about your secession—your *rebellion*—here in Cyclops. I tried hard to get here before any response from the Heart, tried to get in front of it, keep a handle on it, prevent what I was afraid Olympia would order done. And, again, I failed. Commodore Carson and your own people smashed three quarters of Ninth Fleet, but their sacrifice didn't prevent Alaimo from reaching Odysseus, didn't prevent him from butchering the millions of Odyssians who died in the space of only a few days.

"And that was what I found when I got here. Another step towards the thing I most desperately wanted to avoid, the destruction of the Federation. It seemed that no matter what I did, events were avalanching towards that outcome. I was desperate to stop it, but how? Like Governor Ramsay—" he nodded to her "—what I wanted most in the galaxy was to minimize the bloodshed, the death, the destruction. Yet no matter how much I wanted that, it seemed to be slipping through my fingers.

"And then we found Alaimo's orders... and the preemptive pardon he'd been issued. The license to kill he'd been given.

The pardon that would protect him no matter what crimes, what atrocities, he'd committed here on Odysseus or *anywhere else* in the entire sector. The pardon that had been signed by the Prime Minister of the Terran Federation, by every member of her cabinet, by the Chief Justice of the Federation Supreme Court, and by Aristides Fokaides on behalf of the Oval. And when I confronted him with it—when I told him I'd realized it was all intentional, that the people who'd sent him had *wanted* every single one of those deaths simply as a way to terrorize the remainder of their own citizens in the Fringe—he didn't even try to deny it. Worse, you've seen the imagery of Diana Steinbolt *acknowledging* that that was exactly the way Alaimo had explained their mission to her. She actually thought that 'I was covered by my orders and the Five Hundred's pardon' would save her from the firing squad. My God, she almost *boasted* about it."

He paused again, his gray eyes shadowed despite the sunlight, while the silence and the stillness hovered around him. And then he shook his head, his expression like iron.

"That's what I found," he said. "*Who* I found. And when I did, I knew. Or maybe I just finally admitted something I'd known all along and lacked the courage to face.

"I still want to save the Federation," he said softly. "I want that, and I'll fight for that, but I know now that I won't do it through negotiation. Not with a Federation that could send butchers like Alaimo and Steinbolt out to torture and slaughter anyone who got in their way just to 'send a message' to the uppity Fringes that, no, you *aren't* our equals." His voice grew louder. "No, you *aren't* full citizens. You *don't* have the right to live your lives any way except under our terms. Your children are ours to throw into the meat grinder instead of our own, because just like you, they are our chattel property, and you'd better not forget it!"

His final sentence rolled around the conference room like thunder, and his nostrils flared. He let the silence settle once more, then sat back in his chair.

"By my calculations, Vice Admiral Thakore will reach Sol sometime today or tomorrow with word of the Battle of Jalal," he said. "I can't predict exactly how the Five Hundred will react, but based on how they reacted to your secession here in Cyclops— and the fact that they can't realize how disastrously wrong that reaction's gone—I don't expect it to be good. I should reach Jalal no later than March the eighth, and I would really prefer to move directly to Sol from there, but when I sent Vice Admiral Thakore home, I gave the Prime Minister until the second of May to send her own envoy to Jalal in response to my messages to her. If she actually chooses to send that envoy, he'll discover that the Free Worlds Alliance's naval strength is now at least as great as anything immediately available to the Sol System. And he'll also discover that I fully intend to use that naval strength to compel the Five Hundred to meet the just demands of the Fringe and the Free Worlds Alliance.

"Undoubtedly, at this moment we have the strength to compel them to surrender, and if we wait—if we give them that opportunity—we may find that far harder to accomplish afterward. But it's important from the perspective of history that we give Schleibaum and her Five Hundred masters the opportunity to negotiate, to accept our demands, before we resort to military force. And that's even more important because our ultimate success—our ability to rebuild something on the ruin corrupt men and women have made of the Federation instead of simply tearing it apart and walking away—depends on convincing at least a majority of the Heart Worlders who aren't members of the Five Hundred themselves that we did our damnedest to avoid any preventable bloodshed. That we tried the path of reason first and that failure of our efforts was the Five Hundred's fault, not ours.

"But don't mistake me. I never wanted to be a rebel. I never wanted to overthrow the Federation. I never wanted to birth a civil war. Yet what happened here in Bellerophon, here on Odysseus—the message the Five Hundred's Federation chose to send you—tells me that reason *will* fail." His voice was hammered iron and his eyes were harder still. "And if violence and sheer brute force is the only language they understand, then as God is my witness, I will speak to them in a way they'll understand.

"If war is what they want," Terrence Murphy said, in that iron voice, "then war is what they'll have, and I promise you they won't like the way it ends."